Geoffrey de Vinsauf, John de Joinville

Chronicles of the Crusades, contemporary Narratives of the Crusade of Richard Cœur de Lion by Richard of Devizes and Geoffrey of Vinsauf

With illustrative notes and an index

Geoffrey de Vinsauf, John de Joinville

Chronicles of the Crusades, contemporary Narratives of the Crusade of Richard Cœur de Lion by Richard of Devizes and Geoffrey of Vinsauf
With illustrative notes and an index

ISBN/EAN: 9783742887177

Manufactured in Europe, USA, Canada, Australia, Japa

Cover: Foto ©Andreas Hilbeck / pixelio.de

Manufactured and distributed by brebook publishing software
(www.brebook.com)

Geoffrey de Vinsauf, John de Joinville

Chronicles of the Crusades, contemporary Narratives of the Crusade of Richard Cœur de Lion by Richard of Devizes and Geoffrey of Vinsauf

CRUSADERS & SARACENS IN CONFERENCE

CHRONICLES

OF

THE CRUSADES:

CONTEMPORARY NARRATIVES OF THE

CRUSADE OF RICHARD CŒUR DE LION,

BY

RICHARD OF DEVIZES AND GEOFFREY DE VINSAUF;

AND OF THE

CRUSADE OF SAINT LOUIS,

BY

LORD JOHN DE JOINVILLE.

WITH ILLUSTRATIVE NOTES AND AN INDEX.

LONDON: GEORGE BELL AND SONS, YORK STREET,
COVENT GARDEN.
1882.

LONDON ·
PRINTED BY WILLIAM CLOWES AND SONS, LIMITED,
STAMFORD STREET AND CHARING CROSS.

PREFACE.

THE present volume comprises the three most interesting contemporary Chronicles of the Crusades which have been handed down to us; two of them recording very fully the romantic deeds of our lion-hearted Plantagenet; the third the chivalric career of the pious and exemplary Saint Louis of France.

Of the author of the first of these Chronicles, Richard of Devizes, nothing is known beyond what he himself informs us in his preface, by which it appears, that he was in early life a monk of St. Swithin's Priory at Winchester, and subsequently a Carthusian of Witham. Other works have been ascribed to the same writer, but there is great uncertainty as to their authorship. His Chronicle is valuable, because it connects affairs which were passing in England with the events which took place simultaneously in the Holy Land. The original Latin was first published by the English Historical Society, under the editorial care of the Rev. Joseph Stevenson. From that edition, a translation was made by the Rev. Dr. Giles, in 1841, which is here reprinted, with occasional emendations by himself.

The second work in this series is the History of the Expedition of Richard Cœur de Lion to the Holy Land, by Geoffrey de Vinsauf (or Vinosalvo). Little is known of this author, but the peculiarity of his name has given rise to several ingenious conjectures as to its etymology. Some derive it from *Vin* and *sauver*, and suppose he may have

had the custody of wine in his monastery; others from the
German words *Wein* and *sauffen*, which would imply tip-
pling. Others, again, suppose that he may have been su-
perintendent of the vineyard, the wine-pressing, preserving,
&c. Pits, somewhat in confirmation of this latter notion,
cites a MS. which he saw in Caius College, Cambridge,
written by one Geoffrey, on preserving wines and fruits,
and on grafting.

Whatever may be the true derivation of his name, Geoffrey
is generally believed to have been an Englishman by birth,
but of a Norman family. His writings are numerous, and
several of them poetical. The following are the principal:—

> On preserving Wines, Fruits, &c. (De Vinis, fructibus, &c., conser-
> vandis).
> Itinerarium Regis Anglorum Richardi, et aliorum in Terram Hiero-
> solymorum.
> To the Emperor Henry, about liberating King Richard (Ad Cæsarem,
> &c.).
> Monody on the Death of King Richard (Monodia, &c.).
> To William Longchamps, Bishop of Ely, and Chancellor (Ad Wil-
> helmum, &c.).
> Of the State of the Roman Court (De Statu Curiæ Romanæ).
> Manual or Handbook (Enchiridion).
> On New Poetry (De Poetria Nova).
> On Rhetoric (De Arte dicendi).
> On Ethics (De Rebus Ethicis).

But of all his works, the most important and intrinsi-
cally valuable is his History of the Third Crusade, under
Richard the First of England and Philip Augustus of France.
It is the only Chronicle written by an eye-witness, of those
furious assaults which the army of Saladin made upon the
Christians, and of the firmness with which the lion-hearted
Richard withstood and repulsed them. If the reader takes the
trouble of comparing Geoffrey's full and interesting account
of the Crusade with that of Richard of Devizes, he will per-

ceive how much superior it is in every respect. Geoffrey lived to see the death of King Richard, and the accession of his brother John, and it is much to be lamented that he breaks off his history, somewhat abruptly, just at the moment when the Crusaders embark on board ship to leave the Holy Land, at the end of the year 1192. The original of this interesting record was printed for the first time complete in the second volume of Gale and Fell's Collection in 1687, but fragments had previously been given by Bongars in his "Gesta Dei per Francos." The present translation is the conjoint labour of a classical scholar and a gentleman well read in Mediæval history; a mode of proceeding which, after some experiment, it was found advisable to adopt, our author's corrupt Latin being frequently so vague and uncertain as to defy the best scholar who has not made the lore of the middle ages his particular study.

The third and last, and by no means the least interesting work in this volume, is Joinville's Memoirs of Saint Louis, the crusading king of France. The translation is by Colonel Johnes, of Hafod, and is given entire, with all the notes which are really illustrative of the author. Head-lines, dates, and an index have been added; which have, at least, this merit, that no previous edition, either English or French, has any of these useful accompaniments. The Biographical Sketch of Joinville is compiled from Colonel Johnes's materials, the Biographie Universelle, and other sources.

H. G. B.

August, 1848.

CONTENTS.

DESCRIPTION OF THE FRONTISPIECE.

This illumination, which is copied from a fine manuscript, of the fourteenth century, of the *Chroniques de St. Denis*, preserved in the British Museum, represents an event which took place in the year 1270, when Alfonse de Brienne, count of Eu, and great chamberlain of France, and his brother Jean de Brienne, surnamed of Acre, and grand butler of France, the sons of Jean de Brienne, king of Jerusalem, who were on guard near Tunis, were accosted by three Saracen knights requesting baptism. Whilst occupied by them, the count of Eu and his brother were attacked by the Saracens in force, and sixty Christians were slain before the infidels were put to flight.

RICHARD OF DEVIZES.

— · —

PROLOGUE.

To the Venerable Father Robert, his very good Lord, formerly Prior of the Church of Winchester, health to persevere in the good work he has begun, his faithful servant. Richard, surnamed of Devizes, sends greeting :—

SECT. 1. AFTER you had happily proceeded to the Charter House* from our church of Winchester, much and often did I desire to follow you who had thus departed, peradventure to remain with you, but certainly to behold what you were about, how you lived, and whether the Carthusian cell is more exalted and nearer heaven than the cloister of Winchester. It pleased God at length to satisfy my wish. I came, and oh that I had come alone! I went thither making the third, and those who went with me were the cause of my return. My desire displeased them, and they caused my fervour, I will not say error, to grow cold. I saw with you that which elsewhere I had not seen, which I could not have believed, and which I could not sufficiently admire. In each of your cells there is one door according to custom, which you are permitted to open at pleasure, but to go out by it is not permitted, except so much as that one foot should always remain in the cell, within the threshold. The brethren may step out with one foot, whichever they please, but the other must remain in the cell. A great and solemn oath is to be taken that the door by which it is not permitted to enter or depart

* At Witham.

B

should be kept open. I am astonished also at another thing;
abounding in all the good things of this world, as having
nothing, yet possessing all things, more compassionate and
humane than all men, having the most perfect love one to
another, you divide the affection of charity to strangers, you
bless without giving supplies to your guests. Nor do I less
admire, in the third place, that living to yourselves apart out
of society, and singly, you understand all the great things
achieved in the world as they happen, and even sometimes
you know them prior to their being accomplished. Do not,
however, consider it want of respect in me to your more than
Pythagorean taciturnity, if I shall dare presume to address
men of so great gravity, and so arduous profession, rather with
the trifles of the world than mere idle gossip.

Sect. 2. Nevertheless, although, as it is thought, the Om-
niscient God is with you and in you, and through Him you
know all things, and not from man, nor yet by man, you were
pleased, as you said, that my essay would be a solace to you,
inasmuch as in the first place I should write to you a history
of the fresh changes, which the world has produced, turning
squares into circles (more especially since your transmigration
to the celled heaven, by means of which the world may appear
more worthless to you, having its fickleness before your eyes),
and, secondly, that a well-known hand might recal to you the
memory of one beloved.

Oh! what delight! if that holy spirit, if the angel of the
Lord, if the deified man who is become already of the number
of the gods, should deign to remember me before the great
God, me, who am scarcely worthy to be accounted a man. I
have done that which you desired, do that which you have
promised. And that the little book may have a commencement of some importance, I have begun a little higher than
was stipulated, making our Royal house troubled like that of
Œdipus, the bounds of my work, commencing at the latter
part, not daring to hope to unravel the whole. Why, and
how, and when, the father may have crowned his son; how
great things and of what importance thence ensued; who and
how often and what regions they embroiled; with what success they all ended I have left to those who produce greater
works: my narrative serves only for the living.

RICHARD OF DEVIZES

SECT. 3. Now in the year of our Lord's incarnation 1189, Richard, the son of king Henry II. by Eleanor, brother of Henry III.,* was consecrated king of the English by Baldwin, archbishop of Canterbury, at Westminster, on the third of the nones of September (3 Sept.). On the very day of the coronation, about that solemn hour, in which the Son was immolated to the Father, a sacrifice of the Jews to their father the devil was commenced in the city of London, and so long was the duration of this famous mystery, that the holocaust could scarcely be accomplished the ensuing day. The other cities and towns of the kingdom emulated the faith of the Londoners, and with a like devotion despatched their bloodsuckers† with blood to hell. In this commotion there was prepared, although unequally, some evil against the wicked, everywhere throughout the realm, only Winchester alone, the people being prudent and circumspect, and the city always acting mildly spared its vermin. It never did any thing overspeedily; fearing nothing more than to repent, it considers the result of every thing before the commencement. It was unwilling, unprepared, to cast up violently through the parts the indigestion by which it was oppressed to its bodily peril, and it was careful for its bowels, in the mean time tempe-

---

* Henry, son of King Henry II., is frequently styled Henry the Third, in the early Chronicles.
† Jews, so called probably from their usurious practices.

rately concealing its uneasiness, until it should be possible for
it, at a convenient time for cure, to cast out the whole cause
of the disease at once and once for all.

Sect. 4. Not without the anxious solicitude and amaze-
ment of many, a bat was seen, in the middle and bright part
of the day, to flutter through the monastery, inconveniently
recircling in the same tracks, and especially around the king's
throne.

Sect. 5. William de Longchamp, who had been the chancellor of the earl of Poitiers before his accession, when the
earl was crowned king, considered his office to have profited
as much for the better, as a kingdom is superior to an earldom.

Sect. 6. A circumstance happened on the selfsame day of
the coronation in Westminster Abbey, a presage of such por-
tentous omen, as then was hardly allowable to be related even
in a whisper. At Complin, the last hour of the day, the first
peal that day happened to be rung, neither by any agreement,
nor even the ministers of the church themselves being aware
of it, till after it was done; for Prime, Tierce, Sext, Nones,
and the solemn service of vespers and two masses were celebrated without any ringing of peals.

Sect. 7. Stephen de Marzia,* seneschal of Anjou, under the
king lately deceased, he great and mighty, singularly fierce, and
the master of his lord, being taken and cast into chains, was
dragged to Winchester, where being made a gazing-stock to
angels and to men, emaciated with woeful hunger, and broken
with the weight of his irons, he was constrained to the payment of thirty thousand pounds of money of Anjou, and the
promise of fifteen thousand pounds, for his ransom. Ralph de
Glanville, justiciary of the realm of England and the king's
eye, a man not inferior to Stephen, except in manners and
riches, being deprived of authority and given into custody,
redeemed merely his liberty to go and come for fifteen thousand pounds of silver. And whereas this name, Glanville,
had been so great the day before, a name as it were above
every name, so that whosoever, to whom it should be given
by the Lord, would converse among princes, and would be
adored by the people, yet the next morning there remained
not one in the land who could be called by this name. That

* Stephen de Marzia, otherwise called Stephen de Turonia.

was the ruin of those two, to wit, of Stephen and Ralph, which also it is certain has been the ruin of thousands before them, and which hereafter may ruin others, namely, a suspicion arising from the confidence of their former lord.

Sect. 8. John, the king's brother, who alone of the sons of his mother, queen Eleanor, survived his brother, besides the earldom of Mortain, which, by his father's gift, he had long enjoyed, was so greatly enriched and increased in England by his brother, that both privately and publicly it was affirmed by many that the king had no thoughts of returning to the kingdom, and that his brother, already no less powerful than himself, if he should not restrain his innate temper, would, impelled by the desire of sovereignty, endeavour to drive him vanquished from the realm.

Sect. 9. The time of commencing his journey pressed hard upon King Richard, as he, who had been first of all the princes on this side the Alps in the taking up of the cross, was unwilling to be last in setting out. A king worthy of the name of king, who, in the first year of his reign, left the kingdom of England for Christ, scarcely otherwise than if he had departed never to return. So great was the devotion of the man, so hastily, so quickly and so speedily did he run, yea fly, to avenge the wrongs of Christ. However, whilst he kept the greater matter in his mind, giving himself in some little measure to deliberation for the kingdom, having received power from the pope that he might withdraw the cross from such of his own subjects, as he should desire, for the government of his kingdom, he first appointed Hugh Pudsey, bishop of Durham, to be chief justice of the whole realm, and with. design, as is thought by many, further creating him a young earl of Northumberland out of an old bishop, the custody of as many castles as he liked being yielded to him, he diligently cleared from his coffers ten thousand pounds of silver. Geoffrey Fitz Peter, William Briwere, and Hugh Bardulf being permitted to remain at home, the cross being withdrawn from them, the king's treasurer transferred the whole collections of the three as three nuts into the Exchequer. All the sheriffs of the kingdom, on any trivial accusation falling under the king's displeasure, were deprived of their unlucky power, and scarcely permitted to see his face, even by the mediation of inestimable treasure. Ralph de Glanville, than whom none

of his time was more subtle whilst he was in power, now
being reduced to a private person by his prince, was so
stupified through grief, that his son-in-law, Ralph de
Ardenne, utterly lost, by reason of his careless talk, whatever
he had previously acquired by the judgment of his mouth.
He too, himself, because he was an old man, and not able to
bear fatigue, if he had been willing to give the king that little
which remained after the payment of the fine, as a gratuity,
would easily have obtained a remission of the peril of the
journey. The king received security from the tributary
kings of the Welsh and of the Scots, that they would not
pass their borders for the annoyance of England during his
absence.

Sect. 10. Godfrey, son of that renowned Richard de Luci,
Richard (Fitz Neale) the treasurer, Hubert Walter, and
William de Longchamp, four men of no small virtue, and of
no mean praise, were elected at Pippewelle to the four vacant
sees, viz. Winchester, London, Salisbury, and Ely. They all
obtained sufficient canonical nomination, and especially the
elect of Winchester, who obtained his nomination to the
dignity on the seventeenth of the kalends of October
(Sept. 15), while the election of the other three was delayed
till the morrow, the king consenting and the archbishop con-
firming what was done, although at the first he would rather
have had it somewhat otherwise : concerning which it wonderfully happened that he, who had been nominated to one of the
sees by the archbishop's means, died that very day. William,
bishop elect of Ely, retained the king's seal on the payment
of three thousand pounds of silver, although Reginald the
Italian had bid one thousand more. The bishops elect of
Winchester and Salisbury were consecrated at Westminster,
by Baldwin, archbishop of Canterbury, on the eleventh of
the kalends of November (Oct. 22). On that day, Hugh de
Nonante, bishop of Coventry, laid his complaint before the
archbishop and bishops assembled at the consecration of the
bishops elect, against his monks of Coventry, for having laid
violent hands on him and drawn his blood before the altar.
He had also expelled the greater part of the congregation
before his complaint, nor did he cease from his importunity
until he had obtained the sanction of all the bishops in attes-
tation to the pope against the monks.

Sect. 11. Godfrey, bishop of Winchester, mindful of his profession, suing for the restoration of the possessions of his church, which had been taken away, as no one had any right of replevin against the church of Winchester with respect to its two manors, namely Meones and Weregrave, recovered them by judicial decree, three thousand pounds of silver being privately given to the king. Nor did the considerate man omit at the same time to pay a fine to the king for the indemnity of the church's treasure, for his patrimony, for the county of Hampshire and for the custody of the castles of Winchester and Porchester. And because the time for the payment of so much money was nigh at hand, as he could not pass over the day fixed for the payment without detriment to the whole business, and he could find no nearer resource under heaven, although against his will, he laid his hand on the treasure of his church, to restore which, however, he obliged himself and his successors, providing security to the convent by the testimony of a sealed bond. A man of such courtesy and moderation, who not even when angry ever did any thing to those who were under him, but what savoured of mildness: truly of his family, and one of his familiars, of whom it is said, under whom to live is to reign.

Sect. 12. The king readily disburthened all, whose money was a burthen to them, such powers and possessions as they chose being given to anybody at pleasure; wherewith also on a time an old acquaintance in the company joking him, he broke off with this evasion, "I would sell London if I could find a chapman." Many a one might have been forewarned by that expression, had it been uttered sooner, not to learn to be a wise merchant, after the English proverb, "by buying for a dozen, and selling for one and a half."

IN THE YEAR OF THE LORD MCXC.

Sect. 13. In the year from the incarnation of the Lord 1190,* the king crossed the Channel to Neustria (Normandy), the care of the whole kingdom being committed to the chancellor.

Richard, bishop elect of London, and William of Ely, were

---

* December 12, 1189.

consecrated by Archbishop Baldwin at Westminster, the
second of the kalends of January (Dec. 31, 1189). William
de Mandeville, earl of Albemarle, being seized with delirium
in an acute semitertian fever, died at Gisorz: whose relict, a
woman almost a man, who was deficient in nothing masculine
but manhood, William de Fortibus, a knight a thousand times
approved in arms, received to wife by King Richard's gift,
together with all the honours of her former husband.

Sect. 14. William, bishop of Ely, and the king's chancellor,
by nature a second Jacob, although he did not wrestle with
the angel, a goodly person, making up in mind for his shortness in stature, secure for his master's love, and presuming on
his favour, because all power was, is, and will be impatient of
a partner, expelled Hugh de Pusac from the Exchequer, and
barely leaving him even his sword with which he had been
invested as an earl of the king's hand, after a short time, deprived him of the honour of his earldom also. And lest the
bishop of Durham alone should bewail his misfortunes, the
villain, who was now more cruel than a wild beast, and
spared nobody, fell upon the bishop of Winchester also. The
custody of the castles and county is taken away from him,
nor is he even permitted to enjoy his own patrimony. The
kingdom is disturbed, and the discontented are charged with
disaffection to the king. Everybody crosses the sea to importune the king against the tyrant, but he having crossed
first of all, briefly related before the king a partial account of
his entire proceeding and expulsion; by whom also he was
fully instructed in all things to be done; he thus foiled the
adverse wishes of his rivals, and was on his return before
those who assailed him could obtain admission to the king's
presence. So he returns to the English not less powerful and
prosperous, than one who has accomplished all things whatsoever he desired. The king having returned from Gascony,
where he had forcibly put down the thieves, and captured the
holds they had occupied, all those whom the chancellor had
injured assembled before him, who satisfying every one as
then to each seemed good, sent them all back to the chancellor
with such letters as they then desired. John, bishop of
Norwich, being also one of those who threatened Saladin,
amply furnished for his journey and the cause, whilst proceeding on his way in the borders of Burgundy, fell among

robbers, who took from him all his substance; and, as he had no means left wherewith he might proceed, he turned his course towards the pope, and when with his insinuation he had bemoaned his mischance and poverty to him, the clemency of the Holy See dismissed him home, absolved from his vow.

Sect. 15. The bishop of Winchester, being affected with a serious disease, remained some time beyond the sea. The bishop of Durham in haste proceeded direct to London, but not being received by the barons of the Exchequer, he hastily, as if sure to triumph, pursues his way after the chancellor, who at that time had gone on an expedition towards Lincoln; whom having overtaken, he saluted in the king's name, not freely nor without a frown, and then questioned him seriously concerning the affairs of state, and, indeed, as if he would not suffer any thing to be done without his consent. He neglected fine language and long words, and while he boasted too much of power not yet received, not considering with whom he was speaking, he loosely uttered whatever he ought to have kept secret. At the conclusion of his address, the staff is put forth to silence talk, the king's solemn act much to be reverenced is exhibited for recital. The mountains travail, the silly mouse is produced. The observance of strict silence is enjoined during the king's mandate; all were hushed, and attentive held their tongues. The epistle is read in public, which would have been much more to be feared if it had not been so soon read; he (Longchamp), well able to conceal his device, shrewdly deferred to answer what he had heard till the seventh day, appointing their place of conference at Tickhill. On the day appointed the bishop of Durham comes to the castle, and his attendants being commanded to wait for him before the gates, he goes into the chancellor quite alone; he who before had held his peace, speaks first, and compels the deceived to recite with his own mouth letters he had obtained after the former against whatever he had hoped. As he was preparing to answer, he added, " The other day while you were speaking it was time for me to be silent; now that you may discern why I have taken a time for speaking, you being silent; as my lord the king lives, you shall not depart hence until you have given me hostages for all the castles which you hold being delivered up to me, for I do not take you as a bishop

a bishop, but as a chancellor a chancellor!" The ensnared
had neither the firmness nor the opportunity to resist; the
hostages are given, and at the term assigned the castles are
given up for the restoring of the hostages. William, bishop
of Worcester, who succeeded next to Baldwin, went the way
of all flesh.

Sect. 16. The lord bishop of Winchester, at length recovering in Neustria, and also desiring to receive back the
things taken from him, recrossed with all the speed he could,
and found the chancellor besieging the castle of Gloucester.
Whose arrival being known, the chancellor goes forth to
meet him as he comes, and having heartily embraced and
kissed him, says, "You have come at a most desirable time,
dear friend! are we to prosecute the siege or desist?" To
whom the bishop replies, "If you desire peace, lay down
arms." He, quick of apprehension, perceived the force of
the words, and commanded the heralds to sound the retreat;
he also restored to the bishop his patrimony without dispute,
but that only. All the others, who had crossed the sea
against the chancellor, profited less than nothing. William,
legate of the Apostolic See, held a council at Westminster, in
which, lest there should be nothing done to be reported of
him hereafter, he sentenced all religion to be expelled from
Coventry cathedral, and prebendary clerks to be substituted
in place of the monks.

Sect. 17. William, the wonderful bishop of Ely, chancellor
of the king, justiciary of the kingdom, of threefold charge
and threefold title, that he might use both hands as the right,
and that the sword of Peter might succour the sword of the
ruler, took upon himself the office of legate of all England,
Scotland, Wales, and Ireland, which he obtained from the
pope at the instance of the king, who would not otherwise
set out, by Reginald, bishop of Bath. Therefore successful
in every office which he craved, he passed to and fro through
the kingdom with the rapidity of a flash of lightning.

The King of Darkness, that old incendiary, having added
fresh fuel, fanned the ancient spark between the church of
Salisbury and the monastery of Malmesbury into renewed
flames. The abbot is roused not now to make the profession
of pontiff, but to disavow the very title of the bishop as well
as his crosier. Royal letters to the chancellor were obtained,

by which the abbot should be compelled to respond at law to
the motions of the bishop.   Nor did the man whose affairs
were at stake forget himself; no peril could ever overtake
him unprovided, who never knew the loss of any thing through
sloth.   He repelled one nail by another, being presented by
the king with letters invalidating the former letters.   The
chancellor having perceived the shameful contrariety of the
mandates of his prince, lest the king's fame should be injured
by the fact, if he proceeded in the cause, deferred all process
of both the one party and the other till the king's return.

Sect. 18. King Richard exacted an oath from his two
brothers, John, his own brother, and Geoffrey, a bastard, that
they would not enter England within three years from his
departure, the three years to be reckoned from the day of his
starting from Tours; through the entreaties of his mother,
however, dispensing so far concerning John, that passing into
England with the chancellor's approbation, he should abide
his judgment, and at his pleasure he should either remain in
the kingdom, or live in exile.

Queen Eleanor's dowry was recognized throughout the
king's territories by a solemn act, and delivered up to her, so
that she who had before lived on the Exchequer might thenceforward live on her own.

The king's fleet, having left its own shores, sailed round
Spain, and from the ocean having entered the Mediterranean, which further on is called the Grecian Sea, by the
Straits of Africa, steered on to Marseilles, there to await
the king.

The king of France and the king of England, having held
a council at Tours and again at Vezelay, and confirmed the
treaty between themselves and their kingdoms, and having
settled and disposed of all things on both sides according to
their pleasure, depart from each other with their respective
armies.   The Frenchman, being subject to sickness at sea,
marches by land to Sicily; the Englishman, on the contrary,
about to proceed by sea, comes to Marseilles to his ships.
Baldwin, archbishop of Canterbury, and Hubert Walter,
bishop of Salisbury, being the only bishops of all England
who accomplished their vows, follow the king to Sicily, and
arrive first in the land of Juda.

Sect. 19. The monks of the order of Cluni were not wont

to supplant one another in their priories and government
either by entreaty or bribes, and although some of them have
sometimes attempted something of that sort, that however we
have seen visited with condign punishment. There was a
certain venerable man elected prior of Montacute solely on
account of his worth, Josceline by name, in whom you could
discern nothing but what was praiseworthy. To supplant
this so good a man there came a certain one, whose name it is
not necessary to mention, one of his false brethren, with
letters, obtained by great cunning from the abbot of Cluni, by
which it was commanded that the prior should resign to the
bearer of the present letters, and the congregation receive
him for their prelate. The prior by some means foreknew what
commodity the dealer had come to seek, wherefore, without
awaiting the mandate, he vacated his seat in the chapter, and
the congregation being present, addressed him, "Friend, for
what art thou come?" He, having tarried long that he might
appear unwillingly to receive that, which he had come to
take by violence, at length betook himself to his seat, and
anon imprecated himself, saying, "O thou, who with un-
alterable purpose governest the world, whose power takes its
pastime in human affairs, who puttest down the mighty and
exaltest the humble! O thou just judge Jesu Christ, if
wrongfully I here preside, without delay and manifestly do
thou vouchsafe to shew!" Behold the miracle! On that
same day he lost his speech; on the next, his life; on the
third, being consigned to the earth, he learnt by experience,
and taught by example, that sordid plunder is never followed
by prosperous results.

A certain monk of Glastonbury, in hopes of promotion,
courted Earl John with many presents; but just as he should
have come to receive it, a certain beam having suddenly given
way, fell in his face, so that, bruised and wholly disfigured,
he lost both his eggs (qy. expectations) and his money
together.

Sect. 20. The ships which the king found already prepared
on the shore were one hundred in number, and fourteen
busses, vessels of great magnitude and admirable swiftness,
strong vessels and very sound, whereof this was the equipage
and appointment. The first of the ships had three spare
rudders, thirteen anchors, thirty oars, two sails, three sets of

ropes of all kinds, and besides these double whatever a ship can want, except the mast and the ship's boat. There is appointed to the ship's command a most experienced steersman, and fourteen subordinate attendants picked for the service are assigned him. The ship is freighted with forty horses of value, trained to arms, and with arms of all kinds for as many horsemen, and forty foot, and fifteen sailors, and with an entire year's provisions for as many men and horses. There was one appointment for all the ships, but each of the busses received a double appointment and freight. The king's treasure, which was very great and inestimable, was divided amongst the ships and busses, that if one part should experience danger, the rest might be saved. All things being thus arranged, the king himself, with a small household, and the chief men of his army, with his attendants, having quitted the shore, advanced before the fleet in galleys, and being daily entertained by the maritime towns, taking along with them the larger ships and busses of that sea, arrived prosperously at Messina.* So great was the splendour of the approaching armament, such the clashing and brilliancy of their arms, so noble the sound of the trumpets and clarions, that the city quaked and was greatly astounded, and there came to meet the king a multitude of all ages, people without number, wondering and proclaiming with what exceeding glory and magnificence that king had arrived, surpassing the king of France, who with his forces had arrived seven days before. And forasmuch as the king of France had been already received into the palace of Tancred, king of Sicily, within the walls, the king of England pitched his camp without the city. The same day the king of France, knowing of the arrival of his comrade and brother, flies to his reception, nor could their gestures sufficiently express in embraces and kisses how much each of them rejoiced in the other. The armies cheered one another with mutual applause and intercourse, as if so many thousand men had been all of one heart and one mind. In such pastimes is the holiday spent until the evening, and the weary kings departing, although not satiated, return every one to his own quarters. On the next day the king of England presently caused gibbets to be erected without the

* He arrives at Messina, Sept. 23.

camp to hang thereon thieves and robbers.   The judges dele-
gated spared neither sex nor age; the cause of the stranger
and the native found the like law and the like punishment.
The king of France, whatever transgression his people committed, or whatever offence was committed against them, took
no notice and held his peace; the king of England esteeming
the country of those implicated in guilt as a matter of no consequence, considered every man his own, and left no transgression unpunished, wherefore the one was called a Lamb by
the Griffones, the other obtained the name of a Lion.

Sect. 21. The king of England sent his messengers to the
king of Sicily, demanding Johanna his sister, formerly queen
of Sicily, and her dowry, with a golden seat and the whole
legacy which King William had bequeathed to his father,
King Henry, namely, a golden table of twelve feet in length,
a silk tent, a hundred of the best galleys with all their necessaries for two years, sixty thousand silinas of wheat, sixty
thousand of barley, sixty thousand of wine, four and twenty
golden cups, and four and twenty golden dishes.   The king
of Sicily, setting little by the demands of the king of the
English, and still less considering his own exigencies, sent him
back his sister with the ordinary furniture of her bed, having
given her, however, with royal consideration, a thousand
thousand terrini for her expenses.   On the third day following, the king of England, having passed over the great river
Del Far, which separates Calabria from Sicily, entered Calabria in arms, and took therein the well-fortified town which
is called La Banniere, and having expelled the Griffones,
established his sister there, and secured the place with an
armed garrison.   Again the king took a very strong castle,
which is called the Griffones' Monastery, on the same river
Del Far, situated between La Banniere and Messina, and
fortified it when taken; and having without mercy despatched
by various tortures the Griffones who had resisted, caused
them to be exhibited as a gazing-stock to their friends. Wido,
king of Jerusalem, sent word to Philip, king of the French,
and Richard, king of the English, whilst wintering in Sicily,
that the residue of the Christians who lay before Acre would,
on account of their weakness and the violence of the pagans,
either be obliged to depart or perish, unless very shortly sustained.   To aid whom, the kings sent forward Henry, count

of Champagne, and Baldwin, archbishop of Canterbury, and
Hubert, bishop of Salisbury, and Ralph de Glanville, with a
strong army; of whom Archbishop Baldwin and Ralph de
Glanville died at the siege of the city, which the Latins call
Acre and the Jews Accaron, while the kings still remained in
Sicily.

Sect. 22. The Griffones, before King Richard's arrival in
Sicily, were more powerful than all the mighty of that region,
and having moreover always hated the people beyond the
Alps, and now irritated by recent occurrences more inveterate
than ever, kept the peace with all who claimed the king of
France for their master, but sought to wreak the entire vengeance of their wrongs on the king of the English and his
tailed* followers, for the Greeks and Sicilians followed that
king about and called them tailed English.   Thereupon all
intercourse with the country is denied the English by proclamation; they are murdered both day and night by forties and
fifties, wherever they are found unarmed.   The slaughter was
daily multiplied, and it was madly purposed to go on until
they should either destroy or put them all to flight.   The
king of England, excited by these disorders, raged like the
fiercest lion, and vented his anger in a manner worthy that
noble beast.   His fury astounded his nearest friends, and his
whole court, the famous princes of his army sat around his
throne, each according to his rank, and if any one might dare
to raise his eyes to look him in the face, it would be very easy
to read in the ruler's countenance what he silently considered
in his mind.   After a long and deep silence, the king disbur-
dened his indignant lips as follows.

Sect. 23. "O, my soldiers! my kingdom's strength and
crown! who have endured with me a thousand perils, you,
who by might have subdued before me so many tyrants and
cities, do you now see how a cowardly rabble insults us?
Shall we vanquish Turks and Arabs? shall we be a terror to
nations the most invincible? shall our right hand make us a
way even to the ends of the world for the cross of Christ?
shall we restore the kingdom to Israel, when we have turned
our backs before vile and effeminate Griffones?   Shall we,
subdued here in the confines of our own country, proceed

* The origin of this joke is unknown.

further, that the sloth of the English may become a by-word
to the ends of the earth? Am I not right, then, O my friends,
in regarding this as a new cause of sorrow? Truly, methinks
I see you deliberately spare your pains, that perchance you
may the better contend with Saladin hereafter. I, your lord
and king, love you; I am solicitous for your honour; I tell
you, I warn you again and again, if now you depart thus
unrevenged, the mention of this base flight will both precede
and accompany you. Old women and children will be raised
up against you, and assurance will yield a double energy to
every enemy against the runaways. I know that he who
saves any one by constraint, does the same as kill him; the
king will retain no man against his will. I am unwilling to
compel any one of you to stay with me, lest the fear of one
should shake another's confidence in the battle. Let every
one follow what he may have chosen, but I will either die here
or will revenge these wrongs common to me and you. If
hence I depart alive, Saladin will see me only a conqueror;
will you depart, and leave me, your king, alone to meet the
conflict?"

Sect. 24. The king had scarcely well concluded his
harangue, when all his brave and valiant men burst out,
troubled only that their lord appeared to mistrust his men.
They promise that they will comply from their souls with
whatever he shall enjoin; they are ready to penetrate mountains and walls of brass, should he but give a nod: all Sicily,
at his command alone, shall be subjected to him by their
labour; if he should but desire it, as far as the Pillars of
Hercules shall be steeped in blood. As the clamour, hushed
by the ruler's gravity, subsided, "I am pleased," said he,
"with what I hear; you refresh my spirits by your readiness
to cast off your disgrace. And, as delay has always been
hurtful to those who are prepared, we must make haste, so
that whatever we design may be sudden. Messina shall be
taken by me in the first place, the Griffones shall either
ransom themselves, or be sold. If King Tancred do not more
speedily satisfy me for my sister's dowry and the legacy of
King William, which falls to me in right of my father, after
the depopulation of his kingdom, he shall be compelled to restore them fourfold. Whatever belongs to the inhabitants
shall be a prey for everybody to whom it shall fall; only

with my lord the king of the French, who lodges in the city,
and with all his followers, shall perfect peace be preserved.
Let two thousand bold knights,* the choice of the entire army,
and a thousand foot, archers, be made ready within two days.
Let the law be enforced without remission ; let the footman,
who flies full speed, lose his foot, the knight be deprived of
his girdle.   Let every man, according to military discipline,
be disposed in line in exact array, and on the third day, at the
sound of the horn, let them follow me.   I will head them and
shew them the way to the city!"   The assembly separated
with the greatest applause; the king, having relaxed the
sternness of his countenance, was seen returning thanks for
their good-will with his wonted affability of expression.

Sect. 25. It wonderfully fell out that not even the king's
enemy could pretend that his cause was unjust. On the third
day on which the army was to have been led forth to battle,
very early in the morning, Richard, archbishop of Messina,
the archbishop of Montreal, the archbishop of Pisa, Margaritus Admiralis, Jordan de Pin, and many other of King Tancred's familiar friends, having taken with them Philip, king
of the French, the bishop of Carnot, the duke of Burgundy,
the counts of Nevers and Perch, and many followers of the
king of France, also, the archbishops of Rouen and Auch, the
bishops of Evreux and Bayonne, and all who were supposed
to have any influence with the English, came reverently to
the king of England, that they might cause satisfaction for
all his complaints to be given to his content.   The king, after
long and earnest solicitation, is prevailed on by the entreaty of
such honourable men, and commits the matter to be settled by
their arbitration.   They would consider well the enormity of
what he had had to brook, and would provide that the satisfaction should be answerable to the offence.   Whatever their
general deliberation should have determined to be sufficient,
would be satisfactory to him, if only, from that very moment,
none of the Griffones would lay hands on his men.   Those
who had come were even more astonished than rejoiced at
this unhoped-for clemency, and giving him at once what he
had last propounded, they retired from the king's presence,
and were assembled at some distance to treat of the rest.

---

* Literally, men who have not their hearts in their boots.

c

Sect. 26. The king's army having on the previous day been numbered according to the aforementioned order, was with solemn silence in arms before the camp, awaiting the herald, from the rising of the sun, and the framers of the peace, not so easily coming to a determination, had protracted the day till full the third hour, when behold, suddenly and unexpectedly, there was proclaimed by a voice, too distinctly heard, before the gates, "To arms, to arms, men! Hugo Brunus is taken and being murdered by the Griffones, all he has is being plundered, and his men are being slaughtered." The cry of the breach of peace confounded those who were treating for the peace, and the king of France broke forth in the following speech: "I take it that God has hated these men, and hardened their hearts that they may fall into the hands of the destroyer:" and having quickly returned, with all who were with him, to the king's pavilion, he found him already girding on his sword, whom he thus briefly addressed: "I will be a witness before all men, whatever be the consequence, that thou art blameless, if at length thou takest arms against the cursed Griffones." When he had said this, he departed; those who had accompanied him followed, and were received into the city. The king of England proceeds in arms; the terrible standard of the dragon is borne in front unfurled, while behind the king the sound of the trumpet excites the army. The sun shone brightly on the golden shields, and the mountains were resplendent in their glare; they marched cautiously and orderly, and the affair was managed without show. The Griffones, on the contrary, the city gates being closed, stood armed at the battlements of the walls and towers, as yet fearing nothing, and incessantly discharged their darts upon the enemy. The king, acquainted with nothing better than to take cities by storm and batter forts, let their quivers be emptied first, and then at length made his first assault by his archers who preceded the army. The sky is hidden by the shower of arrows, a thousand darts pierce through the shields spread abroad on the ramparts, nothing could save the rebels against the force of the darts. The walls are left without guard, because no one could look out of doors, but he would have an arrow in his eye before he could shut it.

Sect. 27. In the mean time, the king with his troops, without repulse, freely and as though with permission, approached the gates of the city, which, with the application of the battering-ram, he forced in an instant, and having led in his army, took every hold in the city, even to Tancred's palace and the lodgings of the French around their king's quarters, which he spared in respect of the king his lord. The standards of the victors are planted on the towers through the whole circuit of the city, and each of the surrendered fortifications he intrusted to particular captains of his army, and caused his nobles to take up their quarters in the city. He took the sons of all the nobility both of the city and surrounding country as hostages, that they should either be redeemed at the king's price, or the remainder of the city should be delivered up to him without conflict, and he should take to himself satisfaction for his demands from their king Tancred. He began to attack the city about the fifth hour of the day, and took it the tenth hour; and having withdrawn his army, returned victorious to his camp. King Tancred, terrified at the words of those who announced to him the issue of the transaction, hastened to make an agreement with him, sending him twenty thousand ounces of gold for his sister's dowry, and other twenty thousand ounces of gold for the legacy of King William and the observance of perpetual peace towards him and his. This small sum is accepted with much ado and scornfully enough, the hostages are given back, and peace is sworn and confirmed by the nobles of both nations.

Sect. 28. The king of England, now having little confidence in the natives, built a new wooden fort of great strength and height by the walls of Messina, which, to the reproach of the Griffones, he called "Mategriffun." The king's valour was greatly extolled, and the land kept silence in his presence. Walter, who from a monk and prior of St. Swithin's church at Winchester, had been advanced to be abbot of Westminster, died on the fifth of the calends of October.

Sect. 29. Queen Eleanor,* a matchless woman, beautiful and chaste, powerful and modest, meek and eloquent, which is rarely wont to be met with in a woman, who was advanced in years enough to have had two husbands and two sons

---

* Eleanor, queen of Lewis and Henry, mother of Henry and Richard.

crowned kings, still indefatigable for every undertaking, whose power was the admiration of her age, having taken with her the daughter of the king of the Navarrese, a maid more accomplished than beautiful, followed the king her son, and having overtaken him still abiding in Sicily, she came to Pisa, a city full of every good, and convenient for her reception, there to await the king's pleasure, together with the king of Navarre's ambassadors and the damsel.   Many knew, what I wish that none of us had known. . The same queen, in the time of her former husband, went to Jerusalem.   Let none speak more thereof; I also know well.   Be silent.

IN THE YEAR OF THE LORD MCXCI.

Sect. 30. The first conference between the earl of Mortain, the king's brother, and the chancellor, respecting the custody of certain castles and the money out of the Exchequer conceded to the earl by his brother,* was held at Winchester on Lætare Hierusalem.

Robert, prior of St. Swithin's, at Winchester, having left his priory and forsaken his profession, cast himself into the sect of the Carthusians, at Witham, for grief (or shall I say for devotion?)

Walter, prior of Bath, with a like fervour or distraction, had before presumed the selfsame thing; but once withdrawn, he seemed as yet to think of nothing less than a return.

Sect. 31. The king, although he had long ago sworn to the king of France that he would accept his sister as a consort, whom his father King Henry had provided for him, and for a long time had taken care of, because he was suspicious of the custody had of her, contemplated marrying the princess his mother had engaged.   And that he might accomplish the desire without difficulty, with which he vehemently burned, he consulted the count of Flanders, a most eloquent man, and one who possessed an invaluable power of speech, by whose mediation the king of France released the king of England from his oath to marry his sister, and quit-claimed to him for ever the whole territory of Vægesin and Gisorz, having received from him ten thousand pounds of silver.

Sect. 32. The king of France, with his army, departing for

* March 4.

Jerusalem before the king of England, put to sea the third
of the calends of April. The king of England, about to
leave Sicily, caused the fort which he had built to be taken
down, and stowed the whole of the materials in his ships to
take along with him. Every sort of engine for the attack of
fortifications, and every kind of arms which the heart of man
could invent, he had all ready in his ships. Robert, son of
William Fitz Ralph, was consecrated for the bishopric of
Worcester by William de Longchamp, as yet legate, at
Canterbury, on the third of the nones of May. The convent
of Canterbury deposed their prior, whom Archbishop Baldwin
had set over them, and substituted another in the place of the
deposed.

Sect. 33. Walter, archbishop of Rouen, because, as is usual
with the clergy, he was pusillanimous and timorous, having
bidden adieu to Jerusalem from afar, resigned, unasked, all
indignation against Saladin, and gave to the king all the provision he had brought for attacking him, and the cross;
whilst, forgetting shame, he pretended, with that devotion
which diffidence, the most wretched of mothers, brought
forth, that pastors of the church should rather preach than
fight, and that it is not meet for a bishop to wield other arms
than those of virtue. But the king, to whom his money
appeared more necessary than his personal presence, as if
convinced by the overpowering argument, approved the
allegations, and having arranged concerning the three years'
contribution that he should furnish of a certain number of
men and horses, sent him back again into England with his
letters to William the chancellor; this being added at the
end of the letters for honour and for all, that the chancellor
should use his counsel in affairs of state. The king, having
gained experience from the proceedings of this archbishop,
purified his army, not permitting any one to come with him
but such as could bear arms, and with a ready mind would
use them; nor did he suffer those who returned to take back
with them their money, which they had brought thus far, or
their arms. The queen, also, his mother, who had been
received with all honour, as it was meet, and after affectionate
embraces had been led forth with great splendour, he caused
to return with the archbishop; having retained for himself
the princess whom he had sought, and intrusted her to the

safe custody of his sister, who had now returned to the camp
to meet her mother.

Sect. 34. John, bishop of Exeter, closed his last day.

Savaricus, archdeacon of Northampton, being also one of
the many who had followed the king of England out of
England to Sicily, was supplied by the king with letters
patent, in the presence of the king's mother, to the justiciaries
of England, containing the king's assent, and something more
than an assent, that he should be promoted to whatever
vacant diocese he could be elected to. These honourable
acquisitions Savaricus sent to his kinsman, the bishop of
Bath, into England, but he himself retired to Rome as one
who had been best known among the Romans.

Sect. 35. Richard, king of England, in letters destined for
England, taking leave of his whole kingdom, and giving
strict injunction for the chancellor to be honoured by all, his
fleet, more to be prized for its quality than its numbers, being
in readiness, with a chosen and brave army, with his sister
Johanna and the princess he was to marry, with all things
which could be necessary for those going to war, or going to
set out on a long journey, set sail on the fourth of the ides of
April. In the fleet, moreover, there were one hundred and
fifty-six ships, four-and-twenty busses, and thirty and nine
galleys; the sum of the vessels two hundred and nineteen.

Sect. 36. The archbishop of Rouen came to England to the
chancellor, by whom he was received and treated honourably,
and much better than the king had commanded. Others also
followed with many mandates, in all of which the conclusion
was, that the chancellor should be obeyed by all. To his
brother John especially, he sent word by every messenger,
that he should adhere to the chancellor, that he should be
a support to him against all men, and that he should not
violate the oath he had given him. The king of England sent orders to the chancellor, and to the convent of
Canterbury, and to the bishops of the province, that they
should canonically and jointly provide for the metropolitan
see, because, Baldwin being dead, it had been bereft of its
prelate; for the abbacy, however, of Westminster, now
vacant, it is permitted to the chancellor alone to ordain as he
pleases. There happened an eclipse of the sun about the third
hour of the day: those who were ignorant of the causes of

things were astonished, that in the middle of the day, no
clouds obstructing the sun, the sun's rays should give a much
feebler light than usual ; but those whom the motion of the
universe occupies, say that the making deficiencies of the sun
and moon does not signify any thing.

Sect. 37. John, the king's brother, who had long kept his
ears open for it, when he knew for certain that his brother
had turned his back on England, presently perambulated the
kingdom in a more popular manner, nor did he forbid his followers calling him the king's heir. And as the earth is dreary
in the sun's absence, so was the face of the kingdom altered at
the king's departure. The nobles are all stirred up in arms,
the castles are closed, the cities are fortified, intrenchments
are thrown up. The archbishop of Rouen, not foreseeing
more of the future than the fuel of error which was praised,
knew well how so to give contentment to the chancellor, that
at the same time he might not displease his rivals. Writs are
privately despatched to the heads of the clergy and of the
people, and the minds of everybody are excited against the
chancellor. The knights of parliament willingly, though
secretly, consented ; but the clergy, more fearful by nature,
dared not swear obedience to either master. The chancellor,
perceiving these things, dissembled, disdaining to know that
any one would presume any how to attempt any thing against
him.

Sect. 38. At length the pot is uncovered ; it is announced
to him, that Gerard de Camville, a factious man and reckless
of allegiance, had done homage to Earl John, the king's brother, for the castle of Lincoln, the custody whereof is known
to belong to the inheritance of Nicholaa, the wife of the same
Gerard, but under the king. The deed is considered to
infringe upon the crown, and he resolves to go and revenge its
commission. So having quickly collected a numerous army,
he came into those parts, and having first made an attack
against Wigmore, he compelled Roger de Mortimer, im-
peached for a conspiracy made against the king, with the
Welsh, to surrender the castles, and abjure England for three
years. As he departed, he was blamed by his associates for
want of courage, because, while supported by the numerous
soldiery of the castles, and abounding in advantages, he had
given way, without a blow, at the bare threats of the priest.

Reproof was too late after the error ; Roger leaves the kingdom, and the chancellor gives orders to besiege Lincoln. Gerard was with the earl ; and his wife Nicholaa, proposing to
herself nothing effeminate, defended the castle like a man.
The chancellor was wholly busied about Lincoln, whilst Earl
John occupied the castle of Nottingham and that of Tickhill,
both very strong, the warden being compelled to the surrender by fear alone.   He proceeded, moreover, to send word
to the chancellor that he must raise the siege, or otherwise he
would avenge the cause of his vassal ; that it was not proper
to take from the loyal men of the kingdom, well known and
free, their charges, and commit them to strangers and men
unknown ; that it was a mark of his folly that he had intrusted the king's castles to such, because they would expose
them to adventurers ; that if it should go with every barbarian with that facility, that even the castles should be ready
at all times for their reception, that he would no longer bear
in silence the destruction of his brother's kingdom and affairs.

Sect. 39. The chancellor, incredibly troubled at these
threats, having summoned before him the peers and chiefs of
the army, begins : " Never trust me if this man seeks not to
subjugate the kingdom to himself; what he presumes is
exorbitant, even if he had a right to wear the crown by
annual turns with his brother, for Eteocles has not yet completed a full year in his government."   He uttered many
words of anguish after this manner ; and then again having
taken heart, as he was greater in moral courage than in physi-
cal, conceiving great things in his mind, he sent the archbishop
of Rouen to the earl, demanding in an imperative manner
that he should deliver up the castles, and that he should
answer before the court of King's Bench for the breach of his
oath to his brother.   The archbishop, skilful in working with
either hand, praised the constancy of the chancellor ; and
having proceeded to the earl, after the delivery of the mandates, he whispered in his ear, that whatever others might say,
he should dare something great, worthy of Gyara and the
dungeon, if he desired to be any thing.   In public, however,
he advised that the earl and the chancellor should agree to an
interview, and that a reference to arbitration should end their
disagreement.

Sect. 40. The earl, greatly exasperated at the impropriety

of the mandates, was so altered in his whole body that a man
would hardly have known him.   Rancour made deep furrows
in his forehead, his flaming eyes glistened, paleness discoloured
the rosy complexion of his face, and I know what would have
become of the chancellor, if in that hour of fury he had fallen
as an apple into his hands while frantically raging.   His
indignation increased so much in his stifled breast, that it
could not be kept from bursting out at least in part.   " This
son," said he, " of perdition, the worst of the evil ones, who
first borrowed from the peasantry of the French, and introduced among the English, the preposterous practice of kneeling, would not harass me, as you perceive, if I had not refused to learn the new craft offered to me!"   He would fain
have said more, whether true or false, but recalling his presence of mind, and repressing his rage, "If I have spoken
amiss," said he, " O archbishop, I ask pardon."   After these
frivolous expressions, they applied themselves to the weighty
matters.   They consulted about the demands of the chancellor; and the counsel of the archbishop, that there should be
a meeting of them both, was agreed to, about the middle of
the day.   The day was fixed for the fifth of the calends of
August; the place without Winchester.   The chancellor
allowed what they had settled to stand, and, having broken
up the siege, returned to London.

Sect. 41. The earl, however, fearing his craftiness, brought
thither four thousand Welsh, that, if the chancellor should
endeavour to take him during the truce, they, being placed in
ambush close beside the conference, might thwart his endeavours by a sally.   Moreover, he commanded that it should be
summoned, and required that every one of his men, and
others, his adherents, should be prepared to go to battle,
should attend him at the place and on the day of the engagement, so that as the interview between himself and the lord
of the whole land had been undertaken, at least he might
escape alive, if he, who was more than a king, though less in
his eyes, should transgress against the law, or should not consent to an arrangement.   The chancellor, however, on the
other hand, commanded that one-third of the soldiery, with all
the arms of all England, should proceed to Winchester by the
day appointed; moreover, at the expense of the king's revenue
he also hired some Welsh, that if it should come to a contest

with the earl, he might have an equal array, and javelins threatening javelins.

Sect. 42. They came to the interview as was before agreed on, and it happened to terminate better than was feared. The agreement, moreover, made between the earl and the chancellor was thus, and in this way provided. First of all were named the three bishops of Winchester, London, and Bath, in whose fidelity each party considered himself secure. The bishops chose for the chancellor's part the three earls of Warren, of Arundel, of Clare, and certain other eight by name. For the earl's part, Stephen Ridel, the earl's chancellor, William de Venneval, Reginald de Wasseville, and certain other eight by name. These all, some beholding some touching the holy gospels, swore that they would provide satisfaction between the earl and the chancellor concerning their quarrels and questions to the honour of both parties and the peace of the kingdom. And if hereafter any disagreement should happen between them, they would faithfully end it. The earl also, and the chancellor, swore that they would consent to whatever the aforesaid jury should settle; and this was the provision. Gerard de Camville, being received into the chancellor's favour, the custody of the castle of Lincoln was reserved to him in peace and safety; the earl gave up the castles which he had taken, and the chancellor having received them, gave them over to the king's faithful and liege men, namely, to William de Wenn the castle of Nottingham, and to Reginald de Wasseville the castle of Tickhill; and each of them gave an hostage to the chancellor, that they would keep those castles in the safe peace and fidelity of their lord the king, if he should return alive. If, however, the king should die before his return, the aforesaid castles should be delivered up to the earl, and the chancellor should restore the hostages. The constables of the castles of the earl's honours should be changed by the chancellor, if the earl should shew reason for their being changed. The chancellor, if the king should die, should not seek the disherison of the earl; but should promote him to the kingdom with all his power. Concluded solemnly at Winchester, on the seventh of the calends of May.

Sect. 43. The chancellor, by wonderful importunity and earnestness, persuaded first a part of the monks, and afterwards the whole congregation of Westminster, to permit his brother, a monk of Cadomo, to profess a cohabitation in Westminster, and to be elected by all for their abbot for his profession and cohabitation on a day appointed ; and that this election should not be broken, security was taken by a bond, with the church's seal affixed as a testimony.

Sect. 44. Geoffrey, a brother of King Richard and Earl John, but not by their mother, who had been consecrated archbishop of York at Tours, by the archbishop of Tours, by the pope's command, continually solicited by message John the king's brother and his own, that at the least it might be permitted him to return to England ; and having obtained his consent, he prepared to return. The intercourse of the brothers did not escape the chancellor's knowledge, who providing, lest their natural genuine perverseness should increase, commanded the keepers of the coasts, that wherever that archbishop, who had abjured England for the three years of the king's travels, should disembark within the bounds of the kingdom, he should not be permitted to proceed, but by the will of the jury, to whose award the earl and the chancellor had taken oath to stand concerning every thing that should happen.

Sect. 45. A certain Robert, prior of Hereford, a monk who did not think very meanly of himself, and gladly forced himself into other people's business that he might intermix his own, had gone into Sicily to the king on the chancellor's messages, where after the rest he did not forget his own interests ; and having by some means or other worried everybody, succeeded in obtaining the abbacy of Muchelney to be granted to him and confirmed by the king. Into possession of which, by the chancellor's means, he entered, against the will of the convent, neither canonically, nor with a benediction ; and presently on the first day, at the first dinner, by greedily partaking of fresh eels without wine, and more than was proper, he fell into a languor, which the food, undigested and lying heavily on an inflamed stomach, brought on. And lest the languor should be ascribed to his gluttony, he caused the monks of that place to be slandered of having given him poison.

Sect. 46. Geoffrey, archbishop of York, presuming upon the consent of his brother Earl John, his shipping being

ready, came to Dover, and presently having landed, first
sought a church for prayer. There is there a priory of monks
of the profession of Canterbury, whose oratory he entered
with his clerks to hear mass, and his household was intent about
unlading the ships. No sooner had the whole of his goods
been landed, than suddenly the constable of the castle caused
whatever he thought was the archbishop's to be brought into
the town, understanding more in the command of his lord the
chancellor than he had commanded. Certain also of the
soldiers, armed under their tunics, and girt with swords, came
into the monastery, that they might apprehend the pontiff;
whom when he saw, their intention being foreknown, he took
a cross in his hands, and first addressing them and extending
his hands towards his followers, he says, "I am the archbishop; if ye seek me, let these go their way." And the
soldiers reply, "Whether you be an archbishop or not, it is
nothing to us; one thing we know, that you are Geoffrey, the
son of King Henry, whom he begot on some strange bed, who
before the king, whose brother you make yourself, have for-
sworn England for three years; if you are not come into the
kingdom as a traitor to the kingdom; if you have brought
letters of absolution, either say, or take the reproach." Then
said the archbishop, "I am not a traitor, neither will I shew
you any letters." They then laid their hands on him there
before the very altar, and violently dragged him out of the
church against his will, and resisting, but not with force; who
immediately being set without the threshold, excommunicated
by name those who had laid hands on him, both present and
whilst they were still holding him; nor did he receive the
horse that they offered him that he might ride with them to
the castle, because it was the property of the excommunicated.
And so, outraging humanity, they dragged him on foot by the
hands, and carrying the cross, all through the mud of the
streets to the castle. After this they desired of their own
good will to deal humanely with their captive, bringing him
some of the best provisions which they had prepared for themselves; but he, being firmly resolved, by what he had now
suffered, rejected their victuals as if it were an offering to
idols, and refused to live on anything but his own. The
report spread over the kingdom more rapidly than the wind,
those who had followed their lord at a distance came after,

relating and complaining to all that the archbishop, the king's
brother, thus landed, had been so treated and detained in
prison.

Sect. 47. The archbishop was already three days in custody,
and the chancellor, as soon as the case was made known to
him, restored to him all his goods, and set him at liberty to
depart whithersoever he should desire. He wrote, moreover,
to Earl John, and to all the bishops, asserting, with an oath,
that the aforesaid man had suffered the above-written injuries
without his knowledge. The excuse profited little, because the
occasion, which had been long sought and which spontaneously
offered itself against him, was most eagerly and tenaciously
laid hold of. The authors of this daring act, who laid hands
on the archbishop, as well as those who consented thereto, were
all specially excommunicated in every church of the whole
kingdom, that at least the chancellor, who was hateful to
everybody, might be involved in the general malediction.

Sect. 48. Earl John, gnashing his teeth with anger against
the chancellor, whom he hated, brought a weighty complaint
before all the bishops and lords of the kingdom, of the in-
fringement of the convention by the adverse party, by the
arrest of his brother, to his own dishonour. The jurors are
summoned and are sworn to stand by their plighted promise,
and to bring it to pass as quickly as possible, that the perjurer
and breaker of his faith should repair what he had done
amiss by giving ample satisfaction. The affair, hitherto confined to trifles, now bears a serious aspect; the chancellor is
summoned by the powerful authority of all his and the earl's
mediators, to meet him and answer to the earl's accusations,
and to submit to the law, the place at Lodbridge, the day the
third of the nones of October.

Sect. 49. The earl, with the greatest part of the nobility
of the kingdom all favouring him, had awaited the chancellor
two days at the place of meeting, and on the third, in the
morning, he sent on certain of his followers to London, still
waiting at the place of meeting in case he who was expected
should either dare or deign to come. The chancellor, dreading
in himself the earl, and being suspicious of the judges, delayed to come to the place for two days; on the third
(because as every one feels conscious in his mind, so does he
conceive in his breast both hope and fear for his deeds), half-

way between hope and fear, he attempted to go to the meeting. And behold! Henry Biset, a faithful man of his, who had seen the above-mentioned party of the earl's friends passing on, putting frequently the spur to his horse, comes to meet the chancellor, and tells him that the earl, before daylight, had gone in arms to take London; and who was there, on that day, that did not take every thing as gospel, which that honourable man told them? but yet he was not guilty of falsehood, because he thought that what he had said was true. The chancellor, deceived, as all men are liable to be, immediately caused all the force that was with him to arm; and thinking that he was following close upon the earl, came before him to the city. The citizens being asked by him, for the earl was not yet come, that they would close the gates against him when he should come, refused, calling him a disturber of the land, and a traitor. For the archbishop of York, conscious of what would happen, whilst he was tarrying there some days, that he might see the end of the matter, by continual complaints and entreaties had excited them all against him; and then, for the first time, perceiving himself betrayed, he betook himself to the Tower, and the Londoners set a watch, both by land and water, that he might not escape. The earl, having knowledge of his flight, following him up with his forces, was received by the joyful citizens with lanterns and torches, for he came to town by night; and there was nothing wanting in the salutations of the flattering people, save that barbarous Chaire Basileus! which is, "Hail, dear lord!"

Sect. 50. On the next day, the earl and all the nobles of the land assembled in St. Paul's church, and first of all was heard the archbishop of York's complaint; after that, whosoever had aught against him was admitted. The accusers of the absent had an attentive and diligent hearing, and especially Hugh, bishop of Coventry, so prolix in words, who the day before had been his most familiar friend, who, as the worst pest, is a familiar enemy, having harangued more bitterly and perversely than all the rest, against his friend, did not desist until it was said by all, "We will not have this man to reign over us." So the whole assembly, without any delay, elected Earl John, the king's brother, chief justiciary of the whole kingdom, and ordaining that all the castles should be delivered to the custody of such as he should choose, they left only three of the weakest, and lying at a great dis tance from each other, to the now merely nominal chancellor. The chief justice after the earl, the justices itinerant, the barons of the Exchequer, the constables of castles, all new, are appointed afresh.   Amongst others then gainers, both the bishop of Winchester received the custodies which the chancellor had taken from him, without diminution, and the lord bishop of Durham received the county of Northumberland.

Sect. 51. That unlucky day was declining towards evening, when four bishops, and as many earls, sent on the part of the assembly to the chancellor, explained to him, to the letter, the acts of the whole day.   He was horror-struck at such unexpected presumption and arrogance, and, his vigour of mind failing, he fell to the earth so exhausted, that he foamed at the mouth.   Cold water being sprinkled on his face, he revived, and having risen on his feet, he addressed the messengers with a stern countenance, saying, " There is one help for the vanquished, to hope for no help.* You have conquered and you have bound incautiously.   If the Lord God shall grant me to see my lord the king with my two eyes, be sure this day has shone inauspiciously for you. As much as in you lay, you have now delivered to the earl, whatever was the king's in the kingdom.   Say to him, Priam still lives.   You, who forgetful of your still surviving king, have elected to yourselves another to be lord, tell to that your lord, that all will turn out otherwise than he supposes.   I will not give up the castles, I will not resign the seal."   The messengers, having returned from him, related to the earl what they had received, who ordered the Tower to be more closely besieged.

Sect. 52. The chancellor was sleepless the greater part of the night (because he who does not set his mind on honest studies and pursuits will toss about wakeful through hate or love); and at the same time his people disturbed him more than his conscience, falling prostrate at his feet, and entreating with tears that he would yield to necessity, and not stretch forth his arms against the torrent. He, though harder than iron, is softened by the piteous counsel of those who were weeping round him; again and again having fainted with grief, at last, he with much ado assented that that should be done, which, being entirely destitute of aid, he was compelled to do.   One of his brothers, and three, not ignoble, of his adherents, being permitted, not commissioned, announced to the earl at that time of night, that the chancellor, with what readiness it does not matter, was prepared to do and suffer whatever had been determined.   He should avoid delay, because it has always been injurious for those who are prepared to defer.   It should be done the next day, lest the wind should so veer, that it might be deferred for a year.   These return to the Tower, and before day, the earl made known to his adherents that these things had passed.

Sect. 53. Meanwhile, the rising dawn left the ocean, and the sun having now appeared, the earl, with his whole troop, withdrew to the open field, which is without London towards the east ; the chancellor went thither also, but less early than his adversaries.   The nobles took the centre, around whom was next a circle of citizens, and beyond an attentive populace, estimated at ten thousand men.   The bishop of Coventry first attacked the chancellor, rehearsing the several accusations of the preceding day, and ever adding something of his own. " It is not," said he, " either fit or bearable that such gross incapacity of one should so often cause so many noble and honourable men, and from such remote parts, to assemble for nothing.   And since it is better to be troubled once for all, than always, I will conclude all in few words.   It does not please, because it is not convenient, that you should any longer bear rule in the kingdom.   You will be content with your bishopric, and the three castles with which we have indulged you, and the shelter of a great name.   You will in the next place give hostages for giving up all the other castles, and for not seeking increased power or making tumults, and afterwards you will be able to depart freely whithersoever you may desire."   Many spoke much in favour of this, none against ; the lord of Winchester, although he was more eloquent than most of them, alone observed continued silence. At length the chancellor, scarcely permitted to speak, exclaimed, "Am I always to be a hearer only ? and shall I never answer ?*   Before all things, know ye each and every one, that

* Somper ego auditor tantum ?   Nunquamne reponam ?—JUVENAL.

I feel myself guilty of nothing that I should fear the mouth of
any of you.   I solemnly declare that the archbishop of York
was taken, without either my knowledge or my will; that I
will prove in the civil courts if you wish, or in the ecclesiastical.   Respecting the deficiencies of the king, if I have done
any thing amiss in that matter, Geoffrey Fitz-Peter, William
Briwere, and Hugh Bardolf, whom I received from the king
as councillors, would, if it were permitted them to speak, give
satisfaction for me.   Why and in what I have spent the king's
treasure, I am ready to give account to the utmost farthing.   I
do not refuse to give hostages for delivering up the castles,
though in this I ought rather to fear the king; yet as I must,
I must.   The name which you are not able to take away, and
I am still to bear, I do not set light by.   In short, I give you
all to know, that I depose myself from no administration
given me by the king.   You, being many, have besieged me
alone; you are stronger than I, and I, the king's chancellor
and justiciary of the kingdom, am condemned against all form
of law; it is through necessity I yield to the stronger."   The
sun declining to the west, put an end to the allegations of the
parties; the two brothers of the chancellor that was, and a
certain third person, his chamberlain, who had also been his
secretary, were received in hostage.   The assembly is dissolved, the keys of the Tower of London being given up on
the sixth of the ides of October.   The chancellor started for
Dover, one, to wit, of the three castles of which mention was
made; and the earl delivered, to those he chose and whom he
trusted most, all the fortresses of the land which had been
given up to him.

    Sect. 54. Messengers are immediately despatched to the
Land of Promise, to the king himself, both by the condemned
and the condemners, each by his own party, sufficiently instructed to accuse or excuse.   The chancellor, being uncom-
fortable here under the appellation of his lost authority, and
the recollection of his present state, whilst he endeavoured by
all means to elude the prohibition of his going abroad, got
scoffed, not uniformly, nor once only.   I will not recount
how he was taken and detained, both in the habit of a monk
and in that of a woman, because it is enough, and more than
enough, to recollect what inestimable property and immense
treasures the Flemish stripped him of, when at length he

D

arrived in Flanders. His passage over being known, whatever revenue he had possessed in England was confiscated. A most dreadful contention is carried on between the mighty. The chancellor suspends his diocese which had been taken from him, and he denounces his anathema upon all those who trespassed against him. Nor was the archbishop of Rouen more remiss in the same way, for in revenge for his presumptuous excommunication of the Exchequer barons, he commanded it to be announced throughout Normandy that William de Longchamp should be held as excommunicated. He was, however, unwilling to seem to fear the malediction uttered against the invaders of the aforesaid bishopric, nor did he believe that the sentence of a fugitive prelate could find its way before his majesty's throne. So the face of the church of Ely was disfigured, they ceased throughout the diocese from every work of the Lord, the bodies of the dead lay unburied by all the ways. In Normandy, the like being returned, none under the archbishop's authority communicated with the chancellor; on his entry every church was suspended, and on his departure all the bells were rung, and the altars where he officiated cast down.

Sect. 55. Two legates despatched into France by the pope, at the instigation, though secret, as is reported, of the king of the French, came to Gisors to visit Normandy, which they understood was a chief part of the kingdom of the French; but both the constable of the castle and the seneschal of Normandy would not admit them, excusing themselves with this shadow of a reason, that the visitation of any province should not be made unless with the approbation or in the presence of the lord of the land; all the kings of the English, and particularly Richard, being especially indulged with this privilege by the Holy See. No allegation, whether real or probable, availed with the legates; their almost divine power rose and swelled with rage, though against those who heeded them not: the contemned authority of Roman majesty is exercised; they lay aside high-flown sentences and long words. They threaten their adversaries with much bitterness; but, however, as they had not to plead with boys, the castle gates being shut against them, they stood without the doors. But their solace was not wanting, though they were repulsed. They reached with their power, where they

could not approach in person. They excommunicated by
name the constable of Gisorz and the seneschal of Normandy,
there present, and suspended the whole of Normandy from
every administration of the rites of the church. It was
necessary to yield to their power; the church was silent
immediately, and so remained the space of three weeks, until,
the pope being supplicated, both the sentence against those
named was remitted, and the suspension given out against
Normandy. The book of liberty was restored to Normandy,
and the voice of gladness, and the legates were prohibited to
set foot therein.

Sect. 56. The Westminster monks, who before those days
had so greatly excelled in magnanimity, that they would not
stain their deeds for death itself, as soon as they saw a new
era, changed also with the time, putting behind their backs
whatever they had covenanted with the chancellor for his
brother; with the connivance of the earl, they elected the
prior of their house to be abbat, who also received immediately the benediction and staff from the bishop of London.
The chancellor's brother, who by agreement should have
been elected abbat, seeing the convent break their engagement, troubled thereat, departed with his half-modesty, carrying off with him, however, the bond of security, having
made an appeal prior to the second election before legitimate
witnesses, that nothing should be done against his stipulated
promotion.

The monks of Muchelney, after the example of those of
Westminster, though not altogether in a similar way, expelled
their principal, I do not know whether abbat or abbat elect,
whom they had been forced to accept, casting forth the straw
of his bed after him, and thrust him with much insult out of
their island to the four winds of heaven.

Sect. 57. The archbishop of Rouen being constituted by
the earl justiciary of the kingdom, and supreme over affairs,
having convoked, at Canterbury, the clergy and people, as the
king himself had enjoined him, directed them to proceed to the
election of an archbishop. The bishops of London and Winchester, however, were not present, being detained at London
by the king's business, and the question being broached
among the bishops who had assembled, which of them should
be esteemed the greater, whose the election ought to be,

as the two aforesaid of chief dignity were absent, the prior
of Canterbury solving the point of difficulty, made all equal
in choosing a pontiff, and proceeding forth in public with
his monks, in the face of the whole church, elected, as
archbishop, Reginald, bishop of Bath, from the midst of the
clergy.

Sect. 58. Reginald, elect of Canterbury, who would have
proceeded to Rome for his pall, had the fates permitted,
having completed the solemnities which are usually celebrated for the elect at Canterbury, came to set things in
order in the diocese of Bath, which he greatly loved, and
by which he was more beloved. It is reported also, that
he had obtained, as he desired, the assent of the prior and
convent for electing and substituting in his place, Savaricus,
archdeacon of Northampton, and had received the security.
Returning from thence, he fell sick by the way, and was laid
up very ill at his manor of Dokemeresfeld ; and seeing
nothing more likely to happen to him than death, he took
the habit of a monk at the hands of his prior Walter, then
tarrying with him, and receiving it, spoke these words,
" God willed not that I should be archbishop, and I will not ;
God willed that I should be a monk, and I will !"   Moreover.
being in the last extremities, he took the king's letters to the
justices, for conceding to Savaricus whatever diocese he
should be elected to, and gave them to the prior of Bath,
that by the authority of this instrument he might the sooner
be promoted.   Then having accomplished all things which
relate to faith and penitence devoutly and with a sane
mind, he fell asleep in the Lord on the seventh of the calends
of January.*   His

EPITAPH.

Dum Reginaldus erat bene seque suosque regebat ;
Nemo plus quærat ; quicquid docuit faciebat.
Sancti Swithuni nisi pratum præripuisset
Hunc de communi mors tam cito non rapuisset.
Sed, qui pœnituit, minuit mors passa reatum ;
Fecit quod potuit, se dedidit ad monachatum.

Whilst Reginald lived, he well governed both himself and his men.
Let no one ask more; whatsoever he taught, he practised.   If he had

* Dec. 26.

not grasped at Saint Swithin's pasture, death would not have snatched him so soon from the public. But, because he was penitent, a premature death diminished his supposed guilt; he did what he could, he dedicated himself to the monastic life.

Walter, prior of Bath, and his convent, without the clergy, elected to themselves for their future bishop Savaricus, archdeacon of Northampton, who was absent, and as yet ignorant of the decease of his fellow-pontiff; and although the clergy resisted, they carried it out.

Sect. 59. The fleet of Richard, king of the English, put out to sea, and proceeded in this order. In the forefront went three ships only, in one of which was the queen of Sicily and the young damsel of Navarre, probably still a virgin; in the other two, a certain part of the king's treasure and arms; in each of the three, marines and provisions. In the second line there were, what with ships and busses and men-of-war, thirteen; in the third, fourteen; in the fourth, twenty; in the fifth, thirty; in the sixth, forty; in the seventh, sixty; in the last, the king himself, followed with his galleys. There was between the ships, and between their lines, a certain space left by the sailors at each interval, that from one line to another the sound of the trumpet, from one ship to another, the human voice, could be heard. This also was admirable, that the king was no less cheerful and healthy, strong and mighty, light and gay, at sea, than he was wont to be by land. I conclude, therefore, that there was not one man more powerful than he in the world, either by land or sea.

Sect. 60. Now, as the ships were proceeding in the aforesaid manner and order, some being before others, two of the three first, driven by the violence of the winds, were broken on the rocks near the port of Cyprus; the third, which was English, more speedy than they, having turned back into the deep, escaped the peril. Almost all the men of both ships got away alive to land, many of whom the hostile Cypriotes slew, some they took captive, some, taking refuge in a certain church, were besieged. Whatever also in the ships was cast up by the sea, fell a prey to the Cypriotes. The prince also of that island coming up, received for his share the gold and the arms; and he caused the shore to be guarded by all the armed force he could summon together, that he might not

permit the fleet which followed to approach, lest the king
should take again what had been thus stolen from him.
Above the port, was a strong city, and upon a natural rock,
a high and fortified castle. The whole of that nation was
warlike, and accustomed to live by theft. They placed beams
and planks at the entrance of the port, across the passage, the
gates and entrances; and the whole land, with one mind,
prepared themselves for a conflict against the English. God
so willed, that the cursed people should receive the reward of
their evil deeds by the hands of one who would not spare.
The third English ship, in which were the women, having
cast out its anchors, rode out at sea, and watched all things
from opposite, to report the misfortune to the king, lest haply,
being ignorant of the loss and disgrace, he should pass the
place unrevenged. The next line of the king's ships came
up after the other, and they all stopped at the first. A full
report reached the king, who, sending heralds to the lord of
the island, and obtaining no satisfaction, commanded his entire
army to arm, from the first even to the last, and to get out of
the great ships into the galleys and boats, and follow him to
the shore.   What he commanded, was immediately performed; they came in arms to the port. The king being
armed, leaped first from his galley, and gave the first blow in
the war; but before he was able to strike a second, he had
three thousand of his followers with him striking away by his
side. All the timber that had been placed as a barricade in
the port was cast down instantly, and the brave fellows went
up into the city, as ferocious as lionesses are wont to be when
robbed of their young. The fight was carried on manfully
against them, numbers fell down wounded on both sides, and
the swords of both parties were made drunk with blood. The
Cypriotes are vanquished, the city is taken, with the castle
besides; whatever the victors choose is ransacked, and the
lord of the island is himself taken and brought to the king.
He, being taken, supplicates and obtains pardon; he offers
homage to the king, and it is received; and he swears, though
unasked, that henceforth he will hold the island of him as his
liege lord, and will open all the castles of the land to him,
make satisfaction for the damage already done; and further,
bring presents of his own. On being dismissed after the
oath, he is commanded to fulfil the conditions in the morning.

Sect. 61. That night the king remained peaceably in the castle; and his newly-sworn vassal flying, retired to another castle, and caused the whole of the men of that land, who were able to bear arms, to be summoned to repair to him, and so they did. The king of Jerusalem, however, that same night, landed in Cyprus, that he might assist the king and salute him, whose arrival he had desired above that of any other in the whole world. On the morrow, the lord of Cyprus was sought for and found to have fled. The king, seeing that he was abused, and having been informed where he was, directed the king of Jerusalem to follow the traitor by land with the half of the army, while he conducted the other part by water, intending to be in the way, that he might not escape by sea. The divisions reassembled around the city in which he had taken refuge, and he, having sallied out against the king, fought with the English, and the battle was carried on sharply by both sides. The English would that day have been beaten, had they not fought under the command of King Richard. They at length obtained a dear-bought victory, the Cypriote flies, and the castle is taken. The kings pursue him as before, the one by land, the other by water, and he is besieged in the third castle. Its walls are cast down by engines hurling huge stones; he, being overcome, promises to surrender, if only he might not be put in iron fetters. The king consents to the prayers of the supplicant, and caused silver shackles to be made for him. The prince of the pirates being thus taken, the king traversed the whole island, and took all its castles, and placed his constables in each, and constituted justiciaries and sheriffs; and the whole land was subjected to him in every thing just like England. The gold, and the silk, and the jewels from the treasures that were broken open, he retained for himself; the silver and victuals he gave to the army. To the king of Jerusalem also he made a handsome present out of his booty.

And because Lent had already passed, and the lawful time of contract was come, he caused Berengaria, daughter of the king of Navarre, whom his mother had brought to him in Lent, to be affianced to him in the island.

Sect. 62. After these things, having taken again to the ships, whilst sailing prosperously towards Acre, he falls in with a merchant ship of immense dimensions, destined by

Saladin to the besieged, laden with provisions and full of
armed soldiers.   A wonderful ship, a ship than which, with
the exception of Noah's ark, we do not read of any being
greater.   The intrepid king here rejoices, because everywhere
he meets with a fit object for valour ; he, first of his warriors,
having summoned to him, the galleys of his followers, com-
mences the naval action with the Turks.   The ship was fortified with towers and bulwarks, and the desperate fought
furiously, because " the only hope for the conquered is to have
nothing to hope for."   The assault was dreadful and the defence stout ; but what is there so hard, that the sturdy man
who stoutly perseveres shall not subdue ?   The followers of
Mahomet* are vanquished : that ship, the queen of ships, is
shattered and sunk, as lead in the mighty waters, and the
whole property perished with its possessors.

The king, proceeding thence, came to the siege of Acre, and
was welcomed by the besiegers with as great joy as if it had
been Christ that had come again on earth to restore the
kingdom of Israel.   The king of the French had arrived at
Acre first, and was very highly esteemed by the natives ; but
on Richard's arrival he became obscured and without consideration, just as the moon is wont to relinquish her lustre at
the rising of the sun.

Sect. 63. Henry, count of Champagne, whose whole store
that he had brought both of provision and money was now
wasted, comes to his king.   He asks relief, to whom his king
and lord caused to be offered a hundred thousand of Paris
money, if, in that case, he would be ready to pledge to him
Champagne.   To that the count replied, " I have done what
I could and what I ought ; now I shall do what I am compelled by necessity.   I desired to fight for my king, but he
would not accept of me, unless for my own ; I will go to him
who will accept me: who is more ready to give than to
receive."   The king of the English, Richard, gave to Henry,
count of Champagne, when he came to him, four thousand
bushels of wheat, four thousand bacons, and four thousand
pounds of silver.   So the whole army of strangers out of
every nation under heaven bearing the Christian name, who
had already assembled to the siege long before the coming of

* Mocomicolm.

the kings, at the report of so great a largess, took King Richard to be their general and lord; the Franks only who had followed their lord remained with their poor king of the French.

Sect. 64. The king of the English, unused to delay, on the third day of his arrival at the siege, caused his wooden fortress, which he had called "Mate Grifun," when it was made in Sicily, to be built and set up, and before the dawn of the fourth day the machine stood erect by the walls of Acre, and from its height looked down upon the city lying beneath it; and there were thereon by sunrise archers casting missiles without intermission on the Turks and Thracians. Engines also for casting stones, placed in convenient positions, battered the walls with frequent volleys. More important than these, sappers making themselves a way beneath the ground, undermined the foundations of the walls; while soldiers bearing shields, having planted ladders, sought an entrance over the ramparts. The king himself was running up and down through the ranks, directing some, reproving some, and urging others, and thus was he everywhere present with every one of them, so that whatever they all did, ought properly to be ascribed to him. The king of the French also himself did not lightly assail them, making as bold an assault as he could on the tower of the city which is called Cursed.

Sect. 65. The renowned Carracois and Mestocus, after Saladin the most powerful princes of the heathen, had at that time the charge of the besieged city, who, after a contest of many days, promised by their interpreters the surrender of the city, and a ransom for their heads; but the king of the English desired to subdue their obstinacy by force; and wished that the vanquished should pay their heads for the ransom of their bodies, but, by the mediation of the king of the French, their life and indemnity of limbs only was accorded them, if, after surrender of the city and yielding of every thing they possessed, the Holy Cross should be given up.

Sect. 66. All the heathen warriors in Acre were chosen men, and were in number nine thousand. Many of whom, swallowing many gold coins, made a purse of their stomachs, because they foresaw that whatever they had of any value would be turned against them, even against themselves, if

they should again oppose the cross, and would only fall a
prey to the victors. So all of them come out before the
kings entirely disarmed, and outside the city, without money,
are given into custody ; and the kings, with triumphal
banners, having entered the city, divided the whole with all
its stores into two parts between themselves and their soldiers ;
the pontiff's seat alone its bishop received by their united
gift. The captives, moreover, being divided, Mestocus fell by
lot to the portion of the king of the English, and Carracois,
as a drop of cold water, fell into the burning mouth of the
thirsty Philip, king of the French.

Sect. 67. The duke of Austria, who was also one of the
ancient besiegers of Acre, followed the king of the English as
a participator in the possession of his portion, and because, as
his standard was borne before him, he was thought to take to
himself a part of the triumph ; if not by command, at least
with the consent, of the offended king, the duke's standard
was cast down in the dirt, and to his reproach and ridicule
trampled under foot by them. The duke, although grievously
enraged against the king, dissembled his offence, which he
could not vindicate; and having returned to the place where
he had carried on the siege, betook himself that night to his
tent, which was set up again, and afterwards, as soon as he
could, returned to his own country full of rancour.

Sect. 68. Messengers on the part of the captives having
been sent to Saladin for their ransom, when the heathen
could by no entreaty be moved to restore the Holy Cross, the
king of the English beheaded all his, with the exception of
Mestocus only, who on account of his nobility was spared,
and declared openly without any ceremony that he would act
in the same way towards Saladin himself.

Sect. 69. A certain marquess of Montferrat, a smooth-faced
man, had held Tyre, which he had seized on many years ago,
to whom the king of the French sold all his captives alive,
and promised the crown of the region which was not yet conquered ; but the king of the English withstood him to the
face. " It is not proper," said he, " for a man of your reputation to bestow or promise what is not yet obtained ; but
further, if the cause of your journey be Christ, when at length
you have taken Jerusalem, the chief of the cities of this
region, from the hand of the enemy, you will without delay

or condition restore the kingdom to Guy, the legitimate king of Jerusalem. For the rest, if you recollect, you did not obtain Acre without a participator, so that neither should that which is the property of two be dealt out by one hand." Oh! oh! how fine for a godly throat! The marquess, bereft of his blissful hope, returns to Tyre, and the king of the French, who had greatly desired to strengthen himself against his envied ally by means of the marquess, now fell off daily; and this added to the continual irritation of his mind,—that even the scullion of the king of the English fared more sumptuously than the cupbearer of the French. After some time, letters were forged in the tent of the king of the French, by which, as if they had been sent by his nobles out of France, the king was recalled to France. A cause is invented which would necessarily be respected more than it deserved; his only son, after a long illness, was now despaired of by the physicians; France exposed to be desolated, if, after the son's death, the father (as it might fall out) should perish in a foreign land. So, frequent council being held between the kings hereupon, as they were both great and could not dwell together, Abraham remaining, Lot departed from him. Moreover, the king of the French, by his chief nobles, gave security by oath for himself and his vassals, to the king of the English, that he would observe every pledge until he should return to his kingdom in peace.

Sect. 70. On that day the commonalty of the Londoners was granted and instituted, to which all the nobles of the kingdom, and even the very bishops of that province, are compelled to swear. Now for the first time London, by the agreement conceded to it, found by experience that there was no king in the kingdom, as neither King Richard himself, nor his predecessor and father Henry, would have suffered it to be concluded for one thousand thousand marks of silver. How great evils forsooth may come forth of this agreement, may be estimated by the very definition, which is this. The commonalty is the pride of the common people, the dread of the kingdom, the ferment of the priesthood.

Sect. 71. The king of the French, with but few followers, returning home from Acre, left at that place the strength of his army to do nothing, to the command of which he appointed the bishop of Beauvais and the duke of Burgundy. The

English king, having sent for the commanders of the French,
proposed that in the first place they should conjointly attempt Jerusalem itself; but the dissuasion of the French discouraged the hearts of both parties, and dispirited the troops,
and restrained the king, thus destitute of men, from his intended march upon that metropolis. The king, troubled at
this, though not despairing, from that day forth separated his
army from the French, and directing his arms to the storming
of castles along the sea-shore, he took every fortress that came
in his way from Tyre to Ascalon, though after hard fighting
and deep wounds. But to Tyre he deigned not to go, because
it was not in the compass of his part of the campaign.

IN THE YEAR OF THE LORD MCXCII.

Sect. 72. Philip, king of the French, having left his companion, Richard, king of the English, in the territory of
Jerusalem amongst the enemies of the cross of Christ, returned to France, without obtaining either the liberation of the
Holy Cross or of the Holy Sepulchre. Godfrey, bishop of
Winchester, restored to his church a great part of the treasure,
which, as related above, he had appointed, on the third of the
calends of February. The feast of the Purification of the
Blessed Mary was celebrated on the very Sunday of Septua-
gesima* at Winchester. But the Sunday had nothing belonging to Sunday but its memory at vespers and matins, and
the morning mass. One full hide of land at the manse which
is called Morslede, of the village of Ciltecumba, was let to a
certain citizen of Winchester of the name of Pentecuste, to
hold for twenty years for the annual and free service of twenty
shillings, without the privity of the convent.

Sect. 73. Queen Eleanor sailed from Normandy and landed
at Portsmouth on the third of the ides of February.† The
chancellor repaired to the king of the French, and deposed
before him his complaint relative to the loss of his treasures
in Flanders, but he got nothing more there than what makes
men ridiculous.

The king of the French caused all manner of arms to be
fabricated both day and night throughout his whole realm,

* Feb. 1.   † Feb. 11.

and fortified his cities and castles, as was thought, by way of preparation for a struggle against the king of the English, if he should return from his journey.   Which being known in the territories of the king of the English, his constables throughout Normandy, Le Mans, Anjou, Tours, Bourges, Poitou, and Gascony, of themselves fortified every place that could be fortified in the fullest manner.   Moreover, the son of the king of Navarre, to spite the French, ravaged the country about Toulouse.   A certain provost of the king of the French, desiring to become greater than his forefathers, set up a castle on the confines of Normandy and France, where there had never yet been any fortification ; which, ere it was built, the Normans, by the impulse of their natural anger, totally overthrew, and tore the provost himself to pieces.

Sect. 74.   Queen Eleanor, a lady worthy of repeated mention, visited certain houses appertaining to her dower within the diocese of Ely.   To meet her there came out of all the hamlets and manors, wherever she passed, men with women and little children, not all of the lowest class, a piteous and pitiable company, with their feet bare, their clothes unwashed, and their hair unshorn.   They speak in tears, for which, in very grief, they had failed to utter words, nor was there need of an interpreter, as more than they desired to say might be read in the open page.   Human bodies lay unburied everywhere throughout the country, because their bishop had deprived them of sepulture.   The queen, on understanding the cause of so great severity, as she was very compassionate, taking pity on the people's misery for the dead, immediately neglecting her own, and following other men's matters, repaired to London ; she entreated, nay, she demanded, of the archbishop of Rouen, that the confiscated estates of the bishop should be restored to the bishop, and that the same bishop should in the name of the chancery be proclaimed absolved from the excommunication denounced against him, throughout the province of Rouen.   And who could be so harsh or obdurate that that lady could not bend him to her wishes?   She, too, forgetful of nothing, sent word into Normandy to the lord of Ely, of the public and private restitution which she had obtained for him, and compelled him to revoke the sentence of excommunication he had pronounced against the Exchequer barons.   So by the queen's mediation there was peace between

the implacable, though their vexation was apparent, as the
disaffection of their minds, contracted in their former hatred,
could not be changed, without each giving some utterance to
his feelings.

Sect. 75. Earl John, sending messengers to Southampton,
commanded shipping to be made ready for him to depart, as
was thought, to the king of the French; but the queen his
mother, fearing lest the light-minded youth, by the counsels
of the French, might go to attempt something against his lord
and brother, with anxious mind takes in hand with her utmost
ability to divert the intention of her son. The fate of her
former sons, and the untimely decease of both under their op-
pressing sins, recurring to her mind, moved, or rather pierced,
the maternal bowels of compassion. She desired that their
violence might be enough, and that, at least, good faith being
kept amongst her younger children, she, as their mother,
might end her days more happily than had fallen to the lot of
their deceased father. So having assembled all the peers of
the realm, first at Windsor, secondly at Oxford, thirdly at
London, and fourthly at Winchester, she with her own tears
and the entreaties of the nobles with difficulty obtained that
he would not cross the sea for this time. The earl, therefore,
being in effect frustrated of his proposed passage, did what he
could that way, and received the castles from the king's constables of Windsor and Wallingford, whom he had secretly
called to him; and having received them, he delivered them
over to his lieges to keep for him.

Sect. 76. By command of the archbishop of Rouen, there
assembled at London, the pillars of the church, the oracles of
the laws, to discuss either something or nothing, as it often
falls out, in matters of state. There was but one mind among
all, to convene Earl John for the pre-occupation of the castles;
but, because no one of them durst commit himself to another,
every one desired in himself that the question should be proposed rather by a deputy than by his own mouth. So whilst
they all clamour to this end, and with this purpose, Æacus
alone is wanting, to whom they all simultaneously agreed to
resort; but even whilst among other matters they only
casually discoursed of the late chancellor, behold! again is
Crispinus at hand. The messengers of the chancellor, now
again legate, enter the assembly, saluting the queen, who was

present, and all the rest, whom by chance they found together, on the part of their lord, who had safely arrived the day before at Dover. The last clause of the mandates prohibited him from following up the ministration of his legation. Long were they all silent, and greatly astonished, intently kept their peace. At length it came to be the vote of all, that they should humbly entreat him to be their dictator and lord, whom they had assembled to judge as a perjurer and transgressor against their lord. So many of the nobles, of whom one was Echion, are sent, and that repeatedly, to Earl John, then staying at Wallingford, and laughing at their conventions. Humbly, and without austerity, they beg that he would hasten to meet the goat. "Lord!" say they, "he wears horns, beware!"

Sect. 77. The earl, not greatly moved, long suffered himself to be reverently entreated; but at length, satiated with the honour offered him, he came to London with the last intercessors, whom he most loved, sufficiently taught to answer to every question that might chance to be asked. The court rises up and compliments him on his entry, no order either of age or rank being observed; everybody that first can, first runs to meet him, and desires himself to be first seen, eager to please the prince, because to have been acceptable to the great is not the last of praises. The leaders were at a stand. Of the castles, no mention is made; the whole discussion and consultation was about the chancellor. Should the earl advise, all are ready to proscribe him. They strive by all means to soften the earl to consent, but they had a wild beast on their right hand. The earl, on being asked to answer, briefly declares, "The chancellor fears the threats of none of you, nor of you altogether, nor will he beg your love, if only he may succeed to have me alone his friend. He is to give me seven hundred pounds of silver by the seventh day, if I shall not have meddled between you and him. You see I am in want of money. To the wise, a word is sufficient." He said, and withdrew, leaving the conclusion of his proposition in the midst. The court, placed in a great strait, strained its counsel: it appeared expedient to every one to propitiate the man with more than was promised; the gift or loan of the money is approved, but not of their own, and so in the end it all falls upon the treasury of the absent king. Five hundred pounds of silver

sterling out of the Exchequer are lent to the earl by the barons,
and letters to their liking against the chancellor are received.
Nor is there delay; the queen writes, the clergy write, the
people write, all unanimously advertise the chancellor to bolt,
to cross the sea without delay, unless his ears are ticklish to
hear rumours, unless he wishes to take his meals under the
charge of armed soldiers.

Sect. 78. The chancellor stood aghast at the severity of the
mandates, and was as pale as one who treads a snake with
his bare feet. But, on retiring, is reported to have made only
this manly reply :—" Let all who persecute me, know they
shall see how great is he whom they have offended. I am not
destitute of all counsel, as they reckon. I have one who
serves me as a fine ear by true despatches. 'As long as I am
an exile,' said he, ' patiently endure the things which you
suffer. Every land is a home to the brave, believe one who
has found it so by experience; persevere and preserve your
life for a better day. A grateful hour, which is not hoped
for, will overtake both you and me. Unlooked for, I shall
return and triumph over my enemies, and again shall my
victory make thee a citizen in my kingdom, forbidden thee,
and now not obeying me ; haply it may hereafter be gratify-
ing to us to reflect on this event.' "

Sect. 79. Because Winchester ought not to be deprived of
its due reward for keeping peace with the Jews, as in the
beginning of this book is related, the Winchester Jews (after
the manner of the Jews), studious of the honour of their city,
procured themselves notoriety by murdering a boy in Winchester, with many signs of the deed, although, perhaps, the
deed was never done. The case was thus :—A certain Jew
engaged a Christian boy, a pretender to the art of shoe-
making, into the household service of his family. He did not
reside there continually to work, nor was he permitted to
complete any thing great all at once, lest his abiding with
them should apprise him of the fate intended for him ; and,
as he was remunerated better for a little labour there, than
for much elsewhere, allured by his gifts and wiles, he frequented the more freely the wretch's house. Now, he was
French by birth, under age, and an orphan, of abject condition and extreme poverty. A certain French Jew, having
unfortunately compassioned his great miseries in France, by

frequent advice persuaded him that he should go to England, a land flowing with milk and honey; he praised the English as liberal and bountiful, and that there no one would continue poor who could be recommended for honesty. The boy, ready to like whatever you may wish, as is natural with the French, having taken a certain companion of the same age as himself, and of the same country, got ready to set forward on his foreign expedition, having nothing in his hands but a staff, nothing in his wallet but a cobbler's awl.

Sect. 80. He bade farewell to his Jewish friend; to whom the Jew replied, "Go forth as a man. The God of my fathers lead thee as I desire." And having laid his hands upon his head, as if he had been the scapegoat, after certain muttering of the throat and silent imprecations, being now secure of his prey, he continued,—" Be of good courage; forget your own people and native land, for every land is the home of the brave, as the sea is for the fish, and as the whole of the wide world is for the bird. When you have entered England, if you should come to London, you will quickly pass through it, as that city greatly displeases me. Every race of men, out of every nation which is under heaven, resort thither in great numbers; every nation has introduced into that city its vices and bad manners. No one lives in it without offence; there is not a single street in it that does not abound in miserable, obscene wretches; there, in proportion as any man has exceeded in wickedness, so much is he the better. I am not ignorant of the disposition I am exhorting; you have, in addition to your youth, an ardent disposition, a slowness of memory, and a soberness of reason between extremes. I feel in myself no uneasiness about you, unless you should abide with men of corrupt lives; for from our associations our manners are formed. But let that be as it may. You will come to London. Behold! I warn you, whatever of evil or of perversity there is in any, whatever in all parts of the world, you will find in that city alone. Go not to the dances of panders, nor mix yourself up with the herds of the stews; avoid the talus and the dice, the theatre and the tavern. You will find more braggadocios there than in all France, while the number of flatterers is infinite. Stage-players, buffoons, those that have no hair on their bodies, Garamantes, pickthanks, catamites, effeminate sodomites, lewd musical girls,

E

druggists, lustful persons, fortune-tellers, extortioners, nightly
strollers, magicians, mimics, common beggars, tatterdemalions,
—this whole crew has filled every house. So if you do not
wish to live with the shameful, you will not dwell in London.
I am not speaking against the learned, whether monks or
Jews; although, still, from their very dwelling together with
such evil persons, I should esteem them less perfect there than
elsewhere.

Sect. 81. "Nor does my advice go so far, as that you
should betake yourself to no city; with my counsel you will
take up your residence nowhere but in a town, though it
remains to say in what. Therefore, if you should land near
Canterbury, you will have to lose your way, if even you
should but pass through it. It is an assemblage of the vilest,
entirely devoted to their —— I know not whom, but who has
been lately canonized, and had been the archbishop of Canterbury, as everywhere they die in open day in the streets for
want of bread and employment. Rochester and Chichester
are mere villages, and they possess nothing for which they
should be called cities, but the sees of their bishops. Oxford
scarcely, I will not say satisfies, but sustains, its clerks.
Exeter supports men and beasts with the same grain. Bath
is placed, or rather buried, in the lowest parts of the valleys,
in a very dense atmosphere and sulphury vapour, as it were
at the gates of hell. Nor yet will you select your habitation
in the northern cities, Worcester, Chester, Hereford, on
account of the desperate Welshmen. York abounds in Scots,
vile and faithless men, or rather rascals. The town of Ely is
always putrefied by the surrounding marshes. In Durham,
Norwich, or Lincoln, there are very few of your disposition
among the powerful; you will never hear any one speak
French. At Bristol, there is nobody who is not, or has not
been, a soapmaker, and every Frenchman esteems soapmakers
as he does nightmen. After the cities, every market, village,
or town, has but rude and rustic inhabitants. Moreover, at
all times, account the Cornish people for such as you know
our Flemish are accounted in France. For the rest, the kingdom itself is generally most favoured with the dew of heaven
and the fatness of the earth; and in every place there are
some good, but much fewer in them all than in Winchester
alone.

Sect. 82. "This is in those parts the Jerusalem of the Jews, in it alone they enjoy perpetual peace; it is the school of those who desire to live well and prosper. Here they become men, here there is bread and wine enough for nothing. There are therein monks of such compassion and gentleness, clergy of such understanding and frankness, citizens of such civility and good faith, ladies of such beauty and modesty, that little hinders but I should go there and become a Christian with such Christians. To that city I direct you, the city of cities, the mother of all, the best above all. There is but one fault, and that alone in which they customarily indulge too much. With the exception I should say of the learned and of the Jews, the Winchester people tell lies like watchmen, but it is in making up reports. For in no place under heaven so many false rumours are fabricated so easily as there; otherwise they are true in every thing. I should have many things too still to tell you about business; but for fear you should not understand or should forget, you will place this familiar note in the hands of the Jew my friend, and I think, too, you may some time be rewarded by him." The short note was in Hebrew. The Jew made an end of his speech, and the boy having understood all things for good, came to Winchester.

Sect. 83. His awl supplied him, and his companion as well, with food, and the cruel courtesy and deceitful beneficence of the Jew was by the letter unfortunately obtained to their relief. Wherever the poor fellows worked or eat apart by day, they reposed every night in one little bed in the same old cottage of a certain old woman. Days follow days, and months months, and in the same way as we have hitherto so carefully described, our boys hasten the time of their separation that they may meet again. The day of the Holy Cross had arrived, and the boy that same day, whilst working at his Jew's, being by some means put out of the way, was not forthcoming. Now the Passover, a feast of the Jews, was at hand. His companion, during the evening, greatly surprised at his absence, not returning home to bed, was terrified that night with many visions and dreams. When he had sought him several days in all corners of the city without success, he came to the Jew and simply asked if he had sent his benefactor anywhere; whom when he found violently enraged beyond his general disposition, from having been so courteous

the day before, and noticed the incoherence of his words
and change of countenance, he presently fired up, and as he
was of a shrill voice and admirable readiness of speech, he
broke out into abuse, and with great clamour challenged him
with taking his companion away. " Thou son of a sordid harlot," said he; " thou robber, thou traitor, thou devil, thou hast
crucified my friend. Alas, me! wherefore have I not now
the strength of a man! I would tear you to pieces with my
hands." The noise of his quarrelling in the house is heard in
the street, Jews and Christians come running together from
all quarters. The boy persists, and now, deriving courage
from the crowd, addressing those present, he alleged his concern for his companion as an excuse. " O you good people,"
said he, " who are assembled, behold if there is any sorrow
like my sorrow. That Jew is a devil; he has stolen away
my heart from my breast—he has butchered my only companion, and I presume too that he has eaten him. A certain
son of the devil, a Jew of French birth, I neither know nor
am acquainted with; that Jew gave my comrade letters of
his death-warrant to that man. To this city he came, induced,
or rather seduced. He often gave attendance upon this Jew,
and in his house he was last seen." He was not without a
witness to some points, inasmuch as a Christian woman, who,
contrary to the canons, had nursed up the young Jews in the
same house, constantly swore that she had seen the boy go
down into the Jew's store, without coming up again. The
Jew denies it—the case is referred to the judges. The accusers are defective; the boy because he was under age, the
woman because the service of Jews had rendered her ignominious. The Jew offered to clear his conscience of the evil
report. Gold contented the judges. Phineas gave and
pleased, and the controversy ceased.

Sect. 84. The bishop of Chester, who, from his detestation
of religion, had expelled the monks from Coventry, entirely
broke down all the workshops there were in the monastery,
that by the altered appearance of the place, all remembrance
of its past state might be taken away from posterity. And
further, lest the ruin of the walls should some day bespeak
their author, the church of the place, which had not been
finished, was found a ready plea, and having bestowed the
materials upon it, without charge, he began to build. More-

over, he appointed the masons and plasterers their hire out of
the chattels of the monastery. He selected two principal
manors of the monks for his own proper use ; this arrangement
being made for their abuse—that wherever he should eat,
some special delicacy provided out of the issues of the aforesaid manors should be presented to him to eat, that he might
glory in the victory, and might batten, as it were, on the
viscera of the monks, whom he had by his wickedness overcome. But all the rest of their revenues he allotted to the
prebends, some of which he conferred and settled for ever on
the Romish church, appropriated to certain cardinals of the
Apostolic See, appointing them and their canonical successors
in the same titles to be canons of the church of Coventry, that
if by any chance there should be any delay to the transactions
before the pope, he should make the whole court the more
ready in the defence of his part ; he conferred the other prebends on others, but not one on any whom he did not know
for certain to be an advocate of no religion. They built
eagerly, even the absent canons, around the church spacious
and lofty villas, perhaps for their own use, if even once in
their lives any chance should offer a cause for visiting the place.
None of the prebendaries regularly resided there any more than
they do elsewhere ; but doing great things for the gates of
palaces, they have left to poor vicars, induced by a trifling
remuneration, to insult God ; to them have they intrusted the
holy chant and vanquished household gods and bare church
walls.

Sect. 85. This forsooth is true religion ; this should the
church imitate and emulate. It will be permitted the secular
canon to be absent from his church as long as he may please,
and to consume the patrimony of Christ where, and when,
in whatsoever luxuries he may list. Let them only provide
this, that a frequent vociferation be heard in the house of the
Lord. If the stranger should knock at the doors of such, if
the poor should cry, he who lives before the doors will
answer (he himself being a sufficiently needy vicar), " Pass
on, and seek elsewhere for alms, for the master of the house
is not at home." This is that glorious religion of the clerks,
for the sake of which the bishop of Chester, the first of men
that durst commit so great iniquity, expelled his monks from
Coventry. For the sake of clerks irregularly regular—that

is to say, of canons, he capriciously turned out the monks; monks who, not with another's, but with their own mouth praised the Lord, who dwelt and walked in the house of the Lord with unanimity all the days of their life, who beyond their food and raiment knew nothing earthly, whose bread was always for the poor, whose door was at all times open to every traveller: nor did they thus please the bishop, who never loved either monks or their order. A man of bitter jocularity, who even, though he might sometimes spare, never ceased to worry the monks. O what a fat morsel, and not to be absorbed, is a monk! many a thousand has that bit choked, while the wicked at their death have had it for their viaticum. If as often as a monk was calumniated and reproached he was consumed, all religion would be absorbed before many ages. At all times and in every place, whether the bishop spoke in earnest or in jest, a monk was some part of his discourse. Nor did the expulsion of his own monks satisfy him, but ever after, true to himself, he continued censuring the monks as before. But as he could not desist from speaking of them, lest he should incur the opprobrium of a detractor, if in their absence he should carp at their order, he resolved to keep some monk abiding with him in his court; that his conversation about them might be made less offensive, by the presence and audience of one of them. So he took as his quasi chaplain a certain monk, scarcely of age, but yet who had professed at Burton, whom to the scandal of religion he generally took about with him. O excess of sorrow! Even among the angels of God is found iniquity. The monk, wise and prudent, seduced to the delusion, hardened his forehead as a harlot, that he a monk should not blush when monks were reviled. Alas! how great a thirst for roving and riding! Hear me and attend a little; you shall see how the riding of this rider concluded. On a certain day, as the bishop was standing over his workmen at Coventry, his monk attending close by his side, on whom the bishop familiarly resting, said, "Is it not proper and expedient, my monk, even in your judgment, that the great beauty of so fair a church, that such a comely edifice, should rather be appropriated to gods than devils?" And while the monk was hesitating at the obscurity of the words, he added, "I," said he, "call my clerks gods, and monks devils!" And presently putting forth the forefinger of his right hand towards his clerks, who were standing round him, he continued, "I say ye are gods, and ye are all the children of the Highest!" And having turned again to the left, concluded to the monk, "But ye monks shall die like devils; and as one and the greatest of your princes ye shall fall away into hell, because ye are devils upon earth. Truly if it should befal me to officiate for a dead monk, which I should be very unwilling to do, I would commend his body and soul not to God, but to the devil!" The monk, who was standing in the very place that the monks had been plundered of, did not refute the insult on the monks, and because on such an occasion he was silent, met, as he deserved, with the reward of eternal silence being imposed upon him. For suddenly a stone falling from the steeple of the church, dashed out the brains of the monk who was attending on the bishop, the bishop being preserved in safety for some greater judgment.

Sect. 86. The king of the English, Richard, had already completed two years in conquering the region around Jerusalem, and during all that time there had no aid been sent to him from any of his kingdoms. Nor yet were his only and uterine brother, John, earl of Mortain, nor his justiciaries, nor his other nobles, observed to take any care to send him any part of his revenues; but they did not even think of his return. However, prayer was made without ceasing by the church to God for him. The king's army was decreased daily in the Land of Promise, and besides those who were slain with the sword, many thousands of the people perished every month by the too sudden extremities of the nightly cold and the daily heat. When it appeared that they would all have to die there, every one had to choose whether he would die as a coward or in battle. On the other side, the strength of the Gentiles greatly increased, and their confidence was strengthened by the misfortunes of the Christians; their army was relieved at certain times by fresh troops; the weather was natural to them; the place was their native country; their labour, health; their frugality, medicine. Amongst the Normans, on the contrary, that became a disadvantage which to the adversaries brought gain. For if our people lived sparingly even once in a week, they were rendered less effective for seven weeks after. The mingled nation of French and

English fared sumptuously every day, and (saving the reverence of the French) even to loathing, at whatever cost, while their treasure lasted; and the well-known custom of the English being continually kept up even under the very clarions and the clangour of the trumpet or horn, they gaped with due devotion while the chalices were emptied to the dregs. The merchants of the country, who brought the victuals to the camp, were astonished at their wonderful and extraordinary habits, and could scarcely believe even what they saw to be true, that one people, and that small in number, consumed threefold the bread and a hundred-fold the wine more than that whereon many nations of the Gentiles had been sustained, and some of those nations innumerable. And the hand of the Lord was deservedly laid upon them according to their merits. So great want of food followed their great gluttony, that their teeth scarcely spared their fingers, as their hands presented to their mouths less than their usual allowance. To these and other calamities, which were severe and many, a much greater was added by the sickness of the king.

Sect. 87. The king was extremely sick, and confined to his bed; his fever continued without intermission; the physicians whispered that it was an acute semitertian. And as they despaired of his recovery even from the first terrible dismay was spread from the king's abode through the camp. There were few among the many thousands who did not meditate on flight, and the utmost confusion of dispersion or surrender would have followed, had not Hubert Walter, bishop of Salisbury, immediately assembled the council. He obtained by forcible allegations that the army should not break up until a truce was demanded of Saladin. All well armed stand in array more steadily than usual, and with a threatening look concealing the reluctance of their mind, they feign a desire for battle. No one speaks of the indisposition of the king, lest the secret of their intense sorrow should be disclosed to the enemy; for it was thoroughly understood that Saladin feared the charge of the whole army less than that of the king alone; and if he should know that he was dead, he would instantly pelt the French with cow-dung, and intoxicate the best of the English drunkard with a dose which should make them tremble.

Sect. 88. In the meantime, a certain Gentile, called Saffatin, came down to see the king, as he generally did; he was a brother of Saladin, an ancient man of war of remarkable politeness and intelligence, and one whom the king's magnanimity and munificence had charmed even to the love of his person and favour of his party. The king's servants greeting him less joyfully than they were accustomed, and not admitting him to an interview with the king, " I perceive," said he by his interpreter, " that you are greatly afflicted ; nor am I ignorant of the cause. My friend, your king, is sick, and therefore you close his doors to me." And falling into tears, with his whole heart, he exclaimed, " O God of the Christians, if thou be a God, do not suffer such a man, so necessary to thy people, to fall so suddenly!" He was intrusted with their avowal, and thus spoke on : " In truth I forewarn you, that if the king should die while things stand as they are at present, all you Christians will perish, and all this region will in time to come be ours without contest. Shall we at all dread that stout king of France, who before he came into battle was defeated,—whose whole strength, which three years had contributed, the short space of three months consumed ? Hither will he on no account return any more ; for we always esteem this as a sure token (I am not speaking craftily, but simply), that those whom at first we think cowardly, we ever after find worse. But that king, of all the princes of the Christian name whom the round circle of the whole world encompasses, is alone worthy of the honour of a captain and the name of a king, because he commenced well, and went on better, and will be crowned by the most prosperous result, if only he shall remain with you a short time.

Sect. 89. " It is not a new thing for us to dread the English, for fame reported to us his father to be such, that had he come even unarmed to our parts, we should all have fled, though armed, nor would it have appeared inglorious to us to be put to flight by him. He our terror, a wonderful man in his day, is dead ; but, like the phœnix, renewed himself, a thousand times better, in his son. It was not unknown to us how great that Richard was, even while his father lived ; for all the days of his father, we had our agents in those parts, who informed us both of the king's deeds, and of the birth and death of his sons. He was justly beloved for his probity by

his father above all his brothers, and preferred before them to
the government of his states.   It was not unknown to us that
when he was made duke of Aquitaine he speedily and
valiantly crushed the tyrants of the province, who had been
invincible before his grandfather and great grandfather ;—how
terrible he was even to the king of France himself, as well as
to all the governors of the regions on his borders.   None took
of his to himself, though he always pushed his bounds into his
neighbours'.   It was not unknown to us, that his two bro·
thers, the one already crowned king, the other duke of Bre-
tagne, had set themselves up against their dear father, and that
he ceased not to persecute them with the rigour of war, till he
had given them both eternal repose, vanquished as they were
by the length of the prosecution.   Besides, as you will the
more wonder at, we know all the cities of your parts by
name ; nor are we ignorant that the king of your country was
beaten at Le Mans through the treachery of his own people,
that he died at Chinon, and was buried at Fontevraud.

Sect. 90. " It is not through ignorance that I do not relate
who made himself the author of such unusual and mighty
slaughter against us.   O ! if that Richard, whom although I
love yet I fear, if he were despatched out of the way, how
little should we then fear, how very little should we make
account of that youngest of the sons, who sleeps at home in
clover ! It was not unknown to us, that Richard, who nobly
succeeded his great father in the kingdom, immediately set
forward against us even in the very year of his coronation.
The number of his ships and troops was not unknown to us
before his setting forth.   We knew, even at the very time,
with what speed he took Messina, the well-fortified city of
Sicily, which he besieged ; and although none of our people
believed it, yet our fears increased, and fame added false ter-
rors to the true.

Sect. 91. " His valour, unable to rest in one place, proceeded through a boundless region, and everywhere left
trophies of his courage.   We questioned among ourselves
whether he made ready to subdue, for his God, the Land of
Promise only, or, at the same time, to take the whole world
for himself.   Who shall worthily relate the capture of
Cyprus ? Verily had the island of Cyprus been close to
Egypt, and had my brother Saladin subdued it in ten years,

his name would have been reckoned by the people among the
names of the gods. When, however, we at last perceived
that he overthrew whatever resisted his purpose, our hearts
were melted as the hoar frost melts at the appearance of the
approaching sun, forasmuch as it was said of him that he ate
his enemies alive. And if he were not presently, on the very
day of his arrival before Acre, received freely into the city
with open gates, fear alone was the cause. It was not from
their desire to preserve the city, but through dread of the torments promised them and their despair of life that they fought
so bravely, or rather desperately, fearing this more than death,
endeavouring this by all means, namely, that they should not
die unrevenged. And this was not from sheer obstinacy, but
to follow up the doctrine of our faith. For we believe that
the spirits of the unavenged wander for ever, and that they
are deprived of all rest. But what did the rashness and
timidity of the devoted profit them? Being vanquished by
force, and constrained by fear to surrender, they were punished
with a more lenient death than they had expected. And yet,
oh! shame on the Gentiles! their spirits wandered unavenged! I swear to you by the Great God, that if, after he
had gained Acre, he had immediately led his army to Jerusalem,
he would not have found even one of our people in the whole
circuit of the Christians' land; on the contrary, we should
have offered to him inestimable treasure, that he might not
proceed, that he might not prosecute us further.

Sect. 92. "But, thanks be to God! he was burdened with
the king of the French, and hindered by him, like a cat with
a hammer tied to its tail. To conclude, we, though his rivals,
see nothing in Richard that we can find fault with but his
valour; nothing to hate but his experience in war. But what
glory is there in fighting with a sick man? And although this
very morning I could have wished that both you and he had all
received your final doom, now I compassionate you on account
of your king's illness. I will either obtain for you a settled
peace with my brother, or at the least a good and durable
truce. But until I return to you, do not by any means speak
of it to the king, lest, if he should be excited, he may get
worse, for he is of so lofty and impatient a disposition, that,
even though he should needs presently die, he would not consent to an arrangement, without seeing the advantage on his

side!" He would have spoken further, but his tongue, languishing and failing for sorrow, would not continue his harangue, so with his head resting in his clasped hands he wept sore.

Sect. 93. The bishop of Salisbury, and such of the most trusty of the king's household as were present, who had secretly deliberated with him upon this subject, reluctantly consented to the truce which before they had determined to purchase at any price, as if it had been detested, and not desired by them. So their right hands being given and received, Saffatin, when he had washed his face, and disguised his sorrow, returned to Jerusalem, to Saladin. The council was assembled before his brother, and after seventeen days of weighty argument, he with difficulty succeeded in prevailing on the stubbornness of the Gentiles to grant a truce to the Christians. The time was appointed and the form approved. If it please King Richard, for the space of three years, three months, three weeks, three days, and three hours, such a truce shall be observed between the Christians and the Gentiles, that whatever either one party or the other in anywise possesses, he shall possess without molestation to the end; it will be permitted during the interval, that the Christians at their pleasure may fortify Acre only, and the Gentiles Jerusalem. All contracts, commerce, every act and every thing shall be mutually carried on by all in peace. Saffatin himself is despatched to the English as the bearer of this decree.

Sect. 94. Whilst King Richard was sick at Jaffa, word was brought him that the duke of Burgundy was taken dangerously ill at Acre. The day was the day for the king's fever to take its turn, and through his delight at this report, it left him. The king immediately with uplifted hands imprecated a curse upon him, saying, "May God destroy him, for he would not destroy the enemies of our faith with me, although he had long served in my pay." On the third day the duke died; as soon as his decease was known, the bishop of Beauvais, having left the king with all his men, came in haste to Acre; the French out of all the towns assembled before him, all but Henry, count of Champagne, King Richard's nephew by his sister. And the bishop, being made their leader and bully, set forth a proclamation and commanded them all to return home.

Sect. 95. The fleet was made ready, and the glorious prince retreating with his cowardly troop, sails over the Etruscan Sea. Having landed on the German coast, he spreads abroad among the people, during the whole of his journey, that that traitor the king of England, from the first moment of his arrival in Judea, had endeavoured to betray his lord the king of the French to Saladin; that, as soon as he had obtained Tyre, he caused the marquess to be murdered; that he had despatched the duke of Burgundy by poison; that at the last he had sold generally the whole army of the Christians who did not obey him; that he was a man of singular ferocity, of harsh and repulsive manners, subtle in treachery, and most cunning in dissimulation; that on that account the king of the French had returned home so soon; that on that account the French who remained had left Jerusalem unredeemed. This report gained strength by circulation, and provoked against one man the hatred of all.

Sect. 96. The bishop of Beauvais, having returned to France, secretly whispered in the king's ear, that the king of England had sent assassins to France who would murder him. The king, alarmed at that, appointed, though against the custom of his country, a chosen body-guard; he further sent ambassadors to the emperor of Germany with presents, and carefully persuaded his imperial majesty to a hatred of the king of England. So it was enjoined by an imperial edict, that all cities and princes of the empire should take the king of the English by force, if by chance in his return from Judea he should happen to pass through their countries, and present him to him alive or dead. If any one spared him, he should be punished as the public enemy of the empire. All obeyed the emperor's charge; and especially that duke of Austria whom the king of England had dismissed at Acre.

Sect. 97. Henry, count of Champagne, now the only one of the French nobles left in Judea, returned to the king of the English, to Jaffa; and when he announced to him both the death of the duke of Burgundy and the departure of the French, the hope of the king so revived, that he presently experienced a perfect convalescence with a healthy perspiration; and having resumed his strength of body more by the high temper of his mind than by repose or nourishment, he issued a command through the whole coast from Tyre to Ascalon, that

all who were able to serve in the wars should come to the
service at the king's charges.   There assembled before him a
countless multitude, the greater part of whom were foot;
which being rejected, as they were useless, he mustered the
horse, and scarcely found five hundred knights and two
thousand shield-bearers whose lords had perished.   And not
mistrustful on account of their small number, he being a most
excellent orator, strengthened the minds of the fearful in a sea-
sonable harangue.   He commanded that it should be proclaimed through the companies that on the third day they
must follow the king to battle, either to die as martyrs or to
take Jerusalem by storm.   This was the sum of his project,
because as yet he knew nothing of the truce.   For there was
no one who durst even hint to him, who had so unexpectedly
recovered, that which, without his knowledge, they had undertaken through fear of his death.   However, Hubert Walter,
bishop of Salisbury, took counsel with Count Henry concerning the truce, and obtained his ready concurrence in his wishes.
So having deliberated together by what stratagem they might
be able without danger to hinder such a hazardous engagement, they conceived one of a thousand, namely, to dissuade
the people if possible from the enterprise.   And the matter
turned out most favourably; the spirit of those who were
going to fight had so greatly failed, even without dissuasion,
that on the appointed day, when the king, according to his
custom leading the van, marshalled his army, there were not
found of all the knights and shield-bearers above nine hundred.
On account of which defection, the king, greatly enraged, or
rather raving, and champing with his teeth the pine rod which
he held in his hand, at length unbridled his indignant lips as
follows :—" O God !" said he, " O God, my God, why hast
thou forsaken me ?   For whom have we foolish Christians, for
whom have we English come hither from the furthest parts of
the earth to bear our arms?   Is it not for the God of the
Christians ?   O fie !   How good art thou to us thy people,
who now are for thy name given up to the sword ; we shall
become a portion for foxes.   O how unwilling should I be to
forsake thee in so forlorn and dreadful a position, were I thy
lord and advocate as thou art mine !   In sooth, my standards
will in future be despised, not through my fault but through
thine ; in sooth, not through any cowardice of my warfare, art

thou thyself, my King and my God, conquered this day, and not Richard thy vassal."

Sect. 98. He said, and returned to the camp extremely dejected; and as a fit occasion now offered, Bishop Hubert and Henry, count of Champagne, approaching him with unwonted familiarity, and as if nothing had yet been arranged, importuned under divers pretexts the king's consent for making such overtures to the Gentiles as were necessary. And thus the king answered them: "Since it generally happens that a troubled mind rather thwarts than affords sound judgment—I, who am greatly perplexed in mind, authorize you, who have as I see a collected mind, to arrange what you shall think most proper for the good of peace." They having gained their desires, chose messengers to send to Saffatin upon these matters; Saffatin, who had returned from Jerusalem, is suddenly announced to be at hand; the count and the bishop go to meet him, and being assured by him of the truce, they instruct him how he must speak with the lord their king. Saffatin being admitted to an interview with the king as one who before had been his friend, could scarcely prevail with the king not to make himself a sacrifice, and to consent to the truce. For so great were the man's strength of body, mental courage, and entire trust in Christ, that he could hardly be prevailed upon not to undertake in his own person a single combat with a thousand of the choicest Gentiles, as he was destitute of soldiers. And as he was not permitted to break off in this way, he chose another evasion, that, after a truce of seven weeks, the stipulations of the compact being preserved, it should remain for him to choose whether it were better to fight or to forbear. The right hands are given by both parties for faithfully observing this last agreement; and Saffatin, more honoured than burdened with the king's present, goes back again to his brother, to return at the expiration of the term for the final conclusion or breaking off of the above truce.

Sect. 99. Richard, king of England, held a council at Acre, and there prudently regulating the government of that state, he appointed his nephew, Henry, count of Champagne, on whom he had formerly conferred Tyre, to be captain and lord of the whole Land of Promise. Only he thought proper to defer his consecration as king till haply he might be crowned at Jerusalem. King Richard now thinking to return home, when

with the assistance of Count Henry he had appointed chosen
men for all the strongholds that had been taken in his territories, found Ascalon alone without ward or inhabitant for
want of people. Wherefore, taking precaution that it might
not become a receptacle of the Gentiles, he caused the ramparts and fortifications of the castle to be cast down. The
seventh day of the seventh week appeared, and behold Saffa
tin, with many mighty ones who desired to see the face of the
king, drew near; the truce was confirmed on both sides by
oath, this being added to that which had been previously settled, that during the continuance of the truce no one, whether
Christian or Gentile, should inhabit Ascalon, and that the
whole of the tillage pertaining to the town should remain to
the Christians. Hubert, bishop of Salisbury, and Henry,
captain of Judea, together with a numerous band, went up to
Jerusalem to worship in the place where the feet of Christ had
stood. And there was woeful misery to be seen—captive confessors of the Christian name, wearing out a hard and constant
martyrdom; chained together in gangs, their feet blistered,
their shoulders raw, their backsides goaded, their backs wealed,
they carried materials to the hands of the masons and stone-
layers to make Jerusalem impregnable against the Christians.
When the captain and bishop had returned from the sacred
places, they endeavoured to persuade the king to go up; but
the worthy indignation of his noble mind could not consent to
receive that from the courtesy of the Gentiles which he could
not obtain by the gift of God.

GEOFFREY DE VINSAUF'S

ITINERARY OF RICHARD I. AND OTHERS,

TO THE HOLY LAND.

GEOFFREY DE VINSAUF'S

ITINERARY OF RICHARD I. AND OTHERS,

TO THE HOLY LAND.

PROLOGUE

*To the Itinerary of those who went in pilgrimage to the Holy
Land in the time of Saladin, and to the exploits of Richard
king of England, and of the king of France, and of the
emperor of Germany.*

It sometimes happens, that exploits, however well known
and splendidly achieved, come, by length of time, to be less
known to fame, or even forgotten among posterity. In this
manner the renown of many kings has faded, and their deeds
have sunk with them into the grave where their bodies lie
buried—deeds that had been performed with great splendour, and
were much celebrated in their own times, when their novelty
brought them into favour, and unanimous applause set them up
as models before the people. The ancient Greeks, aware of
this, were wise enough to use the pen as a remedy against
oblivion, and zealously stimulated their writers, whom they
termed historiographers, to compile histories of noble deeds.
Thus the silence of the living voice was supplied by the voice
of writing, so that the virtues of men might not die with
them. The Romans, emulating the Greeks, with the view
of perpetuating merit, not only employed the service of the
pen, but also added sculpture : and thus by exhibiting the
ancients they excited their descendants, and impressed the love

F 2

of virtue the more strongly on the minds of its imitators,
conveying it in various ways, both through their eyes and
through their ears. Who would now know anything about
the voyage of Jason, the labours of Hercules, the glory of
Alexander, or the victories of Cæsar, if it had not been for
the service which writers have rendered? And, to adduce
the examples of the Holy Fathers, I may say, that neither
the patience of Job, the liberality of Abraham, nor the gentleness of David, would have remained as an example among
the faithful of after-ages, if antiquity, with a due appreciation
of truth, had not bequeathed history for our perusal. Indeed, kings formerly, when they became the objects of praise,
were most anxious, that, whilst they stood high in the estima-
tion of their contemporaries, they might also descend to the
knowledge of posterity. However numerous have been the
historians, most of them have recorded what they heard ; few
what they have seen. If Dares Phrygius* is more readily
believed about the destruction of Troy, because he was an
eyewitness of what others related only on hearsay, we also,
who treat of the history of Jerusalem, are justly entitled to
credit ; for we testify what we have seen, and celebrate
these deeds with the pen, whilst our memory of them retains its freshness. If the fastidious reader require a more
elegant style, let him consider that we wrote while in the
camp, and that the noise of war did not admit of calm and
silent meditation. Truth has charms enough in herself, and
even though not decked out in pompous array, still possesses sufficient attractions for all who are desirous of learning
her secrets.

* Dares Phrygius, now universally acknowledged to be a forgery, was
nevertheless one of the most popular writers of the middle ages. Historical and literary criticism being then at a very low ebb, few, if any,
suspected the truth of a writer who boasted that he had been present at
the war of Troy.

MASTER GEOFFREY DE VINSAUF.

BOOK I.

CH. I.—IN the year of the Incarnate Word 1187, when Urban III. held the government of the Apostolic See, and Frederic was emperor of Germany; when Isaac was reigning at Constantinople, Philip in France, Henry in England, and William in Sicily, the Lord's hand fell heavy upon his people, if indeed it is right to call those *his* people, whom uncleanness of life and habits, and the foulness of their vices, had alienated from his favour. Their licentiousness had indeed become so flagrant that they all of them, casting aside the veil of shame, rushed headlong, in the face of day, into crime. It would be a long task and incompatible with our present purpose to disclose the scenes of blood, robbery, and adultery, which disgraced them, for this work of mine is a history of deeds and not a moral treatise: but when the ancient enemy had diffused, far and near, the spirit of corruption, he more especially took possession of the land of Syria, so that other nations now drew an example of uncleanness from the same source which formerly had supplied them with the elements of religion. For this cause, therefore, the Lord seeing that the land of his birth and place of his passion had sunk into an abyss of turpitude, treated with neglect his inheritance, and suffered Saladin, the rod of his wrath, to put forth his fury to the destruction of that stiff-necked people; for he would rather that the Holy Land should, for a short time,

be subject to the profane rites of the heathen, than that it
snould any longer be possessed by those men, whom no
regard for what is right could deter from things unlawful.
The approach of future destruction was foretold by divers
events : famine, earthquakes, and frequent eclipses, both of
the sun and of the moon.   And that strong wind also,
which astronomers prophesied would spring out of the conjunction of the planets, became changed to the signification
of this event.   It was a mighty wind indeed ; it shook the
four cardinal points of the earth, and foreshewed that the
whole of the globe was about to be stirred up to troubles and
wars.

Ch. II.—*How Saladin invaded Palestine.*

SALADIN, therefore, having assembled his bands of warriors,
violently assailed Palestine, and sent forward Manafaradin,
admiral of Edessa, with 7,000 Turks, to ravage the Holy
Land.   This man, when he had marched as far as the parts
about Tiberias, was there encountered by Gerard de Riddeford, master of the Templars,* and Roger de Moulins, master
of the Hospital ; one of whom they routed and put to flight,
and slew the other in a sudden attack.   In this battle a few
of our soldiers were cut off and surrounded by an immense
multitude, which led to an achievement of distinction which
deserves to be recorded.   A certain knight of the Temple,
by birth a German, named Jakeline de Maillé, by his extraordinary valour provoked the enemy to turn all their
attacks on him.   His fellow-soldiers, who were estimated
about 500 in number, were all either taken or slain, and he
alone sustained the weight of the whole battle,—a glorious
champion for God's law!   At length, hemmed in by the
enemy's troops, and destitute of all human aid, seeing so
many thousands rushing upon him on every side, he gathered
up his whole courage for an effort, and bravely faced the foe
alone.   His valour attracted the admiration of his enemies ;
they were filled with compassion for him, and called earnestly

* There is some doubt whether the grand master of the Templars at
this time was named Riddeford or Biddeford.   The readings of the MSS.
vary between Riddeford, Biddeford, and Tiddeford, but probability seems
to be in favour of the first.   After the battle, Roger de Moulins was
found dead among a heap of Turks and Saracens whom he had slain with
his own hand.   Jacqueline de Maillé was the maræchal of the Temple.

to him to surrender. He, however, turning a deaf ear to their
exhortations, was not afraid to die for Christ, but overwhelmed
with the load of javelins, stones, and lances, rather than
vanquished, he at length was with difficulty slain, and his
soul fled triumphant, bearing the palm of martyrdom, to the
heavenly kingdom. His death indeed was rendered glorious,
since by his single sword so large a circle of dead bodies had
been heaped around him. It was sweet for a man to die thus,
himself in the centre, surrounded by the unbelievers whom
his brave arm had slaughtered. [And inasmuch as he
rode on a white horse and fought that day in white armour,
the idolaters who knew St. Gregory to have fought in such
costume, boasted that they had slain the knight of the white
armour, who was the bulwark of the Christians.*] There
was, in the place of this conflict, some stubble which the
reaper had left after the ears had been cut off a short time
before, but the Turks had rushed over it in such multitudes, and this single champion had held out so long against
them, that the field in which they stood was wholly trampled
to dust, and shewed no signs of a crop of corn ever having
grown there. It is said, there were some who sprinkled the
limbs of the dead man with dust, which they afterwards placed
on their own heads, believing that they derived force from
the contact; and one man, as is said, more ardent than the
rest, cut off certain members of the man, and kept them for
his own use, that even though dead they might perchance
produce a successor to such distinguished valour.

Ch. III.—Of the origin of Saladin.

At this victory Saladin rejoiced greatly; and fired with
the ambition of gaining the kingdom turned his thoughts
to still greater deeds. But that future ages may know
more of this persecutor of the Christian name, I will
premise a few particulars of his origin, as far as the
brevity at which I aim will allow. He was of the race
of the Mirmuræni, the son of parents who were not noble,
though not a plebeian of obscure birth. His father was
called Job, and his own name was Joseph. For according to

* This passage is omitted in some copies, and is very likely to be
spurious. May we not read St. George instead of St. Gregory?

the tradition of Mahomet, it is customary among many of the heathens, when they circumcise their children, to give them Hebrew names also ; but their princes, that they may be admonished by their names to be zealous defenders of the Mahometan law, take their own names from the very name of that law.   Now, law in their language, is Hadin.   Hence Saladin is so called as the upholder of the law ; and, as our princes are called either emperors or kings, so theirs are called sultans (*soldani*), as it were sold-dominants.*   Now Saladin, under Noradin, sultan of Damascus, as a first omen of his power, began by raising an infamous tribute for himself out of the venal courtezans of that city ; for he would not allow them to exercise their profession until they had first purchased of him a license.   Whatever money he obtained by this base patronage, he lavishly expended on players, and so under the plea of largess, he concealed the design of obtaining the venal favour of the multitude.   He was led to aspire at sovereignty by the prediction of a certain Syrian, that he should obtain the government of Damascus and Babylon.†   Thus he arranged in his own mind the different steps to power, and soon began to aim at more than a kingdom of a small or limited dimensions. In process of time, when his years were matured and he was fit for military service, he came to Enfrid of Toura, the illustrious prince of Palestine, to be mantled, and after the manner of the Franks received from him the belt of knighthood.

CH. IV.—*How Saladin seized on the kingdoms of Egypt and Damascus, with India and other countries.*

AT that time a certain Mahometan, named Sewar, governed all Egypt, under Molanus, whom they called Lord in the language of their country, and he had been compelled to pay tribute to Amalric, the victorious king of Jerusalem.   Now Molanus shewed himself only three times a year to the Egyptians, who made adoration to him on those occasions, and all his subjects thought him so powerful, that it was said the Nile overflowed at his command.   Moreover, in obedience to the statutes of the heathen law, he had as many concubines as there

* This must be considered rather as a monkish pun, than as offered for a derivation of the Saracenic word.

† The Babylon referred to is of course Babylon in Egypt, now Fostat the seat of the Fatimite khalifs.

are days in the year, and so passing his life in his harem, he gave up all the business of his kingdom to Sewar. At this time Saladin, with his uncle, Saracun, was serving in Egypt, and by an act of treachery, he put to death Molanus and Sewar, and thus gained for himself the sovereignty of Egypt. Not long after, Noradin died, and Saladin, marrying the widow, expelled the lawful heirs, and secured for himself through her the possession of their kingdom. Thus the caprice of fortune brought about the establishment of his great power; she is able to make a rich man out of a poor one; a great man out of a little one; and a lord out of a peasant. If things were measured by judgment, and not by opinion, all earthly power, which can be gained by the wicked and the unworthy, would be estimated as dross. That patron of prostitutes, whose power was among stews, his campaigns in a tavern, his studies among dice and garlic, is suddenly lifted up; he sits among princes, and is even greater than princes; he rules on the throne of Egypt; subdues Damascus; occupies the lands of Roasia and Gesyra, and carries his sovereignty to the centre of India Citerior. Wherefore he assails also and subdues the neighbouring kingdoms, at one time by arms, at another time by deceit, and making one monarchy out of several sceptres, arrogates to himself alone the power of so many kings. Neither is the tyrant's cupidity ever gratified; the more he gets the more he covets, and strives with all his power to occupy the land which is the inheritance of our Lord. At length an opportunity arose favourable to his wishes, and he hoped to obtain what he never before presumed to hope for. For Raimund, count of Tripoli, and Guy, the eighth king of the Latins,* quarrelled for the sovereignty, and a fatal sedition arose among the people.

Ch. V.—*Of the immense army with which Saladin attacked the army of the Christians, and captured our Lord's cross with the king Guy, and Acre, and reduced to submission the Land of Promise.*

THE opportunity above mentioned at once roused his ambitious mind, and promised him a brilliant and sure success. Moreover it was not altogether without cause that the sultan

* This was Guy de Lusignan, king of Jerusalem from 1186 to 1191. If we count from Godfrey de Bouillon, Guy was the ninth, and not the eighth, of the Latin kings of Jerusalem.

declared war; Reginald, prince of Antioch, having broken the
terms of truce, which had been agreed upon between our
people and the unbelievers. For once upon a time, when
a large and wealthy caravan of Mahometans were passing
from Damascus to Egypt, and, trusting to the truce, did
not hesitate to pass over the frontiers of the Christian territories, the aforesaid prince suddenly attacked them, and
dishonourably carried them off prisoners, together with all
their baggage. The sultan, excited on one side by his ambition, and on the other moved with indignation at the outrage,
raised all the strength of his kingdom, and assailed with power
and impetuosity the territories of Jerusalem. If the number of
men, the variety of nations, and the diversity of religions were
fully described, as the law of history demands, my plan of brevity
would be interrupted by the ample details of such a narrative:
Parthians, Bedouins, Arabs, Medes, Cordians, and Egyptians,
though differing in country, religion, and name, were all aroused
with one accord to the destruction of the Holy Land. As our
troops were marching to meet them, and the fatal day approached, a fearful vision was seen by the king's chamberlain,
who dreamt that an eagle flew past the Christian army, bearing seven missiles and a balista in its talons, and crying with a
loud voice, "Woe to thee, Jerusalem!" To explain the mystery
of this vision, we need, I think, only take the words of Scripture; "The Lord hath bent his bow, and in it prepared the
vessels of death." What are the seven missiles, but a figure
for the seven sins by which that unhappy army was soon
to perish? By this number, seven, may also be understood the
number of punishments that impended over the Christians,
which was some time after fulfilled by the event, that too faith-
'ul and terrible interpreter of omens. The battle had not begun,
when, the armies having been drawn out at a short distance
from Tiberias, at a place called the Marescallia, the Lord
hemmed in his people with the sword, and as a punishment
for the sins of men, gave over his inheritance to slaughter
and devastation. What need I say more? Neither the plan
of my work, nor the immensity of the calamity, allows me
to find lamentations for all its details. However, to sum all
up in few words, so many were slain there, so many wounded,
and so many cast into prison, that the destruction of our
people drew pity even from the enemies. That vivifying

wood of the cross of our salvation, on which our Lord and
Redeemer hung, and down whose shaft the holy blood of
Christ flowed, the sign of which is adored by angels, vene-
rated by men, and feared by devils, under whose protection
our men have always been victors in war, alas! is now captured by the enemy, and the two bearers of the cross, the
bishop of Acre, and the precentor of our Lord's tomb (the
bishop of St. George), fell with it, the one slain, the other
a prisoner. This was the second indignity, since Chosroes,
king of the Persians, which that holy cross endured for our
sins; it had redeemed us from the old yoke of captivity,
and now it was captured from us, and soiled by the profane
hands of the unbelievers.

Let him that hath intelligence consider how fierce must have
been God's wrath, how great the iniquity of his servants, when
unbelievers were deemed less unworthy than Christians to
become its guardians.   Nothing ever happened so lamentable
in all ancient times; for neither the captivity of God's ark,
nor that of the kings of Judah, can compare with the calamity of
our own times, by which the king and the glorious cross are
taken captive together. Of the other prisoners, whose number
was both extraordinary and lamentable, part were reserved
unhurt to be placed at the victor's disposal, part were dispatched with the sword, and so found a happy and short by-
road to heaven!   Among others was Reginald prince of
Antioch: he was led into the presence of the sultan, and
that tyrant, either following the impulse of his passion, or envious of the great excellence of the man, cut off with his own
hand that veteran and aged head.   All the Templars also who
were taken, except their master, he ordered to be decapitated,
wishing utterly to exterminate those whom he knew to be
valiant above all others in battle.   O what faith, what
fervour of mind was theirs!   How many assumed the ton-
sure of the Templars, and flocked eagerly round their
executioners, joyfully presenting their necks to the sword, in
the pious fraud of this new costume!   Among these soldiers
of Christ was a Templar, named Nicholas, who had so
induced others to aspire to martyrdom, that, by reason of
their emulation to be beforehand with him, he could hardly
succeed in first obtaining the mortal stroke which he coveted.
Nor did the Divine mercy withhold its miraculous manifesta-

tion, for during the three following nights, when the bodies of the holy martyrs were lying still unburied, a ray of celestial light shone over them from above.

When the noise of battle had ceased, Saladin seeing prisoners carried off in all directions, and the ground on all sides covered with the slain, lifting up his eyes to heaven, gave thanks to God for the victory which he had gained. This was his practice in all cases; but at present among other things, he is reported to have said, that it was not his own power but our crimes which had given him the victory; and it was proved to be so by the character of the event. In other engagements, our army, however moderate in size, with the Divine aid always conquered; but now, because we were not with God, nor God with us, our people were altogether defeated, even before the conflict, though they were reckoned at more than 1,000 knights and more than 20,000 footmen: so entirely had the whole force of the kingdom flocked together at the king's command to that fatal campaign, that those only remained to guard the cities and castles, whom weakness of sex or age rendered unfit to bear arms. This disastrous battle was fought on the day of the translation of St. Martin, and in one moment all the glory of the kingdom passed from it and was extinguished. The sultan, therefore, trusting that the fortresses of the kingdom would be easily taken, now that their defenders were slain, carried the captive king in triumph through the castles of Syria, reserving him as a mark for his ridicule, to be shewn to the cities which he wished to take and to enforce their surrender. With this view he marched first to Acre, and took it without a blow, granting the citizens leave to remove themselves and their effects to whatever place they pleased.

CH. VI.—*Of the capture of the Christians, who unwarily put in at the port of Acre.*

MEANWHILE our sailors were proceeding on their customary voyage to Acre, coming from Christian countries, and laden some with merchandise, others with pilgrims. Alas! they had not heard what had happened, and they entered the hostile port to be made prisoners. It was indeed a sad destiny: they hailed the sight of land, where chains were pre-

pared for them on landing : they rejoiced to have passed
the dangers of the sea, and the sword awaited them : they
hoped for repose after their fatigues, and they found per-
secution : some of them were kept as prisoners, many of
them were made objects of derision, a few were allowed to
escape, but designedly naked and helpless, that others might
be deterred by their example.

Ch. VII.—*How the Marquis Conrad escaped being taken in the same snare, and proceeded to Tyre.*

Among others, the marquis, on his way from Constantinople, dropped his sails outside the port of Acre, and, as it
was near sunset, lay to till the morning. For the silence
which prevailed in the city created suspicion, since at other
times there was a general shout of congratulation when any
vessel appeared ; the ensigns of the sultan, seen in different
parts of the city, gave still more cause for apprehension.
Some of the Saracen galleys were now seen approaching,
but the rest of the crew becoming alarmed, the marquis commanded them to be silent, and stood forth as their spokesman.
When, therefore, those who were sent asked who they
were, he said it was a merchantship, and he was the master ;
that he had heard what had happened, and being a devoted
servant of the sultan, would wait on him at break of day
and exhibit his wares. That same night, the wind being
favourable, he sailed to Tyre, and undertook the task of
defending it : his arrival was alike a protection to all other
Christians who should come, and would have contributed to
his own glory, if he had only persevered to the end in the
same line of conduct. This was the marquis Conrad, an
Italian by birth, a man of singular activity, and brave in
all he undertook.* But however noble the beginning, when
it is tarnished by a disgraceful end, it merits shame rather
than glory.

The sultan, after the capture of Acre, followed by the
surrender of Berytus and Sidon, expected to take Tyre
with the same ease, but was shamefully repulsed from its
walls, and raised the siege.

---

* Conrad was the son of William III., marquis of Montferrat ; he had
given powerful assistance in quelling a rebellion at Constantinople, and in
reward had received the hand of the emperor's sister.

CH. VIII.—*How Saladin, after the capture of Berytus and Sidon, was repulsed from the walls of Tyre, and took Ascalon by a false treaty.*

SALADIN, taking the king with him, proceeded thence to Ascalon, and planting his machines for throwing stones, began to assail it. The town is easy to be taken if defended by a weak garrison, though its great strength renders it invincible if sufficiently garrisoned. The insatiable invader, eager above all things to obtain this city, nevertheless distrusted his ability to take it by force, for he did not know how things were within its walls, nor how deficient it was both in arms, men, and victuals. He therefore agreed to a capitulation, by which the citizens were to depart freely with their effects, and the king, with fifteen other distinguished captives, were to be set at liberty as soon as possible. On the same day that this capitulation gave him possession of the city, the sun, as if in sympathy, was eclipsed, and withdrew its light from the city and from the world. The perjured and perfidious tyrant, too, was faithless in the performance of part of his agreement; for the king was carried to Damascus, and was there held in chains until the ensuing month of May; nor was he released from his captivity until he had first consented to abjure his crown.

CH. IX.—*Jerusalem is taken and treated with indignity: the people who ransom themselves are expelled, the rest are made slaves.*

THE fall of Jerusalem was now impending: the victor advancing with speed equal to his hatred, laid siege to the city; and erecting his machines, with sacrilegious irreverence profaned all the holy places. There was a certain cross of stone, which our soldiers formerly, when, after the capture of Antioch, they had gloriously taken this city, had erected on the wall in commemoration of the deed. The ferocious invaders destroyed this cross with a blow from one of their machines, and at the same time struck down a great part of the wall. The citizens interposed such defences as they were able, but all the exertions of our men were ineffectual: bows, balistas, and slings were used to no purpose; both arms and machines visibly declared that the Lord was wroth, and foretold the fall of the city. A large number of people had flocked together to the city from the neighbouring

fortresses, trusting rather in the sanctity of the place than in
the strength of its defences; but in so great a multitude
hardly fourteen knights could be found. The priests and
clerks, although it was contrary to their profession, discharged
the duties of soldiers, according to the emergency, and fought
bravely for the Lord's house, bearing in mind the maxim,
that to repel force by force is allowed by all laws both human
and divine. But the populace, alike ignorant and timorous,
flocked in numbers round the patriarch and the queen, who
were left in charge of the city, bitterly complaining and earnestly entreating that they might treat with the sultan for
peace, as soon as possible. Their capitulation, however, was
one to be deplored, rather than praised: for each of them had
to pay the ransom of his own life; a man was valued at ten
bezants, a woman at five, a child at one; and whoever was
unable to pay, was made a slave. It thus happened that
when many of them, either out of their own property, or
by aids gathered from other sources, had paid the price of
their safety, there remained 14,000, who could not redeem
themselves, and were made slaves for life. To those who
purchased their liberty, the choice was given, either to proceed
to Antioch, or to be carried under safe conduct to Alexandria,
and thence to cross the sea. That day was indeed a bitter day,
on which the exiles separated, each on his different road, and
left that sacred city, that city which had been the queen of
cities, but which was now reduced to slavery; that city
which was the inheritance of its children, but was now in
the hands of strangers, on account of the wickedness of those
who dwelt therein.

Glorious was Jerusalem, the city of God, where the
Lord suffered, and was buried, and where he displayed the glory
of his resurrection; but she is now subject to contamination at the hands of her baseborn foe: nor is there any
grief like that grief, that they should possess the sepulchre,
who persecuted Him that lies buried in it; and those, who had
despised the Crucified, have made themselves masters of his
Cross! This most holy city had been, for about ninety-
six years, in the hands of our people, ever since the victorious
arms of the Christians had taken it, at the same time as
Antioch; when it had been forty years before in the possession of the unbelievers. When the city was taken, the crier

of the Mahometan law proceeded to the summit of the rock of
Calvary, and there published their false law, in the place
where Christ had consummated the law of death upon the
cross.   Another diabolical act was perpetrated by the enemy.
They fastened ropes round a certain cross, which stood upon the
pinnacle of the church of the Hospitallers, and dragged it
to the ground, where they spat upon it, and hacked it, and
drew it, in derision of our faith, through all the filth of the city.

Ch. X.—*How Saladin besieged Tyre by sea and land.*

Now the queen, who was the daughter of King Amalric, and
was named Sibilla, together with Heraclius the patriarch, the
Templars, the Hospitallers, and an immense multitude of fellow-
exiles, directed their course towards Antioch.   How she had a
sad interview at Neapolis with the captive king her husband,
and how the marquis violently carried off to Tyre the ship in
which she intended to embark, brevity compels us to pass
over.   But we must not omit to mention how Saladin, burning
with desire to take the city of Tyre, went against it a second
time with all his army, and not content with besieging it by
land, he blockaded it from the sea with his galleys, and prepared to attack it on every side.   That nothing might be left
untried, he brought forward the marquis's father, whom he had
taken prisoner in the battle before mentioned, trusting that the
son, moved by filial affection, would give up the city in exchange
for his parent.   At one moment he offers him in exchange, at
another he threatens him with death, and tries various means
of working upon his feelings.   All, however, is in vain, for the
marquis, inflexible, derides his offers and despises his threats.
Whenever, to move his compassion, they shew him his father
in chains, he immediately seizes a balista, and aims a shaft
obliquely towards him, intending indeed that his hand shall
err, but feigning to take good aim.   And when the sultan's
messengers came to threaten that his father should be slain,
he replied that he wished it by all means; that the
wicked man, after so many crimes, might at length find a
good end, and he might himself have a martyr for his father.
Thus the tyrant, failing in his expectation of gaining the city
by these means, tried his fortune in another way; and where
art failed, determined to see what could be done by arms.
   Tyre is situated in the heart of the sea, and is surrounded

on all sides by walls. A small part of it, where it is not
washed by the waves, is fortified by several lines of walls.
It was once famous for its kings, and gave birth to the
founders of Thebes and Carthage. When Solomon was king of
Judea, Tyre had her own sovereign, and though she was then
the head of her own dominions, in process of time she became
a part of the kingdom of Jerusalem. This city its eager
foe now assailed by land and sea; and, whilst it suffered
within from hunger, it was exposed to manifold assaults
from without. On the morning after Innocent's day, namely
on the feast of the blessed martyr Thomas,* the citizens
gained an important victory, for at dawn of day they
sailed out with a few small vessels, and in a naval engagement obliged the enemy to raise the siege on the side of the
sea. They seemed indeed more fitted for flight than
fighting; and on the first onset, all the enemy's fleet, by the
power of the Almighty, were so panic-struck, that some of
them were carried into the city with their crews: the rest
in their flight ran aground and there perished. The unbelievers, seeing this engagement by sea, supposed that all the
defenders of the city had left it, and thus, confident of victory,
they attacked the town with impetuosity. Already their troops
had reached the fortifications, and numbers were hasting to
mount them, when the marquis ordered the gates to be thrown
open, and followed by Hugh of Tiberias, with his brothers and
a noble company of men besides, struck down multitudes with
his small band. Saladin seeing the fortunes of the day against
him, gave orders that his remaining engines and galleys should
be burnt, and retreated ingloriously. Afterwards, about the
beginning of May, he released the king from captivity, and,
having broken his former agreement, imposed, as we have
already mentioned, a new and hard condition.

Ch. XI.—*Of the meeting of the king and queen.*

THERE is an island called Arados, having a city named
Antharados, but commonly called Tortosa. Hither the queen
came to meet the king: they kiss and embrace one another,
shedding tears of joy, and rejoice at having escaped the

* Dec. 29, 1187. Thomas Becket, archbishop of Canterbury, was
murdered the 29th of December, seventeen years before.

G

calamities which had caused them so much grief. The
king remained the following year, partly at Antioch, partly
at Tripoli, waiting for the Christians who were preparing
to come from beyond the sea to the succour of the Holy
Land.

Ch. XII.—*Of the money which king Henry formerly deposited with the Templars.*

AMONG other things we think it ought not to be passed
over in silence, that Henry, king of England, had formerly
deposited a large sum of money with the Templars and Hospitallers, to defend Tyre, and provide for other matters concerning the kingdom. This money that magnificent king, by
a provision as pious as necessary, had transmitted to Jerusalem,
during a period of many years, to be used in the service of the
Holy Land : its total, as is said, amounted to 30,000 marks.

Ch. XIII.—*How Saladin, retreating from Tyre, took several towns, both in Palestine, and near Antioch.*

Now Saladin leaving Tyre, occupied several castles
in Palestine, and thence marched with rapidity into the
country round Antioch; and took, by assault rather than by
siege, Gebeli, Laodicea, and several other fortresses of that
province. The city itself was thrown into no small alarm ;
but the patriarch and prince, with the common consent of
the citizens, promised the tyrant to surrender, if they should
not within a given period receive the assistance which
they expected.   Inconsolable would have been the grief
of all Christ's followers, if a city so renowned, and honoured
by the first origin of the Christian name, had again become
subject to the impure heathen, whom, after a long and dreadful
chance of war, our victorious troops had formerly expelled.
But whence are the expected reinforcements to come? and
when or how shall they come ? There is no road open for
them by land, and the sea is blockaded by their enemies.
The ships of the Christians abstain from approaching, for
fear of falling among the galleys of the unbelievers, which they
see lying in wait for them. But what the Lord has resolved
to save, will not be allowed to perish. Behold, the hoped-for
troops arrive! the expected ones are coming! Lo ! William,
the illustrious king of Sicily, sends the first auxiliaries to the

Holy Land, consisting of two earls, five hundred knights, and fifty galleys !

Ch. XIV.—*How William, king of Sicily, sends Margaritus with fifty galleys and five hundred knights to the assistance of the Holy Land.*

To whom else, then, can we give the glory of having saved Antioch, Tripoli, and Tyre, but to Him who preserved from famine and the sword the inhabitants of these cities secure in his strength? At the head of the royal fleet was Margaritus, a very brave man, who, proceeding in advance with the galleys, repressed piratical attempts; and having ascertained that the coast was clear, encouraged the others to follow him. Keeping in check the distant islands, and happily escaping all the dangers of the sea, he had gained such credit by his numerous victories, that he was called the king of the sea, and by some a second Neptune. Already Tripoli appeared in sight to his sailors: the citizens, on the other hand, beheld in the distance his spreading sails. Though they come the heralds of safety, yet fear, that worst prognosticator at critical moments, raises apprehensions. Without delay they man their walls and mount the bulwarks, uncertain, however, whether to offer a surrender or to try the chance of battle. But when the ships arrive near, and the ensigns of the Cross and other emblems of the Christian religion are beheld on their lofty sterns, a loud shout is raised; the waves echo the sound of their mutual congratulations; the shore is covered with the crowds who flock to meet them, and joy unspeakable fills the breasts of all. Among others, Hervy of Dantzic, especially distinguished by the celebrity of his deeds, contributes his veteran wisdom to the defence of that land; and so in a short time, many a valiant band flocked thither, and the coast was preserved from the power of the enemy.

Ch. XV.—*Saladin takes the town Erathrum, and Mount Royal is surrendered to him after a siege of two years, in exchange for Remfrid de Tours, and Girard, the master of the Temple.*

THERE is a castle called Erathrum, where once stood the city of Petras. It is still a metropolitan see, and the prelate of it, retaining his ancient title, is still called the archbishop of Petras. This castle, lying in the innermost parts of the

kingdom, was long held in siege by the admirals of the sultan.
If it were not for famine, which conquers all places however
secure, this fortress would be impregnable.   There is also a
castle called Mount Royal, distant about twenty leagues from
the aforesaid city, lying further towards Egypt.   Against this
also the sultan had sent his admirals at the beginning of the
war ; trusting to reduce it by famine, though he could not by
arms. They did not, therefore, erect machines or try to assault
it ; for it would be ridiculous to try to scale heaven and to
carry by storm a place which could not be approached.   The
siege was protracted two years, when our people began to feel
want, and they endured all the horrors which the Spaniards
are said in ancient times to have suffered at Saguntum or the
Romans at Perusium ; but they still kept up their courage,
nor did they decline to eat food at which man's usual habits
and nature revolt.   Fatherly affection renounces its rights ;
love, too, heeds no longer what it had once delighted in ;
the father rejects his son, the son his decrepit parents, and
the husband his newly-married bride.   They are driven out
weeping from the walls and exposed without protection to the
enemy, that the remaining stock of food may the longer maintain the fighting men.   At last, worn out and half dead with
hunger, they enter into terms of capitulation, but yet such as
honour would sanction ; for they obtained a free passage for
themselves and liberty for their lord Remfrid of Tours who
had been taken prisoner.   By a similar fortune, Gerard de
Riddeford, master of the Temple, was also released on the
surrender of certain fortresses ; and the father of the marquis
obtained his liberty in exchange for some of the Mahomedan
captives.

Ch. XVI.—*How Saladin, extolling the law of Mahomet, is reproved by
a jester.*

SALADIN by these means had got possession of nearly all
the kingdom, and every thing succeeded to his wishes.   Elevated with his proud triumphs, he talked in magnificent terms
of the law of Mahomet, and pointed to the result of his enterprise as a proof that it was superior to the law of Christ.

These insolent vaunts he often threw out in the presence of
the Christians, one of whom, well known to him for his loqua-
city, on a certain occasion, inspired by the Almighty, turned

him into ridicule by the following reply: "God, who is the
father of the faithful, judging the Christians worthy of reproof
and correction for their crimes, has chosen thee, O prince, as
his agent in this matter: thus sometimes a worldly father
in anger seizes a dirty stick out of the mire, wherewith when
he has chastised his erring sons, he throws it back among the
filth where he found it."

Ch. XVII.—*First of Richard, earl of Poitou, then of Henry, king of
the English, and of Philip, king of the French.*

WHILST these things were done in Palestine, the archbishop
of Tyre had embarked on ship-board, and already reported to
Christendom the news of this great calamity, and the affliction
of so small a kingdom was felt as a calamity over many countries.   Fame had carried to the ears of all the kings, and of
all the faithful, that the inheritance of Christ was occupied by
the heathen: some were affected to tears by the news, and
some were stimulated to vengeance.   First of all, Richard the
brave earl of Poitou, assumed the cross to revenge its wrongs,
and took the lead of all, inviting others by his example.   His
father Henry, king of England, was now declining in years;
yet the young man was not deterred by either his father's
advanced age, or his own right to the throne, or the difficulties of so long a voyage: no arguments could deter him
from his purpose.   The Almighty, to reward the valour of
this brave man, whom he had chosen to be the first inciter of
the others, reserved him, after the other princes were dead or
returned to their own country, to achieve his great work.
Some time after, Philip, king of France, and Henry, king of
England, take the cross at Gisors, followed by the nobles of
both kingdoms, with numbers of the clergy and laity,—all,
with equal aspirations, bent upon the same design.   So great
was the ardour of this new pilgrimage, that it was no longer
a question who would take the cross, but who had not yet
taken it.   Several persons sent a present of a distaff and wool
to one another, as a significant hint that whosoever declined
the campaign would degrade himself as much as if he did the
duties of a woman: wives urged their husbands, mothers their
sons, to devote themselves to this noble contest; and they only
regretted that the weakness of their sex prevented themselves
from going also.   The renown of this expedition spread so

extraordinarily, that many migrated from the cloister to the
camp, and exchanging the cowl for the cuirass, shewed themselves truly Christ's soldiers, and quitting their libraries for
the study of arms.   The prelates of the churches publicly
preached to one another the virtue of abstinence, admonishing
all men that, laying aside all extravagance in eating and
dress, they should refrain from their accustomed luxuries.
It was agreed also both among nobles and bishops, by common
consent, that to maintain the pilgrims who were poor, those
who remained at home should pay tithes of their property;
but the flagitious cupidity of many took advantage of this to
lay heavy and undue exactions upon their subjects.   In those
days William, king of Sicily, yielded to the lot of mortality;
and his death was the cause of so much the greater sorrow to
all the faithful, because he had always been prompt and ready
to lend assistance to the Holy Land.

CH. XVIII.—*The emperor of the Romans (Frederic Barbarossa) takes
the cross.*

IN process of time, Frederic, the Roman emperor, assumed
the insignia of the holy pilgrimage, and displayed, both outwardly in his dress, and inwardly in his heart, the form of a
true pilgrim.   So great a king, whose empire was bounded on
the south by the Mediterranean Sea, on the north by the
Northern Ocean, whose glory was augmented by continual victories, whose fortune had experienced no check, resigns every
pleasure and blandishment of the world, and humbly girds on
his sword to fight for Christ.   His bravery, especially in his
declining years, is no less to be wondered at than praised; for
though he was an old man and had sons, whose age and
valour seemed better adapted to military service, yet esteeming
them insufficient, he took upon himself the charge of defending Christianity; but when his sons urged him to let them
discharge the task which he had undertaken, either in his
stead or in his company, he left his eldest son to govern his
empire, and the younger, whom he had created duke of
Suabia, he took with him on the expedition; and because the
imperial majesty never assails any one without sending a defiance, but always gives notice of war to his enemies, a herald
is dispatched from the emperor to Saladin, calling upon him to
give full satisfaction to Christendom, which he has injured, or,
failing to do so, to prepare himself for war.

THE EPISTLE OF FREDERIC TO SALADIN.

Frederic, by the grace of God emperor of the Romans, ever august, the magnificent triumpher over the enemies of the empire, and the fortunate governor of the whole monarchy, to the illustrious Saladin, formerly governor of the Saracens. May he take warning from Pharaoh, and touch not Jerusalem!

The letters which your devotion sent to us a long time ago, on weighty and important matters, and which would have benefited you if reliance could have been placed on your words, we received, as became the magnificence of our majesty, and deemed it meet to communicate by letter with your greatness. But now that you have profaned the Holy Land, over which we, by the authority of the Eternal King, bear rule, as guardian of Judea, Samaria, and Palestine, solicitude for our imperial office admonishes us to proceed with due rigour against such presumptuous and criminal audacity. Wherefore, unless, before all things, you restore the land which you have seized, and give due satisfaction, to be adjudged according to the holy constitutions, for such nefarious excesses, that we may not appear to wage unlawful war against you, we give you, from the first of November, a period of twelve months, after which you shall experience the fortune of war, in the field of Zoan,* by the virtue of the vivifying cross, and in the name of the true Joseph. For we can scarcely believe that you are ignorant of that which all antiquity and the writings of the ancients testify. Do you pretend not to know that both the Æthiopias, Mauritania, Persia, Scythia, Parthia, where our general Marcus Crassus met with a premature death, Judea, Samaria, Maritima, Arabia, and Chaldæa, also Egypt, where, shame to say! a Roman citizen, Antony, a man endowed with signal virtues, passing the bounds of temperance, and acting otherwise than as became a soldier sent from so great a state, submitted to the unchaste love of Cleopatra—do you pretend not to know that Armenia, and other innumerable countries, have been subject to our sway? This is well known to those

---

* The allusion is to Psalm lxxviii. 12. The emperor seems to mean that he will attack Saladin in Egypt.

kings in whose blood the Roman sword has been so often
steeped; and you, God willing, shall learn by experience
the might of our victorious eagles, and be made acquainted
with our troops of many nations—the anger of Germany—
the untamed head of the Rhine—the youth from the banks
of the Danube, who know not how to flee—the towering
Bavarian—the cunning Suabian—the cautious Franconian—
Saxony, that sports with the sword—Thuringia—Westphalia
—the active Brabantine—the Lorrainer unused to peace—
the fiery Burgundian—the nimble mountaineer of the Alps
—the Frison with his javelin and thong—the Bohemian ever
ready to brave death—Bolonia fiercer than her own fierce
beasts—Austria—Byria—Ruwennia—Istria—Rocumphia—
Illyria—Lombardy—Tuscany—the march of Ancona—the
resolute Venetian and the Pisan sailor—and lastly, also, you
shall assuredly be taught how our own right hand, which you
suppose to be enfeebled by old age, can still wield the sword
upon that day of reverence and gladness which has been
appointed for the triumph of Christ's cause.

We think it right to insert in our history the letter which
Saladin sent in reply to the foregoing. The proud boasting
of the tyrant, which he had conceived in his opposition, is
sufficiently manifest in it. However, we give it in the simple
form of words in which it was written, without changing a
syllable of it.

To the great king, his sincere friend, the illustrious
Frederic, king of Germany:—In the name of God the
merciful: by the grace of the one God, the powerful, the
surpassing, the victorious, the everlasting, of whose king-
dom there is no end.

We give continual thanks to Him, whose grace is over all
the world: we pray that he may pour out his inspiration
over all his prophets, and especially on our teacher, his messenger the prophet, Mahomet, whom he sent to teach the true
law, which he will make to appear above all laws. But we
make it known to the sincere and powerful king, our great,
amicable friend, the king of Germany, that a certain man,
named Henry, came to us, professing to be your envoy, and
he gave us a letter, which he said was from your hand. We

caused the letter to be read, and we heard him speak by word of mouth, and to the words which he spake by word of mouth we answered also in words. But this is the answer to your letter:—You enumerate those who are leagued with you to come against us, and you name them and say—the king of this land and the king of that land—this count and that count, and such archbishops, marquises, and knights. But if we wished to enumerate those who are in our service, and who listen to our commands, and obey our words, and would fight for us, this is a list which could not be reduced to writing. If you reckon up the names of the Christians, the Saracens are more numerous and many times more numerous than the Christians. If the sea lies between us and those whom you name Christians, there is no sea to separate the Saracens, who cannot be numbered ; between us and those who will come to aid us, there is no impediment. With us are the Bedouins, who would be quite sufficient singly to oppose our enemies ; and the Turkomans, who, unaided, could destroy them : even our peasants, if we were to bid them, would fight bravely against the nations which should come to invade our country, and would despoil them of their riches and exterminate them. What ! have we not on our side the warlike Soldarii, by whom we have opened and gained the land, and driven out our enemies ? These, and all the kings of Paganism will not be slow when we shall summon them, nor delay when we shall call them. And whenever your armies shall be assembled, according to the import of your letter, and you shall lead them, as your messenger tells us, we will then meet you in the power of God. Nor will we be satisfied with the land which is on the sea-coast, but we will cross over with God's good pleasure, and will take from you all your lands, in the strength of the Lord. For if you come, you will come with all your forces, and will be present with all your people, and we know that there will remain none at home to defend themselves or fight for their country. And when the Lord, by his power, shall have given us victory over you, nothing will remain for us to do but freely to take your lands, by His power, and with His good pleasure. For the union of the Christian faith has twice come against us in Babylon ; once at Damietta, and again at Alexandria : it was also in the coast of the land of Jerusalem while in the hand of the Christians, in the land of Damascus, and in the land of the Saracens; in each fortress there was a lord who studied his own interests. You know how the Christians each time returned, and to what an issue they came.   But these our people are assembled together with their countries, and the Lord has associated with us countries in abundance, and united them far and wide under our power: Babylon, with its dependencies, and the land of Damascus, and Jerusalem on the sea-coast, and the land of Gesireh with its castles, and the land of Roasia with its dependencies, and the land of India with its dependencies —by the grace of God, all this is in our hands, and the residue of the Saracenic kings is in our empire.   For if we were to command the illustrious kings of the Saracens, they would not withdraw themselves from us.   And if we were to admonish the caliph of Bagdad (whom God preserve) to come to our aid, he would rise from the throne of his great empire, and would come to help our excellence.   We have obtained, also, by the virtue and power of God, Jerusalem and its territory; and of the three cities which still remain in the hands of the Christians, Tyre, Tripoli, and Antioch, nothing remains but that we should occupy them also.   But, if you wish for war, and if God so will of his good pleasure that we occupy the whole land of the Christians, we will meet you in the power of the Lord, as is written in this our letter.   But, if you ask us for the boon of peace, you will command the warders of the three places above mentioned to deliver them up to us without resistance; and we will restore to you the holy cross, and will liberate all the Christian captives who are in all our territories; and we will be at peace with you, and will allow you to have one priest at the sepulchre, and we will restore the abbeys which used to be in the time of Paganism,* and will do good to them, and will permit the pilgrims to come during all our life, and we will be at peace with you.   But if the letter which came to us by the hand of Henry be the letter of the king, we have written this letter for answer, and may God give us counsel according to his will. This letter is written in the year of the coming of our prophet Mahomet 584, by the grace of the only God.   And

* This letter has evidently been translated out of the original Saracenic with reference to Christian notions: a Saracen would hardly have described his own faith by the word "paganism."

may God save our prophet Mahomet and his race, and may
he save the salvation of our Saviour, illustrious Lord, and
victorious King; the giver of unity; the true word; the adorner
of the standard of truth; the corrector of the world and of the
law; sultan of the Saracens and Pagans; the servitor of the
two holy houses, and of the holy house of Jerusalem; the
father of victors; Joseph the son of Job; the reviver of the
progeny of Murmurænus! *

Ch. XIX.—*How the emperor Frederic Barbarossa assembled his army,*
throughout Hungary.

This letter of the proud and faithless tyrant, with its ab-
surdities, the magnificent emperor treated with contempt; and,
filled with indignation worthy of a prince, prepared all his
forces for the war.   The princes of all the empire followed
him, and when they were met at Mayence, according to
the imperial edict, all of them joined with one acclaim in
taking the vow of so noble a pilgrimage.   This was the
Lord's doing, of Him whose inspiration bloweth where it
listeth, who inclines the hearts of men at his will.   For these
great princes were neither allured by a desire of vain glory,
nor induced by bribes or entreaties, but solely by desire of
the heavenly reward: by the Lord, and the Lord alone, were
they led to buckle on their armour for this warfare.   For
the loftiness of the heavenly wisdom had provided that, as
they were enlisted of their own free will, they rendered a
service agreeable to God, and the imperial magnificence was
accompanied by a train of worthy followers.   Thus, then, led
by the Holy Spirit, they flocked together on every side; and
whoever could have seen so many nations and princes under
one commander, must have believed that the ancient glory of
Rome was not yet departed.   In this army of Christ were
pontiffs, dukes, earls, marquises, and other nobles, without
number: for if we were to recapitulate their names and territories, the writer would become tedious, his reader be disgusted,
and his plan of brevity be overthrown.   It was determined
by a prudent counsel that no one should go on this expedition whose means could not provide him with supplies for one

* It is hoped the reader may possess some clue to the meaning of this
elegant rhapsody: the translator has given these titles as literally as
possible, and does not venture on a word of comment.

year. A large number of carriages were constructed for the use
of the pilgrims who should be sick, that they might neither
give trouble to the sound, nor be left behind and perish.   It
had long been a question whether the mass of the army should
proceed by sea or land.   But it seemed that any number of
ships, however large, would be insufficient to transport so great
a multitude. The emperor, therefore, urging on the task which
he had undertaken, determined to march through Hungary,
and so, though he was the last sovereign who took the vow
of pilgrimage, he was the first to carry it into effect.

CH. XX.—*Bela, king of the Hungarians, receives the king hospitably.*

THE king of the Hungarians, Bela by name, came out with joy
to meet the emperor. He was a man endowed by nature with
many good qualities ; tall in stature, of a noble countenance,
possessing a combination of virtues, and worthy of the highest
panegyric ; who, if he had no other merit, would be thought
worthy of sovereignty by his dignified appearance.   He
received Christ's army with hospitality, met them in a triumphant procession, and followed them with good will, testifying by his deeds the fervour of his friendship.   The people in
large numbers, burning with their sovereign's example, con-
template the sacred army and are eager to enlist ; they look
forwards to the prizes of the combat, and fear no dangers : at
once they form the wish, they take the vow, and follow with
the army, so that it is evident the workings of Holy Inspiration knew no impediment or delay.   Crossing the Danube
they reached the furthest passes of Bulgaria, where Huns,
Alans, Bulgarians, and Pincenates rushed suddenly from their
ambush upon the Lord's host, encouraged to the attack by the
rugged and inaccessible nature of the ground.

CH. XXI.—*How Frederic, having crossed the Danube, found the Huns and Alans hostile to him.*

THE outlet from Bulgaria into Macedonia is fortified
on both sides by high rocks, covered with thorns and
bushes, through which wind narrow and rugged paths.   To
these the inhabitants have added lofty artificial defences.
These passes were seized by the nations before mentioned,

who had been sent for this purpose by the wicked emperor
Conrad, that they might destroy the army, or at least stop
its further approach. Our soldiers, however, courageously
overcame both the enemy and the road, and passing through
Macedonia, arrived at Philippopolis, a city which had
oefore been called Pulpudeba, but took the name of Philippopolis in honour of the Roman emperor Philip, who first of
all the emperors became a Christian, and by the profession of
the Christian faith conferred additional lustre upon the imperial dignity. The Greeks, hearing of the approach of the
Latin army, deserted the city, fearing where there was no
need of fear ; for which their only reason was that they feared
all whom they did not love : for the pilgrims had not come to
plunder others, as they had sufficient of their own ; nor had they
taken arms against the faithful, but only to crush the errors of
an infidel race. But the ancient and inexorable hatred which
the Greeks entertained of old against the Latins, had been
handed down by the tenacity of ages to their posterity. If
a motive or reason of this enmity be sought—

> " It were no wrong, if it a plea had found."

Yet this may, perhaps, be urged as an excuse, that whereas
the Latins were flourishing in arts and arms, they themselves
were altogether ignorant and unwarlike : this gives a motive
to their enmity, and they pine with jealousy at the prosperity
of others. They are a perfidious race, a wicked generation,
and utterly degenerate : the more illustrious they once were,
the more signal is their degradation ; their gold is converted
into dross, their wheat into chaff, their purity to filth, their
glory to corruption. The old Greeks attempted and achieved
much, both in arts and arms ; but all their zeal for virtue has
chilled in their posterity and has passed over to the Latins, so
that where once were fountains there now are rivulets, or
rather, dry and exhausted channels. Their virtues have found
no heirs, but their crimes many ; they still retain the deceit of
Sinon, the falseness of Ulysses, and the atrocity of Atreus. If I
be asked concerning their military science, this turns on stratagems rather than on battles ; if concerning their good faith, the
man should beware who has them for his friends, though their
hostility can do him no harm. That nation, unable to impede
the march of our army at the aforesaid passes, did what lay

in their power to do it: all the natives fled to the mountain-
tops and carried with them every comfort which we could
have bought of them for money, leaving their empty houses
without an article of furniture in them to our army that was
approaching.   The emperor indeed, on the plea of peace, had
already sent forwards the bishop of Munster, with some
other princes, to Constantinople; but the wicked and cruel
tyrant cast them into prison, daring to violate the sanctity of
an ambassador, which, even among barbarians, has been respected from all antiquity by the sanction of usage and the
laws of honour.   Afterwards, however, influenced more by
fear than a regard for right, he released the ambassadors from
prison; for he feared the destruction of his capital if he
should not speedily pacify our wrath.   It would have been
right, indeed, that the city should have been razed, even to the
ground; for, if we believe report, it was polluted by new
mosques, which its perfidious emperor allowed to be
built, that he might strengthen the league which he had
entered into with the Turks.   The season of the year was now
ripening towards autumn, and the constellation Libra was
balancing the day and night in nearly equal lengths.   The
magnificent emperor of the Romans marched to take up his
winter-quarters at Adrianople, which he found empty and
deserted by its inhabitants.   Here he took up his position,
and waited for the season when he should lead his army
forwards.

CH. XXII.—*Of the emperor Frederic's wintering in Greece, and of th.
peace between him and the emperor Isaac: of the deceitful embassy
sent to him by the sultan of Iconium, and of his passage through St.
George's Arm.*

THE duke of Suabia, son of the emperor, fearing lest ease
should produce luxury, and luxury generate indolence, determined to find employment for the army during the inactivity
of winter; and for this purpose, he formed a plan to storm a
fortress which was situated at no great distance from the
aforesaid city.   The Greeks had assembled together in it,
trusting in its fortifications, that they might from thence
direct their schemes against the Latins; but in this expectation they were confounded, for they were speedily defeated
and vanquished, thrown into chains and kept prisoners.

When the Byzantine emperor heard of these things, he feared that something still worse would happen ; and, apprehending the destruction of all his empire, he hastily sent ambassadors to our emperor, promising hostages for peace, a market for the sale of provisions, and ships to transport all who wished to cross. The emperor, although many of them thought it dangerous to make peace at all with a tyrant, yet preferred to accept the offered treaty rather than longer delay his expedition.   And now that Easter was approaching, he crossed over the narrow sea, generally called by the name of "St. George's Arm." Although but a narrow strait, this sea enjoys no little reputation, because it washes so great a city, and flows between the two divisions of the world, Asia and Europe.   The sultan of Iconium, a deceitful man, and thirsting after Christian blood, under a fraudulent pretext professed friendship towards us, and concealing the malignant venom of his heart, sought thereby to destroy us when off our guard.   He had sent frequent messengers to the emperor, whilst still in Greece, entreating him to cross over; and whilst he accused the Greeks and their prince of treachery, he promised that he would be a devout and faithful servant to the Christians, and that he would place himself and all that he had at their disposal, and furnish to all of them a market to buy provisions, and a safe passage through his dominions.   The emperor, too credulous, and estimating others by his own knowledge of himself, made a proclamation, in which he threatened all with punishment who, when they entered the territories of the Turks, should commit depredations, or fail to observe the peace which had been concluded.   Thus then it happened, that our men passed on without touching the great booty which the sultan had, intentionally, left at the very entrance of his dominions.   Alas, how blind are men and ignorant of the future !   If they could have foreseen the famine which they were about to suffer, the difficulties of the road, and the deceitfulness of the tyrant! Chance had thrown in their way the means of providing for themselves against these great and imminent dangers.   However, our people did not so far listen to the words of that faithless prince, as, neglecting their own security, to march in disorder, or without their arms.   When, therefore, they were about to enter Parthia, all of them seized their arms, in number 3,000 knights ; of the rest there were about 80,000.   There were seven

bishops, one archbishop, two dukes, nineteen counts, and three
marquises; and this splendid army seemed neither to have
had its like before or after. But to prevent disaffection or confusion in so large a mass, the whole army was divided into three
bodies: the first was led by the duke of Suabia, the last by
the emperor, that in the centre was charged with the care
of the sumpter-horses and baggage. The army advanced
judiciously arranged, to the delight of the beholder, neither
crowded together, nor yet dispersedly, but in bodies; and
though there were many officers over each body, yet there was
but one commander-in-chief. This is the best for a camp, au
important circumstance in war; for as an army perishes without a leader, where no one is pre-eminent above the rest, so it
is generally inefficient, where there are many leaders who contend for pre-eminence. Happy empire! happy Germany!
the parent of so many nations, so many brave warriors of Christ,
a source of pride to herself, and destruction to her enemies!

CH. XXIII.—*Of the discomforts which the Christians endured through
the sultan, and how they reached Iconium.*

OUR army, having entered the territories of the Turks, experienced no hostility during several days: the sultan wished
by his forbearance to allure them into the heart of his dominions,
until want of food and the asperities of the road should give
him more ready means of annoying them. That nefarious
traitor had seized the rugged mountain-tops, the thickets of
the woods, and the impassable rivers; and whilst he professed
to observe the treaty which he had made, he opposed arrows
and stones to our passage. This was the market and the
safe-conduct which he had promised us; such is the faith
that must be placed in the unbelievers; they always esteem
valour and treachery as equally praiseworthy towards an
enemy. Moreover, they avoid, above all things, coming to
close quarters and fighting hand to hand; but they shower
their arrows from a distance; and with them it is no less
glory to flee, than to put their enemy to flight. They
attack both extremities of the army, at one time the rear, at
another time the van; that, if by any chance they can separate them, they may attack either the one or the other by
itself. Night brought with it neither sleep nor rest; for a
terrific clamour disturbed the army on every side. A shower

of javelins pierced through their tents, numbers of them were
slain asleep, and the enemy hung on them so incessantly, that
for six weeks, they ate their meals under arms, and slept
under arms, without taking off their coats of mail.   At the
same time they were assailed by such violent hunger and thirst,
that when they lost their horses by the chances of war, it
was to them a consolation and source of delight, to feed on
horse-flesh and drink the blood : in this manner, by the in-
genuity which necessity teaches, they found out an additional
use for the animals on which they rode.

There was a place between high rocks which was rendered
so difficult to pass by reason of the steep ascent and the narrowness of the paths, that when the first division of the army,
led by the emperor's son, had passed through, the Turks suddenly rushed from their ambush on the last division, and
in their confidence of victory, attacked them with lance and
sword.   The alarming news was carried to the duke, who returned with headlong haste upon his march, eagerly retracing
all the difficulties which he had a little before rejoiced
at having surmounted.   His rage heeded not danger ; his
cavalry were made to gallop where they could not even
walk.   In this manner, whilst he was anxiously and incautiously seeking for his father on every side, and incessantly
shouting his father's name, his helmet was struck off by a stone,
and his teeth knocked out, yet he still remained immoveable and
unshaken.   Happy the son, who, to save his father, was so prodigal of his own life, and exposed himself to so many dangers !
As a consolation for the wound which he then received, he
retains a lasting mark of it ; for whenever he opens his mouth,
the bare gum testifies the glory of his victory.   At last, after
many severe attacks, the army arrives at Iconium, where that
wicked traitor had shut himself within the walls of the city :
our soldiers pitched their tents at no great distance, uncertain
what new disaster the morrow might bring with it.   It was now
about the end of Whitsuntide, and that same night so violent and
sudden a storm burst upon them, that its fury was felt even
within the camp.   In the morning, when the clouds were dispersed, the sky became clear, and behold ! the Turkish army
appear around on every side with trumpets, drums, and
horrid clang, ready to attack.   They had never before
been seen in such multitudes, nor could they have been con-

H

ceived to have been so numerous. If any one should read
that there were three hundred thousand or more of them, it
was only an estimate of the amount, for it was impossible to
number them.   All this multitude had been roused to arms by
the sultan's son Melkin, who wished to anticipate his father-
in-law Saladin's victory, and, trusting in the number and
valour of his men, was confident of success.   Meanwhile the
sultan had ascended a lofty tower, where he sat in expectation, eyeing the country beneath him and the armies that were
ready to engage, and hoping in a short time to see accomplished what his sanguine mind had promised.   The emperor,
seeing some of his men alarmed at the unusual multitude
of the enemy, displayed the confidence of a noble chieftain,
and raising his hands to heaven, gave thanks to God in the
sight of all, that the inevitable necessity was at length arrived
for that combat which had so long been deferred by the flight
of the enemy.   At these words, all were inspired with fresh
ardour, as they looked on the emperor's placid countenance ;
and one old man, weak though he was, supplied an incentive
of valour to many who were young and strong,   What
God is so great as our God ?   All that multitude who were
so sure of victory that they brought chains with them rather
than swords, were overthrown in a moment: and at once the
city was taken and occupied, and the enemy without vanquished ; everywhere were blood and death, and heaps of slain.
their number impedes their flight, and they fall by those very
means on which they had counted for triumph.   The battle is
now fought hand to hand; the bows are snapped asunder ; the
arrows no longer fly, and they have scarcely room to wield their
swords.   Thus everything is thrown into confusion by the multitude, and what our enemies intended for our ruin, turns out to
our greater glory ; the flying war, which had been waged among
brambles and the gorges of rocks, is now carried on in a fair
and open field ; the Christians satiate their fury, which had
so often been put forth in vain.   The Turks experience,
against their will, how well their enemies can fight hand to
hand whom they had so often provoked at a distance.

This splendid victory was not granted unworthily by the
Divine excellence to His faithful servants: for they observed
chastity in the camp, and discipline when under arms : in all,
and above all, was the fear of the Lord ; with all was the love

of their neighbour ; all were united in brotherly affection, as they were also companions in danger.   The sultan, when the city was taken, seeing that there remained to him only the tower in which he was, sent hastily to the emperor, throwing all the blame upon his son, and professing his own innocence ; promising, moreover, as much gold as he should demand, and whatsoever persons he should name as hostages for his observance of the treaty.   The emperor, alas ! too easy, accepted what was offered and gave what was asked : in this less worthy of praise, because he let go that man of blood and treachery whom he had almost in his possession, when it would have been more honourable to slay him than to keep alive so great an enemy to the Christian name.   The hostages were given and the treaty confirmed ; but the wickedness of that maliguant traitor did not rest there ; for, whilst the Christians were continuing their march far beyond Iconium, he attacked them, sometimes by ambuscade, sometimes openly in the field.   The hostages were asked what this meant, and they told a falsehood which suited their own purpose : they said that the Turks were a wild race whom no one could govern ; that they wandered about with no fixed habitation, having no property of their own, and always trying to obtain that of others either by robbery or theft.   They attacked us however less boldly, knowing that many of their men had fallen ; for, by a moderate computation, 22,000 of the Turks had been slain in former conflicts.

Ch. XXIV.—*How the Emperor Frederic, arriving in Armenia, is drowned in the river Selesius, and his son, the duke of Suabia, takes the command of the army.*

THE victorious army now enters the Armenian territories : all rejoice at having quitted a hostile kingdom, and at their arrival in the country of the faithful.   But, alas ! a more fatal land awaits them, which is to extinguish the light and joy of all.   Let man take thought and investigate, if he may, the counsels of the Lord, whose judgments are unfathomable. Things will occur sometimes to cause him astonishment, sometimes confusion, yet so that in every circumstance man may recognize the author of all things.   On the borders of Armenia there was a place, surrounded on one side by steep mountains, on the other side by the river Selesius.   Whilst the sumpter-horses and baggage were passing this river, the victorious emperor halted. He was indeed an illustrious man, of stature moderately tall, with red hair and beard ; his head was partly turning grey, his eyelids were prominent and his eyes sparkling ; his cheeks short and wide ; his breast and shoulders broad : in all other respects his form was manly. There was in him, as is read of Socrates, something distinguished and awful ; for his look denoted the firmness of his mind, being always immoveably the same, neither clouded by grief, nor contracted by anger, nor relaxed by joy. He so much reverenced the native language of Germany, that although he was not ignorant of other languages, yet he always conversed with ambassadors from foreign countries by means of an interpreter. This great man, having halted some time, in consequence of the sumpter-horses crossing the river, became at last impatient of the delay ; and wishing to accelerate the march, he prepares to cross the nearest part of the stream, so as to get in front of the sumpter-horses and be at liberty to proceed. O sea ! O earth ! O heaven ! the ruler of the Roman empire, ever august, in whom the glory of ancient Rome again flourished, its honour again lived, and its power was augmented, was overwhelmed in the waters and perished ! and though those who were near him hastened to his assistance, yet his aged spark of life was extinguished by a sudden though not premature death. If love of swimming, as several have asserted, be said to have caused his death, yet the gravity of the man argues the contrary ; nor does it merit belief that, a bad swimmer, he would have committed to the deceitful waters the safety of so many. The conscience is witness that death is less painful than the cause of death, but this is our consolation as it is written : the just, by whatever death he shall be surprised, will be refreshed. If the mountains of Gilboa, where the brave ones of Israel were slain, deserved to be deprived of the dew and rain, what imprecations may we not deservedly utter upon this fatal river, which overthrew a main pillar of all Christendom ? There were some who said that the place had been marked by a fatality from ancient times, and that the nearest rock had long borne upon it these words inscribed, " Here the greatest of men shall perish." The lamentable report of his death was spread around and filled all with dismay. If we search all the annals of antiquity, the traditions of history, and the fictions of romance, concerning the

sorrows of mothers, the sighs of brides, or the distresses of
men in general, the present grief will be found to be without
example, never before known in any age, and surpassing
all tears and lamentations.   There were many of the emperor's domestics present, with some of his kinsmen and his
son ; but it was impossible to distinguish them amid the
general lamentation, with which all and each lamented the loss
of their father and their lord. This, however, was a consolation
to all, and they all returned thanks for it to Divine Providence,
that he had not died within the territories of the infidels.

When his funeral-rites were performed, they left the fatal
spot as soon as possible, bearing with them the body of the
emperor adorned with royal magnificence, that it might be
carried to Antioch.   There the flesh, being boiled from the
bones, reposes in the church of the Apostolic see, and the bones
were conveyed by sea to Tyre, thence to be transported to Jerusalem.   It was fit indeed and wonderfully contrived by God's
providence, that one who had contended gloriously for Christ,
should repose in the two principal churches of the Christian religion, for both of which he had been a champion,—part of him in
the one, and part in the other,—the one that which our Lord's
burial rendered the most distinguished, the other that which
was honoured by being the see of the chief of the apostles. The
Christians arriving at Antioch, after many and long fastings,
gave way too plentifully to their appetites, and died of sudden
repletion : and so, after they had resisted both famine and the
swords of their enemies, repose was fatal to them, and a pernicious abundance cut them off.   In this shameful manner,
then, the greater part of that great army perished, and most
of the survivors returned to their own countries : a small body
of them, ashamed to return, served under the emperor's son,
to whom the prince of Antioch surrendered his city with all
its defences.   For on the plea of greater protection, he offered
of his own accord to commit his city to the duke, that this
brave man might defend his territories against the frequent
assaults of the enemies.

CH. XXV.—*Acre is besieged. King Guy is freed from his oath.*

In the mean time Christ's soldiers, who had been conveyed
by sea to the succour of the Holy Land, were laying siege to
Acre.   That the order of the siege may be better understood,
we will relate it from the beginning.   Guy, king of Jerusa-

lem, after he had been a year in captivity at Damascus, was
released by Saladin on the strict promise that he should abjure his kingdom, and, as soon as possible, go into exile beyond the sea. The clergy of the kingdom determine to release
the king from the bond of his oath; both because what is
done under compulsion deserves to be annulled, and because
the bands of the faithful who were on their way would find
in him a head and leader. It was right indeed that art
should overreach art, and that the treachery of the tyrant
should be deceived by its own example; for one who is
faithless in his promises, gives encouragement to similar faithlessness in him whose promise he exacts. The faithless unbeliever, having broken his previous agreement, had extorted
from the captive king, after many injuries, an oath that
on being restored to liberty he would go into exile. A
sad condition this, of liberty accompanied with exile and
the renunciation of a kingdom. But God so ordered it
that the counsel of Belial was brought to naught; for the
tyrant was baffled in his hopes of retaining the kingdom,
and the king was released by the sentence of the clergy from
the enormity of his promise. Men also had arrived, who
would nobly vindicate the wrongs which had been done to
Christ's cross, distinguished champions, whose devout zeal had
stirred them up to bring consolation to thee, O Jerusalem!
Behold, the whole world is in arms for thy service, and the
word is fulfilled which was spoken by the prophet Isaiah: "I
will bring thy seed from the north, and from the west I will
gather thee together: I will say to the north, Give! and to
the south, Do not forbid." Thus, then, when numbers had
flocked together to meet the king at Tripoli, the minds of all
were inspired with bravery, so that they strove not only to
keep what they had retained, but also to recover what they had
lost. Moreover, whilst they were remaining at Tripoli, they
did not pass the time in idleness; for they assailed the enemies
in that neighbourhood, and defeated at one time three hundred,
at another time a larger number, with their victorious band.
Among the rest was the king's brother who had lately landed:
his name was Geoffrey, and he distinguished himself especially
amongst the combatants by his valour, for, in addition to the
common cause, which influenced all alike, he was roused to
action by his own private wrongs, and the injury which had
been done to his brother.

CH. XXVI.—*How the king, arriving at Tyre, is not received by the marquis, but dissembling the insult, proceeds with the men of Pisa, and a small army to Acre, which the Christians besiege by sea and land.*

AFTER a while the king assembled his army and proceeded to Tyre; but, demanding admittance, was refused by the marquis, though the city had been committed to his custody on the condition that it should be restored to the king and the heirs of the kingdom. Not content with this injury, he adds insult to breach of faith, for whenever the king's messenger, or any pilgrims, endeavoured to enter the town, they were treated harshly, and were in his sight no better than Gentiles and Publicans. But the Pisans, who possessed no small part of the city, would not be induced to consent to his perfidy, but with commendable rebellion stood up for the king's rights. The marquis directed not only insults, but civil war against them, and they, prudently withdrawing for a time, retired with others from the city to the army. The troops had pitched their camp in an open plain; but none of them were allowed to enter the city, even to buy provisions; and they all found an enemy where they had hoped to find an ally. Whilst these events were going on, the marquis was afflicted by a complaint to which he had long been subject; but, as it chanced to assail him this time with greater violence than usual, he conjectured that he had taken poison. Upon this, he issued a harsh edict against physicians who make potions; innocent men were put to death on false suspicions, and those whose province it was to heal others, now found the practice of their art lead to their own destruction. The king was urged by many to attack the city, but he prudently dissembled his own wrong, and hastily marched, with all the army he could collect, to besiege the town of Acre. There were seven hundred knights, and others more numerous still, collected out of all Christendom; but if we were to estimate the whole army, its strength did not amount altogether to nine thousand men. At the end of August, on St. Augustin's day,[*] two years after the city had been taken, they bravely commenced that long and difficult siege which was protracted during two years longer before the city surrendered. The Turks from the battlements of the walls, beheld the army

* Aug. 28, 1189.

approach, but without knowing who they were, or for what
they came. When they learnt the truth, they feared not
their approach, and treated their intentions with derision.
The men of Pisa, who chose to proceed by sea, as shorter
and easier, approached Acre in due order in their ships, and
bravely occupied the shore ; where they had no sooner secured
a station, than they formed the siege on the side towards the
sea with equal courage and perseverance. The king, with
the rest of his army, fixed his tents on a neighbouring hill
commonly called Mount Turon, from which, by the eminence
of the ground, he overlooked the approach both by sea and
land. This hill was higher on the eastern side of the city ;
and, as it allowed the eye to rove freely round, it gave a prospect over the plain on all sides, far and wide.

Ch. XXVII.—*The Christians assault the city, but are attacked by
Saladin in the rear, and whilst they are thus between two enemies,
they are encouraged by receiving a reinforcement of 12,000 northern
warriors.*

On the third day after their arrival the Christians made
an assault upon the town ; and deeming it tedious to await
the effect of engines for throwing stones, together with
other machines, they trusted to the defence of their shields
alone, and carried scaling-ladders to mount the walls. That
day would have put a happy termination to the toil of so many
days, if the malice of the ancient enemy, and the arrival of
false information, had not frustrated their achievement when
it was almost completed ; for it was reported that Saladin
was at hand, and our men returned with speed to the camp ;
but when they perceived that it was only a small body that
had come in advance, they expressed indignation rather than
complaint that the victory had been snatched from them.
They were indeed few that had come, but fear had reported
that an innumerable multitude was at hand : for it is not
unusual, that things should be magnified through terror.
The sultan, at this time, was besieging the castle of Bel-
fort ; and when he heard what was going on, he marched in
haste with a large army to Acre. Our men, unequal to cope
with him, kept themselves within the limits before described.
The Turks assailed them perseveringly, both morning and
evening, trying every means to penetrate to the hill-top ; and

thus, those who came to besiege others, were now besieged
themselves.   In this position, then, were our men, when the
Morning Star visited them from on high ; for behold ! fifty
ships, such as are commonly called cogga, having twelve thousand armed men, on board, are seen approaching,—a grateful
sight to our men, on account of the strait which they were in.
Grateful is that which comes when prayed for ; more grateful
still is that which comes contrary to our hope ; but grateful
beyond all is that which comes to aid us in the last necessity :
yet ofttimes we suspend our belief concerning a thing we so
much long for, and cannot credit what we too much desire.
Our army, from the top of the hill, see the reinforcements
coming, and dare not hope for an event so joyful ; and the
new comers, also, look upon the camp as an object of suspicion.
When, however, they came nearer and saw the ensigns
of the Christian faith, a shout is raised on both sides,—their
joyful feelings find vent in tears : they eagerly flock together
and leap into the waves to go and meet them.   O happy fleet,
which, sailing from the Northern Ocean, and encountering
a voyage never before tried, passed over so many seas, so
many coasts, so many dangers, and came from Europe, along
the shores of Africa, to succour Asia in her distress.   The
crews of these ships were Danes and Frisons, men inured to
labour by the rigours of the north, and having three qualities
good in war—large limbs, invincible minds, and devout fervour for the faith.   They had sailed from their country,
and the kindly breeze had wafted them on : the waves, as
well as winds, were benignant, such as give delight to sailors,
and so the merciful Lord brought his champions safe and
uninjured through so many dangers.   But the inhabitants of
the lands by which these vessels sailed, were excited when
they saw the fleet, and, embarking on ship-board, both
Englishmen and Flemings followed them in haste.   Nor must
I pass in silence a gallant action which was performed by
them as they passed : they courageously attacked a city called
Silvia, on the sea-coast of Spain, and having quickly made
themselves masters of it, and slain the Gentile inhabitants,
they delivered the city up to the Christians, appointed there
a bishop, and proceeded victorious on their voyage.   To Acre,
then, they came ; and having pitched their camp between the
city and Mount Turon, they turned their invincible prowess

to the destruction of the enemy, whom they assailed, not by
frequent skirmishes, but by one continued conflict;—for their
prodigal valour and reckless fury exposed them to so many
dangers that afterwards, when the city was taken, hardly a
hundred men remained alive out of the twelve thousand.

Ch. XXVIII.—*Of the arrival of James d'Avennes: the siege of the
city is pressed with greater vigour: the fiction of Saladin.*

THE night after the landing of the Frisons and Danes,
James d'Avennes reached the desired shore, a man endowed
with threefold qualifications,—in counsel a Hector, in arms an
Achilles, and in honour surpassing Regulus. He pitched his
camp opposite the tower they call the Cursed (Maledicta),
and a little further on lay the Templars; still the greater
part of the city was not besieged, but there was a free communication open to the enemy. Our men, anxious as to their
movements, liked not this freedom of entrance and exit;
but the extended circuit of the walls and the paucity of soldiers allowed not of a continued blockade. They therefore
divided their forces into troops, and by turns watched the
approaches of the city in arms; and thus, for some days,
obstructed the passage of those who would go out. The
Turks, however, issuing from city and camp, and having
collected their strength from all quarters, attacked our men
and prevailed; for a divided line of battle is easily broken
through, and scattered strength quickly yieldeth. On that
day the Hospitallers were on guard, and on giving way,
were relieved by the Templars, who checked the enemy, and
hindered them, though pressed severely, from bursting into
the camp. Moreover, day by day the army of the faithful
increased; and a multitude of ships coming together, struck
no small terror into the Mahometan army. But Saladin, by
means of a fiction, lessened the fears thus excited, asserting
that the Christians took away their ships by night, and
brought them back again at dawn of day as if they were
newly arrived, for the purpose of making a display of
strength. He himself was not, however, ignorant of the
real state of the case, and grieved bitterly at our daily increase of strength; but, dissembling the cloud on his mind
under a haughty aspect, he exhibited a calm and fearless
countenance.

C�componH. XXIX.—*Of the arrival of the French, English, and Germans.*

VERY many indeed had already come from the kingdom
of France; and amongst others the bishop of Beauvais, a
man more devoted to the camp than the closet, and one who
gloried in warfare and strove to be like Turpin if he could but
find a Charles.   There is a part of France called Champagne;
and though the whole country is famous for the pursuit of
arms, this one, by a sort of privilege of chivalry, excels and
surpasses the rest.   Hence its warlike youth marching out
in power displayed the strength which it had exercised in the
gymnasium with greater boldness against the foe; and having
laid aside the playful game of battle, they turned their belli-
cose spirits to the realities of war.   So, indeed, English as
well as French are led on by the warmth of their devotion,
so that not waiting for their own kings they march forward
to perform their duty to the King of kings.   From Germany,
also, there came an illustrious and powerful man, whom in
their language they call Landgrave;* which, according to
the sense of the word, appears to mean count of the land, as
if so entitled *par excellence.*   He persuaded the marquis, who
had a difference with King Guy, to repair to Acre, though at
first he had declined to do so on account of the disagreement.
We know that the rules of history sometimes require us to
commit to writing, seriatim, the names of the chiefs who assist
in the management of affairs, to which, indeed, they themselves, in a sort of itch for glory, sometimes lay claim; whilst,
on the other hand, the fastidious reader may think the work
too long in this particular, and so reject a narrative which
runs to wearisomeness.   We therefore will be as brief as
possible in enumerating the chiefs.   But when the course of
affairs shall offer an opportunity, we will mention the illustrious actions of each.   After the numbers of the faithful
were considerably increased, and when the army was fitter for
setting about its arduous undertaking, it was unanimously determined to attack the neighbouring camp of the unbelievers.
A certain mount stood opposite to Mount Turon, which we
have before described; here the enemy had pitched their
pavilions, and a large intervening space of plain presented far
and wide an area well adapted for battle.   Hither the army

* This was Lewis III., landgrave of Thuringia, who had accompanied
or followed the emperor to the crusade.

descended from the camp to the plain; and there being put
in array, were divided into troops, so that the light-armed
soldiers with the bowmen and arbalesters went first; next to
them followed the body of the army, glittering with horses,
arms, and the various insignia of war. Their countenance and
bearing indicated the disposition of their minds; the faithful
had recourse to prayer, whilst the enemy trembled. There
were those who, abandoning themselves to excessive exultation
at the sight of the battle-array, presumed to say,—" What
power shall prevail, what multitude shall withstand us? Let
the Lord assist neither us nor our adversaries; the victory
rests in our own valour." Certainly a most impious and utterly
detestable sentiment, for it placed the issue of the battle in man
and not in the Deity, when man can do nothing without God;
which, indeed, the issue of affairs proved by sad experience.

The Turks stood resolute for the defence of their camp;
but when our men approached nearer, they opened the body
of their infantry who stood first, and boldly charged the
enemy with their horse. The unbelievers were put to flight,
and abandoned their camp; the Christians desisted from the
pursuit, and were eager after the spoil; the cords of the pavilions were cut, and the tent of the sultan himself was seized
upon by the fiery Count de Bar. Meanwhile, an immense
multitude of the enemy burst out from the city, and marching
from that part which was not besieged, proceeded towards
the mountain by a circuitous path. Indeed, they purposely
marched by a tortuous circuit, that while our men were in
doubt whether they meant to attack the camp or the army,
they might fall suddenly upon the latter, and close them in
from the rear. The Templars, inferior to none in renown,
devoted to slaughter, had by this time burst through the enemies' squares, and, if the remainder of the army had pressed
on in pursuit, they would that day have been the fortunate
conquerors as well of the city as of the battle; but when the
Templars in their ardour had advanced too far in following up
their fortune, they were suddenly attacked by the townsmen;
and although multitudes overcame them, it was not without
great slaughter of their own men that the enemy triumphed.
There Gerard de Riddeford the master of the Templars, of
whom we have made mention before, was slain; happy he on
whom the Lord conferred so great glory, that he should gain the
laurel which he had earned in so many wars, and be admitted

into the fellowship of martyrs. In another part, while the
Germans were too eagerly bent upon plunder, the old deceiver
offered to their view a horse escaping; and seeing them pursue him in a crowd, the rest supposed that they were running
away. By this slight but fatal accident the whole army was
thrown into a panic, and all turned their thoughts to flight.
At the same time, a new rumour increased their fear: for
there was a cry that the townsmen had gone forth to plunder
the baggage. The army was at once thrown into confusion;
the battalions dispersed, and abandoned their standards; even
the commanders fly headlong, and scarce any have courage to
resist.

Ch. XXX.—*The flight and slaughter of the Christians.*

THE Turks, on seeing the confusion of the Christians, wondered at the circumstance, but were ignorant of the cause;
and having regained the victory unexpectedly, they turned
their horses and resumed the courage which they had more
from use than nature, yielding to those who pressed, and pressing on those who yielded; for they will fly from those who
attack, and pursue those who fly. In this lamentable and
disastrous tumult, Andrew de Brienne, while calling upon his
comrades to resume the battle, was slain by the Turks who
were pursuing; this man was so superior to all the other
Frenchmen, that they awarded him the crown of chivalry,
while others were content to strive for the honour of being
second to him. His brother, the Count de Brienne, though he
had seen him fall, passed him as he lay on the ground, and
though called upon, feared to stop, and, like a coward, left him
to his fate. Different from this was the conduct of a soldier,
who, seeing James d'Avennes thrown from his horse, gave
him the one on which he was escaping, and nobly by his own
death saved the life of his lord. King Guy, also, was on the
point of being slain by the foe, had not the marquis come to
his assistance, who forgot the wrongs he had received from him,
to discharge the duties of humanity, though to one undeserving
of it, and rescued him from destruction. Geoffrey, the king's
brother, seeing the army in confusion, and all hastening to fly,
at last abandoned the care of the camp which he had undertaken to defend; and, anxious for his brother's safety, rushed
forward to arrest the fugitives. O miserable change of
affairs! the Christians had gone forth with confidence—they

return in confusion ; they had marched in order—they return
in disorder ; victorious, they had routed the foe—yet they run
back vanquished. Man's presumption at length acknowledged
what man and what man's strength can effect, if it rely not
on the Lord's right hand ; for he powerfully works victory
amongst his own people, who gives confidence to the warrior,
and a crown to the victor.   Our men had presumed on their
own strength, they believed no enemy could be found who
could put them in fear, and yet they found that enemy
too near them, for they lost one thousand five hundred men.
There was a knight named Ferrand, who having been left behind naked and nearly lifeless, after lying hid amongst the
slain, returned by night to the camp, but was so disfigured by
his wounds, that he could not be recognized by his friends,
and with difficulty gained admission.   The license of the poet
or a lengthy dissertation might depict the various incidents of
the battle and the divers modes of death ; but we are obliged
to be brief, and must say, not *how*, but *what* occurred.
Saladin ordered the bodies of the Christians to be collected
and cast into the river which flowed near; that, being carried
down by the current, the sight of them might occasion terror,
or becoming decomposed they might infect the water.

Cʜ. XXXI.—*How our men, increasing in number daily, suffer severely
from the Turks while occupied in carrying a trench round the city.*

AFTER this, our chiefs, thinking it best to abstain for the
present from open war, occupy themselves in strengthening
their camp, and carry round an embankment of turf, with deep
ditches from sea to sea, for the protection of the tents ; while
the marquis and the Hospitallers boldly seized upon the space
free from siege, and thus the city was blockaded by sea and
by land.   While our men were thus sedulously employed in
making the trenches, the Turks harassed them incessantly,
and one party relieving another continued to annoy them from
morn till night.   It was necessary, thus, that one part of our
men should defend the other while at work from their attacks.
Such as we thought worth while to bear with, we did,
without returning them, although the air was darkened
with their missiles and darts, which exceeded all computation.   Our men, however, worked away with their utmost
endeavour and the Turks lamented their progress.   You

might see in their frequent encounters, now these now those (according to the chances of war) overthrown and borne down. While our men were thus for a considerable time struggling, the Lord above grieved over them, and by strengthening and increasing our numbers from day to day, deserted not altogether those who trusted in him. There came together, therefore, from different parts of the world, princes, dukes, counts, besides many of inferior degree ; whose names were the Count of Ferrara, Nargenot du Bourg, Anselm de Montreal, Geoffrey de Grenville, Otho de la Fosse, William Goez, the Viscount de Chatellerauld, the Viscount de Turome, the Chastellan of Bruges, the Archbishop of Pisa, also the Count Bertulf, the Count Nicholas of Hungary, the Count Bernard, the Count Jocelyn, the Count Richard of Apulia, the Count Alebrand, Engelran de Vienne, Hervey de Gien, Theobald de Bar, the Count John of Loegria, another Count John of Seis, with a nephew of the king of Denmark. There came also some chiefs of the Danes, with 400 of their countrymen. At the same time came Guy de Dampierre, the bishop of Verona, and a few Roman citizens. All these, and a great many future martyrs and confessors, were added to the number of the faithful. Martyrs truly they were, a great part of whom died in a short time by the stench of the dead bodies which corrupted the air, and by the fatigue of constant watchings; while others were overcome by the injuries they received, as neither rest nor breathing time was allowed them, for the Turks harassed without intermission those who were working at the ditch, and reduced their spirits by unexpected attacks, until it was at length completed. They then made an attempt to relieve the city from the threatened blockade.

CH. XXXII.—*The description of the city of Acre and the places round about it.*

WE do not think it foreign to our purpose to give at times, as the order of our matter requires, the description of places, in order that a city, so famous for its magnificence, as well as the various incidents of war, may gain additional celebrity by our labours. For if a ten years' war made Troy celebrated ; if the triumph of the Christians made Antioch more illustrious, Acre will certainly obtain eternal fame, as a city for which the whole world contended. In the form of a

triangle, it is narrow on the western side, while it extends in a
wider range towards the east, and full a third part of it is
washed by the ocean on the south and west.   The port,
which is not so convenient as it should be, often deceives and
proves fatal to the vessels which winter there: for the rock
which lies over against the shore, to which it runs parallel, is
too short to protect them from the fury of the storm.   And
because this rock appeared a suitable place for washing away
the entrails, the ancients used it as a place for offering up
sacrifices, and on account of the flies which followed the
sacrificial flesh, the tower which stands above it was called
the Tower of Flies.   There is also a tower called the Cursed,
situated on the wall which surrounds the city; and if we are
to credit common report, it received its name because it is
said that the pieces of silver for which Judas betrayed his
Lord, were made there.   The city, then named Ptolemais, was
formerly situate upon Mount Turon, which is close to the
city, whence, by an error of antiquity, some call Acre Ptolemais.   There is a hill called the Mosque, near Mount Turon,
where the ancients say is the sepulchre of Memnon; but by
whose kind offices he was brought thither, we have learnt
neither by writing nor by hearsay.   The river which flows
by the city is named Belus, and although its bed is narrow,
and not deep, Solinus has rendered it celebrated by number-
ing it amongst the wonders of the world, as being enriched
with glassy sand.   For there was a certain sandy foss, the
sand of which supplied materials for making glass; these, if
taken out, were altogether useless; but, if let in, from the
secret virtue of the place assumed a glassy nature.   Not far
from the river is pointed out a low rock near the city, at
which it is said that the three divisions of the world, Asia,
Europe, and Africa meet; and though it contains separately
the other parts of the world, the place itself, dependent on
none, is distinct from and independent of all three.   Mount
Carmel rises aloft on the southern side of the city, where
Elijah the Tishbite is known to have had an habitation of
modest cost, as his cave still testifies; but although we are
often wont in a description to wander away to the pleasant
parts of the circuit, we must at present overlook the attractions of the surrounding places, while we turn our attention
to the course of the war.

Cʜ. XXXIII.—*How the people of the city were reduced to such starvation that they offered to surrender; the Sultan comes to their assistance with fifty galleys; they capture and put to flight our galleys.*

Wʜᴇɴ therefore our men had encompassed Acre on all sides with a blockade, the townspeople, having consumed their provisions, began to be severely pressed by famine, so that they offered to surrender the city on condition that they should be allowed to depart, with their property, unmolested. These conditions did not satisfy the chiefs, who had determined, either to compel them by extreme necessity to submit to their will, or to gain, by every means in their power, the glory of storming the city. But whilst they were slowly negotiating for the surrender of the city, the sultan had fully equipped at Alexandria fifty galleys, with men, provisions, and arms, which he sent to succour Acre. These arrived on All Saints' Eve, and when they were seen at a distance, vague rumours distracted the people with various forebodings. Some report that the enemy are at hand; others that subsidies are come for the Christians. While they were still doubting, the enemy threw themselves into the city, and even carried with them, by force, one of our ships laden with provisions, which they found in the port; and being long sustained with those provisions, pressed upon us with the greater courage. Not content with plundering our ship of burden, they put to death without mercy the crew and every one else they had found therein, and hung them round the walls on the day of All Saints. Moreover, the galleys of the enemy kept watch over both the exit and entrance of the port of the city, that no one dared to come to our assistance for fear of falling into their hands. And on the morrow of the Nativity of our Lord, one of our galleys deeming the fleet an arrival of Christians, went for the purpose of making inquiries after our succours, incautiously to meet this Babylonian fleet as it approached, and with it a smaller vessel, called a galleon; this taking the lead, owing to its lightness, fell suddenly into the midst of the enemy, instead of meeting with friends as was supposed. The voice of some who answered, and the suspicious silence of others, undeceived them; upon which the terrified sailors cast themselves into the sea, and

escaped, by means of swimming, according as each was able.
Thus then occupying that part of the sea, and our galleys
which were by far the least numerous, having gone away
secretly to Tyre, the enemy had free and open communication with the city by sea.   At that time the Germans,
making a large mill for the grinding of corn, turned by horses,
while the millstones grated as they were drawn round, the
Turks, gazing with great earnestness at the mill at work,
thought that it was some instrument for their destruction, or
for storming their city; for never before had a mill of that
description been seen in that land.

CH. XXXIV.—*Of the sea-fight between the fleet of the marquis and our
men and that of the enemy, and how we gained the victory.*

AT a season of calm, when Easter was close at hand, the
marquis at our request returned from Tyre with a large equipment and supplies of men, arms, and provisions.   For by the
provident care of the chiefs, the king and marquis were pacified on the pretext that the marquis should have possession
of Tyre, Berytus, and Sidon, and on condition that he should
be faithful and strenuous for the interests of the king and his
kingdom. But rash ambition always turns to evil the avaricious
and iniquitous heart; for inflamed with the desire of obtaining
the kingdom, he broke the faith he had pledged; and while
to the outward eye he appeared a friend, within his breast he
concealed the foe.   At length the townspeople liked not
their privation of liberty, and determined to try the issue
of a sea-fight.   They therefore led forth their galleys by
twos, and keeping good order, they rowed into the offing to
meet and attack those that were coming; our men prepared
to meet them as they came on, and since there was no means
of getting away, prepared to face them with greater resolution.
[On the other hand our men got on board our war ships, and
straining to the left by an oblique course, retreated to a distance, and gave the enemy free means of egress.]   And now
that mention is made of a sea-fight, we judge it right to
describe briefly the fleet, and what difference there is between
those of the moderns and ancients.   With the ancients, a
larger number of oars was required in ships of this kind,
which were arranged in stories, so that some plied the oars

at a longer, others at a shorter distance from the sea.
These vessels had frequently three or four banks of oars
each, some even five; and a few of the ships used at the
battle of Actium between Antony and Augustus, are said
to have had six.   Furthermore, ships of war were called
liburnæ; for the ships used in the battle of Actium were
chiefly built at Liburnia in Dalmatia; whence it became
usual among the ancients to call them *liburnæ.*   But all that
ancient magnificence has passed away; for ships of war, which
once had six banks of oars, have now seldom more than two.
But what the ancients used to call a *liburna,* we call a *galea,*
with the middle syllable lengthened; it is long and graceful,
not high out of water, and has a piece of wood at the prow,
which is commonly called the spur; with which the enemy's
ships are struck and pierced.   Galleons are vessels with one
bank of oars, manageable from their shortness, easily turned, and
light for running to and fro; they are better suited for throwing fire.   When, therefore, they went forth on both sides to
fight, our men drew not up their ships in a straight line, but
in the form of a crescent; that if the enemy should charge the
inner ships, he might be shut in and crushed.   They placed their
most powerful ships at the points of the crescent, as against
them would be directed the enemy's most vigorous attack; on
the upper row of benches were arranged shields close together;
and in one the rowers sat, in order that those who were on
deck might have free space for fighting.   The sea was perfectly calm and tranquil, as if it favoured the battle, and the
rippling wave impeded neither the shock of the attacking ship,
nor the stroke of the oars.   As they closed, the trumpets sounded
on both sides.   A terrific clang is roused, and the battle is
commenced by the throwing of missiles.   Our men implore
the Divine assistance, and ply their oars strenuously, and dash
at the enemy's ships with their beaks.   Soon the battle began; the oars become entangled and they fight hand to hand,
having grappled each other's ships together; and they fire the
decks with burning oil, which is vulgarly called Greek fire.
That kind of fire with a detestable stench and livid flames
consumes both flint and steel; it cannot be extinguished by
water, but is subdued by the sprinkling of sand, and put
out by pouring vinegar on it.   But what can be more dreadful than a fight at sea? what more savage, where such

various fates await the combatants? Some are tortured by the
burning of the flames; some falling overboard are swallowed
in the waves; others wounded perish by the enemy's weapons.
One galley, unskilfully managed by our men, exposed its flank
to the foe; and being set on fire, received the Turks as they
boarded her on all sides.   The rowers in their fright fall into
the sea; but a few soldiers, impeded by their heavy armour,
and restrained by ignorance of swimming, took courage from
desperation, and commenced an unequal fight; and trusting in
the Lord's valour, a few of them overcame numbers; and
having slain the foe, they brought back the half-burnt vessel
in triumph.   Another ship was boarded by the enemy, who
had driven the combatants from the upper deck; while those
who were below strove to escape by the help of their oars.
Wondrous and terrible was the conflict; for the oars being
pulled different ways, the galley was drawn first one way, then
the other, as the Turks drove it; yet our men prevailed, and
the enemy, who rowed on the upper deck, being overcome and thrust down by the Christians, yielded.   In this
naval contest, the enemy lost both the galley and a galleon, together with their crews; and our men, unhurt and
joyful, gain a glorious triumph.   Having drawn the captured galley on shore, they gave it up to be plundered by
both sexes who came to meet them.   On this our women,
dragging the Turks by the hair, after treating them shamefully and cutting their throats in a disgraceful manner, beheaded them.   And the weaker the hand to strike, so much the
more lengthened was the punishment inflicted; for they used
knives, and not swords, for cutting off their heads.   A like
sea-fight was never seen, so destructive in its issue, accomplished with so much danger, and completed with so much cost.

CH. XXXV.—*Meanwhile the Turks from without, eager to fill our
breach with earth, fiercely attack our men who were within.*

IN the mean time the Turkish army from without, though
deeply bewailing our victory, persisted in making attacks
upon our men who were within the trench, endeavouring
either to fill up the completed portion by casting back the
earth, or to slay those who resisted.   Our men, sustaining
their attack, though with difficulty, fight under great dis-

advantages, for they seemed unequal to contend against so countless a multitude,—for the numbers of the assailants continually increased, and we had to take precautions on the side of the city 'lest they also should rush in and assault us. There was amongst the assailants a fiendish race, very impetuous and obstinate; deformed in nature as they were unlike to the others in character, of a darker appearance, of vast stature, of exceeding ferocity, having on their heads red coverings instead of helmets, carrying in their hands clubs bristling with iron teeth, which neither helmet nor coat of mail could withstand; and they had a carved image of Mahomet for a standard. So great was the multitude of this evil race, that as fast as one party was thrown to the earth, another rushed forward over them. Thus, by their constant attacks, they confounded our men so much, that we doubted which way to turn ourselves; for as there was neither security nor rest, we were distressed on all sides, at one time guarding ourselves from sallies of the besieged from the city, at another from the incessant attacks of the enemy from without; and again from the side of the sea where their galleys were lying in wait to convey the Turks into the city as they arrived, or to intercept the succours which were coming to us the Christians. At length, by favour of the Divine mercy, our adversaries were driven back and repulsed.

Cr. XXXVI.—*How our men were on the point of assaulting the city with three wooden towers; the townsmen offer to surrender; while we are attacked by the enemy below, our machines are set on fire.*

Our chiefs contribute mutually to the making of machines for storming the city, and construct three moveable towers of dry wood, of which the making of the first fell to the lot of the Landgrave, the second to the Genoese, and the third to the rest of the army. The huge machines raised with zealous emulation, and being carried up by stories, were urged forwards on wheels, which, assisted by mechanical contrivances, moved easily. To prevent their catching fire, the workmen covered them with tarpaulins and raw hides; and that the blow of the *petrariæ* might not injure them, which it does if caught by a softer substance, they suspend twisted ropes in front. And the upper parts of the towers, which were much higher than the walls and bulwarks of the city, contained slingers and darters, while the middle story was occupied by men armed with stakes and poles. Each camp had its *petrariæ*, which stood on the side and afforded protection to the towers as they were drawn along, as well as serving to throw down the opposite walls. The townsmen now entirely despairing, offered to surrender the city if they might be allowed to depart and take away their property with them. Our people refused, and hastened with all their might to bring the machines they had made against the walls, upon which the townsmen resisted, and in turn revenge themselves on their besiegers and assaulters; for, on the Saturday after Ascension-day, when the machines had been brought nearer the walls, after we had assaulted the city from morn till even, behold! the army of the Turks from without came rushing in troops with immense violence upon the trench, to attack from the rear those who were assaulting the city, that they might draw them off if not entirely disperse them. Thus, while our men, held in check on both sides, and having their attention divided, were either defending themselves against the attacks from without, or were engaged in storming the city, and their strength was weakened from having so many objects to contend with, the enemy set fire to our towers, which our utmost endeavours could not extinguish, and being burnt with Greek fire, they were rendered useless. And thus, by an unfortunate accident, our hope of triumph fell,—the more mortifying in the result from being considered so certain at first.

CH. XXXVII.—*Of the famine among the citizens and the succour brought in by the galleys.*

THE besieged were now so sorely pressed from the great want of provisions, that they ate up their horses and spared not beasts of other kinds, forgetful of the Mahometan law, while, reduced by hunger to eat forbidden things, they satisfied their ravening appetites. Meanwhile, they turned out the older Christian captives, whom they reckoned useless, having become speechless and decrepit; but they reserved the younger captives, who were hale and fit for work. While the

Turks were thus straitened, there arrived three vessels of burthen, whose crews suddenly threw themselves into the city, for fear of meeting the Christians, in such haste that some of them were wrecked, but those that carried provisions were saved. Whereupon the besieged, overcome with excessive joy, as if their wishes had been gratified, testify their deliverance by howling in loud tones to the music of cymbals and pipes; they hoped by these rejoicings to confirm the belief that they had not sustained any loss.

Ch. XXXVIII.—*How Saladin, having collected the armies of his kingdom together, attacks our men, who by their bold resistance force him to retire in confusion.*

MEANWHILE, Saladin, having gathered together the forces of all Asia, from the Tigris as far as India, as well as from the parts between the Tigris and Euphrates, and thence to the southern districts, led them forth to war. From Africa too, there came countless tribes; the Nadabaræ, Gætulians, and Numidians, and from the scorching south, the people named Moors or Mauritanians, from the Greek word μαυρος, which means black. Thus two divisions of the globe attacked the third; against both of which Europe entered into conflict, the only one of them which acknowledged the name of Christ. Most of these troops served Saladin as stipendiaries; so that the money which had been raised was no longer sufficient for their pay. For by common agreement the barbarians decreed that whoever died, should leave the third of his property to the defenders of the law. Some, however, served for nothing as a sort of pilgrimage, and instead of performing the ceremonies of the law, went to fight against the Christians. The pouring out, therefore, of these multitudes from all parts, gave the king excessive joy; and falling on our men boldly, he hoped either to carry them all away captive, or to exterminate them with the edge of the sword. And if we read that Darius king of the Persians fought with seven hundred thousand men, we may judge of the multitude on the present occasion; for his army could be numbered, but this army none could count. That large plain, stretching from sea to sea, over which they were spread far and wide, would not hold so many thousands; and had the ground been itself

much more extensive, it would have been narrow compared
with the numbers engaged.   The Christians, though pressed
by the townsmen on one side and by the enemy on the other,
stood their ground manfully ; and having placed guards at the
trenches, repelled the assaults of both. The attack commenced
on the Saturday of Pentecost, and continued for eight days,
the great. slaughter on both sides bearing witness to the fury
of the combat. Our men found the holidays no holidays ; but
their resolute valour strengthened them to the confusion of
the foe ; and He who ordained of old the Apostles to prophecy, now inflamed his soldiers to battle. All had strict
charge not to go beyond the camp ; for there was no need to
go in search of an enemy, when one was at their doors.
And so great was the multitude which came to attack, that
darts thrown at random were not without effect ; nor did any
take aim, when the crowded squadrons afforded so many
objects to wound. · On the eighth day, a blow from a sling
killed one of the sultan's sons, whose death put a stop to the
attack which had begun, and terrified the hostile army.
Very many of them, therefore, returned to their own land in
great dread of coming in contact with the Christians, who
had resisted so great a multitude so boldly.

CH. XXXIX.—*Further of the famine among the citizens and of the*
succours by the galleys.

MEANWHILE, hunger afflicts the townsmen sorely, but the
south wind brings them supplies of corn from the sultan in
Egypt. The vessels were five and twenty in number; of the
three largest of these, two were run aground, while attempting
to push through between the Tower of Flies and the adjacent
rock ; the third got into port unhurt ; for our galleys had
turned them from their intended course ; but one of ours,
in its hasty pursuit of the enemy, struck on a rock and was
dashed to pieces.

CH. XL.—*Of the misfortunes of our men, arising from a battle begun*
without the counsel of their chiefs.

As time wore on, and our army had enjoyed a long repose,
the common soldiers, desirous of a change, began to tax the
chiefs with sloth ; and all excited with one wish, each en-
courages his fellow to battle.   Their indignation is excited

by the proximity of the heathen camp; the greedy are encouraged by the prospect of spoil, and the honour of victory inflames the warlike. They therefore enter into a tumultuous plot, and with eager heat, prepare unanimously for battle, without asking the consent of their chiefs. The latter endeavour, as far as possible, to check the rash daring of the people, and the patriarch forbids them under pain of anathema from provoking the enemy, and incurring the dangers of a battle, without consulting their chiefs; but neither the dissuasions of these, nor the threats of the others, availed; for fury overcame counsel, violence reason, and order yielded to multitudes; whichever way the vulgar are impelled, they think rashness a virtue, and that to be the best which is the object of their wishes; and not weighing the issue of things, they reject him who chideth, and despise him who ruleth. Therefore, on St. James's-day, a mournful and un-propitious one, the ill-fated crowd of common soldiers burst forth; they go forth in arms, it is true, but they oppose themselves without precaution against the coming danger; a fine body of young men, indeed, distinguished for bravery, and that would yield to no victor, had it had a head, or used counsel in its darings, or been as fond of battle as it was of booty. But the army had no leader; every one was his own soldier and guide; they scarcely paid attention to or followed their proper standards; many ran before them, and thought more of the booty than the battle in which they were to perish. The Maho-metans, when they saw the crowd coming forth, whether from fear or design, gave way a little, and as they did not gather up their baggage, they left their tents behind, rich with various things. But under the declivity of an adjacent mount they collected their lost courage, and stopped, while they sent spies to discover the object at which our men aimed, and why they had come forth. Tecadin, the sultan's grand-son, at that time had pitched his tent opposite the camp of Himbert; he was a man of active spirit and bold in arms, but of exceeding wickedness and implacable cruelty, and he hated above all things the name of Christian. Hither the aforesaid multitude hastened; hither the lust for plunder urges every one, and they, who were eager after the spoil, explored not the ambuscades that lay around. Many glutted their appetite with the abundance of food they met with, and having

relinquished their arms, lay down in over security, as if they
had been invited to a feast. The Turks, having learnt what
was going on, soon poured in on all sides, and shouting with
a terrible noise, as is their wont, gained an easy victory over a
scattered and stupified foe. No one dreamt of fighting, every
one thought of flight; but being on foot, laden with arms,
and exhausted with thirst and heat, they could not escape when
pursued by an active and mounted enemy. In all directions
they were routed, and thrown into confusion; no quarter was
given, nor a captive taken; fury could not satisfy its appetite,
and anger recals the sword, which the weariness of the striker
had for a moment laid aside. Wherever fear urged any one,
he was sure to meet with death; an inevitable fate threatened
one and all. The foe and slaughter presented themselves on
all sides; numbers were wounded, and four thousand are
reckoned to have been slain. Though they heard the tumult,
and saw the slaughter, the chiefs pretend to be ignorant of it;
hard-hearted, inhuman, and impious, certainly they were, who
saw their brethren butchered before them, and offered no assistance to them when perishing, whose only crime was the leaving
the camp against orders. At length, when others hesitated
from sloth, rather than from anger, Ralph de Hauterive, archdeacon of Colchester, came to the assistance of those who were
suffering and succoured them when on the point of falling.
He was a man of handsome form and figure, and merited a
twofold laurel for his excellence in both kinds of warfare—
being illustrious for his knowledge, and famous in arms. He
met with a glorious and happy end, after performing many
remarkable actions in the siege in which he was then engaged.
The townsmen on seeing the success of their friends, issued
out boldly, and went so far as to attack and overthrow some
of the nearest tents.

CH. XLI.—*Of the ships and succours which came to our men.*

AFTER this sad slaughter had been brought about, by
which our strength was considerably diminished, fortune
smiled more favourably; and the west wind setting in brought
some vessels laden with soldiers. Meanwhile the barbarian
fleet, mixing itself secretly with ours, got forward, and imitating the language and ensigns of the Christians, made a sudden
and unexpected approach to the city.

CH. XLII.—*What men and warriors of the higher and lower grades of the laity and clergy came to our succour*

WHEN, therefore, our men were utterly purified by the constant fire of tribulation, and the heavy trials which penetrated them to the very soul, the Lord regarded them, and withdrew them from the scourge, for He deserteth not those who hope in Him, and He grieved over them, and brought them powerful allies from the uttermost parts of the earth, illustrious men, mighty in battle, who not only made up for the past valour of the lost army, but also augmented it by numerous additions. Amongst the first that landed was Count Henry of Troyes, count of Champange, with a powerful body of soldiers. There came, also, many others in succession, whose names are given as they arrived. They were: Theobald, Count of Blois, who died within three months after his arrival; next came Count Stephen, the Count of Clairmont, Count of Scalona, Manserius de Garland, Bernard de St. Waleri, John Count of Pontiny, Erard de Castiny, Robert de Buon, Adaunius de Fontaines, Louis de Ascla, Walter d' Arzillieres, Guy de Castellan, with his brother Lovel, Guy de Meisieres, John de Montmirail, John d' Arcy; also the Lord of Camte in Burgundy, Gaubert d'Aspremont, Clarembald de Noyera, the Bishop of Blois, the Bishop of Toulon, the Bishop of Ostia, the Bishop of Mordre (Mordrensis), the Bishop of Brescia, the Bishop of Aste; also the Patriarch of Jerusalem, the Archbishop of Cæsarea, the Bishop of Nazareth; there were also the bishop elect of Acre, and the Archbishop of Besançon, Baldwin, Archbishop of Canterbury, and Hubert Bishop of Salisbury; as well as the Archdeacon of Colchester, Rodolph de Hauteriva, of whom we have spoken before, and the Abbot of Scalona, the Abbot of Esterp. There came, also, a priest, who was incessantly active against the enemy, hurling darts from a sling with indefatigable toil.

There came, also, many from Normandy, such as Walkelin de Ferrars, Robert Trussebot, Richard de Vernon with his son, Guilbert de Tillieres with a strong band of warriors, and Ivo de Vipont, Ranulph de Glanville, formerly justiciary of England, Gilbert de Malines, and Hugh de Gorney. Besides these came many from different parts of the earth, whose

names have not been enumerated; and if we knew them
we would not mention them, for fear of wearying our
hearers.

CH. XLIII.—*How Henry of Champagne was set over the army.*

HENRY count of Troyes at that time landed with a strong
body of soldiers, into whose hands was committed the command of the army, which James d'Avennes and the Landgrave had held hitherto conjointly or by turn; for the
Landgrave being in ill-health left the camp on the pretext
of returning home;—a man who, after performing many
noble actions, to the admiration of all, tarnished the bright
glory of his deeds by his pusillanimous return.

CH. XLIV.—*How the duke of Suabia came to Acre by the persuasion
of the marquis.*

AT this time, the duke of Suabia, shortly after his father's
death, was staying at Antioch with the sons of the emperor,
and the chiefs send to him to remain in that quarter, to make
war upon the neighbouring territory of the barbarians. This
was sound and wholesome policy; for if he had occupied the
enemy by urging the war in many places at once, their
endeavours would have become distracted, and consequently
weaker for individual operations. The marquis, who was
charged with this message, failed to execute his instructions
faithfully, and by an invidious interpretation of them influenced the duke's mind, for he represented that the chiefs
wanted to procure his absence through jealousy, that they
might have the glory of taking the city without him. Some
asserted that the marquis had received from the sultan sixty
thousand byzantines to persuade the duke to depart from
the confines of Antioch. The duke, therefore, on arriving
at Acre, proved a cause of disagreement, for the French had
an old and long-standing quarrel with the Germans, since
the kingdom and empire contended for the supremacy.

CH. XLV.—*How the marquis, by the advice of the duke, aspired to the
kingdom.*

MOREOVER, the marquis, secretly assisting the cause of the
duke, to whom he was related by blood, studiously sought his

presence, that by his means, if he could, he might obtain the throne. An accident also favourable to his wishes made him indulge more confidently in his hopes, for premature death carried off the queen and the offspring she had conceived from King Guy; but in order that this point may be more clearly understood, we will trace the succession of the royal race from its first origin.

Ch. XLVI.—*Of the genealogy of the kings of Jerusalem, and the cause why the marquis aspired to the throne.*

It must be stated that Fulk, father of Geoffrey, count of Anjou, who was chosen king of Jerusalem on account of his singular virtues, had two sons, Baldwin and Almaric, by Melesende, the daughter of King Baldwin, his predecessor. Of these the elder ascended the throne, and bearing his grandfather's name, married Theodora, the daughter [niece] of Manuel, emperor of Byzantium, but died without children after the conquest and capture of Askalon. His brother, who succeeded to his valour and throne, compelled Babylon to pay tribute, and by his two marriages had offspring of both sexes. His first wife, Beatrix, whom he married before coming to the throne, was daughter of the Count of Roasia; but forasmuch as she was related to him by blood, the marriage was set aside by judgment of the clergy, by a formal divorce. He had, however, two children by her, a daughter named Sybilla, and a son called Baldwin, who on his father's death, being presented with the crown, although a minor and afflicted with leprosy, miraculously defeated Saladin and sixty thousand Turks, with a small body of soldiers. He, being removed at an early age from the affairs of this world, appointed as his successor his nephew Baldwin, whose mother had married William, the brother of the marquis; but who died while yet a child in his seventh year. But as the boy's father had been dead some time, Guy, who had come to visit the sepulchre, and was sprung from Poitou, married his mother Sybilla, and in her right assumed the insignia of royalty; by her he had four daughters, whose premature death, and that of their mother, caused Guy to be accused, and gave the marquis the hope of reigning. Furthermore, Maria, whom King Almaric had married after divorcing his first wife, was a kinswoman of the Emperor Manuel, and had two daughters: one of them died

in infancy, but Enfrid of Tours espoused Elizabeth, the second
daughter, before she was of a marriageable age ; but forasmuch
as she was heiress to the throne, the marquis determined to
remove both, and deprive Enfrid of his wife, as well as
Guy of his sceptre.

CH. XLVII.—*The wonders which happened during the siege are
subjoined.*

MEANWHILE, according to the various events of war, as
has been said, success changing from one side to the other,
there occurred manifold incidents not less wonderful than to
be wondered at, which seem worthy of our notice.

CH. XLVIII.—*How a certain petraria of the enemy by its strength destroyed all our machines, and how it struck one of our men without
hurting him.*

ONE of the enemy's *petrariæ*, of which there were a great
number in the city, was of an unusual magnitude and form,
and as the engineers intended it, able to cast stones of immense
weight, the blows of which nothing could resist : for it cast
stones of incredible size to a great distance, and its blow
destroyed everything it struck.   When the stones met with no
obstacle, they were driven into the ground a foot deep.   It
struck and shivered in pieces some of our *petrariæ*, or rendered them useless, and either destroyed our other machines,
or knocked off the part it touched.   In fact there was nothing
so solid or compact, of whatever kind or substance, that
would bear its overwhelming blow, so great was the violence
with which it acted.   This machine struck one of our men
from behind with a stone of enormous size, as he was standing
with his face turned away, quite unsuspicious of danger, not
supposing that a stone could be sent so far, yet it hurt him
not in the least, but, rebounding as from a mountain, fell
close by, and the man, when he saw it, was more horrified at
the sight than injured by the blow.   Who does not see by
this the wonderful works of the Lord, and that his mercy
is ever ready for those who fight for him ?   To the praise of
his mightiness I will subjoin other of his works.

CH. XLIX.—*How a javelin, hurled against one of our men, penetrated his armour, but would not penetrate his breast, where a writing containing the name of God lay.*

FURTHERMORE, one of our body-guard, while walking in the ditch outside the city wall, either for the purpose of reconnoitering the weak parts of the wall, or to strike any of the enemy he could see with his sling, stopped at last; he was armed sufficiently like a foot-soldier, with iron headpiece, coat of mail, and a tunic of many folds of linen, difficult of penetration, and artificially worked with the needle, vulgarly called a *pourpoint*. A Turk from the wall struck him with a dart from a sling with great force on the breast, so that it penetrated all the aforementioned, the iron armour descending from the head, and the coat of mail and *pourpoint*, but it was stopped by a certain writing hanging from his neck on his breast, and fell out blunted and twisted as from an iron plate. Are not the works of God manifest in the dart penetrating many folds of steel, and bounding back blunted from a little scroll? For the man was said to have worn suspended from his breast, the name of God on a scroll, thus proved to be impenetrable to steel. God is a wall of strength to them that hope in him.

CH. L.—*How one of our men unarmed, having retired to satisfy the calls of nature, struck down with a stone a Turk attacking him with a lance.*

AGAIN, as one of our men was stooping down outside the camp, a Turk rode up to attack him unawares, but the soldier on seeing him advance sideways, and scarcely having done what he came for at the aforesaid ditch, rose up hastily, though unarmed, either to avoid him as he came up, or by an impulse from the Lord to receive him in the best way he could. As the Turk struck at him with the point of his lance, he bent down and escaped the blow by the protection of God.

" The horse rode by and passed with scatheless blow."

The Turk annoyed at his ill success, prepared to repeat the attack, and brandishing his lance, bore down upon the soldier. What could the latter do, unarmed as he was? On foot, single-handed, and a ready prey for the foe, he called upon God, who is always by his grace present with his people, and seeing a stone by chance ready at hand, he aimed it at the face of his enemy, which was exposed beneath his helmet, and it struck him on the temple.   The Turk fell stunned from his horse, broke his neck, and died; the soldier caught the horse, mounted, and returned to his friends.   One who saw the occurrence, related it; and it is well known as a fact in the camp.

Ch. LI.—*How a woman on the point of death, while our men were filling the city trench with earth, threw herself in instead of earth.*

ON another occasion, amongst those who were carrying earth to make a mound in the ditch for assaulting the town more easily, was a woman who laboured with great diligence and earnestness, and went to and fro unceasingly, and encouraged others unremittingly, in order that the work might be accomplished; but her zeal put an end to her life and labours; for while a crowd of all sexes and ages were constantly coming and going to complete the work in question, and while the aforesaid woman was occupied in depositing what she had brought, a Turk, who had been lying wait for her, struck her a mortal blow with a dart.   As she fell to the ground, writhing with the violence of her pain, she entreated her husband and many others who had come up to assist her, with tears in her eyes, and very urgently, saying, "By your love for me, my dearest lord, by your piety as my husband, and the faith of our marriage contracted of old, permit not my corpse to be removed from this place; but I pray and beseech you, that since I can do nothing more towards the fulfilment of the work, I may deem myself to have done some good, if you will allow my lifeless body to be laid in the trench instead of earth, for it will soon be earth." This she urged with supplications to all the multitude that stood around, and soon after gave up the ghost.   Oh! wonderful faith of the weaker sex!   Oh! zeal of woman, worthy of imitation, for she ceased not, even dead, to help those who laboured, and in her death continued to shew her zeal in the cause!

CH. LII.—*Of the Turk's horse caught in a net.*

AGAIN, a common fellow of our camp was spreading his net outside the camp, either for the purpose of driving off the Turks or to catch them if they came on; one of them came rushing forward on horseback, and put the man to flight before he had finished what he was about; but unable to overtake him, he gave up the pursuit, when he saw him reach the camp, and in his excessive indignation, he began to pluck up the net. But after pulling up some poles by which the net was fixed with cords, his horse's head was accidentally entangled and caught by the net, which he was trying to roll up in a hasty, incautious manner. The horse, being one of great beauty, was indignant at being thus hampered, and in his wild attempts to get free, became more and more entangled. Some of our men seeing this, rode down in haste toward him. The Turk, finding his horse entangled, quickly dismounted and fled on foot, and although deprived of his steed, escaped his pursuers, for fear added wings to his feet. His valuable horse, which had broken the net in many parts, was with difficulty disentangled, and became an object of contention, but was given to the man who had fixed the net, as compensation for his loss.

CH. LIII.—*Of the Turk's horse that was caught in a foot-trap.*

AT another time, when, on account of the frequent and sudden sallies of the Turks, our chiefs ordered that foot-traps should be made and buried in the earth to escape being seen, it happened one day, that while some of our young men were exercising by appointment in the plain by throwing darts at a mark, some of the Turks, putting spurs to their horses, suddenly attacked them, upon which our young men, being unarmed and inferior in numbers, retreated to the camp. But one of the pursuers, as if trusting in the activity of his horse, too eagerly outstript the others, when the animal was suddenly stopped in its career by being caught in a foot-trap, and no effort or endeavour of his rider could extricate him. The Turk, preferring the loss of his horse to that of his head, escaped on foot, uninjured, to his own friends. The horse was decreed to be given to him whose instrument caught it, viz. Robert Count of Dreux.

K

CH. LIV.—*How Ivo de Vipont slays eighty pirates with a handful of men.*

ON another occasion, as three sailors were conducting Ivo de Vipont with ten companions to Tyre, and had wandered too far from the port, some Turkish pirates, coming out in a galley from an eddy of the sea near the land, bore down upon them; they were about eighty in number, and when the sailors saw them coming near, in their excessive fear they cried out together, "O Lord God, we shall be taken and slaughtered." To whom Ivo de Vipont said, "Why do ye of little faith fear those whom you shall soon see dead?" And when the enemy's galley appeared by force of rowing to be on the point of striking the vessel with its beak, Ivo leapt into it and began to cut down the Turks who pressed upon him, with the axe he carried in his hand. His companions, when they saw his work prosper, gaining heart, leapt into the galley also, and either beheaded whomsoever they found, or led them away captives. Thus these men triumphed who placed their hope in God, who knows not how to be conquered, and with whom a counterfeit faith availeth not, nor a multitude of warriors, for it matters not with the Lord whether the valour of battle and the glory of victory rest with a few or with many.

CH. LV.—*The admiral's genitalia destroyed by the Greek fire with which the enemy proposed to destroy our machines.*

AGAIN, when the townsmen beheld a great multitude of our people going, as was their wont, in search of provender for the animals, they sallied out against them under the command of their admiral Bellegeminus, a famous and powerful man, and rushed without care upon them; but our men withstood the enemy obstinately, and after many were killed on both sides, drove them back into the city. But the admiral stood his ground a long time, as he was a man of greater bravery than the others; while he was doing his best to execute the main object of the attack by cutting to pieces or burning with Greek fire the machines which were ready to move against the walls of the city, and as, while his men fled, he lagged behind to accomplish his purpose, a soldier, coming behind, threw him from his horse, and the vessel in

which he carried the Greek fire being broken by the fall,
the inextinguishable liquid burnt his genitalia. So that
what he had intended for our detriment became his own
destruction.

Ch. LVI.—*How a Turk, while carrying the Greek fire, is caught in a net by our men.*

On one occasion, some of our fishermen were throwing
their nets for fish at no great distance from land,—men who,
being devoted to this pursuit, gained a livelihood for themselves and no small relief by selling the fish. It happened
one day towards sunset, when the nets were stretched out,
that one of our men, sitting on an elevated spot on shore,
saw a man swimming at a distance with his head only above
water, and on his pointing him out, the aforesaid fishermen
closely pursued the swimmer in their boat to ascertain what
this strange appearance might be; and when they approached
nearer they perceived that he was a Turk. He was frightened
at their shouts and tried to escape, but they rowed quickly and
caught him in their net. The man, being an expert swimmer, had already passed their nets with a load which he
carried suspended from his neck, for he had with him in a
skin Greek fire, destined for the besieged in the city. In
this way the Turks used to send Greek fire to the besieged
by skilful swimmers, as they judged it the safest and most
secret plan. The fishermen landed with their captive, and
told their story to those on shore; and then conducted him
with the fire he carried through the midst of the army, and
after scourging him severely and gibing at him, they sadly
mangled, and then decapitated him, and so he had his reward. Thus the Lord shewed that he cared for his people;
for he scattereth the counsels of the heathen and of princes,
and brought to nothing the plans which the malignity of the
enemy imagined.

Ch. LVII.—*How a Turk, who attempted to defile the cross of Christ, died of a wound with a dart in his bowels.*

Again, we think we ought not to pass over the following fact in silence, though irksome of relation and horrible
to listen to: viz. that the Turks were wont, to the scandal

K 2

and disgrace of our faith, to take whatever images and pic
tures representing the mysteries of our religion they could
find in the city, bringing them on the walls in sight of the
Christians, to scourge and beat them with rods as if they were
alive, and spit upon and treat them shamefully in many other
ways as the humour took them.   One day as some of our
men saw a Turk doing this and tossing about a cross with the
image of our Saviour in a shameful and impious manner, and
obscenely giving utterance to blasphemies and impious revilings against our religion, on his proceeding further and
attempting to defile the same, a zealous man cast a dart from
his sling and killed the Turk, and thus proved to him how
man's attempts against the Lord are as nothing.

Ch. LVIII.—*How a Parthian bowman was shot by a Welch bowman,
for not keeping to his agreement.*

IT chanced, moreover, one day that the slingers and
bowmen, and all who were skilled in throwing missiles,
frequently challenged one another on both sides, and discharged their weapons for exercise.   When the rest had
departed from the field in their turns, a Parthian and a
Welchman began to aim their arrows at each other in a
hostile manner, and discharge them so as to strike with all
their might.   But the Welchman, aware of his foe's intention,
repaid like for like; on which the Parthian, making a truce,
approached him, and when within hearing, began a parley.
" Of what country are you," said he, " and by what name
may I be pleased to know you ?   I see you are a good bowman, and in order that you may be more inclined to tell me, I
am a Parthian by nation, brought up from childhood in the
art of shooting, and my name is Grammahyr, of good reputation amongst my people for my deeds of renown, and well
known for my victories."   The Welchman told his name and
nation.   " Let us prove," said the Parthian, " which is the best
bowman, by each taking an arrow, and aiming them against
one another from our bows.   You shall stand still first, and I
will aim an arrow at you, and afterwards you shall shoot in like
manner at me."   The Welchman agreed.   The Parthian having
fitted his arrow, and parting his feet as the art requires, with
his hands stretched asunder, and his eyes fixed on the mark.

" Lets fly the arrow, failing of its aim."

The Welchman, unhurt, demanded the fulfilment of the afore-said condition. "I will not agree," said the Parthian; "but you must stand another shot, and then have two at me." The Welchman replied, "You do not stand by your agreement, nor observe the condition you yourself dictated; and if you will not stand, although I may delay it for a time, as I may best be able, God will take revenge on you according to His will, for your treachery;" and he had scarce finished speaking, when in the twinkling of an eye he smote the Turk with his arrow in the breast, as he was selecting an arrow from his quiver to suit his purpose, and the weapon, meeting with no obstacle, came out at the back, having pierced the Turk's body; upon which he said to the Turk, "You stood not by your agreement, nor I by my word." Animated by these and the like successes, the Christians thought they should pre-serve themselves for good fortune by bearing all their mis-fortunes with more cheerful faith, and more fervent hope.

CH. LIX.—*Of the sea-fight between the Turks and our men, and how, while our men are trying to take the Tower of Flies with towers and machines fixed on the galleys, our machines are destroyed by fire.*

MEANWHILE the Pisans, and others who were skilled in managing ships, to whom had been entrusted the siege of the city from the sea, had built and fitted on their galleys a machine in the form of a castle, with bulwarks, with a great deal of toil, to overlook the walls, and give the power of throwing in their missiles more effectually. They had also built two ladders, with some steps, whereby they might reach the top of the walls. These machines they covered, as well as the galleys, with raw hides, so that it was judged they would not be affected by iron, or any kind of weapon.

Having all things in readiness, they proceeded to lay siege to the Tower of Flies, and fiercely attacked it with slings and missiles. Those who were in the tower manfully resisted them, and being a match for them, both in strength and good fortune, they took immediate revenge on our men for the death of one of their party. And in order to vanquish them or drive them away, nearly two thousand Turks went out from the city against the galleys to give assistance to the be-sieged in the tower, while they harassed the Pisans from the opposite quarter. Our men being skilful and experienced

warriors, moved their machines as conveniently as they could
against the aforesaid tower, and immediately strove to cast
immense anchors on it, and throw on its defenders whatsoever
stones or weapons they had at hand; while others were
appointed to fight by sea, and no less bravely repelled those
who attacked them in that quarter.   With the anchors
they threw on the tower the defences were pulled down,
and the bucklers and shields crushed to pieces.   The
tower was assaulted for a long time with wonderful and
intolerable violence; one party succeeding the other when
tired, in rapid succession and with invincible valour.   Darts
flew with horrid crash, and ponderous missiles rushed whizzing
through the air.   The Turks give way for a time, for they were
not able to withstand the brunt of the battle; and behold! our
men, having fixed the ladders for scaling the tower, were
ready to mount, when the Turks, seeing that it was their
last struggle, and that they must resist our ascent with
all their might, cast masses of enormous size down to crush
our men and throw them from the ladders.   They afterwards
threw Greek fire on our castle, which at last caught fire;
and when those who were in it saw this, they were obliged to
descend and retreat.   An incalculable slaughter of the Turks,
who attacked our men from the sea, was made; and although
the design of our men was defeated on the side of the
tower, those to seaward slew an immense number of the
enemy.   In the end the machines were destroyed by the
devouring fire, together with the turret and the galleys
in which they were placed, and the upright ladders.   The
Turks, overcome with excessive joy, laughed with loud
shouts, making a mockery of us, and wagging their heads
at our misfortune: and the Christians, being disheartened
above measure, were not less annoyed by the revilings that
were heaped upon them, than by the losses they had sustained.   However, their spirits were raised by the constant
arrival of strangers, and they were thus strengthened by the
increase of their numbers.

CH. LX.—*The townsmen, with great loss to themselves, burn the battering-ram of the archbishop of Besançon, with Greek fire.*

MEANWHILE, the archbishop of Besançon had caused to
be built, with great labour and much expense, a machine
to batter down the walls, covered with iron plates, com-

monly called a battering-ram; because by repeated nd frequent blows, after the manner of a ram, it overthrows the
most solid walls. Another very strong ram was built by
Count Henry; and the other princes and heroes, either
singly or conjunctively, had caused to be made different
kinds of machines. Some prepared sows* of different kinds;
others poles; or whatsoever each fancied, or which came
first to hand. A day was then appointed for bringing against
the walls the instruments that each had prepared. The archbishop brought his machine, like a ceiled house, to strike
the walls; it had in front a very long mast of a ship, with
its head covered with iron, which was impelled by many men,
and then being drawn back again, was levelled with greater
force; and thus, by frequent blows, they tried to breach or
cast down the city walls. Those who impelled the machine
below were secure from all injury that came from above.
The Turks defended themselves manfully from the walls, and
collected and threw upon it immense heaps of dry wood, to
set the machine on fire, while, independently of its being
easily assailed by fire, they cast immense masses from the
petrariæ, without ceasing. Last of all, they threw on it
Greek fire, and the dry wood having caught, the men in it
saw it must be inevitably destroyed, and were obliged, by the
intolerable heat, to leave it, and continue their attack with
what instruments they could lay hold of. The Turks were
indefatigable in their efforts to destroy the machine, by
throwing down immense masses on it, or consuming it by
means of liquid oil. Great was the contest and show of
prowess between the Turks and Christians; the latter strove
to extricate the battering-ram, the former to resist their
attempts. The fire, once lighted, and fed constantly by the
Turks, who spared no material for the purpose, reduced the
machine to ashes. The Christians retired, grieving at the
failure of their efforts; while the Turks hastened to and fro,
with dances and shouting, and thought their deeds incomparable. But they did not insult our adversities with impunity,
for they lost eighty of their number, and amongst them, a
certain renowned admiral, at whose command these things
were done; though they concealed their grief, that their loss

* *Sues rostratas, contos, sues.* The sow was a military covering, under
shelter of which the assailants made their approaches to the walls of a
besieged town.

might escape our notice. Our chiefs, observing that their
exertions had not the success they expected, broken down by
their misfortunes, determined to take respite for awhile, and
relax their efforts.

CH. LXI.—*How a fleet of fifteen ships was sent to the aid of the townsmen, of which several perished.*

MEANWHILE, soon after the feast of St. Michael, a fleet of
fifteen ships arrived from Alexandria, glittering in gorgeous
array, and a short distance one from another; they arrived
towards dusk, and being driven by a violent wind, were
unable to slacken their course.   Hence, when they saw
our army, they dreaded lest we should go forth to meet
them, and they could not avoid us; but the Christians did not
venture, as the night was coming on, and the wind high. The
fleet, too, having gathered together, made for the chain, with
all speed: the three largest ships, of the kind called
dromons, came behind; the galleys, which were swifter of
motion, went before.   They bore down violently into port,
and coming into collision with each other, two of them dashed
on the rocks, and most of the men on board perished, amidst
the shouts and laughter of the Christians, who beheaded some
of them that were cast on shore by the fury of the waves.
Besides this, they seized upon the largest of the galleys,
which was driven by the wind into port, laden with provisions; and having killed the crew, they kept the cargo for themselves. The remainder reached the desired haven, below the
chain, in safety; and when the townsmen saw them, they went
out with numberless lamps, and received them with much
pomp into the city, overjoyed at their arrival.   Afterwards, their numbers being thus augmented, they turned out
of the town those of their men who were less fit for fighting, lest their numbers should consume their provisions and
strength; and so the time was protracted.

CH. LXII.—*How, on our men being set in battle array under the command of Archbishop Baldwin against Saladin, Saladin flies to the
mountains.*

THE common men now murmured at the inactivity of the
chiefs, and the continuance of a fruitless blockade, and grew
weary of the siege; and when the chiefs had considered for

some time what had best be done, the result was, that the
enemy on the outside should be challenged to a general engagement; for if the hostile army gave way, the city would
more easily be assaulted and stormed.   On the morrow of
St. Martin's, therefore, our chiefs led out their troops in order
of battle into the plain, in the cold rays of a winter's sun; and
when we saw them come forth, with their various standards,
the Templars, the Hospitallers, and the others, their number,
valour, and varied costumes, created in us mixed sentiments
of admiration, confidence, and pleasure.   The clergy claimed
no small share of military glory; for abbots and prelates
led their own troops, and fought manfully for the faith, joyfully contending for the law of God.   Among and above the
others, the venerable Archbishop Baldwin distinguished himself; and although his advanced age might have inclined him
to inactivity, the perfection of his virtues made up for the de-
fect of nature.   Raising the standard on which was inscribed
the name of the glorious martyr Thomas, he found for it a
meet and worthy company; for two hundred knights and
three hundred followers served in the pay of the holy man.
He himself, with the duke of Suabia, and Theobald, count
of Blois, had charge of the camp; and having performed
the duties of the patriarch, who was ill in bed, he blessed and
gave absolution to the army as it went forth.   Nor could the
noble bishop of Salisbury endure to be absent from the fray,
but he performed the duties of a soldier in the field, a leader
in the camp, and a pastor in the church.   Towards sunset, when the army had advanced and pitched their tents,
the townsmen came into the vacant space, and burst upon
the baggage to plunder it; but our men received them manfully, and putting them to flight, saved their friends without
sustaining any loss.   At night, the sultan ordered all his
tents and property to be carried to the mountains; and what
could not be moved in time was burnt.   It was the part of a
spirit conquered and hesitating, thus declining battle on the
plain, to destroy his own property, change his position, and
retreat to the mountains.   When he found a spot not easy
of access, he halted; and sent out an overwhelming number of
infantry and bowmen to check those who should pursue, that
at least he might annoy from above, those whom he feared to
engage at close quarters.   Our men, therefore, cheated of

their battle in the plain, and unable to follow the foe up the precipitous road, returned equally without hurt and without glory.

CH. LXIII.—*How the Turks fought with a party of our men, who had gone out to Caiffa for provisions, and were returning, and how they yielded.*

AFTER this, hearing that provisions, of which they were much in want, might be procured at Caiffa, the army proceeded in that direction : but when they came to a place called Recordans, behold the Turks suddenly rushing down, made a fierce attack on them, taking them for fugitives ; some of them threw their darts, others pressed on with their spears ; one party made loud shouting, another blew their trumpets like horns, to frighten those who were flying. Our men, having pitched their tents in the plain that night, kept quiet till morning ; and then they saw the Turks in vast numbers surrounding them on all sides. Our men terrified at such a multitude, having taken up their arms, and put themselves in array, went forth in battle array to meet them ; yet the Turks did not venture to attack, but gave way as our men came on, although their own numbers were countless. Having heard that there were no provisions at Caiffa, as they supposed, for the Turks had carried them all away, our men returned towards Acre in order of battle. The Turks constantly harassed them on the road, but they sustained little loss from their attacks. At a certain river, however, which flows from thence to Acre, near a fountain, there was a severe engagement, and great slaughter of noble steeds, before the armies were separated ; our army now proceeded on one side of the stream, while the other was occupied by the enemy, who were constantly engaged in throwing missiles, and threatening them without ceasing, as well as harassing them in the rear. They harassed our men much, for the foot followers and bowmen, who occupied the rear of our army, were forced to keep facing about and discharging arrows at their pursuers without intermission.

On the following night they pitched their camps close by the stream, and had very little rest, but much anxiety ; for they were obliged either to drive off the enemy, who attacked them openly, or watch against hidden ambuscades; for it was not so much by constant, as continued, attacks, that the enemy tried to annoy them with injuries, or provoke them with jeers. There was a bridge over the river, which it was necessary for us to pass, but which was occupied by the Turks before our arrival; this they had not had time to break down, as they intended, but closing together, they placed themselves in the middle of it to check our advance; but when our men saw that nothing but absolute force would remove them, Godfrey of Lusignan, the king's brother, with five other chosen knights, made a fierce attack upon them, and put them to flight in a moment, and by the same assault threw thirty of them into the river, never more to rise, for they were drowned; thus they gained a free passage across the river in spite of all opposition, and returned to the siege of Acre.

CH. LXIV.—*With what guiles the marquis espoused the wife of Reinfred, who was yet alive, in order to gain the heirship of the kingdom.*

Now the marquis, having for some time aspired to the glory of reigning, on seeing a way open to his wishes, made himself confident of obtaining the kingdom, if he could supplant the wife of Reinfred; to this end he strained every effort, and put in practice every art. But adopting an underhand policy, he complained of the condition of the kingdom, that the king was not able to manage affairs, that he was reigning without right, now his wife was removed, and that another daughter of King Amalric still survived. He first set forth these matters among the people, but he sedulously courted the chiefs also, enticing these with gifts, and binding others by the tie of kindred; and all he either allures by his bland manners, or obliges by his gifts, or gains over by his promises. It was easy for so active a man, surpassing Sinon in devices, Ulysses in eloquence, and Mithridates in variety of tongues, to gain all his wishes, armed as he was with such cunning; but forasmuch as the Church forbade the bonds of marriage to be broken asunder, the crafty man found out a new charge to take away the wife of Reinfred; for the chiefs persuaded him that she could be separated from her husband without violation of the law, as having married when too young, and without consent. But Reinfred himself had conceived

the hope of gaining the kingdom in the right of his wife—
a person more akin to a woman than a man, effeminate in
manner and loose in language, and to whom that verse of
Virgil applies,

> " While Nature doubts, if boy or girl be made,
>   You're born, fair boy, to be a pretty jade."

For one day, when, at the mandate of the chiefs, Reinfred
had brought forward his wife, he lost his bride and his
kingdom together by the arts of the marquis.   Oh wickedness worthy of the satirist's pen and of tragic declamation !
For if we condemn the rape of Helen, the present deed is much
more base, and its injustice greater: for Helen was stolen,
surreptitiously stolen, in the absence of her husband, whereas
this one was violently withdrawn in his presence.   But that
the act might lose the infamy of its wrong, the girl is given
into the keeping of a sequestrator, while the judgment of
the clergy is sought for a divorce.   The marquis, therefore,
tampered with the clergy by gifts and wiles ; he sounded all
those whom he believed agreeable to his purpose and effects,
by immense largesses and the fascination of gold, to corrupt
their judicial impartiality.   The report of so great a wickedness was carried to the ears of the most sacred metropolitan of Canterbury ; it arouses his innocence to astonishment, and inflames the anger of the defender of the law.
While he performed with due rigour the duties of the patriarch,
who, as we said, was sick, the friends of the marquis tried
to quash the verdict which was to be given, under the pretext
of appeal.   Three of his chief favourites were Reginald, lord
of Sidon, Pagan, of the castle of Caiffa, and Balisantus ;
and there would have been a fourth, the count of Tripoli,
had he not gone away, who would have formed this consummate council of iniquity.   For in them, as in an abode of
wickedness, were united the treachery of Judas, the cruelty of
Nero, the impiety of Herod, and all that the present or olden
times regarded as abominable and wicked.   Now, Balisantus,
on Amalric's death, had married his wife, this damsel's mother ;
and she, having imbibed from her childhood the lowest Grecian
morals, had a husband similar to herself in cruelty, levity, and
faithlessness.   The marquis wins them both over by presents
and promises, to persuade the girl to prefer a complaint, that she

had married Reinfred against her will, that she had always opposed it, and that the marriage could not stand, because she had never given her consent. This plot is entirely successful, and the woman easily changes her mind; for a female is always variable and changeable, her sex frail, her mind fickle, and she delights in novelty; so she lightly rejects and forgets those whom she knows; the girl is thus easily taught what is bad, and willingly receives evil advice, and so blushed not to say that she was not carried away, but had followed the marquis willingly. Indeed the chiefs themselves, in defiance of justice, used their efforts to bring it about that the marquis should have the kingdom and the damsel. The venerable archbishop of Canterbury seeing that justice and equity were perversely confounded, and that ecclesiastical authority would be rejected; perceiving also that the clergy, with some of the bishops, who had a sounder mind and more fervent zeal, murmured as far as they dared; he pronounced sentence of excommunication on those who had contracted and agreed to this unholy wedlock, and not undeservedly, because he had cohabited with another man's wife, and taken her to his own house and espoused her, by the ministry of the bishop of Beauvais, and because he had a wife in his own country, and another in Constantinople, both of noble birth, young, and beautiful, and suitable to his position; whence the clergy charged him with threefold adultery, and as far as they could, spoke against the act which the holy church deemed impious. Those who favoured him tried to excuse themselves on the plea that the marquis had sworn to supply the army, when in much want, with an abundance of provision from Tyre, on condition of their aiding him in the marriage; but he had set at nought his oath, and transgressed the sanctity of his honour, for he who is faithless in a little, fears not to commit a greater crime. And while the nuptials were celebrated with great festivity, it happened that some of our men, who were guests at the feast, having gone to a short distance from the spot, were set upon by an ambuscade of the Turks, and some taken, others slain. This was the commencement of misfortunes. Here the Butler of St. Lice was taken, and whether the Turks kept him captive or killed him, was never known afterwards. Twenty men were taken prisoners or slain on this occasion.

CH. LXV.—*How the marquis returned to Tyre, and perjured himself,
by not assisting our men when in need of provisions.*

BUT the marquis, having gained his wishes, returned to
Tyre quickly with his wife and his men ; and the army was
disappointed in their expectation of obtaining through him a
supply of provisions. For, on the contrary, either forgetful
of this agreement, or ungrateful for what was done for him,
he did not send so much as an egg when the army was in
danger of starvation ; but, both perjurer and liar, he would
not allow those who wished to sail to Acre with provisions to
depart. Therefore, the want of provisions increased daily
amongst the besiegers ; little or nothing was found to purchase, and nothing was brought by ships.

CH. LXVI.—*How Baldwin, archbishop of Canterbury, died.*

WHEN the archbishop of Canterbury saw what he had
before heard, that the army had become altogether dissolute,
and given to drinking, women, and dice, it afflicted his spirit,
unable to bear such excesses, even to the weariness of life.
And because a disease which is general is difficult to cure,
when one day the worst reports of this kind reached his ears,
knowing that man is charged with the care of things, though
the power of creating is God's, he sighed and uttered these
words, "O Lord God ! now is there need of chastening and
correcting with holy grace, that if it please thy mercy that I
should be removed from the turmoil of this present life, I have
remained long enough in this army." Scarcely fifteen days
after these words, as if heard by the Lord, he began to feel
cold and stiff, and overcome by a fever, a few days after he
slept in the Lord.

CH. LXVII.—*Of the bitterness of the famine amongst our men, and the
enormous price of provisions, which was the cause of their cursing the
marquis.*

MEANWHILE, the want of provisions increased daily, and the
middle and lower classes were tormented at first continuously
rather than constantly by the approaching famine, the more
severely as the marquis prevaricated more shamefully. Nevertheless, he sent provisions secretly to those accomplices and
favourers he had won over to join in his illicit and impious

transaction. And now the higher ranks of the army obtained hardly sufficient food to sustain life, and the winter was drawing near, a period when they were usually more prodigal and luxurious, formerly abundant in all kinds of food, but now with the change of circumstances threatening want; and the hungry stomach, once overloaded, now became satisfied with any food it could procure. The greedy table had consumed their substance, and not satiating the sharp appetite of those who were in search of it, they were worn away by hunger, being without the common necessaries of life; and they felt it so much the more severely, as it was the time when they were accustomed to dainties. The heat of the season, too, added to the horrors of the impending famine, and want is always felt more severely by those who have been brought up in affluence. Why need we say more? A moderate measure of wheat, which a man could carry under his arm, was sold for 100 aurei, a chicken for twelve sols, and an egg for six deniers. By these examples, the rates of all other kinds of provisions may be imagined. The army then cursed the marquis for withdrawing their means of support, and because through him they stood in danger of starvation.

CH. LXVIII.—*How our men, while perishing of famine, ate the dead bodies of their horses, with their intestines.*

FAMINE, as we have said, urges to the commission of crimes, and yet pardonable ones, for the Lord created all things for man, and gave them into his hands to be of service to him, that man should not perish while beasts lived; they therefore slew valuable horses, and without taking off the skins of some of them, ate horse-flesh with joy; even the intestines were sold for ten sols. And wherever it was known a horse was killed, they crowded to it one before the other to buy or steal, and like birds of prey to a corpse, so the starving soldiers rushed in troops to a dead steed, that they might devour the bodies of those that once carried them; and thus the animals who once carried them on their backs were in turn carried themselves; the dead horse sold for more than a living one, and the words of the evangelist seemed to apply to them, "Where the body is, there the eagles are gathered together;" saving the mystical interpretation, from the dignity of which we do not wish to derogate.

None of the intestines of the slain horses were rejected, owing to the pressure of the famine, and the most worthless part was valued at a high rate: they ate up the head with the intestines, so that after all was consumed, nay, devoured with avidity, they licked their fingers with a relish, that while any thing remained, it might be removed with the tongue rather than wiped away with a napkin. Hence they held the marquis in detestation for depriving them of the means of subsistence, since by his means they had been defrauded of their food, and stood in danger of starvation.

Ch. LXIX.—*How he who had some food ate it secretly.*

In progress of time, the famine increased exceedingly for want of provisions, and if any one had any thing appertaining to food, he hid away secretly for his own use that which was enough for more than once, in order that it might not be taken away from him by force ; and thus it happened that little was exposed for sale, and whatsoever they had they did not distribute for common use, but the poor man was everywhere in want. Hence their detestation of the marquis for depriving them of the means of subsistence, as by his means they were deprived of food, and stood in danger of starvation.

Ch. LXX.—*How those who were once delicate ate grass.*

Wherever by chance grass was discovered growing, it was greedily devoured by men who once were brought up delicately, men of high rank and the sons of great men ; they fed on grass like beasts, that the violence of famine might be extinguished by such food, whence many, led to reason by necessity, planted herbs fit for eating and good for driving away the pangs of hunger; and such as they once despised and believed not fit for human use, the greatness of the famine made now most sweet to the starving. Oh! then, the voice of the people, cursing the perfidy of the marquis! because he cared not for the misery of a starving people.

Ch. LXXI.—*How they perish from rain and hunger.*

Moreover, owing to the great quantity of rain that fell, a certain very severe disease spread among the men; for unusual

showers, by their constant and continuous fall, had such an
injurious effect upon the soldiers, that, with the excess of the
affliction, their limbs becoming swollen, the whole body was
affected as with the dropsy, and from the violence of the
disease, the teeth of some of them were loosened and fell out.
O the lamentations of each of them!   O the sorrow of all!
while those who were safe grieved for the sufferings of their
comrades, and day by day saw the funerals of their friends,
for every day they performed the rites of a thousand who had
perished. Some, however (but they were few), recovered from
their disease, and becoming more eager after food, regained
health only to suffer the excessive miseries of famine.   O,
then, the voice of the people, cursing the perfidy of the
marquis, for he cared not for the sufferings of the perishing
people!

Ch. LXXII.—*How our starving men fought at the oven.*

WHEREVER it was known that bread was baking at the
oven, there was a concourse of the people crying out and
saying, " Here is money; we will give what price you please,
so that you give us plenty of bread." For each asked to be
served first, offering a price in exchange for bread, and each
violently struggling to snatch from the others what they had
not yet received, and perhaps never would.   But as often as
it happened that any of the rich bought much bread, then
arose mourning, and sorrow, and clamour among the poor,
united in one voice of wailing, when they saw that quantity
of bread carried away by the rich, which, if distributed in
portions, might have done good to the poor as far as it would
go. They eagerly offered the price of the bread at the will
of the seller; but, because any moderate quantity was not
enough for so great a multitude, there arose frequent and
angry disputes, quarrels, contentions, jealousies, and sometimes
fights around the oven which contained the bread. and they
contended for it like dogs before they were sure of obtaining it.
O. then, the voice of the people, cursing the perfidy of the
marquis, for he cared not for the wretchedness of a perishing
people!

CH. LXXIII.—*How they gnawed and ate up dirty bones which had been already gnawed by dogs.*

BUT who can·write or set forth how great their misery was—how great the general suffering, when some were seen from the pressure of famine running about like rabid dogs and snatching up bones that had been gnawed by dogs for three days together, and sucking and licking them when there was nothing on them to be gnawed, not because they did them any good, but because they gratified the imagination with the remembrance of flesh?   What need we add to these horrors? The enemy, harassing them by constant attacks from both sides, when they slew them suddenly, were held less terrible than the violence of so great a famine; for the former put an end to their lives and their miseries by the edge of the sword and at once, whereas by the famine they pined away in lengthened torments.   Oftentimes, in the sight of all, they whom hunger had stripped of shame, fed upon abominable and filthy things, found by chance, and which cannot be named; yet they deemed them delicious food, though unlawful for man to make use of.   O the voice of the people, cursing the perfidy of the marquis, for he cared not for the wretchedness of a perishing people!

CH. LXXIV.—*How noblemen also, when they had not wherewith to buy bread, stole it.*

FROM some other instances worth relating, the magnitude of the famine may be estimated; for in those who endured it patiently according to the flesh, it may be not undeservedly considered martyrdom, unless perchance by murmuring they diminished the credit which they would thus have received.   The pressure of necessity moreover led to the commission of many disgraceful acts; and some even of noble extraction, who were on that account ashamed to beg openly, feared not to sin in secret to obtain the subsistence so difficult to get honestly, and were in the habit of stealing bread. Thus it happened that one man was caught in this kind of robbery, and was bound tightly with thongs, in which condition he was placed in custody in the house of the man who had caught him, who was a baker; and while the family was

very much engaged in domestic matters, by some movement
or other, the captive managed to get his hands loose, and as
he was placed by chance close by a heap of new loaves, he ate
his full unperceived by any one, and then escaping with one
loaf in his hand, returned unpunished to his friends; and
after telling his story distributed the bread he had in his
hand to them to eat. But what was this among so many?
Want irritated the appetite, and exasperated rather than
quieted hunger. O then the voice of the people, cursing the
perfidy of the marquis, because he cared not for the wretchedness of a perishing people!

Ch. LXXV.—*How many turn apostates from the bitterness of the famine.*

WHAT was still worse, some of our men, and it cannot be
told or heard without great grief, gave way to the severity
of the famine, and in paying attention to their corporeal safety
incurred the damnation of their souls. For after having overcome a great part of their tribulation, some of our men
taking refuge among the Turks, did not hesitate to turn
apostates, and to procure for themselves by wicked blasphemies eternal death, that they might enjoy a little longer this
mortal life. O pernicious exchange! O crime for which no
punishment can suffice! O foolish men like unto senseless
beasts! while ye fled from the death, which must soon come,
you took no care against the death that is without end! For
if a just man liveth by faith, perfidy is accounted death, but
the conscience of all who act foolishly must be purged. Then
they execrate the marquis for breaking his covenant, and imprecate evil on him and mortal woe.

Ch. LXXVI.—*How two friends buy thirteen beans for a denier.*

THERE were two friends, comrades in misfortune as well as
in war, so needy and distressed that the two possessed only
one piece of money, commonly called an angevin, and with
that only they wished to purchase something to eat; but what
could they do? It was a mere trifle, and worth little, even
if there had been abundance of all sorts of good things; and
they had nothing else but their armour and clothing. They

considered for a long time very thoughtfully what they should
buy with that one little piece, and how it could be done to
ward off the pressing evil of the day.   They at last came to
the resolution of buying some beans, since nothing was to be
bought of less value; with difficulty, therefore, they obtained,
after much entreaty, thirteen beans for their denier, one of
which on returning home they found consumed by maggots, and
therefore unfit for eating.   Upon this, by mutual agreement,
they went a long distance in search of the seller, who consented
not without difficulty and after much supplication, to give them
a whole bean in exchange. How strange this exchange of such
a thing after a long search, and at such a distance! From those
beans, which were consumed in a moment, how much benefit
do we think could accrue to the hungry?   We judge that
must be weighed more by the opinion of the hearer than described by the pen.   Then they execrated the marquis for the
violation of his covenant, and prayed for evil on him and
mortal woe.

Ch. LXXVII.—*How the famished ate karrubles, and died from drinking wine.*

There was exposed for sale a kind of fruit growing on
trees; a grain enclosed in a pod like a pea, which the common
people called karruble, sweet to the taste, and very pleasant
to eat.   The hungry were recruited by them, because there
was a greater abundance of them than other things, whence
the way to buy them was much frequented; for although
they were of inferior value, they were something. Of those
who lay weak and ate little, either because they had nothing
to eat, or because they could not eat, the wine which they
drank heated them so much that many were suffocated, either
from the violence of the liquor, which was not tempered with
food, or from being too weak to support its strength and
goodness.   There was a tolerable supply of wine for sale, but
much wine is not good for the preservation of the body with
little food; for it is necessary to proportion the one to the
other.   But inasmuch as the marquis was the cause of the
scarcity, they ceased not to curse him and execrate him for the
violation of his covenant, and invoked evil on him and mortal
woe.

Ch. LXXVIII.—*How the famished ate flesh during Lent.*

SOME were driven by the pressure of the famine to eat flesh in the beginning of Lent, on what is commonly called Ash-Wednesday,—not because they had plenty of it, but because it was more easily obtained : afterwards, however, as the famine slackened, they repented and made proportionate penitence. Above all these things, during the whole of that winter, the charity of all was so cooled by the fear of want of money, that a man did not even share his necessaries with his friend, their little faith leading them to doubt God's love, and to believe that if they shared with others, they themselves would lack the necessaries of life. To such a degree the vice of parsimony, and the concealment of their stores increased, that even they hid what they had, and those that had were thought not to have at all. What did the voice of so many in want then imprecate on the marquis ? Who did not think him the cause of so many being in jeopardy ?

Ch. LXXIX.—*The exhortation of the bishop of Salisbury and some others to the rich, to make collections to assist the poor.*

THE intercourse of the faithful becoming beyond measure checked, and no one taking thought or notice of the poor and needy, the infamy of this want of faith extended itself to all. The bishop of Salisbury was active in shewing that nothing was greater than charity, nothing more acceptable to God, nothing more fruitful than to give ; and to this end he induced all, by his powerful persuasion, to open their hands and distribute to their neighbours, to give to the needy, and support the perishing, lest, if they neglected the wants of others, they should not obtain their own ; for it is said that he who heeds them not when he may, is the cause of death to the languishing : he shewed that he was guilty of another man's death, who refused to assist him when he could ; for we are commanded to give drink to our enemy when thirsty, and to feed him when hungry. And the bishops of Nerrona and Faenza in Italy, earnestly assisted in his exhortation. In consequence of the exhortation and urgency of these men, a collection was made for distribution amongst the poor, and so many and so great were the hearts God moved to con-

tribute to the support of the needy, that the hungry were
greatly recruited; and the substance of the givers, also,
by the grace of God co-operating, was not diminished.
Then arose fresh joy, then the lips of many blessed the
givers, then were benefits multiplied, then it is said that
pity was turned gratefully towards them, whilst the powerful
yearned with compassion over the afflicted. Among the most
active in performing these duties, were Watlin de Ferrars and
Robert Trusebot, and not behind them were Henry count of
Champagne, Jocelin de Montoira, as well as the count of Clairmont; and the bishop of Salisbury, who was the first pro-
moter of these good deeds.

By the care of these men, aided by the others, every one
contributed according to his means to a common fund, that it
might be distributed to each as he had need. Thus, those
whose hearts were before cold under cover of the ashes of
avarice, through God's grace became fervent in deeds of
charity, and because they were converted to compassion the
Lord regarded and magnified his pity with them, according
to his words, "turn unto me and I will turn unto you, saith
the Lord."

Ch. LXXX.—*How a small ship arrived with provisions, and how that
which cost a hundred gold pieces one day, was bought for four on the
morrow.*

For while all were engaged in these works of charity, behold
the Lord sent a ship laden with provisions, by which the
former scarcity of food was very much alleviated. For
so great a want of bread had not existed because there was
no corn, but because the sellers asked such a price for it from
the buyers, that it could scarcely be obtained for a large sum
after much bargaining; for what will not avarice do? The
aforesaid ship, which was but a small one, had arrived, as I
think, on a Saturday; and on the morrow, a measure which had
been sold hitherto for a hundred pieces of gold, by the bounty
of God, the dispenser of all good things, was lowered to four.
Meanwhile there arises among the people an unusual hilarity,
the avaricious merchants being the only persons who grieved,
owing to the decrease of their wonted gain, and with difficulty
concealing it. But why need I say more? There is no
counsel against the Lord, for he doeth whatsoever he will.

Ch. LXXXI.—*How, when a Pisan wished to keep his provisions till the morrow, his house and provisions were consumed by fire.*

A CERTAIN Pisan, a seller of provisions, had kept some corn untouched during the whole year, until he could sell it according to his wishes hereafter, expecting that the famine would increase; and if at any time he sold any, he sold it at his own price, as he liked, to those who could not do without it. But God, by his judgment, shewed the wickedness of this action, for it happened that the house of that Pisan, filled with wheat, suddenly and violently caught fire. And though very many hastened to extinguish the fire, their efforts were ineffectual, for every thing was destroyed.

Ch. LXXXII.—*How all vied in giving away meat, and how a penance was enjoined on those who ate what was unlawful.*

ALL therefore being emulously engaged in such works of piety, strove with all their might to distribute alms; while each one in his zeal was eager to outdo his neighbours in bounty, thinking that he was performing an acceptable duty to God, if he could more abundantly administer what was necessary to the needy. Those also, who from necessity fed on flesh during Lent, as we before said, repenting of their guilt, after each had received penitence from the illustrious and venerable bishop of Salisbury, undertook with a vow to perform proportionate satisfaction as was enjoined them.

BOOK II.

Ch. I.—*Of the kings of England and France.*

AFTER Easter arrived Philip, king of France, and not long after him, Richard, king of England; but in order that the course of their voyage may be more fully known, it seems advisable to commence our history from their first departure from their kingdoms, so that it may be set forth, in the due order of events, until it reaches the period of the siege of Acre.

CH. 11.—*Of the emulation of the French and the English in taking up the Cross.*

WHEN report, then, had spread these events, as we have described, throughout the world, that the cities of the Holy Land were in possession of infidels; that the holy relics were scornfully treated and trodden under foot; and that the Christians were plundered and despoiled, the empires were moved by the most strenuous exhortation of Pope Gregory VIII.; and many men of various nations were aroused, and above all, the French and English devoutly took up the sign of the cross, and prepared with all their strength to hurry to the aid of the Holy Land, being incited like David to take vengeance on the Philistines, who were defying, with their Goliath, the oppressed armies of the God of Jerusalem. For the chief pontiff earnestly stimulated all to obtain by these means pardon for their sins, and according to the authority with which he was invested, gave them absolution from the guilt of their past transgressions, if they would devote themselves to the performance of so pious and so necessary a work; proving to them that they would deservedly be the happier for undertaking the mission at once, in fervent zeal and without delay. Yea, their journey would be the more praiseworthy, and their endeavours many times more excellent, in behalf of a place, though desolate, yet rendered holier by the divine mystical promise, and which was consecrated by the nativity, dwelling, and passion of our Lord. Moreover, it was distinguished, by the divine choice, from every other nation; and being his dwelling, ought to be snatched from the heathen, of whom the Lord had said, "that they should not enter into His Church." They hastened, therefore, with ready zeal and pious emulation to take the cross at the hands of the clergy; so that the question was, not *who* should take it up, but *who* had *not* already done so. The voice of song was now silenced, the pleasures of eating and luxurious habits were abandoned, the quarrels of disputants quieted; new peace was made between old enemies, causes of litigation were settled by mutual agreement, and for this new ground of quarrel, every one who had cause of dispute, even for long-standing enmity, was reconciled to his neighbour. What need is there to say more? By the inspiration of God, all were of one

accord, for one common cause led them to undertake the
labour of this pious pilgrimage.

Ch. III.—*How Henry, king of England, and Philip, king of France,
with an immense multitude, took up the cross between Gisors and Trie.*

RICHARD, then count of Poitou, was the first to take
up the cross, and an immense multitude with him; but they
did not set out on their pilgrimage, owing to some delay,
occasioned by a dispute between Philip, king of France, and
Henry, king of England, the father of Count Richard. An
inveterate dispute had excited them to international war, as
it had done their ancestors, the French and Normans, from
an inexorable and almost uninterrupted feud. The archbishop of the land of Jerusalem, that is of Tyre,* was earnest
to effect a reconciliation between them, and had fixed the day
they were to meet, to take up the cross, at a place between
Gisors and Trie. The aforesaid archbishop had come on a
mission to animate the faithful, and obtain assistance for the deliverance of the Holy Land, having been specially sent to the
king of England, the fame of whose virtues was spread far
and wide above all the other kings of the earth, on account
of his glory, riches, and the greatness of his power. On that
day, after many plans had been proposed, and much spoken on
either side, they both came finally to the determination that
each of them should take up the cross, and depart from his land,
it appearing to each a safe precaution against the one invading
the kingdom of the other, while absent, for neither would venture to go unless the other went also. At length, these conditions having been, with some difficulty, agreed on, the two
kings exchanged the kiss of peace, and assumed the cross
with the blessing of the archbishop, and with them an immense number of both nations, partly from the love of God and
for the forgiveness of their sins, partly from respect for their
king; and so great was the multitude that took up the cross
on that day, that the people, from the crush and intolerable
heat (for it was summer) nearly fainted. The delay in entering upon their march must be reprehended; it was the work
of the enemy of the human race, whose interest it is to
foment discord, and excite inexorable enmity, and by whose

---

* This was William of Tyre, the author of the well-known history of
the earlier period of the Crusades.

instigation, the altercation between the kings was revived, and the seeds of discord sown from a very light occasion, that by their diabolical superstition neither was inclined to forego, lest, as it were, his fame and honour should be derogated thereby; as if it were abject and mean to yield obedience to justice and right.

Ch. IV.—*Henry, king of England, dies.*

THE death of Henry, king of England, put an end to these dissensions, and the vow of making the crusade, which he had deferred fulfilling while in safety, after a lapse of time, could not be performed, by the intervention of his death. As a vow must be entirely voluntary, so when taken, it must irrefragably be discharged; and he who binds himself by a vow is to be condemned for the non-performance of it, as he could not have made it lawfully, but of his own accord and free-will. Now King Henry died on the day of the holy apostles Peter and Paul, in the year of our Lord 1189, and was buried at Fontevrault.

Ch. V.—*How Richard, count of Poitou, was crowned king of England.*

THEREFORE in the same year, after the death of his father, Richard, count of Poitou, having arranged his affairs in Normandy, in about two months crossed over to England, and on St. Giles's day he was received at Westminster, with a ceremonious procession; and three days afterwards, viz., on the 3rd of September, the day of the ordination of St. Gregory the pope, which was a Sunday, he was solemnly anointed king by the imposition of hands, by Archbishop Baldwin, in virtue of his office, who performed the service, assisted by many of his suffragans. At his coronation were present his brother John, and his mother Eleanor, who, after the death of King Henry, had been, by the command of her son Richard, the new king, released from prison, where she had been ten years; and there were also present counts and barons, and an immense crowd of men and soldiers; and the kingdom was confirmed to the hands of King Richard. On the 3rd day of September, in the year of our Lord 1189, Richard was anointed king, on a Sunday, with the dominical letter A.,

viz., in the year after leap year. Many were the conjectures
made, because the day above that was marked unlucky in
the calendar; and in truth it was unlucky, and very much so
to the Jews of London, who were destroyed that day, and
likewise the Jews settled in other parts of England endured
many hardships.   Having therefore celebrated the occasion
by a festival of three days, and entertained his guests in the
royal palace of Westminster, King Richard gratified all, by
distributing money, without count or number, to all according
to their ranks, thus manifesting his liberality and his great
excellence.   His generosity, and his virtuous endowments,
the ruler of the world should have given to the ancient times;
for in this period of the world, as it waxes old, such feelings rarely exhibit themselves, and when they do, they are
subjects of wonder and astonishment.   He had the valour
of Hector, the magnanimity of Achilles, and was equal
Alexander, and not inferior to Roland in valour; nay, he
outshone many illustrious characters of our own times.   The
liberality of a Titus was his, and, which is so rarely found in
a soldier, he was gifted with the eloquence of Nestor and
the prudence of Ulysses; and he shewed himself pre-eminent
in the conclusion and transaction of business, as one whose
knowledge was not without active good-will to aid it, nor his
good-will wanting in knowledge.   Who, if Richard were accused of presumption, would not readily excuse him, knowing
him for a man who never knew defeat, impatient of an injury, and impelled irresistibly to vindicate his rights, though
all he did was characterized by innate nobleness of mind.
Success made him better fitted for action; fortune ever favours
the bold, and though she works her pleasure on whom she
will, Richard was never to be overwhelmed with adversity.
He was tall of stature, graceful in figure; his hair between
red and auburn; his limbs were straight and flexible; his
arms rather long, and not to be matched for wielding the
sword or for striking with it; and his long legs suited the rest
of his frame; while his appearance was commanding, and his
manners and habits suitable; and he gained the greatest celebrity, not more from his high birth than from the virtues that
adorned him.   But why need we take much labour in extolling
the fame of so great a man?   He needs no superfluous commendation, for he has a sufficient meed of praise, which is the

sure companion of great actions. He was far superior to all
others both in moral goodness, and in strength, and memorable
for prowess in battles, and his mighty deeds outshone the most
brilliant description we could give of them. Happy, in truth,
might he have been deemed had he been without rivals who
envied his glorious actions, and whose only cause of enmity
was his magnificence, and his being the searcher after virtue
rather than the slave of vice.

CH. VI.—*How King Richard, having arranged the affairs of his king-*
dom, celebrated the Nativity of Christ at Lions, in Normandy, and
how, by agreement, he and the king of France met on the feast of
St. John the Baptist at Vezelai.

AFTER the coronation-feast was ended, as we before said,
King Richard arose in his father's stead, and, after having
r.us red the oath of allegiance from the nobles, as was the
custom, in the form of homage, and each having submitted
to his sovereignty, he left London and went round his
country; and afterwards he set out on a pilgrimage to
St. Edmund, whose festival was at hand; thence he went to
Canterbury, and at his command some bishoprics, which, having
become vacant, had been kept so by the king his father, were
filled up, and, with the approval of the king, the following
were installed bishops: Richard the treasurer, of London;
Godfrey de Luci, of Winchester; Hubert Walter, of Salisbury,
William de Longchamp, of Ely, whom the king also made his
chancellor and justiciary of all England. In like manner, also,
the king caused bishops to be ordained to the vacant bishoprics
in his other territories. Having prepared every thing necessary for his journey, and having set the kingdom of England
in order as far as time permitted, he returned to Normandy
without delay, and kept the festival of the Nativity of Our
Lord at Lions; for his intention of setting out upon his
journey and the fulfilment of his vow made him unceasingly
anxious, as he judged delay to be dangerous, whilst it was of
consequence to commence the journey which was due: wherefore he wrote to the king of France that he was quite ready
to set out, and urged that he should be ready also, shewing by
his father's example that delay was hurtful when every thing
was prepared. Therefore, in the year of our Lord 1190, with the
dominical letter G, the kings met at Dreux to confer about the
arrangement of their journey. After many had communicated

their opinions, and while the conference was going on, there
suddenly arrived a messenger with the news that the queen of
France was dead. The king, smitten by the bitterness of this
news, was greatly cast down, so that he almost thought of
laying aside his premeditated journey; and to augment this be-
reavement, news was brought that William, king of Apulia,
was likewise dead. Overwhelmed by these adverse occurrences,
and utterly overcome by the belief that they predicted ill,
they abstained from the transaction of the business, and the fire
of their zeal in a measure grew lukewarm. However, by the
favour of the inspiration of God, who guideth the footsteps or
man, and in whose hands are the hearts of kings, to prevent
the ruin of a work planned with so much toil and solemnly
arranged, and the turning into condemnation and disgrace
what had been disposed for the attainment of good, they
recovered their strength, and were animated to proceed · id
set out, and not to grow lukewarm by unpardonable slothfulness. Now they had agreed together to set out on the
Nativity of St. John the Baptist, in order that the kings,
together with their men, should meet on the eighth day
at Vezelai. Whereupon Philip, king of France, setting out
from the city of Paris, which is the capital of France,
with a large quantity of provisions, shortly afterwards
marched by the chapel of St. Denis, to whose prayers and
merits he commended himself, and thus commenced his
journey accompanied by a very large multitude. There
also set out with him on his journey, the duke of Burgundy
and the count of Flanders. Who can relate the progress of
each with their forces? You might meet them on all sides
flocking together and assembling from different parts, and
joining together in one army, amidst pious tears; while those
who went forward with their friends or kinsmen, regarded
them with a look of love, and on their departure were
unable to restrain the tears from bursting forth, as devotion or
sorrow affected them.

CH. VII.—*How King Richard, being at Tours, commanded his fleet to
proceed and go round Spain by the Straits, and wait for him at
Messina.*

KING Richard was at Tours with a chosen body of soldiers.
Both the city and suburbs were so crowded with the multitude
of men that they inconvenienced each other from the crowd

and the narrowness of the streets and roads.   Therefore,
by the command of the king, the royal fleet, being collected together, was ordered to proceed in order, being in
number a hundred and eight, not including the ships that
followed afterwards.   Thus the royal fleet, having been set
forward on its voyage by the command of the king, with a
fair wind and in close company, reached the destined port of
Messina, after having safely escaped the dangerous sandbanks,
and the perils of the terrible rocks, the stormy straits of Africa,
and all the dangers of the ocean.   Here they awaited the
arrival of the king, according to his command, who was
marching with his army by land.   When the king departed
from Tours with his forces, the inhabitants of the land were
terrified by the appearance of so great a multitude.   Who
could relate the numbers of those who accompanied him,
the variety of their arms, the trains of nobles and chosen
bands of combatants?   Or who could describe the troops of
infantry and their bodies of slingers, which those who saw as
they advanced in order, from their inmost hearts, and with
pious zeal forcing out the tears, equally mourned and congratulated their lord the new king, who thus, at the commencement
of his reign, without having tasted the sweets of rest, so de-
votedly and so speedily left all pleasures, and, as if chosen by
the Lord, he undertook a work of so great goodness, so arduous
and so necessary, and a journey so commendable.   O the
miserable sighs for those that left them!   O the groans of
those who embraced at parting! and the good wishes for those
who were going away!   O the eyes heavy with tears, and the
mutual sobs interrupting the words of the speakers amidst the
kisses of those who were dear to them, not yet satisfied with
the conversation of those who were leaving them; and although they grieved, those who were setting out feigned
equanimity by the gravity of their countenances, and separated
from each other, after long conversations, as if choking for
utterance, and often interchanging a farewell, staid a little
longer, and repeated it to gain delay and to appear about to
say something more; and at last, tearing themselves from
the voices of those that cheered them, they bounded forward
and extricated themselves from the hands of those who would
detain them.

CH. VIII.—*How the two kings, according to agreement, met at Vezelai.*

THUS, in the first year of his coronation, Richard, king of England, set out from Tours on his journey. From Tours he marched to Luti, then to Mount Richard ; after that to Cellea, thence to Chapelles, thence to Dama, thence to Vitilia-cum, that is, Vezelai, where the two kings and their forces were to meet. And because the people of both nations were reckoned to be incalculably numerous, the mountains, far and wide, were spread with pavilions and tents, and the surface of the earth around was covered, so that the level of the sowed fields which were occupied, presented to the beholder the appearance of a city, with its effect heightened by a most imposing variety of pavilions, and by the different colours that distinguished them. There you might see the martial youth of different nations equipped for war, which appeared able to subdue the whole length of the earth, and to overcome the countries of all the world, and to penetrate the retreat of different tribes, and judge no place too hard or no enemy too fierce to conquer ; and that they would never yield to wrong while they could aid and assist each other by the help of their valour. That army, boasting in its immense numbers, well protected by the defence of their arms, and glowing with ardour, was scattered by the intervention of disputes, and overthrown by internal discord, which, if com-bined with military discipline and good-will, would have remained invincible to all without ; and thus, by the violation of the ties of fellowship, it met with a heavier downfal, whilst it was distracted by its own friends ; for a house divided against itself is made desolate.

CH. IX.—*How the two kings entered into a treaty at Vezelai, and agreed to wait for each other at Messina, and how they arrived together at Lyons on the Rhone.*

THERE the two kings made a treaty for their mutual security, and for preserving good faith with each other in every respect, and for inquiring into all things according to the rights of war, with a view to their equal division. Be-sides that, it was agreed that he who should arrive first at Messina was to wait for the other to follow ; after which, each of their friends who had followed them so far on

their pilgrimage should return home. The two kings set
forward with their men, and arranged the manner of their
march, holding frequent intercourse with great magnificence,
and paying each other mutual honour; and being also of
one accord, the mighty army, during the progress of their
march, performed their duties without complaint or dissen-
sion,—nay, with joy and alacrity. And as they thus passed
along cities and villages with a mighty equipment and clash
of arms, the inhabitants, observing the multitude, and marking
the distinctions of the men by the place of each nation in the
march, and noticing their discipline, exclaimed, " O heaven !
what meaneth so great a multitude of men, and so mighty an
army ? Who can resist their valour ? O noble soldiery
in the flower of their youth ! O young men, happy in
so much beauty ! Were your parents affected with sorrow
at your departure ? What land gave birth to youths of
so distinguished a mien, or produced such fine young soldiers ? And who are the rulers of so mighty a multitude
that govern with their word such brave legions ? " Uttering
these words, and such like, and following with good wishes
those that passed, they paid the most marked attention to
the people of different nations and those who were fatigued
by the march, by testifying all the devotion in their power.
Thus the army proceeding in order by separate divisions,
went joyfully from Vezelai to St. Leonard of Curbeny,
thence to Mulins, afterwards to Mount Escot, then to Tulnis,
near St. Mary de Bois, thence to Belivi, afterwards to the
village of Furaca, and thence to Lyons on the Rhone ; there
they stopped some days, owing to the difficulty of crossing the
river from its rapidity and unknown depth ; so that the army
which had come in the interim might cross over, and wait the
arrival of those who were to follow. Having at length
crossed the river, the two kings pitched their pavilions on the
other side in the meadows : as many of the army as it
could contain lodged in the town; the others in the fields
in the suburbs. There you might see people of different
nations, distinguished by their proper places and by the
forms of their arms, in countless numbers ; for they were
reckoned to exceed a hundred thousand, and recruits had not
yet ceased to flock in. Afterwards, the king of England followed up his show of friendship and honour to the king of

France, on his departure with all his troops for Genoa. For the king of France had engaged the Genoese, who were good seamen, to carry him over the gulf. For they had agreed, as has been afore said, that whichever first put in at Messina in Sicily, should await the arrival of the other.

CH. X.—*How, after the departure of the king of France to Genoa, the bridge over the Rhone gave way from the pressure of the crowd, and how King Richard embarked at Marseilles and crossed over to Messina.*

WHILE the crowd of pilgrims, who came in constantly from all quarters, was incautiously hastening to cross the bridge over the Rhone, a part of it gave way under their weight, with those who were on it, and, as it was of considerable elevation, about a hundred men fell into the water, which was very violent, and its course rapid, and owing to its depth, it was difficult for any who had fallen in to get out alive. But they who fell in cried out loudly, and implored assistance; and, wonderful to relate, though exhausted, they all escaped save two, who were drowned, and experienced death of the body, though they live spiritually in Christ, in whose service they were. Those who came behind were embarrassed by their numbers, as each sought his own way or means of crossing the Rhone; but they were thrown into despair by the breaking down of the bridge, which seemed to cut off their hopes of reaching the other side. On learning this, King Richard, whose constancy was never shaken, relieved their anxiety by causing a bridge to be made, by collecting as quickly as possible a number of boats together, such as the urgent necessity of the case should suggest; and so they crossed over, after some delay and difficulty. This accident caused a delay of three days to the king and his army: one part then proceeded to the nearest port, Marseilles; part went to Venice; part to Genoa, or Barlata, or Brundusium; and very many set out for Messina, the port where the two kings were to meet. Three days afterwards, the king departed, and on the same day the bridge was broken up. From Lyons we crossed by Vicaria near Alba Ripa, thence to Mount Galonte, afterwards to St. Bernard of Romaux, then by Valence, afterwards by Ariola, after that to Valois, thence to St. Paul of Provence; we afterwards passed through Mount Dragus and Orenge, and then cross-

M

ing Mount Sorgre, we came to Dompas, near Avignon, then by
Tenaiz, then by Salus and Marignan near the sea, and thence
to Marseilles, where we stayed three weeks; then we embarked the day after the Assumption of the Blessed Virgin
Mary, in the first year of King Richard's coronation, and
passed between two islands, of which Sardinia, one of them,
was on our right, Corsica, the other, on our left: here there
is a great strait of the sea. We then passed between two
burning mountains, one called Vulcano, the other Strango,
and by Farus, a very perilous stream, and then arrived at the
city of Messina, where the fleet of King Richard lay, which
he sent forward, as we have said before.

CH. XI.—*Of the city of Messina, and of the queen, sister to King
Richard, and of her dowry from Tancred.*

YOU must know that the city of Messina is filled with
abundance of good things; its situation is pleasant and very
agreeable; it lies on the confines of Sicily and Rass, which
was said to have been given to the famous Agoland, for
his services. Thus the city of Messina stands the first in
Sicily for affluence and wealth; but its inhabitants are a
wicked and cruel race. Their king, Tancred, was very rich
in every kind of wealth, which his predecessors, from the
time of Robert Guiscard, had amassed. At the same time,
the queen of Apulia, having lost her husband, William, was
staying at Palermo; for King William had died without an
heir, and his queen with her dowry was in ward of the same
King Tancred, who had succeeded King William on the throne.
This dowager queen was sister to Richard, king of England,
who taking up her cause, forced King Tancred to give condign
satisfaction, over and above the dowry that was due to her.

CH. XII.—*Of the injuries which the Griffons at Messina did to our men
before the arrival of King Richard.*

THE noble fleet of the king of England, as we have said
before, waited here the arrival of their sovereign,—a fleet
wonderful for its numbers, complement, and the splendour of
its array, and the like of which none was ever seen fitted out
with such labour, and so numerous, besides the various classes
of men that belonged to it, stationed on the shore in pavilions

and tents of different forms; for they kept apart from the city, until the arrival of King Richard, on account of the overbearing insolence of its citizens. For this wicked people, commonly called Griffons, many of whom are of Saracen extraction, hostile to our men, annoyed them by repeated insults, by pointing their fingers into their eyes, and calling them stinking dogs, and mocking them in many other ways, privately killing some of them, and throwing others into the sewers, of which crime many of them were afterwards convicted. In this manner they upbraided our men, and shewed their hatred by doing them every ill turn they dared; and if our men attempted to resist, or retaliate, they threatened to drive them entirely from their city, being strangers, and no match for them in numbers or strength; but the citizens acted in this without foresight, for they forgot that their king was coming.

CH. XIII.—*With what show, first the king of France, then the king of England, arrived in Messina.*

IT is a general custom, that when any particular king or prince of the earth, conspicuous for his glory, might, and authority, comes forth in public, his appearance of power shall not fall short of that with which he is actually invested, —nay, it is but right and becoming that the greatness of a king should be shewn in his display and the homage which is paid him; for a common proverb says, "Such as I see you are, I esteem you." Moreover the general style and manner is taken from the disposition of the chief. When, therefore, the king of France, of so high renown, whose edict so many princes and nations obeyed, was known to be entering the port of Messina, the natives, of every age and sex, rushed forth to see so famous a king; but he, content with a single ship, as if to avoid the sight of men, entered the port of the citadel privately, while those who awaited him along the shore conceived this to be a proof of his weakness, and spoke upbraidingly of him as one not likely to be the performer of any great actions who thus slunk from the eye of man; and being frustrated in their hopes of seeing him, they returned indignant to their homes. But when the report was spread of the arrival of the noble-minded king of England, the people rushed out eagerly

M 2

to behold him, crowding along the shore and seating themselves wherever they were likely to catch a glimpse of him. And lo! they beheld the sea in the distance covered with innumerable galleys; and the sound of trumpets and clarions, loud and shrill, strike upon the ear! Then, as they approached nearer, they saw the galleys as they were impelled onward, laden and adorned with arms of all kinds; their pennons and standards floating in countless numbers in the breeze in good order and on the tops of their spears; the prow of the galleys distinguished from each other by the variety of the paintings, with shields glittering in the sun, and you might behold the sea boiling from the number of oarsmen who plied it, and the ears of the spectators rang with the peals of the instruments commonly called trumpets, and their delight was aroused by the approach of the varied crowd, when lo! the magnificent king, accompanied by the crowd of obedient galleys, standing on a prow more elevated and ornamental than the others, as if to see what he had not seen before, or to be seen by the crowds that densely thronged the shore, lands in a splendid dress, where the sailors whom he had sent before him, and others of his equipage, receive him with congratulations, and bring forward the chargers and horses which had been committed to their care for transportation, that he and his suite might mount. The natives crowd round him on all sides, mixed with his own men, and followed him to his hostel. The common people conversed with each other in admiration of his great glory; and agreed that he was worthy of empire, and deserved to be set over nations and kingdoms, "for the fame of him which we had before heard fell far short of the truth when we saw him." Meanwhile the trumpets blew, and their sounds being harmoniously blended, there arose a kind of discordant concord of notes, whilst the sameness of the sounds being continued, the one followed the other in mutual succession, and the notes which had been lowered were again resounded.

Ch. XIV.—*What injuries our men suffered at Messina at the hands of the Lombards.*

WHEN the Griffons saw the kings land in such strength, their arrogance was in part checked, for they perceived that they were their inferiors in valour and appearance; but

the Lombards * ceased not contumaciously to menace and
revile our men and to provoke them by insults, threatening
even to attack our camp, to slay us and plunder our goods.
They were excited by jealousy on account of their wives, with
whom some of our men had talked, more for the purpose of
irritating their husbands than with the intention of seducing
them. From this quarrel and through envy, the Lombards
were aroused, together with the commune † of the city, and
were always hostile to us as far as they could, chiefly because
they had learnt from their ancestors that they had been subdued by us of yore; whence they did them as much annoyance as they could, at the same time heightening the
battlements of their towers, and deepening the fosses that
surrounded them. To irritate our men still more, they provoked them by repeated revilings and insulted them with
contumelies.

Ch. XV.—*How, owing to a loaf of bread which was sold by a woman, a
fight took place between us and the Lombards.*

By chance one day it happened that one of our men was
bargaining with a woman about a new loaf which she offered
for sale; and while they were conversing together and he
threatened to have the loaf weighed, the woman, because he
would not give her the price she asked, flew into a great passion and insulted him with contumelious and wicked language,
and scarcely restrained her hands from striking him or tearing
his hair. Immediately a concourse of the citizens flocked
together at the noise of the abusive woman, who seized hold
of the man and beat him unmercifully; and after tearing out
his hair and injuring him in many other ways, they trod him
under foot and left him for dead. When complaint was made,
King Richard begged for peace and friendship, asserting that
he had come in peace, and that he had set out merely to
perform a pilgrimage; and he desisted not from praying for
peace, until each party, having given a promise to that effect,
returned quietly to their abodes.

* It is probable that Vinsauf calls this portion of the population
Lombards, because they were occupied in mercantile pursuits. They
were not, of course, Lombards by nation.
† It is hardly necessary to state that the commune was the corporate
body of the city, probably jealous of their municipal privileges, which the
crusaders perhaps had infringed.

Ch. XVI.—*How the Lombards attacked King Richard's men, and how King Richard besieged, assaulted, and stormed the city, and raised his standard on the towers, which gave umbrage to the king of France, who was preparing to assist the Lombards.*

But, by means of that old enemy of the human race, whose part it is to disturb peace and excite sedition, the dispute was renewed on the morrow, so that a more destructive altercation arose between the citizens and the pilgrims. Meanwhile the two kings had a conference with the justiciaries of Sicily and the chief citizens, to treat of peace and security; when behold, a cry arose that the natives were already slaying the men of the king of England; which when the king minded not, chiefly because the Lombards asserted that it was not true, there came a second messenger announcing that the natives had attacked the pilgrims. The Lombards, who had been in the same conflict, persuading him that it was not so, thought to circumvent the king by falsehood: when a third messenger rushed in headlong, exclaiming that such peace was not to be approved of when the sword was actually hanging over their necks. Then the king, hastening without delay from the said conference, mounted on horseback, and went out with the design of putting a stop to the quarrel and making peace between the wranglers. There were two Lombards, very cunning and deceitful, at whose instigation the mob of the city had been excited against the pilgrims; who, to conceal their craft by a lie, asserted that they had come thence, and that no harm had been done: their names were Jordan Luppin and Margarit. When King Richard arrived at the spot, the two parties were already at blows, and strove no longer with words, but with fists and bludgeons; and the Lombards now inflamed with rage, instead of yielding to the king's endeavours to separate the combatants, attacked him with contumelious and profane railings; whereupon he, irritated by their mockeries, took up arms, and besieged them in their city. The French, meanwhile, doubtful what their lord the king would do, ran about in search of him here and there; when they saw him come hastily from the place of conference and enter the palace in which he was lodged. There was a general commotion in the city; every one seized upon what came to hand, and they talked boastingly of defending themselves to the last. The

Lombards went to the king of France to implore his aid
and assistance, offering to give themselves and their property
into his power and will, if he would relieve their city from the
assaults of the king of England, and take it into his own subjection. The king of France immediately took up arms, and
as we were told by one who knew the truth, answered that
he would rather assist the Lombards than the men of the king
of England, although he was bound to him by his oath, and
had pledged his honour to give him aid and to be faithful
to him everywhere. The gates of the city being closed and
guards placed along the battlements, there arose a clamour,
tumult, and commotion from the assaulters without; while
those within ran to arms and seized whatever weapons fury
supplied them with to defend themselves. The French having
joined themselves with the Lombards, they were animated
with one purpose, and acted together as one body. But
those without knew not that their associates had thus become
their adversaries. Some Lombards had gone out before the
gates of the city were shut, to attack the hostel of Hugh le
Brun, and obstinately persevered in fighting. The king
of England, hearing of it, turned his course thither, and
when they saw him coming, they took hastily to flight
and were scattered in a moment, like sheep before wolves;
after which, their attacks and revilings ceased. The king
pursued them as far as a postern of the city, which they
made for, not daring to look at, much less resist, him, though
the king is said to have had only twenty men when he first
attacked them. He slew some of them, however, as they
entered the postern. The Lombards, now seeing that the
attack had become serious, and that they were besieged in
earnest, resisted with all their might, and occupying the
battlements of the walls, they hurled down stones and javelins from bows and slings like showers of rain; and impeded their assailants in every way they could, either to
put an end to their assaults, or cause them to be less formidable; and thus at the commencement of their impetuous
defence, they did much hurt to our men, killing some,
bruising others, wounding and shattering the limbs of many;
for by the shower of darts, javelins, and stones that were
thrown at us, we lost, besides others, three knights, Peter
Tireprete, and Matthew de Saulcy, and Radulph de Roverei.

Indeed, if they had had the true faith of Christ in them, and a due regard for justice, they might have made a great slaughter of our men, and might have conquered by their numbers; but their arrogance and dishonesty deservedly proved hurtful to them, who had wrought such injury without a cause; for the number of the citizens and others who defended the city was said to exceed fifty thousand. You might there see men making most valorous attacks to force an entrance, some showering darts, and others assaulting the gates; while our galleys from seaward occupied the port opposite the palace, and blockaded the city: but the king of France hindered them from entering the port, and some were destroyed in the attempt. But, on the land side, where the king of England was, a man remarkable for his skill in arms, the attack was closely pressed; some essayed to cut the fastenings of the gates, and not succeeding, they ascended a high hill, close by the city, and by means of a postern, which King Richard, on the second day of his arrival, when going round the walls to reconnoitre with two companions, had observed to be neglected by the citizens, they forced an entrance with great boldness and violence, and having broken down the gates, they admitted the rest of the army into the city. Then they slew or made captive all citizens they met who resisted them, and entered the city in a body; and many, as well Lombards as our men, fell in that conflict. For the citizens, not daring to oppose us as we were now entering and occupying the city, threw down darts from the tops of houses and battlements of towers, and tried in every manner they could to annoy us from the solers, in which they had taken refuge. But our men now marched through the captured city as victors, preceded by King Richard, who was the first in every attack: by his own daring example, he at once gave courage to his own men, and carried dismay amongst the foe. About ten thousand men marched in after him, and plundered the whole city. There you might hear horrible clamours, in a variety of confused tones, on the one side, of our men, urging on the pursuit, on the other, of the flying Lombards, screaming for fear, while they redoubled their blows, and mowed down those who met them with their swords, like corn. When our men entered the houses, the Lombards threw themselves from the house-tops and the solers, rather than fall into the hands of their enemies; conscious that by their own inhospitality they had forfeited all claim to mercy. The city was now subdued by force, and no one appeared to make further resistance ; what need we say more ? King Richard captured Messina by one assault, in less time than a priest could chant the matin service. Many more of the citizens would have fallen, had not King Richard, with an impulse of generosity, ordered their lives to be spared. But who could reckon the sum of money which the citizens lost ? All the gold and silver, and whatsoever precious thing was found became the property of the victors. They also set fire to, and burnt to ashes, the enemy's galleys, lest they should escape, and recover strength to resist. The victors also carried off their noblest women. And lo ! after this action had been performed, the French suddenly beheld the ensigns and standards of King Richard floating above the walls of the city; at which the king of France was so mortified, that he conceived that hatred against King Richard which lasted during his life, and afterwards led him to the unjust invasion of Normandy.

Cн. XVII.—*How the king of France being displeased that the standards of the king of England only should be placed on the city walls, King Richard, humbling himself, allowed the standards of both to be placed there together.*

THE king of France, jealous of the successes of the king of England, and misliking his high spirit, very much grieved that he should not have the glory which the other had gained by the force of his own greatness ; for, contrary to the conditions of mutual agreement, and while the army was in the greatest danger, and a great slaughter going on before his eyes, he proffered not a helping hand to the king of England against an obstinate foe, as he was bound by the treaty of alliance. Nay, he resisted as much as he could, and kept him a long time from occupying the entrance of the city where he himself abode. The city being taken, as we said before, and the banners of King Richard planted on the walls, the king of France, by the advice of his council, sent orders to King Richard to take down his standards, and substitute those of France, as an acknowledgment of his superiority. King Richard, indignant at this command, considering what previously occurred, and bearing in mind the rights of their fellowship, sent no answer, lest he should seem to surrender his right, and the victory should be ascribed not only to one who had been inactive, but to a perjured adversary. At the intercession of mediators, however, the anger of King Richard was at length appeased; an end was put to their wrangling, and yielding to the soothings of his friends, with some difficulty, he, who was held invincible, being overcome by his foes, gave way to the request of the king of France, viz., that he should deliver into his custody the towers he had taken, and place in them guards of *both* nations, until they should learn the sentiments of King Tancred as to what had been done; and he who remained angry and obdurate to threats and boastings was moved by prayers and soothing. The standards of both were, therefore, raised above the walls of the city, until he should try the consistency of the king of France, and proved his friendship.

Cᴴ. XVIII.—*How messengers were sent to King Tancred to demand satisfaction and the restoration of the queen's dowry, and how the king of France sends secretly a contrary message.*

It was therefore decreed by common counsel, that King Richard should send messengers to Tancred, king of Sicily, to require satisfaction for the enormous outrage committed by his people, and to ascertain his intentions in regard to what had occurred. Moreover, King Richard commanded King Tancred to give his sister, the queen of Sicily, a sufficient dowry, and the portion of the king her husband's treasure which belonged to her by right, as well as the table of gold, which ought to be equally shared with the wife of him who had possessed it. The duke of Burgundy and Robert de Sabloel, and some others, whose names are lost, were the messengers appointed for this business. Meanwhile, the king of France weighing in his mind the greatness of King Richard, and repining from envy, began to raise a question about the plunder of the city, demanding his portion, according to the covenant they had entered into. Giving vent, therefore, to arrogant and contumelious speeches about these things, because King Richard sternly refused his demand, he ceased not to irritate his spirit to passion by sly insinuations and opprobrious taunts; and he hesitated not to transgress the

terms of the covenant which had been entered into between
them, and to shew the hollowness of his friendship. Whereupon King Richard, more from indignation than from any
other feeling, determined to reject his friendship, and ordered
his ships to be ready to depart with all their baggage ; for
he had rather, under the guidance and direction of the Lord,
proceed alone with his own men to the accomplishment of his
pilgrimage, than have any dealings with an envious man ;
according to the common proverb, " It is better to be alone
than to have a bad companion." When, however, this was
known to the king of France, the latter procured, by means
of mediators, the renewal of their broken friendship and their
association as before, with the condition that every thing
which was gained hereafter should be equally divided.

CH. XIX.—*How King Tancred made an ambiguous reply, on which the
king of England was inflamed with anger ; and how the Lombards
refused his men provisions.*

MEANWHILE the messengers, in discharge of the business
of their mission, inquired the sentiments of King Tancred on
the matters in question. But the king replied in ambiguous
terms, asserting that he would give satisfaction to the kings
by advice of the nobles of the land in proper time, place, and
manner, upon all the subjects specified. It was reported that
the king of France had by letter exhorted King Tancred
not to yield to the demands of the king of England, but to
shew himself firm in defending his right in every thing, with
the assurance that he would not take part with King Richard
against him, but would be faithful to him. If such a message was sent, there was an evidence of it something like the
proverb ; for King Tancred loaded the messengers of the
king of France with presents, while he did not give those of
the king of England so much as an egg. Therefore the
messengers returned, and when they had reported their
answer to the kings, King Richard replied, " There is no
need of much talking or long speeches ; since King Tancred
will not give satisfaction of his own accord, I will endeavour
and labour my utmost to correct his faults myself." These
quarrels restored the courage of the natives, who, incited by
the king of France, endeavoured to injure King Richard and
his men as much as they could, and prohibited the supplying

of provisions necessary for so great an army; and ordered
that nothing should be exposed for sale, in order that they
might thus be compelled to submit themselves to the power of
the natives.

Ch. XX.—*Of the construction of Mategriffin, and of the discord between
the two kings.*

KING RICHARD had expended great labour and diligence in
erecting a castle, to which he gave the name of Mategriffin;
at which the Griffons were very much exasperated, because
this erection they saw was intended for their destruction.
The building was now completed on the hill, close by the
city, and very convenient for retreat. The army would have
suffered much from want of provisions, which were forbidden to
be exposed for sale, had they not used those which were brought
by the fleet as provision against future wants. The enemy,
therefore, did what harm and injury they could to our soldiers; they placed guards over the city by night, and the
army in their turn defended themselves from their attacks by
keeping watch. Moreover, discord again took possession of
the minds of the kings, and the king of France openly shewed
himself a favourer of the enemies of King Richard. But the
great majority of the nobles were earnest for the renewal of
peace, visiting at one time the palace, at another Mategriffin,
to try and pacify their anger: but their labour and endeavours were in vain, for each accused the other, and offered
to prove that the other was the aggressor, and neither of them
would yield to the other's will; the king of France, unwilling
to commit himself to the power of an inferior, and so derogate
from his own dignity; and King Richard, fearful that the
acknowledgment of subjection might lessen the glory of his
own deeds.

Ch. XXI.—*How King Tancred made peace with King Richard, by
giving him 40,000 ounces of gold as a dowry for the queen and the
marriage of Arthur; and how the two kings and the citisens made
peace.*

THUS matters fluctuated, when King Tancred considering
that danger might arise from further discord, and perceiving that King Richard would not desist from his purpose until he had obtained what he wished, sent messengers of
noble birth to offer peace, and beg for reconciliation, asserting—
very appositely for persuading him—that he was unwilling,

as far as lay in him, to bear the ill-will of so great a man,
to the danger of his own people; that he was willing to
purchase his alliance with money, and that he would give
the queen, sister of King Richard, 20,000 ounces of gold
for her dowry, and 20,000 ounces more as a marriage
portion for a daughter of his own, a damsel of talent and
beauty, to become the wife of his nephew, Arthur of Brittany,
if he chose.   King Richard, at the earnest request of the
messengers on both sides, agreed, and the affair was concluded; the money, viz. 40,000 ounces of gold, was paid,
and his sister, the queen, delivered up altogether to her
brother's care.   And thus, after peace had been agreed upon,
and confirmed in writing, all controversy ceased entirely.   So
when King Richard saw that satisfaction had been given him,
as he required, he ordered the money which had been received
from King Tancred to be equally divided, and also the
money which had been given as a dowry for his sister he
divided in like manner, although he was not bound to do so;
but he did it from mere liberality, which redounded to his
glory and praise, and relieved him in part from the hatred of
his adversaries.   Finally, by the advice of Walter, archbishop
of Rouen, all who should not restore entire whatever silver
or gold had been plundered from the city, were laid under
an anathema.   All things having thus been restored, and to
outward appearance peace established, the citizens rejoiced in
their safety, and the pilgrims in their tranquillity; the condition
of the city was thus rendered secure, and penal laws made
against the disturbers of the peace.   The citizens had free
intercourse with the pilgrims, without either quarrelling or
giving offence; all rejoiced exceedingly, and henceforth provisions, for both man and horse, were exposed for sale, at a
very reasonable price.   The friendship of the kings was also
renewed, and by the intervention of justice, universal good-
will was restored.   But though in outward appearance the
king of France dissembled his feelings, the rivalry which had
been once engendered continued immortal in his mind, and
throwing a veil over his envy at the illustrious deeds of King
Richard, he concealed the cunning of the fox beneath an
unmoved exterior.

CH. XXII.—*How King Tancred and King Richard meet at the city of Fatina.*

MEANWHILE, King Tancred, who was residing at that time at Palermo, not a little astonished at the fame of the magnificence and glory of King Richard's deeds, sent ambassadors of noble birth to invite him to an interview at the city of Fatina. He very much desired to behold the face of the man whom he much admired for the report of his magnanimity and valour. Now the city of Fatina was situated midway between Messina and Palermo, and King Richard assenting, went to meet him at the appointed place, with a splendid company of his nobles. And when they had met according to appointment, each was exceedingly rejoiced at the arrival of the other, and strove to shew every mutual civility, and they entered into a treaty of friendship; by which they bound themselves to preserve peace between each other, and having exchanged gifts of royal magnificence, they concluded the ceremony in a becoming manner, and separated, King Tancred returning to Palermo, and King Richard to Messina.

CH. XXIII.—*How King Richard bestows most ample gifts on his soldiers and others who had been impoverished by his stay there.*

MEANWHILE, the soldiers, who had been at great expense during the summer while the aforesaid troubles and disturbances were going on, liked not so long, so idle, and so useless a delay. For they considered that their brethren in Christ were constantly engaged in contests at the siege of Acre, and that they had already spent the greater part of their substance, and had even been compelled to restore what they acquired by plundering the captured city. King Richard, being moved by the prevalence of complaints of this kind, with royal munificence bestowed gifts on all that needed it, beyond their expectation, so that each one was most sufficiently enriched according to his rank. The knights were amply relieved by these gifts, whether of gold or silver, or any other kind; and even noble women of Palestine, who had been deprived of their inheritance and exiled, both widows and virgins, were bountifully enriched. King Richard thus obtained the gratitude and favour of all, for he gave the foot-soldiers and attendants of inferior rank a hundred sols at least. The king of France, also allured by his example,

bestowed very many gifts on his own men.   Hence fresh joy
reigned among the people, and those who had been broken
down by sorrow were raised up by such generous magnificence.

Ch. XXIV.—*Of the great feast given by King Richard at Mategriffin.
on Christmas Day, to which he invited the king of France and all his
people, and of his splendid gifts.*

THE great festival of Christmas was at hand, kept with
the greater solemnity as it was the more needful for the
redemption of the human race.   In honour of this festival,
King Richard invited, with all respect, the king of France
to dinner, and by the public crier called upon every soul to
pass that day with him in joy and gladness.   At his courteous
request, the king of France came with an innumerable band
of nobles, and a crowd of others.   He labours not much
who compels a willing person; and we cannot suppose many
were absent from King Richard's feast.   They were, therefore, received with honour into the castle of Mategriffin,
which he had built against the will of the natives, and
where every one sat down according to his rank.   Who could
count the variety of dishes which were brought in, or the
different kinds of cups, or the crowds of servants in splendid
attire?   which, if any one wishes to do, let him measure in
his mind the magnanimity of King Richard, and then he can
understand the kind of feast which would be prepared.   You
might have seen there nothing unbecoming or inapposite—
nothing which was not of value and commendable; for the
dishes and platters on which they were served were of no other
material or substance than gold or silver, and all the vessels
were of wrought gold or silver, with images of men and beasts
worked thereon with the chisel or the file, and adorned with
precious stones.   Moreover, their joyous countenances were
conspicuous above all, and gave grace to the festival; and the
guests were entertained with the cheerfulness of the enter-
tainers over and above the variety and abundance of meat and
drink.   After the feast was at an end, King Richard set before
the king of France the most beautiful cups, and gave him his
choice in honour of the occasion. and gave to each of the
nobles presents according to his rank; for like Titus, with
whose hand he lavished his wealth, he thought that the day
was lost on which he happened to have given nothing.

CH. XXV.—*How the Pisans and the Genoese attack the guards of King Richard's fleet.*

IT happened at that time that some Pisans and Genoese, heated with wine, and disturbed by some cause or other, attacked the guards of King Richard's fleet in a hostile manner, and from the vehement nature of their assault a great number were killed on both sides. On the morrow, as if grieving that they had not wrought their full malice the day before, they returned to the attack, and while they were fiercely engaged, King Richard came upon them hastily, and with difficulty restraining the combatants, forced them to separate.

CH. XXVI.—*Of the arrival of Queen Eleanor and Berengaria, the future wife of King Richard, and of the departure, first, of the king of France, and then of the king of England, for the Holy Land.*

THEREFORE, in the year of our Lord 1191, with the dominical letter E, after the stormy months of the more idle season of winter, when brighter days were coming on, the people, who were wearied with slothful delay, hailed with joy the arrival of the season for navigation; for the kings had stayed in the city of Messina from the feast of St. Michael until after Lent. They therefore held a conference about the transportation of their men, alleging the inconvenience of further delay, both on account of the presence of fine weather, and because their means would fail if spent in useless idleness, and because their friends at Acre were suffering from want of them, and they were grieved at having given them such tardy help. While, therefore, each was preparing to proceed on his journey, couriers arrived who informed Richard that his mother Eleanor was hastening after him, and having completed her journey, was close at hand; and that she was bringing with her the noble damsel, daughter of the king of Navarre, named Berengaria, the intended wife of King Richard. A long time previous, while yet count of Poitou, he had been charmed by the graces of the damsel and her high birth, and felt a passion for her; on which account her father, the king of Navarre, had committed her to the care of King Richard's mother to be carried to him, in order that he might marry her before crossing the sea as he intended. All rejoiced at their coming. Meanwhile the king of France, having made

ready with all his equipment, taking advantage of a favourable wind, set out with all his fleet, on the Saturday after the
Annunciation of the Blessed Virgin Mary; and King Richard
accompanied him some way in his galleys, with his noblest
peers.   But he himself was not ready to cross the sea, for
he had not yet collected all his transport-ships; and he
thought that they were not sufficiently provisioned: moreover,
he had heard that his mother was coming with the illustrious
Berengaria.   When, therefore, he had let the king of France
go on his voyage in peace, crossing past the Faro he came to
Risa, where he heard that the queen his mother and Berengaria were, and having taken them on board with great joy,
he returned to Messina; where having stayed a short time,
he let his mother depart, and committed to her the care of his
kingdom, together with Walter, archbishop of Rouen, as we
have said before, a man of great virtue.   And with them
returned Guilbert de Gascuil, by whose treachery the king
of France afterwards gained possession of the celebrated castle
of Gisors, situated in a very strong position on the confines of
France and Normandy, which had been committed to his safe-
keeping.   But King Richard retained with him the aforesaid
damsel, whom he was about to marry.   Queen Eleanor returned by Bourges, and thence to Salerna, and thus to Normandy.   But King Richard, having furnished himself with
every thing necessary for the voyage, prepared, according to
agreement, to follow after the king of France as quickly as he
could; and appointed Robert de Torneham to conduct and
take care of the fleet. He sent forward his betrothed, with his
sister the dowager queen of Sicily, in advance, in one of the
ships which are commonly called dromons, keeping a course
direct to the east; he had also placed some knights on board,
and a numerous retinue of servants, for their comfort and safe-
keeping.   These kind of vessels are slower than others, on
account of their burthen, but of stronger make.   The multitude of the galleys remained immoveable, until the king,
having dined, on account of the annoyances which had happened, bade farewell, with all his army, to the natives, and
was on the point of setting out and committing himself to
favourable winds and the waves of the sea.   Then the whole
multitude of ships was launched into the sea, impelled by
numerous oarsmen.   The city of Messina might justly boast

N

that so great a fleet had never in past ages quitted those
shores; and that they never will see there such a one again.
Therefore, on the seventeenth day after the departure of the
king of France, i. e. on the Wednesday after Palm Sunday,
King Richard followed with a numerous fleet of ships, and
passing amid the Faro with a fair breeze, some by sailing,
some by rowing, they came out into the deep,—the dromons,
however, keeping them in the rear as Richard had planned,
in order that, as far as it was possible to avoid it, they should
not part company, unless they were accidentally separated by
the tides; while the galleys purposely relaxed their speed and
kept pace with the ships of burthen, to guard their multitude
and protect the weaker.

CH. XXVII.—*Of the winds that were at one time calm, at another agi-
tating the sea, and the dangers which King Richard sustained as far as
Crete, and from Crete to Rhodes.*

THE wind all at once began to fall gradually, so that the
fleet was compelled to remain motionless at anchor between
Calabria and Mount Gibello; but on the morrow, i. e. the day
of the Lord's Supper, He who withdraws and sends forth the
winds from his treasuries, sent us a wind which continued the
whole day, not too strong, but impelling the fleet at a
moderate speed; but after that it abated altogether on the
following night. But on Holy Friday, a contrary wind
arising, drove it back to the left, and the sea being very much
agitated thereby, boiled up from the very depths, while
the waves beat together, and the storm increased; the roar
of the dashing waves, and the ships creaking with the violence of the wind, struck all with no small terror, and from
the excessive fury of the latter, all management of the ships
was at an end; for no pilot could steer them while tossing to
and fro in such a manner. They were borne hither· and
thither; their line was broken, and they went different ways.
The crews committed themselves to the guidance of the Lord,
despairing of earthly aid; but as far as human weakness permitted, we determined to bear all things with patience, under
the eye of our Saviour, who on that day had suffered so unde-
served a death for our sakes. And as the ships were tossed
to and fro, and dispersed divers ways, men's stomachs began to
feel a qualm, and were affected by a violent nausea; and this

feeling of sickness made them almost insensible to the dangers
around; but towards evening, it grew by degrees calm, and the
fury of the winds and waves abated.   A favourable wind now
springing up, according to our wishes, and the sailors having
recovered their strength and confidence, we strove to keep a
direct course for our voyage.   King Richard, unmoved amid
this state of confusion, never ceased to animate those who
were dispirited, and bid them take courage, and hope for better
fortune; moreover he had as usual a very large wax-light in
a lantern, hoisted aloft in his ship to give light to the rest of
the fleet and direct them in their way.   He had on board most
experienced sailors, who did every thing which human art
could do to oppose the fury of the winds.   All, therefore, as
far as they could, followed the light burning in the king's ship.
The king remained stationary some time to collect his fleet,
which congregated together by seeing the light, so that the
king resembled a hen gathering together her chickens.   After
that, we started with a favourable wind, and sailed along,
without obstacle or injury, on the Saturday of the Passover,
as well as on the day of the festival, and until the following Wednesday.   That day we came in sight of Crete,
where the king put in to repose and collect his fleet.   When
the ships had come together, twenty-five were found missing,
at which the king was much grieved.   Among the steep
mountains of this island of Crete, is one raised above the
others, like a lofty summit, which is called the Camel, which
sailors acquainted with those seas say is exactly midway
between Messina in Sicily, and Acre in Palestine.   On the
morrow, being Thursday, the king and all his army entered
their ships; when the wind began to rise stronger, and though
favourable, was very vehement in impelling us forward, for we
moved rapidly along, with sails swelled out and mast slightly
bent, not unlike the flight of birds.   The wind, which slackened not all night, at dawn of day drove our fleet violently
upon the island of Rhodes: there was no port, and the surf
stretched along the shore; however, we enjoyed there our rest
the better for having wished for it so earnestly, from that day
until the following Monday, when we put in at Rhodes.
Rhodes was anciently a very large city, not unlike Rome;
though its extent can scarcely be estimated, there are so many
ruins of houses and portions of fallen towers still standing,

and such wonderful remains of walls and buildings of admirable workmanship. There are also a few monasteries still remaining out of so many ancient edifices, for the most part deserted, though formerly inhabited by such numerous societies of monks. The site of so great a city, though by time laid waste, proves the former existence of a large population; but very few inhabitants were found there now who could sell us food. But as the king was indisposed, we tarried there a few days, during which he waited the arrival of the ships that had wandered out of their course and lost us, and the galleys which followed him. He made inquiries also about that cruel tyrant, emperor of Cyprus, who was wont to detain the pilgrims who put in at his port.

CH. XXVIII.—*Of the departure of King Richard from Rhodes, through the gulf, and of the arrival of the queen at Cyprus.*

HAVING spent ten days at Rhodes, which is a very fertile and productive island, they went on board, and set out on their voyage on the 1st of May. They were borne on their course into that most dangerous place, called the Gulf of Satalia. There is a mighty strife of currents formed by the junction of four seas, struggled violently together, each dashing against and resisting the other. We were on the point of entering it, when lo! as if apprehensive of our safety, a contrary current carried us back to the place from whence we had started. But in a short time, the wind, which in those parts is constantly shifting, drove us from behind back again into the gulf, with the more danger from its increased violence. Fearing the effects of its fury, we did all we could to guard against the dangers of the place, and pass over the waves that boiled and foamed around. The royal ship was always in advance, and when the king lifted his eyes, he saw beneath a calm sky, a very large ship of the sort called a buss (*buza*) bearing down, which was returning from Jerusalem. The king, therefore, speedily sent men to inquire for intelligence concerning the siege of Acre, from those who were in the ship; who replied that the king of France had already arrived at Acre in safety, and was diligently employed in making machines, until the arrival of the king of England. The king of France had put into the port of Acre on the Saturday of Easter week, and was applying all his energies to the taking of the city. He had therefore caused petrariæ

to be erected, and placed near the tower Maledictum, as well
as other machines for throwing down the walls, for the
king of France lay on the side near to that tower. By means
of filling up and treading in the trenches, and bringing
machines and petrariæ for casting stones, the wall was in
part broken down; but not long afterwards, the machines
were attacked and burnt to ashes by the exertions of the Turks.
When King Richard heard all these things from the aforesaid
sailors, the buss passed on its way, and he made all his
arrangements in high spirits; and as the wind was not fair, he
beat about, and toiled much to master its uncertainty; but the
fleet, from the adverse gales, and the rising and falling of the
waves, was forced back, and driven into the open sea. However, the buss from Lyons, in which the queens were, first put
into the port of the city of Limozin, in the island of Cyprus;
though they did not come to the land, but dropped their
anchors at some distance out at sea.

Ch. XXIX.—*Of the many misfortunes which befel the Holy Land, especially through the emperor of Cyprus.*

WITH what expiation do we deem the Holy Land to have
been punished, or with what scourge smitten, or of what crime
guilty, that so many adversaries should have resisted its succour, whereby assistance should have been so long deferred?
Nay, it began to be believed that the cause of its redemption
being so long delayed was the wickedness of its defenders;
and it is very evident by many proofs that the Divine aid
was withheld in consequence of the iniquity of its inhabitants; whence also it happened that the excellent soldiers of France, who were looked forward to as brave allies,
were unseasonably taken away in the midst. For why need
we speak of the death of the illustrious emperor of Germany,
whose end sullied the glory of his former reign? or who
could relate the grief felt for the death of the once rich and
glorious Henry, king of England? By his money, the city
of Tyre was preserved, and by his wisdom and prudence it
was hoped that the Holy Land would be recovered Lastly,
what might we say of the decease of William, king of Sicily,
who after he had made all the necessary preparations for his
pilgrimage, and had oftentimes sent the wished-for aid, was
cut off by sudden death, and closed his career? All these,
and many other misfortunes, impeded the recovery of the

Holy Land, and each of them was more than enough to
injure the cause. But there was one thing above all others,
we mean that which concerned the island of Cyprus, from
which the land of Jerusalem used annually to gain no small
profit; but now, after shaking off the yoke of subjection, it
disdained to give it any thing, by the direction of the tyrant of
the island, who had usurped the imperial power. Most
wicked of all bad men, and surpassing Judas in treachery, and
Güenelon in treason, he wantonly persecuted all who professed
the Christian religion. He was said to be a friend of Saladin,
and it was reported that they had drunk each other's blood, as
a sign and testimony of mutual treaty, as if by the mingling
of blood outwardly, they might become kinsmen in reality.
This, too, was afterwards evident by certain proofs; for the
tyrant, gaining confidence by this step, and setting at nought
the subjection which he owed, falsely usurped the name of
emperor, and he was accustomed to seize upon every
one who put into the island of his own accord, or was
driven thereto by the violence of the wind, that he might
extract a ransom from the rich, and force the poor to become
slaves. When, therefore, he learnt that a strange fleet had
arrived, he determined, according to his custom, to seize upon
all who were on board, and, having plundered them of their
money, to keep them captives.

Ch. XXX.—*Of the shipwreck and misfortune of some of our men, and
of their capture and imprisonment; also of the attack they made and the
victory they gained over the islanders of Cyprus.*

On the vigil of St. Mark the Evangelist, a little before
sunset, dark clouds covered the horizon, and the spirit of
the storm rushed forth, and the violence of the wind disturbed the waters; some of our ships which had been
dispersed by the shifting of the winds, while attempting
to reach the island of Cyprus before his arrival, were
driven by adverse waves and wind on the rocks; and
though the sailors used their utmost efforts to resist the wind
that assailed them, three of the king's ships filled and went
to pieces, and some of those on board were drowned; but
some who had by chance caught hold of the timbers of the
ship, were by this means, and not without the greatest toil,
from the tossing of the waves, cast on shore naked and penniless. Amongst those who were drowned was Roger, sur-

named Malus Catulus, the king's signet-bearer, and the
signet was lost.   But on the body being cast on shore by the
tide, a man found the signet on him, and brought it to the
army for sale ; and thus it was redeemed, and restored to the
king.   As to the sailors who were cast on shore, the inhabitants, under the garb of peace, hailed their coming with
joy ; and, as if to recruit them, introduced them into a certain
fort close by ; and all those who put to shore in safety, the
Griffons stripped of their arms, and conducted to the same
place, asserting that if they entered in arms, they might appear to be spies, or to have intentions of attacking the island,
and they would wait until they ascertained the will of the
emperor.   But our nobles compassionating the shipwrecked
men who were detained in custody, sent them clothing and
other necessaries.   Also Stephen de Turnham, the king's
steward and treasurer, sent them abundance of provisions,
which, as they were brought to the entrance of the fort for
the captives, were plundered by the Griffons and guards of the
city. However they pacified them with specious language, and
did not yet shew their enmity openly, but they would not
set them at liberty until the emperor had been informed
of what had happened; meanwhile, they promised with crafty
words to supply them with every thing necessary.   They then
convened the nobles of the land, and entered into counsel to
keep captive as many of the pilgrims as they could by stratagem,
and then slay them ; which when it became known to our men,
they shut themselves up of their own accord in the fort,
with the intention of defending themselves, and some of them
were killed by the natives.   Thus, considering that danger
really threatened them, they chose to stand the hazard of a
battle, rather than die of starvation by falling into the hands
of the infidel persecutors of Christians.   Therefore, when
they had come forth from the fort and reached a certain plain,
the natives began to surround and kill them ; but though unarmed, they resisted as much as they could, and effected not
less slaughter than their adversaries, though they had only
three bows to defend themselves with, which they had kept
concealed from the natives.   There was amongst them one
Roger de Hardecurt, who, having found a mare and mounted
her, rode down the crowd that opposed him ; and also
William du Bois, a Norman, and a most skilful archer, scattered first these, then those, by casting darts and arrows

at them incessantly. The soldiers who were yet on board, seeing this, came hastily with their arms to their succour; and the Griffons, with their bows and slings, hindered them as much as they could from landing; but by the protection of the Lord they sallied from their ships and came into port unhurt. At last, after the Griffons had been dispersed and were giving way, the pilgrims, coming out of the aforesaid fort, and defending themselves, came in the rear, and made their way to the port, where they found our men, who had disembarked from their ships, fighting with all their might against the Griffons who opposed them. Having thus formed a junction, they dispersed the Griffons, and gained the port of Limozin, in which was the buss of the two queens that had put in before the arrival of King Richard, 'as has been said before; but owing to their ignorance of the state of the island, and from dread of the cruelty and treachery of the emperor, they had not disembarked.

Ch. XXXI — *Of the arrival of King Richard at Cyprus.*

On the same day, towards evening, on which the pilgrims had made their exit from the aforesaid port, viz. on a Thursday, the emperor of Cyprus, who had been informed of their arrival, came to the city; and when the pilgrims made complaint of the injuries they had received, the emperor promised every kind of satisfaction, and agreed to restore the money taken from the shipwrecked men; and they also obtained entrance and egress into and from the city of Limozin, on condition of a mutual exchange of four men as hostages. Meanwhile, the emperor gave orders that the warriors of all his empire should be assembled, and a mighty army formed. The day after his arrival, the emperor sent a crafty message to the two queens, bidding them put to shore for greater security, and go about as they pleased without fear of molestation or ill-treatment from his people; and on their refusing, he sent them the next day, under pretence of paying them respect, bread and ram's flesh and wine from the vineyards of Cyprus, which are said to have no match for quality throughout the world. On the third day, also, he tried to circumvent and beguile them, by bland and deceptive messages, and on the other hand they were in great state of perplexity, lest the emperor should make

them prisoners, if they should listen to him, or else, if
they obstinately refused, they must fear some violence; for
as yet nothing was known of the expected arrival of
the king, or the good condition of his fleet; but they
kept him in suspense by returning an ambiguous answer,
saying, that on the morrow they would place themselves
at his disposal.   In expectation of the fulfilment of this
promise, the emperor kept quiet; and while the queens
were agitated by intense anxiety, and were questioning and
conversing with each other, that same day, being Sunday, behold! there appeared in the distance, like crows,
on the foaming summit of the curling waters, two vessels,
driven forwards and sailing swiftly towards them. And while
the queens, and those with them, were in doubt as to what they
were, some more ships were espied coming on, and directly
after the whole fleet was seen, bearing down with rapid course
to the port; and conjecturing that it was the king's fleet, they
were so much the more rejoiced that it had come to their
succour, when they were despairing of their desolate position.
And thus King Richard arrived by the guidance of the
Lord, after many dangers overcome, in the port of Cyprus.
Therefore, on the festival of St. John ' before the Latin Gate
(May 6), King Richard put into the port of Limozin, with all
his fleet, but did not go on shore.

Ch. XXXII.—*How King Richard with his forces, routed the emperor
with his forces, first by sea and then by land.*

WHEN the king learnt in what danger the shipwrecked men
had been, and how they were plundered of their property,
and all that had happened in the interim, he was exceedingly
angry; and on the morrow, being Monday, he sent two
knights to the emperor, to ask satisfaction of him, in a peace-
ful manner, for the injuries received, and the money he had
plundered, at his will.   The emperor was very indignant
at this demand, and just as though he himself had been
the injured man, burst out into abusive language, saying,
".Pruht, Sire," and declaring he had nothing to do with a *king;*
boasting, as he did, for the assumption of *imperial* authority,
and wholly confiding in impunity from Heaven, he acted just
as it pleased him.   When the ambassadors brought back
his answer, the king, irritated at the emperor's arrogance, his

abusive reply, and the loss his own men had sustained, shouted
out aloud, "To arms!" a command his men immediately
obeyed. Therefore the king, having armed himself, proceeded, in the boats of the "Esneckars," with his soldiers, to
seize on the port; but the emperor, with a large army, surrounded it, and resisted their landing, and they blocked up
the entrance to the port with every kind of bar and obstacle,
taking the doors and windows from the houses, casks with
hoops, benches and ladders, and long pieces of wood, placed
crosswise; also, bucklers and shields, old galleys, abandoned vessels, dirty from being laid up, and every description of utensil,
to prevent their coming on shore;—in a word, every thing
portable of wood or stone that could be found in the city of
Limozin, the Griffons piled upon the shore to oppose the
assailants.   Moreover, the emperor and his troops marched up
and down the beach.   Oh! how splendidly was the emperor's
host equipped!   They had on costly armour, and very valuable and many-coloured garments, and rode on war-horses
that champed the foaming bit, and beautiful mules; they
marched to and fro, ready for battle, their numberless pennons
and gorgeous banners floating in the breeze, to keep off those
that were advancing, or to give them battle.   As our men
were endeavouring to reach the shore, they tried to frighten
them by horrible shoutings, like growling dogs, and abused
them as if they had been curs, and told them they were
hastening after what it was impossible to accomplish.   They
also had some slingers and archers and five galleys on the shore,
well armed, and filled with young men skilled in sea-
fights.   Our troops, who were making for the port to seize
upon it, blocked up as it was, seemed no match for the enemy,
because they were exposed in small boats, and were also much
fatigued by long tossing about on the sea, and besides, they
were foot soldiers, burdened with their proper arms; the
natives, on the contrary, were in their own country, and could
do every thing at pleasure.   So when our men approached
in their boats, in order, they determined on coming to
close quarters to drive off the slingers and archers in the
galleys, and against them our archers and slingers directed
their attacks; and the Griffons, after losing a great many of
their men, gave way, for they could not withstand the brunt of
the battle.   And when the arrows flew thickly, three or four

at a time leaped out of the galleys into the sea, and dived under
water, where they perished, by knocking against each other in
their attempts to seek refuge in flight. The galleys, therefore,
being captured, and our boats come to shore, our slingers and
archers, gaining courage by success, sent a shower of arrows,
like rain, at those who were guarding the landing-place. The
Griffons not able to stand the charge, retreated from the beach to
firmer ground, while their arbalesters and ours kept constantly
throwing darts, so that the sky was darkened, and the calmness
of day seemed to grow into night from the shower of arrows,
while the whole city swarmed with men, and the neighbourhood was filled with a multitude of men plying their engines.
It was a long time doubtful on which side the victory lay, or
which party was superior; for our troops, though they strove
with all their strength, did not make progress. The king, perceiving that his men were not daring enough to get out of their
boats, and make for the shore, leaped first from his barge into
the water, and boldly attacked the Griffons; and then our soldiers, imitating his example, eagerly sought to put the enemy to
flight; and having made an impression on their troops, forced
them to give way. Then you might see a shower of flying
darts, and the Greeks cut down; and you might hear the
murmurs of the combatants, the groans of the dying, and the
yells of the retreating. Then, also, our men in a body, mowing down the Greeks as they fled in confusion, drove them
first into the city, and from thence to the plains beyond. The
king, pushing on in pursuit of the emperor, found a common
horse, upon which he speedily vaulted by the aid of a
lance, placed behind the saddle, and rode on with cords
for stirrups. The king thus hastily pressed after the emperor, crying out, " My lord the emperor, I challenge you
to single combat;" but, as though he were deaf, he fled
swiftly away. The king, having thus taken the city, caused
the two queens to be landed from the buss and lodged in
Limozin, where, after the fatigues and perils of their voyage,
they recruited themselves in security.

CH. XXXIII.—*Further of the fight between the king and the emperor,
and of the victory of the king and the flight of the emperor to Nicosia.*

THE same night the king lodged in his pavilion, and caused
his horses to be landed by the Esneckars. But the emperor,

not thinking he had any horses, feared him the less, and passed
the night encamped within a distance of two leagues. On the
morrow, about two o'clock, the king mounted his horse, and discovered some Greeks standing not far off in an olive-yard with
their gorgeous banners, and on their taking to flight, he pursued them. But forasmuch as our horses had been injured by
being tossed about on the sea, standing for a whole month, our
men spared them and went at a moderate pace, until they saw
the army of the emperor, which had spent the night in a valley,
and then they stopped in their pursuit. The Greeks, crying
out with a horrible clamour, began to insult our men ; on
which the emperor, aroused from his sleep, mounted his horse,
and marched with his men towards ours gradually, as far as
a neighbouring hill, where he took his station to overlook the engagement. The Greeks making use only of
their bows and slings, cried out that our men were immoveable. Then there came to the king a certain clerk, by
name Hugo de Mara, in arms, and said to the king, " My
lord the king, it appears to be a wise plan to decline for a
time so large and so powerful a multitude." To whom the
king answered, " Sir clerk, as for our profession, you had
better employ yourself in writing, and leave war to us, and
take good care to keep out of the crowd." Others likewise
dissuaded the king from fighting against so mighty a host :
indeed he had not with him at that time more than fifty
men ; but taking courage from the enemy's wavering, he put
spurs to his horse, and was suddenly carried against the
enemy, and piercing through their line, scattered them, and
attacking first one and then the other, he instantly dispersed
them. For when their army perceived that their adversaries
were collecting together, their valour gave way, and they
took to flight ; those who had swift and nimble horses escaped,
but the foot-soldiers and common people, who were less fitted
for flight, were slain in all directions without distinction, and
could not fly further, on account of the arrival of the king.
And while the emperor was encouraging and animating his
men to fight, the king coming suddenly upon him at full
speed, knocked him off his horse with his lance ; but he
quickly procured another, and escaped in the crowd : some of
his companions, however, were lost. Oh ! how many noble
horses might you have seen slain there, and coats of mail, and

helmets, and swords, and lances, and pennons fallen down,
and standards of various shapes, and the bodies of dead men
weltering in their blood, and some yet breathing their last,
in countless numbers.   The emperor, perceiving the boldness of our men, and the flight of his own, and not forgetting his spurs, which he saw were the only thing that remained, fled with the utmost swiftness to the mountains. The
king struck down his banner-bearer, and gave orders that the
splendid and beautiful banner should be kept for him.   Then
our horsemen pursued the fugitives as fast as they could for two
miles; after which, coming back at a moderate pace, they quietly
returned. The people then turning to the booty, took much spoil,
viz. arms, and costly woven vestments, and the tent of the
emperor, with all the vessels of gold and silver which were
found therein, and all his splendid apparel and household
stuff: besides coats of mail, helmets, choice swords, horses
and mules, and also very much plunder in sheep and cattle.
and goats, noble mares and mules, swine, fowls, and hens; and
they also found choice wines and provisions of all sorts, and carried off a host of captives; so that from the immense quantity
of plunder they became fastidious,—in a word, every mind was
satiated with booty, nor would they regard any thing that
was precious when offered them, for they were amply laden.
After these things were done, the king proclaimed an edict
by herald, that whoever of the inhabitants were disposed for
peace, might go and return as they liked without harm from
his men, and enjoy perfect liberty; but that whoever held
the king as an enemy, should take care not to fall into his
hands, or those of the army, for he would certainly treat him
as a foe, and that he would prove himself such as they stood to
him.   By these means the emperor lost very many of his men,
who constantly deserted him.   At last he betook himself to a
very strong fort called Nicosia, in confusion and sorrow at
having failed in his intentions.

Ch. XXXIV.—*Of the arrival of King Guy at Cyprus.*

On the following Saturday three galleys bore in sight,
and all doubted what they could mean, or whence they came.
The king, always prompt, not to say venturous, embarked in a
small vessel impelled with oars, and went to meet them and
inquire who the comers were and whence they came; and
on their answering that it was Guy de Lusignan, the king

returned quickly and ordered supper to be immediately prepared for the guests that were coming.   And when King Guy
landed, he received him with the greatest respect, and entertained him most cordially.   King Guy had come to King
Richard to ask his advice and assistance against the king of
France, who had planned that the marquis, of whom we have
before spoken, should be made king of Jerusalem, and Guy
be deposed.   Then King Richard welcomed him kindly, and
honoured him with gifts, because he was poor and destitute
of means ; for he gave him two thousand marks of silver and
twenty cups of the value of a hundred and five marks, of
which two were of the purest gold.

CH. XXXV.—*Of the nuptials of King Richard and Berengaria, and of
the arrival of the king's galleys.*

ON the morrow, viz. on the Sunday, which was the festival
of St. Pancras, the marriage of King Richard and Berengaria,
the daughter of the king of Navarre, was solemnized at Limozin : she was a damsel of the greatest prudence and most
accomplished manners, and there she was crowned queen.
There were present at the ceremony the archbishop, and the
bishop of Evreux, and the bishop of Baneria, and many other
chiefs and nobles.   The king was glorious on this happy
occasion, and cheerful to all, and shewed himself very jocose
and affable.   The nuptials having been solemnly celebrated
in a royal manner, one day all the king's galleys, which had
been anxiously looked for, arrived in port : they were equipped
and defended with splendid armouries, and no one ever saw
better or safer ships; and he added to them the five galleys
which he had taken from the emperor.   The king had thus
forty armed galleys and sixty others of a very good quality.

CH. XXXVI.—*Of the conference and the manner of making peace
between the king and the emperor.*

THE king, elated with success, thought that fortune smiled
upon him ; he therefore exhorted his soldiers to expedition,
and commanded them to get every thing in readiness, lest
the emperor should make a sudden attack upon them ; and
he caused watches to be kept, and appointed sentinels to
guard the army.   The king proposed with his army to pursue the emperor wherever he was, and so take him by force

or induce him to surrender; but by the mediation and earnest request of the masters of the Hospitallers of Jerusalem, it was determined that a conference should be held between the king and the emperor, who greatly lamented the loss of his men, and that he had been forced to fly in a shameful manner to Nicosia from the face of the king; and he feared pursuit the more, because the natives detested him, and he could not, therefore, trust to their assistance. Wherefore, having called together as many as he could, the king proceeded to a very large plain, between the sea and the highway, close by the city of Limozin. He was mounted on a Spanish charger, of high mettle, of large size and elegant shape, with high shoulder and pointed ears; his neck was long and slender, and his thighs faultless; his feet were broad, and his limbs so perfectly marked, that a painter could not have imitated them with perfect accuracy. As if preparing himself for a swifter movement, he disdained to be checked by his golden curb, and by the alternate change of his feet he seemed at one time to move forward on his hind, at another on his fore legs. The king bounded into his saddle glittering with gold spangles interspersed with red, while on the hinder part two small lions of gold were turned towards each other, with their mouths open, and one pointed to the other on each of the fore legs, as if stretched out to devour. The king's feet were decorated with golden spurs, and he was clothed in a vest of rose-coloured stuff, ornamented with rows of crescents of solid silver, like orbs of the sun shining in thick profusion. The king thus apparelled rode forward, girded with a sword of proved metal with a handle of gold and a woven belt, and the mouth of the scabbard was fastened with silver; on his head he wore a hat of scarlet, ornamented with the shapes of various birds and beasts worked with the hand, and sown in with orfray-work by the needle. He carried a staff in his hand, and the manner of his bearing it proved him to be a soldier of the highest order, and afforded the greatest gratification to all who saw him. After many proposals from both sides, between the king and the emperor, the emperor offered to swear fidelity to him in every thing, and that he would send five hundred knights to the land of Jerusalem, for the service of God, to be at the disposal and command of King Richard; and in addition to all these

things, in order that he might fully satisfy the king and leave no
doubt on his mind, he offered to place all his castles and forts in
the hands of the king's guards, and he gave besides three thousand five hundred marks as satisfaction to those who had lost
their money, or had it plundered; and if the king, according to
the agreement between them, should think that he and his men
fought faithfully, the emperor should have his territory with
his castles and forts restored to him; the friendship between them remaining the same as heretofore. And when the
king referred this offer to his friends for examination, to see
whether there was any thing derogatory to the king's honour
by such an agreement, and whether all were satisfied with it,
they answered that it was in every respect to the king's
honour, and that they were perfectly satisfied with it. And
after the king had heard this, the emperor immediately sware
to observe faithfully all the aforesaid conditions to the king;
and having exchanged the kiss of peace, they made an alliance
in the manner described. The king, returning from the conference, which had been broken up, immediately sent to the
emperor his pavilion, which he had captured in the aforesaid
battle, as a pledge of peace and friendship; he sent, besides,
the vessels which had been plundered from it, and the emperor caused tents to be erected forthwith on the spot where
the abovementioned conference took place.

CH. XXXVII.—*Of the flight of the emperor by night through Famagusta as far as Candoria, and of the capture of Nicosia.*

ON the following night, at the suggestion of a treacherous
knight named Pain de Caiffa, the emperor, trusting to the
darkness, fled away with all speed on a valuable and favourite horse, for the knight told him that King Richard
intended to seize upon him that night, and throw him in
chains; and the emperor, frightened thereat, escaped to
his city of Famagusta, leaving behind him his tents and
chargers, and all his household stuff. On hearing which, King
Richard commenced a pursuit after him, with his galleys,
accusing him of perjury and the violation of his word, and
he entrusted to King Guy the conduct of his army by
land to Famagusta, where he arrived on the third day, and
found it deserted, for the emperor, convinced that it would
not be safe for him to stand a siege, concealed himself in

the woods, where access was difficult, that, if our men should venture to pass through, he might attack them from an ambuscade. The king, on arriving at Famagusta, gave orders that the ports of the sea should be most strictly watched by his galleys, in order that he might take the emperor prisoner, if he attempted to escape. And, after staying there three days, there came as ambassadors, the bishop of Beauvais, and Drogo de Mirle, a nobleman of high renown, to exhort him to cross the sea without delay, and to assure him that the king of France would not proceed to the assault of Acre before his arrival; and they added words of rebuke, that he had neglected necessary matters, and expended his endeavours on vain duties, and was presumptuously persecuting innocent Christians, when so many thousand Saracens were to be attacked in the land adjoining, for whom, even his valour, although so mighty, would be no match on trial. To this message, the king replied in angry terms, by no means suitable for insertion here; but their labour was in vain, although they used every argument to dissuade him from his purpose, for he was busy enough in attacking and pursuing the Greeks as they deserved, as it appeared to be of the greatest consequence to subdue an island so necessary to the land of Jerusalem. Paying no attention to the messengers, he advanced to Nicosia, whither each had brought the provisions necessary for himself, as it was a desert place; they moved forward in order of battle, for they had learnt that the emperor intended to lie in ambush for them. The king marched in the rear, to guard against attacks, when on a sudden, the emperor burst from his hiding-place, and assailed them with about seven hundred Greeks. Their arbalesters exerted all their ability to throw their darts against the foremost of our men; but not even thus did our troops suffer themselves to be broken, for they kept together in good order, while the emperor advancing on the flank to reconnoitre, bore down upon them pell-mell, with a view either to break up our lines, or to find out and shoot the king; and when he found that the king was in the rear, he shot two poisoned arrows at him, which inflamed the king to a pitch of anger, and putting spurs to his horse, he bore down on the emperor, with the intention of striking him with his lance; but the emperor evaded him, and fled as swiftly as possible to his aforesaid fort of Caudaira, in exceeding

o

dismay and confusion, because he had not succeeded according
to his wishes; and the king did not pursue him far, for he
doubted of taking him; for he had a bay horse of such swiftness and perseverance in running, that no one ever saw his
match for speed.   Then the king marched towards Nicosia,
with his army, and an immense booty of noble horses and
men, which had been taken in the encounter; and the citizens
of Nicosia came forth in a body, to congratulate him, and
admitted him as if he had been their lord; and the king
received them in peace, and caused their beards to be shaved
in token of their change of masters.   The emperor, on hearing this, in his fury, caused them to seize upon every one of
our men that they could, and they plucked out their eyes, or
cut off their noses, or mutilated their arms or legs, to satisfy his
revenge and soothe his grief.   The king exacted homage of
the Greek nobles, who appeared to throw off the emperor's
yoke with joy; and feeling himself somewhat afflicted with
sickness, he tarried there to rest and recruit himself.

Cн. XXXVIII.—*Of the capture of the three forts, in one of which was
the emperor's daughter and treasure.*

WITH the army, which had been divided into three parts
by the king, King Guy laid siege to the three forts, Cherimes, Didimus, and Butphenens; the two first he quickly
gained possession of; for, with the help of a guide who knew the
ways and the places of difficult access, the army, approaching
the fort of Cherimes by land and by sea, assaulted it instantly;
and they who were in it, not expecting any aid, surrendered
the fort, in which were found the emperor's daughter, and his
treasure.   When the emperor heard of his loss, he was so
overwhelmed with grief, that it nearly drove him mad.   King
Guy, having hoisted the banners of King Richard on the
battlements of the fort, proceeded to attack the second fort,
called Didimus, very strong by situation, and exposed to attack
on no side; and those who were shut up therein prepared to
defend themselves, and for some days kept throwing stones
and darts at the besiegers, until they were commanded by the
emperor to give it up; and in it the king placed the emperor's
daughter, to prevent her being recaptured.   From thence
King Guy returned to the army at Nicosia, where King

Richard, as has been afore said, lay sick; and immediately on his recovery, he attacked and stormed the fort of Bufferentum, which had hitherto been deemed impregnable.

Ch. XXXIX.—*How the emperor came from Candaira to Nicosia, and prostrating himself at the feet of King Richard, surrendered Cyprus to his power.*

O MIGHTY wealth of the emperor! O land, rich in every good thing! O forts, most strong by position, that were given up, which could never have been stormed by the machines of any enemy, unless obtained by treachery or famine! The emperor considering that he was pressed by misfortune enough; that his daughter, on whom his life hung, had been taken captive; and that his forts had been either seized upon or surrendered, and his people alienated from him; and that he was only tolerated, not beloved by his men; perceiving also, that there was no hope of resistance left, he determined that, although a foe, he would sue for peace and mercy. He therefore sent ambassadors to King Richard, to plead his cause; and in order to incline Richard to feel kindness for him, he followed them in sad attire, and with a dejected countenance; and coming into the presence of King Richard, he fell on his knees in humiliation before him, saying that he submitted himself entirely to his mercy, and that he had neither territory nor fort left: but that he would consider him lord of every thing else, if only he would not throw him into iron chains. The king, moved with pity, raised him up, and made him sit beside him; he also had his daughter brought to him, and when he saw her, he was wonderfully overjoyed, and embracing her most affectionately, covered her with kisses, while the tears started from his eyes. This took place on the Friday after the feast of St. Augustine, and before Pentecost. And the king threw the emperor not into iron chains, but silver ones.

Ch. XL.—*How, after that the king had subjugated Cyprus and set it in order, he made preparations for his voyage, and sent his army to Limosin.*

THUS the king gained possession of Cyprus in fifteen days, and gave it to his men to inhabit. He found all the towers fortified, and the forts filled with much treasure; and various

o 2

riches, in golden cups, and vases, and plates; also in silver
jars, and caldrons, and casks of a large size; with saddles,
bits, and spurs of gold; and a large quantity of precious
stones, of great value. He also found robes of scarlet and
woven cloths, of beautiful pattern, and very costly. Why need
we say more? Whatever different kinds of wealth Crœsus
is said to have possessed, King Richard found that the emperor
had amassed; and being necessary for his expedition, he took
possession of them as if they had been prepared for him; for it
is scarcely possible that means should fail the man who is rich
in courage, or abundance attend on one who is poor in spirit.
Having done all these things, King Richard sent back his
army to the city of Limozin, where the queens were, and the
domestics, with the baggage; and he gave them orders to
give their whole attention to the repair of the fleet, for crossing the sea. He committed the emperor to the custody of
King Guy, and his young little daughter he delivered to his
queen, to bring her up and educate her.

Ch. XLI.—*How, while the fleet of King Richard was sailing towards
Acre, a very large Saracen ship bore in sight; and how the king immediately attacked it, and took it.*

HAVING concluded these operations, the king gave his
attention to the immediate crossing of the sea, and when they
had placed the baggage on board, a favourable wind blowing,
the fleet set sail from the shore; and the queens moved forward in company with the king in person. The king had left
in Cyprus brave and diligent men to secure a supply of necessary provisions hereafter; viz. wheat, corn, and barley; meat
and live stock of various kinds, which abound in that island.
By this time a report was spread that Acre was on the
point of being taken, and when the king heard it, he sighed
deeply and said, " May God defer the taking of Acre till I
come, after it has been so long besieged, and therefore the
triumph will be the more glorious with the assistance of God."
Then getting ready with all speed, he went on board one of
his largest and swiftest galleys, at Famagusta; and as was his
wont, he moved forward in advance, impatient of delay, while
the other ships followed in his wake as quickly as they could,
and well prepared, for there is no power that might not
justly have dreaded their hostility. As they ploughed across
the sea, the holy land of Jerusalem was descried for the first

time, the fort called Margat being the first spot that met the eye; afterwards Tortuosa, situated on the sea-shore; then Tripolis, Nephyn, and Bocion. And soon after appeared the lofty tower of Gibelath. Lastly, on this side of Sidon, opposite Baruth, there bore in sight a vessel filled with Saracens, chosen from all the Pagan empire, and destined by Saladin for the assistance of the besieged in Acre. They were not able to obtain a speedy entrance into the port, because of the Christian army that menaced them, and so were waiting a favourable moment for entering the port by surprise. The king, observing the ship, called Peter des Barres, commander of one of his galleys, and ordered him to row quickly, and inquire who commanded the vessel. And when they answered that it belonged to the king of France, the king in his eager haste approached it; but it had no mark of being French, neither did it bear any Christian symbol or standard; and on looking at it near, the king began to wonder at its immense size and compact make, for it was crowned with three tall masts, and its sides were marked with streaks of red and yellow, and it was well furnished in all manner of equipments, so that nothing could exceed them, and it was abundantly supplied with all kinds of provisions. One of those on board said, that while at Baruth, he saw the vessel laden with all these things; viz. one hundred camel-loads of arms, slings, bows, darts, and arrows: it had also on board seven Saracen admirals, and eighty chosen Turks, besides a quantity of all kinds of provisions, exceeding computation. They had also on board a large quantity of Greek fire, in bottles, and two hundred most deadly serpents for the destruction of the Christians. Others were therefore sent to obtain more exact information who they were, and when, instead of their former answer, they replied that they were Genoese, bound for Tyre, our men began to doubt the truth at this change of reply; one of our galleymen persisted that they were Saracens, and on the king's questioning him, he said, "I give you leave to cut off my head, or hang me on a tree, if I do not prove these men to be Saracens. Now let a galley be sent quickly after them, for they are making away, and let no kind of salute be given them by us, and in this way we shall have certain proof what their intention is, and how far they are to be believed." At the king's command, therefore, a galley was sent at full speed after them. and on reaching their ship, and rowing by its side without giving a salute, they began to throw darts and

arrows at our men. On seeing this, the king ordered the ship
to be attacked forthwith, and after casting a shower of darts
against each other, the ship relaxed in its speed, for the wind
carried it but slowly along. Though our galleymen rowed
repeatedly round the ship, to scrutinize the vessel, they could
find no point of attack : it appeared so solid and so compact, and of such strong materials; and it was defended
by a guard of warriors, who kept throwing darts at them.
Our men, therefore, relished not the darts, nor the great
height of the ship, for it was enough to strive against a foe on
equal ground, whereas a dart thrown from above always tells
upon those below, since its iron point falls downwards. Hence,
their ardour relaxed, but the spirit of the king increased,
and he exclaimed aloud, " Will you allow the ship to get
away untouched and uninjured ? Shame upon you ! are you
grown cowards from sloth, after so many triumphs ? The
whole world knows that you engaged in the service of the
Cross, and you will have to undergo the severest punishment,
if you permit an enemy to escape while he lives, and is thrown
in your way." Our men, therefore, making a virtue of
necessity, plunged eagerly into the water under the ship's side,
and bound the rudder with ropes to turn and retard its progress,
and some, catching hold of the cables, leapt on board the ship.
The Turks receiving them manfully, cut them to pieces as
they came on board, and lopping off the head of this one, and
the hands of that, and the arms of another, cast their bodies
into the sea. Our men seeing this, and glowing with anger,
gained fresh courage from the thirst for vengeance, and crossing over the bulwarks of the vessel, attacked the Turks in a
body with great fierceness, who, though giving way a little, made
an obstinate resistance. The Turks gathering boldness from
despair, used all their efforts to repel those who threatened them,
cutting off the arms, hands, and even heads of our men ; but
they, after a mighty struggle, drove the Turks back as far as
the prow of the ship, while from the interior others rushed
upon our men in a body, preparing to die bravely or repel the
foe ; they were the choice youth of the Turks, fitted for
war, and suitably armed. The battle lasted a long time,
and many fell on both sides ; but at last, the Turks, pressing
boldly on our men, drove them back, though they resisted
with all their might, and forced them from the ship. Upon
which our men retired to their galleys, and surrounding the

vessel on all sides, tried to find a more easy mode of attacking it. The king seeing the danger his men were in, and that while the ship was uninjured it would not be easy to take the Turks with the arms and provisions therein, commanded that each of the galleys should attack the ship with its spur, *i.e.* its iron beak. Then the galleys drawing back, were borne by rapid strokes of the oar against the ship's sides to pierce them, and thus the vessel was instantly broken, and becoming pervious to the waves, began to sink. When the Turks saw it, they leapt into the sea to die, and our men killed some of them and drowned the rest. The king kept thirty-five alive, namely, the admirals and men who were skilled in making machines, but the rest perished, the arms were abandoned, and the serpents sunk and scattered about by the waves of the sea. If that ship had arrived safely at the siege of Acre, the Christians would never have taken the city; but by the care of God it was converted into the destruction of the infidels, and the aid of the Christians, who hoped in Him, by means of King Richard, who by His help prospered in war. The Saracens saw from a distance on the heights what had happened, and sorrowfully carried the news to Saladin, who, on hearing it, seized and plucked out his beard in anger and fury, and afterwards broke out into these words with a sigh, " O God ! have I lost Acre, and my dear and chosen soldiers, in whom I had so much confidence? I am overwhelmed by so bitter a loss." When they who saw it told the tidings to the Saracenic army, there arose long and loud wailings, and bitter lamentations for their misfortune, and they cut off the tresses of their hair, and rent their garments, and cursed the hour and the fate of the stars, by which they had come to Syria. For in the above-mentioned ship they had lost all their choice youth, in whom they trusted.

BOOK III.

Ch. I.—*Of the arrival of King Richard at Acre.*

THUS, after his success by sea, King Richard hastened with joy and alacrity, and with all his suite, towards Acre, whither his eager wishes carried him ; and the next night, with the aid

of a prosperous gale, the fleet anchored off Tyre.   In the morning they weighed anchor, and hoisted sail, and soon afterwards
passed Candalion, of which we have before spoken ; and going
by Casella Ymbrici, the high-tower of Acre came in sight,
and then, by little and little, the other fortifications of the
city.   Around it the besiegers lay in countless multitudes,
chosen from every nation throughout Christendom and under
the face of heaven, and well fitted for the labours and fatigues
of war ;   for the city had now been besieged a long time, and
had been afflicted by constant toil and tribulation, by the
pressure of famine, and every kind of adversity, as we have
before described. Moreover, beyond the besiegers, was seen the
Turkish army, not in a compact body, but covering the mountains and valleys, hills and plains, with tents, the colours of
whose various forms were reflected by the sun. They saw, also,
the pavilion of Saladin, and his brother Safahadin's tent, and
that of Kahadin, the mainstay of Paganism ; he was watching the parts to seaward, and planning constant and vigorous
attacks upon the Christians.   King Richard beheld and computed all their army ; and when he arrived in port, the king
of France and a whole army of natives, and the princes,
chiefs, and nobles, came forth to meet him and welcome him,
with joy and exultation, for they had eagerly longed for his
arrival.

Cн. II.—*Of the joy, songs, and processions which took place on account
of King Richard's arrival.*

On the Saturday before the festival of the blessed apostle
Barnabas, in the Pentecost week, King Richard landed at
Acre with his retinue, and the earth was shaken by the accla-
mations of the exulting Christians.   The people testified their
joy by shouts of welcome and the clang of trumpets ; the day
was kept as a jubilee, and universal gladness reigned around,
on account of the arrival of the king, long wished for by all
nations. The Turks, on-the other hand, were terrified and cast
down by his coming, for they perceived that all egress and return would be at an end, in consequence of the multitude of the
king's galleys. The two kings conducted each other from the
port, and paid one another the most obsequious attention. Then
King Richard retired to the tent previously prepared for him,
and forthwith entered into arrangements about the siege ; for it

was his most anxious care to find out by what means, artifice, and machines, they could capture the city without loss of time. No pen can sufficiently describe the joy of the people on the king's arrival, nor tongue detail it; the very calmness of the night was thought to smile upon them with a purer air; the trumpets clanged, horns sounded, and the shrill intonations of the pipe, and the deeper notes of the timbrel and harp, struck upon the ear; and soothing symphonies were heard like various voices blended in one; and there was not a man who did not, after his own fashion, indulge in joy and praise; either singing popular ballads to testify the gladness of his heart, or reciting the deeds of the ancients, stimulating by their example the spirit of the moderns.   Some drank wine from costly cups, to the health of the singers; while others mixing together, high and low, passed the night in constant dances.   And their joy was heightened by the subjugation of the island of Cyprus by King Richard; a place so useful and necessary to them, and one which would be of the utmost service to the army.   As a further proof of the exultation of their hearts, and to illumine the darkness of the night, wax torches and flaming lights sparkled in profusion, so that night seemed to be usurped by the brightness of day, and the Turks thought the whole valley was on fire.

Ch. III.—*How the Pisans gave themselves up to King Richard, and how the Turks challenged us to battle.*

THE Pisans, admiring the glory and magnificence of King Richard, came before him and did him homage, and took the oath of allegiance that they submitted voluntarily to his authority and service.   But the cunning Turks envied the honour paid him, and some of them, either to feign the assumption of fresh boldness on his arrival, or to provoke a speedy encounter, one Sunday morning exposed themselves to attack outside our camp, wandering up and down as if for the sake of exercise, and throwing their darts at random; and at times they seemed to threaten to cross the ditch in numbers, and annoyed our men, irritating them to a contest unceasingly.

CH. IV.—*Of the gifts of the two kings to their needy soldiers, and of the sickness of King Richard.*

BY the conjunction of the retinues of the two kings, an immense army of Christians was formed : with the king of France, who had arrived on the octaves of Easter, there came the count of Flanders, the count of St. Paul, William de Garlande, William des Barres, Drogo d'Amiens, William de Mirle, and the count of Perche ; and with them also came the marquis, of whom we have before spoken, and who aspired to be king of Jerusalem.   But why should we enumerate them singly ? There was not a man of influence or renown in France who came not, then or afterwards, to the siege of Acre.   And on the following day of Pentecost, King Richard arrived with an army, the flower of war, and upon learning that the king of France had gained the good-will and favour of all, by giving to each of his soldiers three *aurei* a month,—not to be outdone or equalled in generosity, he proclaimed by mouth of herald, that whosoever was in his service, no matter of what nation, should receive four statute *aurei* a month for his pay.   By these means, his generosity was extolled by all, for he outshone every one else in merit and favours, as he outdid them in gifts and magnificence.   "When," exclaimed they, "will the first attack take place, by a man whom we have expected so long and anxiously ?   A man, by far the first of kings, and the most skilled in war throughout Christendom ?   Now let the will of God be done, for the hope of all rests on King Richard."   But after some days' sojourn, the king was afflicted with a severe illness, to which the common people gave the name of Arnoldia, which is produced by change of climate working on the constitution.   But for all that, he caused petrariæ and mangonels to be raised, and a fort in front of the city gates ; and spared no pains to expedite the construction of machines.

CH. V.—*How, while King Richard was sick, the king of France assaulted Acre vigorously ; and how the Turks, upon Saladin attacking our trenches without, made a vigorous resistance, and set the king's machines on fire, upon which the king fell sick.*

THE king of France, not liking the delay in commencing the attack, sent word to King Richard, that a favourable

opportunity now offered itself; and he also warned, by voice
of herald, the army to prepare for an assault.   But King
Richard had signified his inability hitherto to attend to his
duty, both on account of indisposition, and because his men
were not yet come; though he hoped that they would arrive
in the next fleet of ships, and would bring with them
materials for the construction of machines.   The king of
France not thinking fit to desist, on that account, from his
purpose, commanded an assault to be proclaimed, by voice of
herald, throughout the army.   Therefore, on the Monday
after the feast of the Nativity of St. John the Baptist, the
king of France, having erected his machines, gave orders to
his men to arm.   Then might have been seen a countless
multitude of armed men, worthily equipped; and so many
coats of scale armour, gleaming helmets, and noble chargers;
with pennons and banners of various workmanship, and soldiers
of tried valour and courage, as never had been seen before.
Having placed men to defend the trenches against the threatened attack of Saladin from without, the army approached the
walls of the city, and commenced a most vigorous assault, by
casting darts and stones from arbalests and machines, without
ceasing.   When the Turks who were shut up in the city saw
this, they raised a tumultuous clamour, and shouted to the
skies; so that it resembled the crash in the air caused by
thunder and lightning; for some had this sole duty—to beat
basins and platters; to strike timbrels; and by other means,
to make signal to Saladin and the army without; in order that
they might come to their succour, according to agreement.   And
when the Turks from without saw and heard this, they gathered in a body; and collecting every material within their
reach to fill up the ditch, they essayed to cross over, and
attack our men, but failed in effecting their object.   For Godfrey of Lusignan, a man of the most approved valour, opposed them, and drove them back from the barricades, which
they had already seized upon, above our men; and he slew ten
of them with an axe he carried in his hand, in a most glorious
manner; and none he smote escaped; nay, he took some alive;
for such was his courage and activity, that no one since the time
of those famous soldiers, Roland and Oliver, could lay claim
to such distinction, from the mouth of all, as himself.   Our
men regained the barricades, but with much labour and diffi-

culty ; for the Turks kept pouring in, and by their obstinate
persistance, made the issue a long time doubtful. So severe and
insupportable was the struggle, and so horrible the clamour of
the conflict, that the men who were making the assault on the
city, and were intent on filling up the trenches, were forced
to retire, and give up the attempt, for they were not able to
carry on the assault, and at the same time defend their camp
from the Turks without. And many of the French perished by
the darts cast from the arbalests, the throwing of stones, and the
pouring on them of Greek fire ; and there was great mourning
and lamentation amongst the people.   O ! with what earnestness had we expected the arrival of the kings ! How fallen
were our hopes ! They had come, and we profited not ; nay,
we suffered a severer loss than usual ; and those we expected
came to no purpose.   Our men of France having laid aside
their arms, the Turks began to revile them shamefully ; and
reproached them with not being able to accomplish what they
had begun ; moreover, they threw Greek fire on the machines
and other warlike instruments of the king of France, which
had been made with such care, and destroyed them. Whence
the king of France, overcome by fury and anger, sunk into
a state of languid sickness, from sorrow, it was said ; and,
from confusion and discouragement, mounted not on horseback.

CH. VI.—*How, in consequence of the illness of the two kings, the army
    was closely pressed; and how they were comforted by the arrival of
    the Nectars.*

THUS the army pined away from excessive grief and discouragement at the sickness of the two kings ; for they had not
a chief or leader to fight the battles of the Lord.   To add to
the public grief, the count of Flanders died immaturely.   The
arrival of the Nectars (? Esneckars) in some measure consoled
the army, amidst the distress which these circumstances occasioned. There came, after a tranquil voyage, very many bishops
and princes, each accompanied by his own retinue, to the aid
of the Christians, whose names were, the bishop of Eneverria,
Roger de Toony, and many brothers and kinsmen surnamed
de Cornebu ; Robert de Newbury, Jordan de Humez,
the chamberlain of Tancarville, Robert, earl of Leicester ;
Gerard de Talebor, Radulph Taisson ; also the knights named

of Torole; the viscount of Castle Dim, Bertram de Ver-dun, Roger de Hardencort, and the knights of Praels; Garin fitz Gerold, and those of Mara, Henry fitz Nicholas; Ernald de Magnaville, the Stutevilles, William Martel, William Maler, William Bloez, Godard de Loreora, Roger de Satya, Andrew de Chavenguy, Hugo le Brun, Geoffrey de Rancona, Radulph de Mauleon, William des Rocques, Geoffrey de Lancelles; Hugh de Fierte, who was in Cyprus when it was taken, and afterwards came to Acre. The two kings were sick, but the Lord reserved them to succour the Christians, and to recover the city.

CH. VII.—*How the petrariæ of the two kings, and those of the army of the faithful, attacked the tower Maledictum, and shook down and destroyed a great part of the wall.*

THE king of France first recovered from his sickness, and turned his attention to the construction of machines and petrariæ, suitable for attacks, and which he determined to ply night and day, and he had one of superior quality, to which they gave the name of "Bad Neighbour." The Turks also had one they called "Bad Kinsman," which by its violent casts, often broke "Bad Neighbour" in pieces; but the king of France rebuilt it, until by constant blows, he broke down part of the principal city wall, and shook the tower Maledictum. On one side, the petraria of the duke of Burgundy plied; on the other, that of the Templars did severe execution; while that of the Hospitallers never ceased to cast terror amongst the Turks. Besides these, there was one petraria, erected at the common expense, which they were in the habit of calling the "petraria of God." Near it, there constantly preached a priest, a man of great probity, who collected money to restore it at their joint expense, and to hire persons to bring stones for casting. By means of this engine, a part of the wall of the tower Maledictum was at length shaken down, for about two poles' length. The count of Flanders had a very choice petraria of large size, which after his death, King Richard possessed; besides a smaller one, equally good. These two were plied incessantly, close by a gate the Turks used to frequent, until part of the tower was knocked down. In addition to these two, King Richard had constructed two others of choice workmanship and material, which would strike a place at an incalculable distance. He had also built one put together very compactly, which the people called "Berefred," with steps to mount it, fitting most tightly to it; covered with raw hides and ropes, and having layers of most solid wood, not to be destroyed by any blows, nor open to injury from the pouring thereon of Greek fire, or any other material. He also prepared two mangonels, one of which was of such violence and rapidity, that what it hurled, reached the inner rows of the city market-place. These engines were plied day and night, and it is well known that a stone sent from one of them killed twelve men with its blow; the stone was afterwards carried to Saladin for inspection; and King Richard had brought it from Messina, which city he had taken. Such stones and flinty pieces of rock, of the smoothest kind, nothing could withstand; but they either shattered in pieces the object they struck, or ground it to powder. The king was confined to his bed by a severe attack of fever, which discouraged him; for he saw the Turks constantly challenging our men, and pressing on them importunately, and he was prevented by sickness from meeting them, and he was more tormented by the importunate attack of the Turks than by the severity of the fever that scorched him.

Ch. VIII.—*How the Turks burnt with Greek fire all the machines and the cat and cercleia belonging to the king of France, when assaulting the city.*

THE city of Acre, from its strong position, and its being defended by the choicest men of the Turks, appeared difficult to be taken by assault. The French had hitherto spent their labour in vain in constructing machines and engines for breaking down the walls, with the greatest care; for whatever they erected, at a great expense, the Turks destroyed with Greek fire or some devouring conflagration. Amongst other machines and engines which the king of France had erected for breaking down the walls, he had prepared one, with great labour, to be used for scaling it, which they called "a cat;" because like a cat it crept up and adhered to the wall. He had also another, made of strong hurdle twigs, put together most

compactly, which they used to call a "ceroleia," and under its
covering of hides the king of France used to sit, and employ
himself in throwing darts from a sling; he would thus watch
the approach of the Turks, above on the walls, by the
battlements, and then hit them unawares. But it happened
one day that the French were eagerly pressing forward to
apply their cat to the walls, when, behold! the Turks let
down upon it a heap of the driest wood, and threw upon
it a quantity of Greek fire, as well as upon the hurdle they
had constructed with such toil, and then aimed a petraria
in that direction, and all having forthwith caught fire, they
broke them in pieces by the blows from their petraria. Upon
this, the king of France was enraged beyond measure, and
began to curse all those who were under his command; and
rated them shamefully for not exacting condign vengeance of
the Saracens, who had done them such injuries. In the
heat of his passion, and when the day was drawing in, he
published an edict, by voice of herald, that an assault should
be made upon the city on the morrow.

CH. IX.—*How, while the French army were undermining the city walls,
the Christians within the trenches vigorously repelled the Turks, who
had fiercely attacked them from without.*

IN the morning, therefore, all armed themselves, and some
of the bravest soldiers chosen from the whole army were posted
at the trenches towards the exterior, against the repeated annoyances and sudden attacks of the Saracens; for Saladin had
vaunted that on that day he would cross the trenches in force,
and prove his valour in humbling to the dust the army of the
Christians. But he kept not his word, and came not; though
his army, under the command of Kahadin, his vizier, came in
a body to the trenches and attempted to cross them; but
the French were not slow to resist, and endeavoured to drive
them off. The slaughter on both sides was great; and the Turks
dismounting, advanced on foot with greater ease, and having
joined battle, fought most obstinately with swords, hand to
hand, and with poignards and two-edged axes, and some of
them used clubs bristling with very sharp teeth. Their
strokes on the one hand, and cries on the other, were terrific,
and many were slain on both sides. The Turks pressed
on, and the Christians drove them back; the one the most

obstinate, the others the most valiant of men; but they
effected this with so much the more difficulty, as the numbers of the Turks who pushed on was the greater, and
both melted with twofold heat, as it was now summer.
Those who directed their attacks against the city tried by
every means in their power to batter down or undermine the
walls, or else to surmount them with scaling-ladders. The Turks
who were shut up in the city, dreading the spirit of our men,
hoisted a signal to the Turks of Saladin's army without, and
intimated to them, either to make an attack, for the purpose of
removing the French from the walls, or to give them instant
succour. The Turks from without pressed on obstinately, when
Kahadin learnt this, and driving our men back with all their
might, violently filled the ditch; but the Christians, notwithstanding, resisted, and opposed their attacks, so that by God's
aid our men stood as an impenetrable wall, and the enemy was
repulsed.   Meanwhile, the men employed by the king of
France to undermine the wall, advanced so far as to remove
the foundations, and they filled the space thus dug out with
logs of wood, and set them on fire; these ignited the
piles of wood forming the foundations of the wall, which
sunk down gradually, with a slight inclination, and without falling altogether.   A large number of Christians
hastened to that part, in order to enter and drive back
the Turkish army. O! how many banners might then be
seen there, and piles of wood, of different shapes, and on the
other hand the Turks throwing Greek fire; on the one side
were the French applying ladders to the wall, that was but
partially thrown down, and trying to cross over; whilst the
Turks were also mounting with ladders on the other side to
defend the breach which had been made in it.

CH. X.—*How Alberic Clements was slain by the Turks whilst scaling
the walls.*

THERE happened a wonderful event, not to be passed over
in silence.   There was a man of renown for his tried valour
and excellence, named Alberic Clements, who, when he saw the
French toiling to very little purpose, exerted his strength in
the vehemence of his ardour, exclaiming, "This day I will
perish, or, if it please God, I will enter into the city of Acre."
With these words, he boldly mounted the ladder; and as he

reached the top of the wall, the Turks fell on him from all sides and killed him. The French were on the point of following him, but were overwhelmed by the pressure of numbers which the ladder could not hold; and some were bruised to death, and others dragged out much injured. The Turks shouted with the greatest joy and applause when they saw the accident, for it was a very severe misfortune. They surrounded and overcame Alberic Clements, who was left alone on the top of the wall, and pierced him with innumerable wounds. He thus verified what he had before said, that he would die a martyr if he was unable to render his friends assistance by entering Acre. The French were much discouraged by his loss, and ceasing the assault, gave themselves up to lamentation and mourning on account of his death, for he was a man of rank and influence and great valour.

CH. XI.—*How the French from without undermine the tower Maledictum, while the Turks from within carry on a countermine.*

NOT long after, the French miners, by their perseverance, undermined the tower Maledictum, and supported it by placing beams of wood underneath. The Turks also, digging in the same direction, had reached the same part of the foundations; on which they entered into a mutual treaty of peace, that the Turks should depart uninjured; and some of the Christians whom they held captive, were by agreement, in like manner, set at liberty. On discovering this, the Turks were very much chagrined, and stopped up the passages by which they had gone out.

CH. XII.—*How King Richard, though still sick, assaulted the city with his men, slew many by a sling with his own hand, and threw down one of the towers by means of his miners and petraria.*

KING RICHARD was not yet fully recovered from his sickness; nevertheless, anxious for action, and strenuously intent upon taking the city, he made arrangements that his men should assault the city, in the hope that under Divine Providence he should succeed. For this purpose, he caused to be made a hurdle, commonly called a circleia, put together firmly with a complication of interweaving, and made with the most subtle workmanship. This the king intended to be used for crossing over the trench outside the city. Under it he placed his most experienced arbalesters, and he caused himself

to be carried thither on a silken bed, to honour the Saracens
with his presence, and animate his men to fight; and from it, by
using his arbalest, in which he was skilled, he slew many with
darts and arrows. His sappers also carried a mine under the
tower, at which a petraria was directed; and having made a
breach, they filled it with logs of wood, and set them on fire;
when, by the addition of frequent blows from the petraria,
the tower fell suddenly to the ground with a crash.

CH. XIII.—*How the Turks vigorously repelled King Richard's men
who were assaulting the city, and how King Richard slew with his
arbalest one who had on the armour of Alberic Clements.*

PERCEIVING, therefore, how difficult success was, that
he had a most warlike enemy to contend with, and that
there was need of all his strength for the attack, the king
thought it best to incite the minds of his younger soldiers
by rewards, rather than to urge them by severe orders; for
whom will not the love of gain draw on? He therefore
ordered the herald to proclaim a reward of two *aurei*,
afterwards three, and then four, to whoever should overthrow
a petraria from the walls; and for each stone displaced from
the wall, he promised a reward of four *aurei*. Then you
might see the young men bound forward, and soldiers of
great valour press on emulously to draw stones from the
wall, as eager for glory as for gain, and persisting in their
efforts amidst the darts of the enemy. Very many of
them failed in their undertaking, while others were driven
back by fear of death; for the Turks from above vigorously
repelled them, and neither shields nor arms availed to
protect them. The height of the wall was very great, as well
as its thickness; but the men of valour, overcoming all difficulties, extracted very many stones from the solid wall; and
when the Turks rushed upon them in a body, and tried to cast
them down, they strove to repel them, but, having forgot their
arms, they exposed themselves to the darts, in an almost
unarmed condition. One of the Turks, vaunting in the armour
of the aforesaid Alberic Clements, which he had put on, was
shewing himself, to the annoyance of our men, on the highest
part of the wall, in a boastful manner; but King Richard
inflicted on him a deadly wound, piercing him through the
heart with a cast of his arbalest; the Turks, grieving at his fall,

ran together in crowds to avenge his death, and to assuage
the bitterness of their grief by the fierceness of their onslaught.
They boldly exposed themselves, as if they feared not that
the darts and missiles would strike them, and repelled and
pressed on our men like madmen,—never were there braver
warriors of any creed on earth ; and the memory of their
actions excites at once our respect and astonishment.   In the
hottest of the combat, however close the armour fitted, or
whether the coat of mail was twofold, it availed little to resist
the darts from their arbalests.   Nevertheless, the Turks kept
mining from within, so that our men were obliged to retreat ;
and the enemy raised a loud shout, as if they had gained their
purpose.

CH. XIV.—*How our esquires and the Pisans boldly scaled the tower,
which had been shaken, for the purpose of entering the city : and how
the Turks repelled them with spirit, both with arms and Greek fire.*

AT last the aforesaid tower was thrown down by the constant blows of our petrariæ and the pulling away of
stones ; and when King Richard's men had ceased from
undermining, and the assaults were discontinued, our esquires
eager for praise and victory, and fitted and equipped for war,
armed themselves.   Among them were the retainers of the
earl of Leicester, and those of Andrew de Cavegin and Hugo
Brun ; there also came, most nobly arrayed, the bishop of Salisbury, and very many others.   It was about tierce, *i. e.* the
hour of dinner, when the men of valour and the most excellent esquires, prepared to attack the aforesaid tower,
and forthwith boldly mounted it.   The sentinels of the Turks
on seeing them began to shout, and the whole city, being
roused, took up arms with all haste, and ran to oppose
them ; and the Turks pressed in dense numbers upon the squires,
who were nimbly making their way.   While our men
tried to enter the city, and the Turks to drive them back,
they met in a body and fought hand to hand on both sides,
right hand met right hand, and swords flashed against swords ;
some seized hold of each other, others struck each other,—some
were driven back, and others fell.   Our men were few in
numbers ; the multitude of the Turks increased constantly,
and by throwing Greek fire, they forced our men, who could
not withstand it, to retire and descend from the tower ; some of

P 2

them were killed by the enemy and afterwards burnt to ashes by this destructive conflagration. Then the Pisans, either thirsting for praise or revenge, mounted the tower in full force: but the Turks again attacked them like madmen, and although the Pisans made a bold resistance, they were compelled to retire and abandon the tower. For there never was seen any thing like that race of Turks for efficiency in war. The capture of the city would, however, have been accomplished on that day, had the battle been fought with the whole combined army, and on a prudent plan; but the greater part of the army was at dinner at the time, and the attempt was a presumptuous one, and therefore did not succeed.

CH. XV.—*A commendation of the Turks in the city, who sent Mestoc and Caracois in despair to our kings, in order to obtain a respite until they should consult Saladin, but they returned fruitlessly.*

WHAT can we say of this race of unbelievers who thus defended their city? They must be admired for their valour in war, and were the honour of their whole nation; and had they been of the right faith, they would not have had their superiors as men throughout the world. Yet they dreaded our men, not without reason, for they saw the choicest soldiers from the ranks of all Christendom come to destroy them; their walls in part broken down, in part shattered, the greater portion of their army mutilated, some killed, and others weakened by their wounds. There were still remaining in the city 6,000 Turks, with Mestoc and Caracois, their chiefs, but they despaired of succour. They perceived that the Christian army was very much dejected at the death of Alberic Clements, and their sons and kinsmen, who had fallen in battle, and that they were determined either to die bravely or gain the mastery over the Turks, and that they thought a middle course dishonourable. Under these circumstances, by common counsel and assent, the besieged begged a truce in order to inform Saladin of their condition, and to ascertain how far he would afford them security according to the manner of barbarous nations, by either sending them speedy help, or giving them leave to depart from the city with honour. To obtain this object, two of the most noble of the Saracens and of Paganism, Mestoc and Caracois, came to our kings with the promise that if Saladin did not send them speedy assistance, they would give up the city, on the condition that all the besieged Turks should be permitted to depart in freedom, with their arms and property, and go whithersoever they liked.   And on the king of France and nearly all the French giving their assent to this condition at the conference, King Richard absolutely refused his, and said, it was not to be consented to, that after so long and laborious a siege, they should enter a deserted city only.   On his pleasure being known, Caracois and Mestoc returned to the city without effecting their object.   And Saladin, when he learnt that ambassadors had been sent by the besieged, commanded them to persevere and defend their city with as much courage as that which they had hitherto shewn, promising that most ample assistance should soon come to them without a doubt; for he declared to the ambassadors who waited upon him, that he would certainly persevere, and as he was expecting a large body of soldiers from Babylon, they would soon come in ships and galleys; for he had given orders to Muleina to be with him, without fail, in eight days; and if they did not come according to agreement, he promised, with an oath, to procure for them as honourable a peace as he could from the Christians, and the liberty to depart.   On hearing these things, the ambassadors returned to the city, and, repeating the promises of Saladin, persuaded the townsmen to resist, while they looked forward with anxiety for the promised assistance.

Ch. XVI.—*How, while our men were courageously assaulting the city, some of the Turks in despair escaped out of it.*

MEANWHILE, the petrariæ of the Christians never ceased, day and night, to shake the walls; and when the Turks saw this, they were smitten with wonder, astonishment, terror, and confusion; and many, yielding to their fears, threw themselves down from the walls by night, and without waiting for the promised aid, very many sought, with supplications, the sacrament of baptism and Christianity.   There was little doubt, and with good reason as to their merits, that they presumptuously asked the boon more from the pressure of urgent fear than from any divine inspiration; but there are different steps by which men arrive at salvation.   It was now

well known to Saladin, by means of messengers, who passed
backwards and forwards, that to persevere any longer in
defending the city, was dangerous, as it could not be kept
from the Christians.

Ch. XVII.—*How the besieged entered into treaty with the Christians by the advice of Saladin.*

SALADIN, perceiving the danger of delay, at length determined to yield to the entreaties of the besieged : he was,
moreover, persuaded by his admirals, and satraps, and his
influential courtiers, who had many friends and kinsmen
amongst the besieged.   The latter alleged also, that he was
bound to them by his promise made on the Mahometan law,
that he would procure for them an honourable capitulation
at the last moment, lest, perchance, made prisoners at discretion, they should be exterminated or put to an ignominious
death, and thus the law of Mahomet, which had been strictly
observed by their ancestors, be effaced by its dependence on
him ; and nevertheless, very much would be derogated from his
name and excellence if the worshippers of Mahomet should fall
into the hands of the Christians.   They also begged to remind
Saladin of the fact, that they, a chosen race of Turks, in
obedience to his commands, had been cooped up in the city,
and withstood a siege for so long a time ; they reminded him
too that they had not seen their wives and children for three
years, during which period the siege had lasted ; and they
said, it would be better to surrender the city, than that people
of such merit should be destroyed.   The princes persuading
the sultan to this effect, that their latter condition might
not be worse than their former one ; he assented to their
making peace on the best terms they could, and they drew up
a statement of what appeared to them the most proper terms
of treaty.   On the messengers bringing back the resolution
of Saladin and his satraps, the besieged were filled with great
joy ; and forthwith, the principal men of the city went to the
kings, and through their interpreters, offered to surrender
unconditionally the city of Acre, the Cross, and two hundred
and fifty noble Christian captives ; and when they perceived
this did not satisfy them, they offered two thousand noble
Christian captives, and five hundred of inferior rank, whom
Saladin would bring together from all parts of his kingdom, if

they would let the Turks depart from their city, with their
shirts only, leaving behind them their arms and property; and,
as a ransom for themselves, they would give two hundred
thousand Saracenic talents.   As security for the performance
of these conditions, they offered to deliver up, as hostages, all
the men of noble or high rank in the city. After the two kings
had considered with the wisest of the chiefs, the opinion of all
was for accepting the offer, and consenting to the conditions;
that on taking the oath for security, and subscribing the terms
of peace, they might quit the city, without carrying any thing
with them, having first given up the hostages.

CH. XVIII.—*How, on giving hostages for the delivery of the Cross,
money, and captives within a month, the Turks marched out of
the city and the Christians entered it; and how the two kings divided
every thing equally between them.*

THUS, on the Friday after the Translation of St. Benedict,
the principal and noblest of the admirals were given and
received as hostages, and the space of one month fixed for
the delivery of the Cross, and the collecting together of
the captives.   And when it was rumoured abroad that the
city was to be given up, the common people, in their
folly, were inflamed with fury, but the wiser portion rejoiced at gaining so profitably, and without danger, what
they had been so long a time unable to obtain.   Then was
it proclaimed and prohibited, by voice of herald, that any
one should molest the Turks by word or deed, or provoke
them by abuse, or that missiles should any longer be
cast for the destruction of the walls or of the Turks who might
be seen on the battlements.   And when the day came that
the Turks, so renowned for their courage and valour, most
active in the exercise of war, and famous for their magnificence, appeared on the walls ready to leave the city, the Christians went forth to look at them, and were struck with admiration when they remembered the deeds they had done.   They
were also astonished at the cheerful countenances of those who
were thus driven almost penniless from their city,—their de-
meanour unchanged by adversity; and those who but now
had been compelled by extreme necessity to own themselves
conquered, and betake themselves to supplication, bore no
marks of care, as they came forth, nor any signs of dejection

at the loss of all they possessed—not even in the firmness
of their countenances, for they seemed to be conquerors by
their courageous bearing; but the form of superstitious
idolatry, and the miserable error of sinfulness, threw a stain
upon their warlike glories.   At last, when all the Turks had
departed, the Christians, with the two kings at their head,
entered the city without opposition, through the open gates,
with dances, and joy, and loud vociferations, glorifying God,
and giving Him thanks, because He had magnified His mercy
to them, and had visited them, and redeemed His people.
Then the banners, and various standards of the two kings,
were raised on the walls and towers, and the city was equally
divided between them.   They also made a proportionate division of the arms and provisions they found ; and the whole
number of captives, being reckoned, was divided by lot.   The
noble Caracois, and a large number, fell to the lot of the king
of France ; and King Richard had for his portion Mestoc
and the remainder.   Moreover, the king of France had for
his share the noble palace of the Templars, with all its appurtenances ; and King Richard had the royal palace, to which
he sent the queens, with their damsels and handmaids ; thus
each obtained his portion in peace.   The army was distributed
through the city, and after the protracted contest of so long a
siege, gave themselves indulgence, and refreshed themselves
with the rest they needed.   The night following our entrance,
Saladin, through fear of us, retired from the place in which
he was posted, and occupied a most distant mountain.

CH. XIX.—*How vilely and shamefully the Turks, when in possession of
the city, had treated our sacred things.*

FROM the day on which the Saracens first got possession of the city of Acre, to that on which it was restored,
was a space of four years.   It was restored, as has been said,
on the morrow of St. Benedict.   The state of the churches
within the city was not beheld without horror, and it is not
without grief that we relate the unseemly things that had been
perpetrated within them. For who could behold, without tears,
the countenances of the holy images of the crucifixion of the
Son of God, and of many saints, defiled or disfigured in one
way or another? Who would not shudder at the horrible sight of
altars overthrown, and crucifixes cast to the earth, and beaten

in contempt by that insulting and impious nation, the Turks, and their own Mahometan rites exhibited in holy places—all the relics of man's redemption and the Christian religion effaced, and the corruption of the Mahometan superstition introduced?

CH. XX.—*Of the quarrel between the two kings on account of the Marquis and King Guy, and of their reconciliation.*

AFTER this a great discord arose between the two kings, on account of the aforesaid marquis whom the king of France favoured, and to whom he had determined to give his share of all that fell to his lot, present or future, in the Holy Land. But King Richard, who compassionated the distress of King Guy, would not consent to this grant, for he thought that all and every thing belonged to Guy. On this point the kings were at variance for some time; until, by the mediation of the chiefs and leaders of the people, they were reconciled, on the condition that, as the marquis was heir by marriage to the throne, he should have the government of Tyre, *i.e.* Tyre, Sidon, and Baruth, with the title of count, as a recompense for the assistance he had given during the siege, and that Godfrey of Lusignan should be count of Joppa, *i.e.* Joppa and Askalon, as a recompense for his services, being brother to King Guy. And if King Guy died first, the marquis should receive his crown, although he had married in so unlawful a manner the heiress to the throne, as we have before said; but that if the marquis and his wife should happen to die while King Richard was in those parts, it should be left to him to dispose of the kingdom at his pleasure. On these conditions, the disputants were one and all pacified.

CH. XXI.—*How, after the city was restored, the king of France, amidst the wonder, disapproval, and execrations of all, prepared to return home.*

AFFAIRS being in this position, at the end of the month of July, within which the Turks had promised to restore the holy cross, and receive back their hostages, a rumour spread amongst the army, that the king of France, on whom the hope of the people rested, intended to return home, and was making active preparations for his journey. Oh how wicked and how insulting a proceeding, while as yet so much work remained on hand, to wish to go away, when his duty was to rule so large a multitude of people, and when his presence was so necessary to encourage the Christians to so pious a work, and to provide for the progress of so ardoous an undertaking! O why did he come so long a way, with so much toil, if he intended to return almost immediately! O wonderful performance of his vow, by merely entering the Holy Land, and contending against the Turks with such small triumph! But why need we say more? The king of France alleged sickness as the cause of his return; and said that he had performed his vow as far as he was able; most of all, because he was well and sound when he took up the cross with King Henry between Trie and Gieors. But in making this assertion, he produced no one by whose evidence it could be confirmed. It must not be denied, at the same time, that the king of France expended much labour and money in the Holy Land for the assaulting of the city, and that he afforded aid and assistance to very many, and that by the influence of his presence, he procured the more speedy execution and consummation of so great a work in the capture of the city, as the most powerful of Christian kings, and of the highest dignity, should have done: whence, by how much the greater in valour and surpassing in excellence, by so much the more he was held bound to recover a land so cast down and destitute of aid, against which the heathen had come to pollute it; for, according to St. Gregory, when gifts are increased, the reasons for them increase also, and to whom much is given, of the same much will be required. But when the inflexible determination of the king of France to return became known to all, and his refusal to yield to the murmurs of his men, or their supplications to remain, the French would have renounced their subjection to him, if it could have been done, and would have loathed his dominion; and they imprecated on him every kind of adversity and misfortune that could fall to the lot of man in this life. But for all that, the king of France hastened his voyage as much as possible, and left in his stead the duke of Burgundy, with a large number of men. Moreover, he begged King Richard to supply him with two galleys, and the king readily gave him two of his best: how ungrateful he was for this service, was afterwards seen.

CH. XXII.—*How the king of France swore to King Richard that he would observe peace towards his subjects and his territories until the latter returned home.*

KING RICHARD was of opinion that the king of France should enter into a covenant for the preservation of their mutual security; for they, like their fathers, regarded each other with mistrust, under the veil of friendship, which even in the following generation never expelled fear. King Richard was therefore anxious with this uneasy feeling, and required an oath from the king of France to keep his faith not to do injury to his men or territory knowingly or purposely, while he, King Richard, remained in a foreign land; but if on any occasion any thing that should appear reprehensible went unpunished, King Richard on his return should have forty days' notice before the king of France should proceed to obtain redress. The king of France took the oath which was required faithfully to observe all these conditions, and gave the duke of Burgundy and Count Henry as hostages, and five or more others, whose names are lost. How faithfully he stood to his covenant and oath is very well known to all the world; for he had no sooner reached his own country, than he set it in commotion and threw Normandy into confusion. What need we say more? The king of France, having taken leave, retired from his army at Acre, and instead of blessings, he received wishes of misfortune and execrations from all.

CH. XXIII.—*How, on the king of France retiring with his hostages and the Marquis to Tyre, the duke of Burgundy and many others of the French remained with King Richard.*

ON St. Peter's day the king of France embarked and sailed for Tyre, but he left the greater part of his army with King Richard; and with him he took that infamous marquis and Caracois and the other hostages that had fallen to his lot; and he reckoned that he would receive for their ransom a hundred thousand *aurei* or more, which would support his army till Easter. But on the term expiring for ransoming the hostages, the Turks paid no attention to it, and most of them perished: for it was very evident that they would not give an egg or a farthing to release them; and by

their means nothing at all was gained, nor any portion of provisions found in the city; which caused the French to remember
the more frequently that they received no other remuneration
from the king of France. On this account there arose frequent
wrangling and murmuring amongst them, until King Richard,
at the request of the duke of Burgundy, lent him, over and
above his hostages, five thousand marks of silver to support
his men.

BOOK IV.

Ch. I.—*How King Richard bestows gifts on his soldiers, and repairs the walls of Acre.*

KING RICHARD, therefore, perceiving that the consummation of the business and the progress of affairs, together with
the labour and expense, devolved upon him chiefly, made most
ample largesses of gold and silver to the French and to all the
others of every nation, by means of which they might abundantly recruit themselves and redeem what they had put in
pledge. On the king of France returning home with haste as
aforesaid, King Richard turned his attention to the repair of
the walls to a greater height and perfection than before
they were thrown down; and he himself walked about, exhorting the workmen and masons, as if his whole intention
was to strive for the recovery of God's inheritance.

Ch. II.—*How Saladin stood not to his covenant for restoring our Lord's cross, and paying the money; and neglected his men, who were hos-tages.*

HE therefore awaited the term which had been agreed
upon between the Turks and himself as aforesaid, and turned
his attention to the packing up of the petrariæ and mangonels for transportation. For when the time had expired
which had been fixed by the Turks for the restoration of the
cross and the ransom of the hostages, after waiting three
weeks, according to the conditions, to see if Saladin would
stand to his word and covenant, the king looked upon him as
a transgressor, as Saladin appeared to have no care about it;
and perhaps this was by the dispensation of God, that something more advantageous might be obtained. But the Saracens

asked further time to fulfil their promise and make search for
the cross.   Then you might hear the Christians inquiring
for news, and when the cross was coming? but God was
unwilling that it should be restored for those by whom it was
promised, but preferred rather that they should perish.   One
would exclaim, " The cross is coming!" another, that he
had seen it in the Saracen army ; but each speaker was
deceived, for Saladin had not taken any steps to restore
the cross ; nay, he neglected the hostages who were
bound for it, for he hoped, by means of it, to obtain
much more advantageous terms.   Meanwhile, he sent constant
presents and messengers to King Richard to gain delay by
artful and deceptive words, though he fulfilled none of his promises, but tried to keep the king's mind in suspense by crafty
and ambiguous messages.

CH. III.—*How the king of England sent twice to Tyre, before he could
obtain the hostages of Saladin from the Marquis, and how he himself
refused to return.*

IN the meantime messages were sent to Tyre to command the marquis to return to the army, and bring with him
the hostages which had been committed to his charge, in
order to get the ransom for them,—viz., the share of the
payment which belonged to the king of France.   With the
message were sent the bishop of Salisbury, Earl Robert, and
Peter de Pratellis, a very eminent soldier.   To these three
messengers the marquis answered indignantly, that he dared
not venture into King Richard's presence : moreover, he
boasted that if the true cross was ever recovered, he was to
receive the half of it for the king of France ; and that until
this was accomplished he would not resign the hostages.
On ascertaining the obstinate determination of the marquis, the
messengers tried to prevail upon him with soft speeches, offering to leave one of themselves as an hostage to secure his safe
journey to and from King Richard ; but they did not succeed
in persuading him,—nay, he refused with an oath to come.
They therefore returned unsuccessful and empty-handed, and
excited the king's anger by telling him the whole matter.   At his request the duke of Burgundy, Drogo d'Amiens,
and Robert de Quincey, were sent on a second embassy to
request the said marquis to come with them to the army,

as his presence seemed necessary to the progress of the business, especially as he aspired to the kingdom, the acquisition
of which he was preventing; and that he should grant those
who were bringing provisions a free passage from Tyre, for
(according to his former conduct) he had hitherto hindered
them; and on their arrival at Tyre, they set forth their zeal
in behalf of King Richard, and urged him to come to their
aid in Syria, the dominion of which he aspired to obtain.
But he replied arrogantly, protesting that he would not
come, but would maintain the government of his own city.
When they answered each of his assertions, by contrary arguments, the matter was with difficulty brought to this point,—
that the messengers should take back with them the Saracen hostages to King Richard; but they could, by no method
or persuasion, prevail on the marquis to turn from his obstinate
and wicked intentions.

CH. IV.—*How the hostages of Saladin were slain by our men.*

WHEN it became clearly evident to King Richard that a
longer period had elapsed than had been fixed, and that Saladin was obdurate, and would not give himself trouble to ransom the hostages, he called together a council of the chiefs of
the people, by whom it was resolved that the hostages should
all be hanged, except a few nobles of the higher class, who
might ransom themselves, or be exchanged for some Christian
captives. King Richard, aspiring to destroy the Turks root
and branch, and to punish their wanton arrogance, as well as
to abolish the law of Mahomet, and to vindicate the Christian religion, on the Friday after. the Assumption of the
Blessed Virgin Mary, ordered 2,700 of the Turkish hostages
to be led forth from the city, and hanged; his soldiers
marched forward with delight to fulfil his commands, and to
retaliate, with the assent of the Divine Grace, by taking
revenge upon those who had destroyed so many of the
Christians with missiles from bows and arbalests.

CH. V.—*How King Richard ordered his army to move by land and by
sea towards Askalon.*

WHEN evening approached, it was proclaimed by mouth
of herald, that the army should march on the morrow, and
cross the river of Acre in the name of the Lord,—the dis-

penser of all good things—in order that they should proceed
to Askalon and conquer the maritime districts. It was
also ordered that the ships should take on board, for the
army, ten days' provisions,—viz., biscuits, meal, meat,
and wine, and whatever else appeared necessary. The
sailors were strictly enjoined to keep sailing along shore,
with the barges and snacks, which carried the provisions as
well as armed men; and thus the forces advanced in two
divisions, one by sea the other by land; for otherwise it was
not possible to keep possession of the country so completely
occupied by the Turks.

CH. VI.—*How many of our chiefs had died in a year and a half at the
siege of Acre.*

It must be known, that during the two winters and one
summer, and up to the middle of the autumn, when the Turks
were hanged, as they deserved to be in the sight of God and
man, in return for the destruction of our churches and slaughter of our men, many of the Christians who were engaged in
the siege of Acre at a great sacrifice had died. The multitude
of those who perished in so great an army appears to exceed
computation; but the sum total of the chiefs, as a certain
writer has estimated it, omitting the others which he says he
has no means of reckoning, is as follows:—We lost in the
army six archbishops and patriarchs, twelve bishops, forty
counts, and five hundred men of noble rank; also a vast number of priests, clergy, and others, which cannot be accurately
counted.

CH. VII.—*How King Richard compelled the French to quit Acre · and
how he fixed his own tent outside the city.*

After the Turks were hanged, King Richard, having
recovered his health, went out from the city with all his
retinue, and ordered his tents to be pitched in the plain
outside, and compelled all his soldiers, who were not willing,
to quit the city; thus the army took up their quarters
on the aforesaid plain, to be ready for setting out on
its march; of the French some he allured by soft words,
others by entreaties, and many by money, to leave the place,
and some he forced out violently. King Richard thereupon
appointed a large number of guards to lodge about his pavilion in their tents and awnings, for his protection, as the

Turks were making constant irruptions, and all day coming
up and rushing out on them unawares, and it was the king's
custom to be the first to go forth to attack and punish them,
as far as the divine favour would allow him.

CH. VIII.—*How the count of Hungary and the king's marshal, having
put the Turks to flight who had attacked our men, were captured
by them.*

IT happened one day that our camp was put into commotion by the Turks, who were attacking our men, as was their
custom, and making a disturbance. Our men immediately
ran to arms, the king and his cavalry went forth, and also
the count of Hungary, and very many Hungarians with
him, who, having put the Turks to flight, pursued them further
than they ought to have done : for some of our men, although
they behaved themselves most nobly, were taken captive on
the spot and disgracefully treated. The count of Hungary, a
man of tried valour and renown, was taken prisoner by the
Turks and carried off, as well as a man of Poitou, named Hugh,
King Richard's marshal. The king fought recklessly, careless of his own person, and strove with all his might to rescue
Hugh, his marshal ; but he was hurried away too rapidly and
carried off. Oh how uncertain is the fate of war ! Those
who were but now victors are often vanquished, and the vanquished becomes as suddenly victor ; it was fated for those
who had put the enemy to flight to perish themselves, for
the pursuers were now captured by the pursued, and that
which was ascribed to their glory now proved their folly, and
the deed of valour became the cause of danger. In short, the
Turks were not loaded with armour like our men ; but from
their light movements distressed us so much the more
severely, for they were for the most part unarmed, carrying only a bow, or a mace, bristling with sharp teeth, a
scimitar, a light spear with an iron head, and a dagger suspended lightly ; and when put to flight with greater
force, they fled away on horseback with the utmost rapidity, for they have not their equals for agility throughout
the world ; for it is their custom to turn if they see their
pursuers stop ;—like the fly, which, if you drive it away,
will go, but when you cease, it will return ; as long as you
pursue, it will fly, but it reappears the moment you desist ;
so likewise the Turks, when you desist from the pursuit

they will pursue you; if you attack them, they will fly away:
so when the king put them to flight, they fled without stopping; when he was disposed to return, they threatened from
the rear, sometimes not with impunity, and sometimes to the
injury of our men.

CH. IX.—*How our army, being abandoned to pleasures, could scarcely
be forced to quit the city and cross the river of Acre, while the Turks
infested them on all sides.*

KING RICHARD was resting in his tents, waiting for the
army to come out of the city, but they came out slowly and
peevishly, as if they did it against their will; and the numbers of the army did not increase, but the city was crowded
with an immense multitude. The whole army, including those
who were yet in the city, was computed at 300,000 men.
The people were too much given up to sloth and luxury,
for the city was filled with pleasures, viz.—the choicest
wines and fairest damsels, and the men became dissolute by
indulging in them; so that the city was defiled by the
luxury of the sons of folly and the gluttony of its inhabitants, who made wiser faces blush at their shamelessness;
and, in order to blot out this contamination, it was ordained
by the council that no woman should quit the city or go with
the army, except the washerwomen, on foot, who would not be
a burthen to them, nor an occasion for sin. Therefore, on the
morning of the aforementioned day, the soldiers armed themselves, and were arranged in becoming order. The king was
in the rear of the army to check the Turks, who threatened
annoyance; but the duty was a slight one. From the time that
impious race saw our army in motion, they poured down from
the mountains in scattered bands, like rushing waters, and
dispersed themselves in numbers of twenty or thirty, to
find out the best opportunity of harassing us. For they
were exceedingly grieved at the deaths of their parents and
kinsmen, whose slaughtered bodies they saw strewn about as
aforesaid: and they therefore pressed upon our army continuously, and harassed it as much as they could. But, with the
assistance of the Divine Grace, the Turks succeeded not as
they wished; for our army passed over the river of Acre unhurt, and again pitched their tents on the other side the stream
until on Friday, being the vigil of St. Bartholomew, they were

q

all assembled together; and on the following Monday, two
years had elapsed since the Christians first laid siege to
Acre.

CH. X.—*How our army, departing from the city in battle array, boldly
repulsed the Turks, who attacked them in force: the standard is here
described.*

ON the morrow, therefore, of St. Bartholomew, being
Sunday, the army was drawn up, early in the morning,
to advance along the sea-coast, in the name of the Lord.
Oh! what fine soldiers they were! You might there see a
chosen company of virtuous and brave youth, whose equals it
would have been difficult to meet with, bright armour and
pennons, with their glittering emblazonry; banners of various
forms; lances, with gleaming points; shining helmets, and
coats of mail: an army well regulated in the camp, and terrible to the foe! King Richard commanded the van, and kept
the foremost guard. The Normans defended the standard, which
we do not consider it irrelevant here to describe. It was
formed of a long beam, like the mast of a ship; made of most
solid ceiled work, on four wheels; put together with joints,
bound with iron, and to all appearance no sword or axe could
cut, or fire injure it. A chosen body of soldiers were generally appointed to guard it, especially in a combat on the
plains, lest, by any hostile attack, it should be broken or
thrown down; for if it fell by any accident, the army would
be dispersed and put into confusion. For they are dismayed
when it does not appear, and think that their general must be
overcome by faint-heartedness when they do not see his
standard flying; for no people have strength to resist the
enemy if their chief is in alarm from the fall of his standard; but whilst it remains erect they have a certain refuge.
Near it the weak are strengthened; the wounded soldiers,
even those of rank and celebrity, who fall in the battle, are
carried to it, and it is called "Standard," from its standing a
most compact signal to the army. It is very properly drawn
on wheels, for it is advanced when the enemy yields, and
drawn back if they press on, according to the state of the
battle. It was surrounded by the Normans and English.
The duke of Burgundy and the French brought up the
rear, and by their tardy movements and long delay incurred

severe loss. The army marched along the sea-shore, which
was on its right, and the Turks watched its movements
from the heights on the left. On a sudden the clouds grew
dark, and the sky was troubled, when the army arrived at some
narrow roads impassable for the provision-waggons; here,
owing to the narrowness of the way, the order of march was
thrown into confusion, and they advanced in extended line,
and without discipline. The Saracens, observing this, poured
down suddenly on the pack-horses and loaded waggons, slew
both horses and men in a moment, and plundered a great deal
of the baggage, boldly charging and dispersing those who
opposed them as far as the sea-shore. Then there took place
a fierce and obstinate conflict: each fought for his life. Here
a Turk cut off the right hand of Everard, one of the bishop
of Salisbury's men, as he held his sword; the man, without
changing countenance in the least, with his left hand boldly
took the sword, and closing with the Turks, who were pressing
on him, defended himself courageously from them all. By this
time the rear was put into great confusion, and John Fitz-Luke,
alarmed at this mishap, put spurs to his horse, and went to tell
King Richard, who was ignorant of what had taken place. On
hearing it, he rode at full gallop to their assistance, cutting down
the Turks, right and left, like lightning, with his sword. And
quickly, as of yore the Philistines fled from Maccabeus, so were
the Turks now routed, and so did they fly from the face of
King Richard, and make for the mountains; but some of them
remained amongst us, having lost their heads. In that conflict one of the French, William de Bartis, who had been at
variance with King Richard from some old grudge, by his
extraordinary good conduct was reconciled and restored to
the king's former favour. The sultan was not far off with
the whole strength of his army, but owing to the aforesaid
repulse, the Turks, despairing of success, refrained from attacking our men any more, but watched them from the heights.
Our troops, being restored to order, proceeded on their march
as far as a river which they by chance met with, and cisterns,
the excellence of which being ascertained, they pitched their
tents, and rested there on a spacious plain, where they had seen
that Saladin had fixed his camp before, and they judged that
he had a very large army by the extent of the trodden
ground. On the first day there our army fared thus, and by

God's providence they were warned to be more cautious, after having experienced how much loss they might escape if properly on their guard another time.

Ch. XI.—*How our army arrived at Cayphas from the river of Acre.*

SALADIN and the Turks, always on the watch to do us harm, had seized upon some passes between the rugged mountains, by which our army was to proceed; and they intended to kill, seize, or disperse us as we issued forth in an extended line; but when our army had advanced cautiously from the aforesaid river, and by slow march, as far as Cayphas, they pitched their tents there, and waited for the mass of the army who were following. They posted themselves between the town of Cayphas and the sea, and remained there two days, looking into and arranging their baggage, and they threw away what they thought they could dispense with, only retaining what was absolutely necessary, for the common soldiers marched on foot, and were much distressed by the weight of their baggage and provisions; so that in the aforesaid battle they suffered much from fatigue and thirst.

Ch. XII.—*How our army kept along the maritime parts, where they were wounded by the underwood, and met with wild beasts; and how they left Cayphas by way of Capernaum, and reached the passes.*

ON a Wednesday, which was the third day after stopping at Cayphas, the army moved forward in order, the Templars leading the van, and the Hospitallers closing the rear, both of whom by their high bearing gave evidence of great valour. That day the army moved forward with more than wonted caution, and stopped after a long march, impeded by the thickets and the tall and luxuriant herbage, which struck them in the face, especially the foot-soldiers. In these maritime parts there —are also numbers of beasts of the forest, who leapt up between their feet from the long grass and thick copses, ...and many were caught, not by design, but coming in their way by chance. When the king had proceeded as far as Capernaum, which the Saracens had razed to the ground, he dismounted, and took some food, the army, meanwhile, waiting; those who chose took food, and immediately after proceeded on their march to the house called " of the narrow ways," because the road there becomes narrow ; there they halted and pitched their tents. It was the custom of the army each night before lying down to rest, to depute some one to stand in the middle of the camp, and cry out with a loud voice, " Help ! help ! for the holy sepulchre !"   The rest of the army took it up, and repeated the words ; and stretching their hands to heaven, amid a profusion of tears, prayed for the mercy and assistance of God in the cause.   Then the herald himself repeated the words in a loud voice, " Help ! help ! for the holy sepulchre !" and every one repeated it after him a second time, and so likewise a third time, with contrition of heart and abundant weeping.   For who would not weep at such a moment, when the very mention of its having been done would extract tears from the auditors ?   The army appeared to be much refreshed by crying out in this fashion.

CH. XIII.—*How the tarrentes afflicted our people with their venomous stings.*

As each night came round, a sort of reptile attacked us, commonly called *tarrentes*, which creep on the ground, and have most venomous stings.   As the day comes on, they are harmless; but on the approach of night, they used their stings most pertinaciously, and those they stung were instantly swelled with the venom, and tortured with pain.   The more noble and wealthy of those who were attacked applied theriacal ointment on the stings, and the antidote proved efficacious to remove the pain.   At last, the more observant, perceiving that the reptiles were frightened away by loud sounds, raised a great noise at their approach by beating and clashing their helmets and shields together ; also by beating against their seats, poles, casks, flagons, basins, platters, caldrons, and whatever household ware they could lay hands on to make a sufficient sound ; and by these sounds they drove away the reptiles.   The army remained two days at the abovementioned station, where there was plenty of room for their camp, and waited there until the ships arrived which they were expecting ; namely, barges and galleys, laden with provisions, of which they were in need ; for these vessels were sailing in connection with the army along the shore, and carried their provisions on board.

CH. XIV.—*How our men marched from the house of the narrow ways to Merla, and thence to Cæsarea and the Dead River. The Turks, attacking them, were defeated.*

THE army advanced, using all precaution against the Turks, who kept on their flank, to a town called Merla, where the king had spent one of the previous nights: there he had determined that he would lead the van himself the next day, on account of the obstacles in the way, and because the Templars kept guard in the rear; for the Turks continually threatened them in a body on the flank. On that day the king, putting spurs to his horse, charged them furiously, and would have reaped great glory, had it not been for the backwardness of some, which retarded his success; for, when King Richard pursued the Turks to a distance, some of his men suddenly halted, for which they were rebuked in the evening. If the king's companions had followed up their pursuit of the Turks, they would have gained a splendid victory; for the king drove all before him. The army had a very difficult march along the sea-shore on account of the great heat; for it was summer time, and they marched a long day's journey. Many of them, overcome by the fatigue of the march, dropped down dead, and were buried where they died; but the king, from compassion, caused many to be transported in galleys and ships, when they were overcome by the fatigue of the march or sickness, or any other cause, to their destination. The army, after accomplishing its march with much difficulty, arrived that day at Cæsarea. The Turks had been there before them, and broken down part of the towers and walls, and destroyed the city as much as possible; but on the approach of our army they fled. There the army pitched their tents, and passed the night by the side of a river close to the city, called the river of Crocodiles, because the crocodiles once devoured two soldiers while bathing therein. The circuit of the city of Cæsarea is very great, and the buildings are of wonderful workmanship. Our Saviour with his disciples often visited it, and worked miracles there. It was here the king had charged his ships to meet the army. Meanwhile the king caused it to be proclaimed by voice of herald in the city of Acre, that those who had remained behind from slothfulness should embark on board the ships which he had sent, and come to the army, for the love of God, and to promote

the success of the Christian cause, and to perform their vow
of pilgrimage more fully. In obedience to his mandate,
many came to Cæsarea with the fleet, which was amply laden
with provisions; and he arranged that the ships should advance from that place in attendance on the army. A large
number of ships here came together, and when the king had
divided the army into squadrons, they set out one day about nine
o'clock, at a slow pace, on account of the Turks, who continually harassed them when they left their stations, and,
coming up to them as close as they dared, caused them
all the molestation and annoyance in their power. They
troubled us more than usual on this day, but by the help of
God we escaped unhurt, having cut off the head of one of
their admirals, a man of the greatest courage, and renowned
for his valour: he was said to have such strength that no
one could throw him from his horse, or even dare to attack
him; and he carried a lance heavier than two of ours, to
which he gave the name of *aias estog*. The Turks were
overcome with grief and lamentation at his fall, so that they
cut off their horses' tails, and, had they been permitted, would
have carried off the corpse of their chief. After that the army
arrived at a river called the Dead River, which the Saracens
had previously covered over, in order that, not being seen,
our men might endanger their lives by falling into it; but by
the providence of God they were preserved from danger, and,
the river having been uncovered, our men drank thereof, and
passed the night there.

CH. XV.—*How on quitting the Dead River, our army, before they
arrived at the Salt River, were much harassed by the Turks, who slew
many of our men and horses.*

ON the third day the army advanced slowly from the Dead
River, through a country of a most desolate character, and
destitute of every thing; for they were compelled to march
through a mountainous country, because they were unable to
go by the sea-side, which was choked up by the luxuriant
growth of the grass; and the army on its march kept itself
in closer companies than usual. The Templars on that day
had charge of the rear, and they lost so many horses by the
attacks of the Turks that they were almost reduced to despair.
The count of St. Paul also lost many horses; for he himself

opposed the Turks with great valour, when they attacked and
made incursions against us; so that by his exertions the rest
got off in safety, and thus he earned the thanks and favour
of the whole army.   On that day the king was wounded in
the side by a dart while he was driving the Turks; but this
slight hurt only incited him to attack them more vehemently;
for the smarting of the wound made him more eager for vengeance, and during the whole of the day he fought against
them and drove them back.   The Turks, on the other hand,
obstinately annoyed our men, and, keeping by the side of our
army, did them all the injury they could, by throwing darts
and arrows, which flew like hail.   Alas! how many horses
fell transfixed with darts! how many died afterwards of the
wounds which they received! There was such a stream of darts
and arrows, that you could not find four feet of ground, where
the army passed, free from them.   This terrible tempest continued all day, until at night-fall the Turks returned to their
tents and dwellings.   Our people also stopped near what was
called the Salt River, and passed the night there : they
arrived there on the Tuesday after the festival of St. Giles,
and tarried there two days.   Here there was a great throng
on account of the horses who died from their wounds; for the
people were so eager to purchase the horse-flesh, that they
even had recourse to blows.   The king, on hearing this, proclaimed by herald that he would give a live horse to whoever
would distribute his dead one to the best men in his service
who needed it; and thus they ate horse-flesh as if it was
venison, and they reckoned it most savoury, for hunger served
in the place of seasoning.

CH. XVI.—*How our army marched from the Salt River, through the
forest of Assur, in safety, to the river Rochetailie.*

ON the third day, about nine o'clock, our army marched
in battle array from the Salt River; for there was a rumour
that the Turks were lying in ambush for them in the forest
of Assur, and that they intended to set the wood on fire to
prevent our troops from crossing it.   But our men, advancing
in order, passed the place where the ambuscade was said to be,
unmolested; and on quitting the wood, they came to a large
plain that ran along it, and there they pitched their tents, near
the river commonly called Rochetailie.   Here they sent spies to

reconnoitre, who brought back news that the Turks were
awaiting their approach in countless numbers; for their multitudes covered the whole face of the earth around, and were
estimated at 300,000 men, while the Christians were only
100,000 strong. The Christian army arrived at the river
Rochetailie on the Thursday before the Nativity of the
blessed Virgin Mary, and tarried there until the morrow.

Ch. XVII.—*How our army, on advancing from the river Rochetailie
towards Assur, prepared for battle with the Turks, whom they had
vowed to attack on that day with all their might.*

On the Saturday, the eve of the Nativity of the blessed
Virgin Mary, at earliest dawn, our men armed themselves
with great care to receive the Turks, who were known to
have preceded their march, and whose insolence nothing but
a battle could check. The enemy had ranged themselves in
order, drawing gradually nearer and nearer; and our men
also took the utmost care to place themselves in as good
order as possible. King Richard, who was most experienced in military affairs, arranged the army in squadrons,
and directed who should march in front, and who in the rear.
He divided the army into twelve companies, and these again
into five divisions, marshalled according as the men ranked in
military discipline; and none could be found more warlike, if
they had only had confidence in God, who is the giver of all
good things. On that day, the Templars formed the first
rank, and after them came in due order the Bretons and men
of Anjou; then followed King Guy, with the men of Poictou;
and in the fourth line were the Normans and English, who
had the care of the royal standard; and last of all, marched
the Hospitallers: this line was composed of chosen warriors,
divided into companies. They kept together so closely, that
an apple, if thrown, would not have fallen to the ground,
without touching a man or a horse; and the army stretched
from the army of the Saracens to the sea-shore. There you
might have seen their most appropriate distinctions,—
standards, and ensigns of various forms, and hardy soldiers,
fresh, and full of spirits, and well fitted for war. There was
the earl of Leicester, Hugh de Gurnay, William de Borriz,
Walkin de Ferrars, Roger de Toony, James d'Avennes,
Robert count of Druell, the bishop of Beauvais, and William

des Barres his brother, William de Garlande, Drogo de Mirle, and many of his kinsmen.   Henry count of Champagne kept guard on the mountain's side, maintaining a constant look-out on the flank: the foot-soldiers, bowmen and arbalesters, were on the outside, and the rear of the army was closed by the pack-horses and waggons, which carried provisions and other things, and journeyed along between the army and the sea, to avoid an attack from the enemy.   This was the order of the army, as it advanced gradually, to prevent separation ; for the less close the line of battle, the less effective was it for resistance.   King Richard and the duke of Burgundy, with a chosen retinue of warriors, rode up and down, narrowly watching the position and manner of the Turks, to correct any thing in their own troops, if they saw occasion ; for they had need, at that moment, of the utmost circumspection.

CH. XVIII.—*How our armies were much harassed by the Turks, who attacked them incessantly on all sides, and especially in the rear, wounding and cutting them down; and our men would have yielded under the weight of the battle in despair, had not the grace of God assisted them, when they were just on the point of giving way.*

IT was now nearly nine o'clock, when there appeared a large body of the Turks, 10,000 strong, coming down upon us at full charge, and throwing darts and arrows, as fast as they could, while they mingled their voices in one horrible yell. There followed after them an infernal race of men, of black colour, and bearing a suitable appellation, expressive of their blackness.   With them also were the Saracens, who live in the desert, called Bedouins: they are a savage race of men, blacker than soot; they fight on foot, and carry a bow, quiver, and round shield, and are a light and active race.   These men dauntlessly attacked our army.   Beyond them might be seen the well-arranged phalanxes of the Turks, with ensigns fixed to their lances, and standards and banners of separate distinctions.   Their army was divided into troops, and the troops into companies ; and their numbers seemed to exceed twenty thousand.   They came on with irresistible charge, on horses swifter than eagles, and urged on like lightning to attack our men; and as they advanced, they raised a cloud of dust, so that the sky was darkened.   In front came certain of their admirals, as it was their duty, with clarions and trumpets; some had horns, others had pipes and timbrels, gongs, cymbals, and other instruments, producing a horrible noise and clamour. The earth vibrated from the loud and discordant sounds, so that the crash of thunder could not be heard amidst the tumultuous noise of horns and trumpets. They did this to excite their spirit and courage, for the more violent the clamour became, the more bold were they for the fray. Thus the impious Turks threatened us both on the side towards the sea and from the side of the land; and for the space of two miles, not so much earth as could be taken up in one's hand could be seen, on account of the hostile Turks who covered it. Oh! how obstinately they pressed on, and continued their stubborn attacks, so that our men suffered severe loss of their horses, which were killed by their darts and arrows! Oh! how useful to us on that day were our arbalesters and bowmen, who closed the extremities of the lines, and did their best to repel the obstinate Turks. The enemy came rushing down, like a torrent, to the attack; and many of our arbalesters, unable to sustain the weight of their terrible and calamitous charge, threw away their arms, and fearing lest they should be shut out, took refuge, in crowds, behind the dense lines of the army; yielding, through fear of death, to sufferings which they could not support. Those whom shame forbade to yield, or the hope of an immortal crown sustained, were animated with greater boldness and courage to persevere in the contest, and fought with indefatigable valour face to face against the Turks, whilst they at the same time receded step by step, and so secured their retreat. The whole of that day, on account of the Turks pressing them closely from behind, they faced about and went on skirmishing, rather than proceeding on their march. Oh! how great was the strait they were in on that day! how great was their tribulation! when some were affected with fears, and no one had such confidence or spirit as not to wish, at that moment, he had finished his pilgrimage, and had returned home instead of standing with trembling heart the chances of a doubtful battle. In truth, our people, so few in number, were hemmed in by the multitudes of the Saracens, that they had no means of escape, if they tried; neither did they seem to have valour sufficient to withstand so many foes,—nay, they were shut in, like a flock of sheep in the jaws of wolves, with nothing but the sky above, and the enemy all around them.

O Lord God! what feelings agitated that weak flock of
Christ! straitened by such a perplexity; whom the enemy
pressed with such unabating vigour, as if they would pass
them through a sieve. What army was ever assailed by so
mighty a force? There you might have seen our troopers,
having lost their chargers, marching on foot with the foot-
men, or casting missiles from arbalests, or arrows from bows,
against the enemy, and repelling their attacks in the best
manner they were able. The Turks, skilled in the bow,
pressed unceasingly upon them: it rained darts; the air
was filled with the shower of arrows, and the brightness of
the sun was obscured by the multitude of missiles, as if it had
been darkened by a fall of winter's hail or snow. Our horses
were pierced by the darts and arrows, which were so numerous
that the whole face of the earth around was covered with them,
and if any one wished to gather them up, he might take twenty
of them in his hand at a time. The Turks pressed with such
boldness that they nearly crushed the Hospitallers; on which
the latter sent word to King Richard that they could not sustain
the violence of the enemy's attack, unless he would allow their
knights to advance at full charge against them. This the king
dissuaded them from doing, but advised them to keep in a close
body; they therefore persevered and kept together, though
scarcely able to breathe for the pressure. By these means they
were able to proceed on their way, though the heat happened
to be very great on that day; so that they laboured under two
disadvantages,—the hot weather and the attacks of the enemy.
These approved martyrs of Christ sweated in the contest; and
he who could have seen them closed up in a narrow space, so
patient under the heat and toil of the day and the attacks of
the enemy, who exhorted each other to destroy the Christians,
could not doubt in his mind that it augured ill to our success
from their straitened and perilous position, hemmed in, as they
were, by so large a multitude; for the enemy thundered at their
backs as if with mallets, so that having no room to use their
bows, they fought hand to hand with swords, lances, and clubs;
and the blows of the Turks, echoing from their metal armour,
resounded as if they had been struck upon an anvil. They
were now tormented with the heat, and no rest was allowed
them. The battle fell heavily on the extreme line of the
Hospitallers; the more so, as they were unable to resist, but
moved forward with patience under their wounds, returning

not even a word for the blows which fell upon them, and
advancing on their way, because they were not able to bear the
weight of the contest. Then they pressed on for safety upon
the centre of the army which was in front of them, to avoid
the fury of the enemy, who harassed them in the rear. Was it
wonderful that no one could withstand so continuous an
attack, when he could not even return one blow to the numbers who pressed on him? The strength of all Paganism had
gathered together from Damascus and Persia, from the Mediterranean to the East; there was not left in the uttermost
recesses of the earth one man of fame or power, one nation of
valour, or one bold soldier, whom the Sultan had not summoned to his aid, either by entreaty, by money, or by authority, to crush the Christian race; for he presumed to hope he
could blot them from the face of the earth; but his hopes were
vain, for their numbers were sufficient, through the assistance
of God, to effect their purpose. The flower of the chosen youth
and soldiers of Christendom had indeed assembled together
and were united in one body, like ears of corn on their stalks,
from every region of the earth; and if they had been utterly
crushed and destroyed, there is no doubt that there were none
left to make resistance.

Ch. XIX.—*The battle continued, and the wonderful victory of the
Christians.*

A CLOUD of dust obscured the air as our men marched on;
and, in addition to the heat, they had an enemy pressing
them in the rear, insolent, and rendered obstinate by the instigation of the devil. Still the Christians proved good men, and,
secure in their unconquerable spirit, kept constantly advancing, while the Turks threatened them without ceasing in the
rear; but their blows fell harmless upon the defensive armour,
and this caused the Turks to slacken in courage at the failure of
their attempts, and they began to murmur in whispers of disappointment, crying out in their rage, " that our people were
of iron, and would yield to no blow." Then the Turks,
about twenty thousand strong, rushed again upon our men
pellmell, annoying them in every possible manner; when, as if
almost overcome by their savage fury, brother Garnier de
Napes, one of the Hospitallers, suddenly exclaimed, with a loud
voice, " O excellent St. George! will you leave us to be thus

put to confusion? The whole of Christendom is now on the
point of perishing, because it fears to return a blow against
this impious race." Upon this, the master of the Hospitallers
went to the king, and said to him, "My lord the king, we
are violently pressed by the enemy, and are in danger of
eternal infamy, as if we did not dare to return their blows; we
are each of us losing our horses one after another, and why
should we bear with them any further?" To whom the king
replied, "Good master, it is you who must sustain their attack;
no one can be everywhere at once." On the master returning, the Turks again made a fierce attack on them from the
rear, and there was not a prince or count amongst them but
blushed with shame, and they said to each other, "Why do we
not charge them at full gallop? Alas! alas! we shall for
ever deserve to be called cowards, a thing which never happened to us before, for never has such a disgrace befallen so
great an army even from the unbelievers. Unless we defend
ourselves by immediately charging the enemy, we shall gain
everlasting scandal, and so much the greater the longer we
delay to fight." O, how blind is human fate! On what slippery points it stands! Alas, on how uncertain wheels doth it
advance, and with what ambiguous success doth it unfold the
course of human things! A countless multitude of the Turks
would have perished, if the aforesaid attempt had been orderly
conducted; but to punish us for our sins, as it is believed, the
potter's wheel produces a paltry vessel instead of the grand
design which he had conceived.* For while they were treating of this point, and had come to the same decision about
charging the enemy, two knights, who were impatient of
delay, put everything in confusion. It had been resolved by
common consent that the sounding of six trumpets in three
different parts of the army should be a signal for a charge,
viz., two in front, two in the rear, and two in the middle, to
distinguish the sounds from those of the Saracens, and to mark
the distance of each. If these orders had been attended to,
the Turks would have been utterly discomfited; but from the
too great haste of the aforesaid knights, the success of the affair
was marred. They rushed at full gallop upon the Turks, and
each of them prostrated his man by piercing him with his
lance. One of them was the marshal of the Hospitallers, the

* The author here quotes Horace—"currente rotâ cur urceus exit."

other was Baldwin de Carreo, a good and brave man, and the
companion of King Richard, who had brought him in his
retinue. When the other Christians observed these two rushing forward, and heard them calling, with a clear voice,
on St. George for aid, they charged the Turks in a body
with all their strength; then the Hospitallers, who had
been distressed all day by their close array, following the
two soldiers, charged the enemy in troops, so that the
van of the army became the rear from their position in
the attack, and the Hospitallers, who had been the last,
were the first to charge. The count of Champagne also burst
forward with his chosen company, and James d'Avennes with
his kinsmen, and also Robert count of Dreux, the bishop
of Beauvais, and his brother, as well as the earl of Leicester,
who made a fierce charge on the left towards the sea. Why
need we name each? Those who were in the first line of the
rear made a united and furious charge; after them the men of
Poictou, the Bretons, and the men of Anjou, rushed swiftly
onward, and then came the rest of the army in a body: each
troop shewed its valour, and boldly closed with the Turks,
transfixing them with their lances, and casting them to the
ground. The sky grew black with the dust which was raised
in the confusion of that encounter. The Turks, who had purposely dismounted from their horses in order to take better
aim at our men with their darts and arrows, were slain on all
sides in that charge, for on being prostrated by the horse-
soldiers they were beheaded by the foot-men. King Richard, on
seeing his army in motion and in encounter with the Turks,
flew rapidly on his horse at full speed through the Hospitallers who had led the charge, and to whom he was bringing
assistance with all his retinue, and broke into the Turkish infantry, who were astonished at his blows and those of his men,
and gave way to the right and to the left. Then might be
seen numbers prostrated on the ground, horses without their
riders in crowds, the wounded lamenting with groans their
hard fate, and others drawing their last breath, weltering
in their gore, and many lay headless, whilst their lifeless
forms were trodden under foot both by friend and foe. Oh
how different are the speculations of those who meditate
amidst the columns of the cloister from the fearful exercise
of war! There the king, the fierce, the extraordinary king,

cut down the Turks in every direction, and none could
escape the force of his arm, for wherever he turned,
brandishing his sword, he carved a wide path for himself;
and as he advanced and gave repeated strokes with his sword,
cutting them down like a reaper with his sickle, the rest,
warned by the sight of the dying, gave him more ample space,
for the corpses of the dead Turks which lay on the face of the
earth extended over half a mile. In fine, the Turks were cut
down, the saddles emptied of their riders, and the dust which
was raised by the conflict of the combatants, proved very hurtful to our men, for on becoming fatigued from slaying so many,
when they were retiring to take fresh air, they could not recognize each other on account of the thick dust, and struck their
blows indiscriminately to the right and to the left; so that,
unable to distinguish friend from foe, they took their own
men for enemies, and cut them down without mercy. Thus
the Christians pressed hard upon the Turks, the latter gave
way before them: but for a long time the battle was doubtful;
they still exchanged blows, and either party strove for the
victory: on both sides were seen some retreating, covered with
wounds, while others fell slain to the ground. Oh, how many
banners and standards of various forms, and pennons and many-
coloured ensigns, might then be seen torn and fallen to the
earth ; swords of proved steel, and lances made of cane with
iron heads, Turkish bows, and maces bristling with sharp teeth,
darts and arrows, covering the ground, and missiles enough to
load twenty waggons or more! There lay the headless trunks
of the Turks who had perished, whilst others retained their
courage for a time until our men increased in strength, when
some of them concealed themselves in the copses, some climbed
up trees, and, being shot with arrows, fell with fearful groan
to the earth ; others, abandoning their horses, betook themselves by slippery foot-paths to the seaside, and tumbled headlong into the waves from the precipitous cliffs that were five
poles in height. The rest of the enemy were repulsed in so wonderful a manner, that for the space of two miles nothing could
be seen but fugitives, although they had before been so obstinate
and fierce, and puffed up with pride: but by God's grace their
pride was humbled, and they continued still to fly ; for when
our men ceased the pursuit, fear alone added wings to their
feet. Our army had been ranged in divisions when they

attacked the Turks ; the Normans and English also, who had
the care of the standard, came up slowly towards the troops
which were fighting with the Turks,—for it was very difficult to
disperse the enemy's strength, and they stopped at a short distance therefrom, that all might have a rallying point. On the
conclusion of the slaughter, our men paused ; but the fugitives,
to the number of twenty thousand, when they saw this, immediately recovering their courage, and armed with maces,
charged the hindmost of those who were retiring, and rescued
some from our men who had just struck them down. Oh how
dreadfully were our men then pressed! for the darts and
arrows, thrown at them as they were falling back, broke the
heads, arms, and other limbs of our horsemen, so that they
bent, stunned, to their saddle-bows ; but having quickly regained their spirits and resumed their strength, and thirsting
for vengeance with greater eagerness, like a lioness when her
whelps are stolen, they charged the enemy, and broke through
them like a net. Then you might have seen the horses with
their saddles displaced ; and the Turks, who had but just now
fled, returning, and pressing upon our people with the utmost
fury ; every cast of their darts would have told, had our men
kept marching, and not stood still in a compact immovable
body. The commander of the Turks was an admiral, by
name Tekedmus, a kinsman of the sultan, having a banner
with a remarkable device ; namely, that of a pair of breeches
carved thereon, a symbol well known to his men. He was a
most cruel persecutor, and a persevering enemy of the Christians ; and he had under his command seven hundred chosen
Turks of great valour, of the household troops of Saladin, each
of whose companies bore a yellow banner with pennons of a
different colour. These men, coming at full charge, with
clamour and haughty bearing, attacked our men who were
turning off from them towards the standard, cutting at them,
and piercing them severely, so that even the firmness of our
chiefs wavered under the weight of the pressure ; yet our men
remained immovable, compelled to repel force by force, and the
conflict grew thicker, the blows were redoubled, and the battle
raged fiercer than before : the one side laboured to crush, the
other to repel ; both exerted their strength, and although our
men were by far the fewest in numbers, they made havoc of
great multitudes of the enemy ; and that portion of the

R

army which thus toiled in the battle could not return to the
standard with ease, on account of the immense mass which
pressed upon them so severely; for thus hemmed in they began
to flag in courage, and but few dared to renew the attack of
the enemy.   In truth, the Turks were furious in the assault,
and greatly distressed our men, whose blood poured forth in
a stream beneath their blows.   On perceiving them reel and
give way, William de Barris, a renowned knight, breaking
through the ranks, charged the Turks with his men; and such
was the vigour of the onset that some fell by the edge of his
sword, while others only saved themselves by rapid flight.
For all that, the king, mounted on a bay Cyprian steed,
which had not its match, bounded forward in the direction of
the mountains, and scattered those he met on all sides; for the
enemy fled from his sword and gave way, while helmets
tottered beneath it, and sparks flew forth from its strokes.   So
great was the fury of his onset, and so many and deadly his
blows, that day, in his conflict with the Turks, that in a short
space of time the enemy were all scattered, and allowed our
army to proceed; and thus our men, having suffered somewhat, at last returned to the standard, and proceeded in
their march as far as Arsur, and there they pitched their tents
outside its walls.   While they were thus engaged, a large body
of the Turks made an attack on the extreme rear of our
army.   On hearing the noise of the assailants, King Richard,
encouraging his men to battle, rushed at full speed, with only
fifteen companions, against the Turks, crying out, with a loud
voice, " Aid us, O God! and the Holy Sepulchre!" and this
he exclaimed a second and a third time; and when our
men heard it, they made haste to follow him, and attacked,
routed, and put them to flight; pursuing them as far as
Arsur, whence they had first come out, cutting them down
and subduing them.   Many of the Turks fell there also.   The
king returned thence, from the slaughter of the fugitives, to
his camp; and the men, overcome with the fatigues and exertions of the day, rested quietly that night.   Whoever was
greedy of gain, and wished to plunder the booty, returned to
the place of battle, and loaded himself to his heart's desire; and
those who returned from thence reported that they had counted
thirty-two Turkish chiefs who were found slain on that day,
and whom they supposed to be men of great influence and power,

from the splendour of their armour and the costliness of their
apparel.   The Turks also made search for them to carry them
away, as being of the most importance; and besides these the
Turks carried off seven thousand mangled bodies of those who
were next in rank, besides of the wounded, who went off in
straggling parties; and when their strength failed, lay about
the fields and died.   But by the protection of God we did
not lose a tenth, nor a hundredth part so many as fell in the
Turkish army.   Oh the disasters of that day!   Oh the trials
of the warriors! for the tribulations of the just are many.   Oh
mournful calamity and bitter distress!   How great must have
been the blackness of our sins to require so fiery an ordeal to
purify it! for if we had striven to overcome this urgent
necessity by pious long-suffering, and without a murmur, the
sense of our obligations would have been deeper.

CH. XX.—*How the admirable knight James d'Avennes was slain in the
second encounter.*

BUT we had to mourn greatly the loss of James d'Avennes,
who was overpowered by the numbers of the Turks; for
he was thrown by a grievous fall of his horse, while bravely
fighting; and the Turks, gathering round him, after much
labour, put him to death.   But before breathing his last,
he slew fifteen of the Turks, according to the report of those
who were sent to bring his body to the camp, and who found
so many Turkish soldiers lying dead around him.   There
were also found dead along with him three of his kinsmen, to
whom some of our men did not give the assistance which
they ought; but, shame to say, deserted them in their struggle against the attack of the Turks, on which account the
count of Dreux and others who were present obtained the infamy and detestation which they deserved.   Alas for the manifold calamities of war!   How loud were the groans and
sighs of our soldiers on that night for the absence of James
d'Avennes, the excellent soldier and renowned warrior! for
they augured his fall, as they did not see him and his kinsmen
with the rest, and the whole army was afflicted by his ir-
reparable loss.   On the Saturday before the Nativity of the
Blessed Virgin Mary, the aforesaid battle was fought; and
on the Sunday following, it was decreed that a search should
be made for the body, in order that it might be buried.

Therefore, the Hospitallers and knights of the Temple armed themselves, and took with them many of the Turcopoli and others, and, on arriving on the field of battle, they made anxious search, and at last found the body, its face covered with clotted blood, so that it was difficult of recognition until it was washed with water, for it was dyed in gore and swollen with wounds, and very unlike his former self.   Thus, having decently wrapped up the body, they bore it back to Arsur, whence a great multitude of the soldiers came forth to meet it ; and all lamented the death of so great a man, for they called to mind his prowess, bounty, and the many virtues that adorned him, and King Richard and King Guy assisted at his funeral, where a solemn mass was celebrated, with large offerings, in the church of our Lady the Queen of Heaven, whose nativity it was.   After the mass, the funeral rites were solemnly performed, and the nobles, taking his body in their arms, buried it in a grave, erecting a mound thereon ; and there was great wailing, weeping, and lamentation for his death.   When the obsequies were ended, the clergy solemnly performed the service for the day, being that of the Blessed Virgin Mary.

CH. XXI.—*Of the rout of the Turks, who first turned their backs and then fled, and how they left all their baggage about the fields a prey to the Christians.*

Now the emirs and nobles of the Saracens, to whom Saladin had given great territories and riches, had been induced, by his deceitful words and high-flown language, to believe, that on that day, with the aid of Mahomet, he would utterly extirpate the Christians ; but the oracle of Mahomet deceived them, and their insolent boasting was repressed. For according to the report of those who saw it, you might trace the flight of the Turks through the mountains, on the day of battle, by the booty that was thrown aside, the dead horses and camels lying along the way, as they had fallen, and laden with heavy baggage; for the Turkish bowmen had fled from the face of the Christians, and retreated with all that was left them ; and on the day of battle, the more anxiously they hastened their flight, the more surely they failed, and perished, leaving behind them an immense quantity of spoil.   Such was the vigour of our men's last attack, that if the enemy had remained a little longer, and had not taken to flight, they would never again have been in fighting order, and the land would have been left for the Christians to occupy.

CH. XXII.—*Saladin reproaches and derides his men, who excuse themselves by praising King Richard and his troops, beyond all they had ever seen.*

THE sultan, hearing that his choice troops, in whom he had placed so much confidence, were routed in this manner by the Christians, was filled with anger and excitement; and calling together his admirals, he said to them, " Are these the deeds of my brave troops, once so boastful, and whom I have so loaded with gifts? Lo! the Christians traverse the whole country at their pleasure, for there is no one to oppose them. Where now are all their vaunts, those swords and spears with which they threatened to do such execution? where is that prowess which they promised to put forth against the Christians, to overthrow them utterly? They have fought the battle which they desired, but where is the victory they promised? They are degenerated from those noble ancestors who performed such exploits against the Christians, and whose memory will endure for ever. It is a disgrace to our nation, the most warlike in the world, thus to become as nothing in comparison with their glorious ancestors." The admirals held down their heads at these words; but one of them, named Sanscuns, of Aleppo, returned this answer:— " Most sacred Sultan, saving your majesty, this charge is unjust, for we fought with all our strength against the Franks, and did our best to destroy them: we met their fiercest attacks, but it was of no avail; they are armed in impenetrable armour which no weapon can pierce, so that all our blows fell as it were upon a rock of flint. And, further, there is one among their number superior to any man we have ever seen: he always charges before the rest, slaying and destroying our men: he is the first in every enterprise, and is a most brave and excellent soldier; no one can resist him or escape out of his hands: they call him MELECH RIC.* Such a king as he seems born to command the whole earth: what then could we do more against so formidable an enemy?"

* King Richard.

CH. XXIII.—*How Saladin destroyed all the fortresses. except Jerusalem, Crach, and Darum.*

SALADIN, in the heat of his indignation, called to him his brother Saphadin. "It is my wish," said he, "to try what reliance can be placed on my men in this extremity : go and destroy without delay the walls of Ascalon and Gundres, but deliver Darum into the custody of my people, to insure safety to those who pass that way.   But destroy also Galatia, Blancheward, Joppa, the castles of Plans, Maen, St. George, Ramula, Belmont, Toron, the castle of Ernald, Beauverie, and Mirabel : destroy, in short, all the mountain fortresses ; spare neither city, castle, nor fort, except Crach and Jerusalem." Saphadin obeyed these commands, and destroyed all these fortresses without delay.

CH. XXIV.—*The Turks with 15,000 men attack our men on the river Arsur, but without success.*

MEANWHILE, a powerful Saracen prince, named Caysac, urged Saladin to send scouts into the plains of Ramula to reconnoitre the movements of the Franks. "For I hope," added he, "if I have stanch troops, to be able to cut off the greater part of them, and to draw them into the narrow passes, that few of them shall be able to escape us." By his advice, Saladin ordered thirty of his principal admirals, each at the head of five hundred men, to occupy the banks of the river Arsur. Here, therefore, they kept guard, to prevent the Franks from passing. On Monday, the morrow of the Nativity of the Blessed Virgin, and the third day after the battle before mentioned, King Richard marched with his army to the Arsur. The Templars were in the rear, and marched with much order and circumspection, to guard against sudden attacks of the enemy ; but they reached the river without opposition. The Turks now, having kept close in their ambuscade, when the Christians came up, assailed the foremost of them with their javelins and arrows, but failing of success, retreated, and our men encamped that night on the Arsur. In the morning our infantry, who could hardly maintain the march, advanced with the quarter-masters to Joppa, which they found so entirely dismantled, that the army could not find lodgings in it. They therefore encamped in an olive-garden on the left side of the town, about three weeks after they left Acre.

Ch. XXV.—*How our ships brought us provisions from Acre to Joppa.*

THE army remained outside the walls of Joppa, and re-freshed themselves with abundance of fruits, figs, grapes, pomegranates, and citrons, produced by the country round: when lo! the fleet of King Richard, with other vessels, which accompanied the army and went to and fro between Joppa and Acre, brought us necessaries, much to the annoy-ance of the Turks, because they could not prevent them.

Ch. XXVI.—*How King Richard advised to save Ascalon from the Turks, who were dismantling it; but by the sinister counsels of the French they preferred to repair to Joppa, and indulged themselves there in vice and luxury.*

SALADIN, meanwhile, had destroyed the walls of Ascalon. This intelligence was brought by some common soldiers, who escaped, whilst it was in progress; but our people could hardly believe that Saladin had done this in despair, as if so powerful a prince could not or did not dare defend them. To ascertain the truth, King Richard, by advice of his nobles, sent Geoffrey de Lusignan, William de Stagno, and others, in a strong galley to sail to Ascalon, and bring back word how matters stood. This commission they faithfully discharged, and reported that all they had heard was true. King Richard, therefore, and his nobles now deliberated whether they should march to save Ascalon, or proceed at once to Jerusalem: many opinions were given, and the king gave his own, in the presence of the duke of Burgundy and others, in these words: "It seems to me," said he, "that our difference of opinion may be not only useless, but dangerous to the army. The Turks who are dismantling Ascalon, dare not meet us in the field. I think we should endeavour to save Ascalon, as a protection to the pilgrims who pass that way." The French violently opposed this opinion, and recommended rather that Joppa should be restored, because it furnished a shorter and easier route for pilgrims going to Jerusalem. The acclama-tions of the multitude seconded the opinion of the French. Foolish counsel! fatal obstinacy of those indolent men! By providing for their immediate comfort, and to avoid labour and expense, they did what they would afterwards repent of: for if they had then saved Ascalon from the Turks, the whole

land would soon have been clear of them. But the cry of the
people prevailed, a collection was made, and they immediately
began to rebuild the towers, and to clear out the moat of
Joppa. The army remained there long, enjoying ease and
pleasure; their sins grew daily upon them; women came to
them from Acre, to stir up their passions and multiply their
misdeeds: the whole people became corrupted, the zeal of
pilgrimage waxed cold, and all their works of devotion were
neglected.

CH. XXVII.—*How the people returned to Acre, where they spent
their time in taverns, and were led back by King Richard to Joppa,
where they remained seven weeks.*

It was now the end of September, and Joppa partly rebuilt, when the army, issuing from the suburbs, encamped
before the fortress of Habacuc; too small an army, alas! for
many of them had withdrawn to Acre, where they spent
their time in the taverns. King Richard, seeing their idleness and debauchery, sent King Guy to bring them back to
the army at Joppa, but very few of them returned, and King
Richard was obliged himself to sail to Joppa, where he urged
them by exhortations of their duty as pilgrims, and by these
means induced many of them to return to Joppa. He also
conducted back with him the queens and their females. They
now remained seven weeks at Joppa, to assemble and make
ready the army, so that when they came together, they formed
a much more numerous and efficient body than before.

CH. XXVIII.—*How King Richard went out unadvisedly with only a
small escort, and would have been taken by the Turks, if William de
Prateiles had not pretended to be the king, and so secured Richard's
escape.*

About this time King Richard went out hawking with a
small escort, and intending, if he saw any small body of Turks,
to fall upon them. Fatigued with his ride, he fell asleep,
and a body of Turks rushed suddenly upon him to make him
prisoner. The king, awakened at the noise, had hardly time
to mount his bay Cyprian horse, and his attendants were still
getting on their horses also, when the Turks came upon them
and tried to take him; but the king, drawing his sword,

rushed upon them, and they, pretending flight, drew him after them to a place where there was another body of Turks in ambush. These started up with speed and surrounded the king to make him prisoner. The king defended himself bravely, and the enemy drew back, though he would still have been captured if the Turks had known who he was. But in the midst of the conflict one of the king's companions, William de Pratelles, called out in the Saracenic language, that he was the "melech," *i. e.* the king; and the Turks, believing what he said, led him off captive to their own army. In this skirmish were slain Regnier de Marum, a brave knight, but almost unarmed, his nephew Walter, and Alan and Luke du Stable. At the news of this action our army was alarmed, and seizing their arms, came at full gallop to find the king, and when they met him returning safe, he faced about and with them pursued the Turks, who had carried off William de Pratelles, thinking they had got the king. They could not, however, overtake the fugitives, and King Richard, reserved by the divine hand for greater things, returned to the camp, to the great joy of his soldiers, who thanked God for his preservation, but grieved for William de Pratelles, who loyally redeemed the king at the price of his own liberty. Some of the king's friends now reproved him for his temerity, and entreated him not to wander abroad alone, and expose himself to be taken by the ambuscades of the Turks, who were especially eager to make him prisoner; but on all occasions to take with him some brave soldiers, and not to trust to his own strength against such numbers. But, notwithstanding these admonitions on the part of his best friends, the king's nature still broke out; in all expeditions he was the first to advance, and the last to retreat, and he never failed, either by his own valour or the divine aid, to bring back numbers of captives, or if they resisted, to put them to the sword.

CH. XXIX.—*King Richard and his army rebuild the forts of Plans and Maen, and repel the Turks who attack them.*

THE army seemed now by rest to have recovered their vigour, and a royal order was issued for them to march and rebuild the fortress of Plans, which was necessary for the

safety of the pilgrims who passed that way. The king therefore left a garrison in Joppa, with orders that none should
leave it besides merchants bringing provisions. The care of
the town was deputed to the bishop of Evreux, the count of
Chalons, 'Hugh Ribole, and others. On Wednesday, the
feast of All Saints, King Richard was riding in the plains of
Ramula, and seeing by chance some Turkish scouts, he
attacked them bravely, and put them all to the rout, slaying
some of them, and cutting off the head of a noble
Turkish admiral: the rest took to flight. The next day was
the eve of All Saints, and the army, after a short march,
encamped between the forts of Plans and Maen. The Turkish
army was then at Ramula, whence they frequently sallied to
attack us. The army remained fifteen days or more where
they were, during which time the king repaired the fort of
Maen, and the Templars rebuilt the fort of Plans, notwithstanding the attacks of the Turks, who one day assailed them
with an immense multitude of foot and a thousand cavalry; but the king mounting his horse in haste, and the
whole army being roused, the Turks fled, losing twenty in
slain, and sixteen taken prisoners. All the king's attempts to
overtake the others were ineffectual; he pursued them till he
came in sight of Ramula, and then led back his troops to the
camp.

CH. XXX.—*Of the wonderful victory of King Richard and his men, in
defending their men-at-arms who were foraging.*

ON the sixth day after the feast of All Saints, namely, on
the day of St. Leonard's, the esquires and men-at-arms went
out to get fodder for their horses and beasts of burthen. The
Templars were guarding the esquires whilst they dispersed
to find fresh herbage, a duty which sometimes cost them dear,
when they acted without much caution. Whilst the Templars
were thus engaged, about four thousand Turkish cavalry
rushed upon them from Bombrac, in four divisions, and in an
instant the Templars were surrounded by a multitude of
Turks, which was continually increasing. Acting with
promptitude according to the emergency, they dismounted,
and, standing back to back with their faces to the enemy,
defended themselves bravely. Three of them were slain in a
moment, but they still fought bravely, and a fierce conflict

ensued, as the Turks assailed them with the utmost fierceness,
and tried to take them all prisoners. On a sudden, news of
what was going on having been conveyed to the camp, Andrew
de Chamgui galloped up to the rescue with fifteen knights in
his train, and, attacking the Turks, liberated the Templars
from their dangerous position. Andrew bore himself like a
brave knight on that day, as well as his companions bore witness: but the Turks were continually receiving reinforcements,
and sometimes attacked, sometimes retreated, and the battle
still raged, until King Richard, who was busy in rebuilding
Maen, heard of the tumult, and sent the count de St. Paul and
the earl of Leicester to assist the Templars. With them, also,
went William de Cagen and Otho de Pransinges, and the
party soon heard the cries of the men-at-arms for assistance.
Then the king, exhorting the counts to get ready, seized his
arms, and followed them as fast as he was able. As the
counts were galloping onwards, about four thousand Turks
sprang up in four bodies, from the neighbourhood of a certain
river, and half of them attacked the Templars, whilst the
others assailed the two counts. The count of St. Paul then
made an unworthy proposition to the earl of Leicester, that
only one of them should fight with the enemy, whilst the
other should stand by to assist whenever it might be necessary. The earl of Leicester chose to attack the enemy, not
liking to stand by and do nothing. He at once, therefore,
charged the enemy, and rescued from their hands two of our
men whom they had made prisoners, and by his achievements
on that day added greatly to his former reputation. The conflict was raging fiercely when the king came up, and as his
retinue was very small, some of his men said to him, "My
lord, we do not think it prudent or possible, with our small
body, to resist this great multitude, nor shall we be able to
save our men who are fighting with the Turks. It is better
to let them perish, than to expose your person and all
Christendom to certain danger, whilst we have the power
of escaping." The king changed colour with indignation at
these words. "What!" said he, "if I neglect to aid my men
whom I sent forward with a promise to follow them, I shall
never again deserve to be called a king." He said no more,
but spurring his horse, dashed into the middle of the Turks,
overthrowing them on both sides of him, and brandishing his

sword, carved his way to and fro among the thickest ranks, slaying and maiming every one he came near.   Amongst others, he slew a Turkish admiral, named Aralchais, whom chance threw in his way.   In short, the enemy were put to the sword or took to flight, and our men returned with several prisoners to the camp.   This success was gained without any help from the French.   The same day three Turks, from fear of death perhaps, renounced their superstitions, and embracing Christianity, submitted to King Richard.

CH. XXXI.—*How Saladin amused King Richard by false promises, and thereby gained time to destroy certain fortresses.*

THE two castles before mentioned were now partly restored, and King Richard, perceiving that his troops not only hated the Turks, but had less fear of them than before, because they had always, with God's help, defeated them, even when superior in numbers, now sent a distinguished embassy to Saladin and Saphadin his brother, to demand the surrender of the kingdom of Syria, with all that belonged to it, such as the leprous king had last possessed it.   He demanded also tribute from Babylon, as the kings, his predecessors, had received it, together with all the privileges and dues which had at any time before belonged to the kingdom of Jerusalem. The ambassadors unfolded their message before Saladin, who would not, however, acquiesce in the demand.   " Your king," said he, "makes an unreasonable claim, and we cannot, with regard to the honour of Paganism, consent to it ; but I will offer to your king, through my brother Saphadin, to give up to him the whole land of Jerusalem, from Jordan to the sea, without tribute or hinderance, on condition that the city of Ascalon shall never be rebuilt, either by the Christians or the Saracens. When Saphadin came with this message to the king, Richard, who had just been bled, would not converse with him on that day ; but Stephen de Torneham, by the king's order, supplied him with every kind of delicacy for his table, and entertained him in the valley between the castles of the Temple and of Jehoshaphat.   The next day Saphadin sent a present of seven camels and a rich tent, and coming into the king's presence, delivered Saladin's message ; upon which Richard, considering the disturbances and uncertainties of war, determined to have patience for a time, that he might the better make provi-

sion for the future : but, alas! he shewed too little prudence
in not foreseeing the deceit with which they sought to pro-
tract the time until the cities, castles, and fortresses of that
country were destroyed. In short, Saphadin so cunningly
beguiled the too credulous king, that one would have thought
they had contracted a mutual familiarity; for the king
received Saphadin's gifts, and messengers were daily passing
with presents to the king, much to the annoyance of his
friends, who blamed him for contracting friendship with the
Gentiles. But Saphadin pleaded that he wished to make
peace between them, and the king thought he was adopting a
wise policy, by which the bounds of Christianity would be
enlarged, and a creditable peace concluded, particularly since
the departure of the French king, from whom he feared
treachery, for he had always found his friendship hollow and
deceitful. When, however, the king discovered that the
promises of Saphadin were mere words, and likely to produce
no result, particularly in the matter of Fort Erach of Mount
Royal, of which, according to the understood conditions, the
king demanded the demolition, but the Turks would not
consent to it, he at once broke off the negotiations. This
failure of the treaty becoming known, the enemy were soon
again to be seen on our flanks, and King Richard was again
in the field to meet them; and by way of wiping out the former charges which had been made against him, he brought
every day numbers of Turkish heads, to prove that his zeal
had not slackened in the cause of Christianity. The difficulties
thrown in his way, and accusations made against him, had
arisen from those who sought to obtain his money; for it is
rare to find persons not actuated by the desire of gain.

Ch. XXXII.—*Of the annoyance which our men experienced from the
rains and the enemy, whilst they encamped between St. George and
Ramula, and in the town of Ramula itself.*

When the two forts were repaired and garrisoned, Richard
moved his army towards Ramula; which caused Saladin to
order Ramula to be dismantled, because he did not dare
meet the king in the field. He then withdrew with his troops
towards Darum, because he had most confidence in the mountainous districts. Our troops then encamped between St.
George and Ramula, where they remained twenty-two days

waiting for reinforcements and provisions. There also we endured severe attacks from the enemy, and the heavy rains drove
the king of Jerusalem and our people to remove into St. George
and Ramula: the count of St. Paul went to the Castle of
the Baths. We stopped in Ramula seven weeks, not however in
ease, for we had a rough beginning, though it was afterwards
made amends for by a more pleasant termination. The Turks
would not allow us the least repose, but continually attacked
us with their javelins. On the eve of St. Thomas the Apostle,
King Richard had sallied forth with a small retinue towards a
fort called Whitecastle, on some enterprise against the Turks,
but foreboding something wrong, by inspiration as is thought
from heaven, he returned to the camp. The same hour he was
told that Saladin had a little before sent a body of three hundred of his choicest troops to Whitecastle, where Richard was
going. The same day also King Guy went to Acre, whither
he was followed the next day by Stephen de Torneham.
In the middle of the night of the Holy Innocents, the Hospitallers and Templars left the camp, and returned in the
morning with two hundred oxen, which they had driven off
from the mountains near Jerusalem.

Ch. XXXIII.—*Of the glorious victory gained by the earl of Leicester
against the Turks, when our men at last came to his assistance.*

The noble earl of Leicester, one day, followed by a few
men only, endeavoured to drive off a large body of Turks
who were passing by with much arrogance and boasting.
The enemy fled with precipitation, and were followed by three
of the swiftest knights in the earl's train: by this act of
imprudence they placed themselves in the power of the Turks,
who turned back and made them prisoners. The earl, seeing
this, spurred his horse and rode into the midst of more than a
hundred Turks, to rescue the knights. His men, following
him, pursued the enemy over a river, when a fresh force
of about five hundred Turkish cavalry charged them with
bows and lances of reed, and cutting off the retreat of the earl
and his small party, essayed to make him prisoner. Already
was Garin Fitz-Gerald dismounted and severely beaten with
the iron maces. A fierce struggle took place. Drogo de Fonte-
nille Putrell and Robert Nigel were unhorsed, and the Turks
made such exertions to seize the earl that at last they struck

him also from his horse, and almost drowned him in the river.
But the earl defended himself bravely, and dealt his blows
on every side of him, seconded by Henry Fitz-Nicholas and the
brave Robert de Newbury, whose generosity has gained for
him immortal renown; for, seeing the earl hard pressed, in
the midst of his enemies, and engaged in a doubtful contest,
he gave his own horse to the earl, whose safety he deemed
more important than his own.   Few I fear will be led
by his example to do the like, though evil deeds have an
abundance of imitators.   In this manner Robert by his noble
deed saved the earl's life and did not lose his own.   Besides
these, there were with the earl Count Ralph of St. Mary's,
Arnald du Bois, Henry de Mailoc, William and Saul de
Bruil; but what were they among so many?   However,
they defended themselves bravely; but the valour of so few
could do little against such numbers, and as fresh Turks continually came up, they were unable to fight any more, but
holding by the necks of their horses, bore unmoved the blows
which fell upon them.   Thus, as if lost to feeling, they were
led off prisoners towards Darum.   But how good is it to trust
in the Lord, who does not suffer any one to be tempted beyond
what he can bear!   Our army had heard of the skirmish,
and, seizing their arms, were already on the spot: they assail,
vanquish, and rout the Turks.   Andrew de Chamgui, Henry
de Gray, Peter de Pratelles, and other brave men, kill each
his man, the first that came in their way.   The Turk whom
Peter de Pratelles and his companion encountered, was so
powerful that they could not take him prisoner, and had
much trouble to vanquish and slay him.   Andrew de Chamgui
also ran an admiral through the body with his lance; and he
fell, never to lead his men to battle more; but, ere he fell, had
pierced Andrew's arm with his lance of cane.   The Turks,
roused by his fall, rushed to save him, but it was all over with
him, and the infidels turned their rage and their steel-tipped
canes against the Christians.   They would, even now, have
gained the day, if our men had not been reinforced from the
camp.   The battle raged fiercely: the earl was at one time
attacked by the enemy, at another assailing them in turn;
with one blow he cut off their heads, so that a second stroke
was unnecessary.   Two horses were slain under him, and it
may be truly said of him, that so small a man never per-

formed such brave deeds. So many of the best soldiers
sallied from the camp to assist him, that not one of them was
slain, but they repulsed the Turks and pursued them, until,
fatigued with their exertions, they returned quietly to the
camp.

CH. XXXIV.—*Of the annoyances which our soldiers experienced from the
rain and the attacks of the enemy as they marched by Betenoble towards
Jerusalem.*

IN the mean time it became known to Saladin that our
men were preparing to attack Jerusalem, and were only two
miles distant from him ; but, not thinking it safe to fight with
the Christians, he gave orders to destroy Darum, its walls and
towers, and retreated himself to Jerusalem. The Turks, also,
in general left the plains and withdrew to the mountains. In
consequence of this, our men were commanded by voice of
herald to move towards the foot of the mountains, and, when
all the arrangements were completed, they marched towards a
castle called Betenoble. Then the rain and hail began to beat
upon our men, and killed many of their beasts of burthen : the
storm was so violent that it tore up the pegs of the tents,
drowned the horses, and spoiled all their biscuit and bacon.
The armour and coats of mail, also, were so rusted, that the
greatest labour was necessary to restore them to their former
brightness : their clothes were dissolved by the wet, and the
men themselves suffered from the unwonted severity of the
climate. Under all these sufferings, their only consolation
arose from their zeal in the service of God, and a desire to
finish their pilgrimage. To this end each contributed his
share of provisions for the siege, and they came together with
joy prepared for any pilgrimage. Even those who were sick
in bed at Joppa, were carried in litters, so great was their
wish to see Jerusalem. A large number of them, also, were
influenced by a desire to see our Lord's tomb, and this was
their only hope under their great sufferings. But the Turks,
paying no regard to these convoys of the sick, lay in wait for
them and killed both them and their bearers, looking on them
all as enemies alike. But, surely, these are all to be accounted
martyrs, and there is this consolation for them, that though
the Turks slew them with evil intentions, yet they suffered b ut
f ; a moment, and gained the reward of a long service.

CH. XXXV.—*How the army prepare with joy to march on Jerusalem, neglecting the advice of the Templars and other wise men who dissuaded them.*

THE army now rejoiced that they should soon set eyes on our Lord's sepulchre; and all began to brighten up their armour, their helmets and their swords, that there might not be a single spot to spoil their brightness. In short, all were most eager for the enterprise, and boasted that not all the power or assaults of the hostile Saracens should prevent them from accomplishing their plighted vow. But the wiser ones did not acquiesce in these views; for the Templars, Hospitallers, and Pisans, who had sharper eyes on the future condition of that land, dissuaded King Richard from marching at present to Jerusalem, lest, whilst they were besieging Saladin and the garrison of that city, the Turkish army, which was without among the mountains, might attack our men by surprise, and so place them between the attacks of the garrison from within, and the Turkish army from without: and even if they should take the city, it would be necessary to garrison it with some of their bravest troops, which could hardly be done, in consequence of the people's eagerness to complete their pilgrimage and return each to his own home, for they were now all tired out with the privations and disturbances which they had suffered. For these reasons, they advised that the siege should be delayed, and the army be kept together, because their vow would not have been accomplished; for if they could once fulfil their pledge, the army would at once be dissolved. But the advice of the Templars was not listened to.

CH. XXXVI.—*How King Richard, concealing his troops near the Castle of the Baths, surprised and slew the Turks on his march towards Jerusalem.*

IT was now the beginning of a new year, A. D. 1192, being leap-year, and having D for its Dominical letter. On the third day after our Lord's circumcision, the army, bent on their march, were assailed by a multitude of Turks who had lain in ambush during the night near the fort des Plans among the bushes on the line of their route. The two foremost of our men were instantly slain; but God had already prepared to avenge their death, for King Richard had been apprised of the ambuscade, and advanced with all speed in the morning, hoping to rescue the advanced guard. But the Turks who had beheaded them, recognizing the king's banner, took to flight, being about a hundred in number, of whom seven were either killed or taken prisoners by the king in the pursuit. Eighty of the Turks fled towards Mirabel, and were speedily overtaken by the king, who, seated on his bay horse, a charger of incomparable swiftness, slew two of them before any of their friends could assist them. In this skirmish were Geoffrey de Lusignan and some others, who either slew or made prisoners twenty Turks, and if they had pursued them further, there is no doubt that they would have taken many more.

BOOK V.

Ch. I.—*By the advice of the Templars, though much against the inclinations of the army, the march to Jerusalem was abandoned until the walls of Ascalon should first be rebuilt.*

In the year 1192, not many days after the feast of the Epiphany, the councillors of the army, joining with them some of the more discreet of the natives, again consulted about the march to Jerusalem. The Hospitallers, Templars, and Pisans, urged, as before, that the city of Ascalon should first be rebuilt as a check on the Turkish convoys between Babylonia and Jerusalem. To this the majority of the council gave their assent, that Ascalon should be rebuilt to check the arrogance and impede the free passage of the Turks in those parts. When the decision became known the army were much dejected, conceiving that their hopes of seeing the Lord's sepulchre would altogether be frustrated. Their former hilarity altogether disappeared, and was succeeded by despair at what they had just heard. They uttered imprecations on the authors of this counsel as destroyers of all their most ardent wishes. If, however, they had known the penury and destitution of those who dwelt in Jerusalem, they would have derived some little consolation from the tribulation of the enemy. For the Turks in Jerusalem were enduring many severe sufferings from the hail and snow, which, melting in the mountains, caused a flood of water to descend upon the city,

either drowning their cattle, or causing them to perish afterwards from the cold.   So great were their sufferings from the
state of the weather, that if the Christians had known of
them they might certainly have taken the city; though they
could not long have kept it, for the people would have returned home after fulfilling their vow of pilgrimage, and there
could not have been a sufficient garrison left to defend it.

CH. II.—*Of the despondency of the army at the abandonment of their
enterprise, and of their return to Ramula.*

THE feast of St. Hilary was now at hand, and so great was
the disaffection and sorrow of the army that many of them
abandoned their pilgrimage, cursing the day in which they
were born to suffer such a disappointment.   Some of them
also were so worn down by their sufferings and by want, that
they with difficulty could bear up against it.   Their horses
and beasts of burden, also, affected by the cold and rain, were
unable to proceed through the mud, but fell famished and
knocked up beneath their loads.   The drivers, in bitterness of
spirit, raised their hands in anguish to heaven, and uttered
imprecations approaching even to blasphemy. It was impossible
to conceive a severer lot, even in the worst of criminals, than that
which our men now suffered.   Their brave deeds, their prowess
in war, were now succeeded by grief and despair of mind, in
addition to their bodily sufferings ; and whilst all were in this
state, the weak and sick would have been in danger of perishing, if it had not been for the care of King Richard, who sent
out messengers on all sides to collect them together and bring
them to Ramula, where the whole army soon assembled, not
long after they had left it.

CH. III.—*Of the tribulation and anguish which our men endured between
Ramula and Ascalon, from the dangers of the roads and the state of
the weather, and how many of the French left the army.*

WHILST our men remained at Ramula, many of them, either
to avoid the painful march, or from indignation and obstinacy,
deserted from the army, thereby considerably diminishing its
numbers.   The greater part of the French departed out of
indignation ; some of them went to enjoy their ease at Joppa,
others retired to Acre, where there was plenty of provisions. Some joined the marquis at Tyre, as he had often urged

s 2

them to do, others, with the duke of Burgundy, from anger
and indignation turned aside to the fort des Plans, where
they remained eight days. King Richard, angry at the
situation in which things were, proceeded with his nephew,
Henry Count of Champagne, and the army thus reduced in its
numbers, towards Ibelin; but they found the roads so muddy
that it was necessary to halt there, that the army might have
rest; for their misery, both mental and bodily, was so great
that no pen can write, nor tongue tell it. At dawn of day
the men with the tents were sent forwards, and the rest of the
army followed; the sufferings of the day before were nothing
to those which they now endured from fatigue, rain, hail,
and floods, so that it might be thought all heaven had conspired to destroy them. The ground, too, was muddy and
soft beneath them, and the horses and men had the greatest
difficulty to maintain their footing: some of them sunk, never
to rise again. Who can tell the calamities of that day? The
bravest of the soldiers shed tears like rain, and were wearied
even of their very existence for the severity of their sufferings. When the beasts of burden fell, the provisions which
they carried were either spoiled by the mud, or dissolved in
the water. In this manner, cursing the day on which they
were born, and beating their breasts with their hands, they
reached Ascalon, which they found so dismantled by the
Saracens that they could scarcely enter through its gates for
the heaps of stones. This day was the 20th of January, and
they encamped for the night, every man as well as he was
able.

Ch. IV.—*How the army suffered at Ascalon from the weather and want of
provisions.*

THE city of Ascalon lies on the coast of the Grecian sea,
and, if it had a good harbour, could hardly find an equal for
its situation and the fertility of the adjoining country. It
has indeed a port, but one so difficult of access, owing to the
stormy weather in which the army reached it, that for eight
days no vessel could enter it; so that our troops and their
horses, who were greatly in want of provisions, could get nothing for eight days, except what they had brought with them;
for it was not safe, on account of the Turks, to forage for
provisions in the neighbouring country. At last, when the

weather became more favourable, some ships entered the harbour with provisions: but the storm again came on, and the army began again to be in want ; for some barges and galleys, loaded with provisions, perished on the voyage with all their crews: the snakes also, belonging to the king and others, were broken by the storm ; and the king made long vessels out of their materials, vainly imagining that they would serve to cross the sea.

CH. V.—*Saladin, hearing of the return and dispersal of our army, sends his men to their homes until May.*

SALADIN, hearing that our troops were dispersed along the sea-coast, and in part broken up, dismissed his troops to return to their homes, and attend to their domestic affairs, with orders to assemble again in the month of May. The Turks, who had now for four years been serving laboriously in the Sultan's army, now gladly return to see their wives and families. There their admirals and princes, men of renown, recapitulated their adventures, and the disastrous campaigns which they had gone through: men who before had always came off victorious, and got abundance of spoil from all their former wars ; but now, on the contrary, they had suffered both in their own property and by the deaths of their relations slain in the battles which they had fought. They, in particular, grieved for the fate of those princes, admirals, and others, who had been slain by King Richard, as before related, in the siege of Acre, when Saladin failed in his promise to redeem them. For this reason they had conceived bitter anger against Saladin, and now left his army for a time with groans and lamentations.

CH. VI.—*King Richard persuades as many of the French as he can to return, and, by common consent, they rebuild Ascalon.*

THE month of January was now ended, and the sky was becoming brighter. The king, annoyed at the dispersal of the army, sent messengers to persuade the French to return, and so strengthen the army that they might be in a condition for further deliberations. " For," said he, " it is desirable that all the army should be together when we deliberate, for division will only weaken us, and expose us to the attacks of our enemies." The French by these arguments were led to promise that they would rejoin the army until Easter, on condition that they should have leave to depart, and safe conduct at that time, if they should wish it. The king, seeing that it was necessary to use forbearance, assented to these conditions, and the army was thus reunited. It was now agreed by all to rebuild Ascalon; but the princes and nobles were so exhausted, that they found their means insufficient for the purpose. They, nevertheless, began the work as well as they could, and dividing it out amongst them, they dug to the foundations of one of the chief gates, until they came to solid masonry, and removed the rubbish that was lying on the top. All engaged in the work: princes, nobles, knights, esquires, and retainers, might be seen tossing the stones from hand to hand. There was no distinction made between clerks and laymen; nobles and plebeians, princes and their attendants, all worked alike, so that they were even themselves astonished at their own progress. Masons were then brought, the work went on with double vigour, and the walls rose rapidly. Fifty-three of the highest and strongest towers, besides other smaller ones, had been levelled with the ground. Five of these towers had received names from their founders; according to tradition, the first and most powerful, was Ham, the son of Noah, who had thirty two sons: these all reigned after him, and built Ascalon, with the help of the people whom they invited together from all the country under their dominion; and to gain their favour, and a lasting name to themselves, the females built the tower which is called the tower of the "maidens." In the same way the soldiers built the tower of the "shields:" the "Bloody tower" was so called because founded by certain criminals, who, by this work, are said to have saved their lives from the punishment due to their crimes: the fourth tower was erected by the admirals, and is therefore called the "Admirals' tower:" the fifth, called the "Bedouins' tower," was constructed by the race of men bearing that name. Such are the five principal towers of Ascalon, named from their founders. When skilful masons were employed upon it, the work advanced more rapidly. The king, as in all other matters, was conspicuous in promoting the work; and by joining therein with his own hands, encouraging the men, and distributing to each their allotted tasks, he rendered great service. For, at his exhortation, each of the nobles and chiefs undertook the completion of his share in proportion to his means ; and if any one desisted from the work for want of money, the king, more exalted still in heart than in outward dignity, gave to them from his own purse as he knew each had need. And such was his approval and encouragement of the workmen, such his diligence and expenditure, that three-fourths of the city of Ascalon were said to have been rebuilt by his means.

CH. VII.—*How King Richard rescued from the Turks at Darum* 12,000 *Christian captives, who were on their way to Babylon.*

MEANWHILE Saladin had made preparations for sending 12,000 Christians, French, and natives of the Holy Land, captives to Babylon ; and his servants had brought them as far as Darum, and were spending the night there, with the intention of setting forward on their journey on the morrow ; when it happened, by the dispensation of God, that they were rescued by King Richard from slavery. For one day the king chanced to be out, with a chosen body of soldiers, reconnoitering the fortress of Darum, to ascertain how he could take it ; for there was a passage there too convenient for the Turks, who brought provisions from Babylon to Jerusalem. The Turks, who had arrived just before sunset, recognizing the king by his banner, became frightened for their lives, and consulting their own safety, let themselves quickly into the tower of the fort, leaving their captives outside ; and these persons, on seeing this, took refuge with all speed in a church close by. The king, coming up, released them without a moment's delay, and let them go away uninjured ; whilst he and his men slew many Turks, who happened to fall in their way. Then the king took many valuable horses, and captured twenty of the Turkish chiefs alive. Who can doubt but that the king's coming, which turned out so advantageous to those captives, was ordained of God ? Had he not come and rescued them, there is no doubt they would have been condemned to perpetual slavery.

CH. VIII.—*How King Richard sent an order to the marquis and was not obeyed.*

AFTER performing these exploits, King Richard sent messengers to the marquis, whom we have so often already men-

tioned, as he had done many times before, bidding him come
to Ascalon to join in the campaign for the kingdom to which
he aspired; and this he charged him to do by the oath which
he had taken to the king of France, who was a pledge for his
fidelity; but the base marquis replied, with a perverse sneer,
that he would on no account stir unless King Richard first
gave him a meeting. They afterwards held a conference by
appointment at the fort of Ymbric.

Ch. IX.—*How the duke of Burgundy, who had been recalled by King
Richard to Ascalon, again left him, and retired to Acre, because the
king would not lend him money.*

WHILE, therefore, the king and his army were diligently
engaged in the restoration of the walls of Ascalon, a quarrel took place between King Richard and the duke of
Burgundy; for the provisions, being for the most part
consumed, and the substance of each man almost brought
to nothing, the French began to importune the duke of
Burgundy for the pay which was owing to them, alleging that if they were not paid, they could not serve any
longer in the camp. The duke, not being able to meet their
pressing demands, thought it best to ask King Richard to
supply him with a large sum of money. For, on a former
occasion, as before said, the king, at the duke's request, lent
the French an immense sum of money at Acre, which was to
be repaid out of the ransom-money from the captives; but
this had turned out to be nothing, as the captives had paid
no other ransom than their heads; wherefore King Richard
refused his application. It was owing to this, and other
causes of disagreement, that the duke left Ascalon; and for
all his inability to pay them, the French set out hastily with
him towards Acre.

Ch. X.—*How the Pisans at Acre, who favoured King Guy, fought
with the Genoese, who sided with the marquis and the French, and how
they threw the duke of Burgundy from his horse, and compelled
him and the marquis to flee to Tyre; and how they sent for King
Richard, who made peace between them.*

ON their arrival at Acre, the French found the Pisans and
Genoese engaged in a fierce conflict with each other. For
the Pisans, from mere generosity, and a sense of the justice of
his cause, were favourers of King Guy, while the Genoese

were on the side of the marquis,—chiefly on account of the
oath of fidelity by which he was bound to the king of France.
Hence arose discords which ended in bloodshed, and mutual
attacks, as in a civil war, at Acre; and the whole city was
in a state of confusion. On approaching the city the French
heard a great uproar, and the noise of the people, exhorting
each other to fight; upon which they, and the duke of Burgundy, in full armour, hastened to give succour to the
Genoese, who were elated to an insolent pitch by their arrival. For all that, the Pisans, irritated when they saw them
coming, went forth boldly to meet them; for their appearance
was that of men disposed to fight. Falling upon the duke of
Burgundy, who seemed to be their leader, they surrounded
him, and having pierced his horse with a lance, threw him to
the ground; they then retreated to the city, and closed and
bolted the gates, as a precaution against any unforeseen acci-
dents which might happen. For they had heard that the
Genoese had sent to the marquis to ask him to come as
quickly as possible, and seize the city of Acre, which they
promised to deliver over to him. The Pisans, therefore, took
every precaution against this faction, for their own safety and
that of the city. The marquis, without a moment's delay,
came to Acre in his galleys, with a large number of armed
men, in the hope of seizing on the city unawares; and on
their arrival, the Pisans attacked them manfully with petrariæ and mangonels; and confiding in their own valour,
and the justice of their cause, they resisted their adversaries
for three days, and fought bravely with them, until they
sent a message to King Richard to inform him of the state
of affairs, and bid him come with all speed. The king was
then at Cæsarea, on his way to the conference with the marquis, when the messengers arrived, and set forth the whole
matter, and asked of him on the part of the Pisans, to come
quickly and preserve the city: they then returned to Acre
under favour of the darkness of the night. The marquis, on
hearing that King Richard was close at hand, returned
hastily to Tyre, as if conscious that the king's coming be-
tokened ill to himself. For all his haste, the duke of Burgundy and the French reached Tyre first. But King Richard,
on learning the confused state of things on his arrival at
Acre, took upon himself to arrange everything on the day

after Ash Wednesday, as if he were the only man left in
the place; and having called the people together, he persuaded
them, with most convincing arguments, that nothing was
more commendable, amongst comrades, than friendship, nothing pleasanter than good fellowship, or sweeter than peace
and concord, or more lasting than unity; and, on the contrary, that nothing was more dangerous to the continuance of
peace, or more pernicious than ill-will, for it loosened the
bonds of affection: in fine, that whatever was bound by
mutual charity, and strengthened by the graceful ties of
friendship, was always dissolved by the fermentations of
envy. By means of such arguments, King Richard reconciled
the Genoese and Pisans, and caused them to unite in harmony and concord, and re-established their former good
understanding

CH. XI.—*How King Richard held a conference with the marquis at the
castle of Ymbric, and admonished him to return and join the army;
and how, on his refusing, he disinherited him of the lands and revenues
which had been promised to him.*

KING RICHARD, having pacified them in this manner, sent
a messenger to the marquis to return to the conference at
Ymbric, and try if they could, with the help of the divine
grace, come to an amicable understanding about the arrangement of affairs, in order that the government of the kingdom
might be the better administered by their joint efforts. They
therefore met, and held a long conference, but to little purpose. The marquis brought forward, as a pretext for not
performing his duty, the retirement of the duke of Burgundy and the French; and returning to Tyre, concealed
himself in his wife's chambers, away from camps and war.
King Richard, perceiving that the duke of Burgundy and
the marquis, as well as the French, had now voluntarily
absented themselves from the army, and reflecting deeply on
the terms of peace which had been agreed upon, hesitated
for a long time in his mind what it was best to do under
the circumstances, and took into his counsel the leaders and
more discreet men of the army, to ascertain what they thought
most expedient; and they, after carefully weighing the merits
of the whole matter, adjudged that the marquis had forfeited
his claim to the kingdom which had been promised him,

and that, in consequence of his doubtful and prevaricating conduct, he should be deprived of all his revenues. In consequence of this decision, great discord arose between the nobles of the French and King Richard, and especially between him and the marquis; who, as he had often done before, importuned all the French to quit Ascalon, and come to him at Tyre; thus throwing the kingdom and country into such a state of confusion, that King Richard, fully aware of his treachery, remained in Acre from the day after Ash Wednesday until the Tuesday before Easter. For it is the part of a prudent man to take precautions even against an humble foe.

CH. XII.—*How, while King Richard was at Acre, our men at Joppa and Ascalon made an expedition and brought back an immense booty; and how King Richard knighted Saphadin's son.*

ON the third day, before Palm Sunday, a number of young men at Joppa went on an expedition as far as Mirabel; and carried off a large booty of cattle from the Saracens, thirty of whom they killed, and brought back fifty alive, besides an immense spoil. A moiety of it was given to the count, who was governor of the city; the other moiety was sold for eight thousand Saracenic bezants, of good money. Likewise, on the morrow, which was the Saturday before Palm Sunday, all those at Ascalon who had horses made an expedition, and scoured the whole country, as we were told by those who were present, as far as Egypt, four miles beyond Darum; and having collected a large number of cattle, horses, and mares, also twenty asses, thirty camels, and seventy sheep, and other cattle, they formed in a body and returned with all speed to Ascalon, bringing back also with them 200 Saracens, with their wives and children. On Palm Sunday, King Richard, amid much splendour, girded with the belt of knighthood the son of Saphadin, who had been sent to him for that purpose.

CH. XIII.—*How the duke of Burgundy and the marquis, from envy at the successes of King Richard, recalled the French, who were with him at Ascalon and Joppa.*

MEANWHILE, the duke of Burgundy and the marquis, inflamed with envy, which is always jealous of the virtues of a superior, sent ambassadors from Tyre to Ascalon, to charge the residue of the French who remained to come to them at Tyre as quickly as possible, and join in their new schemes and designs, and that they should act together in common concert, in accordance with their former oath of allegiance to the king of France. Then the treachery and premeditated faithlessness with which the marquis had, from the first, himself entered into treaty with the king of France, became manifest; which was, that the marquis should join the French to his party, in order to expedite the accomplishment of his own plans. Hence he strove to withdraw the French, as if they were bound to his service, in order that King Richard might be the less able to carry on the war.

CH. XIV.—*How King Richard returned to Ascalon, and how 700 of the French soldiers, in obedience to the commands of the duke of Burgundy and the marquis, left the king and went to Tyre.*

ON the Tuesday before Easter, King Richard returned to the army at Ascalon, exceedingly sorrowful and disturbed. On the morrow, i. e. Wednesday, the leaders of the French requested of the king to furnish them, according to agreement, with an escort and safe conduct; and the king consenting, assigned to them the Templars, to conduct them on their journey, as well as the Hospitallers, and Count Henry of Champagne, and many others, as their comrades. The king also, anxious to omit no proper mark of attention, escorted them on their way in person; while he entreated them, with tears and soothing words, to stay a little longer with him, and that they should be provided for at his expense if they would succour the Holy Land in its desolation, to the utmost of their power. This, however, they absolutely refused, so he let them go away, and returned to Ascalon; whence he sent messengers at full speed to Acre, to charge the garrison not to admit the French within the city to lodge, but yet not to offer them any insult or annoyance, from which offence might be taken, or an occasion of dispute: so when the French arrived there, they stationed themselves outside the city.

CH. XV.—*How Saladin, hearing of the departure of the French, summoned his army together again.*

THUS on the day of our Lord's Supper the army was dejected at the departure of the French, for it lost no

small portion of its strength thereby, as 700 French knights
had left, men of tried valour and great activity, and the
people were in consequence thrown into much tribulation.
But the Turks were rejoiced on hearing what had taken
place; and Saladin, when he was told of it, sent messengers on horseback to carry letters, addressed to all the admirals and people throughout his dominions, charging them
by edict to lay aside every occupation, and come to the land of
Jerusalem with all speed. "The French," he said, "have,
from ill will, departed, and left the land almost without a
defender, and the strength of the war and the power of
the Christian army are fallen; wherefore we trust that in a
short time we shall gain possession of Acre and Tyre, the
chief cities of the land." The Turks returned at the command of the Soldan, but with less readiness, and in smaller
bodies than before; for they had not forgotten the past: in
comparison, however, with our paucity of numbers, they exceeded us greatly in strength.

CH. XVI.—*How fire from heaven, as usual, lighted the lamp at the
Holy Sepulchre, in the sight of Saladin; and how he had it extinguished three times, and how it was three times relighted.*

ON Easter Eve, Saladin, with his retinue, paid a visit to the
Holy Sepulchre of our Lord, to assure himself of the truth of
a certain fact, namely, the coming down from Heaven of fire,
once a year, to light the lamp. After he had watched for
some time, with great attention, the devotion and contrition
of many Christian captives, who were praying for the mercy of
God, he and all the other Turks suddenly saw the divine fire
descend, and light the lamp, so that they were vehemently
moved, while the Christians rejoiced, and with loud voices
praised the mighty works of God. But the Saracens disbe-
lieved this manifest and wonderful miracle, though they witnessed it with their own eyes, and asserted that it was a fraudulent contrivance. To assure himself of this, Saladin ordered the
lamp to be extinguished; which, however, was instantly re-
kindled by the divine power: and when the infidel ordered it
to be extinguished a second time it was lighted a second time;
and so likewise a third time. God is all-patient. Of what use
is it to fight against the invincible Power? There is no
counsel against God, nor is there any one who can resist

his will. Saladin, wondering at this miraculous vision, and the faith and devotion of the Christians, and exceedingly moved, asserted by the spirit of prophecy, that he should either die or lose possession of the city of Jerusalem. And his prophecy was fulfilled ; for he died the Lent following.

Ch. XVII.—*How King Richard celebrated Easter Sunday at Ascalon.*

King Richard celebrated the feast of Easter, which fell on the fifth of April, at Ascalon, with great magnificence; and he supplied all who needed with abundance of meat and drink. For he caused his pavilions to be pitched in the meadows outside the city, and provided in abundance every necessary for his people to celebrate the occasion with splendour. Nothing, however, was there to be seen more glorious than the ready good-will with which these bounties were dispensed, for courage in action always goes hand in hand with liberality ; and where nobleness of heart harmonizes with deeds of renown,—

> " The stingy mind suits not the bounteous hand,
> But rather checks its givings ; let each gift
> Be e'er attended with a generous heart."

Ch. XVIII.—*How the rebuilding of Ascalon is completed at the king's expense.*

On Easter Monday, King Richard returned with diligence to the work which he had commenced, and continued with all eagerness the rebuilding of the city walls, and familiarly urged the rest to proceed in the work ; so that by his care and co-operation it was all accomplished at his own expense, and without the contributions of the French, who had departed and who ought by right to have shared in the burden.

Ch. XIX.—*How King Richard set out to reconnoitre Gaza and Darum.*

On Easter Tuesday, the king set out with a few followers to reconnoitre Gaza. On the Wednesday he set out to make a close survey of Darum, walking round, and trying to ascertain the best point of assault. But the Turks shut themselves up in Darum, and threw out many missiles from bows and arbalists with much abuse at the king and his men, as if the place were impregnable. When the king had fully surveyed it, he returned to Ascalon.

CH. XX.—*How the French, who were recalled to Tyre, amused them-selves only in luxury and taverns.*

AFTER the French had departed, as aforesaid, those who had been charged by the king to conduct them as far as Acre returned to the camp at Ascalon; but the French, arriving at Tyre, gave themselves up to all kinds of amuse-ments, which we may think worth while here to mention. The very men who were supposed to have been led by their devotion to succour the Holy Land, now left the camp and abandoned themselves to amatory and effeminate songs and debaucheries, for, as was told by those who saw them, they delighted in dancing-women; and their luxurious apparel be-spoke their effeminacy, for the sleeves of their garments were fastened with gold chains, and they wantonly exposed their waists, which were confined with embroidered belts; and they kept back with their arms their cloaks, which were fastened so as to prevent a wrinkle being seen in their gar-ments; and that which was once intended to cover their back, was now forced into the service of other parts of the body, for their bellies, not their backs, were covered by their cloaks; and around their necks they wore collars glittering with jewels, and on their heads garlands interwoven with flowers of every hue: they carried goblets, not falchions, in their hands, and after spending whole nights in drinking and carousing, they went, heated with wine, to the houses of prostitutes, and if by chance they were preoccupied, and the door closed against them, they pulled it down, giving utterance to language and oaths which horrified those who heard them, as is well known from the habits of the French. In a word, their external condition proved their inward levity. Shame on the French for indulging in such excesses! We do not assert that all were guilty of this folly, for there were some who were much concerned at their dissolute habits, and sorry for their discord with King Richard.

CH. XXI.—*How the discord which arose between the Christians, who were now come to the Holy Land, never occurred amongst the ancients.*

THE great King Charlemagne, famous for his deeds and the subjugation of so many kingdoms to his authority, when he set out for the conquest of Spain is said never to have suffered a quarrel to occur in his army. Such was the case

also when he made his expedition against Saxony, where he
performed so many exploits and utterly subdued the famous
Wercelin.* Likewise, when he went from Rome to give
battle to that powerful warrior, Aguland, who had landed at
Pisa, a city of Calabria, with a large body of Saracens, which
would have been invincible but for the divine aid, no discord
ever took place in his army. So also, in the land of Jerusalem, shattered by so many wars, during which so much
slaughter of the enemy was made, and so many battles were
successfully fought, wherever of yore we read of famous
deeds of arms being carried on, there was no quarrel to divide
the army who served under one general, no factious ill-will
to disunite the people of different nations who formed it, nor
did jealousy distract those who were under the guidance of
one prince, nor was reviling or insulting language heard of
amongst them,—nay, they shewed each other every honour
and kindness, and they were called one people on account
of their unity, amongst whom no contention could last long.
This was the reason why the French prevailed in those days
over all foreigners, and so likewise should we moderns imitate
with advantage the example of the ancients.

CH. XXII.—*How the prior of Hereford was sent to the Holy Land.*

WHEN Easter was over, and the season for crossing the sea
came on, the prior of Hereford, an English priory, came with
a message for King Richard which put the whole army in
commotion. The prior brought letters from William, bishop
of Ely, the king's chancellor, informing him that he and the
others whom King Richard had deputed to govern the
country in his absence, had been insolently expelled from
the fortresses of the kingdom, and some of their party killed
in the riots; also, that by the agency of the king's brother,
Earl John, the chancellor, had been driven from England;
that there was no more money in the king's treasury or any
where else, except what was with difficulty kept concealed in
the churches. In addition to this, the prior said that the same
chancellor, priest, and bishop, had been forced to fly to Normandy, after much annoyance and ill-treatment; and that
the said earl rigorously exacted from the earls and nobles of
the land the oath of allegiance, with homage, and the custody

* This appears to be an error for Witekind.

of the castles. He had also arbitrarily laid hands on the king's yearly revenues, namely, those of the exchequer. "And," said the prior, "if your majesty does not take speedy counsel on these matters, and return home with all haste and avenge our wrongs on the insurgents, it will fare worse, and you will not be able to recover your kingdom without the hazard of a war." The king was exceedingly astonished at what he heard, and turning it over in his mind for a long time, said but little, for he thought it incredible and a piece of wickedness exceeding belief. Where is the man who, when his wealth is plundered, bears it patiently? Who endures wrongs without a murmur? Fear, in its anxiety, gives all things, however uncertain, an appearance of probability; and when a confused state of affairs comes to the knowledge of others, they are themselves disturbed, and their minds are apt to be alarmed lest every thing should turn out disordered. The discord of princes is seldom to be allayed; but if King Richard should be obliged to return home, probably not a man would remain in the Holy Land, as there was jealousy and strife between the people of Tyre and Ascalon, and without a doubt the Turks would have possession of the land for ever.

CH. XXIII.—*How the army, on hearing the secret news brought by the king's messenger, took counsel to choose a king for themselves; and how the people preferred the marquis to King Guy.*

ON the morrow, the king having called together the leaders of the army, laid before them the news which he had heard, fully explaining the words of the prior, and at the same time declaring that he must, of necessity, return home directly, but promised to furnish to the campaign in the Holy Land three hundred knights and two thousand chosen foot soldiers, at his own expense. He then inquired who would return with him, and who would stay behind? He would compel no one to do either, but left it entirely to their own choice. Having taken counsel, in common, on this point, they made the following reply to the king's inquiries :—That as the land was suffering from the discord of certain parties, and the issue of events was still uncertain, especially as King Guy had not yet effected his purpose of recovering the kingdom, they thought it absolutely necessary that a new king should be appointed, to

whom all should pay allegiance, and to whose care the land
should be entrusted, that he might fight the battles of the
people ; one, in fine, whom the army could follow and obey ;
and if this should not be settled before the king's departure,
that they would, one and all, depart from the land, for they
should not otherwise be able to guard it against the enemy.
On the king inquiring, in reply to this, which of the two they
would rather have for king, King Guy, or the marquis, the
whole army, high and low, entreated, on their bended knees,
that the marquis should be elevated to the sovereignty, as
much better able to defend the country than any other they
could choose.   The king, listening to their petition, censured
them in gentle terms for their fickleness, for they had before
this often detracted from the character and good qualities of
the marquis.

CH. XXIV.—*How King Richard, to satisfy the people, sent for the
marquis, though known to be seditious and in league with Saladin.*

KING RICHARD, when he had weighed well the petition of
the people for choosing the marquis as their king, gave his
assent, and appointed noble men to go to Tyre, and bring back
the marquis with all due honour.   On the king's giving his consent, a general decree was unanimously issued for the election
of the marquis, and certain men of high rank, viz., Henry
Count of Champagne, Otho de Transinges, and William de
Cague, were sent by sea with a retinue, to impart the good
news to the marquis at Tyre ; but, as the proverb says,
" There is many a slip 'twixt the cup and the lip !" for God
proved the marquis to be unworthy of the kingdom ; and as
a further evidence of his judgment of him, we may add this :—
that after the departure of the French, King Richard had
asked the marquis, as he had often done before, for the aid
which was required to recover the kingdom, as we have
already said, but he refused it obstinately, so that blame must
deservedly be imputed to him ; and over and above this, he was
diligently plotting against the honour of the king's crown,
and the army at Ascalon, by entering into a treaty of peace
with Saladin, on the conditions that he should come to him
and swear to observe concord hereafter, and that the Christians should have a share of the city of Jerusalem ; and that
he should have the fortress of Baruth, and Sidon, and half the

land on this side the river Jordan. To these terms Saladin readily assented in spite of his brother, who opposed them ; and, as we heard afterwards, constantly persuaded Saladin to agree to no conditions of peace with any of the Christians without the consent of King Richard. " There is not a better man than he in Christendom," said Saphadin ; " nor has he his match for probity ; and I will neither advise, nor assent to the confirmation of peace, unless with his consent and privity." By these means the infamous design was abandoned, and the treason failed of success. The existence of this plot was clearly proved afterwards ; for during the time that ambassadors were going to and fro, between Saladin and the marquis, to arrange and negotiate the matter, Stephen de Torneban happened to meet them coming out of Jerusalem from the presence of Saladin. They were men notorious for infamy of character ; one of them was called Baban of Ybelin, the other, Reginald of Sidon ; but we pass them by, for all their anxious endeavours and zeal came to nought, like dust, which a man scatters against the wind.

Ch. XXV.—*How the marquis, on hearing that he had been chosen king, was elated with great joy, as well as his friends ; and how the latter prepared armour for themselves, and every thing necessary for his coronation.*

The ambassadors, who had been sent to fetch the marquis, arriving at Tyre, set forth to him how he had been unanimously chosen king by the whole army, and with the consent of King Richard ; and that the crown of the kingdom had been granted to him, if he would come with his army and perform the duties thereof, vigorously and bravely, against the Turks, and apply himself to the government of the kingdom of Jerusalem in all other matters as his own. On hearing this, it is said, that the marquis, in the excessive joy of his heart, stretched forth his hand to heaven, and prayed thus : " O Lord God ! who has created me, and infused life into my body ; who art a just and merciful King ; I pray Thee, O Lord, if thou thinkest me deserving of the government of Thy kingdom, grant me to see myself crowned ; but if Thou judgest otherwise, consent not thou to my promotion !" When it became well known throughout the city of Tyre. that the marquis was to be crowned king, so great was the joy of the people, that they got in readiness whatever they had, and used their utmost diligence to prepare for celebrating his coronation. They borrowed money to buy robes and armour, for they wished to make the most splendid appearance possible in the service of one so magnificent, who had been raised to so high a dignity. Men were now to be seen cleaning their armour, polishing their rusty arms, sharpening their swords, and rubbing their lances; soldiers and boys engaged in sham battles, and maintaining the appearance of a real conflict of combatants, boasting at the same time of the future destruction of the Turks; and, in fact, they were a brave people, had they not not been without the Divine aid. Thus they indulged in joy, the more unreasonable, for being so intemperate, according to the proverb,—"We should not rejoice too much, nor grieve too much," for all excess is reprehensible.

CH. XXVI.—*How the marquis was stabbed with two-poniards, by two young men, assassins, sent by the old man (senior) of Musse.*

MEANWHILE, Count Henry, after executing his embassy, turned off with his companions to Acre, to equip themselves in becoming attire for the coronation, and were on the point of returning to Ascalon, when the marquis was overtaken by sudden death at Tyre. For it happened one day that he was returning, in a very cheerful and pleasant humour, from an entertainment given by the bishop of Beauvais, at which he had been a guest, and had reached the custom-house of the city, when two young men, assassins,* without cloaks, suddenly rushed upon him, and having drawn two poniards, which they carried in their hands, stabbed him to the heart, and ran off at full speed. The marquis instantly fell from his horse, and rolled dying on the ground; one of the murderers was slain directly, but the second took shelter in a church; notwithstanding which he was captured, and condemned to be dragged through the city until life should be extinct. One of them was closely questioned before expiring, at whose instigation, and for what reason, they had done the deed, when he confessed that they had been sent a long time before to perpetrate the crime, and that they

---

* The origin of the fraternity of Assassins, followers of the Old Man of the Mountain, as he is generally called in the common histories of England, has not been very clearly traced. It appears by the accounts which we have of the Thugs and other tribes in India, that similar associations still exist in the East.

had done it by the command of their superior, whom they
were bound to obey.   This turned out to be true; for these
very young men had been some time in the service of the
marquis, waiting for a favourable opportunity to complete the
deed.   The old man of Musse had sent them over to assassinate
the marquis, whom he thought worthy of death, within a
certain space of time; for every one the old man judged deserving of death, he caused to be assassinated in the same
manner.   The old man of Musse, according to hereditary custom, brought up a large number of noble boys in his palace,
causing them to be taught every kind of learning and accomplishment, and to be instructed in various languages, until
they could converse in them without the aid of an interpreter,
in any nation of the known world.   Cruelty of the greatest
degree was also inculcated with profound secresy; and the
pupils were carefully and anxiously trained to follow it up.
When they reach the age of puberty, the senior calls them to
him, and enjoins on them, for the remission of their sins, to slay
some great man, whom he mentions by name; and for this
purpose he gives to each of them a poniard, of terrible length
and sharpness.   From their devoted obedience, they never
hesitate to set out, as they are commanded; nor do they
pause until they have reached the prince, or tyrant, who has
been pointed out to them; and they remain in his service until
they find a favourable opportunity for accomplishing their
purpose; for by so doing they believe they shall gain the
favour of heaven.   Of this sect were the persons who slew
the marquis.

Now while he was breathing his last, the attendants who
were about him took him up in their arms and carried him to
the palace, mourning and weeping inconsolably; the more so,
as their joy had been, but now, so great.   He enjoined his
wife to attend carefully to the preservation of the city of Tyre,
and to resign it to no one, save King Richard, or to whomsoever
the kingdom should fall by right of heirship.   Immediately
afterwards he expired, and was buried in the Hospital, amidst
great mourning and lamentation.   Thus the former state of
excitement and public joy was cut short; and the dominion
so long desired, but not yet secured, vanished.   The cheer-
ing hopes of that desolate land were destroyed, and intense
grief superseded the former gladness.

CH. XXVII.—*How the French, from envy, accused King Richard of the marquis's death.*

IN the confusion which now prevailed amongst the people, the tares which an enemy had sown sprung up and corrupted the wheat. For it was whispered by certain of the French, who sought to veil their own wickedness by such a falsehood, and they infused it into the minds of all the people, that King Richard had vilely brought about the death of the marquis, and that he had hired these men from the Assassins for that purpose. Oh, infamous and malicious envy, that always carps at virtue, hates what is good, and endeavours to blacken the splendour which it cannot extinguish! Nor were they content with defaming the character of King Richard in those quarters, but also sent a warning to the king of France, to be on his guard against the satellites of the old man of Musse; detailing the manner in which the marquis died, and stating that King Richard had directed four of these ministers of superstition against himself. What did not they deserve who fabricated such misrepresentations, by means of which so many nations are believed to have been confounded, and so many provinces shaken! The infamous authors thought, by the invention of this malicious slander, to add to their own strength, and perhaps palliate their own wickedness.

CH. XXVIII.—*How Count Henry was chosen king at Tyre, and how messengers were sent to report this and the assassination of the marquis to King Richard.*

AFTER the marquis was buried, the French, who lived in tents outside the city, to the number of about 10,000, met together, and after a long discussion, sent orders to the wife of the marquis, bidding her to place the city in their charge, without delay or opposition, for the service of the king of France. But the queen replied, that when King Richard came to see her, she would give it up to him, and to no one else, for such were the commands of her dying lord, as there was no one who had laboured so much to rescue the Holy Land from the hands of the Turks, and restore it to its former freedom; and that the kingdom ought to be given to the bravest man, to dispose of it as he thought fit. The French were exceedingly indignant at this reply, and while they were striving to obtain possession of the city, Count Henry, astonished at what he heard had taken place, came unexpectedly to Tyre; and when the people saw him amongst them, they forthwith chose him as their prince, as if he had been sent by God; and began with much earnestness to entreat him to accept the crown of the kingdom, without excuse or hesitation, and to marry the widow of the marquis, as the kingdom was hers by right of inheritance. To this he replied, that he would act according to the advice of his uncle, King Richard, respecting the settlement of the business, to which it had pleased the Lord to call him; and immediately, ambassadors were sent to announce to King Richard the solemn election of Count Henry by all the people, and the horrible assassination of the marquis.

Ch. XXIX.—*Of the great zeal with which King Richard fought, slew, and made captives of the Turks.*

MEANWHILE, before the messengers from Tyre to King Richard reached their destination, the fair season set in, after the cold winter months; and King Richard began again to attack the Turks, with indefatigable ardour, as before. For there never was a man like him, nor one whom the Turks feared so much; no one had ever before injured them in like manner, falling upon them almost single-handed, and bringing back the heads of his foes, sometimes ten in a day, sometimes twelve, or twenty, or thirty, according as they happened to fall in his way; and besides all this, he would also bring home captives every day in large numbers. There never was a man in the times of the Christians who destroyed so many Saracens single-handed.

Ch. XXX.—*How Mestoc was ransomed, and how some of our men-at-arms, while out foraging, were captured by the Turks.*

ON the Thursday before the feast of Saint Alphage, Mestoc, who, as aforesaid, was taken with many others in the city of Acre, was ransomed and released. Shortly after this, some of our men-at-arms and servants, who had gone out in search of fodder for the beasts of burden, while proceeding incautiously too far, were set upon by an ambuscade of the Saracens, and many were killed and made captives, as well as a large number of horses.

Ch. XXXI.—*Of the fight between King Richard and a boar that he met, and of the king's boldness in the contest*

ON the Wednesday before the feast of St. Mark the evangelist, the king and his army set out to Gadida to protect the city, but found no one there, for the enemy had taken to flight when they heard of his coming. On their way back, the king attacked a fierce boar, which, hearing the noise of the party passing by, had come out and stood in the way. The fierce animal, foaming at the mouth with rage, and with his shaggy hair bristling up, and his ears erect, seemed to be collecting all his strength and fury to receive or make an attack. He did not move from his place when the king shouted; nay, when the king made a circuit round him, he also turned himself in his astonishment round in a circle, and kept in the same place which he had first occupied. The king now making use of his lance for a hunting spear, moved on to pierce him; and the boar, turning a little to one side, prepared to meet him. The animal was of enormous size, and terrible aspect, and the lance which was boldly thrust against his broad breast broke in two, from not being strong enough to bear the pressure of both, as they were closing with each other. The boar, now rendered furious by his wound, rushed with all his might upon the king, who had not an inch of room, or a moment of time to turn away; so putting spurs to his horse, he fairly leapt over the animal, unharmed, though the boar tore away the hinder trappings of his horse; but the activity of the latter frustrated the blow; and the part of the lance which was fixed in the animal's breast prevented him from coming to closer quarters. They then make a simultaneous attack on each other, and the boar made a rapid movement, as if to close with the king; but he, brandishing his sword, smote him with it as he passed, and stunned him with the blow; then wheeled round his horse, and cutting the boar's sinews, he consigned the animal to the care of his huntsmen.

Ch. XXXII.—*Of the capture of some Turks by our men.*

ON the Tuesday before the feast of St. Philip and St. James, Roger de Glanville set out with his soldiers, from Whitecastle, and passing, in force, before the gates of Jerusalem, intercepted some Saracens, whom he put in chains, and brought

back captives.   On the following Wednesday, King Richard
fell in with some Saracens also, between Whitecastle and
Gaza, and slaying some, made prisoners of five of them. whom
he sent to Ascalon.

CH. XXXIII.—*Likewise of the capture of some Turks by King Richard
at Furbia, and by the Templars at Darum.*

WHILE the king was passing the night after the day of the
blessed apostles St. Philip and St. James with a few followers at Furbia, the Turks, early in the morning, came upon
them by surprise, thinking either to capture or destroy them;
but the king was the first to leap from his bed, and seizing
only his shield and sword, took seven of the Turks captive,
and slew four ; the rest fled from before him.   Afterwards
he sent out the Templars and Turcopoles,* as far as the fortress
of Darum, to explore the country, and they found twenty
Saracens, who had come out from the fort, sowing barley ;
these they seized, and sent to Ascalon.

CH. XXXIV.—*How the aforesaid messengers arrived from Tyre, and
how, on their announcing the death of the marquis, and the election of
Count Henry, King Richard was rejoiced at the said election, and
granted the count all he asked for ; and how he sent for the French.*

IN those days, while King Richard was engaged on the
plains of Ramula, in pursuit of the flying Turks, the messengers, who had been sent from Tyre, came to him, and
informed him of the state of affairs there ; of the death of the
marquis, and the choice of Count Henry to be his successor ;
but that the latter would not venture to accept the kingdom
without the king's consent and advice.   King Richard hearing of the death of the marquis, was for a long time silent, with
astonishment, at his violent and untimely end ; but he was
exceedingly rejoiced at the election of his nephew, and the
regal honours so solemnly conferred upon him ; for he knew
that his own people desired it much.   " Wherefore," said he,
" as the marquis, by the inexorable decrees of fate, has ceased
to exist, it is of no use to indulge in sorrow : mourning will
avail nothing to the spirit of the departed !   I congratulate
you on the election of Count Henry ; and I am very desirous,
if it be the will of God, that he should be invested with the

* The Turcopoles seem to have been natives of the country, of cross
breed between Turks and Christians ; they served as light cavalry.

government of the kingdom as soon as we have obtained entire
possession of the Holy Land ; but concerning his marrying the
widow of the marquis, I have no advice to give, for the marquis seized upon her unlawfully while her husband was alive,
and committed adultery by his intercourse with her ; let Count
Henry take the kingdom, and the city of Acre, with all its
appurtenances, Tyre and Joppa, and the whole of the land, if
it so please God, for ever.   Tell him also, in my name, to set
out for the campaign as quickly as possible, and bring the
French with him ; for I purpose to take Darum in spite of all
the opposition of the Turks.

CH. XXXV.—*How on the return of the messengers from King Richard,
and their announcing his pleasure, the count was married to the marquis's widow, to the great joy of all, and how Tyre and other fortresses
were given up to the count.*

AFTER receiving the instructions of King Richard, the
ambassadors returned to Tyre to the count, their future king,
and reported the message entrusted to them.   Then the joy
and exultation of all was revived, and the principal persons
persuaded the count to marry the marquis's widow, who was
heiress to the kingdom ; but he refused, lest he should offend
King Richard.   Upon this, the French, and the nobles of
the kingdom, urged him to it, alleging that his position would
be strengthened thereby ; and by their influence, the lady
came of her own accord to offer him the keys of the city.
This was done at the instance of the French, who were for
hurrying on the matter.   The marriage was solemnized in
the church in the presence of the clergy and laity.   Those
who persuaded the count to this step were not supposed to
have had much difficulty ; for there is no trouble in persuading a willing man.   The nuptials were solemnized with royal
magnificence, and all were rejoiced at the accomplishment of
the affair, which was wished for by every one ; the French
exulted, and the Normans were equally joyful, for the count
was a nephew of both the kings of France and England ; and
by this union happier times were hoped for, and a return of
those who differed to peace and concord.   On the completion
of his nuptials, the count immediately sent persons to assume
the government of Acre, Joppa, and other cities and forts, in
his name ; and to take possession of all his dominions, which

they were to hold under him as their lord.   He then published
an edict, calling on all to get ready for the expedition against
Darum.

Ch. XXXVI.—*With what joy Count Henry was received at Acre on his
way, with the duke of Burgundy and his army, to aid King Richard.*

HAVING, therefore, left fit persons to guard the city of Tyre,
and the rest of the land, Count Henry, in company with the
duke of Burgundy, moved forward his army towards Acre, in
order to hasten the campaign and provide what was necessary;
and he also brought his wife with him, as he could not yet
endure to be without her.   When the count's coming was
known to the people of Acre, they came out, with dances, to
meet and applaud their new lord; and crowding round him,
they accompanied him into the city, which was adorned on
every side like a temple, with curtains and silken cloths;
burning censers were filled with frankincense, and carried
about the roads and streets; and women led the dance
with joy and exultation.   Why need we enter into
detail?   An immense number of people, calculated at
60,000, went forth in full armour to meet the count, and
testify their joy and regard for him.   The clergy led him by
the hand into the church before the altar, and offered him the
Holy Cross, and other relics, to kiss.   The count himself, and
several others, made many precious offerings there; after
which he was conducted to the royal palace, where he ordered
a banquet to be prepared, and every one, according to his
means, strove to do honour to their new lord.

Ch. XXXVII.—*How King Richard, moved with pity, gave to King
Guy the island of Cyprus as a reward for his prowess in war, and to
console him for the loss of his kingdom.*

BUT since it is hardly possible for one man to rise without
another's downfall, so that the loss of the one turns to the
advantage of the other, King Guy was now deprived of
the kingdom, in the acquisition of which Count Henry
gloried, and for which he had fought so many battles.   He
now dwelt therein like a private man, not because he was
undeserving of the kingdom, for there was not another king
to be found of more royal habits or character than he, but for
this only reason, that he was simple-minded and unversed in

political intrigue; instead of being esteemed the more on this
account, as he should have been, he was considered the more
contemptible.   He was a soldier of great prowess, and conducted the siege of Acre, when occupied by the Turks, with
the greatest vigour and perseverance; but owing to the increasing numbers of the enemy on the side towards the sea,
he could not storm the city, which two kings afterwards with
difficulty gained possession of.   Ought, then, the simplicity of
his character to have injured him in obtaining his rights?
For such was the perversity of the age, that he whoever was
known to be most inhuman in his actions was thought worthy of greater honour and glory; and thus while craftiness
gained respect, piety sunk into disrepute, because prudence
is the reigning virtue of the present age.   Thus, then, Guy
became a king without a kingdom, until King Richard,
moved with pity for him and his well-known probity, gave
him the unconditional sovereignty of the island of Cyprus,
although the Templars had previously bought it of him; and
thus the condition of purchase by the Templars being set
aside, Guy was made emperor of Cyprus.

CH. XXXVIII.—*How messengers arrived frequently from England, and
how the news they brought made King Richard doubtful what to do.*

At the time that the marquis was assassinated at Tyre as
aforesaid, many messengers arrived from England, soliciting
the king to return; some of them said that every thing was
safe, others that England was on the point of being taken from
him; some begged him to return home, while others used all
their endeavours to persuade him to accomplish his pilgrimage
in the land which he had come to; and thus their different
assertions disturbed his mind, and made him doubtful to
which he should lean. But he measured the spirit of the king
of France by his former experience, for, according to the
proverb, "He who has a bad man for his neighbour, is sure
to find something wrong in the morning."

CH. XXXIX.—*How King Richard, without the aid of the French, and
with his own army alone, took Darum by storm in four days, and
captured 300 Turks therein.*

In the meantime, while Count Henry and the French at
Acre were proceeding to the siege of the fort of Darum, King

Richard, who hated delay, started with his men from Ascalon, and sent his stone-engines, which had been placed piece-meal on board the ships, to proceed thither by sea. The king deputed men to guard the city, and hired others, at the most lavish price, to keep a good look-out by day towards the neighbouring forts, and a careful watch by night to prevent the Turks from carrying supplies as before to Darum, or whatever might be wanted by the army at Jerusalem, or from any longer having a safe retreat to Darum, whence they frequently planned ambuscades against our men. Then the king, with his own soldiers only, set out armed for the fort of Darum, and arriving there on a Sunday, he pitched his tent and those of his followers at a short distance from it. Owing to the paucity of our men, it was doubted which part of the fort they should attack, as they were unable entirely to surround it; for if our small numbers were scattered, they would not be able to storm the tower, or withstand the attack of the Turks; wherefore they retired in a body towards a village situated in a plain, where they drew up. The Turks, on seeing so small an army, came forth from the castle, as if to solicit and challenge them to battle, and then retired again, and having barred their gates very strongly, prepared to defend themselves. Immediately afterwards, the king's stone-engines arrived in his ships, which being disjointed, and in different pieces, the king, his princes, and nobles, carried on their shoulders from the shore, not without much sweating, as we ourselves saw, for nearly a mile. At last, when the engines were put together, and men placed to work them, the king took upon himself to manage one of them, and with it to attack the principal tower of the fort, the Normans had the second, and the men of Poictou the third; and all of them were put in motion for the destruction of the fort. The Turks saw that utter destruction was close at hand; but for all that, they endeavoured to defend themselves manfully. King Richard caused his engines to be plied day and night. Darum had seventeen strong and compact towers, one of which was higher and stronger than the others, and externally it was surrounded by a deep ditch, which was built on one side of layers of paving stones, and a natural rock hung over the other. And now cowardly fears came upon the un-believing race, lest they should not be able to defend them-

selves effectually, or even to escape with their lives. On the
morrow, the king caused the sappers to carry a mine very
cleverly underground, in order to break up the pavement,
and make a hollow in the wall; and the stone-engines, being
plied in common, broke in pieces, by their frequent blows,
one of the enemy's mangonels, erected on the principal tower,
at which the enemy were very much discouraged. At first
the Turks drove back our men with stones and darts, which
fell in dense showers from their slings and bows; but our
slingers, to the great destruction of our foes, wherever they
saw any one exposed to their attack on the battlements, threw
missiles at him, and wounded and killed so many of them,
that the enemy scarcely dared to move for fear; and their
condition began now to be far from enviable, when on a sudden, one of the gates of the fort was broken down, set on fire,
and utterly destroyed by the blows of the king's stone-
engines. The Turks, now driven to desperation, by this continuous and harassing attack, were not able to make a longer
defence, and many were killed, while others lay wounded on
the ground. It was now clear that King Richard was invincible in every operation he commenced; and that by undermining the towers, and plying his engines, he was sure to
succeed. Three, therefore, of the Saracens came from the fort
to the king, and sued for peace, offering to surrender the fort,
and every thing belonging to it, on condition that they should
be allowed to go away with their lives; but the king refused, and told them to defend themselves to the utmost of
their power. They returned therefore to the fort, and the
king's engine was kept constantly at work; and directly afterwards, a tower, which had been weakened by a subterranean
passage, made by the king's miners, after repeated blows, fell
to the ground with a dreadful crash. The Turks in escaping
from the ruins became mingled with our men, who pursued
them with slaughter, till they took refuge in the principal tower,
having first performed the horrible act of cutting the sinews of
their horses, to prevent their being of service to the enemy. The
Turks now fled, and our men boldly approached the fort. The
first who entered it were Seguin Borret, and his armour-
bearer, named Ospiard; the third was Peter of Gascony, and
after him, many others, whose names are lost. The banner
of Stephen de Longchamp was the first that was raised above

the walls; the second was that of the earl of Leicester; and
the third, that of Andrew de Chavegui; the fourth was that of
Raimund, son of the prince; and then the Genoese and Pisans
raised on the wall their standards of various forms. Thus the
banners of our men were raised, and those of the Turks thrown
down. And now the Turks might be seen flying towards the
tower, or falling to the earth, smitten with the sword or
transfixed with darts, before they could reach it; all whom our
men found still standing their ground on the battlements,
they hurled down to the earth below. Sixty Turks were
killed in different parts of the fort. Those who had taken
refuge in the tower, seeing the slaughter of their troops, and
that their place of refuge would be demolished (for, at the
instance of the king, men were already setting to work to
overthrow it), and that there was no longer any safety in
opposing the king, in their extremity, on the Friday before
Pentecost, gave themselves up to the royal clemency to be
slaves for ever; especially as one of their most powerful
admirals, by name Caisac, to whose care the fort had been
intrusted, had failed in his promise to give them succour.
The fort of Darum being thus taken, nearly forty Christian
captives were found there in chains, and were now set at liberty.
On the following Saturday night, King Richard caused his men
to keep guard over the Turks who still survived in the tower,
until the morning; and on the Whitsuntide eve he ordered
them to come down therefrom, having their hands tied behind
their backs with thongs, so that their limbs became stiff.
Their number amounted to 300, besides boys and women.
Thus King Richard, with his own soldiers, gained possession
of the fort of Darum with great credit, after assaulting it for
four days; for our men were very desirous of accomplishing
this without the French, in order that they might gain the
greater glory.

Ch. XL.—*How King Richard gave Count Henry the fort of Darum on
his arrival there, and returned to Furbia.*

Thus Darum was taken; but meanwhile Count Henry, with
the French, and the Duke of Burgundy, were coming in great
haste, that they might be present at its capture, but it was
already taken. The king received the count on his arrival
with special manifestations of joy; and leading him to the

fort, gave it over to him, in the presence of all, as the first fruits of the kingdom, which he was to obtain, with the appurtenances thereof, present and future. All remained in the fort of Darum on the great day of the feast of Pentecost. On the Monday after, they placed some of the count's men as guards in the fort, and set out for Ascalon, passing through the midst of Gaza, till they came to Furbia. Here the king tarried three days, but the rest set out for Ascalon, where the French solemnized the festival of Pentecost.

CH. XLI.—*How King Richard, on hearing that Caisac, the admiral, was fortifying the castle of Figs with 1,000 Turks, went thither to storm it, and how the enemy fled at his approach.*

ONE of the king's spies, in returning to Furbia, from the direction of the castle of Figs, reported that a thousand Saracens, or more, were with the chieftain, Caisac, posted in that fort, and were actively engaged in fortifying it against the Christians, in case they should come to attack it. On hearing this, King Richard started thither immediately, and the army followed him. At nightfall, they stopped at the fort of Reeds, or the "Cane-brake of starlings" (cannetum sturnellorum), and at dawn of day set out for the castle of Figs, as they had proposed, but they found no one there save two Turks, whom they took away captive with them, for the Turks had levelled the gates of the fort to the ground, and fled rapidly away on hearing of the approach of King Richard and his army. They were also not a little frightened at the capture of the fort, and the men who were found therein; and mindful of their loss, took precautions lest they should themselves fall into a like predicament. Our men, therefore, finding the fort deserted, mounted the highest of the battlements, and took a survey around, to see if any enemy was in sight, that they might attack him; but not finding any one to fight with, they returned to the house of starlings to spend the night.

CH. XLII.—*How on hearing the news of the disturbed state of his kingdom, through the intrigues of Earl John, his brother, King Richard was much moved, and declared his wish to return home.*

WHILE Richard was at this place, there arrived a messenger from England, a clergyman, by name John de Alençon, to inform the king of the disturbed state of

England, owing to Earl John, his brother, who would not listen to the persuasions of his mother the queen, nor to those of any other person, but was led on by his own will, and the frequent solicitations of the king of France ; and be assured the king that unless the infamous treason was put a stop to by some means or other, England stood in danger of being alienated from the dominion of King Richard.   The king was troubled at hearing this news, and reflected in his mind, for a long time, what would be the best course to adopt ; at last he confessed that he must return home, if he would not have his native land, and the kingdom of his fathers, wrested from him.   As the report of the king's intention was not made public, some said he was going away ; others said that he would remain, and not allow uncertain reports to call him away from the accomplishment of so pious an undertaking; an act which would neither promote the recovery of the Holy Land, nor redound to his own honour.

Cʜ. XLIII.—*How the whole army unanimously agreed that Jerusalem should be besieged, whether King Richard should return home directly or not.*

Wʜɪʟᴇ people differed in opinion as to the departure of King Richard, all the leaders and officers of the army, English, French, Normans, men of Poictou, Maine, and Anjou, met together, and agreed with each other, that whether King Richard returned or not, they would proceed to the siege of Jerusalem, and that nothing should prevent them.   When this was known in the army, the people were filled with exceeding joy, and all, rich and poor, high and low, rejoiced in common ; and there was not a man in the army but evinced by outward signs the most immoderate joy each in his own peculiar manner ; wherefore they made a brilliant illumination, and danced and sang nearly all the night ; and thus

They passed the livelong night in wakeful glee.

The king was the only one troubled with care from what he had heard, and he fell into a long train of thought, until, overcome with the weight of it, he threw himself, in an angry mood, upon his bed.   It was now the beginning of

U

June, and the whole army was animated with the desire of
setting out for Jerusalem.

CH. XLIV.—*How the flies called cincenelles stung the soldiers in the
face, at Ybelin, so that they looked like lepers.*

THE king and the army started from the Brake of Starlings,
and proceeded through the plains to Ybelin, of the Hospitallers, by Hebron, near the valley, where Anna, the mother
of the Virgin Mary, is said to have been born. Here, the
army made a halt, exceedingly rejoiced at the prospect of
proceeding towards Jerusalem. And here the men were
beset with swarms of small insects, which flew about like
sparks of fire, and were called cincenelles. The whole
region round swarmed with them, and they annoyed the
pilgrims horribly, with their sharp stings in the hands,
neck, throat, forehead, and face, and in whatever part
of the person happened to be exposed; their stings were
immediately followed by burning and swelling, and those who
were stung looked like lepers. They could scarcely keep off
their troublesome attacks with veils thrown over the face
and neck. But they were in high spirits, and thought they
should bear these annoyances with patience; for they were
all pledged to advance to the siege of Jerusalem, and
the king was the only one troubled at the news which he had
received from England.

CH. XLV.—*How one of King Richard's chaplains addressed him, and
dissuaded him, by every argument in his power, from returning
home.*

ONE day a chaplain from Poicton, named William, saw
the king sitting alone in his tent, with his eyes fixed on the
ground, in meditation, and he felt grieved for him, for he
knew that he was exasperated at the news brought from
England; but he did not venture to come up to him, to
lighten his mind of the cares which oppressed him; so he
regarded him with a respectful look, and shed tears, but
without uttering a word. When the king saw by his
manner that the man was desirous of addressing him, he
called him, and thus spoke to him: "Sir Chaplain, I pray
you, by your allegiance to me, tell me, without delay or dissimulation, what is the cause of your weeping, and if the

occasion of your distress has any reference to me." The
chaplain, with eyes swollen with tears and humble voice,
replied, " I will not speak before I know that your high-
ness will not be angered with me for what I say." The king,
with an oath, gave him free leave to speak. Upon which,
the chaplain, taking confidence, thus began : " My lord the
king, I weep on account of the ill repute in which you
stand with the army, because you intend to return home,
and especially amongst those who are the most solicitous for
your honour ; but may God forbid that you be turned from
the recovery of this desolated land, by doubtful or uncertain reports, for we believe it would tend to your eternal
disgrace ; let not then the glory of a most splendid enterprise be overcast by a hasty retreat ; nor let it be charged
against you hereafter, that you returned home in idleness, while your enterprise was still unfinished. How
unlike will the end be to the beginning, if you thus derogate from your former glory ! I pray you to take heed,
lest your glory, so well earned at first, fade and tarnish
in the end ! My lord the king, remember what God hath
done for you, and how he hath prospered all your acts, to
be recorded by immortal fame. Never did king of your age
perform so many or such glorious deeds ! Remember, O
king, that even when you were but count of Poicton, you
never had a neighbour for a foe, whatever might be his
valour or courage, but he was subdued and conquered by
your might. Remember, O king, the multitudes of Bra-
baçons whom you so often routed and dispersed, with a small
band of soldiers. O king, remember how gloriously you
raised the siege of Hautefort, when the count of St. Giles
besieged it ; how you drove him off, and put him to
ignominious flight. O king, remember how you obtained
possession of your kingdom, peacefully and quietly, without
opposition, or need of shield or helmet. O king, remember
how many and mighty nations you have subdued, how bravely
you captured the city of Messina, and how nobly you
behaved yourself when the Greeks ventured to provoke
and make war against you, and how you crushed them,
and the divine mercy rescued you out of their hands,
whilst they were confounded and destroyed. Remember,
O king, the qualities with which God has endowed

you, according to the riches of his grace, when you subdued the island of Cyprus, which no one had dared to
attack before, and which you subjugated in the short
period of fifteen days; which you were only able to do
by the assistance of God himself. Remember how you then
captured the emperor; and that ship of extraordinary size,
which could not put into the port of Acre by reason of a
contrary wind, you met and overwhelmed her with the
eighty armed Turks, and cast into the waves of the sea
the serpents which were therein. Remember, my lord
the king, the siege of Acre, to the capture of which you
arrived in good season, and which was surrendered when
you assaulted it. Remember how you then fell ill of the
sickness called arnalia, and how you suffered much, but, by
the mercy of God, recovered when so many princes died
of the same complaint. O king, remember that land which
God hath committed to your care, and whose eye is turned
to you only, for the king of France has departed, like a
coward. O king, remember the Christian captives whom
you released from the bonds with which the Turks had
fettered them, in the fort of Darum, and to whose succour
you were sent by God. How deeply should you reflect
on the numberless triumphs with which God has honoured
you, and the successes with which he has magnified you,
so that there is not a king or prince who can venture to
resist you. Has it also escaped your memory that you
have lately captured the fort of Darum in four days?
And what shall we think of that hour, when you were
lying asleep incautiously, and were nearly seized by the
wicked infidels, had not God aroused you, and rescued
you from their hands? Why need I detail the foes whom
you have subdued throughout the world, the cities that
have fallen before you, and the successful issues of all
your undertakings? Remember, that when you came
hither from the western world, you were everywhere
victorious, and your enemies lay in chains at your feet; for
before your face,

> In vain Antæus rose refreshed from earth,
> Or Hydra's heads were multiplied.

And now the sultan trembles at your name, the hearts of
the people of Babylon are astonished, and the Turk is

struck with awe. Need I say more? All agree in declaring that you are the father, the champion, and the defender of Christianity, and if you desert them, it is the same as if you gave them up to be destroyed by the enemy. O king, continue to be their chief, bravely as you have begun; succour this people, for their hope is entirely in you : you are their natural protector, and may you, with the aid of Christ, still continue to prosper!"

CH. XLVI.—*How King Richard caused it to be proclaimed, by voice of herald, throughout the army, that he would not return until after Easter.*

THE king attended to the words of the chaplain, and deliberated within himself some time in silence. He had held his peace while the chaplain was speaking, and they also who were sitting with him in his tent had listened with the utmost attention. The king's heart was changed by this address, and his intention was confirmed as to the certainty of the course which he should pursue ; and therefore, he and his army returned at three o'clock on the morrow to Ascalon, and stopped in the orchards outside the city, while every one supposed that he was on the point of returning home, and that in reality he was hastening his departure. But the king had changed his purpose by the inspiration of God, through the agency of the chaplain; and he told Count Henry, the duke of Burgundy, and others of the nobles, that he would not leave before Easter for the solicitations of any messenger, or any reports or complaints whatever. On the fourth of June, therefore, in Trinity week, he summoned Philip, his herald, and commanded him to proclaim throughout the army, that the king would not depart from the Holy Land before Easter ; and that all should equip themselves according to their means, and prepare for the siege of Jerusalem.

CH. XLVII.—*How the army was rejoiced on hearing the king's determination, and how they prepared for the siege of Jerusalem.*

WHEN the army heard the words of the herald, they were as delighted as a bird at dawn of day, and all immediately set themselves in readiness, packing up their luggage, and preparing for the march. Then, with hands lifted up to heaven, they prayed thus : " O God, we adore and thank thee that we shall

soon see thy city of Jerusalem, in which the Turks have dwelt
so long!   O how blessed are our expectations, after this long
delay!   How deserved have been the sufferings and tribulations of each of us!   The much longed-for sight of thy
city will recompense us for all!"   These and the like prayers
were offered up by each; their only care and anxiety being
now to proceed on their march.   Moreover, the crowd of the
lower class of people, made active by hope, took the provision
baggage on their shoulders, asserting that they were fully able
to carry a month's supply, so eager were they to proceed to
Jerusalem; for there is nothing the mind of a willing man
cannot overcome, if he only has the inclination; and zeal in
the service of God softens the hardships of his toil.

Cн. XLVIII.—*How King Richard and the army set out from Ascalon
towards Jerusalem, and arrived at the White Custody; and how two of
our men died from the bite of serpents.*

While, therefore, each was getting ready for the campaign,
every thing that happened seemed to be done in harmony with
their intentions.   The king and army, therefore, who were
encamped outside the city, being now thoroughly prepared for
the march, set out from Ascalon on Sunday, the octave of the
holy Trinity, towards Jerusalem at dawn of day.   A chosen
people, and nobly arrayed, were they who now issued forth,
advancing slow on account of the heat.   The richer classes
supplied with lowly generosity the poor pilgrims who were on
foot with means of conveyance—horses, and every kind of
beast of burden, to carry them; while the light-armed and
robust young soldiers followed spontaneously behind them on
the march.   Then might you have seen many a banner and
pennon of various forms floating in the breeze; many a
mother's son, people of various nations, arms of various shape,
and helmets with crests, brilliant with jewels, and shining
mails, and shields, emblazoned with lions or flying dragons in
gold; mules and horses, eager to move at full speed, and
burning with indignation at being held in by the foaming bit;
many a lance with its sharp point glittering; the air sparkling
with the gleaming of swords, and so many soldiers, choice
men, good and true, who, in my opinion, were quite sufficient
to crush or withstand the Turkish host, or even a much larger
number than they could shew.   They made such progress

on their march, that after crossing a river of sweet water, they arrived at the White Custody, and having pitched their tents in the plain outside, they spent the night there. On the first night of their stay, a soldier and his armbearer died from the bites of two serpents, within a small space of ground; and may God, in whose service they were taken, give their souls absolution. The army tarried in that place two days.

CH. XLIX.—*How the king and his army arrived in three days at Beto-noble from the White Custody, and there waited for the arrival of the people one month.*

ON the third day, *i. e.* the ninth of June, the army arrived at "Turon of the Soldiers," without obstacle or misfortune. On that night, our men captured fourteen Parthians who had come down from the mountains to plunder. On the morrow, after dinner, the army moved forward, the king going first, with his own private soldiers, as far as the castle of Arnald, where he ordered his tent to be pitched on the right and higher side of the castle. On the morrow, the French arrived, and the whole army set out for Betenoble, where they stayed some time in expectation of Count Henry, whom King Richard had sent to Acre to fetch the people who were living there in idleness; wherefore, it was necessary for the army to stay a whole month or more at the foot of the mountain, which the pilgrims are obliged to cross in going to and returning from the Holy City. While in the valley, we saw many things happen which we do not think we ought to pass over in silence. On the morrow of St. Barnabas, which was Friday, the king was informed by a spy that the Turks were on the mountains, lying in ambush for those who should pass by, and at earliest dawn he set out in search of them, and coming to the fountain of Emaus, he caught them unawares, slew twenty, put the others to flight, and captured Saladin's herald, who was accustomed to proclaim his edicts;—he was the only one King Richard saved alive. He also took three camels, and horses, mules, and beautiful Turcomans; and also two mules laden with costly silken coverings, and different species of aloes, and other things. The rest of the Saracens he pursued over the mountains, routing and slaying them, until he came to a valley, where, after piercing one of the enemy, and casting him dying from his horse, he looked up and beheld in the distance the city of Jerusalem.

CH. L.—*How the Turks in Jerusalem, on hearing that King Richard was coming fled away in terror, and how Saladin prepared for flight.*

WHEN, therefore, news was brought by the fugitive Turks to those who dwelt in Jerusalem, that King Richard was approaching, they were struck with terror, and there is no doubt that had the king and his army moved forward at this critical juncture of their panic, the Turks would have abandoned Jerusalem, and let the Christians take undisputed possession of it; for the Saracens one and all had left it and fled, and not a man who could defend it even ventured to remain in the city; nor was any one deterred by the threats of the sultan, or allured by the hope of reward; for all that the sultan himself demanded was to be supplied with his swiftest charger, that he might flee from the face of King Richard, whose arrival he dared not await.

CH. LI.—*How, while the French were at Betenoble, they would have been routed in a conflict with 200 Turks, had not the bishop of Salisbury come to their succour.*

ON the same day on which the king was thus employed, two hundred Saracens came down from the mountains to the plain opposite the tents of the French, and threw the whole army into confusion before they could be put to flight. They had killed two of our guards, who had gone some distance in search of fodder for the beasts of burden; at whose cry, the French rushed forth with the Templars and Hospitallers, but the Turks defended themselves manfully at the foot of the mountain, and boldly returned their blows, refusing to fight with our men on level ground, but turning to resist as soon as they reached the declivity of the mountain; they also unhorsed one of our knights, from which the French obtained no small disgrace. On this occasion a knight would have performed an act of memorable valour, had he not transgressed the rule of his order, and his exploit was ascribed more to rashness than real courage. He was an Hospitaller, by name Robert de Bruges, who, having passed the royal standard, spurred with violence the valuable charger on which he sat, and in his eagerness to close with the enemy, issuing from the ranks, contrary to dis-

cipline, charged the Turks alone, before the others came up in
order; and urging at full speed against a Turk who was most
splendidly armed, he pierced him through his coat of mail
and body with such force, that the lance came out at his back.
The Turk fell to the ground, but his body was not left behind;
and then our men made a simultaneous charge upon the enemy.
After this, Gervier, the master of the Hospitallers, commanded Robert to dismount, and attend to the discipline of
his order; Robert obeyed his commands, and dismounting,
returned on foot, and waited patiently until some nobles and
men of influence prayed Gervier, the master, on their knees,
to forgive him, and remit his transgression, warning him not
to behave in like manner for the future.   Both sides now
laboured in the contest with doubtful success.   The heavens
resounded with the shouts of war; the earth was moist with
blood; swords rung as they clashed together, shields rattled,
and each side was agitated by equal fury.   Our men, fatigued
by the weight of the battle, began to waver, when, by divine
providence, the count of Perche, hearing the noise of the
combat, came up; yet he shewed himself but a timid man,
and the French would have been routed on that day, had not
the bishop of Salisbury, hearing the tumult, come quickly to
their succour.

CH. LII.—*How, while the army was staying at Betenoble, a large
   number of our men, who had the charge of the caravans from Joppa,
   were vilely treated and most roughly beaten by the Turks, and how
   they were rescued by the earl of Leicester.*

ON the seventeenth of June, i. e. on St. Botolph's day,
being Wednesday, our caravan was on its way from Joppa
to the army, laden with provisions and other necessaries.
Ferric of Vienna was deputed to conduct it, in the place
of Count Henry, who should have protected the rear,
but who had been sent to Acre.   Ferric had that day asked
Baldwin de Carron and Clarenbald de Mont Chablon, to
take charge of the caravan, lest the people should straggle too
widely, or be incautiously separated; but they nevertheless fell
into this error, and paid the penalty of their negligence.
These were Manassier de Lisle, Richard de Erques, The-
oderic Philip, and some comrades of Baldwin de Carron,
Otho, and many squires, with their relations and friends, who
proved their friendship in the hour of need.   The foremost

of our men moved quickly forwards, but the hindmost followed with a slow and unwilling pace ; when suddenly, not far
from Ramula, the Turkish horse from the mountains, bursting from their ambush, rushed upon the latter at full speed,
and endeavoured to get before them ; they therefore penetrated and passed through the horses, which formed the hindmost of the caravan.   There Baldwin de Carron was thrown
from his horse ; but brandishing his drawn sword and mul-
tiplying his blows in all directions, he proved inaccessible to
the enemy.   In that encounter Richard Torques and The-
odoric were thrown from their horses, but Baldwin fought
with great courage until his men brought him a horse, and
helped him to mount it. There was then a very severe conflict,
and honourable to both sides ; drawn swords flashing, the one
side attacking, and the other defending themselves most
bravely ; horses wandering up and down without riders ; the
Turks rushing about, and our men fighting stoutly.   As
often as the Turks felled a man to the ground, our men
closed round him, and raising him up, helped him to mount his
horse, each assisting one another.   But our men fought at
great odds, for they were very few compared with the hosts
of the enemy, and each contended separately with the foe,
and was hid as it were by the multitude of his adversaries ;
whence it was not to be wondered that the enemy's numbers
excluded our men ; for whenever one of our bravest men was
thrown from his horse, he was overpowered by numbers, and
the horses were wounded and much weakened by the showers
of darts that were thrown at them.   Moreover Baldwin was
soon after thrown a second time from his horse, and he immediately commanded one of his men-at-arms to dismount from
the horse on which he sat, and himself mounted on it, immediately after which, the man, who had behaved himself with
great prowess, had his head cut off.   Our men now stood on the
defensive, and Philip, the comrade of Baldwin, who behaved
himself with great distinction, was taken prisoner, and with
him the Turks took another man-at-arms of great prowess,
and killed the brother of Richard.   The timid would dread a
renewal of such a combat.   Baldwin and his comrades fought
with their swords and defended themselves with all their
might.   But Clarembald de Mont Chablon deserted his
men, and took to flight as soon as he saw the numbers of
the Turks increase.   Then the conflict was renewed with

fresh vigour, and Baldwin was a third time thrown from his horse, and so beaten with clubs, as almost to be rendered lifeless; the blood flowed in streams from his nose and ears, whilst his sword was blunted from constant use, and was unserviceable from its point being broken. Then Baldwin, on finding himself surrounded by a dense mass of Turks, cried out to Manassier de Lisle, a knight of great prowess, and who crushed all he met:—" Manassier," said he, " do you then desert me ?" On hearing this, Manassier flew with all speed to rescue him from the Turks; but the enemy were so many, that these two could do nothing against them, though they fought bravely for a long time against overwhelming numbers; until Manassier was thrown from his horse, and when he was on the ground they beat him cruelly with their iron maces, made rough with teeth, and, standing round, they so mangled him, that they broke off his leg, bone and all, from his body; and thus Baldwin and Manassier were being destroyed by the enemy, while their own men were ignorant of their fate. But, at this moment, God sent the valiant earl of Leicester, who had been ignorant of their danger, to rescue and protect them. The earl, on his arrival, dashed at the enemy and cast the first man he encountered from his horse; upon which, Anscun, the comrade of Stephen de Longchamps, cut off his head, and hurled it to a distance. Stephen also behaved himself manfully, and our people increasing in numbers, the enemy were routed, and fled with speed to the mountains, except those whom our men overtook. Those of our army who were wounded were placed carefully on horses, and carried to the army. Thus then we have thought that day's action worthy of mention, on account of the brave deeds of the earl of Leicester, who put the Turks to flight, killed some, and captured others.

CH. LIII.—*How, while Richard was at Betenoble, the Syrian bishop of St. George gave him a piece of the Lord's Cross.*

A CERTAIN Syrian bishop of St. George, who had been a tributary to Saladin for himself and his flock, when, after the destruction of the country, the Saracens first came to Jerusalem, brought a piece of the Holy Cross to King Richard. He was accompanied by a large number of men and women, belonging to his own people, and gave the piece of the Cross to the king.

Ch. LIV.—*Likewise, how while King Richard was there, an abbat came to him, and told him he had hidden a piece of the Holy Cross in a certain spot: and how the king went thither with the abbat, and found it, and.how the people worshipped it.*

It also happened, on the third day before the feast of St. John the Baptist, i. e. St. Alban's day, that while the army was staying there, they were much comforted by news which was brought to the king; for a devout man, the abbat of St. Elie, whose countenance bespoke holiness, with long beard and head of snow, came to the king, and told him, that a long time ago he had concealed a piece of the Holy Cross, in order to preserve it, until the Holy Land should bo rescued from the infidels, and restored entirely to its former state; and that he alone knew of this hidden treasure, and that he had often been pressed hard by Saladin, who had tried to make him discover the Cross, by the most searching inquiries; but that he had always baffled his questioners by ambiguous replies, and deluded them with false statements; and that on account of his contumacy, Saladin had ordered him to be bound; but he persisted in asserting that he had lost the piece of the Cross during the taking of the city of Jerusalem; and had thus deluded him, notwithstanding his anxiety to find it. The king, hearing this, set out immediately, with the abbat and a great number of people, to the place of which the abbat had spoken; and having taken up the piece of the Holy Cross with humble veneration, they returned to the army; and together with the people, they kissed the Cross with much piety and contrition.

BOOK VI.

Ch. I.—*How, when the French were desirous of proceeding to Jerusalem, King Richard would not agree, without the advice of the Templars, Hospitallers, and natives of the country.*

When the army had worshipped the Cross for a long time, in their exceeding great joy, the lower order and common people complained, and said, "O Lord God, what shall we do? Shall we still proceed to Jerusalem? What more shall we undertake? Shall we be able to hold out

until we have accomplished our pilgrimage?" Thus loud
murmurs and complaints arose amongst the people. On which
account, the king and the leaders of the army assembled together, to consider whether it was expedient to proceed to the siege
of Jerusalem or not. The French earnestly entreated, and even
exhorted the king to proceed; but he replied, that it could
not be done. "For," said the king, "you will not see me
acting as the guide and leader of the people in this matter;
for I might incur disgrace thereby, as it would be the height
of imprudence now to press on this enterprise. If it please
you to proceed to Jerusalem, I will not desert you; I will
be your comrade, but not your commander; I will follow,
not lead you. Does not Saladin know all that goes on in our
camp; and do you think that our weak condition has escaped
his notice? He is aware of our precise strength, and that
we are so distant from the sea-coast, that if the enemy were
to come down with force from the mountains to the plains of
Ramula, to watch the roads, and block up the passage,
against those who convey our provisions, the consequences
would be most disastrous to the besiegers. When too late, we
should repent, and pay the penalty of our foolhardy enterprise. Moreover, the walls of Jerusalem, to which we propose to lay siege, are, as we hear, very great in circuit; and
were we to attempt to blockade it with our troops, few as
they now are, and proportionably divided, their number
would not be sufficient to carry on the siege, or to protect
those who brought in the supplies, in case the Turks should
attack them; nay, they would, one and all, be utterly destroyed to a certainty, if they had none to relieve them.
Should I, therefore, undertake this hazardous enterprise,
and should any misfortune befal when I was general (which
God forbid), I alone should be blamed for my blind infatua-
tion; and should alone be responsible for the danger, were I, in
these circumstances, to conduct the troops to the siege of
Jerusalem. But there is no doubt, and I am well aware, that
there are persons here at present, as as well as in France,
who have long wished, and very much desired, that I should
exert my utmost efforts in this matter, without due and proper caution; and that I should perform daring acts, which
might justly be questioned, and bring infamy on my hitherto
spotless name. Wherefore, in so hazardous an undertaking,

with such doubtful issue, I should deem it wrong to rush
rashly forward, without great precaution.   Moreover, we,
and our people, are ignorant of the locality of this region, of
the roads and defiles ; which, if we were better acquainted
with, we should be able to proceed with greater safety ; until
we attained, with joy and triumph, the long-desired success.
But I am of opinion, that the best course to pursue, is to ask
the advice of the natives of the soil, who long to recover their
lands and former possessions, and endeavour to ascertain
from them what they deem best to be done, as they are fully
acquainted with the nature of the roads.   I think also we should
consult the Templars and Hospitallers, and take their judgment and opinion, as to whether we should proceed, first, to
the siege of Jerusalem, or to Babylon, or Baruth, or Damascus ; and thus our army will not continue, as now, to be
divided into parties, from diversity of opinion."

CH. II.—*How it was agreed by common consent, that twenty discreet
men should be appointed, and that all should abide by their opinion ;
and how the king assented and the French opposed it.*

IT was therefore agreed, by the king's recommendation,
and by common consent, that twenty trusty men should be
sworn, and that all should follow their advice, without further
opposition.   There were chosen five of the Templars, five of
the French nobles, five of the Hospitallers, and five of the
natives of Syria.   These twenty met together, and after con-
ferring for some time on the aforesaid matter, they gave it as
their decided opinion, that it was the most eligible plan to
proceed direct to the siege of Babylon.   On hearing this, the
French stoutly opposed it, and protested that they would
march nowhere else but to the siege of Jerusalem.   The
king, on hearing of the obstinacy and defection of the French,
was troubled thereat, and remarked : " If the French will
accede to our plan, and agree to proceed to the siege of
Babylon, according to their oath of obedience, I will give
them my fleet, which lies at Acre, fully equipped, to carry
their provisions and necessaries, and the army can then
march along the coast with confidence.   I will also conduct
thither, at my own charge, 700 knights, and 2,000 of their followers, in the name of the Lord ; and if any one has need
of the assistance of my money or means, he may be assured

that he shall be supplied according to his wants; and if any
one doubts my doing this, I will march with my own soldiers
only, and without other help." Then he immediately ordered
that inquiries should be made at the tents of the Hospitallers,
which were contiguous to his own, what they could supply
for the completion of the siege, and how many men they
could furnish. The chiefs also came there, and agreed to make
an ample contribution towards the expenses of the siege,
though they had very little in their pockets. But at that
doubtful and critical juncture, they seemed too eager to
undertake so venturous an enterprise, with even less precaution than they evinced in commencing the siege of Jerusalem, from which the jurors had so earnestly dissuaded
them.

Cⁿ. III.—*How, while the army was at Betenoble, Bernard, the king's
spy, brought news of the approach of some very large caravans from
Babylon, and how King Richard sent out men to capture, and Saladin
sent on the other hand to guard them.*

Wₕₗₑ therefore they were anxiously inquiring what each
ought to contribute towards the expenses of the siege, there
arrived Bernard, a spy of King Richard's, and two others,
all of whom were natives of the country, and came from the
neighbourhood of Babylon. They were attired in the Turkish
costume, and differed in nowise from the Saracens, and it was
their business to report to King Richard the condition of the
enemy. No one spoke the Turkish language with greater
ease, and King Richard had given to each of the three 100
marks of silver for his services. They signified to the king
that he should set out, with all his men, as quickly as possible, to intercept the caravans, which were coming from
Babylon, and to which they promised to conduct him. The
king, delighted at what he heard, charged the duke of Burgundy to join him immediately in the enterprise, and bring
the French to assist; and they agreed to go, on condition
that they should receive the third part of the booty, to which
the king assented. Then about 500 soldiers instantly set out,
well armed, and the king took with him a thousand hired
serving-men. At evening they pursued their march, the king
preceding them, and advancing all night, by the light of a
splendid moon, they arrived at Galatia. There they rested a

short time, and sent to Ascalon for provisions. Meanwhile,
they carefully prepared their arms, until the servants, who had
been sent for the provisions, arrived. But our men had no
sooner started, as we have said, to capture the caravans, than
a spy informed Saladin, at Jerusalem, that he had seen King
Richard set out, with his people, in great haste, to intercept
his caravans ; and thus the secret of our expedition was re-
vealed. Saladin then hastily sent off 500 chosen Turks, who,
on joining with the others that were intrusted with the protection of the caravans, formed a body of 2,000 horsemen,
besides a numerous company of foot-soldiers.

Ch. IV.—*How King Richard fought bravely with the Turks, and took a
caravan full of costly things, of inestimable value, camels, dromedaries,
horses, and asses.*

WHILST King Richard and his people were staying at
Galatia, a spy informed the king, that one of the aforesaid caravans was passing by a round cistern, and advised him to proceed at once and capture it, recommending that he should keep
back his troops ; " for," said he, " whoever shall capture
that caravan, will gain an immense booty." But as the spy
was a native of the country, the king did not think he ought
to place implicit confidence in his sole assertion. Therefore,
the king straightway sent a Bedouin and two cautious
Turcopolite servants, to inquire into the truth of the matter,
and ascertain its accuracy ; and he caused them to be clothed
after the fashion of Bedouins, to look like Saracens. These
men set out by night across the hills, which were covered
with watch-towers, and descended to the valley, by turns,
until they saw some Saracens on the higher ground, who
were themselves spies, and lying in wait for those who might
cross the mountains; and when our Bedouin approached,
with stealthy steps, to reconnoitre them, the Saracens asked
him, who they were, whence they came, and whither they were
going? The Bedouin, beckoning the other two to be silent, lest
the Saracens should recognize them by their speech, answered,
" that they were returning from the neighbourhood of Ascalon,
whither they had gone for the sake of plunder :" but one of the
Saracens said to him, " You are come to look out for us, and
you belong to the king of England." The Bedouin answered,
" that he lied," and then proceeded hastily in the direction of

the caravan, followed for some time by the Saracens, with
their bows and lances, until they ceased in their pursuit from
weariness. They, however, strongly suspected that they were
of their own country, and not belonging to the enemy. Our
spies, therefore, having ascertained the truth, as to the before-
mentioned caravans, returned with all speed to the king, and
told him that he might easily capture the caravans if he would
make haste. On learning this, the king, after refreshing his
horses with provender, set out with his men, and they walked
during the following night until they came to the place where
the caravan and its guards were resting : a short distance
from it they halted, armed themselves, and formed into
companies ; the king being in the front rank, and the French
in the rear. The king forbade, by mouth of herald, any one
from turning to plunder ; and commanded, that all should
endeavour, by their utmost means, to break and destroy the
Turkish lines. When, therefore, day arrived, and they were
engaged in forming their ranks, another spy came up at full
speed, and informed the king that the caravan was preparing
to hasten forwards at dawn of day, for the king's intention to
attack it had become known to its guards. On hearing this,
the king sent forward the lightest of his slingers and bowmen
to retard their march ; and by feigning to challenge them to
battle, keep them in check until he and his troops should come
up. In this manner the Turks were harassed and delayed by
these attacks ; whilst our army approached in battle array.
When the Turks perceived them, they immediately began to
ascend a certain mountain, in order that the higher ground
might afford them a firmer position ; but their bearing was less
arrogant than usual. Then the Turks, making a fierce onset,
threw their darts and arrows, like hail, upon our ranks : the
caravan, meanwhile, standing motionless. King Richard now
having placed his army in two divisions, suddenly charged the
Turks, and with his followers, penetrated and routed the foremost rank. Such was the fury of his onset, that they fell to
the ground almost without a blow ; and he pressed so hard
upon the fugitives, that there were none left to make further
resistance, except that several of those who fled turned back
and shot their arrows behind them. Thus all of them took to
flight, like hares before the hounds, and were routed in every
direction, while the caravan stood at the mercy of the pur-

suers, who slew all they met with; so that the enemy lay
dead in heaps upon the sand. Those who were thrown from
their horses by our knights, were put to death by their
squires.   There might be seen horses with their saddles
twisted round; the conquered were miserably destroyed, and
the king's men fought nobly.   The French, too, fought with
the utmost spirit, like men accustomed to battle.   The king
was conspicuous above all the rest by his royal bearing, surpassing all of them: he was mounted on a tall charger, and
charged the enemy singly; his ashen lance gave way from
his repeated blows, and was shivered in pieces; but drawing
his sword instantly, and brandishing it, he pressed upon the
fugitives, and mowed them down, sweeping away the hindmost, and subduing the foremost; thus he thundered on, cutting
and hewing every one he came up with; no kind of armour
could resist his blows, for the edge of his sword cut open the
heads from the top to the teeth: thus waving it to and fro,
he scared away the routed Turks, as a wolf, when he pursues
the flying sheep.   While the king was thus scattering the
fugitives, who were flying with all their speed over the mountains, some of them despairing of escape from his persevering
pursuit, for he had come up with the foremost, turned aside
out of their road, and returned to our nearly deserted camp,
hoping to effect something against the guards in the king's
absence, for their courage failed them when he was in sight,
and not without reason, for the life or death of the enemy was
always in his hands.   About thirty, therefore, of the fugitives came round upon our men by a circuitous route, and
made a violent charge on Roger de Toony, whose horse they
killed under him; and they were near capturing himself, but
he was rescued from their hands by one of his comrades, Jakel
of Maine, who however was also thrown from his horse; but
Roger stoutly defended him on foot, and succeeded in rescuing
him.   Meanwhile, our men-at-arms came up, and the earl of
Leicester, who attacked them to the right and left, also Gilbert
Malemain, with four companions, Alexander Arsi, and others,
to the number of about twenty; Stephen de Longchamp also
generously offered his services to Roger de Toony, in the
midst of the hostile Turks, and supplied him with a horse to
mount.   Then the slaughter was renewed; swords flashed in
the air; and the ground was covered with blood; arms rung and

clashed together; bodies were torn limb from limb; heads, arms,
feet, and hands, and other limbs, lay scattered about ; and our
men were interrupted as they walked along by the bodies of
the enemy, which lay along the fields in great numbers, and
caused them to stumble at every step.   The men of Poictou
and Anjou, together with the French and Normans, distinguished themselves in the battle; but King Richard, the
flower of valour, and the crown of chivalry, bore away the
prize from all ; and any praise that I could give him would
fall far short of his merits.   The slaughter of the Turks was
greater than our ancestors had ever seen ; and such was their
confusion and dismay in the encounter, that a boy might have
killed ten of them, or, in fact, as many of them as came in his
way.   By this defeat the pride of the Turks was entirely
cast down, and their boldness effectually repressed ; whilst
the caravan, with all its riches, became the spoil of the victors.
Its guards surrendered to our soldiers themselves, their beasts
of burden, and sumpter horses ; and stretching forth their
hands in supplication, they implored for mercy, on condition
only that their lives should be spared.   They led the yoked
horses and camels by the halter, and offered them to our men,
and they brought mules loaded with spices of different
kinds, and of great value ; gold and silver ; cloaks of silk ;
purple and scarlet robes, and variously-ornamented apparel,
besides arms and weapons of divers forms; coats of mail,
commonly called *gariganz ;* costly cushions, pavilions, tents,
biscuit, bread, barley, grain, meal, and a large quantity of
conserves and medicines ; basins, bladders, chess-boards ;
silver dishes and candlesticks ; pepper, cinnamon, sugar,
and wax ; and other valuables of choice and various kinds ;
an immense sum of money, and an incalculable quantity of
goods, such as had never before (as we have said) been taken
at one and the same time, in any former battle.

Ch. V.—*How many camels and dromedaries were taken, and how many
Turks were slain.*

THE slaughter of the infidels being finished, and the caravan
captured, our army was harassed with new toils in gathering
together the runaway camels and dromedaries, by which the
whole army was thrown into confusion, for they avoided the
pursuit of our horses with such great fleetness, that no other

kind of animal appeared to be of so active and swift a nature.
These animals appeared slothful and tardy until the pursuers
were within a short distance, and then they moved at full
speed.   At last, by one means or another, 4,700 camels and
dromedaries were collected together, though the number is not
quite certain.   They took so many mules of both sexes, and
laden asses, that they could not reckon the number, for they
appeared more abundant than the number of men could possibly require.   Moreover, the number of Turkish horsemen
who were that day slain, exceeded 1,700, besides very many
foot soldiers, who were trodden to death in the mêlée.

Ch. VI.—*How while King Richard was returning with his spoil to
Betenoble. whence he had started, Count Henry from Acre met him
with the army for which he had been sent.*

HAVING accomplished all these things, and prepared the
baggage for returning, the king and his army set out, laden
with spoil, at an easy pace, and reached Bethaven, which was
only four miles distant from Joppa.   There they shared the plunder, and then proceeded on the second day to Ramula.   Here
Count Henry came up with the troops, and the people he had
brought with him from Acre, and thence they all set out for
Betenoble, from which place they had started.   Here the universal joy was renewed, and all flocked together in astonishment at the numbers of beasts of burden with which the army
was accompanied.   On arriving, the noble king distributed the
camels, which were larger than any that had ever been seen
there, as well to the soldiers, who had remained to protect the
camp, as to those who had joined in the expedition, in equal
proportions.   In this respect, he graciously imitated the example of that renowned warrior, King David, who gave an
equal share of the spoil to the soldiers who went forth to
battle, and to those who remained in the camp ; and he also
divided the asses amongst his serving men.   By these means
the army was supplied with so plentiful a number of camels
and other beasts of burden, that it was with difficulty they
were kept together.   The flesh of the young camels they
stuffed with lard and roasted for the table, and they found it
very white and palatable.

CH. VII.—*How the people murmured at being prohibited, however reasonably and prudently, from going to Jerusalem.*

SHORTLY after the distribution of the plunder, the people grew discontented, and complained that the beasts of burden consumed too much barley and provender, and that on this account the price of grain was become higher. Besides this, there arose much complaint and sorrowing amongst the people, because it was not thought expedient to proceed to the siege of Jerusalem, as they wished, owing to the opposition of the twenty counsellors aforesaid, who had given their reasons for deciding to the contrary. They thought it a difficult and impossible enterprise, from the want of water, which the men and cattle could not do without, especially as the festival of St. John was close at hand; a time when, from the increasing heat of the summer, all things were naturally dry, particularly around Jerusalem, which is situated in the mountains. Besides this, the Turks had blocked up all the cisterns, so that not a drop of drinkable water could be found within two miles of the city, and it would be unsafe to go in search of it to a distance when the siege had once begun ; and the small stream of Siloe, which runs down at the foot of the Mount of Olives, would not be sufficient for the army. These were the reasons why the counsellors dissuaded the king from the siege of Jerusalem at that time, and when it became known to the army that they were not to proceed thither, but were on the point of turning away from that city, they cursed this delay in the hopes they had conceived, and asserted that they only wished to live until Jerusalem and the Holy Land and Cross were once more in the possession of the Christians alone. But God, who is the just judge of men's feelings, governeth time and actions ; and to his mercy and kindness is it to be ascribed that he chastens sinners and punishes them for all the inventions of their hearts.

CH. VIII.—*Of the jealousies and discords of the French, and how they separated themselves from the rest of the army, and how Henry, duke of Burgundy, composed a satirical poem against King Richard.*

WE must not wonder that the pilgrims who were thus harassed without any good result, grieved at the failure of their wishes, for discord grew rife amongst them ; nor that

the vacillating character of the French, which distinguished
them from all other nations, should have been here displayed.
For at evening, when the army advanced on their march, the
French separated themselves from the rest, and took up a
distinct position, as if they disdained their company. They
were not, however, content with separating only, but they fell
to quarrelling among themselves, and gave utterance to ironical
jests and abusive language, each vaunting his own superior
prowess, while they disparaged that of the others. Above all,
Henry, duke of Burgundy, whether instigated by a spirit of
arrogance, or influenced by envy and jealousy, composed and
caused to be recited in public, a song, which if he had any
sense of shame, he would never have allowed to be published;
and those songs were sung not only by men but by immodest
women. By which means, they shewed the real character of
those who indulged in such indecent folly, and the nature of
their hearts was sufficiently manifest from this fact, for the
stream is clear or turbid according as is its source. On this
composition becoming current amongst the soldiers, King
Richard was much annoyed, but he thought that a similar
effusion would be the best mode of revenging himself on the
authors, and he had not much difficulty in composing it, as
there was abundance of materials; why then should he hesitate to reply to such a false and scurrilous composition?
Moreover, the king's high honour was so evident in all his
actions, that his rivals, who could not equal him, assailed him
with foul and gratuitous aspersions. For they were not like
the pilgrims of yore who besieged and captured Antioch, and
whose famous deeds and victories are still recited in song.
Such were Boemund, Tancred, and Godfrey of Bouillon, and
other princes of high renown, who gained so many triumphs,
and whose exploits are like food in the mouths of their narra-
tors. Men, who because their hearts were true to the service
of God, received from the Lord the reward of their labours,
who magnified them by giving them an immortal name,
which posterity should regard with the deepest veneration.

CH. IX.—*Of the return of the army from Betenoble to Joppa.*

THE army remained in this state for some days after the
capture of the caravan, and were in great sorrow and distress
in consequence of the check put on their progress to visit the

Holy Sepulchre at Jerusalem, from which they were only four miles distant.   The dejection which their return caused was never before equalled in a people of the like valour.   Our men, on setting out on their march, were attacked by the Turks from the mountains, and some of our camp-followers were slain, though they were repulsed by our horsemen, from not having good horses.   The army afterwards arrived at a place between Saint George and Ramula, where they spent the night, the French posting themselves on the left, the king and his men on the right.   Next day they proceeded on their march in separate divisions, and arrived at night at a castle midway; this was on the 6th of July.   Here some in disgust deserted the army, on account of the tediousness and penury to which they were exposed in the expedition: these went to Joppa.

CH. X.—*How Saladin, learning the discord and departure of the Christians, collected an immense army.*

WHEN the state and intention of the Christians were made known to Saladin, his hopes revived, and his joy was unbounded.   He immediately sent messengers bearing despatches, sealed with his own ring, to the admirals, princes, satraps, and prefects of his dominions, informing them of the internal discord which had broken up the Christian army and forced them to retire ; and that whoever wished to serve in his pay, should come forthwith to Jerusalem.   So large a number flocked thither in consequence, that the cavalry was estimated at 20,000 strong, besides a countless multitude of foot soldiers.

CH. XI.—*How King Richard, seeing the defection of his men, sought to obtain the truce which had been first offered him, but in vain; and how in consequence he destroyed Darum and fortified Ascalon, and then returned to Acre by way of Joppa.*

MEANWHILE our men moved off by degrees, and many went to Joppa.   The king, perceiving his inability to check them on account of the diversity of opinion which prevailed, thought the best line of policy was to send to Saphadin at this juncture, and agree to the truce, which had been before offered between him and Saladin, in the plains of Ramula, for a certain period, in order that he might have time to return from

his own country.   But Saladin, who knew well the condition
of our army, and that it was daily growing weaker and weaker,
absolutely refused, unless Ascalon was razed to the ground.
The king, learning Saladin's answer, was not at all discom-
posed; nay, he gave immediate orders to the Templars, Hospitallers, and others, to the number of three hundred, to mount
their horses and proceed to the destruction of Fort Darum ;
and he set guards to watch over and fortify Ascalon as
strongly as possible.   They hastened to obey the king's orders, and levelled Darum with the ground.   The army then
returned in dejected mood as far as Joppa, and thence the
king and the rest proceeded in all haste to Acre, but many
remained from ill health and weakness at Joppa.   Thus the
army returned to Acre, broken up, with a heavy heart, for
God did not as yet judge them worthy of the higher bounties
of his grace.

CH. XII.—*Of the great army with which Saladin came to Joppa.*

WHEN Saladin heard that the men of Joppa were without
the presence of King Richard to protect them, he ordered his
army should proceed thither, in the hope that he would easily
take the city during the king's absence.   He therefore led an
immense army having 20,000 horse in that direction ; and he
had with him the powerful admiral of Bala, and the son of
Arcisus, together with about one hundred and six admirals,
and an immense multitude of infantry from the mountains,
who covered the face of the earth like locusts.   The army,
leaving Jerusalem, descended into the plains of Ramula,
rushing on in troops and squadrons as if impelled by the
furies to the utter destruction of the Christians.

CH. XIII.—*How Saladin assaulted Joppa so vigorously, that he would
have taken it, if the townsmen had not asked for a cessation of arms
until the next day.*

ON the same Sunday, next preceding the feast of St. Peter
ad vincula, being the same day on which King Richard
came with his army to Acre, Saladin advanced with his
troops to assault Joppa.   On the Monday following they
began to attack the castle ; but the citizens issuing forth into
the suburbs, resisted them the whole day, and prevented them
from approaching the town.   Tuesday and Wednesday also

passed away in the same manner; nor was it till Thursday, that the Turks, ashamed of being baffled by so few, made a great exertion, and formed the siege at once. By the command of Saladin, four powerful petrariæ were erected, and two mangonels of great efficiency for casting missiles. The besieged were about 5,000 in number, and they now began to be afflicted at their desperate condition, and to call out upon the Lord to save them. They also turned their thoughts towards the king of England, and to wish that he had not gone to Acre, leaving them there to be destroyed. Meanwhile, the Turks pressed on the siege; and it would have melted any one to tears to have seen the distracted state of the townspeople, who offered the bravest resistance, though they were overwhelmed with a thousand cares at once in the defence of their city. The petrariæ and mangonels played without intermission; though the latter instruments were worked the most successfully. At last, by the exertions of the Turks, the gate leading to Jerusalem was broken open on the Friday by the frequent strokes of their petrariæ, and the wall on the right-hand side was shattered, about two poles in width. The conflict was then fierce, whilst the besieged resisted the entrance of the Turks, who at length, however, became so reinforced by numbers, that the Christians were driven back, and followed even as far as the citadel of the fortress. What a terrific slaughter then took place! The Turks put to death without mercy all those whom they found in the houses sick and lying in their beds. Some of our people fled down to the seashore and escaped; whilst the enemy plundered every thing; and knocking out the heads of the casks which they found in the houses, let the wine run about the streets. Some of them, however, attacked the principal tower of the fortress; and others pursued those who fled down to the seaside. Numbers of the hindmost were cut off; and Alberic of Rheims, whose duty it was to defend the town, fled on board ship to escape being slain; but his companions reproaching him for his cowardice, recalled him to a sense of duty, and absolutely forced him into one of the towers; where, seeing nothing but danger on every side surrounding him, he exclaimed, " Here then we shall devote our lives to God's service ;" for it was the only thing that remained for him to do. The Turks now

fiercely assaulted the tower, and the arrows flew like hail, so
as to darken the sky: the besieged knew not which part
first to defend, and so the attack lasted the whole day; and
the besieged would certainly have at length yielded to its
violence, if by God's good pleasure the newly-elected patriarch
had not been present : and he proved himself, at that moment,
a man whom no fear of death could vanquish, nor any danger
terrify.   This man, instigated by the necessity of the case,
proposed to Saladin and his brother to grant them a respite
from the attack until the next day, on condition, that if before three o'clock, they should not receive assistance, each of
those who were in the tower, should pay Saladin ten bezants
of gold, every woman five, and every child three bezants, in
return for the respite which he had granted them; and that
the patriarch, with others of the nobles, should be given up
to Saladin to be kept in chains as hostages, until the hour
agreed on should arrive.   Saladin assented ; and when the
guarantee was completed for observing the conditions of the
truce, the following hostages were given over to Saladin:
the patriarch, Alberic of Rheims, Theobald of Trèves, Augustin of London, Osbert Waldin, and Henry de St. John,
besides others, whose names we do not remember, all of whom
were carried off prisoners to Damascus; for the besieged had
now conceived hopes of obtaining succour from the king, for
which, indeed, they had already sent, the moment they first
saw Saladin approaching.

CH. XIV.—*How King Richard, though on the point of embarking to
return home, and refused aid by the French, no sooner heard of the
message from Joppa, than he proceeded thither immediately by sea,
having first sent on his troops by land.*

MEANWHILE King Richard was busily engaged in preparing to leave Acre for his own country, and his ships were
all but ready : he had also obtained consent and a blessing
from the Templars and Hospitallers, and had sent forward
seven of his galleys, with troops to dislodge the enemy from
Baruth, by which he would pass; and the expedition had
succeeded, for the enemy fled in alarm.   The king was in his
tent, talking with his officers about embarking for their homes
on the morrow, when, lo ! the messengers from Joppa entered,
and tearing their garments, related to the king how the

enemy had taken Joppa, all but the citadel, in which the remnant were besieged, and unless he should render them speedy assistance, they would all be involved in one common fate, according to the conditions which had been entered into with Saladin. The king, hearing of the danger to which the besieged were exposed, and pitying their condition, interrupted the messengers: "As God lives," said he, "I will be with them, and give them all the assistance in my power!" The words were hardly out of his mouth, before a proclamation was made that the army should be got ready. But the French would not vouchsafe even to honour the king with an answer, exclaiming proudly that they should never again march under his command; and in this they were not disappointed, for they never again marched under anybody's command, for in a short time they all miserably perished. Meanwhile, however, the soldiers of all nations, whose hearts God had touched, and the sufferings of their fellow-creatures excited to compassion, hastened to set out with the king; namely, the Templars, the Hospitallers, and several other valiant knights, all of whom marched by land to Cæsarea; but the noble king trusting for his safety to his own valour, embarked on board his fleet of galleys, which were equipped with every thing that could be necessary. With him were the earl of Leicester, Andrew de Chaveguy, Roger de Satbeya, Jordan de Humez, Ralph de Mauleon, Achus de Fay, and the knights of Pratellea, companions of the king, together with many others of illustrious names, besides Genoese and Pisans. Those who went by land to Cæsarea, halted there some time for fear of an ambuscade, which they heard had been laid by Saladin for all such as should pass that way; and there was no better way for them to go by, on account of the son of Arcisus, who guarded the maritime district between Cæsarea and Arsur: and besides this, a contrary wind arose, which detained the king's ships three days at Cayphas, where they had put in. The king, vexed at this delay, exclaimed aloud, "O Lord God, why dost thou detain us here? consider, I pray thee, the urgency of the case, and the devoutness of our wishes." No sooner had he prayed thus, than God caused a favourable wind to spring up, which wafted his fleet before it into the harbour of Joppa, in the midst of the night of Friday immediately preceding the Saturday on which they

had agreed to surrender, and all of them would have been
given over to destruction. Alas, for the perfidy of that
wicked race! Early on the morning of that day, which was
the day of St. Peter *ad vincula*, the besieged were importuned
by the Turks to fulfil the conditions of the truce. They accordingly began at the ninth hour to pay in part the bezants
which they had promised; when the wicked Turks, behaving
worse than brute beasts, and with no feeling of humanity
about them, cut off the heads of those who paid them the
money; and thus seven of them had already perished, and
their heads were thrown into a ditch. But those in the
town who were still alive, discovering the treachery, were
struck with terror, and began to send forth cries of lamentation and distress. Seeing certain death before them, they
bent their knees, and confessed their sins to one another,
thinking no longer of their lives which were doomed, but of
their souls; whilst to delay their fate for some few moments
longer,—for who is there that does not fear death?—they fled
up the fortress as far they were able, and there awaited the
stroke of martyrdom, shedding tears, and supplicating the
mercy of the Almighty, who at length was appeased, and
deigned to listen to their petition: their deliverer was already
come, his fleet was riding in the harbour, and his soldiers
were eager to land for their rescue!

CH. XV.—*Of the fierce conflict by which the king recovered the castle of
Joppa, and liberated the besieged.*

THE Turks, discovering the arrival of the king's fleet,
sallied down to the seaside with sword and shield, and sent
forth showers of arrows: the shore was so thronged with
their multitude that there was hardly a foot of ground to
spare. Neither did they confine themselves to acting on the
defensive, for they shot their arrows at the crews of the ships,
and the cavalry spurred their horses into the sea to prevent
the king's men from landing. The king, gathering his ships
together, consulted with his officers what was the best step to
take. "Shall we," said he, "push on against this rabble
multitude who occupy the shore, or shall we value our lives
more than the lives of those poor fellows who are exposed to
destruction for want of our assistance?" Some of them replied that further attempts were useless, for it was by no

means certain that any one remained alive to be saved, and how could they land in the face of so large a multitude? The king looked around thoughtfully, and at that moment saw a priest plunge into the water and swim towards the royal galley. When he was received on board, he addressed the king with palpitating heart and spirits almost failing him. "Most noble king, the remnant of our people, waiting for your arrival, are exposed like sheep to be slain, unless the divine grace shall bring you to their rescue." "Are any of them still alive, then?" asked the king, "and if so, where are they?" "There are still some of them alive," said the priest," and hemmed in and at the last extremity in front of yonder tower." "Please God, then," replied the king, "by whose guidance we have come, we will die with our brave brothers in arms, and a curse light on him who hesitates." The word was forthwith given, the galleys were pushed to land : the king dashed forward into the waves with his thighs unprotected by armour, and up to his middle in the water ; he soon gained firm footing on the dry strand : behind him followed Geoffrey du Bois and Peter de Pratelles, and in the rear came all the others rushing through the waves. The Turks stood to defend the shore, which was covered with their numerous troops. The king, with an arbalest which he held in his hand, drove them back right and left ; his companions pressed upon the recoiling enemy, whose courage quailed when they saw it was the king, and they no longer dared to meet him. The king brandished his fierce sword, which allowed them no time to resist, but they yield before his fiery blows, and are driven in confusion with blood and havoc by the king's men until the shore was entirely cleared of them. They then brought together beams, poles, and wood, from the old ships and galleys to make a barricade ; and the king placed there some knights, servants, and arbalesters, to keep guard and to dislodge the Turks, who, seeing that they could no longer oppose our troops, dispersed themselves on the shore with cries and howlings in one general flight. The king then, by a winding chair, which he had remarked in the house of the Templars, was the first to enter the town, where he found more than 3,000 of the Turks turning over every thing in the houses, and carrying away the spoil. The brave king had no sooner entered the town, than he caused his banners to be hoisted on an eminence, that they might be seen by the Christians in the tower, who taking courage at the sight, rushed forth in arms from the tower to meet the king, and at the report thereof the Turks were thrown into confusion. The king, meanwhile, with brandished sword, still pursued and slaughtered the enemy, who were thus enclosed between the two bodies of the Christians, and filled the streets with their slain. Why need I say more ? All were slain, except such as took to flight in time; and thus those who had before been victorious were now defeated and received condign punishment, whilst the king still continued the pursuit, shewing no mercy to the enemies of Christ's Cross, whom God had given into his hands ; for there never was a man on earth who so abominated cowardice as he.

Ch. XVI.—*Of the severe conflicts by which the king made Saladin raise the siege, and fixed his own tents where those of Saladin had been.*

But the king had only three horses with him, and what were three among so many ? If we examine the deeds of the ancients, and all the records left us by former historians, we shall find that there never was a man who so distinguished himself in battle as King Richard did this day. When the Turks leaving the town saw his banners floating in the air, a cry was raised on right and left as he sallied forth upon them, and no hail-storm or tempest ever so densely concealed the sky, as it was then darkened by the flying arrows of the Turks. Saladin, hearing of the king's arrival, and of his brilliant contest with the Turks, of whom he had slain all who opposed him, was seized with sudden fear, and like that timid animal, the hare, put spurs to his horse and fled from before his face. The king, with his men, still continued the pursuit, slaying and destroying, whilst his arbalesters made such havoc of the horses, that for two miles the traces of their flight were visible. He now therefore pitched his tent in the same place where those of Saladin had been, and thus by the divine grace so small a body of men had defeated this large army of the Turks. Saladin called together his admirals and thus addressed them : " Has he then beaten all of us ? Has the Christian army returned from Acre to slaughter and defeat us thus ? By what superior disposition have they been able to accomplish this? In infantry, as well as cavalry, our army was decidedly superior." To these words, one of those perverse ones who were present, conscious of the state of our army, replied: " My lord, it is not as you think; they have neither horses nor beasts of burden of any kind, except three horses only, which their wonderful king found in Joppa. I think, however, that the king himself could easily be surprised, for he lies almost alone in his tent, and fully worn out with fatigue. Whoever seizes him will at once put an end to our labours and to the whole campaign." It was then given out among the Turks what a reproach it was to them, and lasting scandal, that so large an army and so many thousands of the Turks had been defeated by so small an army, and that Joppa had been recovered from them by force of arms. In this manner they murmured to one another at what had taken place, and trembled with confusion.

Ch. XVII.—*How the Christians acted in the matter of the swine which the Turks had killed.*

Now the execrable Turks, who were surprised in Joppa, had made an immense slaughter of those who were too weak to resist, and in particular had killed a large number of swine, in fact, all they could find; for it is against the law of Mahomet to eat them; wherefore they naturally abominate swine as unclean, because swine are said to have devoured Mahomet. The Turks, therefore, in contempt of the Christians, had collected into one mass the bodies of the swine, together with the bodies of the Christians, whom they had slain. But the corpses of the Christians were now buried in peace, whilst those of the Turks were in their turn cast out to rot with those of the swine.

Ch. XVIII.—*Of the rebuilding of the walls of Joppa.*

On the next day, being Sunday, the king diligently set to work to repair the walls of Joppa, and continued his exertions on Monday and Tuesday, that some protection at least might be furnished by them such as it was, though the repairs were made without either lime or cement: but this could not be avoided, for an immense army of Turks was close at hand.

CH. XIX.—*How certain men called Menelones and Cordivi boasted that they would surprise the king, asleep or otherwise, unawares.*

MEANWHILE a certain depraved set of men among the Saracens, called Menelones of Aleppo and Cordivi, an active race, met together to consult what should be done in the existing state of things. They spoke of the scandal which lay against them, that so small an army, without horses, had driven them out of Joppa, and they reproached themselves with cowardice and shameful laziness, and arrogantly made a compact among themselves that they would seize King Richard in his tent, and bring him before Saladin, from whom they would receive a most munificent reward.

CH. XX.—*How Count Henry arrived at Joppa from Cæsarea, and of the number of his soldiers.*

IN the mean time Count Henry came in a galley with his followers from Cæsarea, where the rest of our army was detained, on account of the ambuscades of the Turks, who lay in wait at all the roads, bridges, and wells, so that the king could not, on this emergency, bring with him out of all his army more than fifty-five knights, with a strong body of infantry, arbalesters, and retainers; besides, about two thousand Genoese and Pisans and others; whilst of horses he had no more than fifteen, whether good or bad.

CH. XXI.—*How the aforesaid Menelones and Cordivi would have surprised the king in his tent, as they had boasted, if a certain Genoese had not perceived them, and awakened the king.*

MEANWHILE the Menelones and Cordivi aforesaid prepared themselves in the middle of the night to surprise the king, and sallied forth armed, by the light of the moon, conversing with one another about the object which they had in hand. O hateful race of unbelievers! they are anxiously bent upon seizing Christ's steadfast soldier, while he is asleep: they rush on in numbers to seize him, unarmed and apprehensive of no danger. They were now not far from his tent, and were preparing to lay hands on him, when, lo! the God of mercy, who never neglects those who trust in Him, and acts in a wonderful manner even towards those who know him not, sent the spirit of discord among the aforesaid Cordivi and Menelones. The Cordivi said, "You shall go in on foot, to take the king and his followers, whilst we will remain on horseback to prevent their escaping into the castle." But the Menelones replied, "Nay, it is your place to go in on foot, because our rank is higher than yours: we are content with the service which is our duty; but this service on foot belongs to you rather than us." Whilst thus the two parties were contending which of them were the greatest, their continued dispute caused much delay, and when at last they came to a decision how their nefarious attempt should be achieved, the dawn of day appeared, viz. the Wednesday next following the feast of St. Peter *ad vincula*. But now, by the providence of God, who had decreed that his holy champion should not be seized whilst asleep by the infidels, a certain Genoese was led by the divine impulse to go out early in the morning into the fields, where he was alarmed at the noise of men and horses advancing, and returned speedily, but just had time to see helmets reflecting back the light which now fell upon them. He immediately rushed with speed into the camp, calling out "To arms! to arms!" The king was awakened by the noise, and leaping startled from his bed, put on his impenetrable coat of mail, and summoned his men to the rescue.

CH. XXII.—*Of the marvellous bravery of the king in this never-to-be-forgotten skirmish.*

GOD of all virtues! lives there a man who would not be shaken by such a sudden alarm? The enemy rush unawares, armed against unarmed, many against few, for our men had no time to arm, or even to dress themselves. The king himself therefore, and many others with him, on the urgency of the moment, proceeded without their cuishes to the fight, some even without their breeches, and they armed themselves in the best manner they could, though they were going to fight the whole day. Whilst our men were thus arming in haste, the Turks drew near, and the king mounted his horse, with only ten other knights, whose names are as follows: Count Henry, the earl of Leicester, Bartholomew de Mortimer, Ralph de Mauleon, Andrew de Chavegni, Gerald de Finival, Roger de Sacy,

Y

William de l'Etang, Hugh de Villeneuve, a brave retainer, and Henry le Tyois, the king's standard-bearer. These alone had horses, and some even of those they had were base and impotent horses, unused to arms: the common men were skilfully drawn out in ranks and troops, with each a captain to command them. The knights were posted nearer to the sea, having the church of St. Nicholas on the left, because the Turks had directed their principal attack on that quarter, and the Pisans and Genoese were posted beyond the suburban gardens, having other troops mingled with them. O who could fully relate the terrible attacks of the infidels? The Turks at first rushed on with horrid yells, hurling their javelins and shooting their arrows. Our men prepared themselves as they best could, to receive their furious attack, each fixing his right knee in the ground, that so they might the better hold together, and maintain their position; whilst there, the thighs of their left legs were bent, and their left hands held their shields or bucklers; stretched out before them in their right hands they held their lances, of which the lower ends were fixed in the ground, and their iron heads pointed threateningly towards the enemy. Between every two of the men who were thus covered with their shields, the king, versed in arms, placed an arbalester, and another behind him to stretch the arbalest as quickly as possible, so that the man in front might discharge his shot whilst the other was loading. This was found to be of much benefit to our men, and did much harm to the enemy. Thus every thing was prepared as well as the shortness of the time allowed, and our little army was drawn up in order. The king ran along the ranks, and exhorted every man to be firm and not to flinch. "Courage, my brave men," said he, "and let not the attack of the enemy disturb you. Bear up against the frowns of fortune, and you will rise above them. Every thing may be borne by brave men; adversity sheds a light upon the virtues of mankind, as certainly as prosperity casts over them a shade; there is no room for flight, for the enemy surround us, and to attempt to flee is to provoke certain death. Be brave, therefore, and let the urgency of the case sharpen up your valour: brave men should either conquer nobly, or gloriously die. Martyrdom is a boon which we should receive with

willing mind: but before we die, let us whilst still alive do
what may avenge our deaths, giving thanks to God that it has
been our lot to die martyrs. This will be the end of our
labours, the termination of our life, and of our battles."
These words were hardly spoken, when the hostile army
rushed with ferocity upon them, in seven troops, each of
which contained about a thousand horse. Our men received
their attack with their right feet planted firm against the sand,
and remained immovable. Their lances formed a wall against
the enemy, who would assuredly have broken through, if
our men had in the least degree given way. The first
line of the Turks, perceiving, as they advanced, that our men
stood immovable, recoiled a little, when our cross-bow-
men plied them with a shower of missiles, slaying large
numbers of men and horses. Another line of Turks at once
came on in like manner, and were again encountered and
driven back. In this way the Turks came on like a whirl-
wind, again and again, making the appearance of an attack,
that our men might be induced to give way, and when they
were close up, they turned their horses off in another direction. The king and his knights, who were on horseback,
perceiving this, put spurs to their horses, and charged into
the middle of the enemy, upsetting them right and left, and
piercing a large number through the body with their lances;
at last they pulled up their horses, because they found that
they had penetrated entirely through the Turkish lines. The
king now looking about him, saw the noble earl of Leicester
fallen from his horse, and fighting bravely on foot. No sooner
did he see this than he rushed to his rescue, snatched him out
of the hands of the enemy, and replaced him on his horse.
What a terrible combat was then waged! a multitude of
Turks advanced, and used every exertion to destroy our
small army: vexed at our success, they rushed towards
the royal standard of the lion, for they would rather have
slain the king than a thousand others. In the midst of
the mêlée the king saw Ralph de Mauleon dragged off prisoner by the Turks, and spurring his horse to speed, in a
moment released him from their hands, and restored him to
the army; for the king was a very giant in the battle,
and was everywhere in the field.—now here, now there,
wherever the attacks of the Turks raged the hottest. So

bravely did he fight, that there was no one, however gallant,
that would not readily and deservedly yield to him the pre-
eminence. On that day he performed the most gallant deeds
on the furious army of the Turks, and slew numbers with
his sword, which shone like lightning; some of them were
cloven in two from their helmet to their teeth, whilst others
lost their heads, arms, and other members, which were lopped
off at a single blow. While the king was thus labouring with
incredible exertions in the fight, a Turk advanced towards
him, mounted on a foaming steed. He had been sent by
Saphadin of Archadia, brother to Saladin, a liberal and munificent man, if he had not rejected the Christian faith. This
man now sent to the king, as a token of his well-known
honourable character, two noble horses, requesting him earnestly to accept them, and make use of them, and if he
returned safe and sound out of that battle, to remember
the gift and recompense it in any manner he pleased. The
king readily received the present, and afterwards nobly
recompensed the giver. Such is bravery, cognizable even
in an enemy; since a Turk who was our bitter foe, thus
honoured the king for his distinguished valour. The king,
especially at such a moment of need, protested that he would
have taken any number of horses equally good from any one,
even more a foe than Saphadin, so necessary were they
to him at that moment. Fierce now raged the fight, when
such numbers attacked so few: the whole earth was covered
with the javelins and arrows of the unbelievers; they threw
them several at a time against our men, of whom many were
wounded. Thus the weight of the battle fell heavier upon
us than before, and the galley-men withdrew in the galleys
which brought them, and so in their anxiety to be safe,
they sacrificed their character for bravery. Meanwhile a
shout was raised by the Turks, as they strove who should
first occupy the town, hoping to slay those of our men whom
they should find within. The king, hearing the clamour,
taking with him only two knights and two cross-bow-men,
met three Turks, nobly caparisoned, in one of the principal
streets. Rushing bravely upon them, he slew the riders in
his own royal fashion, and made booty of two horses. The
rest of the Turks who were found in the town, were put to
the rout in spite of their resistance, and dispersing in

different directions, sought to make their escape even where
there was no regular road. The king also commanded the
parts of the walls which were broken down to be made
good, and placed sentinels to keep watch lest the town should
be again attacked.

Ch. XXIII.—*Of the wonderful acts of the king in battle, by which,
with the Divine aid, he overthrew numbers of the enemy, and returned
safe out of the midst of them to his own army.*

THESE matters settled, the king went down to the shore,
where many of our men had taken refuge on board the
galleys. These the king exhorted by the most cogent arguments to return to the battle, and share with the rest whatever
might befal them. Leaving five men as guards on board
each galley, the king led back the rest to assist his hard-
pressed army; and he no sooner arrived, than with all his fury
he fell upon the thickest ranks of the enemy, driving them
back and routing them, so that even those who were at a distance and untouched by him, were overwhelmed by the throng
of the troops as they retreated. Never was there such an
attack made by an individual. He pierced into the middle of the hostile army, and performed the deeds of a
brave and distinguished warrior. The Turks at once closed
upon him and tried to overwhelm him. In the meantime our
men, losing sight of the king, were fearful lest he should have
been slain, and when one of them proposed that they should
advance to find him, our lines could hardly contain themselves.
But if by any chance the disposition of our troops had been broken, without doubt they would all have been destroyed. What
however was to be thought of the king who was hemmed in by
the enemy, a single man opposed to so many thousands? The
hand of the writer faints to tell it, and the mind of the reader
to hear it. Who ever heard of such a man ? His bravery was
ever of the highest order, no adverse storm could sink it ; his
valour was ever blooming, and if we may, from a few instances,
judge of many, it was ever indefatigable in war. Why then
do we speak of the valour of Antæus, who regained his
strength every time he touched his mother earth, for Antæus
perished when he was lifted up from earth in the long wrest-
ling match. The body of Achilles also, who slew Hector, was
invulnerable, because he was dipped in the Stygian waves ; yet

Achilles was mortally wounded in the very part by which he
was held when they dipped him.   Likewise Alexander, the
Macedonian, who was stimulated by ambition to subjugate the
whole world, undertook a most difficult enterprise, and with a
handful of choice soldiers fought many celebrated battles, but
the chief part of his valour consisted in the excellence of his
soldiers. In the same manner, the brave Judas Maccabeus, of
whose wars all the world discoursed, performed many wonderful
deeds, worthy for ever to be remembered, but when he was
abandoned by his soldiers in the midst of a battle, with thousands of enemies to oppose him, he was slain, together with
his brothers.   But King Richard, inured to battle from his
tenderest years, and to whom even famous Roland could not
be considered equal, remained invincible, even in the midst of
the enemy, and his body, as if it were made of brass, was impenetrable to any kind of weapon.   In his right hand he
brandished his sword, which in its rapid descent broke the
ranks on either side of him.   Such was his energy amid that
host of Turks, that, fearing nothing, he destroyed all around
him, mowing men down with his scythe as reapers mow down
the corn with their sickles.   Who could describe his deeds?
Whoever felt one of his blows, had no need of a second. Such
was the energy of his courage, that it seemed to rejoice at
having found an occasion to display itself. The sword wielded
by his powerful hand, cut down men and horses alike, cleaving
them to the middle. The more he saw himself separated from
his men, and the more the enemy sought to overwhelm him, the
more did his valour shine conspicuous.   Among other brave
deeds which he performed on that occasion, he slew by one marvellous stroke an admiral, who was conspicuous above the rest
of the enemy by his rich caparisons.   This man, by his gestures seemed to say that he was going to do something wonderful, and whilst he reproached the rest with cowardice, he
put spurs to his horse and charged full against the king, who
waving his sword as he saw him coming, smote off at a single
blow not only his head, but his shoulder and right arm.   The
Turks were terror-struck at the sight, and giving way on all
sides, scarcely dared to shoot at him from a distance with their
arrows. The king now returned safe and unhurt to his friends,
and encouraged them more than ever with the hope of victory.
How were their minds raised from despair when they saw him

coming safe out of the enemy's ranks! They knew not what
had happened to him, but they knew that without him all the
hopes of the Christian army would be in vain. The king's person was stuck all over with javelins, like a deer pierced by the
hunters, and the trappings of his horse were thickly covered
with arrows. Thus, like a brave soldier, he returned from
the contest, and a bitter contest it was, for it had lasted
from the morning sun to the setting sun. It may seem
indeed wonderful and even incredible, that so small a body
of men endured so long a conflict; but by God's mercy
we cannot doubt the truth of it, for in that battle only one or
two of our men were slain. But the number of the Turkish
horses which lay dead on the fields is said to have exceeded
fifteen hundred; and of the Turks themselves more than
seven hundred were killed, and yet they did not carry back
King Richard, as they had boasted, as a present to Saladin;
but, on the contrary, he and his brave followers performed so
many deeds of valour in the sight of the Turks, that the
enemy themselves shuddered to behold them.

CH. XXIV.—*How Saladin ridiculed his men for having boasted that
they would seize King Richard, and how they, in self-defence, replied
that they had never seen so brave a soldier.*

IN the meantime, our men having by God's grace escaped
destruction, the Turkish army returned to Saladin, who
is said to have ridiculed them by asking where Melech
Richard was, for they had promised to bring him a prisoner? "Which of you," continued he, "first seized him,
and where is he? Why is he not produced?" To whom
one of the Turks that came from the furthest countries of the
earth, replied: "In truth, my lord, Melech Richard, about
whom you ask, is not here: we have never heard since the
beginning of the world that there ever was such a knight, so
brave and so experienced in arms. In every deed at arms,
he is ever the foremost; in deeds, he is without a rival, the
first to advance, and the last to retreat: we did our best to
seize him, but in vain, for no one can escape from his sword;
his attack is dreadful; to engage with him is fatal, and his
deeds are beyond human nature."

CH. XXV.—*How the king was ill from his fatigue and exertions in the battle.*

FROM the toil and exertion of the battle, King Richard and several others who had exerted themselves the most, fell ill, not only from the fatigue of the battle, but the smell of the corpses, which so corrupted the neighbourhood, that they all nearly died.

CH. XXVI.—*Saladin sends word to the king, whilst he was sick, that he was coming to seize him. Richard sends to Cæsarea for assistance from the French, who refuse to come.*

IN the meantime Saladin sent word to the king that he would come with his Turks and seize him, if he could only be sure that Richard would await his approach. The king replied instantly, that he would wait for him there, without stirring one foot from where he was, provided only that he had strength, to stand upright and to defend himself. Such was the king's courage, that it could not be overcome by any disasters. When the king, however, came to reflect on his actual situation, and the illness by which he was disabled, he thought it not expedient to be too secure when the serpent was in his neighbourhood; he therefore sent Count Henry to Cæsarea, with a message to the French, who had previously come thither, that they should join him and assist in defending the Holy Land, signifying also to them his present complaint, and the aforesaid message of Saladin. But the French refused to render him the least assistance; indeed, as far as they were concerned, he might have been destroyed by the multitude of the enemy, if he had not agreed to a truce which in some particulars was open to reprehension. So great was the multitude of the Turks, that what chance could so small a body of men have had against them, even if they had not been sick? It was therefore agreed that Ascalon should be destroyed, rather than that so dangerous a hazard should be run; for if the enemy, meeting with no opposition, had seized the king lying ill upon his bed, Ascalon would of course have been taken possession of without resistance; but would Tyre or Acre have been safe?

CH. XXVII.—*How the king wished to return to Acre to be cured, but, on the people opposing it, he asked of Saladin a truce for three years, which was granted.*

IN the meantime the king began to be anxious about his health, and after long reflection he sent for his relation Count Henry, with the Templars and Hospitallers, to whom he explained the enfeebled state of his body, and protested that in consequence of the vitiated atmosphere, and the bad state of the fortifications, he must immediately leave the place. He then appointed some of them to go and take charge of Ascalon, and to others to guard Joppa, whilst he went himself to Acre to be cured, as was now absolutely necessary for him. To this proposition they all with one heart and one voice made objection, saying, that they could not possibly guard Joppa or any other fortress after he was gone ; and persisting in this refusal, they kept aloof, and no longer acted in concert with the king. Richard was vexed and embarrassed by this conduct, and it gave him the most bitter pain that none of them sympathized with his intentions or wishes. He then began to waver as to what he should do, but in all his deliberations he came only to the same conclusion, that there was none of them to sympathize with his misfortunes. Seeing, then, that all left him, and that none took the slightest interest in the common cause, he ordered proclamation to be made, that whoever wished to receive the king's pay should come together to give him their help. At once two thousand footmen and fifty knights came forward. But the king's health now began to get so bad, that he despaired of its being re-established ; wherefore, in his anxiety both for the others and for himself, he thought it best, of all the plans which suggested themselves, to ask a truce, rather than to leave the land a prey to devastation, as many others had done, by sailing home in numbers to their own country. Thus the king, perplexed and hesitating what he had best do, requested Saphadin, the brother of Saladin, to mediate between them, and obtain the most honourable terms of truce in his power. Now Saphadin was a man of extraordinary liberality, who on many occasions paid great honour to the king for his singular virtues ; and he now with great zeal procured for Richard a truce on the following conditions ; namely, that Ascalon,

which had always been a cause of annoyance to Saladin's
government, should be destroyed, and not rebuilt for the space
of at least three years, beginning at the following festival of
Easter; but at the end of that time, whoever could get possession of it might fortify it; that the Christians should be
allowed to inhabit Joppa without let or molestation, together
with all the adjoining country, both on the sea-coast and in
the mountains; that peace should strictly be observed between
the Christians and Saracens, each having free leave to come
and go wherever they pleased; that pilgrims should have free
access to the Holy Sepulchre, without any payment or pecuniary
exaction whatever, and with leave to carry merchandise for
sale through the whole land, and to practise commercial pursuits without opposition. This treaty was presented in writing
to King Richard, who gave it his approbation, for in his weak
condition, and having so few troops about him, and that too
within two miles of the enemy, he did not think it in his
power to secure more favourable terms. Whoever entertains
a different opinion concerning this treaty, I would have him
know that he will expose himself to the charge of perversely
deviating from the truth.

Ch. XXVIII.—*How the king and Saladin corresponded amicably with one another by means of messengers.*

WHEN therefore the king, in his present emergency, had
settled matters in the way described, he, in his magnanimity,
which always aimed at something lowly and difficult, sent ambassadors to Saladin, announcing to him, in the presence of
numerous of his chiefs, that he had only asked for a truce of
three years for the purpose of revisiting his country, and collecting more men and money, wherewith to return and rescue all
the land of Jerusalem from his domination, if indeed Saladin
should have the courage to face him in the field. To this
Saladin replied, calling his own Holy Law and God Almighty
to witness, that he entertained such an exalted opinion of
King Richard's honour, magnanimity, and general excellence,
that he would rather lose his dominions to him than to any
other king he had ever seen, always supposing that he was
obliged to lose his dominions at all. Alas! how blind are
men, whilst they lay plans for many years to come, they
know not what to-morrow may bring forth: the king's mind

was looking forward into the future, and he hoped to recover
the sepulchre of our Lord ; but he did not

> Reflect how every human thing
> Hangs pendent on a slender string.

Ch. XXIX.—*How the king went to Cayphas for his health.*

THE truce having been reduced to writing, and confirmed
by oaths on both sides, the king went to Cayphas in the best
manner he could, to take medicine and get himself cured.

Ch. XXX.—*How the French, by the king's agency, for their malice, were forbidden to visit the Holy Sepulchre, whilst the others had permission.*

IN the meantime the French, who had been long enjoying
a holiday at Acre, were getting ready to return home ; but
though they had venomously opposed the truce, they now,
before leaving the country, wished to complete their pilgrimage
by visiting our Lord's sepulchre. The king, remembering
their backwardness to assist him at Joppa, as we have related,
and also on many other occasions, sent messengers to request
that neither Saladin nor Saphadin, his brother, would allow
any one to visit the Holy Sepulchre who did not bring a passport from either himself or Count Henry. The French were
much vexed at this, and foiled of their object, soon afterwards
returned to their own country, carrying back nothing with
them but the reproach of ingratitude. The king, hearing that
the greater part of the French who did their utmost to defame
him were gone home, and that the mouths of his slanderers
were stopped, caused it to be announced by proclamation,
that whoever wished might visit our Lord's tomb, and bring
back their offerings to help in repairing the walls of Joppa.

Ch. XXXI.—*Of the first company who made the pilgrimage to Jerusa-lem, led by Andrew de Chavegui, and of the alarm occasioned by their indiscretion on the way.*

THE people were now arrayed to visit Jerusalem in three
companies, each of which was placed under a separate leader.
The first was led by Andrew de Chavegui ; the second by
Ralph Teissun ; and the third by Hubert bishop of Salisbury.
The first company then advanced under Andrew bearing
letters from the king. But, for their sins, they fell into a

suare on the journey; for when they reached the Plain of
Ramula, they by common consent despatched messengers
to inform Saladin that they were coming with letters from
King Richard, and that they wished to have a safe-conduct,
coming and going. The messengers were noble men, and
energetic in character, but on this occasion they well nigh incurred the charge of neglecting their duty; their names were
William des Roches, Girard de Tourneval, and Peter de
Pratelles. When they came to "the Tower of the Soldiers,"
they halted there to procure the authority of Saphadin for
proceeding further; but there they fell asleep, and slept till
sunset, and found on awaking that all the pilgrims, on whose
behalf they came, had passed by and were gone on before
them. The whole number crossed the plains and were approaching the hills, when Andrew de Chavegui and the rest,
looking behind them, saw their own messengers coming after
them as fast as they were able. Seeing this, they halted in
much alarm, considering that they were in great danger of
being put to death, for the army of the Turks had not yet
departed, and their messengers, who ought to have brought
back for them a safe-conduct from the Saracens, were now
behind them. When therefore these came up, the others
blamed them for their neglect, and told them once more to make
haste on before, and do as they had been instructed. The
messengers went on with all speed to Jerusalem, and found
about 2,000 Turks, or more, encamped without the city.
They inquired for Saphadin, and when they had found him,
they explained what had happened, and he, rebuking them
smartly, said it was evident that they did not value their
lives a rush, as they had come into the middle of a hostile
army without passport or safeguard of any kind. It was now
sunset, and the other pilgrims came up, not knowing what they
ought to do, and having no arms to defend themselves. The
Turks grinned and frowned on them as they passed, and it was
manifest by their looks what enmity they harboured in their
hearts, for the face is after the index of the mind; and our
men at that moment were so confounded that they wished
themselves back again at Tyre, or even Acre, which they had
just left. Thus they passed the night, near a certain mountain, in a state of great alarm.

CH. XXXII.—*How the Turks wished to take vengeance on our pilgrims, but Saladin and his chiefs would not allow it.*

THE next day certain of the Turks appeared before Saladin, and earnestly entreated of him that they might be allowed to take vengeance on the Christians who were now in their power, for the death of their friends, fathers, brothers, sons, and relations who had been slain, first at Acre, and afterwards at other places, now, as they said, that they had so good an opportunity. Saladin sent for the Turkish chiefs to consult about this request, and Mestoc, Saphadin, Bedridin, and Dorderin were speedily in attendance. When the subject was placed before them, it was their unanimous opinion that the Christians should have leave to come and go, without injury or hinderance. "For," said they to Saladin, "it would be a deep stain upon our honour, if the treaty which has been made between you and the king of England should, by our interference, be broken, and the faith of the Turks for ever afterwards be called in question." In consequence of these observations, Saladin gave orders immediately that the Christians should be taken care of, and escorted to the city and back again without molestation. To discharge this commission, Spahadin was at his own request deputed; and under his protection the pilgrims had free access to the Holy Sepulchre, and were treated with the greatest liberality, after which they returned joyfully to Acre.

CH. XXXIII.—*Of the second company of pilgrims who went to Jerusalem, escorted by Ralph Teissun.*

ON their return, the second company of pilgrims stationed between the castle of Arnald and Ramula, set forth, led by Ralph Teissun. Now Saladin, as we have before stated, had posted his men to keep diligent guard over the roads whenever any of the pilgrims were on their way to Jerusalem. In consequence of this precaution, we travelled freely and unmolested, and crossing the hill country, arrived at the Mountain of Delight, where, seeing in the distance the city of Jerusalem, we knelt down and gave humble thanks to God, as is the custom of pilgrims. From the same spot we saw also Mount Olivet: after which all advanced with joy, and those who had horses rode forward with speed, that they might the

sooner gratify their desire of saluting the Holy Sepulchre.
Moreover, as those horsemen who had gone before told us,
Saladin allowed them to see and kiss the true Cross of our
Lord, which formerly had been carried to battle.   But we
who were on foot, and came in the last, saw what we could,
viz. : in the first place we saw our Lord's monument, where
oblations were made : but, as the Saracens took these away,
we did not offer much, but gave part to the French and
Syrian slaves, whom we there saw in servitude, labouring in
the duties assigned to them.   From thence we proceeded to
Mount Calvary, where our Lord was crucified, and where
there was a stone in which our Lord's cross had been fixed in
Golgotha.   When we had kissed this with reverence, we proceeded to the church built on Mount Sion, on the left side of
which was the place from which Mary, the Holy mother of
God, passed from this world to the Father.   This spot we
saluted with tears running down our cheeks, and then hastened
to see the holy table at which Christ condescended to eat
bread.   This also we kissed fervently, and then we all departed
together, in haste ; for it was no longer safe for us to go
anywhere, except in a body, on account of the treachery of
the unbelievers, for the Turks had secretly strangled three or
four of our men who had strayed into the passages of the
crypts.   From thence we hastened to the sepulchre of the
Blessed Virgin Mary, mother of God, in the middle of the
valley of Jehoshaphat, near Siloe, and kissed it with devout
and contrite hearts.   After which, with minds not altogether
free from apprehension, we entered the vaulted chamber in
which our Lord and Redeemer was kept prisoner during the
night, to be crucified the next morning.   This we saluted
devoutly, whilst the tears ran down our cheeks, and then took
our leave in haste, and the Turks also spurned us from them
not a little, and we grieved for the pollutions with which the
holy places were defiled by the horses of the unbelievers who
used them for stables.   We now took leave of Jerusalem and
returned to Acre.

Cn. XXXIV.—*Of the third company of pilgrims, led by Hubert Walter, bishop of Salisbury, to whom Saladin shewed much honour, and granted every thing he asked for.*

THE third company, led by the bishop of Salisbury, was now not far from Jerusalem, and Saladin sent out his people to receive the bishop honourably, and to conduct him wherever he pleased, to visit the holy places. Moreover, in acknowledgment of his prudent and honourable character, and his other merits, which had long before been known to Saladin, he was requested to take up his residence in the sultan's palace, and to be entertained at his expense. The bishop refused, saying, "By no means, for we are but pilgrims." Saladin enjoined his servants to shew every attention to the bishop and his men, and sent him many presents; afterwards, also, he invited them to an interview, that he might behold his manner and deportment, and he allowed him to have a sight of the Holy Cross; and they sat and conversed together a long time. Saladin, therefore, asked him about the king of England, and what the Christians said of his Saracens. To which the bishop replied, "In truth, as concerns my lord the king, I will only say what justice demands, that he has no equal among all the knights in the world, either for valour or for liberality in giving; for he is in every thing distinguished for every excellent quality. In short, my lord, in my humble opinion, if any one, bating your majesty's sins, were to bring your virtues into comparison with those of King Richard, and were to take both of you together, there would not be two other men in the world that could compete with you." Saladin listened patiently to the bishop, and at last replied, "I have long since been aware that your king is a man of the greatest honour and bravery, but he is imprudent, not to say foolishly so, in thrusting himself so frequently into danger, and shews too great recklessness of his own life. For my own part, of however large territories I might be the king, I would rather have abundance of wealth, with wisdom and moderation, than display immoderate valour and rashness." The conversation then took a familiar turn between the two, and Saladin told the bishop to ask for any thing he liked, and it should be given him. The bishop in reply, asked if he might have until the next day to consider what he should ask. Which being granted, he then

requested, that, whereas divine service was but half performed before at our Lord's tomb, which he had just visited,
in the barbarous way of the Syrians, it might be allowed
for the future, that two Latin priests with two deacons,
to be maintained by the offerings of the faithful, should
perform divine service in conjunction with the Syrians;
and an equal number at Bethlehem, and also at Nazareth.
This petition was one of great importance, and as we believe,
agreeable to God.   The sultan assented to the request; and
the bishop instituted two priests in the aforesaid places, together with two deacons, rendering to God a service where
there had been none before. After this, the pilgrims obtained
the sultan's license, and returned from Jerusalem to Acre.

Ch. XXXV.—*How the pilgrims, having fulfilled their pilgrimage, set
sail for their own country, but suffered many shipwrecks and hardships
on the way.*

The people had now completed the pilgrimage to which
they had devoted themselves, and preparing their fleet to
return home, they spread their sails to the winds, and committed themselves to their ships.   The fleet speedily set sail,
and the ships were wafted in different directions, according to
the variety of the winds.   For a long time they were tossed
about on the waves, and some of them reached different ports
in safety; others were driven about, and in danger of being
shipwrecked; others, again, died on their voyage, and found
their grave in the depths of the ocean; others also were
seized with incurable diseases, and never recovered or returned
to their own country.   Others, moreover, who endured in
safety to the end, through the loss of their fathers, brothers,
relations, and friends, who had perished of disease or by the
sword, are believed to have endured a severe species of martyrdom, and diverse passions pierced their breasts as with a
sword.   Each, in his own way, we must admit it, endured a
kind of martyrdom; every one, in short, of those, who with
simple and devout hearts had exposed themselves for the
love of God to this distant pilgrimage.   Some, however,
with loquacious garrulity, were accustomed afterwards to
complain that the pilgrims had done little good in the land of
Jerusalem, because they had not freed the city; but they did
not know what they were saying, for they were inquiring

about things of which they have no personal knowledge or
experience. We, however, who have seen, and who know
all of it by our own eye-sight, claim to be believed in our
accounts of the tribulations and miseries which those men
endured. Wherefore, we state confidently, in the hearing of
those also who were present, that 100,000 Christians perished
in that pilgrimage, for the sole reason that, in the hope of
divine reward, they had separated themselves from women,
deeming it wicked by sacrificing their purity to obtain bodily
health ; and thus they opposed patience even to the corruption of the flesh, that the purity of their minds might remain
unimpaired. We know also, for certain, that by sickness
and famine combined, there died more than 300,000, in the
siege of Acre, and afterwards, in the same city. Who, however, can doubt of the salvation of the souls of such noble
and excellent men, who daily heard divine service from the
lips of their own chaplains? These surely may be supposed
to have gone to heaven.

CH. XXXVI.—*How the king, before setting sail for home, exchanged
ten noble Turkish captives for William de Pratelles, who had suffered
himself to be captured to save the king, saying that himself was Melech.*

MEANWHILE King Richard's ship was made ready, and
every thing necessary, both in arms and provisions, prepared for the voyage. The king then, out of mere liberality,
and impelled by his nobleness of mind alone,[*] redeemed
William de Pratelles, who, as we have before related, suffered
himself to be captured to save the king, by exchanging for him
ten of the most noble Turks, though they would gladly have
given a large sum of money to retain him ; but the king's
generosity would not condescend in any way to be tarnished.

* Such may be the opinion of Geoffrey de Vinsauf, a narrow-minded
priest of the twelfth century ; but every liberal-minded and enlightened
man will believe, and probably no one knew it better than the noble
King Richard, that his escutcheon would have been for ever dishonoured,
if he had left the Holy Land without redeeming from slavery the noble
knight who had sacrificed himself for his sovereign.—See Book ii. c. 20.

CH. XXXVII.—*How King Richard set sail to return home, and of the misfortunes which he met with.*

EVERY thing was now settled, and the king was already on the point of embarking, when determining before he went, to leave nothing behind him that might detract from his honour, he ordered proclamation to be made that all who had claims on him should come forward, and that all his debts should be paid fully, and more than fully, to avoid all occasion afterwards of detraction or complaint. What sighs and tears were there when the royal fleet weighed anchor! A blessing was invoked on the king's many acts of benevolence, his virtues and his largesses were set forth, and the numerous excellences combined in one man. How then did the lamentations of all resound as they exclaimed, "O Jerusalem, bereft now of every succour! How hast thou lost thy defender! Who will protect thee, should the truce be broken, now that King Richard is departed?" Such were the words of each, when the king, whose health was not yet fully re-established, and who was the subject of all their anxious wishes, went on board and set sail. All night the ship ran on her way by the light of the stars, and when morning dawned, the king looked back with yearning eyes upon the land which he had left, and after long meditation, he prayed aloud, in the hearing of several, in these words, "O holy land, I commend thee to God, and if his heavenly grace shall grant me so long to live, that I may, in his good pleasure, afford thee assistance, I hope, as I propose, to be able to be some day a succour to thee." With these words he urged the sailors to spread their canvass to the winds, that they might the sooner cross over the expanse of sea that lay before them; ignorant indeed of the tribulations and sorrows that awaited him, and the calamities that he was to suffer from the treachery that had long before been transmitted to France, by which it was contrived that he should be wickedly thrown into prison, though he justly suspected no such evil in the service of God, and in so laborious a pilgrimage. O how unequally was he recompensed for his exertions in the common cause! His inheritance was seized by another, his castles in Normandy were unjustly taken, his rivals made cruel assaults upon his

rights without provocation, and he only escaped from captivity
by paying a ransom to the emperor of Germany.   To gather
the money for his ransom, the taxes were raised to the
uttermost;   a large   collection was levied upon all his
land, and every thing was distracted; for the chalices
and hallowed vessels of gold and silver were gathered from
the churches, and the monasteries were obliged to do
without their utensils; neither was this unlawful according to
the decrees of the holy fathers, nay, it was even a matter
of necessity, inasmuch as no saint, many though there be,
ever during life suffered so much for the Lord as King
Richard in his captivity in Austria and in Germany.   He
who had gained so many triumphs over the Turks was
nefariously circumvented by the brethren of his own faith,
and seized by those who agreed with him in name only as
members of the creed of Christ.   Alas, how much more are
secret snares to be feared than open discord, according to
the proverb. "It is easier to avoid a hostile than a deceitful
man."   Oh, shame be it said, that one whom no adversary
could resist, nor the whole force of Saladin could conquer,
was now seized by an ignoble people, and kept a prisoner
in Germany.   Oh, how painful is it for those who have been
nurtured in liberty, to be placed at the beck of another!   But
out of that captivity, by God's usual mercy, his own activity,
and the care of his faithful servants, he was at length set
at liberty for a large sum of money, because he was known
to be a man of great power.   At last restored to his native
soil and the kingdom of his ancestors, in a short time he
restored all to tranquillity.   He then crossed over into
Normandy, to avenge himself on the wanton aggressions of
the king of France, his rival; and when he had more than
once defeated him, he powerfully recovered with sword and
spear his alienated rights, even with augmentation.

HERE ENDS THE BOOK OF KING RICHARD'S EXPEDITION TO

THE LAND OF JERUSALEM.

MEMOIRS

OF

LOUIS IX. KING OF FRANCE,

(COMMONLY CALLED SAINT LOUIS.)

BY

JOHN LORD DE JOINVILLE,

HIGH SENESCHAL OF CHAMPAGNE

BIOGRAPHICAL NOTICE OF JOINVILLE.

THE family of Joinville was, in the thirteenth century, one of the most distinguished in Champagne. About the middle of the preceding century, Etienne, surnamed Devaux, an ancestor of the author of these memoirs, became very powerful. He espoused the countess de Joigny, who brought him the fief so named, together with several other manors, as a marriage portion; and he was the first who built the castle of Joinville.

The uncle and father of Joinville covered themselves with glory; the first, during the reign of Philip Augustus, when in attendance upon the count of Flanders, at the conquest of Constantinople: the second, during the minority of St. Louis, in defending the town of Toyes against the joint efforts of almost all the lords of France.

John lord of Joinville, author of the following memoirs, was eldest son to Simon lord of Joinville, by Beatrice of Burgundy, his second wife. Biographers differ as to the date of his birth. Du Cange places it in 1220; De la Ravaliere in 1224; and De la Bastie as late as 1228. The authors of the "Biographie Universelle" decide in favour of the middle period. He was betrothed during the life of his parents to Alicia, daughter of Henry count de Grand Pré, by Marie de Garlande. The articles of marriage were agreed to in the month of June, 1231, in the presence of Thibaud count of Champagne, the principal conditions of which were, that the countess and her son Henry should give, in consideration of this alliance, three hundred livres yearly, in land, and that in return Alicia should renounce all claim to the succession of her father and mother.

It was likewise stipulated that Simon lord of Joinville, father to John, should so manage that Geoffry de Joinville, his son, should approve of and ratify the sentence of separation which the archbishop of Rheims had pronounced between him and the countess of Grand Pré; from which we may conjecture, that this marriage was concluded to appease the quarrel which this divorce had caused between the two families.

The articles were only signed by the countess of Grand Pré, in the absence of her son; but the count of Champagne pledged himself for his duly executing them. This was not, however, so soon accomplished, nor was the marriage completed until after the year 1239; at which period John lord of Joinville having succeeded his father in his estates, and in the seneschalship of Champagne, was unmarried; for in this year he promised Count Thibaud, king of Navarre, not to ally himself with the count de Bar, nor take his daughter to wife. Beatrice, mother to John, made the count a similar promise for her son.

His marriage with Alicia must have taken place instantly afterward; for, in a deed of the year 1240, the lady of Joinville is styled sister to Henry count de Grand Pré. It had probably been deferred until then on account of the youth of the lord de Joinville, who thus speaks of himself: "That when the treaty between the king, Saint Louis, and the

count de la Marche, was concluded, he had not then put on his helmet."
That is to say, he had not then borne arms, nor received the order of
knighthood; and that when he put on the cross to march to the Holy Land
with his king, he was very young.

That was the first occasion he made use of to display his valour, and
shew to all the world that he was no way degenerated in courage and
virtue from his ancestors. The crusade had been proclaimed throughout
France, and St. Louis, his queen and children, with the brothers to the
king, and the principal barons of the realm, had already put on their
armour, and covered their shoulders with the mark of our redemption, to
recover the Holy Land from the hands of the infidels, and to carry the war
into their country.

John lord of Joinville followed the examples of his ancestors, who had
signalized themselves in these illustrious conquests, took the cross, and
determined to accompany the king. But as this enterprise was attended with
danger, and would probably be of long duration, he wished, before he set
out, to make a settlement of his affairs, and leave every one satisfied with
his conduct, so that he might be in the proper condition to deserve the
fruits and pardons which these crusaders merited through the concessions
of the sovereign pontiff. Having assembled his friends and neighbours,
he gave them to understand, that if any one had the smallest subject
of complaint against him, or if he had wronged him in the slightest manner, he was ready to make him all the satisfaction that could be wished
for. On the other hand, as his mother, Beatrice, was still living, and
enjoyed the greater part of his fortune as her dower, he found himself
obliged to mortgage the principal part of the remainder of his lands, to
supply the expenses of his equipment for so long a voyage, and of so
considerable an enterprise, so that there scarcely remained to him twelve
hundred livres of yearly rent in land.

He set out from his castle of Joinville after the Easter of 1248, accompanied by ten knights, whom he kept in his pay; among whom were
three bannerets,—namely, Hugh de Landricourt, Hugh de Til-châtel, lord
of Conflans, and Peter de Pontmolain. He journeyed in company with
John lord d'Aspremont, Gosbert d'Aspremont and his brothers, who
were his cousins, and the count de Sarrebruche, all of whom had in like
manner put on the cross. They embarked at Marseilles and sailed to
Cyprus, where they found the king of France, who had arrived there a
short time before. It was there the lord de Joinville first entered
into the service and pay of this great king, whose good graces and affection he so much gained that this prince would have him always near his
person, employing him in the most important negotiations, and considering him as one of his confidential and faithful counsellors. From
the day he entered into the service of the king, in the island of Cyprus,
he scarcely ever quitted him until his death, and was always attendant on
him for the space of twenty-two years.

This would be the place to relate his adventures, his combats, and his
travels; how he landed in Egypt, and was attacked by the Saracens, how
he repulsed them; how he was wounded, and then caught the epidemical
disorder of the army; how he was made prisoner by the enemy, saved
and delivered from their hands; how he accompanied the king to Acre,

who again retained him and his knights in his pay : in short, after having been absent on these expeditions the space of seven years, he returned to France with the king. But as this narration would be of considerable length, and as he himself has written the history, I pass it over, and shall only mention some others of his principal actions. On his return to France, he took leave of the king at Beaucaire, whence, having visited the dauphiness of Vienne his relation, the count de Châlons his uncle, and the count de Bourgogne his cousin-german, he arrived at his castle of Joinville. After residing there some time, he went to Soissons to meet the king, who received him with so much kindness and friendship that the whole court was surprised and became jealous of him. It was about this time that Thibaud II. king of Navarre and count of Champagne, employed him to request of the king his daughter Isabella ; and this negotiation he managed with so much address and prudence that, in spite of great difficulties, the marriage was concluded, and celebrated at Melun with royal magnificence, in the year 1255.

This service, in addition to others, gained him the affections of the king of Navarre, who presented him with many gifts, among which was the donation to him and his heirs, dated January 1258, of all the rights and royalties of the village of Germay, as an augmentation of fief, on condition of paying homage liege. In the following year he subscribed the testament of Ebles de Geneva, son to Humbert count of Geneva, in which, however, he adds no title to his name, which may cause a doubt whether this John de Joinville, or de Genville, as he is called, be our seneschal.   He was, afterward, almost constantly at the court of the king of Navarre, his lord, and accompanied him, in the year 1267, when this prince did homage to the bishop of Langres for the towns of Bar sur Aube, Bar sur Seine, and some others, which he held under the church, in presence of William lord de Grancey, Renier Vitardore, and Eustache de Conflans, marshals of Champagne, and other lords of that country.

The king, St. Louis, having convoked at Paris all his barons, on the subject of a new crusade, summoned thither the lord de Joinville, at that time suffering under a quartan ague. On his arrival, the king, and Thibaud king of Navarre, pressed him to put on the cross, and undertake, with them, an expedition to Africa ; but he excused himself on the plea of the poverty and distress of his subjects and vassals, who had been harshly treated by the exactions made on them by the king of France's officers during his former expedition. He acted sometime afterward as president in the extraordinary assemblies and assizes held at Troyes, as the person best qualified, in the year 1271. During the journey which was made to Arragon in 1283, by King Philip the Hardy, who had the wardship of Jane queen of Navarre and countess of Champagne, sole daughter to King Henry, he was appointed by him governor and guardian of that country. He was present likewise at the assizes of Champagne in the years 1291 and 1296 ; and in the year 1303 he is named, with John de Joinville lord of Ancerville, Ansean de Joinville, and other great barons of France and Champagne, in the summons of Philip the Fair to meet him at Arras the 5th of August, and attend him in his war against Flanders.

He was also one of the lords and barons of Champagne, who formed a

league, in the month of November, 1214, against this same king, on
account of a subsidy which he had undertaken to raise from the nobles of
his realm. This dispute was settled the ensuing year by the king, Louis
Hutin, who, by his letters, dated from the Bois de Vincennes, the 17th
day of May, 1315, appointed commissioners to inquire into their privileges. The king immediately after issued a summons for the nobles of
his realm to assemble at Arras in the month of August, to assist him in
his war against the Flemings ; but the lord de Joinville was ordered, by
a private letter from the king, to be at Authie by the middle of June.
This was, however, too short notice for him to make his preparations,
and he wrote to the king his excuses, alleging the impossibility of being
at the appointed place by the time fixed, and promising at the same time
to join the army as speedily as he could. And in the list of those men-
at-arms who were in the company of my lord the count of Potiers, and
received at Arras and elsewhere by his two marshals, M. Regnaut de
Lor and the Borgne de Ceris, his name appears, with one knight and six
esquires. .

The letter which he wrote to the king on the subject of this summons
was as follows :—

" To his good lord, Louis, by the grace of God, King of France and
Navarre, John lord of Joinville, seneschal of Champagne, sends health
and his willing service. Dear sire, it is indeed true, as you inform me,
that it has been reported you had made up matters with the Flemings ;
and, as we believed it, sires, we have not made any preparations to obey
your summons, which you sent me, sire, acquainting me that you should
be at Arras to redress the wrongs the Flemings have done you; and in
this I think you act well, and may God give you his assistance ! And as
you have ordered me and my people to be at Authie by the middle of
June, sire, I inform you that that cannot well be done ; for your letters
only arrived the second Sunday in June, eight days before we ought to
have been at the rendezvous. My people shall be got ready as soon as
possible, to go whithersoever you please. Sire, do not be displeased that
at the beginning of this letter I have only called you my good lord, for I
have never done otherwise to my lords your ancestors and predecessors
in the government, whose souls may God pardon ! Written the second
Sunday of June, the same day that your letter was brought me, in the
year 1315."

This letter was folded, and sealed with a seal of yellow wax, of the size
of a large golden crown, having an impression of a knight armed with his
sword and shield, and the coat of arms and housing of his horse blazoned
with the arms of Joinville: around it, instead of an inscription, was a
border of flowers de luce, similar to that which is on the coins of St. Louis.
The lord de Joinville must have been ninety or ninety-two years old in
this year of 1315 ; for since his marriage was arranged in 1231, and consummated in 1240, he could not then have been younger than twenty
years. A late author assures us, that he lived upwards of one hundred
years ; and in a title-deed of the abbey of St. Urbain, near Joinville, dated
on the morrow of Easter, in the year 13 . . ., by which he grants to Robert,
the abbot, and to the monks of that monastery, certain fields and woods,
he says, that he had been engaged so long in the country of the infidels,

where he had remained seven years with the king, Saint Louis, and in other parts; for which God, out of his mercy, had preserved his body and mind in greater health and vigour to a longer period of time than had been allotted to any of his predecessors.

Although no deed has been found that marks precisely the time of his death, it must have been about the year 1318; for in that year his son Anceau was in possession of the estate of Joinville, and of the office of seneschal of Champagne, as we shall see hereafter. There is a tradition at Joinville, that this lord was of an extraordinary stature and strength of body, and that his head was of an enormous size, as large again as that of any of his contemporaries, and that it may now be seen at Joinville with one of his thigh-bones. This agrees with what he writes himself of his constitution and habit of body, saying that he had " la tête grosse, et une froide fourcelle," meaning a cold stomach; for which cause, his physicians had ordered him to drink his wine pure, and to warm it. With regard to the qualities of his mind, it will be sufficient to say, that the great king, Saint Louis, appointed him one of his principal counsellors and ministers of state; besides, he says of himself that he had a subtle wit.

These memoirs, which Joinville finished in 1309, and published after the death of Philip the Fair, have always been highly esteemed by the public. Although they include a space of but six years, they give us sufficient information respecting the military system of those days, and the principles of administration adopted by St. Louis. They present to us a faithful picture of the customs and manners of our ancestors: they charm us by the affecting simplicity of style, which is one of its greatest merits; and if we wish to become acquainted with the noble mind of St. Louis, it is in them displayed with the most exact truth.

Among the different editions of these memoirs (in French), the two most approved of are that of Du Cange, printed in 1668, and the one published by the late Mr. Capperonnier in 1761. Whatever may be the merit of the edition of 1761, we prefer that of Du Cange. The public opinion, as well as that of several learned friends, has determined us to make this choice. It is not surprising that the edition of Du Cange has preserved its great reputation; for that of 1761, notwithstanding the glossary which has been added to it, would not be intelligible for three-fourths of its readers, who, unless perfectly well versed in the old French language, would be fatigued and disgusted with it.

The remarks with which Du Cange has enriched this edition, clear up a number of important facts contained in the memoirs of Joinville, and throw the greatest light on many points connected with the customs and institutions of that period. They seemed too precious to be withheld from our readers, and are, therefore, subjoined to the present edition.

A DISSERTATION

ON

JOINVILLE'S LIFE OF ST. LOUIS.

By M. le Baron de la Bastie.

———

Tʜᴇ life of St. Louis, written by the lord de Joinville, has always been considered as one of the most precious monuments of our history ; and as a work that contains many of those qualifications which we are accustomed to wish for in the lives of private persons. The author was of very considerable rank by his birth, his connections, his employments, and still more from his personal merit. He had not only lived under the reign of the prince whose life he has written, but was moreover personally attached to him for twenty-two years, and, by consequently following him in his expeditions, had participated in the most important events of his reign. The air of candour and good faith that accompanies his recitals prejudices the reader in his favour ; the scrupulous attention he shews not to mention facts of which he was not a witness, and only to touch on such as he relates from the report of others, as his history requires ; this attention, I repeat, ought to convince us, that the lord de Joinville had no other intention than to transmit to posterity nothing but what he was perfectly well informed of.

His history is not, like the greater part of the chronicles of those times, a simple recital of what passed in France and elsewhere during the reign of St. Louis ; it makes us intimately acquainted with that monarch : it gives us a just idea of his heart and head, and paints equally well the great man, the great saint, and the great king. The friendship and confidence with which St. Louis honoured the lord de Joinville ; the intimate familiarity, if I may be allowed the expression, to which he had admitted him, have furnished many curious details, which, although improper for a general history, are not the less agreeable or instructive, since they more distinctly display the characters of the principal persons whom the historian successively offers to our view.

So many interesting motives to the French will not suffer them to see with indifference the attempt that has been made to tear from their hands one of their principal historians, by endeavouring to make the history of the lord de Joinville pass for a romance, not composed till the fifteenth century. For upwards of two hundred years, when it was first printed, no one had ever thought of suspecting its authenticity, when an unjust criticism appeared in the posthumous works of a learned man (Jo. Hardouin), more celebrated, however, for the singularity of his ideas, than for the extent of his erudition. He maintains, that the Life of St. Louis, generally attributed to the lord de Joinville, is the work of an author very much posterior to him, who has forged the name of the supposed author of it.

I pass over these objections in silence ; they will have no weight, until it shall be granted that the greater part of ecclesiastical and profane authors have been supposititious writers.

DEDICATION.

To the most noble, most excellent, and most potent prince, Louis, son to the King St. Louis, of most renowned and holy memory, by the grace of God, King of France and Navarre, and Count Palatine of Champagne and Brie, John Lord of Joinville, Seneschal of Champagne, sends health, wishing that, at his prayer, Jesus may anoint him with holy love.

MAY it please you to know, most noble and potent lord, that my late most excellent lady, your mother, whose soul may God pardon, from the great affection she bore me, and from her knowing with how much loyalty and love I had served and attended the deceased king, St. Louis, her spouse, in several countries, had most earnestly entreated me, that in honour to God, I would collect and write a small book or treatise of the holy actions and sayings of the above-mentioned King St. Louis. This I very humbly promised her to execute to the best of my power ; and because you, my most excellent and potent lord, are his eldest son and heir, and have succeeded to the crown and kingdom of our late lord and king, St. Louis, I send this book to you, not knowing any one living to whom it can more properly belong, in order that you and all others who may read it, or hear it read, may profit by imitating the examples and deeds which it contains, and may God our Father and Creator be worshipped and honoured by it.

JOINVILLE'S PREFACE.

IN the name of the most holy and most sovereign Trinity, the Father, Son, and Holy Ghost, I, John lord of Joinville, high steward of Champagne, do indite and cause to be formed into a book, the life and most pious acts and sayings of my late lord, St. Louis, king of France, from what I personally saw or heard during the space of six whole years that I was in his company, as well in the holy expedition and pilgrimage beyond sea as since our return thence. This book will be divided into two parts. The first will shew how the above-mentioned king, St Louis, governed himself according to the precepts of God and of our holy mother the church, to the profit and advancement of this kingdom.

The second part will speak of his gallant chivalry and deeds of arms, that the one may follow the other, to enlighten and exalt the understandings of such as shall read or hear it. The contents of both parts will shew plainly that no man of his time, from the beginning of his reign unto the end of it, ever lived a more godly or conscientious life than he did.

It seems however to me, that sufficient respect has not been shewn him, inasmuch as he has not been ranked among the martyrs, for the great vexations he suffered on his pilgrimage for the honour of the cross during the six years that I attended him ; for, as our Lord God died for the human race on the cross, so in like manner died the good king St. Louis, at Tunis, with the cross on his breast. Because nothing is to be preferred to the salvation of the soul, I shall begin this first part which speaks of his righteous doctrine and holy conversation, which is food for the soul.

MEMOIRS

OF

LOUIS IX. KING OF FRANCE,

(COMMONLY CALLED SAINT LOUIS.)

BY JOHN LORD DE JOINVILLE,

HIGH SENESCHAL OF CHAMPAGNE.

FIRST PART.

THIS holy man, King St. Louis, loved and feared God during his life above all things, and, as is very apparent, was in consequence favoured in all his works. As I have before said that our God died for his people, so in like manner did St. Louis several times risk his life and incur the greatest dangers for the people of his realm, as shall be touched on hereafter.

The good king, being once dangerously ill at Fontaine-bleau, said to my Lord Louis, his eldest son,[*] "Fair son, I beseech thee to make thyself beloved by the people of thy kingdom; for, in truth, I should like better that a Scotsman,[†] fresh from Scotland, or from any other distant and unknown country, should govern the subjects of my realm well and

---

[*] He was born in the year 1244, and died when sixteen years old, in 1260.

[†] I know not if the lord de Joinville here speaks of the Scots as of a people very distant from France, and who inhabit what was called the Ultima Thule, or whether he wished to mark the character of this nation, which delighted so much in travelling to different countries, that there was scarcely a kingdom wherein great numbers of them were not to be found. This is noticed by Walfridus Strabo in the forty-sixth chapter of the second book of his Life of St. Gall. Owing to this love of emigrating, we read that in almost every part of France there were hospitals founded for them, of which mention is made in the capitularies of Charles le Chauve, tit. 6 and 23; in Synodo Meld. can. 14, and in the charter of the foundation of the abbey of Walcourt, in the diocese of Namur, published by Miræus in Diplom. Belg. lib. 2, cap. 22. See also, on this subject, Innocent. Ciron. lib. 1; Observat. Jur. Canon. cap. 13.

loyally, than that thou shouldst rule them wickedly and re-
proachfully."

The holy king loved truth so much, that even to the
Saracens and infidels, although they were his enemies, he
would never lie, nor break his word in any thing he had
promised them, as shall be noticed hereafter. With regard
to his food, he was extremely temperate ; for I never in my
whole life heard him express a wish for any delicacies in
eating or drinking, like too many rich men ; but he sat and
took patiently whatever was set before him.

In his conversation he was remarkably chaste ; for I never
heard him, at any time, utter an indecent word, nor make
use of the devil's name, which, however, is now very commonly uttered by every one, by which I firmly believe is so
far from being agreeable to God, that it is highly displeasing
to him.

He mixed his wine with water by measure, according to
the strength of it, and what it would bear. He once asked
me, when at Cyprus, why I did not mix water with my
wine. I answered what the physicians and surgeons had
told me, that I had a large head and a cold stomach, which
would not bear it. But the good king replied, that they had
deceived me, and advised me to add water ; for that if I did
not learn to do so when young, and was to attempt it in the
decline of life, the gout and other disorders, which I might
have in my stomach, would greatly increase ; or, perhaps, by
drinking pure wine in my old age, I should frequently intoxicate myself ; and that it was a beastly thing for an
honourable man to make himself drunk.

My good lord the king asked me at another time, if I
should wish to be honoured in this world, and afterward to
gain paradise ; to which I answered, that I should wish it
were so. "Then," replied he, "be careful never knowingly
to do or say any thing disgraceful, that should it become
public, you may not have to blush, and be ashamed to say I
have done this, or I have said that." In like manner he
told me never to give the lie, or contradict rudely whatever
might be said in my presence, unless it should be sinful or
disgraceful to suffer it, for oftentimes contradiction causes
coarse replies and harsh words, that bring on quarrels,

which create bloodshed, and are the means of the deaths of thousands.

He also said, that every one should dress and equip himself according to his rank in life, and his fortune, in order that the prudent and elders of this world may not reproach him, by saying such a one has done too much, and that the youth may not remark, that such a one has done too little, and dishonours his station in society. On this subject, I remember once the good lord king, father to the king now on the throne, speaking of the pomp of dress, and the embroidered coats of arms that are now daily common in the armies. I said to the present king, that when I was in the Holy Land with his father, and in his army, I never saw one single embroidered coat or ornamented saddle in the possession of the king his father, or of any other lord. He answered, that he had done wrong in embroidering his arms; and that he had some coats that had cost him eight hundred Parisian livres. I replied, that he would have acted better if he had given them in charity, and had his dress made of good sendal,* lined and strengthened with his arms, like as the king, his father, had done.

The good king, once calling me to him, said he wanted to talk with me, on account of the quickness of understanding he knew I possessed. In the presence of several, he added, " I have called these two monks, and before them ask you this question respecting God:" " Seneschal, what is God ?" " Sire," replied I, " he is so supremely good, nothing can exceed him." " In truth," answered the king, "that is well said, for your answer is written in the little book I have in my hand. I will put another question to you, whether you had rather be 'mezeau et ladre,'† or have committed, or be about to commit,

* Sendal or cendal, is what we call taffety. In the account of Stephen de la Fontaine, who was silversmith to the king, in the year 1351, which is in the Chamber of Accounts at Paris, there is a charge " For two bundles of scarlet cendal, 120 crowns. For one bundle of yellow cendal, 52 crowns," &c.

† These two words are synonymous, and signify lepers, of whom, at that period, there were numbers, more especially in the Holy Land. Philippes de Beaumanoir, chap. 62. says,—" When lepers call to them a holy man, or a holy man calls to a leper, the leper may put himself in a state of defence, because he is out of the protection of the law." In an old manuscript law-book of Normandy, it is declared, " that the mezel

a mortal sin?" But I, who would not tell a lie, replied
" that I would rather have committed thirty deadly sins than
be a leper."

When the two friars were gone away, he called me to him
alone, making me sit at his feet, and said, " How could you
dare to make the answer you did to my last question?"
When I replied, "Were I to answer it again, I should repeat
the same thing," he instantly said,—" Ah, foul musart!*
Musart, you are deceived; for you must know there can be
no leprosy so filthy as deadly sin, and the soul that is guilty
of such is like the devil in hell. It is very true," he added,
" that when the leprous man is dead, he is cured of that
disorder; but when the man who has committed a deadly sin
dies, he is not assured for certain that he had sufficiently repented of it before his death, to induce the goodness of God
to pardon him: for which cause he must have great fears lest
this leprosy of sin may endure for a length of time, even so
long as God may remain in paradise.

" I therefore entreat of you, first for the love of God, and
next for the affection you bear me, that you retain in your
heart what I have said, and that you would much rather prefer having your body covered with the most filthy leprosy
than suffer your soul to commit a single deadly sin, which is
of all things the most infamous."

He then inquired if I washed the feet of the poor on
Holy Thursday. On which I said, "Oh, for shame, no;
and never will I wash the feet of such fellows." "This
is in truth," replied he, "very ill said, for you should
never hold in disdain what God did for our instruction; for
He who is lord and master of the universe, on that same
day, Holy Thursday, washed the feet of all his apostles,
telling them, that he who was their master had thus done,
that they, in like manner, might do the same to each other.
I therefore beg of you, out of love to him first, and then
from your regard to me, that you would accustom yourself to
do so."

(leper) cannot be heir to any one, since the disorder is visibly increasing,
but that he may possess the inheritance he had before he became a leper."
In the Assizes of Jerusalem, ch. 128—" Whoever pleases may challenge
and claim at the assizes any male or female slave he had bought, whether
leper or not, or afflicted with any other filthy disorder."

* Idler, one who amuses himself by doing nothing.

He loved every one who, with uprightness of heart, feared and loved God; insomuch that from the great reputation he had heard of my brother Sir Gilles de Bruyn, who was not a Frenchman, for his fear and love of God, as was the truth, he appointed him constable of France.

In like manner, from the favourable report which he had heard of Master Robert de Sorbon being a courageous and discreet man, he made him one of his personal attendants, and permitted him to partake of his table. One time, as we were sitting near each other, and eating and drinking at the king's table, we conversed together in a low voice, which the good king observing, reprimanded us by saying, "You act wrong thus to whisper together; speak out, that your companions may not suspect you are talking of them to their disadvantage, and railing at them. When eating in company, if you have any things to say that are pleasant and agreeable, say them aloud, that every one may hear them: if not, be silent."

When the good king was in a cheerful mood, he frequently put questions to me in the presence of Master Robert; and once he said, "Seneschal, now tell me the reason why a discreet man is of more worth than a valiant man." Upon this a noisy dispute arose between Master Robert and me; and when we had long argued the question, the good king thus gave his judgment. "Master Robert, I should not only like to have the reputation of a discreet man, but to be so in reality, and your other distinctions you may keep; for discretion is of such value, that the very word fills the mouth. On the contrary," added the good king, "it is most wicked to take the goods of others; for the surrendering of them to their rightful owners is so grievous that the pronouncing of it tears the palate, from the number of rrr's that are in the word; which rrr's signify the rents of the devil, who daily draws to him all those who wish to give away the chattels of others they have seized upon. The devil does this with much subtlety, for he seduces the usurers and despoilers, and urges them to give their usuries and rapines to the church, in honour of God, which they ought to restore to the proper owners, who are well known to them." When thus conversing, he told me to say in his name to King Thibaut, his son-in-law, that he must look well to his actions, and not overcharge his soul,

2 A 2

thinking to acquit himself by the large sums which he gave, or should leave to the monastery of father-preachers in Provins; for the discreet man, as long as he lives, ought to act like to the faithful executor of a will.* First, he ought to restore and make amends for any wrongs or misdeeds done to others by the deceased; and from the residue of the fortune of the dead he should give alms to the poor, in the name of God, as the Scripture plainly sheweth.

The holy king was, one Whitsun holidays, at Corbeil, accompanied by full 300 knights, and also by Master Robert de Sorbon and myself. After dinner, the king went into the meadow above the chapel, to speak with the earl of Brittany,† father to the present duke, whose soul may God receive, when Master Robert, taking hold of my mantle, in the presence of the king and the noble company, asked my opinion, whether, if the king should seat himself in this meadow, and I were to place myself on a bench above him, I should, or should not, be blameable; to which I answered, " Yes, most certainly."   " Why, then," added he, " do not you think yourself blame-worthy for being more richly dressed than the king?"   " Master Robert," replied I, " saving the king's honour and yours, I am in this respect blameless; for the dress I wear, such as you see it, was left me by my ancestors, and I have not had it made from my own authority. It is you, on the contrary, that deserve being reprimanded; for you are descended from bondmen, on both sides, have quitted the dress of your ancestors, and have clothed yourself in finer camlet than what the king now wears."

I then took hold of his surcoat‡ and compared it with what

---

* The lord de Joinville is laughing at those who, having committed atrocious acts of plunder during their lives, imagine they may acquit themselves before God by giving alms to some monasteries or churches.

† John I. of the name, and who is noticed in several parts of this history. He died the 8th of October, 1286, and was father to John II., duke of Brittany, deceased in the year 1305. It is apparent from this, that the lord de Joinville wrote his history, or at least augmented or corrected it at different times; for in this part he says, that John II. was still alive, and elsewhere he speaks of Guy de Dampierre, earl of Flanders, and of his death, which happened at Compeigne in this same year 1305.

‡ A sort of dress or robe common to men and women. In the accounts quoted in the preceding note is an article,—" For three pieces and a half of fine velvet in grain, given to the aforesaid Eustache, to make a surcoat,

the king had on, saying, "Now see, if I did not tell the truth." The king, upon this, undertook the defence of Master Robert, and to save his honour as much as he could, declared the very great humility he possessed, and how kind he was to every one.

After this conversation, the good king called to him my Lord Philip, father to the king now on the throne, and King Thibaut, his son-in-law, and seating himself at the door of his oratory, he put his hand on the ground, and said to his sons, "Seat yourselves here near me, that you may be out of sight." "Ah, sir," replied they, "excuse us, if you please; for it would not become us to sit so close to you." The king, then addressing me, said, "Seneschal, sit down here," which I did, and so near him that my robe touched his. Having made them sit down by my side, he said, "You have behaved very ill, being my children, in not instantly obeying what I ordered of you; and take care that this never happen again." They answered, that they would be cautious it should not.

Then turning towards me, he said, that he had called us to him to confess to me that he had been in the wrong in taking the part of Master Robert; "but," continued he, "I did so from seeing him so much confounded, that he had need of my assistance; you must not, however, think or believe that I did it from the conviction of his being in the right; for, as the seneschal said, every one ought to dress himself decently, in order to be more beloved by his wife, and more esteemed by his dependants." The wise man says, we ought to dress ourselves in such manner that the more observing part of mankind may not think we clothe ourselves too grandly, nor the younger part say we dress too meanly.

You shall now hear a matter of information which the good king made me to understand. When returning from Asia, we

a dress mantle, and a hat lined with ermines for the king, against the feast of the Star, &c. For the said surcoat, a fur lining of 346 ermines, for the sleeves and wristbands, 60, for the frock, 336," &c. Isaacus Pontanus, in the description of Denmark, page 801, remarks, that among the Danes the word *serk* signifies a woman's dress. It may be that the French have borrowed this term from the Normans, who frequently ravaged France; but it is more probable that this dress was so called from being worn over the coat. This name was afterwards given to the robes of the men.

were driven near to the isle of Cyprus by a wind called
Garbun,* which is not one of the principal winds that rule the
sea; and our vessel struck with such force on a rock as
frightened our sailors, who, in despair, tore their clothes and
beards. The good king leaped out of his bed barefooted,
with only a gown on, and ran to throw himself on his knees before the holy sacrament, like one instantly expecting death.
Shortly after, the weather became calm. On the morrow, the
king called me and said, " Seneschal, know that God has
shewn to us a part of his great power; for one of these trifling
winds, which scarcely deserves a name, had almost drowned
the king of France, his queen, children, and family; and St.
Anceaune declares, they are the menaces of our Lord, as if
God had said, ' Now see and feel that if I had willed it, you
would all have been drowned.'" The good king added, " Lord
God, why dost thou menace us? for the threat thou utterest
is neither for thy honour nor profit; and if thou hadst drowned
us all, thou wouldst not have been richer nor poorer: thy
menaces, therefore, must be intended for our advantage, and
not for thine, if we be capable of understanding and knowing
them. By these threatenings," said the holy king, " we
ought to know, that if we have in us the smallest thing displeasing to God, we should instantly drive it from us; and, in
like manner, we should diligently perform every thing that we
suppose would give him pleasure and satisfaction. If we thus
act, our Lord will give us more in this world and in the next
than we ourselves can imagine. But should we act otherwise,
he will do to us as the master does to his wicked servant; for
if the wicked servant will not correct himself, in consequence
of the menaces he receives, his master punishes him in his
body, and in his goods until death, or farther were it possible.
In suchwise will our Lord punish the perverse sinner who
shall not be reclaimed by the threats which he hears; and he
will be the more heavily stricken in body and goods."

This holy king, and good man, took infinite pains, as you
shall hear, to make me firmly believe the Christian laws
which God has given us. He said, we should so punctually
believe every article of the faith, that for any thing that may
be done against us personally, we ought not to act or say any
thing contrary to them   He added, that the enemy of man-

---

* In Italian *garbino*, called by English sailors a south-wester.

kind, the devil, is so subtle, that when any persons are near dying, he labours with all his power to make them depart with doubts of the articles of our faith; for he knows well that he cannot deprive a man of the good works which he may have done; and that he loses the soul if the man die in the true belief of the Catholic faith. For this reason every one should be on his guard, and have such a steady belief, that he may say to the enemy when he comes to tempt him, "Go thy way, thou enemy of mankind; thou shalt never take from me what I so firmly believe, namely, the articles of my religion; I had rather that thou shouldst cut off all the members of my body; for I am determined to live and die in the faith." Whoever acts thus, conquers the enemy with the staff with which he meant to slay him.

The good king, however, said that faith in God was of such a nature that we ought to believe in it implicitly, and so perfectly as not to depend on hearsay. He then asked me if I knew the name of my father; I answered, that his name was Simon. "And how do you know that?" said he. I replied, that I was certain of it, and believed it firmly, because my mother had told it me several times. "Then," added he, "you ought perfectly to believe the articles of the faith which the apostles of our Lord have testified to you, as you have heard the Credo chanted every Sunday." He told me that a bishop of Paris, whose Christian name was William,* informed him that a very learned man in sacred theology once came to converse with, and consult him, and that when he first opened his case he wept most bitterly. The bishop said to him, "Master, do not thus lament and bewail, for there cannot be any sinner, however enormous, but that God has the power to pardon." "Ah," replied the learned man, "know, my lord bishop, that I cannot do any thing but weep; for I am much afraid that, in one point, I am an unbeliever, in not being well assured with respect to the holy sacrament that is placed on the altar, according to what the holy church teaches and commands to be believed. This is what my mind cannot receive; and I believe," added he, "that it is caused by the temptation of the enemy."

"Master," answered the bishop, "now tell me, when the

* Who has left behind him several works, and under whom the question of plurality of benefices was agitated.

enemy thus tempts you, or leads you into this error, is it pleasing to you?" "Not at all," said he; "on the contrary, it is very disgusting, and displeases me more than I can tell you."

"Well, I ask you again," said the bishop, "if ever you accepted of money or worldly goods, to deny, with your mouth, the holy sacrament on the altar, or the other sacraments of the church?" "You may be truly assured," answered the learned man, "that I have never accepted money, or worldly goods, for such purposes; and that I would rather have my limbs cut off, one by one, while I was alive, than in any way to deny these sacraments."

The bishop then remonstrated with him on the great merit which he gained in the suffering of such temptations, and added, "You know, master, that the king of France is now carrying on a war against the king of England. You know, likewise, that the castle situated nearest to the frontiers of each monarch is La Rochelle, in Poitou; now tell me, if the good king of France was to nominate you governor of the castle of La Rochelle, on the frontiers, and to make me governor of the castle of Montlehery, which is in the heart of France, to whom would the king, at the end of the war, feel himself most obliged, you or me, for having prevented the loss of his castles?"

"Certainly, sir," replied the learned man, "I should suppose it would be me, and for this good reason, that I had well guarded La Rochelle, as being in a more dangerous situation." "Master," answered the bishop, "I assure you that my heart is like the castle of Montlehery; for I am perfectly convinced of the truth respecting the holy sacrament displayed on the altar, as well as the other sacraments, without having the most trifling doubt on their subject. I must however tell you, that whatever good-will God the Creator bears me, because I believe his commandments without doubting, he will have double satisfaction in you, for having preserved to him your heart in the midst of perplexity and tribulation; and that for no earthly good, nor for any distress that adversity might bring on your body, you would ever deny or abandon your faith in his religion. It is for this reason, I say, that your state is more pleasing to him than mine; and I am much rejoiced thereat, and entreat that you will keep it in your remembrance, for he will succour you in your distress."

The learned man, on hearing these words, threw himself on his knees before the bishop, and felt his mind much at ease, and was well contented with the bishop's comfortable advice.

The holy king related to me * that the Albigeois once came to the count de Montfort, who was guarding that country for the king, and desired he would come and see the body of our Saviour, which had become flesh and blood in the hands of the officiating priest, to their very great astonishment. But the count replied, "Ye who have doubts respecting the faith may go thither; but, with regard to me, I implicitly believe every thing respecting the holy sacrament, according to the doctrines of our holy mother church. In return for this faith, I hope to receive a crown greater than the angels, who see the Divinity face to face, which must make them firm in their belief."

At another time, the holy king told me, that during a great disputation at the monastery of Clugny, between the monks and Jews, an ancient knight happened to be present, who requested the abbot of the monastery to allow him to say a few words, which with difficulty was granted him. The old knight, raising himself on his crutches, desired the most learned clerk and the first rabbi of the Jews to come near him, which being done, the knight put the following question to the rabbi: "Do you believe in the Virgin Mary, who bore our Saviour JESUS CHRIST in her womb, and then in her arms, and that she was a virgin when delivered, and is now the mother of God?" The Jew replied, that he did not believe one word of all this. The knight said, "Very stupidly hast thou answered, and foolhardy art thou, when disbelieving all I have asked, thou hast entered the monastery and house of God, for which truly thou shalt now pay;" and lifting up his crutch, he smote the Jew such a blow on the ear as felled him to the ground. The other Jews, seeing their rabbi wounded, fled away, and thus ended the disputation between the monks and the Jews.

The abbot advanced to the knight, and said, "Sir knight,

* Giovanni Villani, 1. 6, ch. 7. attributes this history to St. Louis himself, and not to the count de Montfort.

you have done a foolish thing, in thus striking the Jew;" but the knight answered, "You have committed a much greater folly in permitting such an assembly, and suffering such a disputation of errors; for here are numbers of very good Christians, who might have gone away unbelievers in consequence of the arguments of the Jews."

"I therefore tell you," continued the king, "that no one, however learned or perfect a theologian he may be, ought to dispute with the Jews; but the layman, whenever he hears the Christian faith contemned, should defend it, not only by words, but with a sharp-edged sword,[*] with which he should strike the scandalizers and disbelievers, until it enter their bodies as far as the hilt."

The king's mode of living was such, that every day he heard prayers chanted, and a mass of requiem, and then the service of the day, according to what saint it was dedicated to, was sung. It was his custom to repose himself daily on his bed after dinner, when he repeated privately, with one of his chaplains, prayers for the dead, and every evening he heard complines.

One day a good Cordelier friar came to the king, at the castle of Hieres, where we had disembarked, and addressed him, saying, that he had read in the Bible, and other good books which spoke of unbelieving princes; but that he never found a kingdom of believers or unbelievers was ruined but from want of justice being duly administered. "Now,"

---

[*] It was the maxim of those days that heretics should be exterminated by fire and sword. We frequently read of heretics being burnt alive, especially in the reign of St. Louis, who carried on an incessant war against the Albigeois. See what two learned Greeks of that age have written on the subject:—Nicolaus Almannus in not. ad Procopii Hist. Arcanam. p. 55, et Leo Allatius, lib. 2, de Concord. utriusque Eccl. cap. 13, n. 2. But Agathias, in lib. 1 of his History, holds errors in religious matters pardonable:—"Forasmuch," says he, "as those who embrace these erroneous and heretical opinions commonly do so from the firm belief which they have of their truth." Theodore Balsamon, on the Nomocanon of Photius, tit. 9, ch. 25, says, that he cannot conceive how the council held at Constantinople, under the patriarchate of Michael Oxistus, could have condemned to the flames the Bogomiles, who were heretics of those times, since at that period there did not exist any canon of the church which decreed the punishment of death against heretics. Several learned persons have therefore endeavoured to prove, by solid reasoning, that heretics ought to be reclaimed by gentle means instead of rigorous ones.

continued the Cordelier, "let the king, who I perceive is
going to France, take care that he administer strict and
legal justice to his people, in order that our Lord may suffer
him to enjoy his kingdom, and that it may remain in peace
and tranquillity all the days of his life."

It is said that this discreet Cordelier, who thus lessoned the
king, is buried at Marseilles, where our Lord, through him,
does many fair miracles.

This Cordelier would not remain longer with the king than
one day, in spite of all the entreaties that were made him.
The good king was not forgetful of what the friar had told
him, to govern his realm loyally according to the laws of God,
but was anxious that justice should be done to all, according
to the manner you shall hear.

It was customary after the lord de Neeles,* the good lord
de Soissons,† myself, and others that were about the king's
person, had heard mass, for us to go and hear the pleadings
at the gateway, which is now called the Court of Requests, in
the palace at Paris. When the good king was in the morning
returned from the church, he sent for us, and inquired how
things had passed, and if there were any matters that required
his decision. And when we told him that there were some,
he sent for the parties, and asked them why they would not
be contented with the sentence of his officers, and then instantly
made their differences up to their satisfaction, according to
the custom of this godly king.

Many times have I seen this holy saint, after having heard
mass in the summer, go and amuse himself in the wood of
Vincennes; when, seating himself at the foot of an oak, he
would make us seat ourselves round about him, and every one
who wished to speak with him came thither without ceremony,
and without hindrance from any usher or others. He then
demanded aloud if there were any who had complaints to
make ; and when there were some, he said, " My friends, be

---

* Simon, son of Raoul de Clermont, lord of Ailly, and of Gertrude,
lady and heiress of Neelle. He was regent of the kingdom of France
during the second expedition of Saint Louis to the Holy Land.

† John, the second of the name, surnamed le Begue, son to Raoul de
Neelle count of Soissons, by Jolande de Joinville, his second wife, and
consequently cousin-german to our lord de Joinville, as he thus styles
him some pages hence.

silent, and your causes shall be despatched one after another."
Then, oftentimes, he called to him the lord Peter de Fontaines, and the lord Geoffroy de Villette,* and said to them,
"Despatch these causes;" and whenever he heard any thing
that could be amended in the speeches of those who pleaded
for others, he most graciously corrected them himself. I have
likewise seen this good king ofttimes come to the garden of
Paris, dressed in a coat of camlet, a surcoat of tyretaine,†
without sleeves, and a mantle of black sendal, and have car-
pets spread for us to sit round him, and hear and discuss the
complaints of his people with the same diligence as in the
wood of Vincennes.

I remember all the prelates of France‡ once assembled at
Paris, to speak with the good St. Louis, and to make him a
request ; which, when he was told, he went to the palace to hear
what they had to say. The meeting being full, it was the
bishop Guy d'Auxerre, son to the lord William de Melot,
who addressed the king, by the unanimous assent of the other
prelates, as follows :—"Sire, know that all these prelates, who

* This lord was bailiff of Tours in the year 1261, as we learn from a
list of the bailiffs of France at Candlemas in that year, and which is in the
Chambre des Comptes at Paris. In another of the year 1268, he is mentioned as having been sent ambassador to the republic of Venice.

† Tyretaine, tiretaine,—a woollen stuff used in the present times, that
took its name from the town of Tyre.

‡ This assembly of the prelates of France was induced, according to
the lord de Joinville, to remonstrate with the king on the contempt
in which the heretics, that is to say, the Albigeois, held the excommuni-
cations of the bishops, and to request that they should be compelled to
undergo absolution and return by this means to an union with the church
under the penalty of seizure and confiscation of their goods, imploring,
to effectuate this, the aid and support of the royal authority. The
assembly must have been held between the year 1247, when Guy de
Mello, bishop of Auxerre, the president of the meeting, took possession
of the episcopal throne, and the year 1270, which was the year of his
death. Thus we cannot refer to this assembly the ordinance of St. Louis,
which he issued on the same subject in the year 1228, and which is to be
found in the register of the Trésor des Chartes, Nos. 10, 26, and 27,
from which I should be inclined to believe, that the bishops only required
in this assembly that this ordinance should be put into execution. The
chronicle of the abbots of Castres, published by Dom Luc d'Achery (in the
7th volume of his Spicilegium), reports some verses which shew that the
bishops and other ecclesiastics forced by imprisonment such as were
excommunicated to resort to absolution ; but as temporal punishments
concerned the secular arm, the royal judges always opposed this mode of
punishment, and maintained that it belonged to their sole jurisdiction.

are here assembled in your presence, instruct me to tell you that you are ruining Christendom, and that it is sinking in your hands."

The king, upon this, crossed himself, and said, " Bishop, inform me how this happens, and by what cause." " Sire," answered the bishop, " it is because no notice is taken of excommunicated persons ; for at this moment a man would rather die in a state of excommunication than be absolved, and will no way make satisfaction to the church. It is for this reason, sire, that they unanimously call on you, in the name of God, and in conformity to your duty, that you would be pleased to command your bailiffs, provosts, and other administrators of justice, that wherever in your realm they shall find any one who has been excommunicated a whole year and a day, they constrain him to be absolved by the seizure of his goods."

The holy man replied, that he would most cheerfully order this to be done to every one who should be found unjust towards the church, or towards his parents. The bishop said, it only belonged to them to be acquainted with their own cause of complaint. To this, the good king said, he would not act otherwise, and that it would be blameable before God, and against reason, to force those who had been injured by churchmen to absolve themselves without being heard in their own defence. And he quoted, as an example, the count of Brittany, excommunicated as he was, having pleaded for seven years against the prelates of Brittany, and at last brought the business before our holy father the pope, who gave judgment against them in favour of the count. " Now, should I have constrained the count to seek absolution instantly after the expiration of the first year, he would have been forced to allow to these prelates their demands whether he would or not, and I should, by so doing, have behaved wickedly towards God and towards the count of Brittany."

After the prelates had heard this, they were satisfied with the favourable answer the king had made them ; and from that time I have never heard that there was further question about it.

The peace which St. Louis made with the king of England*

* The preliminaries of this peace were settled at London on the Monday after St. Valentine's Day in the year 1258, between Guy, dean of St. Martin's church in Tours, Odo, treasurer of the church of Bayeux, and

was contrary to the opinion of his whole council, who said to him, " Sire, it seems to us that you are doing wrong to your realm by giving up so much of its territory to the king of England, to which he appears to us not to have any right, since his father lost it by a legal sentence." The king replied, that he knew well the king of England had no right to it; but that, for a good reason, he thought he was bound to give it to him, adding, "We have married two sisters : our children, therefore, are cousins-german, and it is fitting that there should be union among us. It has likewise given me great pleasure to make peace with the king of England, for he is at present my vassal, which was not the case before."

The uprightness of this good king was very apparent in the case of the lord Reginald de Trie,* who brought to the holy

---

Sir Richard de Menon, the king of France's knight, as commissioners from the said king, on the one part, and Humphrey de Bohun, earl of Hereford and Essex, constable of England, and William de Fortibus, earl of Albemarle, commissioners from the king of England, on the other part. This preliminary treaty is now to be seen in the Trésor des Chartes du Roi, with the seals of these two earls attached to it. It is similar to the one which Claude Menard has given in his Observations, both in terms and substance, excepting that it is drawn up as a plan on which the definitive treaty of peace was afterwards formed. The arms of William de Fortibus, earl of Albemarle (whose family was originally from Normandy, where the lordship of Fors is situated), represented on his seal, have a cross pattée of Vair, which proves an error made by Ralph Brook, and Vincent, Rouge Croix, his corrector, in the Collections which they have made of the arms of the English dukes and earls, wherein they have given this earl " un écu d'argent au chef de gueules." They have been again mistaken, in giving to the two Stephens, earls of Albemarle, of the house of Blois or of Champagne, the cross pattée de Vair, which are the arms of de Fortibus. The arms of Stephen, first of the name, being an escutcheon plain, with a bordure componée, as Andrew du Chesne has noticed in respect to the seal of this earl, in his Genealogical History of the House of Bethune, page 152.

* The countess of Boulogne, of whom our author is speaking, was Matilda, only daughter and heiress of Reginald, count de Dammartin, by Ide, countess of Boulogne. She was twice married; first to Philip of France, surnamed Hurepel, son to Philip Augustus by Agnes de Meranie. From this union was born Jane, an only daughter, who was married to Gaucher de Châtillon, lord de Saint Agnan, and died childless. The countess Matilda married, secondly, Alfonso, afterwards king of Portugal, who in like manner died without posterity in the year 1258. After his decease, there were many disputes relative to the succession, which are fully discussed in the History of the House of Châtillon, book 3, ch. 8.

man letters which declared he had given to the heirs of the countess of Boulogne, lately deceased, the county of Dammartin, which letters were disfigured and the seals broken. All that remained of the seals were one-half of the legs of the king's effigies and the chantel* on which the royal feet were placed.

The king shewed these letters to us who were of his council, to have our advice on the occasion. We were unanimously of opinion that the king was not bounden to put these letters into execution, and that the persons mentioned in them ought not to enjoy that county. The king instantly called to him John Sarrazin, his chamberlain, and asked for the letter which he had commanded him to draw up. When he had examined it, he looked at the seal, and at the remains of that on the letters of Sir Reginald, and then said to us, "My lords, this is the seal I made use of before I went to the Holy Land, and the remnant on these letters so much resembles the whole seal that I dare not, without sinning against God and reason, retain the county of Dammartin." He then called for the lord Reginald de Trie, and said, "My fair sir, I restore to you the county which you demand."

SECOND PART.

HERE begins the second part of this present book, in which, as I have before said, you shall hear of grand feats of chivalry.

In the name of the all-powerful God, this good king, St. Louis, as I have frequently heard say, was born† on the feast-

The county of Dammartin fell to the family of Trie, as being the nearest heirs on the side from whence that estate came.

* *Le chantel* or *chanteau* was that side of the seal on which the foot-stool of the king was. Philippes Mouskes, in the Life of Robert, king of France, says,—

"La lance et l'escu en cantiel ;"

that is to say, on the side shields and bucklers were commonly worn, namely, on the left side. The romance of Guerin uses other terms :—

"An col ly pendant un escu de cartier."

† St. Louis came into this world on the festival of Saint Mark, the 25th of April, in the year 1215, at Poissy, where is still to be seen, in the chapel called by the name of St. Louis, in the cathedral church, a large

day of St. Mark the apostle and evangelist. On this day, crosses were carried in processions in several parts of France, and were called "the black crosses,"[*] a sort of superstition among the people, in commemoration of the great multitudes who died as it were crucified in the expeditions of their holy pilgrimages ; that is to say, in Egypt and before Carthage. This caused much grief and moaning in this world, and at present there is great joy in paradise among those who died for the faith of God in these devout pilgrimages.

He was crowned [†] the first Sunday in Advent, on which Sunday the mass begins with these words, "Ad te levavi animam meam," which is as much as to say, "Good Lord God, I have raised my heart and soul toward thee: I put my trust in thee." In these words the good king had great con-

vase of freestone, elevated on a high pedestal, which is said to be the font wherein St. Louis was baptized.

* Durandus, in Rationali Divinor. Offic. lib. 6, cap. 102, remarks, that this procession, which is annually made on the feast of St. Mark, and which the whole church acknowledges, under the name of Litania major, was instituted by Pope Gregory the Great, is now known under the name of the Black Crosses, from the altars and crosses being that day covered with black, in remembrance of the great mortality which happened at Rome in consequence of the plague, and which caused this great pope to institute public prayers. With regard to what the lord de Joinville says, that in certain places this procession was called the Black Crosses, it is only the mode of expression of those times, when all sorts of processions were called Crosses.

† On the first day of December, 1226, by the hands of the bishop of Soissons, the archbishopric of Rheims being then vacant. I found in an old roll in the Chamber of Accounts at Paris a state of the expenses of this coronation, entitled, "Expensæ pro Coronatione Regum," in these terms :—"Expenses incurred for the coronation of the king Saint Louis, in the month of November, 1226."

Bread	896 livres.	
Bread for the king, pies, and making ..	38	
Wine	991	
Kitchen expenses	1356	4 sols.
Wax and fruit	138	
The king's chamber	914	10
The queen's expenses	320	
Wages and deliveries for the king's household, and for the king when beyond sea	400	
Sum total ..	5053	14

fidence, as respecting himself personally, for the great charge he had just undertaken. He had the fullest trust in God from his infancy to his death; for at the end of his latter days, he called upon God and his saints, and especially on St. James and St. Genevieve as his intercessors. In return be was protected by God, in regard to his soul, from his earliest years to his death, and also in respect to the good doctrine he received from his mother, who taught him to believe in God, and to love and fear him in his youth; and he has, ever since that time, lived a virtuous and holy life. His mother caused him to be attended by religious persons, who preached to him the word of God on Sundays and feast-days. Many times has he related that his mother should frequently say that she would rather he was in his grave, than that he should commit a mortal sin.

It was needful that God should help him in his youth; for his mother was from Spain, a foreign country, and remained in France without any of her own family, relations, or friends. The barons of France thus seeing him an infant, and his mother a foreigner, without any support but from God, made the count of Boulogne, uncle to the king just dead, their leader, and considered him as their lord and master. It happened therefore, after the coronation of this good king, that by way of beginning the rebellion, some of these great barons of France required of the queen-dowager, that she would give them lands appertaining to the crown of France; and because she would not consent, urging, as an excuse, that it was not for her to dismember the kingdom of France contrary to the will of her son, who was now crowned king, these barons assembled at Corbeil. The holy king told me that when he and his mother were at Montlehery, they dared not go to Paris until the inhabitants came with a large force of men-at-arms to escort them thither; and he added, that the whole road from Montlehery to Paris was filled on all sides with men-at-arms, who besought the Lord that he would grant the king long life and prosperity, and that he would defend him against all his enemies. And this God did in different places, and at different times, as you shall hear in the course of this history.

While the barons were assembled at Corbeil they practised among themselves, and resolved, with one accord, to raise up

2 B

the count of Brittany* against the king. They promised
him, in order to act more treacherously to the good king, that
they would obey the royal summons; and if the king should
send them to make war against the earl of Brittany, they
would not bring with them more than two knights each,
that the count might the more easily conquer the good king
Louis, and his mother, who was a foreigner, as you have
before heard.

This plot the barons put into execution, according to the
engagement which they had entered into with the count of
Brittany; and I have heard many say, that the count would
have destroyed and subdued the king and his mother, if it had
not been for God's assistance, which never failed him. The
count Thibaut de Champagne, as it were by divine permission,
put himself and his forces in motion, to wait on the good
king when he was in such distress and danger. In good
truth, he set off with full three hundred knights, perfectly
well equipped, and, through God's grace, arrived in good
time; for, by this timely reinforcement of the count of Champagne, the count of Brittany was forced to surrender himself
to the king, and beg his mercy. The good king had no desire
of revenge, and considering the victory he had obtained was
gained through the power and will of God, in sending to
him so opportunely the count of Champagne, received the
count of Brittany into favour, and thenceforward the king
travelled throughout his kingdom in security.

Because incidents frequently happen that deserve mention,
I shall at times leave the principal matter of my history to
relate them; but, notwithstanding this, you shall hear of
some things necessary to be related, for the better understanding the matters I treat of. I will therefore advance
with truth.

The good count Henry le Large had, by the countess Mary
his wife, who was sister to the king of France, and to Richard
king of England, two sons; the elder was called Henry, and
the second Thibaut. Henry had put on the cross, and had
accompanied King Philip and King Richard to the Holy
Land, where these three besieged the city of Acre, and
took it.

* Pierre de Dreux, surnamed Mauclerc, who had withdrawn himself
from the king's homage.

Immediately after the capture, King Philip returned to France, for which he was greatly blamed. King Richard remained in Palestine, and performed very great feats of arms against the unbelievers and Saracens. They were so much in dread of him, that, as it is written in the history of this expedition to the Holy Land, whenever Saracen children cried, their mothers said to them, " Be quiet, be quiet; here is King Richard* coming to fetch you;" and, instantly, through the fear which these Saracen children had of the name of King Richard, they became quiet. In like manner, when the Saracens or Turks were riding in the fields, and their horses started at a bush or shadow, and took fright, they said to their horses, sticking spurs into their sides, " What, dost think King Richard is there?" All this clearly proves that he performed grand deeds of arms against them, to make him so much dreaded

This King Richard gained so great renown by his valour that he gave to Count Henry of Champagne, who, as I have before said, had remained with him, the queen of Jerusalem for his wife. Henry of Champagne had by her two daughters, the elder of whom was queen of Cyprus, and the other was married to Sir Ayrart de Brienne, from whom a noble progeny descended, as is apparent in France, and in Champagne.†

* Raoul de Coggeshall, whose manuscript is in the library of St. Victor at Paris, Matthew Paris, John Brompton, and other English historians of the year 1172; Jacques de Vitry, l. 1, ch. 99; Sanudo, l. 3, part 11, ch. 1; Le Moine de Saint Marian d'Auxerre, and others, speak most amply of the great actions and deeds of arms of King Richard I. in the Holy Land; but they have all omitted this circumstance mentioned by the lord de Joinville, who has taken it, as he says himself, from the history of the holy wars written in the vulgar tongue, which I have read in manuscript, and which relates the same thing in these terms :—" From whence it happened, &c., King Richard was so feared in the country that whenever a Saracen mother perceived her children crying, she said to them, ' DO NOT MAKE A NOISE, FOR HERE IS KING RICHARD !' and he was so dreaded that the children gave over crying instantly."

Matthew of Westminster relates that in the year 1240, when Richard earl of Cornwall arrived in the Holy Land, the Saracens began to dread exceedingly the experience and power of Richard, as well because his name had always been held up as that of the bitter enemy of the Saracens, as because he abounded in gold and silver.

† See the list of nobles who went on the expedition to the Holy Land, ch. 1, Vignier; Du Chesne, in the histories of the families of Châtillon and of Bethune.

Of the wife of my beforesaid lord, Sir Ayrart de Brienne, I will not say more at present, but speak of the queen of Cyprus,* because it is right to continue my subject properly, and thus proceed.

After the good king had conquered the count of Brittany, through the aid of Count Thibaut de Champagne, the barons of France, indignant against Count Thibaut, agreed among themselves to disinherit him, as being a son of the second son of Champagne, and to send for the queen of Cyprus. This, however, did not seem to them to be for their advantage ; and for this reason, and because some of the barons foreseeing they could not accomplish their ends, undertook to be mediators of a peace between Count Peter of Brittany and Count Thibaut of Champagne, the matter was so warmly pushed forward, that for greater solidity of peace, Count Thibaut promised to espouse the daughter of Count Peter of Brittany.† A day was fixed on for this ceremony, when the young lady was to be conducted to an abbey belonging to the Preaching Friars near Château Thierry, called Valserre, when the count of Champagne was to marry her. And thus, as I have heard, the count of Brittany set out attended by the barons of France, who were almost all his relations, to conduct the damsel to the monastery of Valrerry, and sent to summon the count of Champagne, then at Château Thierry, to come and marry the lady, according to his engagement, which he was well inclined to do. But suddenly there came to him Sir Geoffrey de la Chappelle bringing letters from the king, the contents of which were as follows.

"Sir Thibaut de Champagne,—I have learnt that you have entered into engagements to marry the daughter of the count Peter of Brittany. I therefore send to require of you, that for the sake of all you love in France, you do not perform them. The reason of my desiring it is well known to you : I have never found any one more willing to do me evil than the count of Brittany."

When Count Thibaut had read these letters, although he had left Château Thierry, he instantly returned thither.

---

* Alicia, eldest daughter of Henry, count of Champagne, by the queen of Jerusalem.

† Joland, who was afterward married to Hugh XI., count de la Marche et d'Angouléme.

The count Peter of Brittany, and the French barons, in
opposition to the king of France, were waiting for the count
of Champagne at Valserre; and perceiving that he had deceived them, in the first burst of their rage against him, they
sent for the queen of Cyprus, who shortly afterward joined
them.

Immediately on her arrival, they, with one accord, having
discussed the matter, sent each of them to collect as many men-
at-arms as they possibly could, and resolved to make an inroad by way of France into the territories of Count Thibaut,
even into Champagne and Brie.

They had a good understanding with the duke of Burgundy,
who had for his wife the daughter of Robert, count de Dreux;
and who likewise engaged, on his part, to enter the county of
Champagne from Burgundy.   A day was appointed for their
assembling all together before the city of Troyes, in order to
take it; but all this was known to good King Louis, who, in
like manner, summoned his men at arms to accompany him to
the aid of Count Thibaut de Champagne.

The barons, in fact, burnt and pillaged the whole country
they marched through, as did their ally the duke of Burgundy.   When the count of Champagne thus saw himself
and his country attacked on all sides, he burnt and destroyed
several of his towns, such as Epernay, Vertus, and Sezanne,
that his enemies might not find them well furnished with provisions and stores, and turn them against him.

The citizens of Troyes, finding their good master and lord,
the count of Champagne, had left their town, instantly sent
to Simon, lord of Joinville, father to the lord de Joinville of
the present day, and whose name is inscribed in the prologue
of this book, to desire that he would come to their assistance.
That good gentleman did so.   His people were immediately
informed of the intelligence that had been brought him, and
before day they were in the city of Troyes, where, for his
part, he performed such wonders in aiding the citizens, that
the barons failed to take it.

The barons were forced to march beyond the town, and fix
their quarters in the meads with the duke of Burgundy.
When the king of France knew where they were lodged, he
marched his army straight to combat them; which the barons
learning, they sent to entreat that he would withdraw his

army, for that they were going to fight the count of Champagne, and the duke of Lorraine and their forces, with 300 knights less than were with the count and the duke of Lorraine.   But the king replied, that they should no way fight with his vassals without his being personally engaged in their defence.   This answer threw the barons into confusion, and speedily after, they sent again to say, they would cheerfully persuade the queen of Cyprus to offer terms of peace to Count Thibaut of Champagne.   The king's answer was, that he would not listen to any proposals for peace, nor suffer the count of Champagne to do so, until they should have quitted the county of Champagne.

On hearing this, they instantly marched away, and at one march quartered themselves under Juilli.   The king lodged at Ylles, whence he had driven them ; and the barons perceiving the king was so closely pursuing them, they decamped from Juilli, and quartered at Langres, which is in the county of Nevers, and attached to their party.   Thus did the good king, St. Louis, make up the differences between the queen of Cyprus and the count of Champagne, in spite of the enterprise of the barons ; and peace was concluded between them in such wise, that the count of Champagne gave to the queen of Cyprus, for her rights of succession, 2,000 livres of landed annual revenue ; and the king paid her, in behalf of the count of Champagne, the sum of 40,000 livres for the reimbursement of her expenses.   To repay these 40,000 livres the count of Champagne sold to the king the following fiefs and lordships ; namely, the fief of the county of Blois ; the fief of the county of Chartres ; the fief of the county of Sancerre ; the fief of the viscounty of Châteaudun.   Some said that the king held them only as a security for the repayment, but that is not the truth, for I put the question to the good king in Palestine, and he told me he held them by purchase.

The lands which the count de Champagne gave to the queen of Cyprus were part of the present county of Brienne and the county of Joigny, because the grandmother of the count de Brienne was daughter to the queen of Cyprus, and wife to the great count, Walter de Brienne.   And that you may know whence came the fiefs which the count of Champagne sold to the king, I shall inform you, that the great count Thibaut, who is interred at Laigny, had three sons, the eldest of whom was named Henry, the second Thibaut, and the third Stephen. Henry was afterwards count of Champagne and of Brie, and surnamed Henry the Liberal; for generous and liberal was he towards God and man.   Towards God he was apparently liberal, by his founding the church of St. Stephen at Troyes, as well as many other, to each of which he daily made great gifts, as is well known throughout Champagne.

Towards man he was equally generous, as is notorious from his conduct to Arthault of Nogent, and in many other instances too tedious to relate; but I must mention that of Arthault of Nogent.   This Arthault was a citizen in whom, for a time, Count Henry had the greatest confidence; and Arthault increased so much in riches that he built the castle of Nogent.   Now it chanced that Count Henry was desirous of descending from his castles of Troyes to hear mass at St. Stephen's church on Whitsunday: on the lower steps of the entrance to the church, he found a poor knight on his knees, who with a loud voice cried out, "Sir count, I request of you, in the name of God, that you would give me wherewith to portion my two daughters that are by my side for I am unable to do it."   Arthur de Nogent, who was behind the count, replied to the knight, "Sir knight, you do wrong to make such a request to my lord; for he has given away so much, he is no longer able to be generous."

The count, on hearing this, turned round to Arthault and said, "Sir Vilain, you do not speak truth when you say I have no longer wherewithal to give, for I have you in my disposal, and I give you to him.   Here, sir knight, I give this man to you, and warrant him your bondsman."   The poor knight was greatly surprised, and instantly seizing the citizen by his hood, said he would not let him go until he should have ransomed himself handsomely.   Arthault was forced to pay a fine of 500 livres.

The second brother to Henry the Liberal was Thibaut count de Blois, and the third, Stephen count de Sancerre; but these two brothers held their counties and lordships under their elder brother Henry the Liberal, and after him under his heirs, who possessed the county of Champagne until this Count Thibaut sold them to the king, St. Louis, as has been mentioned.

Let us now return to our more immediate subject, and say,

that shortly after this King Louis held a great and open court
at Saumur in Anjou, which I shall speak of, having been
present. I can assure you that it was the grandest sight I
ever witnessed, the best ornamented and prepared. At the
king's table were seated the count de Poitiers,* whom he had
knighted on the last St. John's day; the count John de
Dreux,† whom he had lately knighted; the count de la
Marche,‡ and the count Peter of Brittany.

At another table, before that of the king on the side where
count de Dreux was seated, the king of Navarre dined. He
was most richly dressed in cloth of gold, in coat, mantle,
girdle, clasp,§ and cap of fine gold, to whom I was the carver.
The count d'Artois‖ served the king, St. Louis, and his brother, and the count de Soissons cut up the meat. Sir Ymbert
de Beljeu, who was afterwards constable of France, Sir
Honourat de Coucy, and Sir Archibald de Bourbon were
the guards of the king's table; and there were behind these
barons, full thirty of their knights in cloth of silk, to serve
under them. There were likewise behind these knights a
great many ushers of arms, and of the apartments, who bore
the arms of the count de Poitiers, worked on fendal.

The king was dressed as magnificently as it was possible,

---

* Alphonso, brother to St. Louis, who had been created a knight by
the king on the feast of the Nativity of St. John the Baptist, in the year
1241, at which time he likewise gave him the county of Poitou.—See M.
Paris, p. 313.

† Son of Robert III., count de Dreux, by d'Aënor de St. Valery, the
first who bore the name of John. He died at Cyprus.

‡ Hugh X., surnamed le Brun, count de la Marche and d'Angoulême.

§ Clasp or fermail was a sort of medal or ornament, like the diamond
ornaments now in fashion, which was fastened not only to the shoulder
where the folds of the mantle met, in like manner to the latus clavus
of the Romans; but also to the front of the cap, as diamonds are now worn.
In war it was fastened to the hood, on the coat of arms, or in some other
conspicuous place. Women wore them on their breast. Froissart, in the
154th chapter of the 2nd volume, says, " he received, as the prize,
a clasp of precious stones, which the duchess of Burgundy detached from
her breast." It is for this reason, that the Latin and French MS.
Glossary translates the word *monile* clasp or fermail. Elsewhere
redimiculum a female ornament, as a clasp, chaplet, or girdle.
Johannes de Janua calls it " Fibularium." But I suspect he intended to have called it *fibulatorium*, which the Greek and Latin
Glossary defines to be the diminutive of *fibula.*

‖ Robert, brother to the king.

but it would be tedious to enter into the particulars of his habiliments. I have heard several persons declare, that they never before saw at any feast so many surcoats and other dresses of cloth of gold as at this.

After this feast, the king conducted the count of Poitiers to that city, to recover the fiefs and lordships. It happened immediately after the king's arrival there, that the count de la Marche, who had even dined at the king's table at Saumur, secretly assembled a large body of men-at-arms to wage war against the king until he should gain his object, and kept himself at Lusignan near to Poitiers. The good king wished to have been in Paris, but he was forced to remain at Poitiers fifteen days without daring to venture beyond its walls. It was said that the king and the count of Poitiers had made a disadvantageous peace with the count de la Marche. It was necessary, therefore, for the king, in order to make up matters with the count de la Marche, to hold a parley with him and the dowager queen of England his wife, mother to the monarch on the throne.

It was not long after the king was returned from Poitiers to Paris, that the king of England and the count de la Marche united together to make war on good St. Louis, and to collect as large a body of men-at-arms as they could. They assembled in Gascony, before the castle of Taillebourg, which is situated on a dangerous river called the Charente, near which there was only one narrow stone bridge that could be passed over.

King Louis, on hearing this, marched an army against them towards Taillebourg; and his men no sooner saw the host of the enemy, who had the castle of Taillebourg on their side, than with great peril they hastened to cross the bridge, and others passed over the river in boats, and began to charge the English. Heavy blows were given on each side, which the good king beholding, he with much danger joined them: indeed, the risk was very considerable, for the English were more numerous than the French who passed the river, by one hundred to one.

Notwithstanding this superiority, when the English found that the king of France had crossed the river, they took fright, as it seemed God willed, and made for the city of Saintes, which they entered. It happened in the confusion, that several of our men entered that city with them, and were made prisoners.

I have heard from some among them, that during that night there was much discord between the king of England and the count de la Marche in Saintes,* as they were informed; and that the king of England should tell the count that he had sent for him, under promise that he would find great aid in France; and that, perceiving the fallacy of his information, he should return to Gascony, whence he had come. The count de la Marche thus deserted, and knowing that he could not amend himself for the evil he had done, surrendered himself, his wife and children, prisoners to the king, who gained, on consenting to a peace, many considerable territories from the count. I know not what quantity, for I was not present at the treaty, not having then put on the coat of mail;† but I have heard, that with the lands the king acquired, the count de la Marche gave him an acquittance for ten thousand livres parisis, which he was wont to receive from him annually.

Shortly after this, the good king was taken grievously ill at Paris;‡ and so bad was his state, that I have heard that one of the ladies who nursed him, thinking it was all over, wanted to cover his face with a cloth, but that another lady, on the opposite side of the bed (so God willed it), would not

---

* See William Guiart and Matthew of Westminster, among others, respecting the treaty, and this new war of the count de la Marche.

† John, lord of Joinville, was not a knight in the year 1243, and consequently had not attained the age of twenty-one, which was the age to receive the order of knighthood, and put on the hauberk, which was a species of armour peculiar to knights. Hence it comes that those who possessed fiefs of hauberk in Normandy, "qui per loricas terras suas serviebat," to the terms of the laws of William I., king of England, were obliged to have horse and arms, and from the time they were twenty-one years of age to be created knights, in order that they might join the armies of their prince or other superior lord, on the first summons, as is noticed in the ancient MS. Coutumier of Normandy, 1, P. sect. 3, chap. 8. When the term *loricati* is met with in ancient Latin authors, it must be understood to mean such knights alone as were entitled to wear the hauberk, for previously they wore but the arms of squires.

‡ The lord de Joinville says this happened at Paris; but Nangis and the author of the Chronicle of Saint Denis say that it was at Pontoise. William Guiart particularly mentions the king being ill at the monastery of Maubuisson, and marks the year 1243 for the period, while the others place it in the following year.

suffer his face to be covered, or buried as it were, declaring continually that he was alive.

During the conversation of these ladies, our Lord worked upon him, and restored to him his speech. The good king desired them to bring him a crucifix, which was done; and when the good lady, his mother, heard that he had recovered his speech, she was in the utmost possible joy; but when she came and saw that he had put on the cross* she was panic-struck, and seemed as if she would rather have seen him dead.

In the like manner as the king had put on the cross, so did Robert, count d'Artois; Alphonso, count of Poitiers; Charles, count d'Anjou, who was afterwards king of Sicily; all three brothers to the king; Hugh, duke of Burgundy; William, earl of Flanders; his brother Guion de Flandres, who died shortly after at Compiegne; the valiant count Hugh de St. Pol; his nephew, Sir Walter, who behaved most gallantly beyond sea, and would have gained great renown had longer life been granted him. The count de la Marche, whom we have lately mentioned, was also of the number; Sir Hugh le Brun and his son; the count de Salebruche; Sir Gaubert d'Apremont and his brothers, in whose company, being my cousins, I, John de Joinville, crossed the sea in a small ship which we hired. We were twenty knights: ten of whom accompanied me, and ten came with my cousins. This event took place after Easter, in the year of grace 1248.

Before my departure, I summoned all my men and vassals of Joinville, who came to me the vigil of Easter-day, which was the birthday of my son John, lord of Ancarville, by my first wife, sister to the count of Grand Pré. During that whole week I was occupied in feasts and banquets with my brother de Vaucouleur, and all the rich men† of that part of

* Richer, monk of Sens, says in his Chronicle, ch. 10, that the king put-on the cross in consequence of a vision that he had during this illness. Matthew Paris mentions several circumstances of this illness.

† Our author makes use of this mode of expression in several parts of his history, to point out the barons and great lords of a country, in imitation of the Spaniards, who divide their nobility into three orders, *ricos ombres, cavalleros,* and *infançós*. These are called in France, barons, knights, and squires. The term baron is generally understood to mean all those who have a right to bear a banner in the

the country, where, after eating and drinking, we amused
ourselves with songs, and led a joyous life.   When Friday
came, I addressed them thus:—"Gentlemen, know that I
am about to go to the Holy Land, and it is uncertain whether
I may ever return : should there be any of you,* therefore,
to whom I have done wrong, and who thinks he has cause
for complaint, let him come forward; for I am willing to
make him amends, as I am accustomed to do to those who
have complained of me or my people."

I did this according to the usual manner of my country
and my lands; and in order that they might not be awed by

wars, and are commonly called bannerets, but to whom the Spaniards
give a more specific name, *ricos hombres de senera.* Hier. Blanca in
Comment. Rer. Arragon. often speaks of these rich men, or rather of these
Spanish *ricombres*, who are usually styled *rici homines* in Latin deeds.
Many have thought that the *ricombres* were thus named in Spain from
the syllable *ric*, which is found to terminate the names of the greater
part of the Gothic kings; but I believe it more probably originates from
another word which was common to the northern nations. *Ric*, which is
the termination of most of the names of their chieftains, signifies rich,
whence the Germans have formed the word *rück*, the French *riche*, and
the Spanish *rico*, to mark a person of opulency; and because great lords
are commonly rich and powerful in land, they have been thus styled,
besides that all who abounded in landed property did not come under the
title of *ricos ombres*, for birth, fiefs, and distinguished lordships alone
gave this qualification.

* Those who had put on the cross, and were preparing for these long
and troublesome expeditions to the Holy Land, were accustomed, before
their departure, to settle their affairs, to make their wills, and to fix portions for their children. And as their return was very uncertain, both
from the difficulties of the journey, and the hazards and perils of war, the
events of which are always doubtful, they commonly performed all such
acts as those who are on the point of death usually observe; such as
making restitution of whatever they may have seized or usurped from the
church, or from private persons, for the discharge of their consciences.
Title-deeds abound with these restitutions made to the church by knights
before the departure for the Holy Land. The lord de Joinville,
although he did not feel himself guilty of any such usurpations,
yet to satisfy the duty of his conscience, made preparations, before
he set out on this expedition, to repair whatever wrongs he might have
done to his neighbours, should there be any of them that made complaint
against him. Many persons imagine that the greater part of the monasteries built towards the end of the eleventh century, and in the following ones, were solely founded from the restitutions which the great
lords had made prior to their undertaking expeditions to such a great
distance.

my presence while they consulted together, I withdrew, and would only listen to what they might say to me without the restraint of fear. I likewise adopted this measure, because I was unwilling to carry with me one single penny wrongfully; and to fulfil any demands that might be made, I had mortgaged* to friends a great part of my inheritance, so that there did not remain at the utmost more than twelve hundred livres of yearly revenue from my lands; for my lady-mother was still living, who held the best of my estate in dower.

I set out, I before said, with my nine knights, having three banners: and I have mentioned the things above, because if it had not been for the aid and assistance of God, who never forgot me, I should never have been able to support such a burden as I bore for six years, the time I was on my pilgrimage in the Holy Land.

When I was on the point of departure, John, lord d'Apremont, and the count de Salebruche, sent to me to inquire if I were willing to join parties, and embark together, for that they were ready to march, and their company consisted of ten knights. I cheerfully assented, and we ordered a

---

* The devotion of our first crusaders in the Holy Land, added to their courage and desire of acquiring glory and reputation in the wars, were so extraordinary, that they not only made no difficulty in abandoning their families and country, but even alienated or mortgaged the fairest parts of their possessions. The history of these wars informs us, that Godfrey de Bouillon; Raymond, count de St. Gilles; William, duke of Normandy; Boëmond, duke de la Puglia; Harpin, count de Bourges, and other great lords, sold or mortgaged their duchies or counties, to supply the means for the expense of so great an enterprise. Such was the height of their fervour; and in imitation of them, and following the example of his ancestors, the lord de Joinville did not fail to mortgage the better part of his estates, although they were then but small, on account of his mother's enjoying the larger share for her dower. The facility with which the crusaders sold or mortgaged their lands, to afford them the means of undertaking these expeditions, gave rise to the spirited reply which king Philip Augustus made to John, king of England, who having put on the cross, afterwards sent his ambassadors to Philip, to demand " that he would be pleased to restore to him some portion of the land, which he had gained from him in war, for a fixed amount of money." The king gave them this witty answer: " It is a strange and unheard-of thing, for one marked with the cross to wish to become a purchaser; when he ought rather to sell, if he entered upon his pilgrimage as became him."

vessel to be hired for us at Marseilles, which carried us, our arms and horses.

You must know, that before the king left the realm, he summoned all the barons to Paris, and there made them renew their fealty and homage,* and swear loyalty to his children, should any unfortunate event happen to himself during this expedition to the Holy Land. He summoned me also; but I, who was not his subject, would not take the oath: besides, it was not my intention to remain behind.

When I was nearly ready to set out, I sent for the abbot of Cheminon, who was at that time considered as the most discreet man of all the White Monks, to reconcile myself with him. He gave me my scarf and bound it on me, and likewise put the pilgrim's staff in my hand. Instantly after, I quitted the castle of Joinville without ever re-entering it, until my return from beyond sea. I made pilgrimages to all the holy places in the neighbourhood; such as Bliecourt, St. Urban, and others near to Joinville, on foot without shoes, and in my shirt. But as I was journeying from Bliecourt to St. Urban, I was obliged to pass near to the castle of Joinville; I dared never turn my eyes that way for fear of feeling too great regret, and lest my courage should fail on leaving my two fine children and my fair castle of Joinville, which I loved in my heart. Being suddenly called upon by the count de Salbrucha, my brother in arms, with our knights and attendants, we went to dine at La Fontaine Archevêque before Dongeux: and there the abbot of St. Urban, to whom may God shew mercy! gave to me and my knights very handsome jewels. We then took our leave of him, and went straight to Auxonne, where we embarked with our armour on the Soane for Lyons: our cavalry and war-horses were led along its banks. When we came to Lyons, we embarked on the river Rhône to go to Arles le Blanc. I remember well that on its banks we saw the remains of a castle called La Roche-gluy, which castle the king had caused to be demolished on account of the lord of it, named Roger, having a very ill-famed reputation

---

* The king, Louis VIII., father to St. Louis, when taken ill of a grievous disorder at Montpensier, of which he died, exacted a similar oath from those barons who were then at court, as the letters of this king inform us, which remain in the cartulary of Champagne, in the Chamber of Accounts at Paris.

of stopping and plundering all merchants and pilgrims that
passed that way

It was the month of August in this same year that we
embarked at the rock of Marseilles,* and the ports of the
vessel were opened to allow the horses we intended carrying
with us to enter.   When we were all on board, the port
was caulked and stopped up as close as a large tun of wine,
because when the vessel was at sea, the port was under
water.   Shortly after the captain of the ship cried out to his
people on its prow, "Is your work done?   Are we ready?"
They replied, "Yes: in truth, we are."

When the priests and clerks embarked, the captain made
them mount to the castle of the ship, and chant psalms in
praise of God, that he might be pleased to grant us a prosperous voyage.   They all, with a loud voice, sang the beautiful hymn of "Veni Creator," from the beginning to the
end; and while they were singing, the mariners set their sails
in the name of God.   Instantly after, a breeze of wind filled
our sails, and soon made us lose sight of land, so that we
only saw sea and sky, and each day we were at a farther
distance from the places from which we had set out.

I must say here, that he is a great fool who shall put
himself in such dangers, having wronged any one, or having
any mortal sins on his conscience; for when he goes to sleep
in the evening, he knows not if in the morning he may not
find himself under the sea.

I will tell you the first marvel that befel us at sea.   It was
a great round mountain which we met with about vespers, off
Barbary : when we had passed it, we made all the sail we
could the whole night, and in the morning we supposed we
must have run fifty leagues, or more, but we found ourselves
again off this large mountain.   We were, of course, much
alarmed, and continued to make all the sail we could that day
and the following night, but it was all the same, we still had
the mountain near at hand.   We were more astonished than
ever, and thought we ran great risk of our lives; for the
sailors told us that the Saracens of Barbary would come and
attack us.   A very discreet churchman, called the dean of

* He thus calls the promontory which encloses the port of Marseilles,
where the fort of Notre Dame de la Garde is placed.   The writers of the
middle ages often use the word rock to signify a fort or castle.

Mauru, came forward and said, "Gentlemen, I never remember any distress in our parish, either from too much abundance, or for want of rain or any other plague, but that God and his mother delivered us from it, and caused every thing to happen as it could be wished, when a procession had been made three times with devotion on a Saturday." Now this day was a Saturday, and we instantly began a procession round the masts of the ship. I remember well that I was forced to be supported under my arms, because I was at the time very sick. Immediately afterwards we lost sight of this mountain, and arrived at Cyprus the third Saturday after we had made our procession.

We found, on our landing at Cyprus, that the good king, St. Louis, was already there, and had laid in provisions in great abundance.* You would have taken his cellars, at a distance, for great houses formed of casks of wine, placed one on the other, which his purveyors had bought two years before, and had left in the open fields. In like manner was the wheat, barley, and other grain in large heaps, which, from their immense size, appeared like mountains; and in truth many would have supposed them such; for the rains which had battered their sides had made the corn grow, so that there was nothing to be seen but green corn. When the army of the king came to remove the grain, in order to its being sent to Egypt, and to take off the crust of green corn, they found the corn underneath as fine and fresh as if it had been just threshed.

The good king was impatient to set sail, so that if it had not been for his barons, and near relations, who prevailed on him to wait the arrival of forces that were daily expected, he would have embarked alone, or with a very small company.

While the king remained in Cyprus, the great cham of

---

* Matthew Paris writes, then when the king's army was in want of provision, the Venetians and the inhabitants of some other towns, which he does not name, brought succour. The emperor Frederick also sent him assistance, for which the king felt so much obliged, that he wrote in his favour to the pope to obtain his absolution. Queen Blanche likewise thanked him by her letters, and sent him various presents, as an acknowledgment to him from France, assuring him that the whole French army was indebted to him for its preservation.

Tartary* sent him an ambassador, who paid him many fine compliments; among others, the cham of Tartary sent him word that he was ready and at his command to assist him in the conquest of the Holy Land, and to deliver Jerusalem from the hands of the Saracens and Pagans. The king received this embassy with kindness, and, in return, sent ambassadors to the cham of Tartary, who were two years before they returned. The king of France sent likewise to the cham a tent in the form of a chapel; it was of fine scarlet cloth, very rich, and handsomely made, with the intent to see if he could induce the cham and his subjects to embrace our faith and religion; and, as a further inducement, he had embroidered on the inside of the tent the Annunciation of the Virgin mother of God, with other mysteries of our faith. Two Black Monks, who understood the Saracen language, had charge of this tent, and to exhort the Tartars, and shew how they ought to put their belief in God.

The two monks shortly returned, thinking to meet the king at Acre; but he was already in Cæsarea, upon which they went back to France. To say how the other ambassadors, whom the king had sent to the king of Barbary, were received, would be to tell of wonders, as I heard them related to the king from their own mouths. I have likewise frequently inquired of them concerning their adventures; but I will not say any thing of them at present, for fear of breaking in upon the principal matter, which I had already begun.

You must know that when I quitted France, to join this expedition to the Holy Land, I did not possess more than 1,200 livres of yearly revenue, and yet I took charge of nine other knights and three banners. On my arrival at Cyprus I had but twelve score livres in gold and silver, after paying the freight of the ship, so that many of my knights told me they would leave me if I did not better provide myself with money. I was somewhat cast down in courage on hearing this, but had ever my confidence in God; and when the good king St. Louis heard of my distress, he sent for me, and

* This king was not the great cham of Tartary, but a prince over his subjects, whose name was Ercatar as we see in the additions to Matt. Paris, p. 116.

retained me in his service, allowing me, like a kind lord, 800 livres Tournois. · I instantly returned thanks to God, for I had now more money than I had need of.

It is now necessary that I speak of the state and power of the princes beyond sea, and I shall first begin with the sultan of Connie.* This sultan is the most powerful king of all pagan land, and had a most marvellous work achieved; for he had melted part of his gold, and made it into large vessels after the manner of the earthen pots in which wine is preserved in those countries, each of which held about a tun of wine. He afterwards had these pots broken, and the pieces lay in one of his castles, which was open for every one to see and touch these broken masses of gold. It was said that he had six or seven of these large golden pots. His great riches were apparent in a pavilion which the king of Armenia sent to the king of France when he was at Cyprus, for it was estimated at 500 livres. The king of Armenia sent word, that it had been given to him by one of the serrais of the sultan of Connie. Now you must know that these serrais have the care and management of the pavilions of the sultan, and their employment is to clean every day the apartments of his different palaces.

This king of Armenia was vassal to the sultan of Connie; and went to the grand cham of Tartary to complain that the sultan had made war upon him, and kept him in vassalage, and at the same time to entreat he would support and succour him. He consented to become vassal to the cham of Tartary, if he would supply him with a large body of men-at-arms against the sultan of Connie.

The cham of Tartary was willing to do this, and sent him a considerable force, with which the king of Armenia marched against the sultan, whose army was nearly equal to his; but the Armenians and Tartars defeated the troops of their enemy; and in consequence of this the king of Armenia was no longer vassal nor subject to the sultan. This victory, which he had gained by the assistance of the Tartars, increased his renown

* This sultan of Iconium, a town in Cilicia or Caramania, which the Turks at this day call Coni, had the name of Azatines, and was a Christian. There is a letter from him to Pope Gregory IX., who wanted to persuade him to embrace the Christian religion, in the Ecclesiastical Annals of Odoricus Raynaldus, in the year 1235, n. 37, in which he is called Alatinus.

so much in Cyprus, that many of our people went to Armenia
to seek for profit in these engagements; but of them we had
never after any intelligence.

Of the sultan of Babylon* I shall say, that he imagined the
king was about to make war on the sultan of Hamault,† his
ancient enemy: he was therefore waiting for the king to join
his forces against the sultan of Hamault; but when he perceived that the king did not advance, he departed, and went
to lay siege to the city of Hamault, in which the sultan
resided.

The sultan, thus finding himself besieged, knew not how to
act; for he was aware, that if the sultan of Babylon should
remain long, he must conquer and overthrow him.   He,
however, practised so successfully by gifts and promises with
one of the varlets of the chamber of the sultan of Babylon
that he poisoned his master.   The manner of his doing it was
as follows:—The varlet, who in their language is officially
called Serais, knowing that the sultan after playing at chess ‡
was frequently used to lie down on mats that were at the foot
of his bed, poisoned one of these mats; and it chanced that
the sultan, having thrown aside part of his dress, lay on the
mat with his naked legs, and turning about rubbed a sore he
had on one of them against the poisoned part.   The venom

* According to the Arabian Chronicle given to the public by Abraham
Echellensis, his name was Saleh Nagem-addim Aiiub, and he was son to
the king Alcamel Mahomet, whom Vincent de Beauvais calls Soldanus
Klemel.

† It should be of *Haman*. This sultan was lord of Aleppo, as we
learn from the monk Aython, ch. 38 and 39, and from Vincent de
Beauvais, l. 32, ch. 89 and 95, wherein he relates also the difference
between the two sultans.

‡ This game has been always very much in vogue among the Turks and
Saracens, as we learn from Elemacin, l. 2, ch. 7, from Aython, ch. 53,
and from Ducas, in his History, ch. 16.   The game has even taken its
name from a Turkish or Arabic word Scach, which signifies king, because
the principal piece of chess is the king, as is noticed in the Pandect of
Leunclavius, n. 1, 102, 179.   The Greeks of the middle ages, and those
of the present day, call it Ζατ6ίκιον, as Saumaise in his observations
on Pliny, and Meursius in his Glossary, have observed.   Anna Comnena,
in the 22nd book of her Alexiade, makes use of this word, and remarks, that it was invented by the Assyrians.   See the Chronicle of
Hainault, by Jacques de Guyse, vol. i. pp. 53 and 54, and M. Menage
in his Glossary of the French Language.   Lucanus in Paneg. ad Pisonem
has elegantly described the game of chess, and after him Hieronymus
Vidas.

instantaneously took effect through this sore, and his whole body became so much affected that he lost the use of that side. When the venom was come towards the head, he continued for two days without eating or drinking, and this was the cause that the sultan of Hamault remained in peace, for the sultan of Babylon was obliged to be carried back to his own country by his people.

As soon as the month of March was come, it was proclaimed, by orders of the king, that all vessels should be laden and ready to sail whenever the king should command. All things being ready, the king, the queen, and their households embarked on board their different ships. On the Friday preceding Whitsunday, the king ordered every one to follow him on the morrow, and proceed to Egypt; and on the morrow, being Saturday, every vessel made sail, which was a pleasant sight to see, for it seemed as if the whole sea, as far as the sight could reach, was covered with cloth, from the great quantity of sails that were spread to the wind, there being 1,800 vessels great and small.

The king, followed by the other vessels, came on Whitsunday to the point of Lymesson, where he landed, and heard mass; but of full 2,800 knights, who had embarked to follow the king, there were now only 700 with him on shore. A horrible wind that blew from Egypt had made the remainder alter their course, and had separated them from the company of the king, and driven them on the coast of Acre and other strange countries at a great distance, so that the king did not see them again for a long time. He and his companions were much grieved at their loss, for they believed them drowned, or in great danger at least.

On the morrow of Whitsunday, the wind was favourable, and the king and we who were with him made sail, in God's name, to pursue our route. It happened that in our course we met the prince of Morea* and the duke of Burgundy,† who has sojourned in the Morea. The king arrived with his

* William de Villehardouin, prince of Achaia and of the Morea, seneschal of Romania.

† The duke of Burgundy had passed the winter in the Morea, according to Vincent de Beauvais, l. 32, ch. 97, and, as I presume, then returned to Constantinople, which he undertook in consequence of a promise he had made the emperor Baldwin so long ago as the year 1238, to succour him in case of need, as we read in Albericus.

fleet on the Thursday after Whitsuntide at Damietta, where a great company were waiting for us.

On the shore we saw the whole force of the sultan, who were handsome men to look at. The sultan wore arms of burnished gold of so fine a polish, that when the sun shone on them, he seemed like a sun himself. The tumult and noise they made with their horns and nacaires* was frightful to hear, and seemed very strange to the French.

The king, perceiving this, called together his barons and counsellors to consult on what should be done. They advised him to wait until the whole of his force should arrive; for he had not now with him a third part, owing, as I before said, to the contrariety of the wind. But the king would not consent, saying, that by such conduct he should encourage the enemy; and likewise because there was not any port near in those seas whither he might retire, and wait in safety the return of those who had been dispersed by the storm. He added, that a strong gust of wind might arise and separate them from each other in these foreign countries, as had happened to his other knights on Whitsunday last. They acceded, therefore, to his proposal, that on the Friday preceding Trinity Sunday the king should disembark, and combat the Saracens, if it were not their fault. The king ordered the lord John de Belmont to cause a galley to be given to the lord Airart de Brienne, with whom I was, to land us and our men-at-arms, because the large ships could not approach near enough to the shore. Thus was it the will of God that I should quit my ship, and enter a small galley, which I thought I had lost, and wherein were eight of my horses. This galley had been given me by Madame de Baruth, cousin-german to the count de Montbelial.

The lord Airart de Brienne and I, fully armed, went to the

---

* The Italians call them *naccara* and *gnaccara*. Philippo Venuto says, that it is a "Stromento musico, col quale i fanciulli cantano il san Martino." Pietro de la Valle, in his Travels, ep. 6, says, that a sort of drum is called by this name which is used by the German cavalry, and which we commonly call *tymbale*. Jean d'Oronville, in his History of Louis, Duke of Bourbon, chap. 76, attributes in like manner the naccaires to the Saracens of Africa. "The king of Tunis, the king of Tremeçen, and the king of Bugia, came before the town of Africa with their array, and, according to custom, attended by their naccaires, drums, cymbals, flutes, and shoutings."

king on the Friday, to ask for the galley which he had
ordered for us ; but Sir John de Belmont replied, in the presence of the king, that we should not then have it ; from
which may be known, that the good king had as much trouble
in keeping his own people in peace together, as in his ill-for-
tunes and losses.

When our people saw that we were not bringing back the
galley, they dropped into the boat with all their weight, and
when the sailors perceived the boat was gradually sinking,
they retired into the ship, abandoning my knights in the boat.
On seeing this, I called out to the captain, and asked how
many there were overweight for the boat. He said, too
many by eighteen so armed. I then instantly discharged so
many from the boat, and put them in the ship with my horses.
As I was thus arranging these men-at-arms, a knight, belonging to the lord Airart de Brienne, named Plouquet, wanting
to descend from the ship to the boat as it was pushing off, fell
into the sea and was drowned.*

We then began to sail after the boat of the king's large ship,
and made for land ; but when those attached to the king, who
were hastening to land like ourselves, saw that we made more
speed than they, they cried out for us to wait for the arrival
of the standard of St. Denis ;† but I would not attend to

---

* After these words the Poitiers edition adds, " And I must relate a
marvellous event which happened in my little boat. I had taken with me
two valiant knights bachelor, whose names were Villains de Vergy and
William de Dammartin. They bore so great a hatred to each other, that
it could not be exceeded, insomuch that they had several times fought,
and there was no way of appeasing their rage. But when my boat was
on the point of leaving the ship for land, on a sudden these two bachelors,
without saying one word, ran and embraced each other, weeping through
affection, and mutually asking pardon for their offences. I mention this
to shew that the danger of death extinguishes all hatred and rancour."

† That is to say, the vessel which bore the standard of St. Denis, for,
farther on, " the galley arrived with the standard of St. Denis ;" and
directly afterward, " when the good king Saint Louis knew that the
standard of St. Denis was landed." This standard of St. Denis was no
other than the oriflamme. This name was given to it because it was slit up
from the bottom to resemble flames, or perhaps from its being of a red
colour ; when it fluttered in the wind, it appeared at a distance like flames ;
and, beside, the lance to which it was fixed was gilded. The oriflamme was
the particular banner of the abbot and monastery of St. Denis, which was
borne in their wars by their proxies, who, in quality of defenders or pro-
tectors of monasteries and churches, undertook to lead their vassals in the

them, and continued advancing towards a large battalion of
Saracens and Turks, consisting of 6,000 men, at least, on
horseback. The moment they saw us on shore they spurred
their horses full gallop toward us; but we struck our spears
and shields into the sand with their points against them,
which as soon as they perceived, and that we were advancing
inland, they suddenly wheeled about and fled.

That discreet man Sir Baldwin de Rheims, as soon as I
was landed, sent one of his squires to desire I would wait for
him. I made answer, by his messenger, that I would cheerfully do so, for that so valiant a man as he was well deserved
waiting for; and he was thankful for this attention as long
as he lived. He shortly after joined our company, with a
thousand knights at least. You must know that when I
first landed I had not any one person with me, neither friend
nor servant, of all those I had brought from France. Notwithstanding this, God always assisted me with his grace, for
which I ever praise him.

On our left the count de Japhe,* cousin-german to the
count de Montbelial, and of the lineage of the house of Joinville, drew up his men. This count Japhe had disembarked
in a most grand manner; for his galley was all painted
withinside and without with escutcheons of his arms, which
were a cross patée gules on a field or. There were full three
hundred sailors on board the galley, each bearing a target of

---

defence of their rights, and to bear their standards in war: hence they have
been called standard-bearers to the church, "Signiferi Ecclesiarum." The
counts of Vexin and of Pontoise had this title in the monastery of St.
Denis, of which they were the proxies and guardians, and in this quality
they bore the oriflamme in the wars which they undertook in the defence
of its property. From this the banner has been by authors more commonly called the standard of St. Denis, not because it was preserved in
the church of that monastery, but because it was the banner usually borne
in the wars in which this abbey was concerned. We may therefore conclude
that it was not borne by our kings in their wars until they were become
proprietors of the counties of Pontoise and Mante; that is to say, of the
Vexin, which happened during the reign of Philippes I. or of Louis le
Gros, his son.

* This count was the person who had succeeded Count Walter de
Brienne, made prisoner by the sultan of Persia, about the year 1244. His
name was John d'Ibelin, and he was lord of Baruth, by descent from his
father, Balian d'Ibelin. His mother was Eschive de Montbeliard, by
reason of which alliance John d'Ibelin was a cousin, once removed, from
Germain de Richard, count de Montbeliard, son of Peter.

his arms, and on each target was a small flag with his arms
likewise, of beaten gold. It was a sight worthy to be viewed
when he went to sea, on account of the noise which these flags
made, as well as the sounds of the drums,* horns, and Saracen
nacaires, which he had in his galley.

The moment his vessel grounded on the sand, and as near
as she could be brought to the land, he himself, his knights,
and men-at-arms disembarked, well armed at all points, and
posted themselves by our side. The count de Japhe instantly
ordered his pavilions to be pitched, which when the Saracens
saw was about to be done, they again returned, spurring
their horses against us; but finding we were not any way in-
timidated, and that we were firmly waiting for them, they
turned their backs and galloped away.

On our right, the galley bearing the standard of St. Denis
arrived within a crossbow-shot of us; and it happened, that
as she was touching the ground, a Saracen rode against the
crew full speed. I know not why he did so, whether he
could not stop his horse, or expected support from his countrymen, but the poor creature was very soon destroyed and
cut to pieces.

When the good king St. Louis learnt that the standard of
St. Denis was landed, he quitted his vessel, which was
already close to the shore, without waiting until he could

---

* The Saracenic horn is mentioned in the extract I have made from
the roll in the Chamber of Accounts of Paris. The manuscript chronicle
of Bertrand du Guesclin mentions it likewise:—
　　　" Trompes et chalemelles et cors Sarazinois."
I have already spoken of nacaires: it remains only that I say a few
words respecting drums, the use of which we have also borrowed from the
Saracens. The lord de Joinville shews us, that in his time they were
called tabours, which is confirmed by the romance of Garin:—
　　　" Les tabours sonnent por les chevaux lesdir."
And by William Guiart in the year 1202:—
　　　" Ne mena trompes ne tabours."
Jacques Millet, in his Destruction of Troy:—
　　　" Faites ces trompettes sonnor,
　　　Tabours, menestriers, et clarons."
Sanuto, l. 2, part 4, ch. 21, uses the word tamburtam. The Spaniards
call them altambors. Bonaventura Pistofilo, i. part. della Oplomachia,
supposes these words to have been formed from the Greek ταμβος,
these instruments having been invented to astonish and strike dismay; but
it is certain that the word, as well as the use of drums, has originated
with the Saracens and Arabians.

disembark from it, and against the will of the legate, who
was with him, leaped into the sea, which was up to his
shoulders, and advanced to the land, his shield on his neck,
his helmet on his head, and lance in hand.*   On joining his
men, he observed the Saracen army, and asked who they
were.   On being told they were Turks and Saracens, he
wanted to make a course alone against them, but his attendants would not permit it, and made him remain quiet until
his whole army should be assembled and armed.

A messenger, called Coullon, was sent thrice to the sultan
of the Saracens, to inform him of the arrival of the king of
France ; but no answer was returned, because the sultan was
ill.   The Saracens, hearing of this, abandoned the city of
Damietta, believing their sultan was dead.†   When the king
heard this news, he sent one of his knights to Damietta to
know the truth of it, who, on his return, related that the
sultan was really dead, and that the Saracens had fled from
Damietta, for he had entered their houses that were empty.

Upon this, the king had the legate called, with all the
prelates of the army, and ordered the " Te Deum laudamus "
to be sung throughout.   The king and his army, shortly
after, mounted their horses, and went to take up their quarters in Damietta.   The Turks were ill advised to retreat so
suddenly without destroying the bridges which they had
made of boats, which would have distressed us much.   But
in another way they did us great mischief, by setting fire to
all parts of the Soulde,‡ where their merchandise and plun-

* Froissart, vol. i. ch. 12, and the Chronicle of Flanders, pp. 55, 99,
&c., mention this usage.
† The Oriental Chronicle says, that the sultan of Babylon was not
deceased when St. Louis took Damietta, but that he died the day the king
left it to encamp before Massoura, which was the 25th of November.
‡ According to the lord de Joinville, the Soulde was a row of trades-
men's shops; but it is an error, and la Soulde must be changed to
la Fonde, as it is printed in the edition of Bordeaux.   In the treaty
concluded by the patriarch Guermond, and the barons of Jerusalem,
with Dominico Michial, doge of Venice, relative to the undertaking
the siege of the city of Tyre in the year 1123, as reported by William, archbishop of Tyre, in his History, l. 12, ch. 25 :—" Ipse rex
Hierusalem et nos omnes duci Venetorum de funda Tyri ex parte regis
festo apostolorum Petri et Pauli trecentos in unoquoque anno Byzantios
Saracenatos ex debiti conditione persolvere debemus."   Now the words
funda Tyri mean nothing else than the revenue afforded by commerce,

der had been deposited, which they burnt, for fear we might make any advantage of them. It would be the same thing if fire were set to the Petit Pont of Paris, which God preserve from such an accident!

Now let us ask ourselves, what grace did not God the Creator shew us in preserving us from death and danger on our landing, and when we joyfully advanced to our enemies who were on horseback? What other greater grace did not our good Lord shew us in delivering up Damietta without any risk of our lives, and which we never could have gained but by starving the garrison? These graces, we may say, were wondrous great, and apparent to every one.

King John had indeed taken it by famine in the times of our ancestors: but I doubt if the good Lord God may not say as much of us as he did of the children of Israel, when he had conducted and led them into the land of promise; for which he reproached them, saying, "*Et pro nihilo habuerunt terram desiderabilem, et quæ sequuntur.*" He said this, because they had forgotten him, who had showered down on them so much good. He had saved them, and brought them out of the captivity of Pharaoh, and given them the land of promise. Thus may he say of us, who forgot him, as shall hereafter be told.

I shall begin with the person of the king himself, who assembled all the barons and prelates that had accompanied him, and asked their advice what he should do with the riches he had found in Damietta, and how he should divide them? A patriarch who was present* spoke first, and said,

and taken from the common purse of the merchants, for *funds* signifies a purse, in Macrobius, l. 2, Saturnal. c. 4; and in some Greek authors, quoted by Meursius in his Glossary, v. φουνδα. This may be the cause that, in some of the towns of Germany, the Low Countries, and in England, the public places for the meetings of merchants have retained the name of Bourse, or Purse, on account of its being the common purse of the companies of merchants.

* It was the patriarch of Jerusalem, of whom mention is made hereafter, and who, according to the account of the lord de Joinville, was eighty years old at the time of this expedition. His name was Guy, and a native of La Puglia. Pope Gregory IX. promoted him to the bishopric of Nantes in Brittany after the death of the patriarch Girold. Albericus in the year 1236. The epistle of Pope Gregory, mentioning his promotion to this dignity, may be found in the Annals of Odoricus Raynaldus, anno 1240, n. 47.

—"Sire, it seems right to me, that you should reserve the wheat, barley, rice, and all other provisions, in order that the city may not suffer famine; and that you should order proclamation to be made throughout the army, that all other goods and furniture should be carried and deposited in the house of the legate, under pain of excommunication." This advice was acceded to by the barons and all present, and put in execution.

The furniture that was carried to the legate's house was found, on valuation, not worth more than six thousand livres. When all had been brought thither, the king and the barons sent to seek for the good and discreet man, Sir John de Valeri. On his arrival, the king told him what had been done, and that his council had advised that the legate should give him the six thousand livres at which the goods had been valued, which he would carry to his house, in order that he might dispose of them in the manner he should see right, and where he should think them best employed.

"Sire," replied Sir John, "I most humbly thank you for the honour you do me; but, under your good pleasure, I will not accept your proposal: never, please God, will I alter good and ancient customs, and such as our predecessors have followed in the Holy Land; for, whenever any city, or other considerable booty, was gained from the enemy, the king never received but one-third of all the riches or goods that were found in the city, and the pilgrims had two parts. This was the custom followed by King John, when formerly he took Damietta: and thus, as I have heard my elders say, did the king of Jerusalem act before King John's time, without failing in any one point. Now, consider if you be willing to give me two parts of the grain and other provisions which you have retained, and most cheerfully will I divide and distribute them among the pilgrims, in honour of God."

The king did not agree to this advice, and matters remained as before, which made many discontented with the king, because he had broken through good ancient customs.

The king's officers, when they were at their ease, and comfortably lodged in the city of Damietta, instead of well treating and entertaining the merchants, and those who followed the army with provisions, hired out to them stalls and workmen at as dear a rate as they possibly could. This conduct was spread abroad to distant countries ; and those who would have supplied the army with provisions delayed doing so, which was a great evil and loss.

The barons, knights, and others, who ought to have attended to their money concerns, and to have practised economy, as a resource in times of need, began to give sumptuous banquets in rivalship to each other, with the utmost abundance of the most delicious meats. The commonalty likewise gave themselves up to debauchery, and violated both women and girls. Great were the evils in consequence ; for it became necessary for the king to wink at the greatest liberties of his officers and men. The good king even told me, that at a stone's throw round his own pavilion were several brothels,* kept by his personal attendants. Other disorders were going forward, and to a greater extent than any person had hitherto seen.

But let us return to our principal object. After we had remained some time in this city of Damietta, the sultan laid siege to it on the land side, with a numerous army. The king and his men-at-arms were soon properly drawn out. In order to prevent the Turks from taking possession of the camp we had on the plain, I went to the king fully armed, whom I found in the same state of preparation, as well as all his knights seated around him on benches,† and most humbly requested that he would permit me and my people to make a course against the Saracens. But the moment Sir John de Belmont heard me, he cried out with a loud voice, commanding me, in the king's name, not to dare to quit my quarters until I should be so ordered by the king.

You must know that there were with the king eight good and valiant knights, who had several times won the prize of

---

* The word *bordel*, which signifies a place of infamy, *brothel*, takes its origin from loose women and suchlike characters inhabiting small houses, which in the old French language were called *bordels*, from the diminutive of *borde*, a house, and is probably borrowed from *bord* of the English Saxons, with whom this word has the same meaning. See likewise Spelman's Glossary. From the word *borde* comes *bordel*, to mark a small house. There are some who conceive that the word *bort*, which the Gascons formerly used to signify bastard, took its rise from the term bordel, as born " incerto patre," and in places of public resort.

† That is to say, mounted on their war-horses.

arms, as well on this side of the sea as on the other, and they were usually called the good knights. Among them were Sir Geoffroy de Sargines,* Sir Mahom de Marly,† Sir Philip de Nantuel, and Sir Ymbert de Beaujeu, constable of France; but these were not present when I made my request, being on the plain without the city, as well as the master of the cross-bows, with a large body of men-at-arms to prevent the Turks from approaching our main army. It happened that Sir Walter d'Entrache having caused himself to be well armed, and his lance and shield to be given to him, mounted his horse; and one of the sides of his pavilion being raised, stuck spurs into his horse, and rode full gallop against the Turks. He thus quitted his pavilion, attended only by one of his people, named Castillon; but his horse flung him to the ground, and ran off, covered with his arms, full speed to the enemy; for the greater part of the Saracens were mounted on mares, which caused the horse to play these tricks and run away. I heard from those who said they had witnessed it, that while the lord d'Entrache lay on the ground, four Turks came to him and, as they crossed him backward and forward, gave him heavy blows with their clubs, and would have killed him, if the constable of France had not gone to his succour with a body of king's troops which were under him. He was led back to his pavilion, but so much bruised by the blows he had received, that he was speechless. He was soon attended by the physicians and surgeons; and because they did not think him in any danger of death, they bled him in the arm, from which fatal consequences ensued.

Towards evening, Sir Aubert de Nancy desired I would accompany him on a visit to him, for that he was a man of great renown and valour: this I very willingly did, and we went together. On our entering his tent, one of his squires came to us, and desired we would tread softly, lest we might awaken him. We followed this advice, and found him lying on his mantle of minever,‡ which covered him; but, on approaching his face, we saw he was dead.

* He is called Gaufridus de Sarcinis, in an epistle of Pope Urban IV. in the fifth vol. of the Historians of France, p. 870. This letter informs us that he remained in the Holy Land after the departure of St. Louis.

† Mahieu de Marly, who was a nobleman descended from a branch of the Montmorenci family.

‡ In those days, the coverlids of beds usually consisted of skins of

We, and several more, were much grieved at the loss of such a man; but when it was told the king, he replied, that he did not wish for any one's service who would not attend to him, and obey his orders better than the lord d'Entrache had done; and that through his own fault he had caused his death.

I must inform you that the sultan gave for every head* of a Christian that was brought to him a besant of gold; and these Saracen traitors entered our camp during the night, and wherever they found any asleep they cut off their heads. They once surprised the watch† of the lord de Courtenay, and cut off his head, leaving the body lying on a table. They were likewise well informed of the manner of our encampment: for the engagements between us brought each party near to the other in the evenings; and the Saracens, in

value; whence ancient writers have included them among the richest furniture. In the last will of Jane, queen of France and Navarre, in the year 1304, sheets, coverlids, and counterpanes are named among the furniture of value; but our old writers particularly speak of those rich coverlids of exquisite skins when on the subject of the ceremonies used in times of peace on the creation of knights; for after they had been bathed, they were laid in a rich state bed under the finest coverlids, and were there visited by their friends. The author of the "Ordene de Chevalerie," after telling us how Saladin was put into the bath by Huês Tabarie, before he gave him the order of knighthood, adds, "that he led him to his new bed, and having laid him therein, said to him, 'Sire, this bed gives you .... to the great city of Paradise, which you must conquer by your chivalry;' and when he had reposed himself, he made him rise, and clothed him with a white robe of fine linen or silk." The same ceremonies are observed in creating knights of the Bath, according to the customs of England, related by Edward Bisse, in his notes on Nicholas Upton, page 21. "This done, the squires directors take the noviciate out of the bath, and put him to bed, until he be dry; and this bed must be plain, and without curtains."

* The Turks to this day follow the same custom, as our countrymen witnessed when they signalized their valour in the last wars between the emperor of Germany and the Grand Signor. See Gaufrid. Malaterra. L 2, ch. 46.

† In the Chronicle of Bertrand du Guesclin :—
     "Y avoit une gaite toute jour à journée,
     Qui sonnoit un bacin, quant la pierre est levée."
These verses inform us, that he who acted as sentinel on the watchtowers, and rang the alarm bell in cases of danger, was thence called Bachinator, in some of the ordinances of King Edward, relative to the office of seneschal of Gascony.

consequence of this knowledge, entered the camp as soon as
the guard had made its round, and committed many disorders
and murders.

The king, when he heard of this, gave orders for those
who were wont to go the rounds on horseback henceforward
to do so on foot; by this means the army was in security; for
we were so closely encamped that we touched each other, and
there were no void spaces.

We remained a long time in and before Damietta; for the
king had none in his council who advised him to march
further, until his brother, the count de Poitiers, whom the
storms had driven, as before mentioned, to Acre, was returned: for he had with him the arriere ban of France.   From
fear that the Turks might force the camp with their cavalry,
the king ordered it to be surrounded with deep ditches; and
on their banks there were numerous parties of cross-bows
and others, who watched during the nights.

The feast of St. Remy had passed without the army receiving any news from the count de Poitiers or his men.
This alarmed the king greatly, and the army were in much
distress; for they began to fear, from his not coming, that he
was either dead, or in very great danger.   I then recollected
the worthy dean of Mauru, and told the legate how, by means
of the three processions which he made us perform when at
sea, we were delivered from the great peril we were in, as I
have already related.   The legate believed what I said,
and ordered three processions to be proclaimed throughout the
army, to be put into practice the three following Saturdays.

The first procession began at the house of the legate, and
proceeded to the church of our Lady in the town of Damietta.   This church had been a mosque of the Turks and
Saracens; but the legate had consecrated it to the honour
of the Mother of God, the glorious Virgin Mary.   Thus
was it continued for two Saturdays: and each time the
legate preached a sermon.   The king and the great lords
attended, to whom, after they had heard the sermon, the
legate gave absolution.   Before the third Saturday, the count
de Poitiers arrived with his men, and fortunately for him
he did not come earlier; for during the space of the two
proceding Saturdays there were such continued storms at sea

before Damietta, that twelve score vessels, great and small, were wrecked and sunk, and their crews drowned. Had the count de Poitiers arrived at that time, he would have run great risk of suffering a similar fate; and I believe it would have been so, if God had not assisted him.

There was much joy in the whole army on the arrival of the count de Poitiers, the king's brother; and shortly after the king assembled his barons and council, and asked them what route he should pursue, whether to Alexandria or to Babylon? The count Peter of Brittany, with several other barons, were of opinion that the king should march to Alexandria, because there was a good harbour for boats and vessels, to bring provision to the army. But this plan was not approved of by the count d'Artois, who said he would never march to Alexandria until he should have been at Babylon, which was the seat of empire in Egypt. He added, among other reasons, that whoever wished to kill a snake, should begin with the head. To this opinion the king assented, and gave up the former plan.

At the beginning of Advent, the king and his whole army began their march toward Babylon, according to the advice given by the count d'Artois. On the road near to Damietta, we met a branch of the great river; and the king was advised to halt a day, until a dam should be thrown across, that the army might pass. This was easily done; and the river was stopped so level that it did not overflow, and might be crossed with facility.

What did the sultan do? He sent craftily to the king five hundred of his best-mounted troops, saying they were come to assist him, but in reality to delay him as much as possible. On St. Nicholas's day, the king commanded his army to mount their horses, and forbade any of his people to dare to hurt, in any way, one of the Turks or Saracens whom the sultan had sent to him. Now it happened, that when the Saracens perceived the king's army was in motion, and heard that the king had forbidden any one to touch them, they advanced with great courage in a body toward the Templars, who had the van of the army. One of these Turks gave a knight in the first rank so heavy a blow with his battle-axe as felled him under the feet of Sir Reginald de Bicher's horse, who was marshal of the Templars.

The marshal, seeing this, cried out to his men-at-arms,—
" Now, companions, attack them, in the name of God ! for I
cannot longer suffer thus."   He instantly stuck spurs into his
horse, and charged the Saracens, followed by the whole
army.   The horses of the Turks were worn down and tired,
while ours were fresh and hearty, which caused their misfortune ; for I have since heard that not one escaped being slain
or drowned in the sea.

It is proper that I say something here of the river which
runs through Egypt, and which comes from the terrestrial
paradise ; for such things should be known to those who
are desirous of understanding the subject I am writing on.
This river differs from all others, for the more brooks fall
into a large river, the more it is divided into small stream-
lets, and spread over a country ; but this river has not such
aids, and seems always the same.   When arrived in Egypt, it
spreads its waters over the country.   About the period of
St. Remy's day, it expands itself into seven branches, and
thence flows over the plains.   When the waters are retired,
the labourers appear, and till the ground with ploughs without
wheels, and then sow wheat, barley, rice, and cummin, which
succeed so well that it is not possible to have finer crops.

No one can say whence this annual increase of water comes,
except from God's mercy.   Were it not to happen, Egypt
would produce nothing, from the very great heat of that country ; for it is near to the rising sun, and it scarcely ever rains
but at very long intervals.

This river is quite muddy, from the crowds of people of that
and other countries who, towards evening, come thither to
seek water to drink.   They put into their vessels which hold
it four almonds or four beans, which they shake well, and on
the morrow it is wondrous clear and fit to drink.   When this
river enters Egypt, there are expert persons, accustomed to
the business, who may be called the fishermen of this stream,
and who in the evenings cast their nets into the water, and in
the mornings frequently find many spices in them, which they
sell into these countries dearly, and by weight ; such as cinnamon, ginger, rhubarb, cloves, lignum-aloes, and other good
things.   It is the report of the country, that they come from
the terrestrial paradise, and that the wind blows them down
from these fine trees, as it does in our forests the old dry

2 D

wood.   What falls into the river is brought down with it, and collected by merchants, who sell it to us by weight.

I heard in the country of Babylon, that the sultan had frequently attempted to learn whence this river came, by sending experienced persons to follow the course of it.   They carried with them a bread called biscuit, for they would not have found any on their route, and on their return reported, that they had followed the course of the river until they came to a large mountain of perpendicular rocks, which it was impossible to climb, and over these rocks fell the river.   It seemed to them, that on the top of this mountain were many trees; and they said they had seen there many strange wild beasts, such as lions, serpents, elephants, and other sorts, which came to gaze at them as they ascended the river.   These travellers, not daring to advance further, returned to the sultan.

Now, to pursue my subject, this river, on entering Egypt, spreads its branches over the plain : one of them flows to Damietta, another to Alexandria, another to Tunis, and another to Rexi.   To this branch which runs by Rexi, the king of France marched with his whole army, and encamped between the Damietta branch and that of Rexi.*   We found the sultan encamped with his entire force on the opposite bank of the Rexi branch, to prevent and oppose our passage. It was easy for him to do this, for none of us could have crossed unless we had stripped ourselves naked, as there were no other means to pass.

The king determined to have a causeway made, to enable him to pass over to the Saracens; and to guard those employed on it, he had built two beffrois,† called *chas-cha-*

---

* All the historians who relate this passage call the river Thanis, which is the name of one of the branches of the Nile that flows by a place of the same name, and is called at this day Tanes or Tenes. It will-therefore be necessary to correct our author, and make it Tanis instead of Tunis.

† The beffroy was a warlike machine in the form of a tower, made of wood, having different stories, which was drawn near to the walls of a town, and the stories filled with a proper number of soldiers, who shot from their bows and cross-bows over the walls, against the defenders of the place.   These machines were usually moved on four wheels, and to prevent the Greek fire from hurting them, they were covered with boiled horse or bullock skins.   Froissart, in his first volume, chap. 108, thus describes the bef-

*teils.** There were two towers in front of these beffrois, and two
houses in their rear, to receive the things the Saracens threw
upon their machines, of which they had sixteen that did
wonders. The king ordered eighteen machines to be constructed, under the direction of a man named Jousselin de
Courvant, who was the inventor and undertaker; and with
these engines did each army play on the other. The king's
brother was on guard over the cats in the daytime, and we
other knights guarded them at night.

These chas-chateils were finished the week before Christmas, and then the causeway was set about in earnest; but as
fast as we advanced, the Saracens destroyed it. They dug, on
their side of the river, wide and deep holes in the earth, and
as the water recoiled from our causeway it filled these holes
with water, and tore away the banks; so that what we had
been employed on for three weeks or a month, they ruined in
one or two days; they also very much annoyed, by their
arrows, our people who were carrying materials for the dam.

The Turks, after the death of their sultan, who died of the
disorder he was seized with when before Hamault, chose for
their chief a Saracen named Sacedun, son of the sheik,
whom the emperor Ferrait had made a knight.

Shortly after this, Sacedun sent part of his army to cross
near Damietta, and to a small town called Sourmesac, which

---

frois : " The English had constructed two large towers, of great beams of
wood, three stories high ; each tower was placed on wheels, and covered
over with prepared leather, to shelter those within from fire, and from
the arrows : in each story were 100 archers." William of Malmesbury,
in the fourth book of his History of England, calls this machine *berfroy.*
This word *beffroy* (belfry) has since been applied to the highest towers
of frontier towns, wherein a sentinel is placed to watch for their security,
and with a bell for him to strike on to alarm the inhabitants and guards at
the gates. This bell has afterwards been employed to mark the hour for
the retreat of the inhabitants to their houses, and the garrisons to their
quarters, and other public uses.

* The cat was properly a machine made in the form of a covered
gallery (whence Anna Comnena, in her Alexiade, page 383, gives it the
name of στοα), which was fastened to the walls to afford shelter to the
sappers. Ravedicus, in the second book of the History of Frederic I. c.
63, describing the siege of Crema, says that the inhabitants, to defend themselves against those who scaled the walls, or who descended on their walls
from beffrois and towers of wood, made use of cats to enable them to
attack the enemy within their machines.

is on the Rexi branch, that from that quarter they might fall
on us. On Christmas day, whilst I and all my people were at
dinner with my companion Pierre d'Avalon, the Saracens
entered our camp, and slew many of our poor soldiers who had
strayed into the fields.

We instantly mounted our horses to attack them; and well
timed was it for my lord Perron, our host, who had quitted
the camp on the first alarm; for before we could overtake
him, the Saracens had made him prisoner, and were carrying
him off with his brother, the lord Du Val. We pushed our
horses forward, attacked the Saracens, and rescued these two
good knights, whom they had already, by their blows, struck
to the ground, and brought them back to the camp. The
Templars, who were within hearing, formed a bold and
determined rear-guard.

The Turks continued to make repeated attacks on us in
that quarter with much courage, until our army had closed
up the canal toward Damietta, from that branch to the one of
Rexi.

This Sacedun, chief of the Turks, was held to be the most
able and courageous of all the infidels. He bore on his banners the arms of the emperor who had made him a knight; his
banner had several bends,* on one of which he bore the same
arms with the sultan of Aleppo, and on another bend on the
side were the arms of the sultan of Babylon. His name was,
as I said before, Sacedun, son of the sheik, which signifies the
same in their language as to say the son of the old man. His
name had great weight with them; for they are a people, it
is said, who pay much honour to such old men as have in
their youth been especially careful to preserve their characters
from reproach. This chief, as it was told the king by his
spies, boasted, that on St. Sebastian's day next coming, he
would dine in the king's tent.

When the king heard this, he replied, that he would take
good care to prevent it. He then drew his army in closer
array, orders for which were given to the men-at-arms; and
to the count d'Artois, brother to the king, was given the com-

---

* It results from this passage that armorial bearings were in use
among the Mahometans, and that their sultans or princes had them
painted on their banners.

mand of the beffrois and machines. The king, and the count
d'Anjou, who was afterwards king of Sicily, took on them
the guard of the army, on the side of Babylon; and the count
de Poitiers, with me, seneschal of Champagne, had the guard
on the side towards Damietta.

Not long after this, the chief of the Turks, before named,
crossed with his army into the island that lies between the
Rexi and Damietta branches, where our army was encamped,
and formed a line of battle, extending from one bank of the
river to the other. The count d'Anjou, who was on the spot,
attacked the Turks, and defeated them so completely that
they took to flight, and numbers were drowned in each of
the branches of the Nile.

A large body, however, kept their ground, whom we dared
not attack, on account of their numerous machines, by which
they did us great injury with the divers things cast from
them. During the attack on the Turks by the count d'Anjou,
the count Guy de Ferrois, who was in his company, galloped
through the Turkish force, attended by his knights, until they
came to another battalion of Saracens, where they performed
wonders. But at last he was thrown to the ground with a
broken leg, and was led back by two of his knights, supporting him by the arms.

You must know there was difficulty in withdrawing the
count d'Anjou from this attack, wherein he was frequently
in the utmost danger, and was ever after greatly honoured
for it.

Another large body of Turks made an attack on the count
de Poitiers and me; but be assured they were very well
received, and served in like manner. It was well for them
that they found their way back by which they had come;
but they left behind great numbers of slain. We returned
safely to our camp without having scarcely lost any of our
men.

One night the Turks brought forward an engine, called by
them *la perriere*, a terrible engine to do mischief, and placed
it opposite to the chas-chateils, which Sir Walter de Curel and
I were guarding by night. From this engine they flung such
quantities of Greek fire,* that it was the most horrible sight

* This fire was so called, because it was first invented among the

ever witnessed. When my companion, the good Sir Walter,
saw this shower of fire, he cried out, " Gentlemen, we are

Greeks by Callinicus the architect, a native of Heliopolis, a town in
Syria, under Constantinus Barbatus; and likewise because the Greeks
were for a long time the only people who preserved the use of it, which
they very rarely communicated to any of their allies. Anna Comnena
says, that this fire was made with pitch and other gums from trees, mixed
with sulphur, and the whole ground together. Abbon, in the first book
of the Wars of Paris, has given the composition of it in these verses :

> " Addit eis oleum, ceramque, picemque ministrans,
>   Mixta simul liquefacta foco ferventia valde,
>   Quæ Danis cervice comas uruntque trahuntque."

The author of the History of Jerusalem, p. 1167, makes oil a part of
the composition : at least, he names it, " oleum incendarium, quod ignem
Græcum vocant." It may perhaps be naphtha, which Procopius, in the
fourth book of the War of the Goths, ch. 11, says, the Greeks call
Μηδειας ελαιον, and the Medes naphtha, which Lambecius, in his observations on Codinus, thinks should be corrected to Μηδιας ελαιον, oil of
Media, and that for this reason the same Greeks have given to this artificial fire the name of Μηδικον πορ, which is met with in Cinnamus,
p. 308, and in Codinus, p. 7 of the royal edition. There are others,
however, who imagine naphtha was called Μηδειας ελαιον, or πορ,
because Medea, according to Pliny (l. 2, ch. 105), burnt her husband
Jason with this fire. Whatever may be thought of this, Procopius,
in the part quoted, informs us, that in the composition of this artificial fire, there was a mixture of naphtha with sulphur and bitumen.
Vanoccio Biringuccio, in the tenth book of his Pyrotechny, chap. 9,
has described all the materials that form part of the artificial fireworks
which the Greeks made use of to burn the vessels of their enemies. The
Greeks made use of this fire when at sea, in two ways; first by fire-ships
filled with this fire, that were floated among the enemies' fleet, and thus
set them on fire. Fire-ships were used before the time of the emperor
Constantinus Barbatus, for Theophanes informs us, p. 100, that under
the empire of Leon le Grand, Genseric, king of Africa, burnt with
vessels that were filled with dry wood and other combustibles, and which
he floated down the stream, the whole of the Grecian fleet. Secondly, by
artificial fires on the prows of these vessels, placed in large tubes of
copper, through which they blew them into the enemy's ships. With
regard to the use of the Greek fire in battles on land, it was different,
for soldiers were then supplied with copper tubes, and blew it through
them on their enemies.—See Anna Comnena, in the 13th book of her
Alexiade.   Sometimes they threw sharp bolts of iron, covered with
tow, well oiled and pitched, with which they set fire to the engines.
Joinville speaks of this fire, " and they opened a very quick fire upon
us with balls made of the Greek fire." Sometimes this fire was put into
phials and pots, and it was also discharged from perrieres and cross-
bows. Albert d'Aix, l. 7, ch. 5, remarks, that " hujus ignis genus
aqua erat inextinguibile;" but there were other materials by which it

all lost without remedy ; for should they set fire to our chas-chateils we must be burnt ; and if we quit our post we are for ever dishonoured ; from which I conclude, that no one can possibly save us from this peril but God, our benignant Creator ; I therefore advise all of you, whenever they throw any of this Greek fire, to cast yourselves on your hands and knees, and cry for mercy to our Lord, in whom alone resides all power."

As soon, therefore, as the Turks threw their fires, we flung ourselves on our hands and knees, as the wise man had advised ; and this time they fell between our two cats into a hole in front, which our people had made to extinguish them ; and they were instantly put out by a man appointed for that purpose.   This Greek fire, in appearance, was like a large tun, and its tail was of the length of a long spear ; the noise which it made was like to thunder ; and it seemed a great dragon of fire flying through the air, giving so great a light with its flame, that we saw in our camp as clearly as in broad day.   Thrice this night did they throw the fire from la perriere, and four times from cross-bows.

Each time that our good king St. Louis heard them make these discharges of fire, he cast himself on the ground, and with extended arms and eyes turned to the heavens, cried with a loud voice to our Lord, and shedding heavy tears, said, "Good Lord God Jesus Christ, preserve thou me, and all my people ;" and believe me, his sincere prayers were of great service to us.   At every time the fire fell near us, he sent one of his knights to know how we were, and if the fire had hurt us.   One of the discharges from the Turks fell beside a chas-chateil, guarded by the men of the Lord Courtenay, struck the bank of the river in front, and ran on the ground toward them burning with flame.   One of the knights of this guard instantly came to me, crying out,—"Help us, my lord, or we are burnt ; for there is a long train of Greek fire, which the Saracens have discharged, that is running straight for our castle."

could be extinguished, namely, vinegar and sand.   Jacques de Vitry, l. 3, ch. 84, adds urine as an extinguisher ; and Cinnamus, in the place before quoted, says that ships were frequently covered with cloths dipped in vinegar, to prevent the bad effects of this fire.

We immediately hastened thither, and good need was
there; for as the knight had said, so it was. We extinguished the fire with much labour and difficulty; for the
Saracens, in the mean time, kept up so brisk a shooting from
the opposite bank, that we were covered with arrows and
bolts.

The count of Anjou, brother to the king, guarded these
castles during the day, and annoyed the Saracen army with
his cross-bows. It was ordered by the king, that after the
count of Anjou should have finished his daily guard, we, and
others of my company, should continue it during the night.
We suffered much pain and uneasiness; for the Turks had
already broken and damaged our tandies and defences.
Once these Turkish traitors advanced their perriere in the
daytime, when the count d'Anjou had the guard, and had
brought together all their machines, from which they threw
Greek fires on our dams, over the river, opposite to our
tandies and defences, which completely prevented any of the
workmen from shewing themselves; and our two chas-
chateils were in a moment destroyed and burnt. The count
d'Anjou was almost mad at seeing this; for they were under
his guard, and like one out of his senses, wanted to throw
himself into the fire to extinguish it, whilst I and my knights
returned thanks to God; for if they had delayed this attack
to the night, we must have all been burnt.

The king, on hearing what had happened, made a request
to each of his barons, that they would give him as much of
the largest timbers* from their ships that were on the coast
as they could spare, and have them transported to where the
army lay; for there was not any timber near fit to make use
of. After the king had made this request, they all aided
him to the utmost; and before the new chas-chateils were
finished, the timber employed was estimated to be worth
upwards of 10,000 livres. You may guess from this that
many boats were destroyed, and that we were then in the
utmost distress.

When the chas-chateils were completed, the king would
not have them fixed, or pointed, until the count of Anjou
resumed the guard: he then ordered that they should be

_____
* Materials of beams of wood.

placed on the exact spot where the others had been burnt.
This he did to recover the honour of his said brother, under
whose guard the two others had been destroyed.   As
the king had ordered, so it was done; which the Saracens
observing, they brought thither all their machines, and,
coupling them together, shot at our new chas-chateils vigorously.   When they perceived that our men were afraid of
going from one castle to the other, for fear of the showers of
stones which they were casting, they advanced the perriere
directly opposite to them, and again burnt them with their
Greek fires.   I and my knights returned thanks to God for
this second escape.   Had they waited until night to make
the attack, when the guard would have devolved to us, we
must all have been burnt with them.

The king, seeing this, was, as well as his army, much
troubled, and he called his barons to council, to consider what
should be done; for they now perceived themselves that it
would be impossible to throw a causeway over the river to
cross to the Turks and Saracens, as our people could not
make such advance on their side, but they were more speedily
ruined by the Turks on the other.

Sir Humbert de Beaujeu, constable of France, then addressed the king, and said, that a Bedouin had lately come
to him to say, that if we would give him 500 golden besants,
he would shew a safe ford, which might easily be crossed on
horseback.   The king replied, that he most cheerfully granted
this, provided he spoke the truth; but the man would on no
account shew the ford before the money demanded was paid.

It was determined by the king, that the duke of Burgundy, and the nobles beyond sea his allies, should guard the
army from the alarms of the Saracens; whilst he, with his
three brothers, the counts of Poitiers, Artois, and Anjou, who
was afterward king of Sicily, as I have said before, should
with their attendants on horseback make trial of the ford
the Bedouin was to shew them.   The day appointed for this
purpose was Shrove-Tuesday, which, when arrived, we all
mounted our horses, and armed at all points, followed the
Bedouin to the ford.

On our way thither, some advanced too near the banks of
the river, which being soft and slippery, they and their

horses fell in and were drowned. The king seeing it, pointed it out to the rest, that they might be more careful and avoid similar danger. Among those that were drowned was that valiant knight Sir John d'Orleans, who bore the banner of the army. When we came to the ford, we saw, on the opposite bank, full 300 Saracen cavalry ready to defend this passage. We entered the river, and our horses found a tolerable ford with firm footing, so that by ascending the stream we found an easy shore, and, through God's mercy, we all crossed over with safety. The Saracens, observing us thus cross, fled away with the utmost despatch.

Before we set out, the king had ordered that the Templars should form the van, and the count d'Artois, his brother, should command the second division of the army ; but the moment the count d'Artois had passed the ford with all his people, and saw the Saracens flying, they stuck spurs into their horses and galloped after them ; for which those who formed the van were much angered at the count d'Artois, who could not make any answer, on account of Sir Foucquault du Melle, who held the bridle of his horse ; and Sir Foucquault, being deaf, heard nothing the Templars were saying to the count d'Artois, but kept bawling out "Forward, forward !"

When the Templars perceived this, they thought they should be dishonoured if they allowed the count d'Artois thus to take the lead, and with one accord they spurred their horses to their fastest speed, pursuing the Saracens through the town of Massoura, as far the plains before Babylon ; but on their return the Turks shot at them plenty of arrows, and other artillery, as they repassed through the narrow streets of the town. The count d'Artois and the lord de Coucy, of the name of Raoul, were there slain, and as many as 300 other* knights. The Templars lost, as their chief informed me, full fourteen score men-at-arms and horses. My knights, as well as myself, noticing on our left a large body of Turks who were arming, instantly charged them ; and when we were advanced into the midst of them, I perceived a sturdy Saracen mounting his horse, which was held by one of his esquires by the bridle, and while he was putting his

* The Oriental Chronicle says, that the French lost in this defeat, beside the brother of the king, fourteen hundred knights.

hand on the saddle to mount, I gave him such a thrust with my spear, which I pushed as far as I was able, that he fell down dead. The esquire, seeing his lord dead, abandoned master and horse; but, watching my motions, on my return struck me with his lance such a blow between the shoulders as drove me on my horse's neck, and held me there so tightly that I could not draw my sword, which was girthed round me. I was forced to draw another sword which was at the pommel of my saddle, and it was high time; but, when he saw I had my sword in my hand, he withdrew his lance, which I had seized, and ran from me.

It chanced that I and my knights had traversed the army of the Saracens, and saw here and there different parties of them, to the amount of about 6,000, who, abandoning their quarters, had advanced into the plain. On perceiving that we were separated from the main body, they boldly attacked us, and slew Sir Hugues de Trichatel, lord d'Escoflans, who bore the banner of our company. They also made prisoner Sir Raoul de Wanon, of our company, whom they had struck to the ground. As they were carrying him off, my knights and myself knew him, and instantly hastened, with great courage, to assist him, and deliver him from their hands. In returning from this engagement the Turks gave me such heavy blows, that my horse, not being able to withstand them, fell on his knees, and threw me to the ground over his head.* I very

---

* After these words, as far as " to the walls of this ruined house," the Poitiers edition has, " and the Saracens would have killed me, had it not been for Sir Arnaud de Commenge, viscount de Couzerans, who came most valiantly to my succour, and the vigorous gallantry he displayed. He had left the cross-bows, which he was conducting to the camp with the duke of Burgundy, and had followed the count de Poitiers, whom he would never abandon in any serious affair. From the time he gave me this timely assistance, there never was a day of my life that I did not most affectionately love him. " After I was thus rescued from the Saracens, the viscount de Couzerans and myself retired towards a house that had been destroyed to wait for the king, who was coming, and in the mean time I found an opportunity of recovering my horse. But while we were waiting near this house, a fresh troop of Saracens appeared, who seeing the main body of our people in our rear, pushed by us to attack them: in their passage, they flung me to the ground with my shield over my neck, and galloped over me, thinking me dead, which was nearly the case. When they had passed, Sir Arnaud de Commenge, after having courageously fought the Saracens, returned to me, and raised me from the ground, and then we went to the walls of this ruined house."

shortly replaced my shield on my breast, and grasped my spear, during which time the Lord Errat d'Esmeray, whose soul may God pardon! advanced towards me, for he had also been struck down by the enemy; and we retreated together towards an old ruined house to wait for the king, who was coming, and I found means to recover my horse.

As we were going to this house, a large body of Turks came galloping towards us, but passed on to a party of ours whom they saw hard by: as they passed, they struck me to the ground, with my shield over my neck, and galloped over me, thinking I was dead; and indeed I was nearly so. When they were gone, my companion, Sir Errart, came and raised me up, and we went to the walls of the ruined house. Thither also had retired Sir Hugues d'Escosse, Sir Ferreys de Loppei, Sir Regnault de Menoncourt, and several others; and there also the Turks came to attack us, more bravely than ever, on all sides. Some of them entered within the walls, and were a long time fighting with us at spear's length, during which my knights gave me my horse, which they held, lest he should run away, and at the same time so vigorously defended us against the Turks, that they were greatly praised by several able persons who witnessed their prowess.

Sir Hugues d'Escosse was desperately hurt by three great wounds in the face and elsewhere. Sir Raoul and Sir Ferreys were also badly wounded in their shoulders, so that the blood spouted out just like to a tun of wine when tapped. Sir Errart d'Esmeray was so severely wounded in the face by a sword, the stroke of which cut off his nose, that it hung down over his mouth. In this severe distress, I called to my mind St. James, and said, "Good Lord St. James, succour me, I beseech thee; and come to my aid in this time of need." I had scarcely ended my prayer, when Sir Errart said to me, 'Sir, if I did not think you might suppose it was done to abandon you, and save myself, I would go to my lord of Anjou, whom I see on the plain, and beg he would hasten to your help." "Sir Errart," I replied, "you will do me great honour and pleasure, if you will go and seek succour to safe our lives; for your own also is in great peril;" and I said truly, for he died of the wound he had received. All were of my opinion that he should seek for assistance; and

I then quitting hold of the rein of his bridle, he galloped towards the count d'Anjou, to request he would support us in the danger we were in.

There was a great lord with him who wished to detain him, but the good prince would not attend to what he urged, but, spurring his horse, galloped towards us followed by his men. The Saracens, observing them coming, left us; but when on their arrival they saw the Saracens carrying away their prisoner, Sir Raould de Wanon, badly wounded, they hastened to recover him, and brought him back in a most pitiful state.

Shortly after, I saw the king arrive with all his attendants, and with a terrible noise of trumpets, clarions, and horns. He halted on an eminence, with his men-at-arms, for something he had to say; and I assure you I never saw so handsome a man under arms. He was taller than any of his troop by the shoulders; and his helmet, which was gilded, was handsomely placed on his head; and he bore a German sword* in his hand.

Soon after he had halted, many of his knights were observed intermixed with the Turks: their companions instantly rushed into the battle among them; and you must know, that in this engagement were performed, on both sides, the most gallant deeds that were ever done in this expedition to the Holy Land; for none made use of the bow,† cross-bow, or

---

* William Guiart, in the Life of Philip Augustus, speaks of these German swords :—

"A grans espées d'Allemagne
Leur tranchent souvent les poins outre."

In his description of the battle of Bovines, he says that the Germans fought with short and sharp swords. The emperor Nicephorus Phocas reproaches the Germans, through his ambassador Luitprandus, for their long swords. In some old ordinances of the town of Paris mention is made of the swords of Lubec. The French, on the contrary, used short swords. William Guiart :—

"Li François espées reportent,
Courtes et roides, dont ils taillent."

† To kill an enemy by the bow, cross-bow, or other artillery, has never been esteemed by the French an action of valour. They only valued blows from the hand, sword, or lance, which required address and skill; and it was for this reason, that, in process of time, they forbade the use of cross-bows, arrows, and poisoned darts: it was not sufficient to destroy the enemy by any means whatever, it was necessary that he should be conquered by fair force, and with such arms as displayed the dexterity of the person using

other artillery.   But the conflict consisted of blows given to
each other by battle-axes, swords, butts of spears, all mixed
together.   From all I saw, my knights and myself, all
wounded as we were, were very impatient to join the battle
with the others.

Shortly after one of my esquires, who had once fled from
my banner, came to me, and brought me one of my Flemish
war-horses : I was soon mounted, and rode by the side of the
king, whom I found attended by that discreet man, Sir John
de Valeri.   Sir John seeing the king desirous to enter into
the midst of the battle, advised him to make for the river-
side, on the right, in order that in case there should be any
danger, he might have support from the duke of Burgundy
and his army, which had been left behind to guard the
camp ; and likewise that his men might be refreshed, and
have wherewith to quench their thirst ; for the weather was
at this moment exceedingly hot.

The king sent orders for his barons, knights, and others
of his council, to quit the Turkish army, and on their arrival,
demanded their counsel, what was best to be done.   Several
answered, that the good knight, Sir John de Valeri, now by
his side, would give him the best advice.   Then, according
to the former opinion of Sir John de Valeri, which many agreed
was good, the king turned to the right hand, and advanced
toward the river.

As this was doing, Sir Humbert de Beaujeu, constable of
France, came up, and told the king that his brother, the
count d'Artois, was much pressed in a house at Massoura,
where, however, he defended himself gallantly, but that he
would need speedy assistance ; and entreated the king to go
to his aid.   The king replied, "Constable, spur forward,

---

them.   It is certain that the above-mentioned arms have been forbidden
at various times by the popes, and particularly at the council held at Rome
under Pope Innocent II. in the year 1139, ch. 29.   The emperor Conrad
was one of the Christian princes who forbade their use for similar reasons.
From whence it is easy to judge, that we must interpret favourably the
terms of the Breton poet, when, in the second book of his Philippiade, he
says that Richard I., king of England, invented cross-bows ; it must
be explained by his meaning that King Richard revived the use of them
during his reign.   This is so strictly true, that in every action we read of
in the histories of the first crusades, they made use of bows and cross-
bows.

and I will follow you close." I also, the lord de Joinville, said to the constable, that I would be one of his knights, and follow him in such a case as this.

All of us now galloped straight to Massoura, and were in the midst of the Turkish army, when we were instantly separated from each other by the greater power of the Saracens and Turks. Shortly after, a serjeant at mace of the constable, with whom I was, came to him, and said the king was surrounded by the Turks, and his person in imminent danger. You may suppose our astonishment and fears, for there were between us and where the king was full one thousand or twelve hundred Turks, and we were only six persons in all. I said to the constable, that since it was impossible for us to make our way through such a crowd of Turks, it would be much better to wheel round and get on the other side of them. This we instantly did. There was a deep ditch on the road we took between the Saracens and us; and, had they noticed us, they must have slain us all: but they were solely occupied with the king, and the larger bodies: perhaps also they might have taken us for some of their friends. As we thus gained the river, following its course downward between it and the road, we observed that the king had ascended it, and that the Turks were sending fresh troops after him. Both armies now met on the banks, and the event was miserably unfortunate; for the weaker part of our army thought to cross over to the division of the duke of Burgundy, but that was impossible from their horses being worn down, and the extreme heat of the weather. As we descended the river, we saw it covered with lances, pikes, shields, men and horses, unable to save themselves from death.

When we perceived the miserable state of our army, I advised the constable to remain on this side of the river, to guard a small bridge that was hard by; "for if we leave it," added I, "the enemy may come and attack the king on this side; and if our men be assaulted in two places, they must be discomfited."

There then we halted; and you may believe me when I say, that the good king performed that day the most gallant deeds that ever I saw in any battle. It was said, that had it not been for his personal exertions, the whole army would have been destroyed; but I believe that the great courage he naturally possessed was that day doubled by the power of God, for he forced himself wherever he saw his men in any distress, and gave such blows with battle-axe and sword, it was wonderful to behold.

The lord de Courtenay and Sir John de Salenay one day told me, that at this engagement six Turks caught hold of the bridle of the king's horse, and were leading him away; but this virtuous prince exerted himself with such bravery in fighting the six Turks, that he alone freed himself from them; and that many, seeing how valiantly he defended himself, and the great courage he displayed, took greater courage themselves, and abandoning the passage they were guarding, hastened to support the king.

After some little time, the count Peter of Brittany came to us who were guarding the small bridge from Massoura, having had a most furious skirmish. He was so badly wounded in the face that the blood came out of his mouth, as if it had been full of water, and he vomited it forth. The count was mounted on a short, thick, but strong horse, and his reins and the pommel of his saddle were cut and destroyed, so that he was forced to hold himself by his two hands round the horse's neck for fear the Turks, who were close behind him, should make him fall off. He did not, however, seem much afraid of them, for he frequently turned round, and gave them many abusive words, by way of mockery.

Towards the end of this battle, Sir John de Soissons and Sir Peter de Nouille, surnamed Cayer, came to us: they had suffered much from the blows they had received by remaining behind in the last battle. The Turks, seeing them, began to move to meet them, but observing us who were guarding the bridge, with our faces towards them, suffered them to pass, suspecting that we should have gone to their succour, as we certainly should have done. I addressed the count de Soissons, who was my cousin-german: "Sir, I beg that you will remain here to guard this bridge. You will act right in so doing; for, if you leave it, the Turks whom you see before you will advance to attack us, and the king may thus have his enemies in front and rear at the same moment." He asked, if he should stay, would I remain with him? to which I most cheerfully assented.

The constable, hearing our conversation and agreement, told

me to defend this bridge, and not on any account to quit it, and
that he would go and seek for succour.   I was sitting quietly
there on my horse, having my cousin Sir John de Soissons on
my right and Sir Peter de Nouille on my left hand, when a
Turk, galloping from where the king was, struck Sir Peter de
Nouille so heavy a blow with his battle-axe on the back as
felled him on the neck of his horse, and then crossed the
bridge full speed to his own people, imagining that we would
abandon our post and follow him, and thus they might gain
the bridge.   When they perceived that we would on no
account quit our post, they crossed the rivulet, and placed
themselves between it and the river; on which we marched
towards them in such-wise that we were ready to charge them,
if they had further advanced.

In our front were two of the king's heralds: the name of
one was Guillaume de Bron, and that of the other John de
Gaymaches; against whom the Turks, who, as I have said,
had posted themselves between the rivulet and river, led a
rabble of peasants of the country, who pelted them with clods
of earth and large stones.   At last, they brought a villanous
Turk, who thrice flung Greek fires at them; and by one of
them was the tabard of Guillaume de Bron set on fire; but he
soon threw it off, and good need had he, for if it had set fire
to his clothes, he must have been burnt.   We were also covered
with these showers of stones and arrows which the Turks discharged at the two heralds.

I luckily found near me a gaubison* of coarse cloth which
had belonged to a Saracen, and turning the slit part inward,
I made a sort of shield, which was of much service to me;
for I was only wounded by their shots in five places, whereas
my horse was hurt in fifteen.   Soon after, as God willed it,
one of my vassals of Joinville brought me a banner with my
arms, and a long knife for war, which I was in want of; and
then, when these Turkish villains, who were on foot, pressed
on the heralds, we made a charge on them, and put them instantly to flight.

* It should be *gambison*, which is the name of this sort of dress.
Roger Hoveden, in the year 1181, uses the word *wambasis*, and in
page 614 that of *wanbais*.   The gamboison was a quilted dress, well
stuffed with wool, that had been soaked in, and beat up with vinegar,
which Pliny, in the 48th chapter of his 8th book, says resists iron.

Thus when the good count de Soissons and myself were returned to our post on the bridge, after chasing away these peasants, he rallied me, saying, "Seneschal, let us allow this rabble to bawl and bray; and, by the 'Cresse Dieu,'" his usual oath, "you and I will talk over this day's adventures in the chambers of our ladies."

It happened that towards evening, about sunset, the constable, Sir Hymbert de Beaujeu, brought us the king's crossbows that were on foot; and they drew up in one front, while we, horsemen, dismounted under shelter of the cross-bows. The Saracens, observing this, immediately took to flight, and left us in peace. The constable told me that we had behaved well in thus guarding the bridge; and bade me go boldly to the king, and not quit him until he should be dismounted in his pavilion. I went to the king, and at the same moment Sir John de Valeri joined, and requested of him, in the name of the lord de Chastillon, that the said lord might command the rear guard, which the king very willingly granted. The king then took the road to return to his pavilion, and raised the helmet from his head, on which I gave him my iron skull-cap, which was much lighter, that he might have more air.

Thus as we were riding together, Father Henry, prior of the hospital of Ronnay, who had crossed the river, came to him and kissed his hand, fully armed, and asked if he had heard any news of his brother, the count d'Artois. "Yes," replied the king, "I have heard all;" that is to say, that he knew well he was now in paradise. The prior, thinking to comfort him for the death of his brother, continued, "Sire, no king of France has ever reaped such honour as you have done; for with great intrepidity have you and your army crossed a dangerous river to combat your enemies; and have been so very successful, that you have put them to flight and gained the field, together with their warlike engines, with which they had wonderfully annoyed you, and concluded the affair by taking possession this day of their camp and quarters."

The good king replied, that God should be adored for all the good he had granted him; and then heavy tears began to fall down his cheeks, which many great persons noticing, were oppressed with anguish and compassion, on seeing him thus weep, praising the name of God, who had enabled him to gain the victory.

When we arrived at our quarters, we found great numbers of Saracens on foot holding the cords of a tent which some of our servants were erecting, and pulling against them with all their might. The master of the Temple, who had the command of the vanguard, and myself, charged this rabble, and made them run away. The tent remained, therefore, with us; not, however, that there was any great fight, for which reason many boasters were put to shame. I could readily mention their names, but I abstain from doing so because they are deceased; and we ought not to speak ill of the dead. Of Sir Guyon de Malvoisin I am willing to speak, for the constable and I met him on the road, returning from Massoura, bearing himself gallantly, although hard pressed by the Turks, who closely pursued him; for after they had dispersed the count of Brittany and his battalion, as I have before said, they followed the lord Guyon and his company. He had not suffered much in this engagement, for he and his people had most courageously behaved; which is not to be wondered at, when, as I have heard from those who knew him and his family, almost all his knights were of his kindred and lineage, and his men-at-arms his liege vassals. This gave them the greater confidence in their chief.

After we had discomfited the Turks, and driven them out of their quarters, the Bedouins,† who are a powerful people, entered the camp of the Saracens and Turks, and seized and carried off whatever they could find, and all that the Saracens and Turks had left behind them. I was much surprised at this; for the Bedouins are subjects and tributary to the Saracens; but I never heard that they were treated the worse by the Saracens for what they had thus pillaged. They said it was their usual custom to fall on the weakest, which is

---

* He is called Frère Guillaume de Sonnac in the additions to Matt. Paris, p. 110.

† The lord de Joinville has here confounded, as elsewhere, the Bedouins with the Assassins. Jacques de Vitry says positively they were Arabians, that their residence was near Aleppo and Crach, in Arabia, and that the Assassins inhabited a canton of the province of Phœnicia, enclosed by mountains near Tortosa. However this may be, every writer agrees that the Bedouins were a wandering and vagabond people.

the nature of dogs; for when there is one dog pursued by
another, and a shouting made after him, all the other dogs
fall on him.

As my subject requires it, I shall say something concerning these Bedouins, and what sort of people they be. The
Bedouins reside in deserts and mountains, and have no great
faith in Mahomet, like the Turks, but believe in the religion
of Aly,* who, they say, was uncle to Mahomet. They are
persuaded that when any one of them dies for the service
of his lord, or when attempting any good design, his soul
enters a superior body, and is much more comfortable
than it was before; this makes them ready to die at the
command of their superiors or elders. These Bedouins do
not reside in town or city, but always lie in the fields and
deserted places, where, whenever the weather is bad, they,
their wives and children, make themselves an habitation,
by sticking into the ground poles connected by hoops, like to
what women use in drying their washed clothes; and over
these hoops they throw skins of their large sheep, which
they call skins of Somas, tanned with alum. The Bedouins
have large pelisses of coarse hair, which cover their whole
bodies, and when evening comes, or when it is cold or wet,
they wrap themselves up in them, and retire to rest.
Those who follow war have their horses feeding near them
during the night, and have only to take off their bridles,
and let them eat. In the morning they spread their pelisses
to the sun, and, when dry, rub them, so that they do not
appear as if they had been wetted. They never are armed
for combat, for they say, and believe, that no one can die but
at his appointed hour : they have likewise a mode of cursing,
alluding to their faith, when they swear at their children,
saying, "Be thou accursed, like him who arms himself
for fear of death." In battle they use only a sword, made
after the Turkish manner, and are clothed in linen robes like
to surplices. They are an ugly race, and hideous to look

---

* Aly was not uncle to Mahomet, but his cousin, and son-in-law,
having married his daughter Fatima. The writers of the Mahometan
histories relate at length the difference of the religion established by
Mahomet, and that introduced by Aly, the latter of which was embraced
by the caliphs of Egypt, who for that reason are called *Fatimites* in the
Eastern Chronicle, from the name of *Fatima*, wife of Aly.—See Ockley's
History of the Saracens.

at; for their hair and beards are long and black. They live on the superabundance of the milk from their herds; and their numbers are not to be counted; for they dwell in the kingdoms of Jerusalem, Egypt, and throughout all the lands of the Saracens and infidels, to whom they are tributary.

Now I am on the subject of the Bedouins, I must say that I have seen, since my return from the Holy Land, some calling themselves Christians, who hold similar faith with the Bedouins; for they maintain that no man can die before his determined time, happen what may, which is a falsehood. I consider such a belief the same as if they should say that God had not the power to assist or hurt us, nor to lengthen or abridge our lives, which is heresy. On the contrary, I declare that we ought to put our whole faith in him who is all-powerful, and may, according to his good pleasure, send us death sooner or later. This is the opposite to the faith of the Bedouins, who firmly believe the day of death to each person is determined infallibly, without any possibility of prolonging or shortening the time.

To return to the original matter, and continue my history. In the evening of this severe engagement that I spoke of, and when we had taken up our quarters in those from whence we had driven the Saracens, my people brought me, from the main army, a tent, which the master of the Templars, who had the command of the van, had given me. I had it pitched on the right of those machines we had won from the enemy, as each of us was eager for repose: indeed we had need of it, from the wounds and fatigues we had suffered in the late battle.

Before daybreak, however, we were alarmed by the cries of "To arms, to arms!" and I made my chamberlain rise, who lay by my side, to go and see what was the matter. He was not long in returning, much frightened, and crying out, "My lord, up instantly; for the Saracens have entered the camp, both horse and foot, and have already defeated the guard which the king had appointed for our security, and to defend the engines we had won from them."

These engines were in front of the king's pavilions, and of us who were near to him. I immediately rose, threw a cuirass on my back, and put my iron skull-cap on my head;

and having roused our people, wounded as we were, we drove the Saracens from the engines which they were so anxious to recover.

The king, seeing that scarcely any of us had armour on, sent Sir Walter de Chastillon, who posted himself between us and the Turks, for the better guard of the engines. After Sir Walter had several times repulsed the enemy, who made frequent attempts during the night to carry off these engines, the Saracens, finding they could not succeed, retreated to a large body of their horse, that were drawn up opposite to our lines, to prevent us from surprising their camp, which was in their rear.

Six of the principal Turks dismounted, armed from head to foot, and made themselves a rampart of large stones, as a shelter from our cross-bows, and from thence shot volleys of arrows, which often wounded many of our men. When I and my men-at-arms who had the guard of that quarter saw their stone rampart, we took counsel together, and resolved that, during the ensuing night, we would destroy this rampart, and bring away the stones.

Now I had a priest called John de Waysy,* who, having overheard our counsel and resolution, did not wait so long, but set out alone towards the Saracens, with his cuirass on, his cap of iron, and his sword under his arm. When he was near the enemy, who neither thought of nor suspected any one coming against them thus alone, he rushed furiously on, sword in hand, and gave such blows to these six captains, that

---

* Anna Comnena, in the 292nd page of the tenth book of her Alexiade, reproaches the Latins for their clergy putting on armour, and with sword and lance hastening to the field of battle when they have but just received the order of priesthood, which is directly forbidden by the Greeks. Petrus Diaconus, in the fourth book of the Chronicle of Monte Cassino, makes the same charge. Doubtless it is not without reason that the Greeks have so often made this reproach to the Latins; seeing that although it has been forbidden by all the councils for priests to handle arms, or interfere in battles as combatants, yet notwithstanding they are there to be found fighting like seculars. Thus we read that Ebles, abbot of St. Germain des Prés, and Gosselin, bishop of Paris, fought valiantly against the Normans, who had besieged the capital of France. The clergy not only fought against the infidels, but against the Christians; witness the bishop of Beauvais, who, at the battle of Bovines, struck the earl of Salisbury to the ground with his battle-axe.

they could not defend themselves, and took to flight, to the great astonishment of the other Turks and Saracens.

When the Turks saw their leaders fly, they stuck spurs into their horses, and charged the priest, who was returning to our army, whence had sallied fifty of our men to oppose them, as they were pursuing him on horseback: the Turks would not meet them, but wheeled off two or three times. It happened, however, that during these wheelings, one of our men threw his dagger* at a Turk, and hit him between the ribs: he carried off the dagger, but it caused his death. The other Turks, seeing this, were more shy than before, and never dared to approach while our men were carrying away the stones of the rampart. My priest was well known ever after by the whole army, who said when they saw him, "That is the priest who, single-handed, defeated the Saracens."

These things happened during the first day of Lent; and this same day the Saracens elected another chief, in the place of their late chief, Secedun, of whom mention has been made, and who died in the battle of Shrove-Tuesday; at the same time, probably, that the good count d'Artois, brother to the king St. Louis, was slain. This new chief found among the other dead the body of the count d'Artois, who had shewn great intrepidity in this battle, magnificently dressed, becoming a prince; and this chief took the count's coat of armour, and, to give courage to the Turks and Saracens, had it hoisted before them, telling them it was the coat-armour of the king their enemy, who had been slain in battle; adding, "My lords, this should make you exert yourselves the more, for body without head is nothing, nor is an army without prince or chief to be feared. I advise, and you ought to have confidence in me, that we increase the force of our attacks on them; and on Friday next we must conquer and gain the battle, since they have now lost their commander." All who heard him cheerfully agreed to follow his advice.

You must know that the king had many spies in the Saracen army, who, having overheard their plans, knew their inten-

* The word *dagus* is still in use for a small knife or dagger. The Spaniards call it *dagas*, the English *dagger*. The statutes of William, king of Scotland, cap. 23 :—" Habeat equum, habergeon, capitium e ferre et cultellum, qui dicitur dagger."

tions, and how they meant to act. Some of them informed
the king of the intended attack of the enemy, and that they
believed him dead and the army without a leader.

Upon this, the king summoned all his captains, and commanded them to have their men-at-arms completely armed,
and ready drawn up before their tents at midnight, and then
to advance as far as the lines which had been made to prevent the Saracens entering the camp on horseback, although
they were so constructed that they might pass them on foot.
This was punctually executed according to the king's orders.

You may suppose that the plan the Saracen chief had proposed and adopted he lost no time in putting into execution.

On the Friday morning, by sunrise, 4,000 knights, well
armed and mounted, were drawn up in battalions, alongside
our army, which lay on the banks of the river toward Babylon, and extending as far as a town called Ressil. When
the Pagan chief had thus drawn up his 4,000 knights in
front of our army, he then brought another large body of
Saracens on foot, and in such numbers that they surrounded
all the other side of it. After doing this, he drew up at a
short distance other bodies in conjunction with the power of the
sultan of Babylon, to succour and aid each of the two former,
as occasion might occur.

The chief of the Saracens, having now completed the arrangement of his army, advanced on horseback alone, to view
and make his observations on the manner in which the king's
army was formed; and where he saw ours was the strongest
or weakest, he strengthened or diminished his own. After
this he ordered 3,000 Bedouins, whose nature and character
I have described, to march in front of the troops under the
command of the duke of Burgundy, which were posted between the two branches of the Nile, thinking that part of the
king's army might be under the duke, and his own so much
the weaker, and that these Bedouins would effectually prevent the duke from affording any support to the king.

All these operations of the infidel chief took him up until
about mid-day. This done, he ordered the nacaires and
drums to be loudly sounded, according to the mode of the
Turks, which is certainly very surprising to those who have
not been accustomed to hear them; and then both horse and
foot began to be in motion on all sides. I will speak first of

the battalion under the count d'Anjou, which received the
first attack, being posted the nearest to Babylon.   The
enemy advanced in a chequered manner, like to a game of
chess : for their infantry ran towards our men, and burnt
them with Greek fires, which they cast from instruments
made for that purpose.   On the other hand, the Turkish
cavalry charged them with such rapidity and success, that
the battalion of the count d'Anjou was defeated.   He himself
was on foot among his knights, very uncomfortably situated.

When news was brought to the king of the danger his
brother was in, nothing could check his ardour ; nor would
he wait for any one, but, sticking spurs to his horse, galloped
into the midst of the battle, lance in hand, to where his
brother was, and gave most deadly blows to the Turks,
hastening always to where he saw the greatest crowd.   He
suffered many hard blows ; and the Saracens covered all his
horse's tail and rump with Greek fires.   You may be assured
that at such a time he had God in his heart and mind ; and
in good truth our Lord in this distress befriended him, and so
far assisted him, that the king rescued his brother, the count
d'Anjou, and drove the Turks before him without the lines.

Next to the battalion of the count d'Anjou was that commanded by Sir Guy de Guivelins, and his brother Baldwin,
which joined the battalion of that bold and gallant man Sir
Walter de Chastillon.   He had with him numbers of chivalrous knights ; and these two battalions behaved so vigorously against the Turks, that they were neither any way
broken nor conquered.

The next battalion, however, fared but badly, under the
command of Friar William de Sonnac, master of the Temple,
who had with him the remnant of the men-at-arms that had
survived the battle of Shrove-Tuesday, which had been so
severely murderous.   The master of the Temple, having but
few men, made of the engines that had been taken from the
enemy, a sort of rampart in his front ; this, nevertheless,
availed him nothing, for the Templars having added to them
many planks of fir-wood, the Saracens burnt them with their
Greek fires ; and seeing there were but few to oppose them,
they waited not until they were destroyed, but vigorously
attacking the Templars, defeated them in a very short time.
It is certain, that in the rear of the Templars there was about

an acre of ground so covered with bolts, darts, arrows, and
other weapons, that you could not see the earth beneath them,
such showers of these had been discharged against the Templars by the Saracens. The commander of this battalion had
lost an eye in the preceding battle of Shrove-Tuesday ; and
in this he lost the other, and was slain : God have mercy on
his soul !

Sir Guy de Malvoisin, a bold and valiant captain of another
battalion, was severely wounded in the body ; and the Saracens perceiving his gallant conduct and address, shot Greek
fire at him incessantly, so that at one time when he was hit
by it, his people had much difficulty to extinguish it. But
notwithstanding this, he stood bold and firm, unconquered by
the Pagans.

From the battalion of Sir Guy de Malvoisin, the lines
which enclosed our army descended to where I was, within a
stone's cast of the river, and passed by the division of the
lord William earl of Flanders, which extended to that branch
of the river which entered the sea. Our battalion was posted
opposite, and on that bank of the river where Sir Guy de
Malvoisin was. The Saracens, observing the appearance of
the division of the earl of Flanders fronting them, dared not
make any attack on us, for which I thanked God, as neither
my knights nor myself could put on any armour, on account
of the wounds we had received in the engagement of the Tuesday, which rendered it impossible to wear any defensive
clothing.

The Lord William of Flanders and his battalion did wonders ; they gallantly and fiercely attacked the Turks on
horseback and on foot, and performed great deeds of arms.
Seeing their prowess, I ordered my cross-bows to shoot
strongly at the Turks, who were on horseback at this engagement ; and the moment they felt themselves or horses wounded
by the arrows, they instantly took flight, and abandoned their
infantry. The earl of Flanders and his division, observing
the Turks fly, passed the lines, and charged the Pagans, who
were on foot, killing great numbers, and bringing off many
targets. Among others, Sir Gaultier de la Horgne, who bore
the banner of the count d'Aspremont, displayed much
courage.

Adjoining this battalion was that of my lord the count de

Poitiers, brother to the king; it was composed solely of infantry, and the only person on horseback was the count, which was unfortunate for him; for the Turks defeated this battalion, and made the count prisoner. They would surely have carried him away, had not the butchers, and all the other traffickers, men and women, who supplied the army with provision, hearing that the Turks were carrying off the count de Poitiers, set up a great shout, and rushed on the Saracens with such fury that they rescued the count de Poitiers, and drove the Turks beyond the lines.

The next battalion to that of the count de Poitiers was the weakest of the whole army, and commanded by Sir Josserant de Brançon, whom my lord de Poitiers had brought with him to Egypt. This division was also formed of dismounted knights, Sir Josserant and his son Sir Henry being the only persons on horseback. The Turks broke this battalion on all sides, on which Sir Josserant and his son fell on the rear of the Turks, and cut them down with their swords. They pressed the enemy so much that they frequently turned on them again, leaving the main body of his men. In the end this would have been fatal; for the Turks must have slain the whole, if Sir Henry de Cone, a wise and valiant knight of the division under the duke of Burgundy, well knowing the weakness of the lord de Brançon's battalion, had not, every time he saw the Turks make their charge on it, ordered the king's cross-bows to shoot at them. He exerted himself so effectually that the lord de Brançon escaped from this danger, but lost twelve of the twenty knights whom it was said he had, without counting other men-at-arms. He himself, however, was the victim of the wounds he received in the service of God, who, we are bound to believe, has well rewarded him for it.

This lord was my uncle, and I heard him on his death-bed say, that he had in his time been in thirty-six battles or warlike skirmishes, and had borne off the prize of arms in most. Of some of them I have a remembrance; for once being in the army of the count de Mascon, who was his cousin, he came to me and a brother of mine on a Good Friday, and said to us, " Come my nephews with all your men, and join us in charging these Germans, who are destroying the monastery of Mascon."

We were instantly on horseback, and hastened to attack the Germans, whom, with hard blows of sword and lance, we drove from the monastery, where many were killed and wounded. When this was done, the good man fell on his knees before the altar, and cried with a loud voice to our Lord, praying that he would be pleased to have mercy on his soul, that he might die for his service, to the end that he might be entitled to the reward of paradise. I have related this, that you may know, as I firmly believe, that God has granted to him the request he then made.

After this battle was ended, the king summoned all his barons, knights, and other great lords, to whom, when assembled, he thus kindly addressed himself: "My lords and friends, you have all now witnessed the great grace which God our Creator has of late shewn us, and continues to do so daily, for which we are bounden to return him our thanksgiving. Last Tuesday, which was Shrovetide, we, aided by him, dislodged our enemies from their quarters, of which we have gained the possession. This Friday, which is now passed, we have defended ourselves against them, very many of us being without arms, while they were completely armed on horseback, and on their own ground." Many more fair speeches did he make; and the good king dwelt much upon what had passed, to comfort and give them courage and faith in God.

In pursuing the subject-matter of my book it is necessary now and then to make digressions, and to inform you of the manner in which the sultan supported his men-at-arms, and how his armies were supplied. It is true that the greater part of his chivalry was composed of foreigners, whom the merchants trading by sea had bought when young, and whom the Egyptians purchased by order of their sultan. They came mostly from the east; for when an eastern king* had defeated in battle another neighbouring monarch, the victor, and

* It is still the custom of the Turks to compose their principal military force, the Janizaries, from tributary children, sent for this purpose every fifth year by commissaries established in the provinces. These children are carried off from Christians, and are instructed in the Turkish religion, and trained up to military exercises. Soldiers, thus educated, and unacquainted with their parents and birth, only acknowledge the Grand Signor for their father and protector, which is one of the best political maxims of the infidels, although contrary to the law of nature.

his people, seized the subjects of the vanquished, whom they sold to merchants, who bought them, as I have said, to sell again in Egypt. The children born from these captives the sultan supported and educated, and when their beards appeared, they were taught to draw the bow, by way of amusement; and when he was in a jocund mood they displayed their skill before him.

As they increased in strength, their small bows were exchanged for others of greater weight, and proportioned to their powers. These youths bore the arms of the sultan, and were called his *Bahairiz.** When their beards were grown, the sultan made them knights; and their emblazonments were like his, of pure gold, save that to distinguish them, they added bars of vermilion, with roses, birds, griffins, or any other difference as they please. They were called the band of *La Hauleca*, which signifies the archers of the king's guard; and were always about the person of the sultan to defend him. When the sultan went to war they were quartered near him as his body-guard.

He had, beside these, other guards still nearer to his person, such as porters and minstrels, who played upon their instruments from the break of day until the sultan rose; and in the evenings sounded the retreat. Their instruments made so loud a noise, that those who were near them could not hear each other speak; and their notes were distinctly heard throughout the army. During the daytime, they dared on no account play on them, without express orders from the commander of the Hauleca.

* Bahairiz.—This word comes from Bahr, which the Arabians use to express the sea, or any great collection of water. The name of Bahairiz was first given to a thousand youths, whom Melik-Ussali had bought of the Tartars who ravaged the Turquestan, and whom he had educated in all military exercises in a castle, built by his orders, opposite to Cairo, on an island of the Nile called Revdbah. This fort was called Bahriieh, or the Maritime Fortress, on account of the Nile surrounding it. It was in this castle that Melik-Ussali, who had not forgotten the cowardly conduct of his troops at the siege of Napoulous, fixed his residence. He gave his whole confidence to these Bahairiz, loaded them with favours, and named from among them the governors of provinces, the commanders of his armies, and the first officers of the state. The remainder were reserved for the guard of his new palace, and to attend on him wherever he went, during peace or war. It is this body of troops the lord de Joinville means under the name of La Hauleca.

When the sultan wanted any thing, or wished to give orders to his men-at-arms, he mentioned it to the above commander, who ordered the minstrels to sound their Saracen horns, drums, and nacaires; and to this sound the whole of the chiefs drew up before their sultan's tent, to whom the commander of the Hauleca told the good pleasure of the sultan, which they instantly obeyed to the utmost of their power. Whenever the sultan went personally to war, he nominated from such of the knights of the Hauleca as shewed the most courage and abilities an admiral,* or captain over the men-at-arms, and according as they rose in merit, the more the sultan gave them; by which means every one of them tried who should surpass the other to the utmost.

The manner of the sultan's acting towards them was, that whenever any one of the knights of the Hauleca had, by his prowess and chivalry, gained a sufficiency, so that he was no longer in want, and could live independent, the sultan, for

---

* That is to say, as the lord de Joinville explains this word, captain or governor of a province or place, chief of an army or smaller body of troops. The word is derived from the Arabic *emir* or *amir*, which signifies *lord*. The same thing is observed by the lord de Villerval in his manuscript travels, in the chapter on the condition and nature of the sultans, of their admirals and slaves, &c. "Item. The sultan of Babylon has always, as they tell me, as well in Cairo as in the environs, about ten thousand slaves in his pay, who fight for him when war makes it necessary, some with two horses, and others with more or less, according to their circumstances. It must be known, that these slaves are from foreign nations, such as Tartary, Turkey, Bulgaria, Hungary, Sclavonia, Wallachia, Russia, Greece, and other countries, as well from those of the Christians, as elsewhere. They are not called the sultan's slaves unless they be bought with his money, or sent to him as presents from distant countries. In these slaves he trusts wholly for the guard of his person, and he gives them women, houses, horses, and robes, and places them, when young, under masters, to teach them the art of war. According to their different abilities, he appoints one captain of ten lancemen, another of twenty, another of fifty, another of one hundred; and, thus rising, they are made, one governor of Jerusalem, another king, or ruler, of Damascus, another chief governor of Cairo, and thus with other officers of that country."

The word *admiral* is printed by different writers various ways. This officer is called by the Greeks, αμκραι, αμηραιοι, and by the Latins of the middle ages, *admirabiles*, *admiraldi*, &c. This much is however certain, that we have borrowed the word from the infidel nations, and commonly style the chiefs of naval armaments admirals, because those from whom we have adopted it thus applied the word.

fear he should dethrone or kill him, had him arrested and thrown into prison, where he was secretly put to death, and then he took possession of all the fortune his wife and children might have had left to them. An example of this happened while I was in that country; for the sultan had imprisoned those who, by their valour and address, had made prisoners of the counts of Montfort and Bar; and from envy and jealousy, and from his dread of them, had them put to death. He acted in like manner to the Boudendars, who are his subjects; for when they had defeated the king of Armenia, and came to inform him of the event, they found him hunting wild beasts. Having dismounted to make their obeisance, and thinking, as they had behaved so well, they should be recompensed, he eyed them maliciously, and said he should not return their salute, for they had made him lose his chase; and ordered their heads to be struck off.

To return to our subject. The sultan, lately deceased, had left a son, who was twenty-five years old, well informed, prudent, and already full of malice. The last sultan, fearing he might dethrone him, kept him at a distance from his person, and had given him a kingdom in the East; but the moment his father was dead, the admirals of Babylon sent for him, and made him their sultan. On taking possession of his dignity, he deprived the constable, marshals, and seneschals of his father of their golden wands, and the offices which they held, and gave them to those whom he had brought with him from the East.

This caused great discontent in those who had been removed, as also in those of the council of his late father, who suspected strongly that he would act by them, after seizing their wealth, in the same manner as the sultan had done by those who had taken the counts of Montfort and of Bar, as already related. They therefore unanimously agreed to put him to death, and found means of obtaining from those called La Hauleca, who were the sultan's guard, a promise to murder him.

After the two battles I have mentioned, which were marvellously sharp and severe, the one on Shrove-Tuesday, and the other the first Friday in Lent, another great misfortune befel our army. At the end of eight or ten days, the bodies of those who had been slain in these two engagements,

and thrown into the Nile, rose to the top of the water.
It was said, this always happens when the gall is burst and
rotten.   These bodies floated down the river until they came
to the small bridge that communicated with each part of our
army; and the arch was so low it almost touched the water,
and prevented the bodies passing underneath.   The river
was covered with them from bank to bank, so that the water
could not be seen a good stone's throw from the bridge up-
ward.

The king hired one hundred labourers, who were full eight
days in separating the bodies of the Christians from the
Saracens, which were easily distinguishable : the Saracen
bodies they thrust under the bridge by main force, and
floated them down to the sea; but the Christians were buried
in deep graves, one over the other.   God knows how great
was the stench, and what misery it was to see the bodies
of such noble and worthy persons lying so exposed.   I witnessed the chamberlain of the late count d'Artois seeking the
body of his master, and many more hunting after the bodies
of their friends ; but I never heard that any who were thus
seeking their friends amidst such an infectious smell ever
recovered their healths.   You must know, that we ate no
fish the whole Lent but eelpouts, which is a gluttonous fish,
and feeds on dead bodies.   From this cause, and from the
bad air of the country, where it scarcely ever rains a drop,
the whole army was infected by a shocking disorder, which
dried up the flesh on our legs to the bone, and our skins became tanned as black as the ground, or like an old boot that
has long lain behind a coffer.   In addition to this miserable
disorder, those affected by it had another sore complaint in
the mouth, from eating such fish, that rotted the gums, and
caused a most stinking breath.   Very few escaped death that
were thus attacked ; and the surest symptom of its being
fatal was a bleeding at the nose, for when that took place
none ever recovered.

The better to cure us, the Turks, who knew our situation,
fifteen days afterward attempted to starve us, by means I
shall now tell you.   These villanous Turks had drawn their
galleys overland, and launched them again below our army,
so that those who had gone to Damietta for provision never
returned, to the great astonishment of us all.   We could not

imagine the reason of this, until one of the galleys of the earl of Flanders, having forced a passage, informed us how the sultan had launched his vessels, by drawing them overland, below us, so that the Turks watched all galleys going toward Damietta, and had already captured fourscore of ours, and killed their crews.

By this means all provision was exceedingly dear in the army; and when Easter arrived, a beef was sold for eighty livres, a sheep for thirty livres, a hog for thirty livres, a muid of wine for ten livres, an egg for sixpence, and every thing else in proportion.

When the king and his barons saw this, and that there was not any remedy for it, they advised the king to march the army from near Babylon, and join that of the duke of Burgundy, which was on the other bank of the river that flowed to Damietta. For the security of his retreat, the king had erected a barbican in front of the small bridge I have so often mentioned; and it was constructed in suchwise that it might be entered on each side on horseback. As soon as this barbican was finished, the whole host armed; for the Turks made a vigorous attack, observing our intentions to join the duke of Burgundy's army on the opposite side of the river.

During the time we were entering the barbican, the enemy fell on the rear of our army, and took prisoner Sir Errart de Valeri; but he was soon rescued by his brother, Sir John de Valeri. The king, however, and his division never moved until the baggage and arms had crossed the river; and then we all passed after the king, except Sir Gaultier de Chastillon, who commanded the rear-guard in the barbican.

When the whole army had passed, the rear-guard was much distressed by the Turkish cavalry; for from their horses they could shoot point blank, as the barbican was low. The Turks on foot threw large stones and clods of earth in their faces, without the guard being able to defend themselves. They would infallibly have been destroyed, if the count d'Anjou, brother to the king, and afterwards king of Sicily, had not boldly gone to their rescue, and brought them off in safety.

The day preceding Shrovetide I saw a thing which I must relate. On the vigil of that day died a very valiant and

2 r

prudent knight, Sir Hugh de Landricourt, one under my
banner; and during his burial, six of my knights talked so
loud they disturbed the priest as he was saying mass: on
this I arose, and bade them be silent; for it was unbecoming
gentlemen thus to talk whilst the mass was celebrating.   But
they burst into laughter, and told me they were talking of
marrying the widow of Sir Hugh, now in his bier.   I rebuked them sharply, and said such conversation was indecent
and improper, for that they had too soon forgotten their
companion.

Now it happened on the morrow, when the first grand
battle took place, although we may laugh at their follies, God
took such vengeance on them, that of all the six not one
escaped death, and remained unburied.   The wives of the
whole six re-married.   This makes it credible, that God
leaves no such conduct unpunished.   With regard to myself,
I fared little better, for I was grievously wounded in the
battle of Shrove-Tuesday.   I had, besides, the disorder in
my legs and mouth before spoken of, and such a rheum in
my head it ran through my mouth and nostrils.   In addition,
I had a double fever, called a quartan, from which God
defend us! and with these illnesses was I confined to my bed
the half of Lent.

My poor priest was likewise as ill as myself; and one day
when he was singing mass before me as I lay in my bed, at
the moment of the elevation of the host, I saw him so exceedingly weak that he was near fainting; but when I perceived he was on the point of falling to the ground, I flung
myself out of bed, sick as I was, and taking my coat, embraced him, and bade him be at his ease, and take courage
from him whom he held in his hands.   He recovered some
little; but I never quitted him until he had finished the mass,
which he completed, and this was the last, for he never after
celebrated another, but died.   God receive his soul!

To return to our history.   It is true there were some
parleys between the councils of the king and of the sultan,
respecting a peace; and a day was appointed for the further
discussion of it.   The basis of the treaty was agreed on,—
namely, that the king should restore to the sultan Damietta,
and the sultan should surrender to the king the realm of
Jerusalem.   He was also to take proper care of the sick in

Damietta, and to give up the salted provision that was there, for neither Turk nor Saracen eat of it, and likewise the engines of war; but the king was to send for all these things from Damietta.

The end of this was, that the sultan demanded what security the king would give him for the surrender of Damietta; and it was proposed that he should detain as prisoner one of the king's brothers, either the count de Poitiers, or the count d'Anjou, until it were effected. But the Turks refused to accept of any other hostage than the person of the king.

To this the gallant knight, Sir Geoffry de Sergines, replied, that the Turks should never have the king's person; and that he would rather they should all be slain than it should be said they had given their king in pawn; and thus matters remained.

The disorder I spoke of very soon increased so much in the army that the barbers were forced to cut away very large pieces of flesh from the gums, to enable their patients to eat. It was pitiful to hear the cries and groans of those on whom this operation was performing; they seemed like to the cries of women in labour, and I cannot express the great concern all felt who heard them.

The good king, St. Louis, witnessing the miserable condition of great part of his army, raised his hands and eyes to heaven, blessing our Lord for all he had given him, and seeing that he could not longer remain where he was, without perishing himself as well as his army, gave orders to march on the Tuesday evening after the octave of Easter, and return to Damietta. He issued his commands to the masters of the galleys to have them ready to receive on board the sick, and convey them to Damietta. He likewise gave his orders to Josselin de Corvant, and to other engineers, to cut the cords which held the bridges between us and the Saracens; but they neglected them, which was the cause of much evil befalling us.

Perceiving that every one was preparing to go to Damietta, I withdrew to my vessel, with two of my knights, all that I had remaining of those that had accompanied me, and the rest of my household. Towards evening, when it began to grow dark, I ordered my captain to raise the anchor, that we might float down the stream; but he replied, that he dared not obey me, for that between us and Damietta were the large galleys of the sultan, which would infallibly capture us.

The king's seamen had made great fires on board their galleys, to cherish the unfortunate sick; and many others in the same state were waiting on the banks of the river for vessels to take them on board. As I was advising my sailors to make some little way, I saw, by the light of the fires, the Saracens enter our camp, and murder these sick that were waiting on the banks of the Nile; and as my men were raising the anchor, and we began to move downward, the sailors who were to take the sick on board advanced with their boats; but seeing the Saracens in the act of killing them, they retreated to their large galleys, cut their cables, and fell down on my small bark.

I expected every moment they would have sunk me; but we escaped this imminent danger, and made some way down the river. The king had the same illness as the rest of his army, with a dysentery,* which, had he pleased, he might have prevented, by living on board his larger vessels; but he said, he had rather die than leave his people. The king, observing us make off, began to shout and cry to us to remain, and likewise ordered some heavy bolts to be shot at us, to stop our course until we should have his orders to sail.

I will now break the course of my narration, and say in what manner the king was made prisoner, as he told me himself. I heard him say, that he had quitted his own battalion and men-at-arms, and, with Sir Geoffry de Sergines, had joined the battalion of Sir Gaultier de Chastillon, who commanded the rear division. The king was mounted on a small courser, with only a housing of silk; and of all his men-at-arms, there was only with him the good knight Sir Geoffry de Sergines, who attended him as far as the town of Casel, where the king was made prisoner. But before the Turks could take him, I heard say, that Sir Geoffry de Sergines defended him in like manner as a faithful servant does the cup of his master from flies; for every time the Saracens approached him, Sir Geoffry guarded him with vigorous strokes of the blade and point of his sword, and it seemed as if his courage and strength were doubled.

* In the lapidary manuscript, in the chapter of Amethysts, it is said, " that it destroys dead flesh from wounds, and stops the dysentery."

By dint of gallantry he drove them away from the king, and thus conducted him to Casel, where, having dismounted at a house, he laid the king in the lap of a woman who had come from Paris, thinking that every moment must be his last, for he had no hopes that he could ever pass that day without dying.

Shortly after arrived Sir Philip de Montfort, who told the king that he had just seen the admiral of the sultan, with whom he had formerly treated for a truce, and that if it were his good pleasure, he would return to him again, and renew it. The king entreated him so to do, and declared he would abide by whatever terms they should agree on.

Sir Philip de Montfort returned to the Saracens, who had taken their turbans* from their heads, and gave a ring, which he took off his finger, to the admiral, as a pledge of keeping the truce, and that they would accept the terms as offered, and of which I have spoken.

Just at this moment a villanous traitor of an apostate sergeant, named Marcel, set up a loud shout to our people, and said, " Sir knights, surrender yourselves ; the king orders you by me so to do, and not to cause yourselves to be slain." At these words, all were thunderstruck ; and thinking the king had indeed sent such orders, they each gave up their arms and staves to the Saracens.

The admiral, seeing the Saracens leading the king's knights as their prisoners, said to Sir Philip de Montfort, that he would not agree to any truce, for that the army had been made prisoners. Sir Philip was greatly astonished at what he saw, for he was aware that, although he was sent as ambassador to settle a truce, he should likewise be made prisoner, and knew not to whom to have recourse. In Pagan countries, they have a very bad custom, that when any ambassadors are despatched from one king or sultan to another, to demand or conclude a peace, and one of these princes dies,

---

* Turbans are commonly made of napkins or other linen wrapped round the head. The lord de Joinville, in another part, says, "And know that they received heavy blows on these towels : they, however, wore them when going to battle, and they are tightly wrapped round one over the other." The Latin authors of the middle ages have differently written this word *touaille;* the Chronicle of Fontenelle uses *toacula,* Odoricus de Frioul *toalia,* the Roman Ceremonial in MS. *tobalea,* Johannes de Janua *togilla.*

and the treaty is not concluded before that event takes place,
the ambassador is made prisoner, wherever he may be, and
whether sent by sultan or king.

You must know, that we who had embarked on board our
vessels, thinking to escape to Damietta, were not more fortunate than those who had remained on land ; for we were
also taken, as you shall hear.   It is true, that during the time
we were on the river, a dreadful tempest of wind arose, blowing towards Damietta, and with such force that, unable to
ascend the stream, we were driven towards the Saracens.
The king, indeed, had left a body of knights, with orders to
guard the invalids on the banks of the river ; but it would
not have been of any use to have made for that part, as they
had all fled.   Towards the break of day, we arrived at the
pass where the sultan's galleys lay, to prevent any provisions
being sent from Damietta to the army, who, when they perceived us, set up a great noise, and shot at us and such of our
horsemen as were on the banks, with large bolts armed with
Greek fire, so that it seemed as if the stars were falling from
the heavens.

When our mariners had gained the current, and we attempted to push forward, we saw the horsemen whom the
king had left to guard the sick flying towards Damietta.
The wind became more violent than ever, and drove us
against the bank of the river.   On the opposite shore were
immense numbers of our vessels that the Saracens had taken,
which we feared to approach ; for we plainly saw them murdering their crews, and throwing the dead bodies into the
water, and carrying away the trunks and arms they had thus
gained.

Because we would not go near the Saracens, who menaced
us, they shot plenty of bolts ; upon which, I put on my armour, to prevent such as were well aimed from hurting me.
At the stern of my vessel were some of my people, who cried
out to me, " My lord, my lord ; our steersman, because the
Saracens threaten us, is determined to run us on shore, where
we shall be all murdered."   I instantly rose up, for I was
then very ill, and, advancing with my drawn sword, declared
I would kill the first person who should attempt to run us on
the Saracen shore.   The sailors replied, that it was impossible
to proceed, and that I must determine which I would prefer,

to be landed on the shore, or to be stranded on the mud of
the banks in the river. I preferred, very fortunately, as you
shall hear, being run on a mud bank in the river to being
carried on shore, where I saw our men murdered, and they
followed my orders.

It was not long ere we saw four of the sultan's large galleys
making toward us, having full a thousand men on board. I
called upon my knights to advise me how to act, whether to
surrender to the galleys of the sultan or to those who were on
the shore. We were unanimous, that it would be more advisable to surrender to the galleys that were coming, for then we
might have a chance of being kept together; whereas, if we
gave ourselves up to those on the shore, we should certainly
be separated, and perhaps sold to the Bedouins, of whom I
have before spoken. To this opinion, however, one of my
clerks would not agree, but said it would be much better for
us to be slain, as then we should go to paradise; but we
would not listen to him, for the fear of death had greater influence over us.

Seeing that we must surrender, I took a small case that
contained my jewels and relics, and cast it into the river.
One of my sailors told me, that if I would not let him tell the
Saracens I was cousin to the king, we should all be put to
death. In reply, I bade him say what he pleased. The first
of these galleys now came athwart us, and cast anchor close to
our bow. Then, as I firmly believe, God sent to my aid a
Saracen, who was a subject of the emperor. Having on a
pair of trousers of coarse cloth, and swimming straight to my
vessel, he embraced my knees, and said, "My lord, if you
do not believe what I shall say, you are a lost man. To save
yourself, you must leap into the river, which will be unob-
served by the crew, who are solely occupied with the capture
of your bark." He had a cord thrown to me from their galley
on the escot of my vessel, and I leaped into the water followed by the Saracen, who indeed saved me, and conducted
me to the galley; for I was so weak I staggered, and should
have otherwise sunk to the bottom of the river.

I was drawn into the galley, wherein were fourteen score
men, besides those who had boarded my vessel, and this poor
Saracen held me fast in his arms. Shortly after, I was
landed, and they rushed upon me to cut my throat: indeed, I

expected nothing else. for he that should do it would imagine he had acquired honour.

This Saracen who had saved me from drowning would not quit hold of me, but cried out to them, "The king's cousin! the king's cousin!"

I felt the knife at my throat, and had already cast myself on my knees on the ground ; but God delivered me from this peril by the aid of the poor Saracen, who led me to the castle where the Saracen chiefs were assembled.

When I was in their presence, they took off my coat of mail ; and from pity, seeing me so very ill, they flung over me one of my own scarlet coverlids, lined with minever, which my lady-mother had given me. Another brought me a white leathern girdle, with which I girthed my coverlid around me. One of the Saracen knights gave me a small cap, which I put on my head; but I soon began to tremble, so that my teeth chattered, as well from the fright I had had as from my disorder.

On my complaining of thirst, they brought me some water in a pot ; but I had no sooner put it to my mouth, and began drinking, than it ran back through my nostrils. God knows what a pitiful state I was in ; for I looked for death rather than life, having an imposthume in my throat. When my attendants saw the water run thus through my nostrils, they began to weep and to be very sorrowful.

The Saracen who had saved me asked my people why they wept ; they gave him to understand, that I was nearly dead, from an imposthume in the throat which was choking me. The good Saracen, having always great compassion for me, went to tell this to one of the Saracen knights, who bade him to be comforted, for that he would give me something to drink that should cure me in two days. This he did; and I was soon well, through God's grace, and the beverage which the Saracen knight gave me.

Soon after my recovery, the admiral of the sultan's galleys sent for me, and demanded if I were cousin to the king, as it was said. I told him I was not, and related why it had been reported, and that one of my mariners had advised it through fear of the Saracens in the galleys, for that otherwise they would put us to death. The admiral replied, that I had been very well advised, or we should have been all murdered

without fail, and thrown into the river.   The admiral again
asked me, if I had any acquaintance with the emperor
Ferry* of Germany, then living, and if I were of his lineage;
I answered truly, that I had heard my mother say I was his
second cousin.   The admiral replied, that he would love me
the better for it.

Thus, as we were eating and drinking, he sent for an inhabitant of Paris to come to me, who, on his entrance, seeing
what we were doing, exclaimed, "Ah, sir, what are you
about?"   "What am I about!" replied I.   When he informed me, on the part of God, that I was eating meat on a
Friday.   On which, I suddenly threw my trencher behind
me; and the admiral, noticing it, asked of my friendly Saracen, who was always with me, why I had left off eating.   He
told him, because it was a Friday, which I had forgotten.
The admiral said, that God could never be displeased, because
I had done it unknowingly.   You must know, that the
legate who had accompanied the king frequently reproached
me for fasting when thus ill, and when there was not any
statesman but myself left with the king, and that I should
hurt myself by fasting.   But notwithstanding this, and that I
was a prisoner, I never failed to fast every Friday on bread
and water.

A CONTINUATION OF THE SECOND PART OF THE MEMOIRS OF JOHN LORD DE JOINVILLE,

&c. &c. &c.

On the Sunday after we had been made prisoners, the admiral ordered all that had been taken on the Nile to be
brought from the castle, on the banks of the river.   In my
presence, my chaplain was dragged from the hold of the
galley; but, on coming to the open air, he fainted, and the
Saracens killed him instantly before my eyes, and flung him
into the stream.   His clerk, from the disorder he had caught
when with the army, being unable to stand, they cast a mortar
on his head, killed him, and flung him after his master.

* The emperor Frederic II.

In the like manner did they deal with the other prisoners; for as they were drawn out of the hold of the galleys wherein they had been confined, there were Saracens purposely posted, who, on seeing any one weak or ill, killed him and threw him into the water. Such was the treatment of the unfortunate sick. Seeing this tyranny, I told them, through the interpretation of my Saracen, that they were doing very wrong, and contrary to the commands of Saladin the pagan, who had declared it unlawful to put to death any one to whom they had given salt and bread. They made answer, that they were destroying men of no use, for that they were too ill with their disorders to do any service.

After this they brought before me my mariners, and said they had all denied their faith. I replied I did not believe it, but that their fears of death might have caused them to say so, and that the moment they found themselves in another country they would return to their own religion.

The admiral added to this, that he believed firmly what I said, for that Saladin had declared, that a Christian was never known to make a good pagan, nor a good Saracen a Christian. The admiral, soon after, made me mount a palfrey, and we rode side by side over a bridge to the place where St. Louis and his men were prisoners.

At the entrance of a large pavilion we found a secretary writing down the names of the prisoners by orders of the sultan. I was there forced to declare my name, which I no way wished to conceal, and it was written down with the others. As we entered this pavilion the Saracen, who had preserved my life, and had always followed me, said, "Sir, you must excuse me, but I cannot follow you further. I advise and entreat that you will never quit the hand of this young boy whom you have with you; otherwise the Saracens will murder him." The boy's name was Bartholomew de Montfaucon, son to the lord Montfaucon de Bar.

When my name was written down, the admiral led me and the little boy to the tent where were the barons of France, and more than ten thousand other persons with them. On my entrance, every one seemed to testify great pleasure at seeing me again; and for some time nothing could be heard for their noisy joy, as they concluded I had been murdered.

Thus as we were together, hoping, through the grace of God, we should not long remain in this state, a rich Saracen led us into another tent, where we had miserable cheer. Numbers of knights and other men were confined in a large court, surrounded with walls of mud. The guards of this prison led them out one at a time, and asked each if he would become a renegado: those that answered in the affirmative were put aside, but those who refused, instantly had their heads cut off.

Shortly after, the council of the sultan sent for us, and demanded to whom it was most agreeable they should deliver the sultan's message. We unanimously answered, by means of an interpreter, who spoke both French and Saracen, to the count Peter of Brittany. This was the message: " My lords, the sultan asks by us if you wish to be free, and what you are willing to give for your liberty ? "

To this the earl of Brittany replied, that we all heartily wished to be delivered from the hands of the sultan, who had made us suffer most unreasonably. But when the council of the sultan asked if we would not be willing to give for our ransom some of the castles of the barons of the Holy Land, the earl of Brittany answered, that we could not possibly comply ; for these castles and strong places belonged to the emperor of Germany,* now on the throne, and who would never consent to the sultan holding any fiefs under him.

The council then asked if we would not surrender some of the castles belonging to the Knights Templars, or to the hospital of Rhodes, for our deliverance. The earl replied, that that was equally impossible ; for it would be contrary to the accustomed oath which the governors or lords of such castles take on their investiture, when they solemnly swear to God that they will never surrender these castles for the deliverance of any man whatever.

The Saracens then spoke together, saying, that it did not appear we had any desire to regain our liberty ; and that they would send us those who well knew how to use their swords, to treat us as the others had been dealt with, and on that they left us.

Not long after the sultan's council had departed, a tall old Saracen, of goodly appearance, came to us, accompanied by a great multitude of young Saracens, each of whom had a large sword by his side, which alarmed us much. The old Saracen

* Frederic II., who had been crowned king of Jerusalem, and held all the places in the kingdom.

asked us, by means of an interpreter, who spoke and understood our language well, if it were true that we believed in
one only God, who had been born for our salvation, was crucified to death, and after three days rose again to save us.
We answered, that what we had heard was perfectly true.
On this he replied, that since it was so, we ought not to be
cast down for any persecutions we might suffer for his sake;
and that we had not as yet endured death for him, as he had
done for us; and since he had the power to raise himself from
the dead, it would not be long before he would deliver us.

The old Saracen then went away with all the young men,
without doing any thing more, which rejoiced me exceedingly;
for I really thought the intent of his visit was to cut our
heads off.   It was not long after this before we heard news
of our deliverance.

The sultan's council soon returned to us again, and said the
king had exerted himself so effectually, that he had succeeded
in obtaining our liberty.   They ordered us to send four of
our company to hear and know the terms on which we were
to have our freedom.   To this end we deputed the lords John
de Valeri, Philip de Montfort, Baldwin de Ebelin, seneschal
of Cyprus, and his brother, the constable of Cyprus, who was
one of the handsomest and best-informed knights I ever knew,
and who loved greatly the people of that country.

These four knights were not long in bringing us the terms
of our liberty.   In order to try the king, the sultan's council
had made the same demands from him as from us; but it
pleased God that the good king, St. Louis, made similar
answers to what we had done through the mouth of Count
Peter of Brittany.   The council, seeing the king would not
comply with their demands, threatened to put him in the
bernicles,* which is the greatest torture they can inflict on
any one.   The bernicles are formed of two thick blocks of
wood, fastened together at the top; and when they use this
mode of torture, they lay the person on his side, between these

---

* This engine of torture appears to have been made of pieces of wood
pierced with holes, into which the legs of criminals were put: they were
placed at such distances from each other, and forced to so great an exten-
sion of the legs as caused very great pain, for the criminals could not
draw them back again. The holes in these pieces of wood were at various
distances, and the legs of the criminal were inserted into those that extended them to a greater or lesser distance, according to the heinousness
of the crime or the pains to be inflicted.

two blocks, passing his legs through broad pins; they then fix
the upper block on the sufferer, and make a man sit on him, by
which means all the small bones of his legs are broken or dislo-
cated. To increase the torture, at the end of three days they
replace his legs, which are now greatly swollen, in the bernicles, and break them again, which is the most cruel thing ever
heard; and they tie his head down with bullock's sinews, for
fear he should move himself while in them.

The good king held all their menaces cheap, and said, that
since he was their prisoner they might do to him whatever
they pleased. The Saracens finding they could not conquer
the king by threats, came to him, and asked how much money
he would give the sultan for his ransom, in addition to Damietta, which was to be surrendered. The king replied, that if the
sultan would be contented with a reasonable ransom, he would
write to the queen to pay it for himself and his army. The Saracens asked why he wanted to write to the queen. He answered,
that it was but reasonable he should do so, for that she was
his wife and companion. The council then went to the sultan
to know what sum he required from the king; and on their
return told the king, that if the queen would pay a million of
golden besants, equal at that time to 500,000 livres, she
would, by so doing, obtain the king's liberty. The king then
asked them, on their oath, should the queen pay these 500,000
livres, would the sultan consent to his deliverance. On this
they again returned to the sultan to know if he would bind
himself by such a promise, and brought back his answer, that
he was very willing so to do.

The council then took their oaths to the punctual fulfilment
of this agreement, which, when done, the king engaged to pay
cheerfully, for the ransom of his army, 500,000 livres; and
that for his own ransom he would surrender the town of
Damietta to the sultan; for he was of a rank whose bodily
ransom could not be estimated by the value of money.

When the sultan heard the good disposition of the king, he
said, " By my faith, the Frenchman is generous and liberal,
when he does not condescend to bargain about so large a sum
of money, but has instantly complied with the first demand.
Go, and tell him from me," added the sultan, " that I make
him a present of 100,000 livres, so that he will have only to
pay 400,000."

The sultan then commanded that all of the principal nobles.

and great officers of the king, should be embarked in four of
the largest galleys, and conducted to Damietta. In the
galley on board of which I was shipped, were the good count
Peter of Brittany, William count of Flanders, John, the good
count de Soissons, Sir Hymbert de Beaujeu, constable of
France, and those two excellent knights and brothers, Sir
Baldwin and Sir Guy d'Ebelin.

The captain of the galley made us land before a large house
which the sultan had erected on the banks of the river, where
there was a handsome tower made of poles of fir-wood, and
covered with painted cloth. At the entrance a great pavilion
had been pitched, where the admirals of the sultan left their
swords and staves whenever they wanted to speak with him.
Passing this pavilion, there was another very handsome gateway, that led to the great hall of the sultan, and adjoining
was a tower like unto the first, by which they mounted to the
chamber of the sultan. In the midst of this lodgment was a
handsome lawn, on which was another tow erlarger than the
others, whence the sultan made his observations on the surrounding country, and on each army. There was in this lawn
an alley that led to the river, at the end of which the sultan
had made a summer-house on the strand to bathe himself.
This summer-house was formed of trelliswork, covered with
Indian linen, to prevent any one seeing what passed withinside.
All the towers were likewise covered with cloth.

We arrived before this lodging on the Thursday preceding
the feast of the Ascension of our Lord. Near to it the king
had landed, to hold a parley with the sultan in a pavilion, and
it was then agreed that the ensuing Saturday the king should
go to Damietta.

Just as we were on our departure for Damietta, to surrender to the sultan, the admiral of the present sultan's father
shewed great dissatisfaction with the reigning monarch.
Although he had been the principal author of his having been
sent for on his father's death at Damietta, to succeed to the
throne, he had much disappointed the admiral by dismissing
him from his office of constable, and others from their mar-
shalships and seneschalships, to provide for those who had
accompanied him to Egypt.

They therefore held a council, when he said,—" My lords,
you see how much the sultan has dishonoured us, by depriving us of those governments and honours with which his father

had entrusted us. Such conduct, you may be assured, will induce him, when once master of the castle and fortresses of Damietta, to have us arrested and put to death in his prisons, through fear that in process of time we may take our revenge on him; as his grandfather did to the admiral and the others who had made the counts de Bar and de Montfort prisoners. It will be therefore more to our advantage that we destroy him before he escape out of our hands."

This was unanimously assented to; and they instantly went to practise with the band of the Hauleca, who, as I have said before, are those who have the guard of the sultan's person. They made to them remonstrances on the subject similar to those which they had made among themselves, and required of them to slay the sultan, which they promised to do.

One day the sultan invited the knights of the Hauleca to dine with him. After the dinner, when he had taken leave of his admirals, and was about to retire to his chamber, one of these knights, who bore the sultan's sword, struck him a blow on the hand, which cut up his arm between the four fingers. The sultan, turning to his admirals, who had been the instigators of it, said, "My lords, I make my complaint to you against the knights of the Hauleca, who have endeavoured to kill me, as you may see by my hand." They all replied, that it was much better he should be slain than that he murder them, as he would assuredly do if once in possession of the fortresses of Damietta.

The conspirators acted with great caution, for they ordered the sultan's trumpets and nacaires to sound for the assembling of the army to know the sultan's will. The admirals and their accomplices told them, Damietta was taken, that the sultan was marching thither, and ordered them to arm and follow him. Instantly all armed, and set off, full gallop, towards Damietta. We were much frightened, on noticing what was going forward, for we really believed Damietta had been stormed.

The sultan, though wounded, being aware of the malice of his enemies, who had conspired against his person, fled to the high tower near his chamber which I mentioned; for those of the Hauleca had already destroyed his other pavilions, and were surrounding that in which he had hidden himself. Within this tower were three of his ecclesiastics, who had dined with him, who bade him descend. He replied, he would willingly descend, if they would answer for his safety; but they replied that they would make him come down by force. for that he was not yet arrived at Damietta. They then discharged some Greek fire into the tower, which being made only of fir and linen cloth, as I have before said, the whole was in a blaze; and I promise you, I never beheld so fine nor so sudden a bonfire.

When the sultan saw the fire gaining ground on all sides, he descended into the lawn, of which I have spoken, and ran for the river; but in his flight one of the Hauleca struck him a severe blow on the ribs with a sword, and then he flung himself, with the sword in him, into the Nile. Nine other knights pursued and killed him while in the water, near the side of the galley.*

One of the foresaid knights, whose name was Faracataic, seeing the sultan dead, cut him in twain, and tore the heart from his body. On coming to the king with his hands all bloody, he said, "What wilt thou give me who have slain thine enemy, who, had he lived, would have put thee to death?" But the good king St. Louis made no answer whatever to this demand.

The deed being done, about thirty of them entered our galley with their swords drawn, and their battle-axes on their necks. I asked Sir Baldwin d'Ebelin, who understood Saracenic, what they were saying. And he replied, that they said they were come to cut off our heads; and shortly after I saw a large body of our men on board confessing themselves to a monk of La Trinité, who had accompanied the count of Flanders. With regard to myself, I no longer thought of any sin or evil I had done, but that I was about to receive my death: in consequence, I fell on my knees at the feet of one of

* A Chronicle, published by M. Catel, of the year 1249, says, that the sultan was killed by his own people, in a dispute about the ransom of St. Louis. The lord de Joinville writes, that he was slain by those of the Haulequa. Matt. Paris says, that he was poisoned by his chamberlains. Aython, in ch. 52, says it was done by the Comains; and the Oriental Chronicle, by the Mamelukes. This difference is easily reconciled, for the lord de Joinville has before said, that the knights of the Haulequa formed part of the military force of the sultans of Egypt, composed of children sent as tribute; and Aython adds, that these tributary children were from Comania. These foreign soldiers were, in the Arabian language, called Mamelukes, as we learn from William of Tyre, l. 2, ch. 23.

them, and, making the sign of the cross, said, " Thus died St.
Agnes." Sir Guy d'Ebelin, constable of Cyprus, knelt beside me, and confessed himself to me ; and I gave him such
absolution as God was pleased to grant me the power of
bestowing ; but of all the things he had said to me, when I
arose up I could not remember one of them.

We were confined in the hold of the galley, and laid heads
and heels together. We thought it had been so ordered because they were afraid of attacking us when we were in a
body, and that they would destroy us one at a time. This
danger lasted the whole night. I had my feet right on the
face of the count Peter of Brittany, whose feet, in return,
were beside my face. On the morrow we were taken out of
the hold, and the admirals sent to inform us that we might
renew the treaties we had made with the sultan. Those who
were able went thither ; but the earl of Brittany, the constable of Cyprus, and myself, who were grievously ill, remained on board.

The earl of Flanders, the count de Soissons, and the others
who had gone to parley with the admirals, related to us the
convention for our delivery ; and the admirals promised, that
as soon as Damietta should be surrendered to them, they
would give liberty to the king and the other great personages
now prisoners.

They told them, that had the sultan lived, he would have
had the king beheaded, with the others ; and that, contrary
to the treaties entered into, and the promises made to the
king, he had already transported to Babylon several of their
most considerable men ; that they had slain the sultan,
because they knew well that the moment he should have been
master of Damietta he would have had them instantly murdered, or would have put them to death when in confinement.

By this new agreement, the king was to swear to leave at
their disposal 200,000 livres before he quitted the river, and
the other 200,000 he should pay in Acre. They declared
they would detain, for their security, all the sick in Damietta,
the cross-bows, armours, machines, and salted meats, until
the king should send for them, and should have paid the
balance of his ransom.

The oath, which was on this occasion to be taken by the
king and the admirals, was drawn up ; and on the part of the

2 G

admirals it ran thus; that in case they failed in their conventions with the king, they would own themselves dishonoured like those who for their sins went on a pilgrimage to Mecca, bareheaded, or like to those who divorced their wives, and took them again. By their law, no one can divorce his wife and cohabit with her again, before he has witnessed some other person lying in bed with her. The third oath was, that they would own themselves blasted and dishonoured, like a Saracen who should eat pork.

The king accepted the above oaths, because Master Nicolle, of Acre, who knew their manners well, assured him they could not swear more strongly. After the admirals had taken the oath above mentioned, they had one such as they wished him to take written down, and gave it to the king. This oath had been drawn up according to the advice of some renegade Christians, whom they had with them. It ran thus, that in case the king did not fulfil the conventions he had entered into with them, he might be deprived for ever of the presence of God, of his worthy mother, of the twelve apostles, and of all the saints of both sexes in Paradise. This oath the king took. The other was, that if the king broke his word he should be reputed perjured, as a Christian who had denied God, his baptism, and his faith; and in despite of God would spit on his cross, and trample it under foot. But when the king heard this oath read, he declared he would never take it.

The admirals, hearing the king had refused to take the oath which they had required of him, sent in haste for Master Nicolle, of Acre, to tell him they were greatly dissatisfied with him, and discontented with the king; for that they had sworn every oath he had desired, and now, in his turn, he had refused to comply with the oaths offered to him on their part. Master Nicolle told the king that he was certain, that unless he took the oaths as prescribed, the Saracens would behead him and all his people.

The king replied, that they might act according to their pleasure, but that for his part he would rather die a good Christian than live under the anger of God, his blessed mother, and his saints. At that time, the patriarch of Jerusalem was with the king; he was eighty years old, or thereabout, and had once before gained the good-will of the Saracens for the king, and was then come to him to assist in his delivery from them. It was the custom among the Pagans and Christians, that in case any two princes were at war with each other, and one of them should die during the time ambassadors were sent to either, the ambassadors were, in such case, to remain prisoners, whether in pagan land or in Christendom; and because the sultan, lately murdered, had granted a safe-conduct to this patriarch, he was become a prisoner to the Saracens as well as ourselves.

The admirals perceiving the king was not to be frightened by their menaces, one of them said to the others, that it was the patriarch who had thus advised him; and if they would allow him to act, he would force the king to take the oath, for he would cut off the head of the patriarch, and make it fly into the king's lap. The rest would not agree to this; but they seized the good patriarch, and tied him to a post in the presence of the king, and bound his hands behind his back so tightly, that they soon swelled as big as his head; and the blood spouted out from several parts of his hands. From the sufferings he endured, he cried out, "Ah! sire, sire, swear boldly; for I take the whole sin of it on my own soul, since it is by this means alone you may have the power to fulfil your promises." I know not whether the oath was taken at last; but however that may be, the admirals at length held themselves satisfied with the oaths of the king and his lords then present.

When the knights of the Hauleca had slain the sultan, the admirals ordered their trumpets and nacaires to sound merrily before the king's tent; and it was told the king, that the admirals had holden a council and were very desirous to elect him sultan of Babylon. The king one day asked me, if I were of opinion, that if the kingdom of Babylon had been offered him, he ought to have taken it? I answered, that if he had, he would have done a foolish thing, seeing they had murdered their lord. Notwithstanding this, the king told me he should have scarcely refused it.

This project only failed from the admirals saying among themselves, that the king was the proudest Christian they ever knew; and that, if they elected him sultan, he would force them to turn Christians, or have them put to death. This they said from observing, that whenever he quitted his

lodgings, he made the sign of the cross on the ground, and
crossed his body all over.   The Saracens added, that if their
Mahomet had allowed them to suffer the manifold evils that
God had caused the king to undergo, they would never have
had any confidence in him, nor paid him their adorations.

Not long after the conventions had been completed between
the king and the admirals, it was determined that on the
morrow of the feast of the Ascension of our Lord, Damietta
should be surrendered to the Turks, and the king and all the
other prisoners set at liberty.   Our four galleys were anchored
before the bridge of Damietta, where a pavilion had been
pitched for the king's landing.

About sunrise of the appointed day, Sir Geoffry de Sergines
went to the town of Damietta* to deliver it to the admirals,
and instantly the flags of the sultan were displayed from the
walls.   The Saracen knights entered the town, and drank of
the wines they found there, insomuch that the greater part
were drunk.   One of them came on board our galley with
his naked sword reeking with blood, telling us that he had
killed six of our countrymen, which was a brutal thing for
any knight or other to boast of.

Before the surrender of Damietta, the queen had embarked
with all our people on board the ships, except the poor sick,
whom the Saracens were bound by their oath to take care of,
and give up on the payment of 200,000 livres, as has been
mentioned.   They were also to restore the war machines,
salted meats, which they never eat, and our armour; but these
infidel dogs, on the contrary, killed all the sick, and cut to
pieces the machines and other things which they had promised to take care of and restore at the proper time and
place.   They made a great heap of the whole, and set it on
fire; and it was so immense, the fire blazed from the Friday
to the Sunday following.

After they had thus killed, destroyed, and set fire to all
they could lay hands on, we that ought to have had our

---

* It was then under the guard of the duke of Burgundy and Olivier
de Termes, in which the legate and a number of prelates had saved themselves; as did likewise the queen of France, according to Matt. Paris.
Aython, ch. 24, says, that when it had been surrendered to the Saracens,
they completely destroyed it, and made it a desert, building another town
farther distant from the river and sea, to which they gave the name of
New Damietta.

liberties at sunrise remained until sunset without eating or drinking, and the king suffered equally with us. The admirals were disputing together, and seemed inclined to put us to death. One of them, addressing the others, said, " My lords, if you will believe me and these beside me, we will kill the king and all the great persons with him, and then for forty years to come we need not fear them ; for their children are young, and we have possession of Damietta, which will likewise be our security."

Another Saracen, named Scebrecy, a native of Morentaigne,* opposed this, and remonstrated with the others, that if they should slay the king, just after they had killed their sultan, it would be said that the Egyptians were the most disloyal and iniquitous race of men in the world. The admiral, who was desirous of our deaths, replied by palliating arguments. He said, that indeed they had been to blame in slaying their sultan, because it was contrary to the law of Mahomet, who had commanded them to guard their sovereign as the apple of their eye, and he shewed them this commandment written down in a book which he held in his hand. " But," added he, " listen, my lords, to another commandment," and, turning over the leaves of his book, read to them the commandment of Mahomet, that for the security of the faith, the law permitted the death of an enemy. Then, turning his speech to his former purpose, he continued, " Now consider the sin we have committed in killing the sultan, against the positive command of our prophet, and the great evil we shall again do if we suffer the king to depart, and if we do not put him to death, in spite of the assurances of safety he may have had from us, for he is the greatest enemy to our law and religion."

One of the admirals that were against us, thinking we should be slain, came to the bank of the river, and shouted out in Saracen to those who were on board our galleys, and taking off his turban made signs, and told them, they were to carry us back to Babylon. The anchors were instantly raised, and we were carried a good league up the river. This caused great grief to all of us, and many tears fell from our eyes, for we now expected nothing but death.

However, as God willed it, who never is forgetful of his

* Mauritania.

servants, it was agreed among the admirals, about sunset, that we should have our liberty, and we were in consequence brought back to Damietta. Our galleys were moored close to the shore, and we requested permission to land; but they would not allow it until we had refreshed ourselves, for the Saracens said it would be a shame for the admirals to discharge us fasting from their prison.

Shortly after they sent us provision from the army; that is to say, loaves of cheese that had been baked in the sun to prevent the worms from collecting in them, with hard eggs, which had been boiled four or five days, and the shells of which, in honour to us, they had painted with various colours. When we had eaten some little, they put us on shore, and we went towards the king, whom the Saracens were conducting from the pavilion where they had detained him, toward the water-side. There were full 20,000 Saracens on foot surrounding the king, girded with swords.

It chanced that a Genoese galley was on the river opposite to the king, on board of which there appeared but one man, who, the moment he saw the king, whistled, and instantly fourscore cross-bows, well equipped, with their bows bent and arrows placed, leaped on the deck from below. The Saracens no sooner saw them, than, panic struck, they ran away like sheep, and not more than two or three stayed with the king.

The Genoese cast a plank on shore, and took on board the king, his brother the count d'Anjou, who was afterward king of Sicily, Sir Geoffry de Sergines, Sir Philip de Nemours, the marshal of France, the master of the Trinity, and myself. The count de Poitiers remained prisoner with the Saracens until the king should send the 200,000 livres which he was bound to pay before he quitted the river.

The Saturday after the Ascension, which was the morrow of our deliverance, the earl of Flanders, the count de Soissons, and many other great lords, came to take leave of the king. He entreated them to delay going until his brother, the count de Poitiers, should have his liberty; but they replied it was not possible, for their galleys were on the point of sailing.

They embarked on board their galleys on their return to France, and with them was the earl of Brittany, who was grievously sick. He did not live three weeks, but died at sea.

The king, uneasy at the situation of his brother, was very anxious to pay the 200,000 livres; and the whole of Saturday and Sunday were employed in it. They paid the money according to weight,* and each weighing was to the amount of 10,000 livres. Towards evening of the Sunday, the king's servant, occupied in this payment, sent him word they still wanted 30,000 livres. There were then with the king only the count d'Anjou, the marshal of France, the master of the Trinity and myself, all the rest being engaged in paying the ransom. I said to the king it would be much better to ask the commander and marshal of the Knights Templars to lend him the 30,000 livres to make up the sum, than to risk his brother longer with such people.

Father Stephen d'Outricourt, master of the Temple, hearing the advice I gave the king, said to me, "Lord de Joinville, the counsel you give the king is wrong and unreasonable; for you know we receive every farthing on our oath; and that we cannot make any payments but to those who give us their oaths in return."

The marshal of the Temple, thinking to satisfy the king, said, "Sire, don't attend to the dispute and contention of the lord de Joinville and our commander. For it is as he has said; we cannot dispose of any of the money entrusted to us, but for the means intended, without acting contrary to our oaths, and being perjured. Know, that the seneschal has ill-advised you to take by force, should we refuse you a loan; but in this you will act according to your will. Should you, however, do so, we will make ourselves amends from the wealth you have in Acre." When I heard this menace from them to the king, I said to him, that if he pleased I

---

* What Louis Lasseré, purveyor to the college of Navarre, has introduced in the life of St. Louis, is only a vulgar error; namely, that when the ransom of the king was fixed at 800,000 golden besants, there were instantly coined a similar number at Paris from gold which he had exacted from the people, and sent off by Charles, count of Anjou, whom his brother, the king St. Louis, had ordered to return to France expressly for this purpose. It is also another vulgar error, that St. Louis paid for his ransom his weight in gold, and that he put himself into the scales for this purpose, the word *besans* having caused the mistake.

would go and seek the sum, which he commanded me to do.

I instantly went on board one of the galleys of the Templars, and, seeing a coffer, of which they refused to give me the keys, I was about to break it open with a wedge in the king's name; but the marshal, observing I was in earnest, ordered the keys to be given me. I opened the coffer, took out the sum wanting, and carried it to the king, who was much rejoiced at my return. Thus was the whole payment of the two hundred thousand livres completed for the ransom of the count de Poitiers. Before it was all paid, there were some who advised the king to withhold it until the Saracens had delivered up his brother; but he replied, that since he had promised it, he would pay the whole before he quitted the river.

As he said this, Sir Philip de Montfort told the king, that the Saracens had miscounted one scale weight, which was worth ten thousand livres. The king was greatly enraged at this, and commanded Sir Philip, on the faith he owed him as his liege man, to pay the Saracens these ten thousand livres, should they in fact not have been paid. He added, that he would never depart until the uttermost penny of the two hundred thousand livres were paid.

Several persons, perceiving the king was not as yet out of danger from the Saracens, often entreated him to retire to a galley that was waiting for him at sea, to be out of their hands, and at length prevailed on him so to do, for he said that he believed he had now fulfilled his oath.

We now began to make some way at sea, and had advanced a full league without saying a word to each other on the concern we felt to have left the count de Poitiers in prison. In a very short time, Sir Philip de Montfort, who had remained to make good the payment of the ten thousand livres, approached us, calling out to the king, "Sire, sire, wait for your brother the count de Poitiers, who is following you in this other galley." The king then said to those near him, "Light up, light up!" and there was great joy among us all on the arrival of the king's brother. A poor fisherman having hastened to the countess of Poitiers, and told her he had seen the count at liberty from the Saracens, she ordered twenty livres parisis to be given him, and each then went to his galley.

Before I quit the subject of Egypt, I wish not to forget any occurrences that happened while we were there. I shall first speak of Sir Gaultier de Chastillon, and say, that I heard from a knight, that he had seen him post himself with his drawn sword in a street at Casel, where the king was made prisoner, and, whenever any Turks passed that street, he attacked and drove them before him with hard blows; as they fled, they discharged arrows at him, with which he was covered; and, when Sir Walter had put them to flight, he picked the arrows out of his body, and re-armed himself. He was a long time thus engaged; and the knight saw him rise in his stirrups, and call out, "Ha! Chastillon, chevalier, where are my good companions?" but not one was with him.

One day afterward, as I was conversing with the admiral of the galleys, I inquired of all his men-at-arms if there were any one who could give me an account of what was become of him, but I could hear nothing. At length, I met with a knight called Sir John Frumons, who told me, that as they were carrying him prisoner, he saw a Turk on the horse of Sir Gaultier de Chastillon, whose tail and rump were covered with blood; and when he asked him what was become of the knight to whom that horse belonged, he replied, that he had cut his throat while on horseback, and that he was thus covered with his blood.

There was a most valiant man in our army whose name was Sir James du Chastel, bishop of Soissons, who when he saw we were going towards Damietta, and that every one was impatient to return to France, preferred living with God to returning to where he was born. In consequence, he made a charge on the Turks, as if he alone meant to combat their army; but they soon sent him to God, and placed him in the company of martyrs, for they killed him in a very short time.

Another thing I witnessed. As the king was waiting on the river the completion of the payment of the ransom for his brother, the count de Poitiers, a handsome and well-dressed Saracen came up, and presented him with some lard in pots, and a variety of sweet-smelling flowers, telling the king it

was the children of the nazac of the sultan of Egypt,
who had been murdered, that sent him this gift.

The king, hearing the Saracen address him in French,
asked him where he had learnt it. He replied, that he was a
Christian renegado : on which the king bade him withdraw,
for he would not say any more to him. I took him aside,
and inquired who he was, and why he had become a renegado. The Saracen told me, " that he was born in Provence,
and had followed King John to Egypt, where he was
married, and had a very considerable property." I said to
him, " And do you not know, that if you were to die in such
a state, you would descend straight to hell, and be damned for
ever ?" He replied, " that he knew it well, and that there
was not a better religion than that of the Christians; but I
fear, were I to return with you, I should suffer great poverty,
and be continually reproached all my days by being called
' Renegado, renegado !' I had rather, therefore, live at my
ease, like a rich man, than become such an object of
contempt."

I remonstrated with him, that it was much better to suffer
the scorn of the world, since at the day of judgment every evil
deed would be made manifest to all, and then damnation would
follow. But all this was to no purpose, and when he quitted
me I never saw him more.

You have had related the great persecutions and miseries
the good king St. Louis and we all suffered in Egypt. You
must know also, that the good queen was not without her
share, and very bitter to her heart, as you shall soon hear.
Three days before she was brought to bed, she was informed
that the good king, her husband, had been made prisoner,
which so troubled her mind, that she seemed continually to
see her chamber filled with Saracens ready to slay her; and
she incessantly kept crying out, "Help, help;" when there
was not a soul near her. For fear the fruit of her womb
should perish, she made a knight watch at the foot of her bed
all night without sleeping. This knight was very old, not
less than eighty years, or perhaps more ; and every time she
screamed he held her hands, and said, " Madam, do not be
thus alarmed ; I am with you : quit these fears."

Before the good lady was brought to bed, she ordered
every person to leave her chamber except this ancient knight,

when she cast herself out of bed on her knees before him, and requested that he would grant her a boon. The knight, with an oath, promised compliance. The queen then said, " Sir knight, I request, on the oath you have sworn, that should the Saracens storm this town and take it, you will cut off my head before they seize my person." The knight replied, that he would cheerfully so do, and that he had before thought of it, in case such an event should happen.

The queen was, shortly after, delivered of a son in the town of Damietta, whose name was John, and his surname Tristan,* because he had been born in misery and poverty. The day she was brought to bed it was told her, that the Pisans, the Genoese, and all the poorer commonalty that were in the town, were about to fly and leave the king.

The queen sent for them, and addressed them,—"Gentle-men, I beg of you, for the love of God, that you will not think of quitting this town ; for you well know if you do, that my lord the king, and his whole army, will be ruined. At least, if such be your fixed determination, have pity on this wretched person who now lies in pain, and wait until she be recovered, before you put it into execution.

They answered, they could not remain longer in a town where they were dying of hunger. She said, they should never die of hunger ; for that she would buy up all the provision that was in the place, and retain it henceforward in the name of the king. This she was obliged to do ; and all the provision that could be found was bought up, which, on her recovery a little time after, cost her upwards of three hundred and sixty thousand livres to feed these people. Notwithstanding this, the good lady was forced to rise before she was perfectly recovered, and set out for the city of Acre, for Damietta was to be surrendered to the Turks and Saracens.

It should be known, that although the king had suffered such a variety of woes, his attendants, when he embarked, had not made any preparations for him on board, such as robes, bed, bedding, and other necessary things. He was thus forced, for six days, to sleep on mattresses, until we arrived at Acre. The king had not any other habiliments but two robes which the sultan had caused to be made for

* Tristan died in 1270, at Tunis, aged twenty years.

him; they were of a black silken stuff, lined with squirrel
skins, with a number of golden buttons.

While we were on our voyage to Acre, on account of illness, I was always seated near the king; and it was then he
related to me how he had been taken, and how, through the aid
of God, he had accomplished his own ransom and ours. I
was likewise obliged to tell him how I had been captured on
the river, and how a Saracen had saved my life. The king
said, I ought to feel myself under the greatest obligations to
our Lord, who had delivered me from such imminent dangers.
At times, the good and holy king bewailed bitterly the death
of his brother the count d'Artois.

He one day inquired what his brother the count d'Anjou
was doing, and complained, that notwithstanding they were
in the same galley, he never once thought of being in his
company a single day. When the king was told that he was
playing at tables* with Sir Walter de Nemours, he arose
hastily, though from his severe illness he could scarcely stand,
and went staggering to where they were at play, when, seizing
the dice and tables, he flung them into the sea, and was in a
violent passion with his brother for so soon thinking of thus
amusing himself by gaming, forgetful of the death of his
brother the count d'Artois, and of the great perils from which
the Lord had delivered them. But Sir Walter de Nemours
suffered most, for the king flung all the money that lay on the
tables after them into the sea.

[After these words, the Poitiers edition contains a whole
chapter, which is wanting in the edition of Menard, in the
following terms :—

" When we arrived before Acre, the citizens came out to
meet the king as far as the shore with grand processions. and
received him joyfully.

" I attempted to mount the palfrey that had been brought
for me from the town; but I was no sooner mounted than I
fainted, and should have fallen to the ground had it not been
for him who brought the horse, who held me tight, and with

---

* Among the orders laid down for the more regular discipline that was
to be observed in these expeditions to the Holy Land, all playing with
dice was strictly forbidden : " Statutum est etiam, ut nullus enormiter
juret, et quod nullus ad aleas, vel ad decios ludat." In William de
Neubourg, l. 3. ch. 23.

much difficulty I was led to the king's house. I remained
some time at a window without any one taking the least
notice of me, and of all those whom I had brought to Egypt
I had on'y with me, a young boy, called Bartholomew, the
bastard-son of the lord Amé de Montbelliar, lord of Montfaucon, of whom I have before spoken.

"As I was there waiting, a youth came to me dressed in
scarlet striped with yellow, and, having saluted me, asked if
I did not know him. On my saying I did not, he told me he
was a native of Chasteau-Descler, that belonged to my uncle.
He asked if I would take him into my service, for he was with-
odt a master. This I readily agreed to, and retained him as my
varlet. He soon after brought me clean coifes, and combed my
hair exceedingly well. At this time, the king sent for me to
come to dinner; I went, attended by my new varlet, who
carved before me, and found means to get a sufficiency for
himself and the young boy.

"After the dinner this varlet, whose name was Guillemin,
obtained for me a lodging near the baths, that I might wash
and clean myself from the filth I had gained in prison.
Towards evening, he put me into a bath; but I had no sooner
entered it than I again fainted and fell backwards in the
water, so that with much trouble they drew me out alive, and
carried me to my chamber. You must know, that I had
only a poor jacket for my dress, nor any money in my
pocket to buy better clothing, or to support me in my illness.
This affected me very much, and I suffered more from the extreme indigence I was in, than from the pains of my disorder.

"As I was in this distress, most fortunately a knight came
to visit me, whose name was Sir Peter de Bourbrainne, and
seeing my miserable state, he comforted me to the best of his
power, and caused cloth to be given me to new-dress myself,
by a merchant o Acre, to whom he gave his own security for
the due payment.

"At the end of three days, when I was somewhat better
and stronger, I went to the king, who blamed me much for
having been so long absent, and charged me, as I valued his
love, not to fail partaking of his meals morning and evening,
until he should determine to remain there, or return to
France. While with the king, I complained to him of
the lord Peter de Courcenay, who owed me 400 livres

of my pay, and refused to give it me; and the king ordered
the 400 livres to be instantly paid me, to my great joy, for I
did not possess a single farthing.

" When I had received my money, Sir Peter de Bourbrainne advised me to keep only forty livres for my expenses,
and to give the remainder to the governor of the palace of
the Templars to keep for me, which I willingly did. Having
spent the forty livres, I sent for as much more; but this
governor bade them tell me, that he had not any money of
mine, and, what was worse, that he did not know me.

" On the receipt of this answer, I went to the master of
the Templars, whose name was Father Regnaut de Vichiers,
to whom I carried intelligence of the king, and then told him
the treatment I had met with, and complained to him of the
governor of the palace, for not restoring to me the money I
had entrusted to his care. But I had no sooner ended, than
he flew into a violent passion, and said, ' Lord de Joinville,
I love you very much, but I shall cease doing so, if you hold
such language, for it seems to be insinuated, by what you
complain of, that our brotherhood are all thieves.' I replied, that
so far from being silent, I would make the matter public, for
that I was in such want of my money I had not a penny to
support me, and, without a word more, left him.

" I can assure you I was during four days in the utmost
uneasiness about my money, and knew not to what saint to
make my vows, to recover it. These four days I did nothing
but run about, seeking means to regain it. On the fifth the
master of the Templars accosted me with a smile, and told
me he had found my money, and instantly gave me the
amount, to my great joy, as I was in very great need of it;
and I took good care, in future, not to trouble these monks
with the keeping of my cash."]

At this place I must relate some great persecutions and
evils that befel me when at Acre, but from which those two,
in whom I had my whole confidence, our Lord God and the
blessed Virgin Mary, relieved me. This I say as an encouragement to such as may read my book, to have a perfect
confidence in God, and patience in their adversities and tribulations, when he will aid them, as he has done me, many
and many times.

On the king's arrival before Acre, the inhabitants of that

city came out in grand procession to meet him on the sea-shore, and received him with much joy. Soon after, the king sent for me, and expressly commanded me, as I valued his love, to come and eat with him morning and evening, until he should determine whether to return to France or to remain there.

I was lodged with the rector of Acre, for there the bishop had fixed my residence, and was most grievously ill. Of all my servants, there was but one that was not confined to his bed with sickness like myself ; nor had I any to comfort me, by once offering me something to drink. The more to enliven me, I saw daily pass my window twenty corpses for burial ; and when I heard the chant, " Libera me Domine," I shed floods of tears, and cried out to God that he would mercifully save me and my household from the pestilence that then raged. And this he did.

Not long after the king's arrival at Acre he summoned his brothers, and all the other nobles, on a certain Sunday, and, when assembled, he addressed them: " My lords, I have called you together, to give you some news from France. In truth, my lady-mother, the queen, has sent for me, and it is necessary that I return with the utmost haste, for my kingdom is in great danger, inasmuch as there exists neither peace nor truce with the king of England. The people here wish to detain me, assuring me that if I depart their country will be destroyed, and insist on following me. I beg you will maturely consider what I have said, and give me your opinions within eight days."

On the Sunday following, we all presented ourselves before the king to give him our opinions, as he had charged us, whether he should depart or stay. Sir Guion de Malvoisin was our spokesman, and said, " Sire, my lords your brothers, and the other nobles now present, have fully considered your situation, and they are of opinion, that you cannot remain longer in this country with honour to yourself or profit to your kingdom. For, in the first place, of all the knights whom you led to Cyprus, amounting to 2,800, not one hundred remain. Secondly, you have not any habitation in this country, nor have your army any money ; for these reasons, which we have maturely weighed, we unanimously advise that you return to France to reinforce yourself with

men-at-arms, and supply yourself with money, so that you
may hastily repair again hither, and take vengeance on the
enemies of God and of his holy religion."

The king was not pleased with this advice of Sir Guy, but
demanded from each person his private opinion on the business, beginning with the counts d'Anjou, de Poitiers, and the
other nobles near him. All of them replied, they agreed in
the advice of Sir Guy de Malvoisin. The count de Japhe
was hard pressed to give his opinion, for he had castles and
possessions in those countries; but when the king insisted on
having it, he said, that if the king could keep the field, it
would redound more to his honour to remain, than thus discomfited to return. I, who was the fourteenth in rank,
answered in my turn that I was of the same opinion with
the count de Japhe; moreover, giving these additional reasons,
that it was reported the king had not as yet expended any of
the money from the royal treasury, but had employed that
which was in the hands of the clerks of finance; and that
the king should send to the Morea, and the adjoining countries, to seek powerful reinforcements of men-at-arms, who,
when they should learn the high pay the king was willing to
give, would hasten to join him from all parts, and by this
means the king might deliver the multitude of poor prisoners
who had been captured in the service of God, which would
never be the case unless it were done as now proposed.

You must know, that at this moment none reproved me
for my opinion, but many began to weep, for there was
scarcely one among us who had not some of his relations in
the prisons of the Saracens.

Sir William de Belmont* spoke next, and said that my
advice was very good, and that he agreed in it. When all
had delivered their opinions, the king was much confounded
at their diversity, and took eight days more to declare which
he should follow. When we had left the presence of the
king, the great nobles made a violent attack on me, and,
through jealousy and envy, said, " Ha! certainly the king
must be mad, if he do not follow your opinion, lord de Join-

* I believe this to be the same whose name appears in the cartulary of
the bishopric of Paris, wherein he is mentioned as doing homage to that
see, in the year 1263, for his lordship of Pierre Fitz.

ville, in preference to that of the whole French council.* But
to this I made not any reply.

The tables were soon after laid for dinner, and the king,
who had usually made me sit down near him when his brothers were absent, and during the repasts had conversed with
me, did not now open his lips, nor even turn his face toward
me.   I then thought he was displeased with me for having
said that he had not employed his own money, when he had
expended such very large sums. After he had said grace,
and returned thanks to God for his dinner, I retired to a
window near the head of the king's bed, and, passing
my hand through the grating, remained there musing. I
said to myself, that if the king should now return to France,
I would go to the prince of Antioch,* who was a relation of
mine.

While I was thus meditating, the king leant on my
shoulders, and held my head between his hands. I thought
it was Sir Philip de Nemours, who had been fretting me all
the day for the advice which I had given the king, and said
to him, " Sir Philip, do leave me quiet in my misfortune."
As I turned round, the king covered my face with his hands,
and I then knew it was the king from an emerald on his
finger.   I wished to make some reparation, as one that had
improperly spoken ; but the king made me be silent, and continued, " Now, lord de Joinville, tell me how you, who are so
young a man, could have the courage to advise me to remain
in these countries contrary to the opinion of all my greatest
nobles?" I replied, that if I had advised him well, he should follow it ; if the contrary, he ought not to think more on what I
had said.   " And will you remain with me, if I should stay?"
" Yes, certainly," answered I, "were it at my own or at
another's expense."   The king said, that he was pleased with
the advice I had given, but ordered me to tell this to no one.

I was so rejoiced that whole week with what he had told
me, that I was insensible to my illness, and defended myself
boldly against the other lords when they attacked me.

You must know, in these countries the peasant is called

* Boëmond V., prince of Antioch, and count of Tripoly, who died in
the year 1261.

2 H

Poulain,* and I was told by my cousin Sir Peter d'Avallon, that I was called Poulain, because I had advised the king to remain with the Poulains. This information he gave me, that I might defend myself against those who should call me so, and tell them that I would rather be a Poulain than such recreant knights as themselves.†

On the Sunday we all again assembled in the presence of the king, who began by signing himself with the cross, saying that it was from the instructions of his mother he did so, who

---

* *Poulain*,—a child born of an European mother by a Syrian father.— *Gloss. to Louvre edit.* The author of the Life of Louis le Gros explains the force of this word in his 24th chapter, as follows : " Pullani dicuntur, qui de patre Syriano et matre Francigena generantur." It is probable that Frenchmen gave this name to such as had sprung from these irregular connections, because they resembled young wild colts, that could not be caught. During the time the French possessed the empire of Constantinople, they called Gasmoules (Γασμουλοι) those born from a French man and Greek woman ; or more probably *Gastemoules*, by way of derision ; as if such children by these irregular marriages, on account of the difference of nations, and even religions, had in some sort sullied and debased the womb of their mothers, which is the mould wherein children are formed. Thus in Antioch, the issue of Armenian or Greek inhabitants of that town by Turkish women were called *Turcati*.

† That is to say, one who owned himself conquered, for that is the meaning of the word *recreu*, which is taken from the usage of duelling. When one of the combatants was overpowered by his adversary, and confessed himself unable to continue the fight longer, he owned that he was *recreant* or *recrue*; that is, that he was exhausted, and could do no more, and confessed himself vanquished. * * * In those parts of the MS. Assizes of the kingdom of Jerusalem which speak of "wager of battle," the appellant or defendant is introduced as saying these words before the judge of the field : " I am ready to prove it by my body against his body, and to fight until death, or till I own myself recreant any hour of the day, and here is my glove," &c. * * * The same Assizes say, chap. 94, on the subject of trial for the cause of murder : " The judges of the field must attend, and be as near the combatants as possible, that if one of them should utter the word *recreant*, he may be heard, and in that case, the moment it shall be heard, they will order his adversary to cease, and say that he has done enough. They will then take the body of the vanquished, and give it up to the pleasure of the lord, who will order it to be dragged thence to the gallows, and hanged by the neck. The same will be done to him that shall be slain in the duel, although he may not have said the word *recreant*." * * * So that the lord de Joinville, on this occasion, returned abuse for abuse, and, as they called him " Poulain," he retorted on these knights " recreant knights," that is to say, cowards and base. * * *

had thus ordered him, and likewise to invoke the name of God and the aid of his Holy Spirit, whenever he was about to make a speech. He then continued: "My lords, I feel equally thankful to those who have advised our return to France as to those who have recommended our stay here. But, since I last saw you, I have fully considered this matter, and believe, that should we remain here, my kingdom will not the sooner be in great danger from it; for my lady-mother the queen has a sufficiency of men-at-arms to defend it. I have thought much on what the knights of this country say, that if I depart, the kingdom of Jerusalem will be lost, since no one will remain here after me. Now, my lords, having told my resolution, let such speak out boldly who wish to remain with me; and I promise to give them emoluments, that the fault shall not be mine but their own, if they do not remain. Those that may not choose to stay, God be with them."

When the king had done speaking, several were as if thunderstruck, and began to weep bitterly. After the king had declared his resolution, he gave permission to his brothers to return to France; but I know not if he did this at their requests, or whether it was the will of the king. This passed about St. John Baptist's day.

Shortly after the departure of his brothers for France, the king was impatient to learn what success those who had stayed with him had met with in recruiting his men-at-arms. On the feast-day of St. James, whose pilgrim I was, for the manifold kindness he had shewn me, the king, after mass, retired to his chamber, and called to him the chiefs of his council, namely, Sir Peter the chamberlain,* who was the most loyal and upright man I ever saw of the king's household, that good knight Sir Geoffry de Serginea, the discreet Sir Giles le Brun, and others, among whom was that prudent man, to whom the king, after the death of Sir Hymbert de Beaujeu, had given the constable's sword. He asked them what numbers and sort of men they had collected for the reinforcement of his army, and with warmth continued,—"You know that it is about a month since I have declared my intention to stay

* Peter de Nemours, or de Ville-Beon, chamberlain of France, under the reign of St. Louis, whom he accompanied in his expedition to Tunis, and died there. He was buried at the king's feet, in the abbey of St. Denis.

here, and I have not as yet had intelligence that you have raised any reinforcements of knights or others."

To this Sir Peter the chamberlain replied, in the name of the council,—"Sire, we have not hitherto done any thing, nor do we think we shall ever accomplish it; for every one demands such a price, and so great pay, that we are afraid of promising to give them what they ask." The king would know to whom they had spoken, and those who had demanded such great pay. They unanimously replied, that it was I, and that I would not be satisfied with a trifle. All this I overheard, as I was in the king's apartment; and the council had told the king these things of me, because I had advised him, contrary to their opinion, to remain, and had thus prevented their return to France.

The king sent for me; on my entrance, I cast myself on my knees before him; when, making me rise and seat myself, he said,—"Seneschal, you know full well the confidence I have in you, and how much you are beloved by me. My council, notwithstanding this, assure me, that you are so hard to deal with, that they cannot satisfy you in regard to the pay they are willing to give you. How is this?"

"Sire," replied I, "I know not what they may have reported to you; but in regard to myself, if I demand a good salary, I cannot avoid it; for you know, that when I was made prisoner on the Nile, I lost every thing I had, except what was on my body, and I cannot maintain my people on a little."

The king then asked, how much I would have for the support of my company until next Easter, which was nearly half a year. I answered, two thousand livres. "Now tell me," continued the king, "have you no knights here with you?" "Yes, sire, I made Sir Peter de Pontmolain remain, who is the third under my banner; and he costs me four hundred livres." The king, then reckoning on his fingers, said, "Your knights and men-at-arms then cost you twelve hundred livres." I then said, "Consider, sire, if I must not require full eight hundred livres to equip myself with horses and armour, and to provide a table for my knights until Easter." The king then told his council that he could not think my demands extravagant; and said to me, that he retained me in his service.

Not long after this, the emperor of Germany sent an embassy to the king, with credential letters, to say that he had written to the sultan of Babylon, of whose death he was ignorant, to give credit to those he sent to him, and, cost what it would, to deliver the king of France and his army from their captivity. But I well remember, that several said they believed the emperor wished to find them still prisoners; for they suspected, that his motive in sending this embassy was to cause us to be more straitly confined, and more heavily oppressed. When the ambassadors found us at liberty, they returned to the emperor.

After this embassy was departed, there arrived at Acre another from the sultan of Damascus to the king. The sultan complained, in his letter, of the admirals of Egypt, for having put to death their sultan, who was his cousin. He offered, if the king would assist him against them, to deliver up the kingdom of Jerusalem, which they held. The king replied to these ambassadors, that if they would retire to their lodgings, which had been prepared for them, they should shortly have an answer on the subject on which the sultan of Damascus had written to him. To this they consented; and the king resolved, in council, to send his answer by the ambassadors: but that they should be accompanied by a monk, called Father Yves le Breton, who was of the order of Preaching Friars.

Father Yves was sent for, and despatched to the ambassadors of the sultan, to say, the king had ordered him to accompany them to Damascus, to inform the sultan what were the king's intentions respecting the Saracens. This Father Yves did; but I must relate an incident which I heard from him. On going from the king's residence to the lodgings of the ambassadors, he met a very old woman in the street, having in her right hand a porringer full of fire, and in her left a phial of water. Father Yves asked, "Woman, what art thou going to do with this fire and water which thou art carrying?" She replied that with the fire she wished to burn paradise, and with the water to drown hell, so that there should be never

more a paradise or hell. The friar asked why she uttered
such words. "Because," she said, "I wish not that any
one should do good for the reward of paradise, nor avoid
evil from fear of hell; but every good ought to be done
from the perfect and sincere love we owe to our Creator,
God, who is the supreme good, and who loved us so much
that he suffered death for our redemption; which death he
submitted to for the sin of our first father, Adam, and for our
salvation."

During the king's residence at Acre, there came likewise to him ambassadors from the prince of the Bedouins, called the Old Man of the Mountain. After the
king had attended mass in the morning, he would hear
what these ambassadors had to say. On their entrance,
the king caused them to be seated, to deliver their message;
when one of the chiefs began by asking the king if he were
acquainted with their lord, the prince of the mountain. The
king said he was not; he had never seen him, although he
had heard much spoken of him. The chief continued: "Sire,
since you have heard my lord spoken of, I wonder much that
you have not sent him such of your people as should have
made him your friend, in like manner as the emperor of
Germany, the king of Hungary, the sultan of Babylon, and
many other princes have yearly done; for they know well
that they would not be allowed to exist or reign, but during
his good pleasure. For this cause he has despatched us
hither to advertise you, that he wills you should act in the
like manner, or at least that you acquit him of the tribute
he pays annually to the grand master of the Temple, or of
the Hospital, and if you do this, he will consider it as
paid to himself. My lord says truly, that should he destroy
the master of the Temple, or of the Hospital, there would
soon be others as good, and for this reason he is unwilling
o risk his people's lives where little is to be gained."

The king replied, that he would consider what they had
said, and if they would return in the evening they should
have his answer. When they came again before the king,
it was about vespers, and they found the master of the
Temple on one side of him, and the master of the Hospital
on the other. The king, on their entrance, ordered them

to repeat what they had before said to him, as well as the demand which they had made in the morning. They replied, that they should not think it right to repeat what they had said, except in the presence of such as had heard them in the morning. The masters of the Temple, and of the Hospital, on this ordered them to repeat it. The chief then repeated what he had said before to the king, as has been mentioned.

The masters, on hearing it, bade them come and confer with them in the morning, and they should then know the king's pleasure. On the morrow, when they were before the masters of the Temple and Hospital, they told them, that their lord had very foolishly and impudently sent such a message to the king of France, and had used such harsh expressions, that were it not unbecoming the honour of the king, on the account of their being invested with the character of ambassadors, he would have had them thrown into the filthy sea of Acre, and drowned, in despite of their master. "And we command you," continued the masters, "to return to your lord, and to come back within fifteen days with such letters from your prince, that the king shall be contented with him and with you."

Before the fifteen days were expired, the same ambassadors returned from the prince of the mountain, and addressing the king, said, "Sire, we are come back from our lord, who informs you, that as the shirt is the part of dress nearest to the body, he sends you this, his shirt, as a gift, or a symbol that you are the king for whom he has the greatest affection, and which he is most desirous to cultivate; and, for a further assurance of it, here is his ring that he sends you, which is of pure gold, and hath his name engraven on it; and with this ring our lord espouses you, and understands that henceforward you be as one of the fingers of his hand."

Among other presents sent to the king were an elephant of crystal, figures of men of different crystals, the whole set in fine pieces of amber with borders of pure gold. You must know, that when the ambassadors opened the case that contained all these fine things, the whole apartment was instantly embalmed with the sweet odour of their perfumes.

The king desirous not to be behindhand in making a

return for these presents from the old prince of the mountain,* sent to him, by his ambassadors, and by Father Yves Le Breton, who understood the Saracenic, great quantities of scarlet robes, cups of gold, and other vessels of silver. When Father Yves was in the presence of the prince of the Bedouins, he conversed with him on the articles of his faith; but, as he afterward reported to the king, he found he did not believe in Mahomet, but followed the religion of Aly, who was, he said, the uncle of Mahomet. He told him, that it was Aly to whom Mahomet was indebted for all the honours

---

* All the writers on the holy wars agree, that the Old Man of the Mountain, who is called "Vetulus," or "Senex de Montanis," ruled over the Assassins, who inhabited, as I have elsewhere remarked, the mountains of Phœnicia, whence he was called prince of the mountains. The lord de Joinville confounds the Bedouins, in this place, with the Assassins. Arnold de Lubeck, l. 7, ch. 10, speaks thus of them: "In terminis Damasci, Antiochiæ, et Alapiæ, est quoddam genus Saracenorum in montanis, quod eorum lingua vulgari Heissesim vocatur." He then describes the palace, and the behaviour of this prince, which is conformable to what the lord de Joinville and the greater part of those who have written on the holy wars relate. Among others, William of Tyre, l. 14, c. 19; l. 20, ch. 21; Matthew Paris, in the year 1150; William de Neubourg, l. 4, c. 24; l. 5, ch. 16. From these authors, the author of the MS. "Traité de la Terre d'Outremer" has drawn all he has written of the Assassins and their prince in these terms:—"In the lands near Damascus and Antioch, live a sort of Saracens, called by some 'Haussassis,' by others 'the people of the Old Man of the Mountain.' These people live a lawless life, and eat pork, contrary to the religion of the Saracens, and lie with every woman they meet, whether mothers or sisters. They inhabit great towers, which they have built among the mountains. The country is full of wild beasts, on which they live. Their prince is very cruel, and very different from other Saracens and Christians, for he is accustomed to put many to death without reason. He has several fine and strong palaces, surrounded by high walls, and he has them very well guarded, so that no one can enter them but at one gate. In these palaces he confines the children of his subjects, and none of these youths appear before him, unless so ordered by their masters, who teach them various languages and other things: they must obey the commands of their prince, believing that through him alone they can obtain paradise, and not otherwise. When once confined, they are never to come into his presence without his permission, and when he asks them if they be willing to obey his orders in hopes of gaining paradise, they make him such answers as their masters have taught them. The prince then gives them a large and sharp knife, and sends them whither he lists to assassinate those he hates; and know that they will, if possible, execute this commission, whatever may happen to them in life or death"

he enjoyed; and that, when Mahomet had made his great
conquests over mankind, he quarrelled with and separated
from Aly, who perceiving the pride of Mahomet, and that he
wished to trample upon him, began to draw as many as he
could to his doctrines, and retired to a part of the deserts and
mountains of Egypt, where he gave them a different creed
from that of Mahomet. Those who support the religion of
Aly call those who follow Mahomet unbelievers, as the Mahometans in like manner style the Bedouins infidels. Each
party, in this respect, says the truth, for in fact they are both
unbelievers.

One of the points of doctrine of Aly consists in the belief,
that when any one is killed by the command or in the service
of his superior, the soul of the person so killed* goes into
another body of higher rank, and enjoys more comforts than
before. It is for this reason that the Bedouins of the mountain are ambitious to be killed in the service of their prince,
in the expectation of enjoying the above recompense.

Another point is, that no man can die before his pre-
determined day. This the Bedouins so firmly believe, that
they never go in armour to battle; for, if they did, they
would think they were acting contrary to the dogmas of their
faith. When they swear at their children, they usually say,
" Mayest thou be cursed like him who arms himself for fear
of death," which, they think, every one should be ashamed
of. This is an absurd error; for it supposes that God, who
is all-powerful, cannot abridge or lengthen life at his pleasure.
It is also false, for in Him alone resides omnipotency.

While Father Yves Le Breton was on his embassy to the
Old Man of the Mountain, he one day found at the head of
the prince's bed a small book,† in which were written many
of the excellent words that our Saviour had said to Peter
during his residence on earth, and prior to his passion. Father
Yves, having read them, said, " Ah! my lord! the frequent
reading of this book will do you much good; for, small as it
may be, it contains many excellent things."

---

* They had borrowed from the Arabians the doctrine of the Metem-
psychosis.

† This prince had, in this respect, followed the example of his predecessors, who had made themselves acquainted with the mysteries of our
religion, by reading the Evangelists and Epistles of St. Paul.

The Old Man of the Mountain replied, that he frequently read it, as he had great faith in St. Peter. He continued, "In the beginning of the world, the soul of Abel, after his brother Cain had murdered him, entered the body of Noah; and the soul of Noah, on his decease, went into the body of Abraham; and after Abraham it entered the body of St. Peter, who is now under the earth."

Father Yves, hearing him thus talk, argued with him on the absurdity of his belief, and shewed him many fair promises and commandments of God, but he would never have any faith in them. Father Yves reported to the king, that when the prince of the Bedouins took the field, he was preceded by a man carrying his battle-axe, the handle of which was covered with silver; and this handle served as a case for a number of sheep knives. The bearer cried out with a loud voice in his language, "Turn back! fly from before him who carries the deaths of kings in his hands."

I have delayed informing you of the answer which the king made to the ambassadors from Damascus. It was to this effect; that the king would send to the admirals of Egypt to know if they were willing to re-establish the truce they had promised, but which they had already broken, as has been said, and, should they refuse, the king would very willingly join his forces, and assist him in revenging the murder of his cousin the sultan of Babylon.

After this, the king, during the time he was at Acre, sent Sir John de Vallance to the admirals in Egypt, to require them to make such satisfaction to the king for the outrages they had committed, contrary to treaty, that he should be contented with them. This the admirals promised to do, but on condition that he would unite himself with them against the sultan of Damascus before mentioned. To gain the king's heart, after that wise man Sir John de Vallance had strongly remonstrated with and severely blamed them for the wrongs they had done contrary to their law, and for breaking the truce they had solemnly sworn to keep, they sent to the king all the knights whom they had detained in their prisons. They likewise sent him the bones of the count Walter do Brienne, that they might be buried in consecrated ground.

Sir John de Vallance brought back with him 200 knights, without including great numbers of common people who had been confined in the Saracen prisons. On his arrival at Acre, Madame de Secte, cousin-german to the count de Brienne, received his bones, and had them interred well and honourably in the church of the Knights Hospitallers at Acre. The funeral service was grand, and attended by every knight, who made his offering of a waxen taper and a silver penny. The king offered a taper, and a golden bezant of the coinage of Madame de Secte,* which caused every one to wonder, for he was never before known to make an offering of any coin but his own. He did this, however, out of compliment to Madame de Secte.

Among the knights whom Sir John de Vallance had brought with him from Egypt, I was acquainted with forty at least, attached to the count of Champagne, who were in a most ragged and dirty condition. These forty I had new dressed at my own expense, and, clothed in coats and sur-coats of green, I conducted them to the presence of the king, and entreated that he would detain them in his service.

The king, having heard my request, made not a word of reply; but one of his council then present reproved me, say-ing, that I did very ill to make such requests to the king, who had already exceeded the state of his income by 7,000 livres. I replied, that misfortunes make people speak; for that among us of Champagne we had lost in the service of the king at least five-and-thirty knights bannerets of the count of Champagne, adding, that the king would not act properly if he did not retain them, seeing the want he was in of knights. As I said this, I began to weep, when the king appeased me, by granting what I had asked; he retained all the knights, and added them to my battalion.

When the king had given audience to the ambassadors from the admirals of Egypt who had accompanied Sir John de Vallance, and learnt that they were impatient to return, he told them, that he would not enter into any negotiation with them for a truce until they should have restored all the heads of the Christians which were hanging on the walls of Quassere,† from the time the counts of Montfort and of Bar

---

* Of the number of the great barons of the kingdom of Jerusalem, who among other rights, had that of coining money, was the lord de Sajette.

† The Poitiers edition has *Quahere*. and the lord de Joinville gives us

were made prisoners. They were likewise to send him all
children whom they had taken when young, and had forced
to deny the Christian religion and believe in their faith ; and,
beside these two articles, they were to send an acquittance
for the 200,000 livres which were still owing to them.

The king ordered Sir John de Vallance to return with the
ambassadors, on account of his consummate wisdom and
valour, to announce this answer to the admirals.

About this time the king left Acre, and went to Cæsarea
with all his people, and had the walls and fortifications of
that place repaired, which the Saracens had broken down
and destroyed. Cæsarea is full twelve leagues from Acre,
on the road to Jerusalem. I know not how it happened,
except by the will of God, who can do as he lists, but
during the year that the king stayed at Cæsarea to repair
it, no attack was made upon him, nor harm done to him,
nor to the few men-at-arms that were left at Acre.

I have before said that ambassadors had come to the
king from the great cham of Tartary during our residence at Cyprus. They assured the king they were come
to assist him in the conquest of Jerusalem from the Saracens. The king sent them back, and with them two notable
Friars Preachers, who carried as a present to the cham of
Tartary a tent in the form of a chapel, the lining of which
was of scarlet cloth, embroidered over with the history of
our religion ; the Annunciation of the angel Gabriel, the
Nativity, the Baptism of our Lord, the Passion, the Ascension, and the Descent of the Holy Ghost. The king sent
also chalices, books, ornaments, and every thing necessary
for saying mass ; and, as I have since heard these ambassadors tell the king, they embarked for the port of Antioch,
and in going from thence to the place where the cham of
Tartary resided, they were occupied for a whole year, travelling ten leagues a day. They found the country through
which they passed subject to the Tartars, and saw in
different towns on their road large mounds of bones.

The ambassadors inquired how they could have conquered

to understand, further on, that he means the town of Cairo. The Eastern
Chronicle also informs us, that the heads of those slain at the battle of
Massoura were brought to Cairo, and affixed to the points of lances, on
the gate of Zualia, which is a suburb of Cairo.

so large a tract of country, and destroyed such numbers of people, whose bones they had seen piled up. The Tartars described to them their manners, beginning from their first origin, saying they were sprung from a great berrie,* in a plain where nothing grew. This berrie was placed under a rock, so very high that no one could pass it, and pointed toward the east. The Tartars told them, that between this, and other rocks towards the extremity of the earth, were enclosed the people of Gog and Magog,† who were to attend Antichrist when he should come, at the end of the world, to make a general destruction.

From this same berrie came the Tartars that are subject to Prester John‡ on the one side, and to the emperor of

---

* A flat country. Sanuto, 1. 2, part 4, c. 28, " in quo habitant Arabes, qui Bedwini vocantur, in beria continue habitantes, seu in locis campestribus, sub tentoriis mansiones suas omni tempore facientes." Spelman has thought that the word " beria," or " de berry," which is found at the termination of the names of some towns in England, signified " a burgh ;" but it is more probable they were thus called from their being built on extensive plains. Matthew Paris speaks in the year 1174 of the berry of St. Edmund, " beria S. Edmundi," which is nothing more than the plain belonging to the monastery of St. Edmund.

† In the list of the Aijubite Caliphs, in the *Chronicon Orientale*, it is said, that these people of Gog and Magog inhabited the country adjoining China : " Anno 613 fuit irruptia Tartarorum, qui colebant planitiem Sinarum contermimam, quae dicitur Hagin-Magin." Marco Polo, 1. 1, ch. 64 : " Sunt etiam ibi regiones Gog et Magog, quas illi nominant Lug et Mungug."

‡ It was an ancient error, now no longer believed, that the empire of Prester John was the kingdom of the Abyssinians in Africa. The kingdom of Prester John was in Asia, and meant the empire of India. William of Tripoly relates, that at the time of the capture of Antioch by the French in the year 1098, Coiren Cham was lord or king of the eastern parts of Asia. After his death, a certain Nestorian priest seized the kingdom, and was called Priest John. Albericus, in the year 1145, has fully spoken of him, and said that it was believed he was of the race of the Magi mentioned in the Scriptures. He may, however, have advanced this opinion, from what he had read, that he governed the country called in the Scriptures Gog and Magog. In the year 1165, he says, that this prince sent ambassadors to the emperors of Germany, Manuel and Frederick. He speaks of him again in the year 1170. His brother, Wth Cham, succeeded him, but was defeated by Genghis, cham or king of the Tartars, prior to the year 1200, as Paolo Veneto tells us in l. 1, chapters 51 and 52. This king of India was called David, and the son of Prester John. The Tartars having subdued the kingdom of India, and killed the king, established another, who was of the race of Prester John,

Persia on the other, which empire was joined to them also by a narrow tract of land.

There were many infidel nations intermixed with them, to whom they were forced to pay a yearly tribute, for themselves and for the pasturage of their herds, which were their sole nourishment.

The Tartars added, that this Prester John, the emperor of Persia, and the other kings to whom they were tributary, held them in great abhorrence and hatred; for when they carried them their tribute, they would not receive it in their presence, but turned their backs on them. This conduct was the cause that one of their wise men went from berrie to berrie, stating to the inhabitants the wretched condition they were in, and remonstrating on the base slavery they were suffering from various princes, and recommended that they should take counsel together on the best means of extricating themselves from the debasing condition in which they were now kept. This wise man worked so effectually on their minds, that there was a general assembly appointed at the berrie nearest to the lands of Prester John. After many remonstrances, this wise man prevailed on them to act as he should advise: they only requested him to be prudent in adopting the best means to accomplish his purposes.

He told them, they would never be successful until they should have a king to be master and lord over them, and

and made him tributary to them. Vincent de Beauvais says, that this king was a Christian, and adds, that Ghengis Cham married his daughter, which last part is confirmed by Thomas de Cantinprè and Sanuto. Our ancient heralds even go so far as to give for arms, to Prester John, a shield or, with a crucifix azur, having on each side two thongs of the same. There are some writers who do not agree that this prince, who was the origin of, and gave his name to these kings of India, was a priest; and they suppose the error to have arisen from his being called in the Persian language *prestegiani*, which means in Latin *apostolicus*, or a Christian orthodox king, and that in this quality he had a cross borne before him, like the archbishops and primates, to shew his people that he was the protector and defender of the Christian religion. This is the opinion of Joseph Scaliger, in lib. 7, de Emendat. Tempor. and of some others. But it is not very certain what were the provinces of Asia which these princes possessed, whose dominions were so extensive, that it was said the first Prester John subjugated and rendered tributary seventy-two kings.

whom they must obey in whatsoever he commanded. The manner in which he proposed they should elect a king was as follows: of the fifty-two tribes of which the Tartars were composed, each tribe should bring him an arrow* marked with the name and seal of the tribe. This was agreed to by all the people; and when done, the whole fifty-two arrows were placed before a child of five years old, and from the tribe whose arrow the child should pick, the king was to be chosen.

The child having taken an arrow, all the tribes were ordered to retire; and fifty-two men, the most learned and valiant, were selected from the tribe to whom the arrow belonged, among whom was their adviser; and each of them holding an arrow apart signed with his name, they made a child of five years old take one of these arrows, the owner of which was to be their king or ruler. By accident the choice of the child fell on the arrow of him who had proposed the measure, to the great joy of the whole nation. Having caused silence to be proclaimed, he said,— "Gentlemen, if you wish that I should be your lord, you will swear by Him who made the heavens and earth, that you will obey my commands." And they all took the oath.

After this, he gave them many useful instructions, very excellent for keeping a nation in peace at home. One of his regulations was, that no one should seize the goods of another without his will, nor to his loss; and that no one should strike another, under pain of his hand being cut off. Another, that no one should force the wife or daughter of any one, under penalty of death. Many other good laws did he promulgate for the preservation of peace among them.

Having given them these instructions, he remonstrated with them on their ancient enemy Prester John, and how great his hatred was against them; and, in conclusion, said,—

---

* The lord de Joinville has made a mistake by attributing to the Tartars the election of their king by the number of arrows. This circumstance is told of the Turks and Turcomans by William of Tyre, who lived before the name of Tartars was heard of, in the first book and seventh chapter, and by Albericus in the year 1059, when they possessed themselves of the lands of the king of Persia.

" Now, as I am determined to attack him, I order you all
to be ready to-morrow to follow me. Should it so happen
that we be defeated, which God forbid, each of you must
do the best he can to save himself. Should the victory be
ours, I strictly command that it be followed up with courage, should the combat last three days and three nights,
without any one daring to think of pillage, but all must
be solely occupied with destroying and putting to death
the enemy; for when the victory shall be completely gained,
I will so honourably divide the plunder among you, that every
one shall be satisfied." He was heard with pleasure, and his
orders unanimously obeyed.

On the morrow, according to what had been proposed, so
did they act. They made a very severe inroad on their
enemies, and according to the will of God, who is all-
powerful, they defeated them, and put to death every one
that had defensive arms in his hand. But those that wore
a religious dress, and the priests, were spared. The rest of
the nation, under Prester John, who were not engaged in
battle, submitted, and placed themselves under their dominion.

A wonderful thing happened after this conquest. A
great chief of one of the tribes before spoken of was missing from the Tartars three days, without any thing being
known of him. On his return, he told his people that he
thought he had been absent but one night, and that he
had not suffered hunger or thirst. He related, that he had
ascended a marvellous high hill, where he had seen the
handsomest race of men, and the finest dressed, that he
had ever beheld in his life. In the centre of this hill a
king was seated on a throne of gold, who was superior in
beauty and dress to all the others: on his right and left
were six kings richly adorned with jewels, and with crowns
on their heads. Near to him, on his right, was a queen
on her knees, who begged and entreated him to consider
his people. On his left a most beautiful youth knelt,
having two wings as brilliant as the sun; and around the
king were great numbers of handsome winged attendants.

The king called him to him, and said, "Thou art come
from the host of the Tartars." "Sire," replied I, " I am."
"Thou wilt return thither and tell the cham of Tartary
that thou hast seen me, who am the Lord of heaven and

earth; and that I order him to render me thanks and praise for the victory I have granted him over Prester John and his nation; and thou wilt tell him from me, that I give him power to subdue the whole earth." "Sire," answered the chief, "how will the cham of Tartary believe me?" "Thou wilt tell him he shall believe in thee from the following circumstance; that thou shalt go and combat the emperor of Persia with three hundred of thy men, and that, through me, thou shalt vanquish the emperor of Persia, although he will advance to combat thee with three hundred thousand men-at-arms and upwards. But before thou thinkest of fighting with the emperor of Persia, thou wilt demand of the cham of Tartary, that he give up to thee all priests, the monks, and the commonalty who have remained of those taken in the battle with Prester John; and thou wilt believe all they shall say and show to thee, for they are my people and my servants." "Sire," replied the Tartar chief, "I shall never find my way, unless you cause me to be conducted." The king, on this, turned round, and said, "Come hither, George; go and conduct this man to his quarters, and let him be restored safe;" and instantly this chief was transported among the Tartars.

On his return, all the host of the Tartars came to see him, and made him good cheer. He very soon demanded the priests and monks from the cham of Tartary, according to the instructions he had received from the king on the mount, who were granted to him. This prince of the Tartars received very kindly the doctrines they taught, and all his people were baptized. When this ceremony was over, he selected 300, made them confess themselves and get ready, and thence marched to attack the emperor of Persia, whom he defeated, and drove out of his kingdom and possessions. He fled as far as Jerusalem; and it was he who vanquished our people, and made the count Gautier de Brienne prisoner, as you shall hear related. The subjects of this Christian prince increased so much, according to the information I had from those whom the king had sent as ambassadors to Tartary, that they counted in his army 800 chapels on wheels.

But let us now return to my principal subject. During the time the king was fortifying Cæsarea, as I have before noticed, there came to him a knight called Sir Elenars de

2 I

Seningaan, who said he had set out from the kingdom of
Norone, where he had embarked, and coasting Spain, had
passed the Straits of Morocco ; and that he had run great
hazards and suffered much evil before he could come to us.
The king retained this knight, with ten others of his companions. I heard him say, that the nights in the land of
Norone, during the summer, were so short, that you could
see in the latest part of them. When this knight became
acquainted with the country, he and his people began to hunt
the lions, many of which they took, but not without much
bodily danger.

Their manner of hunting was on horseback ; and when
they found a lion, they shot at him at a proper distance from
their bow or cross-bow. On the lion being wounded, he ran
at the first he saw, who instantly spurred his horse to a full
gallop, dropping as he fled some piece of old cloth or coverlid,
which the lion seized and tore to pieces, imagining it was the
man he was in pursuit of. As the lion was employed in tearing
the cloth, others advanced and shot at him, which made him
again pursue them : they kept dropping old cloths, and shooting at him alternately, until they killed him. Thus did they
destroy many lions.

Another most noble knight came to the king when he was
at Cæsarea, who said he was of the house of Coucy. The king
said, he was his cousin by his descent from one of the sisters of
King Philip, who had been married to the emperor of Constantinople. The king retained this knight, and nine others,
for one year ; on the expiration of which, he returned to Constantinople, whence he had come. While he was with us, I
heard him tell the king, that the emperor of Constantinople
had once formed an alliance with the king of the Commains,
to have their assistance to conquer the emperor of Greece,
whose name was Vataiche ; and he added, that the king of
the Commains, to have greater faith in the professions of the
emperor of Constantinople, caused him and their people on
both sides to be blooded, and made each drink alternately of
the other's blood, in sign of brotherhood, saying they were
now brothers of the same blood. It was thus we were forced
to do with this knight and his companions ; and our blood,
being mixed with wine, was drunk by each party, as consti-
tuting us all brothers of the same blood.

They performed another ceremony, by driving a dog between them and us, as we were divided into two bodies, and then cutting him to pieces with their swords, saying, "Let those be thus mangled who shall fail in their engagements to each other."

Another wonderful story this knight of Coucy told the king. He said, that in the country of the Commains, when a great and powerful prince died, on his decease an immense grave was made, and the dead person, most richly adorned, was seated in a magnificent chair within the grave, and the finest horse he had possessed, together with one of his officers, were let down alive in the grave. The officer, before he descended, took leave of the king and the other great personages present, when the king gave to him a large quantity of gold and silver coin, which he placed in a scarf round his neck, the king making him promise that on his arrival in the other world he would restore to him his money, which he faithfully engaged to do. After this, the king gave him a letter addressed to the first of their monarchs, in which he told him, that the bearer of it had well and faithfully served him, and on that account entreated he would properly reward him. When this was done, the grave was filled up over the corpse, the living officer, and the horse, and covered with planks well nailed together. Before night there was a considerable mound of stones piled over the grave, in memory of those whom they had interred.

When it was near Easter I left Acre, and went to visit the king at Cæsarea, where he was employed in fortifying and enclosing it. On my arrival, I found him in conversation with the legate, who had never left him during this expedition to the Holy Land. On seeing me, he quitted the legate, and coming to me, said, "Lord de Joinville, is it really true that I have only retained you until this ensuing Easter? Should it be so, I beg you will tell me how much I shall give you from this Easter to that of this time twelve months."

I replied, that I was not come to him to make such a bargain, and that I would not take more of his money; but I would offer other terms, which were, that he should promise never to fly into a passion for any thing I should say to him, which was often the case, and I engaged that I would keep my temper whenever he refused what I should ask.

2 I 2

When he heard my terms, he burst into laughter, and said that he retained me accordingly; then, taking me by the hand, he led me before the legate to his council, and repeated the convention that had been agreed to between us. Every one was joyous on hearing it, and consequently I remained.

I will now speak of the acts of justice, and the sentences of the king, which I witnessed during his stay at Cæsarea. The first was on a knight who had been caught in a house of ill fame : he gave him the alternative,* that the prostitute with whom he had been found should lead him in his shirt through the army, with a cord tied to his private parts, one end of which cord the prostitute was to hold ; or, should he not like this, he should forfeit his horse, armour, and accoutrements, and be driven from and banished the king's army. The knight preferred the loss of his horse and arms, and banishment from the army. When I saw the horse was forfeited, I requested to have him for one of my knights who was a poor gentleman ; but the king said my request was unreasonable, for that the horse was well worth from fourscore to a hundred livres, which was no small sum. I answered, " Sire, you have broken our convention in thus replying to my request." The king laughed, and said, " Lord de Joinville, you may say what you please, but you shall not put me in a passion the sooner." However, I did not get the horse for my poor gentleman.

The second act of justice I witnessed was on some of my knights who, one day, had gone to hunt the animal called an antelope, which is something like a roe-buck. The Knights Hospitallers had sallied out to meet my knights, fought with them, and did them much mischief, for which outrage I went to lay my complaints before their commander, taking with me those of my knights who had been wounded. The commander, having heard my accusation, promised to do me justice, according to the rules and customs of the Holy Land, which were, to make the brethren who had been guilty of this

---

* Matthew of Westminster relates, in the year 1253, another instance of the severity of St. Louis in the punishment of knights found guilty of crimes. He tells us, that the king having ordered a knight to be hanged, the father was so outrageous at it, that he retired to the Saracens, and, changing his religion, embraced that of Mahomet.

outrage, eat upon their cloaks, in the presence of those who had been ill-used, who should afterwards carry away their cloaks.

The commander did indeed make the guilty eat on their cloaks before me and some of my knights, but when we demanded of the commander that they should rise up, he wanted to refuse; however, he was forced to it at last; for we seated ourselves to eat with the brethren, which they would not suffer, and they were obliged to rise with us to eat with the other brethren at table, leaving us their cloaks.

Another act of justice was on a king's serjeant called Goullu, who laid his hands on one of my knights, and rudely pushed him. I went to complain of this to the king, who told me I might as well be quiet, since the serjeant had only pushed the knight. But I replied, that I would not be quiet, and would quit his service unless justice were done me; for that it was highly indecent for any serjeant to lay his hands on a knight. The king, hearing this, did me the usual justice, which was, that, according to the custom of the country, the serjeant should come to my lodgings, barefooted, and in his shirt, with a sword hanging on his wrist, when, having knelt before the knight whom he had injured, he was to offer the sword by the hilt, and say to him,—" Sir knight, I crave your mercy for having laid hands on you, and have brought this sword, which I now offer to you for you to cut off my hand, if it shall so please you." I then entreated the knight to pardon him, which he did. Several other judgments I witnessed, that were executed according to the rites and customs of the Holy Land.

You have before heard how the king had sent to inform the admirals of Egypt, that unless they made him satisfaction for the outrages they had committed, he would not abide by any truce that had been made with them. Ambassadors, in consequence, had arrived from the admirals, with letters, to assure the king that they would do all he had desired.

A day was appointed for the king and these ambassadors to meet at Jaffa, when they were to promise the king, on their oaths, that they would surrender Jerusalem up to him. In return, the king and his nobles were to swear, on their part, to aid and assist the admirals against the sultan of Damascus. It happened, that on the sultan of Damascus hearing that we

were become the allies of his enemies in Egypt, and that a
day was appointed for the ratification of the treaties at Jaffa,
he sent upwards of 20,000 Turks to guard the passes ; but
this did not prevent the king from putting himself in motion
to march to Jaffa.

When the count of Jaffa learnt that the king was coming,
he put his castle into such a good state, that it resembled a
well-defended town : at each bulwark of his castle were
posted 500 men, each with a target and penoncel with his
arms.   It was a beautiful sight to see ; for his arms were of
fine gold, with a cross-patée gules, richly worked.

We encamped on the plain, near to this castle of Jaffa,
which was situated on an island near the sea-shore ; and the
king began to fortify and enclose a village adjacent to the
castle, wherever the shore would permit it.   The king, by
way of encouraging his workmen, said to them, " I have more
than once carried the hod myself to gain a pardon."   The
admirals of Egypt were afraid to advance, on account of the
passes being so well guarded by the sultan of Damascus :
however, they sent to the king all the heads of the Christians
that had been exposed on the walls of Cairo, in compliance
with the demand which he had made for them.   Those heads
he caused to be buried in consecrated ground.   They likewise
sent him all the children they had detained, and whom they
had forced to abjure their faith to God, together with an elephant, which last the king had transported to France.

As the king and his whole army were lying before Jaffa,
fortifying themselves against those in the castle, news was
brought the king that the army of the sultan of Damascus
had taken the field, and was in ambush waiting to attack
him ; and that one of their admirals had advanced to reap
and despoil the corn of a Karet, within three leagues of the
army.   The king instantly sent thither to reconnoitre, and
followed in person ; but the admiral no sooner saw us appear
than he took to flight, pursued by some of our men full
gallop.   A young gentleman of our army came up with them,
and gallantly unhorsed two Turks with the point of his lance,
without breaking it.   The admiral perceiving that this gentleman was alone, turned about, but he received such a stroke
from him with his spear as wounded him desperately in the
body, when the young man returned to the army.

The admirals of Egypt, learning that the king and his army were at Jaffa, sent other ambassadors to him, to appoint a day when they would meet him without fail. The king having fixed on a day, they promised faithfully to be punctual in concluding all the different businesses that were in agitation. While we were waiting for this day of meeting with the admirals from Egypt, the count d'Eu came to the king bringing with him the good knight Arnold de Guynès, and his two brothers, whom, with eight other knights, the king retained in his service, and created the count d'Eu a knight, who was at that time but a very youth.

At the same time, the prince of Antioch and his mother waited on the king, to whom he paid much respect, and received them with every honour. The king made the prince of Antioch a knight, though but sixteen years old; but I never saw, at that age, so discreet a youth. When he was knighted, he requested the king to allow him and his mother a private audience, which being granted, he spoke as follows: " Sire, it is very true that my mother here present keeps me in ward, and has the power of so doing for four years to come,* by which she has the enjoyment of all things, and I have nothing. I think, however, that she ought not to suffer my lands to be wasted; and this I say because my city of Antioch is falling to ruin in her hands. I therefore supplicate you, sire, to remonstrate with her on this matter, and to prevail on her to allow me money and men that I may succour my people who are in that city, as she is bounden in justice to do."

When the king had heard the prince's demand, here monstrated so effectually with his mother that she complied with his wishes, and the prince returned to Antioch, where he did wonders. From that time, in honour to the king, he quartered his arms, which are gules with the arms of France.

* Whence it may be inferred, that in the principality of Antioch, at least in regard to princes, the same custom was followed that was universal through France, which fixed the age of majority, and the period judged proper for the uncontrolled management of estates, and the holding of fiefs, at twenty-one years. Elsewhere, according to the Assizes of Jerusalem, the age of majority for males was fifteen years, and for females twelve years complete. Neither could hold fiefs until they had attained these years, and during their minority their guardian or tutor managed their estates.

As it is very praiseworthy and pleasant to relate, in order that they may be known, the deeds and virtues of any excellent prince, we will here speak of the good count of Jaffa, Sir Gautier de Brienne. He performed in his lifetime most gallant deeds of chivalry, and kept possession of his county of Jaffa for many years, although continually attacked by the Egyptians, and without enjoying any revenues but what he gained in his excursions against the Saracens and other enemies of the Christian faith.

He once defeated a large body of infidels, who were transporting many bales of different sorts of silken cloths, which having taken and brought home, he divided the whole among his knights, without keeping any part for himself. His way of life was, after parting with his knights in the evening, to enter his chapel, where he was long employed in prayer and thanksgiving to his God. He afterwards went to bed to his wife, who was a wondrous good lady, and sister to the king of Cyprus.

You have before heard of the Tartar prince having, through the aid of God, defeated the emperor of Persia and his army of 300,000 men, with only 300, and afterwards driving him out of his kingdom. We now know the road that this emperor of Persia, whose name was Barbaquan, took. He fled to the kingdom of Jerusalem, and on his arrival did great damage to it; for he took the castle of Tabarie, that belonged to Sir Eudes de Montbeliar, and put to death as many of our people as he could find in the hospitia without Acre, and without Jaffa. After doing as much mischief as he could, he marched toward Babylon, to receive succours from the sultan of Babylon, who was to join his forces and attack us. Upon this, the barons of the country assembled with the patriarchs, and determined to offer combat to the emperor before he should form his junction with the sultan of Babylon. They sent to the sultan of La Chamelle for his assistance, who was one of the best and most loyal knights in all pagan land. He came to them, and was most honourably received at Acre, which they left together, and sat down before Jaffa.

When this army arrived at Jaffa, the chiefs entreated the count Gautier to join them, and march against the emperor of Persia. He replied, that he would cheerfully do so if the patriarch would absolve him from an excommunication which he had lately denounced against him, because he would

not surrender a tower of his castle of Jaffa called the Tower of
the Patriarch, and which the patriarch claimed as belonging to
him.   The patriarch would not absolve him: nevertheless, the
count did not fail to accompany us.   The army was divided into
three battalions: the first was given to Count Gautier, the
second to the sultan of La Chamelle, and the third to the
patriarch and barons of the country.   In the battalion of Sir
Gautier were the Knights Hospitallers.

When these three battalions had been properly arrayed,
they moved forward, and advanced within sight of the enemy;
who, on noticing their approach, formed their army likewise
into three divisions.   Count Gautier de Brienne, observing
this manœuvre, cried out, " My lords, what are we about?
We allow our enemies time to draw up their men in array,
and increase their courage by seeing us thus remain inactive.
I beg of you, in the name of God, instantly to charge them."
But not one would pay him the least attention, or advance.
He then went up to the patriarch, and again demanded absolution, but it was refused him.

With the count was a most learned man, the bishop of
Ranid, who had done many gallant deeds of chivalry in
company with the count.   The bishop said to him, " Do not
let your conscience be uneasy at this excommunication of the
patriarch, for he is very much in the wrong ; and, from the
powers I possess, I absolve you from it, in the name of the
Father, Son, and Holy Ghost.   Amen."   He then added,
" Come now, let us charge the enemy."   Sticking spurs into
their horses, they fell on the battalion of the emperor of
Persia that formed the rear, but it was too numerous for those
who had followed the count.   Very many were slain on each
side : notwithstanding this, the count was made prisoner, for
his battalion most shamefully fled, and several, from despair,
threw themselves into the sea.   One cause of this despair was
owing to a battalion of the emperor of Persia falling on that
of the sultan of La Chamelle, who fought and defended himself with such great valour, although he was much weaker in
numbers than the enemy, that out of 2,000 men there did
not remain more than fourscore, so that he was forced to make
his retreat to the castle of La Chamelle.

The emperor of Persia, concluding that his victory was
complete, resolved to besiege the sultan in his castle of La

Chamelle.   But the sultan, observing his approach, like a wary soldier, assembled his garrison, and said, "Gentlemen, if we allow ourselves to be besieged we are undone: it will be better therefore that we attack them." In consequence, he ordered out a party, badly armed, to march in the hollow of a valley, and to fall on the rear of the enemy. This was executed, and a great slaughter made of women and children. The emperor hearing a sudden noise in his rear, as he was advancing near the castle, turned about, with the intent to put a stop to it, but this was no sooner done, than the sultan made a sally with his whole garrison, and fought them so desperately, that the emperor's army, which at first consisted of 25,000 men, being attacked in front and rear, was defeated, and not one man or woman escaped being put to death.

You must know, that the emperor of Persia, before he marched to lay siege to the castle of La Chamelle, had carried the good count of Jaffa, Sir Gautier de Brienne, before the city of Jaffa, and had him hung by the arms to a gallows that was in front of the castle, declaring publicly that he would never take down their count until they should have surrendered to him the castle. As the poor count was thus suspended, he cried with a loud voice to his people never to surrender the castle for any thing they might see done to him; for should they so do. the emperor would put them all to the sword.

The emperor, perceiving he could not gain any thing more, sent Count Gautier to the sultan of Babylon as a present, with the commander of the Knights Hospitallers, and many other noble personages whom he had made prisoners. He ordered 300 of his knights to escort Count Gautier and the other prisoners as far as Babylon, which turned out fortunately for them; since by this they avoided being included in the butchery of the emperor of Persia and his army before the castle of La Chamelle, as has been before told.

When the merchants of Babylon heard that their sultan detained Count Gautier in his prisons, they assembled, and made a clamorous petition to the sultan, that he would execute the count of Jaffa, for that he had destroyed several of their companions, and had frequently done them much mischief. In compliance with their request, the sultan ordered the body of Count Gautier to be delivered to them, in order that they might take their own revenge on him. These traitorous dogs entered the prison of the count and cut him into pieces, making him thus suffer martyrdom, for which we may imagine he is now glorious in paradise.

But to return to the sultan of Damascus. He withdrew the men he had at Gadres, and, entering Egypt, made an attack on the admirals. By the fortune of war, one of his battalions defeated one of the admirals, and in another instance the chance was just the reverse. On this account, the sultan of Damascus returned to Gadres, very badly wounded in the head and other places. While he stayed there, the admiral sent him ambassadors, who made a peace between them, so that we seemed a subject of mockery to both sides; for, from that time forward, we enjoyed neither peace nor truce from the sultan, nor from the admirals. You must know, that we could never muster in our army more than about 1,400 men-at-arms fit for service.

As soon as the sultan of Damascus had concluded a peace with the admirals of Egypt, he collected all his men from Gadres, and marched his whole army, amounting to 20,000 Saracens and 10,000 Bedouins, within sight of us. They passed within two leagues, but never made any attack. The king, the master of his artillery, and the whole army were on the watch for three days, lest they should attempt to fall on us when we were unprepared.

On St. John's day, next after Easter, while the king was at sermon, one of the men attached to the master of the artillery entered the king's chapel armed and told him that the Saracens had surrounded the master of the cross-bows in the plain. I instantly requested of the king permission to go thither, to which he consented, and gave me 500 men-at-arms, whom he named. As soon as we were without the camp, and were perceived by the Saracens who were pressing round the master of the cross-bows, they retreated to an admiral that was posted on a small hillock with at least 1,000 men. The battle now began between the Saracens and the company of the master of the cross-bows; and as the admiral saw his men fail, he sent thither fresh reinforcements, in like manner did the master of the cross-bows to his men. While they were thus fighting, the legate and the barons of

the country told the king, it was great madness to allow me
to take the field; and he thereon sent to order me back, together with the master of the cross-bows.

The Turks now retired, and we returned to the army; but
many were much surprised that the Turks let us return
quietly without an attack, and accounted for it by saying,
that their horses were almost starved by having remained a
whole year at Gadres.

Some other Turks, who had left Jaffa, came to Acre, and
sent to inform the lord d'Asur, who was constable of Jerusalem, that if he did not send them 50,000 besants, they
would destroy the gardens round the town. The lord d'Asur
made answer, that he would give them nothing. Upon this,
they drew up their battalions, and advanced along the sands
so near to the town of Acre as to be within cross-bow shot.
The lord d'Asur then quitted the town and marched to the
mount, where was the church-yard of St. Nicholas, to defend
the gardens; and when the Turks approached, a body of
foot sallied out of Acre, and kept up a brisk discharge of
arrows against them; but for fear of the dangers they might
incur, the lord d'Asur sent them orders by a young knight
from Genoa to retire within the walls.

As the Genoese knight was retiring with his body of
infantry, a Saracen, suddenly moved by his courage, came
boldly up to him, and said·in his Saracenic tongue, that if
he pleased, he would tilt with him. The knight answered
with pride that he would receive him; but, when he was on
the point of beginning his course, he perceived on his left
hand eight or nine Saracens, who had halted there to see the
event of the tournament. The knight, therefore, instead of
directing his course toward the Saracen who had offered to
tilt with him, made for this troop, and striking one of them
with his lance, pierced his body through, and killed him dead
on the spot. He retreated to our men, pursued by the other
Saracens, one of whom gave him a heavy blow on his helmet
with a battle-axe. In return, the knight struck the Saracen
so severely on the head that he made his turban fly off.
You must know, that these turbans save them from many
hard blows; and for this reason, they always wear them
when they go to battle. Another Saracen thought to have
given the knight a mortal blow with his Turkish blade, but

he twisted his body in suchwise that it missed him; and
the knight, by a back-hand blow on the Saracen's arm, made
his sword fall to the ground, and he then made a good retreat
with the infantry.   These three famous actions did the
Genoese knight perform in the presence of the lord d'Asur,
and before all the principal persons of the town, who were
assembled on the battlements.

The Saracens withdrew from before Acre; and as they had
heard the king was strengthening and enclosing Sajecte, and
had but few men-at-arms with him, they marched thither.
As soon as the king learnt their intentions, not having a
sufficient force to oppose them, he retired with the master of
his artillery, and as many as the place would hold, into the
castle of Sajecte, which was very strong, and well enclosed:
few, however, could be lodged within it from the smallness
of its extent.   The Saracens arrived soon after, and entered
Sajecte without any opposition, for the walls were not then
finished, and slaughtered full 2,000 of the poorer sort of our
army: having done this, and pillaged the town, they marched
off toward Damascus.

The king was much grieved on hearing that the Saracens
had destroyed all his works at Sajecte, but he could not help
it; on the contrary, the barons of the country were rejoiced
at it; and the reason was, that the king intended, after he
had finished at Sajecte, to enclose a mound, on which formerly had stood a castle in the time of the Maccabees, and
which was on the road from Jaffa to Jerusalem.   The barons
opposed its being enclosed, because it was five leagues from
the sea, and they said, and said truly, that it could never
be victualled without certain risk of the provision being
seized on the road thither by the Saracens, as they were
more numerous.   The barons remonstrated with the king,
that it would be preferable in point of honour, and in all
other respects, to repair Sajecte, than to undertake a large
and new building so far from the sea.   To this the king
assented.

During the king's stay at Jaffa, he was told that the
sultan of Damascus would allow him to visit Jerusalem in
perfect security.   The king would most willingly have gone
thither, but his great council dissuaded him from it, as it
would leave the city in the hands of the enemy.   The lords

of the country likewse were unwilling to consent to this,
and cited to him the example of King Philip, who, when
he departed from Acre on his return to France, left the
command of his whole army to Hugh, duke of Burgundy,
grandfather to the duke lately deceased.*

In those times, and when Duke Hugh of Burgundy and
King Richard of England were residing in Acre, they
received intelligence that they might take Jerusalem on
the morrow, if they pleased; for that a large army of knights
from Egypt was gone to the assistance of the sultan of
Damascus, in his war at Neasa against the sultan of that
place. The duke of Burgundy and the king were soon
prepared to march thither; and when they had divided
their army, the king of England led the first battalion, followed by the duke of Burgundy, and by such of the king of
France's army as had remained after his departure. But
when they were near to Jerusalem, and on the point or
taking it, intelligence came from the duke of Burgundy's
division, that he had turned back merely out of envy, and
to prevent its being said, that the English had taken Jerusalem. As this intelligence was discussing, one of the king
of England's officers cried out, "Sire, sire, only come hither,
and I will shew you Jerusalem." But the king, throwing
down his arms, said with tears, and with hands uplifted to
heaven, "Ah! Lord God, I pray thee that I may never
see thy holy city of Jerusalem, since things thus happen,
and since I cannot deliver it from the hands of thine
enemies."

This example was laid before the king St. Louis, because
he was the greatest monarch in Christendom; and if he
should perform a pilgrimage to Jerusalem, without delivering
it from the enemies of God, every other king, who might
wish to make a similar pilgrimage, would think he had

---

* Henry III., duke of Burgundy, father to Duke Eudes III., and
grandfather to Duke Hugh IV., died in the year 1272. Sanuto, l. 3,
part 10, ch. 6, seems to speak of the retreat of the duke of Burgundy
with less bitterness than the lord de Joinville; for he says, that as the
Christians were advancing towards Jerusalem, the duke represented to the
French, that the whole flower of French chivalry was in his battalion;
whereas King Richard had but few in number, to whom, nevertheless, the
honour of the victory would be given, which would be to the disadvantage
and shame of France.

amply performed it without seeking to do more than the king of France had done.

This Richard, king of England, performed such deeds of prowess when he was in the Holy Land, that the Saracens, on seeing their horses frightened at a shadow or bush, cried out to them, "What, dost think King Richard is there?" This they were accustomed to say, from the many and many times he had conquered and vanquished them. In like manner, when the children of the Turks or Saracens cried, their mothers said to them, "Hush, hush! or I will bring King Richard of England to you;" and from the fright these words caused they were instantly quiet.

I must say something more of this Hugh, duke of Burgundy. He was personally brave and chivalrous, but never reputed very wise toward God or man, as appears from what has just been told of him; and, in allusion to him, the great king Philip said, when he was told that the count John de Châlons had a son whom he had christened Hugh, "May God, out of his goodness, make him a *preuhomme* as well as a *preudhomme*."* There is much difference between these two characters, for many a knight among the Christians and Saracens is bold enough, but of little discretion, who neither fears nor loves God; and it was said that God had been very gracious to that knight, who, by his actions, shewed he united both these qualities. But the person of whom I am speaking might well be called a preudhomme, for he was sufficiently bold and personally enterprising, but not mentally so, for he feared not to sin, nor to behave ill toward his God.

Of the immense sums it cost the king to enclose Jaffa, it does not become me to speak, for they were countless. He enclosed the town from one side of the sea to the other; and there were twenty-four towers, including small and great. The ditches were well scoured, and kept clean

---

* Saint Louis made this distinction between *preuhomme* and *preudhomme*. The first was valiant and personally bold; the second, prudent, discreet, having a good conscience, and the fear of God. The words *preu* and *preuhomme* are derived from the Latin *probus*, which, in the writers of the middle ages, signified a "valiant man;" and from this the French have formed their word *preux*. From this word we have formed "prousee," the English "prowess," the Spaniards "prozza," the Italians "prodezza."

both within and without. There were three gates, one of
which the legate was ordered to build, as well as the wall
that connected it with the next gate. To form some estimate of what the king's expenses might have been, I was
once asked by the legate how much I thought the gate
and wall he had erected cost him. When I replied that
I estimated the gate at five hundred livres, and the wall
three hundred, he told me I was very far from the amount,
and added, that as God might help him, the gate and
wall had cost him full thirty thousand livres. We may
guess from this sum how great was the expense for the
remainder.

When the king had finished the fortifications of Jaffa,
he was desirous of doing the same to Sajects, and repairing
its walls, to put it in a similar state to what it had been
in before the Saracens destroyed it. In consequence, he
gave orders for the march of the army thither on the festival of St. Peter and St. Paul. While the king and his
army were before the castle of Asur, he summoned his
council in the evening, and told them he was very anxious
to take from the Saracens the city of Naples, which is
called in the Holy Scriptures Samaria.

The Knights Templars, barons and admirals of the country,
advised him to it, as what he was in duty bound to do;
but added, that he ought not personally to expose himself
there, for fear of any unfortunate accident, saying that if he
were made prisoner or killed, the whole country would be
lost.

The king replied, that he would not allow his army to
march thither without his accompanying it, and from this
disagreement the enterprise was no more thought of. We
continued our march along the sands to Acre, where the king
and his whole army were lodged that night.

On the morrow, a great troop of Armenians, who were on
their pilgrimage to Jerusalem, came to me, and entreated,
through a Latin interpreter, that as I was about the king's
person, I would shew them the good king Louis. I went
to the king, and told him that a large body of people,
from Upper Armenia, going to Jerusalem, were very desirous to see him. He burst into laughter, and bade me
bring them to him. I instantly obeyed, and they followed

me eagerly. When they had seen him, they recommended him to God, as he did the same to them in return.

The next day the king and his army marched to a place called Passe-poulain,* about a league distant from Acre, where are many beautiful springs of water, with which the sugar-canes are irrigated.

When I was lodged, one of my knights said to me, " Sir, you are now much better quartered than you were before Saint Sur." Upon which another of my knights, who had fixed on my lodgings the preceding day, replied, "You are too foolhardy in thus blaming me to my lord;" and having said this, he sprang on the other knight, and seized him by the hair. Astonished at the presumption of the knight, who had thus in my presence seized his companion, I ran to them, and gave the aggressor a hard blow between the shoulders, which made him quit his hold of the knight's hair. I then ordered him to quit my lodgings instantly, for that never more, as God might help me, should he be of my household.

The knight went away making great moan to Sir Gilles le Brun, then constable of France, who shortly after came to me to entreat I would take my knight again, for that he was sorely repentant of his folly. I told him I could not do any thing until the legate had absolved me from my oath. The constable then went to the legate, told him the case, and requested him to give me absolution from the oath I had sworn; but the legate said, he had not the power to absolve me, seeing that I was justified in making such an oath, and that the knight had richly deserved it by his conduct. This story I wished to introduce into my book, as an example to all not to make any oaths without very sufficient grounds for so doing; for the wise man says, that those who swear on every occasion will probably as often forswear.

On the day following, the king marched his army before the city of Sur, which is called Thiry in the Bible. When there, the king was pressed to march and take a city hard by called Belinas; his council advised him to it, but not to go thither in person, to which, with some difficulty, he was persuaded. It was determined that the count d'Anjou should march thither, with Sir Philip de Montfort, the lord

* See note at page 466.

2 K

of Sur, Sir Gilles le Brun, constable of France, Sir Peter
the chamberlain, the masters of the Temple and of the
Hospital, and their men-at-arms.   During the night we
armed ourselves, and a little before day saw the plain in
which was situated the city of Belinas,* called in Scripture
Cæsarea Philippi.   There is within the city a beautiful
fountain named Le Jour, and on the plain before the place,
another fine spring, called Dain.   From these two springs
issue rivulets, which unite at some distance and form the
river Jordan, in which our Lord Jesus Christ was baptized.

By the advice of the count d'Anjou, and the masters of the
Templars and Hospitallers, it was ordered, that the battalion
of the king, in which I then was, with my knights, as were
also the forty knights from Champagne, whom the king had
put under my command, Sir Geoffry de Sergines, and the
other brave men that were with us, should march between the
castle and town; that the barons and landholders of the
country should enter the town on the left, the Hospitallers on
the right, and the master of the Templars, with his division,
was to enter the place from the road by which we had come.
Each body was now in motion; and as we approached the
back parts of the city we found many of our countrymen
dead, whom the Saracens had killed and thrown over the
walls.   You must know the line we were to take was very
dangerous; for, in the first place, there were three walls to
pass, and a bank so steep and broken, that no one could keep
his saddle.   On the top of this bank, which we were to ascend,
was a large body of Turks on horseback.   Perceiving that
our people were at one place breaking down the walls, I
wished to advance towards them skirmishing.   As I was
doing this, one of our men attempted to leap the wall, but he
fell under his horse, which was also thrown down.   When I
saw this I dismounted, and, taking my horse by the bridle,
ascended boldly towards the Turks; but, as God willed it,
they fled and left us the place.   On the top there was a
road out in the rock which led to the city; and the Saracens
within the place no sooner saw us masters of the rock than
they took to flight, and gave up the city without opposition
to our army.

* Called by the ancients " Paneas," and " Cæsarea Philippi." Noradin
captured it from Humphrey de Toron in the year 1177.

While I was on the top of this mount, the master of the Templars, hearing that I was in great danger, hastened to me. I had with me the Germans, who, when they saw the Turks fly for the castle, which was at some distance from the town, began to pursue them, in spite of me, and although I cried out to them they were doing wrong, for we had accomplished what we had been ordered to perform.

The castle was seated above the town, but without the suburbs, and nearly half a league up Mount Libanus. There are very high rocks to pass before you arrive at the castle ; and when the Germans found they were very rashly pursuing the Turks, who had gained the castle, well knowing all the turnings of the rocks, they returned to rejoin us ; but the Saracens, observing them retreating, dismounted, and, falling on them as they descended the rocks, gave them many severe blows with their battle-axes, insomuch that they drove them back in disorder to where I was. My men seeing the mischief the Saracens did to the Germans, whom they closely pursued, began to be frightened, and to take alarm ; but I told them that if they quitted their position I would break them, and prevent them ever after from receiving the king's pay. They replied, " Lord de Joinville, we are much worse off than you are ; for you are on horseback, and can escape when and where you please ; but we who are on foot are in the greatest danger of being killed, should the Saracens come hither." Upon this I dismounted among them, to give them more courage, and sent my war-horse to the battalion of the Templars, which was a long cross-bow-shot distant.

As the Saracens were thus driving the Germans before them, one of my knights received a bolt from a cross-bow in the throat that laid him dead at my feet, upon which another of my knights, called Sir Hugh d'Escossé, uncle to the dead knight, desired I would assist him to carry his nephew down from the mount, that he might be buried : but I refused, for the knight had joined the Germans in pursuing the Saracens, contrary to my will and orders. If, therefore, he suffered for it, I was no way to blame. So soon as Sir John de Valenciennes heard the danger we were in, and that my division was in disorder, he hastened to Sir Olivier de Termes, and the other captains from Languedoc, and addressed them, " My lords, I beg of you,

2 K 2

and indeed command, in the king's name, that you join me to assist the seneschal of Champagne."

A knight, whose name was Sir William de Beaumont, came to him, and said that I was killed; but, notwithstanding this, the good Sir Olivier de Termes did not the more spare himself, for he was determined to know the truth, whether I was alive or dead, that he might give the king certain information of it, and gallantly ascended the mount, when I went to him. Sir Olivier, when on the mount, saw the great danger we were in, and that we could not descend the way we had got up; he therefore gave us good advice, and made us descend a slope of the hill, as if we were going to Damascus, saying that the Saracens would suppose, by this manœuvre, that we meant to fall on their rear. When we had got into the plain, Sir Olivier ordered a large heap of corn, that was stacked on the ground, to be set on fire, and by this means, and our own exertions, through the good counsel of Sir Olivier de Termes, we escaped, and arrived on the morrow in safety at Sajecte, where the king was. We found the good and holy man had ordered the bodies of those Christians that were slain to be buried, and that he himself had assisted in carrying their corpses to the grave. Some of the bodies were in such a state of corruption, that divers of the carriers were obliged to stop their nostrils, but the good king never did this. When we came to him, he had caused our lodgings and quarters to be ready prepared for us.

* [" While we were before Sajette, some merchants came to the king, and brought him intelligence that the king of Tartary had taken the city of Baldac, with the apostle of the Saracens, who was lord of the town, and was called the Caliph of Baldac.

" The manner of its capture was as follows :—The king of Tartary had laid his plans with much secrecy and caution, and after he had besieged the place, sent to inform the caliph, that in order to preserve peace and be on good terms with him, he was desirous that a marriage should

---

* The chapter, which is here given, is omitted by Menard, but is contained in the Poitiers edition. As it bears every appearance of having been written by Joinville, it has been thought proper to insert it in its place.

take place between their two children. The caliph, having consulted his council, replied, that he was satisfied with the proposal. In return, the king of Tartary requested that he would send to him forty of his principal counsellors to treat of and agree to this marriage. This the caliph complied with; but the king of Tartary detained them, and sent word they were not enough, and that forty more of the richest of the caliph's subjects must also be sent for the greater security of the articles of the marriage. The caliph, believing what he said was the truth, sent him forty more, as he had desired, and even a third time the same number of his principal subjects.

"When the Tartar king had thus got six score of the best captains, and the principal and most wealthy of the caliph's subjects, he thought the remainder must consist of such common people as could not resist him, and would be unable to defend themselves.

"Upon this, he ordered the six score personages to be beheaded, and attacked the town so briskly that he took it, with the caliph its lord.

"Having gained the town, he wished to cover his disloyalty and treason by throwing the blame on the caliph, whom he confined in an iron cage. He made him fast until the last extremity, when the king came to him, and asked if he were hungry. 'Yes, indeed, am I,' replied the caliph, 'and not without cause.' The king then ordered a large golden platter filled with jewels and precious stones to be offered to him, and asked him, 'Caliph, dost thou know these rich jewels and treasure which thou seest before thee?' 'Yes,' said the caliph, for they had been his own. The king again asked, if he much loved these jewels; and on the caliph answering in the affirmative, he replied, 'Well, since then thou lovest these treasures so much, take of them as much as thou wilt, and eat them, to appease thy hunger.' The caliph said they were not food to eat. 'Now,' answered the king of Tartary, 'thou mayest at present see thy great fault; for if thou hadst given of thy treasures, which thou lovest so dearly, to subsidize soldiers in thy defence, thou mightest have held out against me; but that which thou prizedst the most has failed thee in thy need.'"]

During this time, being one day in the presence of the king, I asked his leave to make a pilgrimage to our Lady of Tortosa, which was then very much in request. Great numbers of pilgrims went thither daily, for it was said to have been the first altar erected in honour of the mother of God. Our Lady performed there many wonderful miracles; and one in particular on a poor man that was a demoniac, having lost his senses, for he was possessed by a wicked spirit. It happened, that one day he was brought to this altar of our Lady at Tortosa; and as his friends who had brought him were praying to our Lady to cure him, and restore his senses, the devil whom the poor creature had in his body replied, "Our Lady is not here but in Egypt, whither she is gone to aid the king of France and the Christians, who land this day on the Holy Land, to make war on the Pagans, who are on horseback to receive them."

What the devil had uttered was put down in writing; and when it was brought to the legate, who was with the king of France, he said to me that it was on that very day we had arrived in Egypt; and I am sure the good Lady Mary was of the utmost service to us.

The king very readily gave me leave to make this pilgrimage, and at the same time charged me to buy for him a hundred-weight of different coloured camlets, which he was desirous to give to the Cordeliers on his return to France. From this, I guessed that it would not be long before he set out on his return thither.

When I arrived at Triple,* the end of my pilgrimage, I made my offerings to God, and to our Lady of Tortosa, and afterward bought the camlets according to the king's orders. My knights, seeing me thus occupied, asked what I intended doing with so many camlets. I induced them to believe that I made these purchases to gain a profit from reselling them.

The prince of that country, hearing of our arrival, and knowing that I was come from the king's army, gave us a most honourable reception, and offered us magnificent presents. We returned him our most humble thanks, but would accept of nothing but a few relics, which I brought to the king with his camlets.

* Qy. Tripoli.

You must know, that the queen had heard that I had been on a pilgrimage, and had brought back some relics. I sent her by one of my knights four pieces of the camlets which I had purchased; and when the knight entered her apartment, she cast herself on her knees before the camlets, that were wrapped up in a towel, and the knight, seeing the queen do this, flung himself on his knees also. The queen, observing him, said, " Rise, sir knight, it does not become you to kneel, who are the bearer of such holy relics." My knight replied, that it was not relics, but camlets, that he had brought as a present from me. When the queen and her ladies heard this, they burst into laughter, and the queen said, " Sir knight, the deuce take your lord for having made me kneel to a parcel of camlets."*

Soon after the king's arrival at Sajecte, he received the news of the death of the queen his mother, which caused him such grief that he was two days in his chamber without suffering any one to see him. On the third, he sent one of his valets to seek me; and, on my presenting myself, he extended his arms, and said, " Ah, seneschal, I have lost my mother!"

" Sir," replied I, " I am not surprised at it, for you know there must come a time for her death; but I am indeed greatly so, that you who are considered as so great a prince should so outrageously grieve; for you know," continued I, " that the wise man says, whatever grief the valiant man suffers in his mind, he ought not to shew it on his countenance, nor let it be publicly known, for he that does so gives pleasure to his enemies and sorrow to his friends."

I thus appeased him a little; and he gave orders that most magnificent religious services should be performed in the country in which he then was, for the salvation of the soul of the late queen. He sent likewise to France a load of jewels and precious stones to the national churches, with

* After these words, what follows is in the edition of Poitiers: " I forgot to say, that whilst the king was at Sajette, a great person in Egypt sent him a most curious stone, the like was never seen. It split into scales, and when one scale was taken off, there was seen the perfect resemblance of a sea-fish was deeply impressed between two stones, to which neither colour nor form was deficient, in similar matter to the stone. The king gave me a part of it, and, when it was divided, there was the exact form and colour of a tench, such as it is in nature."

letters from him to entreat they would pray to God for him,
and for the soul of the late queen his mother.

[The Poitiers edition adds : "After I had quitted the apartment of the king, the lady Mary de Bonnes-Vertus came
to entreat that I would wait on the queen to comfort her,
for that she was in marvellous great grief. When I was in
her chamber, and saw her weeping so very bitterly, I could
not refrain from saying to her, that the proverb was very
true which said, ' We ought never to believe in the tears of
women,' for that the lamentation she was making was for
the woman she hated the most in this world. She replied,
that it was not for her she wept, but for the extreme melancholy of the king, as well as for her daughter, afterwards
queen of Navarre, who would now be under the guardian-
ship of men. The reason why the queen disliked the queen
dowager, was the continued rudeness of her behaviour to
her ; for she would not suffer her son to keep company with
his queen, and prevented it as much as lay in her power.
When the king made any excursions through his kingdom,
in company with the two queens, Queen Blanche had him
separated from his queen, and they were never lodged in
the same house. It happened one day, during a stay which
the court made at Pontoise, that the king was lodged in
the story above the apartments of his queen, and he had
given orders to his ushers of the chamber, whenever he
should go to lie with his queen, and his mother was coming
to his, or to the queen's chamber, to beat the dogs until
they cried out : when the king heard them, he hid himself
from his mother. Now one day Queen Blanche went to
the queen's chamber, where her son had gone before to comfort her, for she was in great danger of death, from a bad
delivery, and he hid himself behind the queen to avoid
being seen ; but his mother perceived him, and, taking him
by the hand, said, ' Come along : you will do no good
here,' and put him out of the chamber. Queen Margaret
observing this, and that she was to be separated from her
husband, cried aloud, ' Alas ! will you not allow me to see
my lord, neither when I am alive nor dying?' In uttering
these words she fainted, and her attendants thought she
was dead : the king likewise believed it, and instantly returned to her, and recovered her from her fainting-fit."]

Not long after this the king attended to his affairs, but was undetermined whether to remain longer where he was, or to return to France. While he was thus hesitating, and during his stay at Sajecte, which he had almost enclosed, he called the legate, who had accompanied it, and bade him make many processions, requesting God to enlighten him, and let him know his will, whether he should return to France or remain in Palestine. Some little time after these processions were over, the principal persons of the country and myself were going to amuse ourselves in a meadow, when the king called me to him. The legate was with him, who said to me, in the presence of the king,—" Seneschal, the king is very much satisfied with the good and agreeable services you have done him, and earnestly wishes for your honour and advancement. He orders me to tell you, as he knows it will give you much pleasure at heart, that his intention is to return to France on this side Easter that is coming."

I replied, " May our Lord induce him to act alway according to his will." When I had said this, the legate left the king, and desired I would accompany him to his lodgings, to which I willingly assented. He made me enter his closet, when, bursting into tears, he clasped my hands and said,— " Seneschal, I am greatly rejoiced, and thank God for that you have thus escaped from the imminent dangers you have been in during your stay in this country; and, on the other hand, I am much concerned and grieved at my heart, that I shall be forced to quit such good and religious companions, to return among such a set of wretches as the court of Rome consists of. But I will tell you that my intention is to remain one year, after your departure, at Acre, to expend all money in enclosing the suburbs of that place, which I shall continue to do as long as my means shall last, to avoid having any reproaches made against me."

On my return to the king the next day, he commanded me to arm myself and my knights on the morrow. When I was armed, I asked him what was his pleasure for us to do. He then said, to escort the queen and his children to Sur, which was full seven leagues distant. I would not say any thing against this, in spite of the great dangers we should run, for at that time we had neither peace nor truce with the

Egyptians, nor with those of Damascus. We set out, and through the mercy of God, arrived in the evening at Sur without any accident or hinderance.

Soon after the patriarchs and barons of the country who had for a length of time attended on the king, seeing that he had enclosed Sajecte with high walls and large towers, and that the ditches were well cleansed within and without, waited on him to render him their most humble thanks and praise for the great good and the honour he had conferred on Palestine ; for he had rebuilt, from the ground, Sajecte, Cæsarea, Jaffa, and had greatly strengthened the city of Acre with high walls and towers.

They addressed him as follows : " Sire, we perceive very clearly that your stay with us cannot be much prolonged, with any kind of profit to the kingdom of Jerusalem. We would therefore advise you to go to Acre, where you may make your preparations for departure during this ensuing Lent, so that you may secure a safe passage to France."

The king followed their counsel and went to Sur, whither we had escorted the queen and his family, and at the beginning of Lent we all arrived at Acre.

During the whole of Lent, the king was making his fleet ready for his return to France, which consisted of fourteen ships and galleys. On the vigil of St. Mark, after Easter, the king and queen embarked on board their ship, and put to sea, having a favourable wind for their departure. The king told me he was born on St. Mark's day ; and I replied, that he might well say he had been born again on St. Mark's day, in thus escaping from such a pestilent land, where he had remained so long.

On the Saturday following, we arrived at the island of Cyprus ; and there was a mountain hard by the island, called the Mountain of the Cross, which marked at a great distance the situation of the island. On this Saturday, about vespers, there came on such a thick fog from the land that our sailors thought themselves at a greater distance from the shore than they were, for they lost sight of this mountain ; and it happened, that as they were eager to reach the shore, they struck on the extremity of a sandbank which was clear of the island : fortunately it was so, for had we not struck on this bank, we should have run against some dangerous half-covered rocks, and should have been in the utmost peril of being all drowned. We were even now in much danger. All thought themselves lost, and that the vessel must be wrecked; but a sailor, casting the lead, found we were no longer aground, on which every one rejoiced and returned thanks to God.

Many on board were kneeling before the holy sacrament that was on the ship's altar, adoring and begging pardon of God, for each expected nothing but death. When day appeared, we saw the rocks on which we should have struck, had it not been for the good fortune of the sandbank. In the morning the king sent for the principal of the ships' captains, who brought with them four divers, fellows who dive naked to the bottom of the sea like fish. The captains ordered the divers to plunge into the sea at this place, who did so, and passed under the king's ship. On their reappearance on the opposite side to where they had gone down, we heard each ask the other what he had found. They all reported, that on the part where our vessel had struck on the sand three fathoms of its keel had been beaten off, which account surprised very much the king, and all who heard it. The king asked the mariners for their advice on the occasion, who replied,—"Sire, if you will believe us, you must remove from this ship to another. We know well, that since the keel has suffered such damage, all the ribs of the vessel will have been started, and we very much fear that she will be unable to bear the sea, should there be any wind, without danger of sinking. When you sailed from France, we saw an accident just similar happen to a vessel which had struck on a bank; and when she was afterward in a gale of wind she could not withstand it, but opened her sides and was lost; all on board perished but a young woman, with an infant child in her arms, who had accidentally remained on one of the ship's timbers, and was saved."

The king having listened to what the mariners said, and the example they brought, I testified to the truth of it; for I had seen the woman and child, who had arrived at the city of Baphe, in the house of the count de Joigny, who had all care taken of them for the honour of God.

The king summoned his council to deliberate on what was to be done, and they unanimously agreed to what the mariners had proposed ; but the king called the captains again to him, and asked them, on the faith and loyalty which they owed him, whether, if the ship were their own, and full of merchandise, they would quit it.   They all said they would not ; for that they would prefer risking their lives to the loss of such a vessel, which would cost them from forty to fifty thousand livres.   " Why then," said the king, " do you advise me to quit her ? "   They replied,—" Sire, you and we are two different sorts of things ; for there is no sum, however great, that can be had in compensation for the loss of yourself, the queen, and your three children ; and we will never advise that you should put yourself in such risk."

" Now," said the king, " I will tell you what I think of the matter.   Suppose I quit this ship, there are five or six hundred persons on board, who will remain in the island of Cyprus for fear of the danger that may happen to them should they stay on board ; and there is not," added the king, " one among them who is more attached to his own person, than I am myself, and if we land they will lose all hopes of returning to their own country.   I therefore declare, I will rather put myself, the queen, and my children, in this danger, under the good providence of God, than make such numbers of people suffer as are now with me."

The great mischief that would have happened, if the king had landed, was very apparent, from what befel that puissant knight Sir Olivier de Termes, who was on board the king's ship.   Sir Olivier was one of the bravest knights, and most enterprising men of all I was acquainted with in the Holy Land ; he was, however, afraid of remaining on board, and therefore went on shore ; but, rich and mighty as he was, he met with so many difficulties, that it was upwards of a year and a half before he could again rejoin the king.   Now, if so rich a man found so many difficulties, what would the number of inferior personages have done, who could not have money to defray their expenses and support themselves ?

After God had saved us from this peril, near the island of Cyprus, another befel us ; for there arose so violent a storm, that in spite of all our efforts we were driven back again to the same island, after we had long left it.   The sailors cast four anchors in vain, for the vessel could not be stopped until they had thrown out the fifth, which held.   All the partitions of the king's cabin were obliged to be destroyed ; and so high was the wind, that no one dared stay therein for fear of being blown overboard.

The queen came into the king's chamber, thinking to meet him there, but found only Sir Gilles le Brun, constable of France, and myself, who were lying down. On seeing her, I asked what she wished. She said, she wanted the king, to beg he would make some vows to God and his saints, that we might be delivered from this storm, for that the sailors had assured her we were in the greatest danger of being drowned. I replied to her,—"Madam, vow to make a pilgrimage to my lord Saint Nicholas, at Varengeville, and I promise you that God will restore us in safety to France." "Ah ! seneschal," answered she, "I am afraid the king will not permit me to make this pilgrimage for the accomplishment of my vow." "At least, then, madam, promise him, that if God shall restore you in safety to France, you will give him a silver ship of the value of five marcs, for the king, yourself, and your children ; and if you shall do this, I assure you that, at the entreaties of St. Nicholas, God will grant you a successful voyage ; and I vow for myself, that, on my return to Joinville, I will make a pilgrimage to his shrine barefooted."

Upon this, she made a vow of a silver ship to St. Nicholas, and demanded that I would be her pledge for her due performance of it, to which I assented. She shortly after came to us, to say that God, at the intercession of St. Nicholas, had delivered us from this peril.

On the queen's return to France, she caused the ship to be made that she had vowed, and had introduced in it the king, herself, her three children, with the sailors, mast and steerage, all of silver, and the ropes of silver thread. This ship she sent me with orders to convey it to the shrine of my lord Saint Nicholas, which I did. I saw it there a long time afterward, when we conducted the king's sister to the emperor of Germany.

We will return to our principal subject, and continue the account of our voyage home. When the king perceived we had escaped from these two perils, he rose from a bench of the vessel, and said to me,—"Now see, seneschal, if God has not clearly manifested his great power, when by a blast of one

of these four winds, the king, the queen, our children, and so
many other persons, might have been drowned?   For our deliverance from this danger, we ought to pay him our sincerest
thanks."

The good king talked incessantly of the imminent danger
we had been in, and of the power which God had displayed.
He said to me, " Seneschal, when such tribulations befal mankind, or other misfortunes of sickness, the saints say they are
threatenings from our Lord.   I therefore maintain, that the
perils we have been in are the same kind of threatening from
our Lord, who might say, ' Now consider how very easily I
might have suffered you all to be drowned, had I so willed
it.'   "For this reason," continued the holy king, " we should
examine ourselves well that there be nothing in our conduct
displeasing to God our Creator ; and whenever we may find
there is any thing wrong, we ought instantly to make ourselves
clear of it.   When we thus act, God will love us and preserve us from all perils; but, should we follow a contrary behaviour after having noticed these menaces, he will afflict us
with some grievous malady, perhaps death, and permit us to
descend to hell, without hope of redemption."

The good and holy king continued,—" Seneschal, that
good man Job said to God, ' Lord God, wherefore dost thou
afflict us ? for if thou destroy us, thou wilt not be the poorer ;
and if thou wert to call us all to thee, thou wouldst not be
more powerful nor   more   rich.'   Whence we may see,"
added he, " that the menaces of God are uttered against us
from his great love to us, and for our welfare, not for his own ;
that we may the more clearly discover our faults and de-
merits, and purify our consciences from all that may be displeasing to him.   Let us therefore act in this manner, and we
shall be the wiser and better for it."

After having taken water on board at the island of Cyprus,
and some other necessary articles, we again set sail when the
tempest had ceased, and saw another island called Lampedosa.*   We landed on it, and catched a great many rabbits.

* This is the island of Lampedosa, called by Ptolemy *Lapadusa*, by
the Italians *Lampadousa*, and by Ariosto in his fourth canto *Lipadusa*,
who represents it as being uninhabited, as well as the lord de Joinville.
It is 100 miles distant from Malta.   Geographers remark, there is at
present a church called Sancta Maria de Lampedusa, divided into two
parts, as described by our author.

We found there a hermitage among the rocks, with a handsome garden planted with olives, figs, vines, and other fruittrees, with a fine spring of water, that ran through it. The king and his company went to the upper part of the garden, where was an oratory, the roof of which was painted white, with a red cross in the centre. In another chamber, more retired, we found two dead bodies with their hands on their breasts, and only the ribs which held them together. These bodies were laid towards the east, as is the usual custom at interments.

When we had seen and examined every thing, the king and his company returned on shipboard; but one of our sailors was missing, and the captain, after considering a while, said he guessed who it was, and that it was one who was desirous of living there henceforward as a hermit. The king, hearing this, ordered three sacks of biscuit to be left on the shore of this island, in order that the sailor might find them, and they might serve for his sustenance.

[The Poitiers edition to this adds: "Afterward, in the course of our voyage, we passed another island, called Pantaleone, which was peopled with Saracens, a part of whom were subject to the king of Sicily, and part to the king of Tunis. When we first saw this island at a distance, the queen entreated the king to have the goodness to order three galleys to bring fruit for her children, which he did, commanding them to make haste, that they might meet him when he should pass the island.

"It fell out, that when the king was opposite to the port of this island, he could not see his galleys. The sailors, to his questions about them, answered, 'that very probably the Saracens had captured them and their crews; but, sire, we would not advise you to wait for them, for you are near the kingdoms of Sicily and Tunis, neither of whose kings bears you any great love; and if you will allow us to make sail, we will, before night, place you out of danger from them, for we shall, in a short time, have passed the straits.' 'In truth,' replied the king, 'I shall not follow your advice, but order you to turn the helm, that we may seek our people.' And, happen what would, we were obliged so to do, and thus lost full eight days in waiting for them, on account of their gluttony, which they were impatient to satisfy.

" This island, which is here called ' Pantaleone,' is that
named by geographers ' Pantalarea,' situated between Sicily
and Africa, pretty near to Sousa, a town in the kingdom
of Tunis.   It belongs to the king of Spain, and is subject to
the viceroy of Sicily.   The inhabitants, although Catholic
Christians, wear the dress and speak the language of the
Moors."]

Shortly after, an accident happened on board the ship of
the lord d'Argones, one of the most powerful lords of Provence.
He was annoyed one morning in bed by the rays of the sun
darting on his eyes through a hole in the vessel, and calling
one of his esquires, ordered him to stop the hole.   The esquire,
finding he could not stop it withinside, attempted to do it
without, but his foot slipping, he fell into the sea.   The ship
kept on her way, and there was not the smallest boat alongside to succour him.   We, who were in the king's ship, saw
him, but as we were half a league off, we thought it was
some piece of furniture that had fallen into the sea, for the
esquire did not attempt to save himself, nor to move.   When
we came nearer, one of the king's boats took him up, and
brought him on board our vessel, when he related his accident.   We asked him why he did not attempt to save himself
by swimming, nor call out to the other ships for help.   He
said he had no occasion so to do, for, as he fell into the sea,
he exclaimed, " Our Lady of Valbert ! " and that she had
supported him by his shoulders until the king's galley came to
him.   In honour of the blessed Virgin Mary, and to per-
petuate this miracle, I had it painted in my chapel of Joinville, and also on the windows of the church of Blecourt.

At the end of ten weeks that we had been at sea, we
arrived in the port of Hieres, in front of the castle that
belonged to the count de Provence, afterward king of Sicily.

The queen, and the whole of the council, advised the king
to disembark there, as it was on his brother's land ; but he
declared he would not land before he came to Aigues
Mortes, which was his own territory.   On this difference,
the king detained us there Wednesday and Thursday, without
any one being able to prevail on him to land.   On the Friday,
as he was seated on one of the benches of the ship, he called
me to him, and demanded my opinion, whether he ought
to land or not.   I replied, " Sire, it seems to me that you

ought to land; for Madame de Bourbon, being once in this
very port, and unwilling to land, put again to sea, to disembark at Aigues Mortes, but she was tossed about for upwards
of seven weeks before she could make that harbour." Upon
this, the king consented to follow my advice, and landed at
Hieres, to the great joy of the queen and all on board.

The king, the queen, and their children took up their residence in the castle of Hieres until horses should be provided
for the further continuance of their journey. The abbot of
Cluny, who was afterward bishop of Olive, sent the king two
palfreys; one for himself, and the other for the queen. It
was said at the time, that they were each well worth 500
livres. When the king had accepted of these two fine horses,
the abbot requested an audience of him on the morrow, on the
subject of his affairs. This was granted, and the next day
the abbot conversed a long time with the king, who listened
to him very attentively.

When the abbot was gone, I asked the king if he would
answer a question I wished to put to him. On his replying
in the affirmative, I said, "Sire, is it not true that you have
thus long listened to the abbot for the sake of the horses
he gave you?" The king said, "It was certainly so." I
then continued, that I had asked the question, that he might
forbid, on his return to France, those of his council, on their
oaths, to receive the smallest gifts from any one who had
business to transact in his presence; "for be assured," added
I, "that if they take presents, they will listen and attend to
the givers, even longer than you have done to the abbot
of Cluny." The king, calling his council, told them the
request I had made, and the reason for my making it. His
council, however, said that I had given very excellent
advice.

While we were at Hieres we heard of a very good man,
a Cordelier friar, who went about the country preaching: his
name was Father Hugh. The king being desirous of hearing and seeing him, the day he came to Hieres, we went out
to meet him, and saw a great company of men and women
following him on foot. On his arrival in the town, the king
directed him to preach, and his first sermon was against the
clergy, whom he blamed for being in such numbers with
the king, saying they were not in a situation to save their

souls, or that the Scriptures lied. This was true; for the Scriptures do say that a monk cannot live out of his cloister, without falling into deadly sins, any more than fish can live out of water without dying. The reason is plain; for the religious, who follow the king's court, eat and drink many meats and wines which they would not do were they resident in their cloisters, and this luxurious living induces them more to sin than if they led the austere life of a convent.

He afterwards addressed the king, and pointed out to him, that if he wished to live beloved and in peace with his people, he must be just and upright. He said, he had carefully perused the Bible and other holy books, and had always found, that among princes, whether Christians or infidels, no kingdoms had ever been excited to war against their lords, but through want of proper justice being done to the subject. "The king, therefore," added the Cordelier, "must carefully have justice administered equally to every one of his subjects, that he may live among them in peace and tranquillity to his last day, and that God may not deprive him of his kingdom with dishonour and shame.

The king had him several times entreated to live with him during his stay in Provence; but he replied that he would not on any account remain in the company of the king. This Cordelier only stayed with us one day, and on the morrow departed. I have since heard that his body is buried at Marseilles, where it performs many fine miracles.

After this, the king set out from Hieres, and came to the city of Aix in Provence, in honour of the blessed Magdalen, who is interred a short day's journey off. We visited the place of Le Baume, which is a deep cave in a rock, wherein, it is said, the holy Magdalen resided for a long time, at a hermitage. We passed the Rhône at Beaucaire; and when the king was in his own realm I took my leave of him, and went to my niece the dauphiness of Viennois, thence to my uncle's the count de Châlons, and to the count of Burgundy his son, whence I went to Joinville.

Having made a short stay there, I set out to meet the king, whom I found at Soissons. On my arrival, he received me with such joy as surprised every one. I met there Count John of Brittany, and his wife, the daughter of King Thibault. On account of the dispute that was between the king of Navarre and the heiress of Champagne, for some claims the king of Navarre pretended to have on the country of Champagne, the king ordered them all to Paris, that each side might be heard, and justice properly done between them.

At this parliament King Thibault of Navarre demanded in marriage Isabella, the king's daughter; and they had brought me with them that I might in suitable terms make this proposal of marriage, for they had observed the high favour I was in with the king when at Soissons. I went purposely to speak on this subject to the king, who replied, "Seneschal, go first and make peace with the count of Brittany, and when that is done, we will settle the marriage." I answered, "Sire, you should not neglect this matter on any account." But he said, he would not marry his daughter without the consent of his barons, nor until peace were concluded with the count of Brittany.

I immediately returned to Queen Margaret of Navarre, the king her son, and their council, to tell them the king's answer: which having heard, they set about concluding a peace with all diligence with the count of Brittany; and when that was done, the king gave his daughter Isabella in marriage to the king of Navarre. The wedding was celebrated with pomp and magnificence at Melun, whence King Thibault conducted her to Provins, where they were most splendidly received by the barons.

I will now speak of the state and mode of living of the king, after his return from Palestine. In regard to his dress, he would never more wear minever or squirrel furs, nor scarlet robes, nor gilt spurs, nor use stirrups. His dress was of camlet or Persian, and the fur trimmings of his robes were the skins of garnutes or the legs of hares. He was very sober at his meals, and never ordered any thing particular or delicate to be cooked for him, but took patiently whatever was set before him. He mixed his wine with water according to its strength, and drank but one glass. He had commonly at his meals many poor persons behind his chair, whom he fed, and then ordered money to be given to them. After dinner, he had his chaplains who said grace for him; and, when any noble person was at table with him, he was an excellent companion, and very friendly. He was considered

2 z 2

as by far the wisest of any in his council ; and as a proof of
his wisdom, whenever any thing occurred that demanded
immediate attention, he never waited for his council, but gave
a speedy and decided answer.

Soon after, the good king St. Louis negotiated so successfully that he prevailed on the king and queen of England to
come to France with their children to conclude a peace.   His
council, however, were much against this peace, and said to
him, " Sire, we marvel greatly how you can consent to the
king of England keeping so large a tract of your territories,
which your predecessors have conquered from him for ill
conduct, and which it seems you have not duly considered,
nor will he be any way grateful for it."

To this the king answered, that he was well aware the king
of England and his predecessor had mostly forfeited the lands
he held, and that he never meant to restore any thing but
what he was in justice bounden to do.   But he should make
this restoration in order to confirm and strengthen that union
which ought to exist between them and their children, who
were cousins-german.   The king added, " And by thus
acting, I think I shall do a very good work ; for, in the first
place, I shall establish a peace, and shall then make him my
vassal, which he is not yet, as he has never done me homage."

The king, St. Louis, was the man in the world who
laboured most to maintain peace and concord among his subjects, more especially between the princes and barons of his
realm, in particular between my uncle, the count de Châlons,
and his son, the count of Burgundy, who carried on a violent
war after our return from Palestine.   To make a peace between
the father and son, he sent several of his council, at his own
costs and charges, into Burgundy, and took such pains, that
at length he concluded a peace between them.   Through his
interference, in like manner, was peace made between the
second king Thibault of Navarre, and the counts of Châlons
and Burgundy, who carried on a very disastrous war ; but he
sent part of his council thither, who appeased their differences,
and concluded a peace.

After this peace another serious war broke out between
Count Thibault de Bar and the count of Luxembourg, who
had married his sister.   They fought a duel with each other
below Pigny, when the count de Bar made prisoner the count

de Luxembourg, and won the castle of Ligney, that belonged
to the latter in right of his wife. To put an end to this
war, the king, at his own expense, sent thither his chamberlain, the lord Perron, in whom, of all his courtiers, he put the
greatest confidence, who, in conjunction with the king,
laboured so effectually that peace was restored.

His council sometimes reproved him for the great pains he
took to make up the quarrels of foreigners, for that he acted
wrong in preventing them from making war on each other,
as peace would in consequence be more securely maintained.
The king, in answer, told them, they did not advise what was
right ; " for," added he, " if the princes and great barons,
whose territories join mine, perceive that I suffer them to
make war on each other with indifference, they may say
among themselves, that the king of France allows them thus
to act, through malice and ingratitude, and on that account
they may unite and make an attack on my kingdom, which
may suffer from it ; and I shall, besides, incur the anger of
God, who expressly says, ' Blessed are peacemakers, for theirs
is the kingdom of heaven.'"

The Burgundians and Lorrainers perceiving so much
goodness in the king, and the great pains he took to keep them
at peace, had such an affection for him that they were willing
to obey his commands, and with much pleasure pleaded their
private disputes in his presence. I saw them frequently come
on this business to Paris, to Rheims, to Melun and elsewhere,
as the king might happen to be.

The good king loved God and the blessed Virgin with such
sincerity, that he severely punished every one that was guilty
of villanous swearing, or of having used any indecent or
beastly expression. I saw him once at Cæsarea order a silversmith to be pilloried* in his shirt and breeches, to the disgrace
of the criminal ; and I heard that, after his return from
Palestine, while I was at Joinville, he caused a citizen of
Paris to be burnt, and marked with a hot iron on the nose and
under-lip, for having blasphemed. I heard also, from the
king's own mouth, that he would willingly be seared with a

* This ladder of punishment was used in ancient times, and, according
to the Glossary of Du Cange, is similar to our pillory. The criminal
was forced to mount it, and be exposed to public view, to make him
suffer the shame his crime deserved.

red-hot iron, and he was little able to bear such an operation, if he could banish from his kingdom all blasphemies and swearings.

I have been constantly with him for twenty-two years, but never in my life, for all the passions I have seen him in, did I hear him swear or blaspheme God, his holy mother, or any of the saints. When he wished to affirm any thing, he said, " Truly it is so ;" or, " In truth, it is not so." It was very clear that on no earthly consideration would he deny his God; for when the sultan and admirals of Egypt wanted to make that the condition, should he break the treaty, he would never consent ; and when he was told this was the last proposal of the Turks, he replied, that he would rather die than commit such a crime.

I never heard him name or mention the word devil,* if it was not in some book that made it necessary ; and it is very disgraceful to the princes and kingdom of France to suffer it, and hear the name ; for you will see that in any dispute one will not say three words to another in abuse, but he will add, " Go to the devil," or other bad words. Now it is very shocking thus to send man or woman to the devil, when they are by baptism become the creatures of God. In my castle of Joinville, whoever makes use of this word is instantly buffeted, and the frequency of bad language is abolished there.

The holy king once asked me if I washed the feet of the poor on Thursday before Easter. I said I did not, for that I did not think it very becoming such a person as I was. The good king instantly replied, ' Ah, Lord de Joinville, you ought not to disdain nor think unbecoming that which God has done for our example, when he washed the feet of his apostles, he who was their Lord and Master. I believe you would very unwillingly perform what the king of England, now with us,

---

* Our first Christians, and the devout who served God, held the devil in such abhorrence, as the enemy of mankind, that they were scrupulous even of naming him. It is for this reason that we find the fathers of the church have affected to call him the wicked one, by simply naming him Malus. Several imagine that this is understood in the words of the Lord's prayer, " Deliver us from evil." St. Chrysostom thinks so, with Euthymius, Theophylactes, Origen, and others, on this prayer. Our ancient poets call him almost always Maufez, because he does evil, and is the author of it ; or because he is deformed and ill made, whence we have the word mauvais at present in use.

does.   On this Holy Thursday, he washes the feet of lepers,
and then kisses them."

Before this good king went to bed he was often accustomed
to have his children brought to him, and then related to them
the brilliant actions and sayings of kings and other ancient
princes, telling them to retain them well in their memory, to
serve as examples.   In like manner, he told them the deeds of
wicked men, who, by their luxury, rapine, avarice, and pride,
had lost their honours and kingdoms, and that their deaths
had been unfortunate.   " Such things," added the king, " you
will cautiously avoid doing like them, that you may not fall
under the displeasure of God."   He likewise taught them
their prayers to the blessed Virgin, and heard them daily
repeat the prayers for the day, according to the seasons, in
order to accustom them to do the same when they should be
more advanced in years, and govern their country.

He was a most liberal almsgiver; for, whenever he travelled through his kingdom, he always visited the churches,
the infirmaries, and hospitals.   He sought out distressed
gentlemen, poor widows, and unmarried girls without fortune ;
and every place where he found distress or want, he gave
large sums of money.   To poor beggars he ordered meat and
drink, and I have often seen him cut the bread and pour out
drink to them himself.

During his reign, he built and endowed several churches,
monasteries, and abbeys ; such as Reaumont, the abbey of St.
Anthony at Paris, the abbey Du Lis, the abbey De Malbois-
son, and many more for the Cordeliers and Friars-preachers.
He also erected the Maison Dieu at Pontoise, that of Vernon,
the house of the Quinze-vingts at Paris, and the abbey of
Cordeliers at St. Cloud, which the princess Isabella, his sister,
founded at his request.   When any benefices became vacant
and were in his gift, before he provided for them, he made
strict inquiry of proper persons respecting the situation and
condition of those who asked for them, and whether they were
men of letters and well informed.   He would never allow
those to whom he gave benefices to hold more than was becoming their state, and he never gave them without having
duly consulted those well qualified to give him good advice.

You will see below how he punished his bailiffs, judges,
and other officers when in fault, and the handsome new esta-

blishments he formed for the benefit of his kingdom of France. His ordinance runs thus:

"We Louis, by the grace of God, king of France, order that all bailiffs, provosts, mayors, judges, receivers, and others in whatever office they may be, do each henceforth make oath that, during the time he shall hold such office, he will do strict justice to every one, without exception of person, as well to the poor as to the rich, to the stranger as well as to the resident, and will follow such laws and customs as have been found good and approved of. Should any one act contrary to his oath, we will and expressly command that he be punished in body and estate, according to the exigency of the case. We reserve to ourselves, and to our own discretion, the punishments that may be due to our bailiffs, judges, and other officers, and also to those employed under them.

"Our treasurers, receivers, provosts, auditors of accounts, and other officers concerned in our finances, will swear that they will well and loyally guard our rents and domains, with all our rights, liberties, and privileges, without suffering them in any way to be infringed upon or abridged.

"They will not themselves accept of any gift or present, nor permit their clerks or other persons under them to do the same, nor consent to any presents being made to their wives or children, in order to gain their favour. Should any gift have been made, they will instantly and without delay restore it, or have it sent back. In like manner, they will not make any presents to any persons their superiors, to gain their favour and support. They will also swear, that whenever they shall discover any officers, sergeants, or others, who are robbers, and abuse their offices, for which they ought to be dismissed from them, and our service, they will not conceal or disguise their guilt for any gift, favour, promise, or otherwise; but that they will punish and correct them, as the case may require, with good faith and equity, and without any malice.

"We will, that the aforesaid oaths be taken before us, and that afterward they be proclaimed publicly before clerks, knights, lords, and the commonalty, in order that they may be better observed, and that those who have taken these oaths may be afraid of committing the sin of perjury, not only for the punishment that may ensue at our hands, but for fear of public disgrace and the judgment of God hereafter.

"We likewise forbid and prohibit all our said bailiffs, provosts, mayors, judges, and others our officers, either to swear by or blaspheme the name of God, his holy mother, or the blessed saints in paradise, or to game with dice, or to frequent taverns, or houses of ill-fame, under penalty of deprivation of office and undergoing such other punishment as their crimes may deserve. We order, likewise, that common prostitutes and women too free of their favours, be put out of private houses, and separated from others of a different behaviour; and that no person let to hire any house or habitation for them to carry on their libidinous trade and vicious habits of luxury.

"We also forbid and prohibit any of our bailiffs, provosts, mayors, or others our officers, to have the boldness to acquire or purchase, by themselves or others, any lands or possessions in the districts over which they have been appointed to administer justice, without our being previously made acquainted therewith, and our leave and license first had and obtained. Should they act otherwise, we will and declare that such lands and possessions, so acquired, be confiscated to our benefit.

"In like manner, we forbid any of our aforesaid superior officers, so long as they shall be in our service, to marry their sons, daughters, or other relations they may have, to any persons within their bailiwicks or district, without our special permission first obtained. We also include within the above prohibitions of acquisitions of property and marriage, all other inferior judges, or other subalterns of office.

"We likewise forbid any bailiff, provost, or other, to have too great a number of sergeants or beadles, so that the people may be aggrieved thereat.

"We also forbid any of our subjects to be personally arrested or imprisoned for any debts of theirs, but what may be owed to the crown, and that any fine be levied on any of our subjects for debt.

"We likewise ordain that those who may hold our provostships, viscountships, or other offices, do not sell nor transfer them to any other person without our consent. And when several are in one office, we order that one of them do its duties for all.

" We forbid, likewise, any disseizure of possession without assigning a proper reason for it, or having our special commands to that purpose. We order that there be no additional taxes raised, nor any other imposts or customs whatever.

" We will that our bailiffs, provosts, mayors, viscounts, and other our officers, who shall at any time be deprived of their offices, and dismissed our service, do remain after such dismission forty days within the districts where their appointments lay, either personally, or by sufficient proxy, to answer to those who shall be their successors, to such questions as they shall ask touching their evil deeds and the complaints made against them."

By these regulations, the king greatly improved the state of his kingdom, insomuch that every one lived in peace and security. You must know that in former times the office of the provostship of Paris was sold to the highest bidder; whence it happened that many robberies and other crimes were committed, and justice was corrupted at its source, by favour of friends, gifts, or promises. The common people were afraid of dwelling in the open country of France, which, by this means, was almost a desert. Oftentimes there were not ten prisoners when the provost held his assizes, notwithstanding the multitude of crimes that were daily committed. For this he would not that the provostship should be sold, as it was an office he would give to some wise and upright man with a sufficient salary for his expenses, and to support his dignity. He also abolished all the heavy taxes, that had before weighed on the common people.

He made inquiry throughout the realm for a learned and honest man, who understood the laws, and would rigorously punish malefactors, without regarding the rich more than the poor. In consequence of this, Stephen Boileau was brought to him, to whom he gave the provostship of Paris, and who ever after did wonders in the said office, so that henceforth no robber, murderer, or other malefactor could remain in Paris without his having instant knowledge thereof, and he was sure to be hanged or punished very severely according to the greatness of his guilt. No friends, relations, or money could prevent him from acting on every occasion with the strictest justice.   In a short time, population increased so much throughout the realm, from the justness and upright-ness that reigned, that the estates, rents, and revenues of the kingdom were in one year nearly doubled, and the country was very much improved.

From his earliest youth he was very compassionate to the poor and those under misfortune; which so much increased as he grew up, that, during his reign he was accustomed to feed daily six score poor people at his table in whatever part of the kingdom he might be.   In Lent the numbers of the poor were greater; and ofttimes I have seen him serve them himself, and from his own table.   On the vigils of annual festivals, before he had eaten or drunk, he served the poor, who, when fed, carried away a certain sum of money each. In short, the king St. Louis gave away such immense sums in alms that they cannot be told nor counted.   Some of his household murmured at these great gifts and alms, saying he was too extravagant in these expenses; but the good king re-plied, that he had rather spend such large sums in alms than in follies and vanity.   However, for all this expense in alms, he did not keep the less grand household, which was costly and liberal, and such as became so great a prince.   He was naturally generous; and, during the parliaments and councils that were held for the establishment of his new regulations, he entertained daily at his court all the lords and knights that attended them, with greater magnificence than any of his predecessors had done.   He was attached to all who served God, and in consequence founded many monasteries and religious houses in various parts of his realm, and even surrounded Paris with different orders of religion, whose houses he founded and endowed with his own money.

After he had arranged his new establishments, he summoned all the barons of his realm to meet him during the Lent at Paris.   He sent for me at Joinville, and I thought to excuse myself from going on account of a quartan ague that I had; but he sent me word, that he had enough of people who knew how to cure a quartan ague, and that from the love I bore him I must come to Paris.   I obeyed, but when I was there I could never find out why he had thus summoned all the great barons of his kingdom.   It happened, on the festival of our Lady in March, that I fell asleep during matin service. In my sleep, I thought I saw the king on his knees before an altar, and that he was surrounded by many prelates who clothed him with a red chasuble, that was of serge of Rheims. When I awakened, I told one of my chaplains, who was a learned man, my dream, who informed me that the king was the next day to put on the cross. I asked him how he knew this : he replied, by what I had told him of my vision ; and that the red chasuble I had seen him clothed with signified the cross of our Lord Jesus Christ, which was dyed with the precious blood he had shed for us ; and, as the chasuble was of serge of Rheims, the croisade would be of a short duration ; and the truth of what he said I should be witness to on the morrow.

Now, on the next day, the king and his three sons did put on the cross ; and the croisade was a trifling business, as the chaplain had foretold to me the preceding day. This made me consider it as a prophecy. When this was done, the king of France and the king of Navarre pressed me strongly to put on the cross, and undertake a pilgrimage with them ; but I replied that when I was before beyond sea, on the service of God, the officers of the king of France had so grievously oppressed my people that they were in a state of poverty, insomuch that we should have great difficulty to recover ourselves ; and that I saw clearly, were I to undertake another croisade, it would be the total ruin of my people. I have heard many say since, that those who had advised him to this croisade had been guilty of a great crime, and had sinned deadly. As long as he remained in his kingdom of France, every thing went on well, and all lived peaceably and in security, but the moment he left it things began to decline. They were criminal in another respect, for the good king was so weakened in his body that he could not support the weight of his armour, nor remain long on horseback. I remember that I was once forced to carry him in my arms from the house of the count d'Auxerre as far as the convent of the Cordeliers, when we landed on our return from Palestine.

Of his expedition to Tunis I will say nothing, for I was not of it, and am resolved not to insert any thing in this book but what I am perfectly certain is true. But I will say, that during the time the good king Saint Louis was at Tunis, and before the castle of Carthage, he was seized with a dysentery; the lord Philip, his eldest son, was attacked with the same disorder, and a quartan ague. The good king took to his bed, and, well knowing he was about to quit this life for another, called to his children, and, addressing himself to his eldest son, gave them instructions, which he commanded them to consider as his last will, and the objects which they were to attend to when he should be deceased. I have heard that the good king had written out these instructions with his own hand, and that they were as follow:

"Fair son, the first advice that I shall give thee is, that with all thy heart, and above all other things, thou love God, for without this no man can be saved. Be most careful not to do any thing that may displease Him; that is to say, avoid sin. Thou oughtest to desire to suffer any torments rather than sin mortally. Should God send thee adversity, receive it patiently, give him thanks for it, and believe that thou hast well deserved it, and that it will turn out to thine honour. Should he grant thee prosperity, be humbly grateful for it; but take care thou do not become worse, through pride or presumption, for it behoves us not to make war against God for his gifts. Confess thyself often, and choose such a discreet and wise confessor as may have abilities to point out to thee the things necessary for thy salvation, and what things thou oughtest to shun; and mayest thou be such a character, that thy confessor, relations, and acquaintance may boldly reprove thee for any wrong thou mayest have done, and instruct thee how thou shouldest act. Attend the service of God, and of our mother church, with heartfelt devotion, more particularly the mass, from the consecration of the holy body of our Lord, without laughing or gossiping with any one. Have always a compassionate heart for the poor, and assist and comfort them as much as thou canst.

"Keep up and maintain good manners in thy kingdom: abase and punish the bad. Preserve thyself from too great luxury; and never lay any heavy imposts on thy people, unless through necessity forced to it, or for the defence of thy country. If thy heart feel any discontent, tell it instantly to thy confessor, or to any sober-minded person, that is not full of wicked words: thou mayest thus more easily bear it, from the consolation he may give thee. Be careful to choose

such companions as are honest and loyal, and not full of
vices, whether they be churchmen, monks, seculars, or others.

"Avoid the society of the wicked; and force thyself to
listen to the word of God, and to retain it in thy heart. Beg
continually in thy prayers for pardon, and the remission of
thy sins. Love thine honour. Take care not to suffer any
one to dare utter words in thy presence that may excite to
sin, nor any calumny of another, whether he be present or
absent; nor any thing disrespectful of God, his holy mother,
or of the saints.

"Offer thanks frequently to God for the prosperity and
other good things he gives thee. Be upright, and do justice
strictly to all, to the poor and to the rich. Be liberal and
good to thy servants, but firm in thy orders, that they may
fear and love thee as their master. If any controversy or
dispute arise, inquire into it until thou comest to the truth,
whether it be in thy favour or against thee. If thou possess
any thing that does not belong to thee, or that may have
come to thee from thy predecessors, and thou be informed
for a truth that it is not thine, cause it instantly to be restored to its proper owner. Be particularly attentive that
thy subjects live in peace and security, as well in the towns
as in the country. Maintain such liberties and franchises as
thy ancestors have done, and preserve them inviolate; for by
the riches and power of thy principal towns thy enemies will
be afraid of affronting or attacking thee, more especially thy
equals, thy barons, and such like.

"Love and honour all churchmen, and be careful not to
deprive them of any gifts, revenues, or alms which thy
ancestors or predecessors may have granted to them. It is
reported of my grandfather Philip, that when one of his
counsellors told him that the churchmen were making him
lose his revenues, royalties, and even his rights of justice,
and that he was surprised how he suffered it, the king replied, that he believed it was so, but that God had shewn
him so much favour, and granted him such prosperity, that he
had rather lose all he had, than have any dispute or contention with the servants of his holy church.

"Be to thy father and mother dutiful and respectful, and
avoid angering them by thy disobedience to their just commands. Give such benefices as may become vacant to dis-

creet persons of a pure conversation, and give them with the advice of well-advised, prudent persons.   Avoid going to war with any Christian power, without mature deliberation, and if it can in anywise be prevented.   If thou goest to war, respect churchmen and all who have done thee no wrong. Should contentions arise between thy vassals, put an end to them as speedily as possible.

"Attend frequently to the conduct of thy bailiffs, provosts, and others thy officers: inquire into their behaviour, in order that if there may be any amendment to be made in their manner of distributing justice, thou mayest make it.   Should any disgraceful sin, such as blasphemy or heresy, be prevalent in thy kingdom, have it instantly destroyed and driven thence.   Be careful that thou keep a liberal establishment, but with economy.

"I beseech thee, my child, that thou hold me, and my poor soul, in thy remembrance when I am no more, and that thou succour me by masses, prayers, intercessions, alms, and benefactions, throughout thy kingdom, and that thou allot for me a part of all the good acts thou shalt perform.

"I give thee every blessing that father ever bestowed on son, beseeching the whole Trinity of paradise, the Father, the Son, and the Holy Ghost, to preserve and guard thee from all evils, more particularly that thou die not under any deadly sin, and that we may, after this mortal life, appear together before God, to render him praise and thanksgiving, without ceasing, in his kingdom of paradise.   Amen."

When the good king St. Louis had finished giving the above instructions to the lord Philip, his son, his disorder so greatly increased, that he asked for the sacraments of the holy church, which were duly administered to him, whilst he enjoyed full life and perfect memory.   This was very apparent when they came to the unction; for when they chanted the seven penitential psalms, he himself repeated the responses with the assistants, who replied to the priest that was anointing him.   I have since heard from my lord the count d'Alençon, his son, that while the good king was in the agonies of death, he made efforts to call on all the saints in paradise to come and aid him in his distress.   He in particular called on my lord St. James, in repeating his prayer, which begins "Esto Domine."   He prayed to my lord St. Denis of France, in words that were nearly as follow :—" Lord God, give us grace to have the power of despising and forgetting the things of this world, so that we may not fear any evil." He called, likewise, on St. Genevieve. He then ordered his body to be placed on a bed of ashes, and, crossing his hands on his breast, with eyes uplifted to heaven, rendered his soul back to his Creator, at the very same hour that our Lord Jesus Christ expired on the cross for the salvation of his people.

The death of this holy prince was a melancholy event and worthy of lamentation ; for he had lived like a saint, had well taken care of his kingdom, and done many religious acts towards God. As an author has his book finely illuminated, that greater honour and respect may be paid to it, so our late holy king had illuminated his country by his great alms, and by the churches and monasteries that he had erected and founded in his lifetime, in which, at this moment, God is praised and adored day and night. The good king departed from this life to another on the morrow after the feast of St. Bartholomew, and his corpse was brought to St. Denis in France, and was buried in the spot he had some time before fixed for his sepulture; in which place, God has, through his intercessions, done many and great miracles.

Soon after, by orders from the holy pontiff at Rome, a prelate of France, who was archbishop of Rouen, in company with another bishop, came to St. Denis, where they remained a long time, making inquiries into the life of the good king St. Louis. They summoned me before them, and I stayed there two days in relating all I knew of his life and manners. When they had made every necessary inquiry respecting this good king, they carried with them their report to Rome ; where, having thoroughly canvassed it, they placed him among the saints in paradise. This was undoubtedly joyful news to France, and ought to be so to the whole kingdom, and a great honour to his descendants, particularly such as may follow his example, but dishonourable to those who shall not ; and they will be pointed at by the fingers of the public, who will say, the holy man, had he been alive, would never have done such disgraceful acts.

When intelligence of his canonization was brought from Rome, the king appointed a day for the raising of his holy

body,* which was done by the then archbishop of Rheims,
and it was borne by Sir Henry de Villiers, archbishop of
Lyon, and by several archbishops and bishops, whose names
I do not remember. After its translation, Friar John de
Semours preached a public sermon. Among the many traits
of the life of this holy king which he dwelt upon, was one
which I had told him : I mean, his great fidelity to his word ;
for, as I have before said, whenever he had simply given his
word to the Saracens on any subject, there was nothing that
could prevent him from most strictly keeping it, whatever
might be the consequences ; nor, for 100,000 livres would he
have broken his word. Friar John, in his sermon, detailed the

---

* The body of St. Louis was taken from its tomb in the church of
St. Denis, and transferred to the holy chapel in Paris in the year 1298,
Pope Boniface having granted indulgences to all who should assist at this
elevation by his bull, given at Rome the first day of June, in the fourth
year of his pontificate. This translation was performed on the morrow
of the feast of Saint Bartholomew, not in the year 1299, as Walsingham
writes, but in the preceding year. A manuscript chronicle, which ends
at the year 1322, has these words :—" In this year King Philip had the
fair body of Saint Louis, formerly king of France, brought from the
church of St. Denis with great solemnity, and attended by multitudes of
people, on the morrow of Saint Bartholomew, which was just eighteen
years after he had departed this life." Stephen, archbishop of Sens,
performed the service on the day of this translation, in the church of St.
Denis, in the presence of the prelates. The expenses of this ceremony
were very great, as may be collected from a journal of the king's treasury,
beginning the first day of January, 1297, to the last day of December,
1301, which is in the Chamber of Accounts at Paris. It informs us
that there were public festivals attended with great pomp ; that Raoul de
Beaumont, director of the kitchen, spent 100 livres parisis ; Robert de
Meudon, pantler, 1,500 livres for tablecloths ; Alain Breton, horse-ser-
geant to the Châtelet, 10 livres for setting to music the history of Saint
Louis ; Master Guillaume, the silversmith, 300 livres for the workmanship of the shrine or bier ; Guillaume de Flavacourt, knight, 60 livres
for the expenses of divers works that were made for this festival ; the
king's fruiterers, 2,000 livres tournois for lights ; Raoul de Beaumont,
king's cook, 1,500 livres parisis for plate ; Geoffry Coquatrix different
sums, as for wine delivered, and other things. In short there were given
to the proprietors of houses and stalls, which were pulled down at Saint
Denis for this feast, 255 l. 13 s. 6 deniers parisis. The king commanded
several persons to write the life of this holy king ; namely, Monsieur
Geoffroy, chaplain to the lord James de St. Paul, whose history is in print,
and Master Peter de la Croix of Amiens. Geoffroy received 30 livres and
Peter de la Croix 10 livres. There is likewise mention made, under the
date of the 16th March, 1299, of Arthur of Florence, notary-public, to
whom was given the sum of 200 livres tournois.

2 M

whole life of this good king, as I have indited it. On the
sermon being ended, the king and his brothers carried the
corpse of their father * to the church of St. Denis, assisted by

---

* His head was afterwards separated and carried to the holy chapel
in Paris. Guillaume Guiart, as well as Louis Lasseré, says, that this
translation took place in the year 1306. The MS. chronicle, before
quoted, which ends with the year 1322, says it took place the preceding
year. " In this year, the head and one of the ribs of St. Louis were
brought to Paris, without the chin and gums, by King Philip, attended
by numbers of prelates and barons, with the permission of the sovereign
pontiff. The rib was placed in the church of Notre Dame, in Paris,
and the head in the king's chapel, on the Tuesday preceding Japhe."
Among the chattels which had personally belonged to St. Louis, and
which our kings most carefully preserved as relics, were his missal and his
cup of gold, out of which, from respect to him, no one afterward drank.
In the account of the disbursements of the queen's household from
the 25th December, 1329, to the 8th of April, 1330, is the following :—
" Expenses of the chapels. To the almoner, for having bound and
cased the missal that had belonged to our lord St. Louis, 20 livres." In
the inventory of the furniture of King Louis Hutin, which is in a roll in
the Chamber of Accounts : " This is the inventory of the butlery, &c.
Item, the golden cup of St. Louis, out of which no one drinks."
It is to be remarked, that from the time this great monarch was
enrolled among the saints, our kings, his successors, have chosen him for
the protector of their sacred persons and their kingdom. This is the
title which Charles VIII. gives him, in letters of mortmain issued at
Pont de Cé in the month of April, 1487, the original of which was communicated to me by M. d'Herouval. " By and at the request and
prayer of his uncle and cousin, the duke of Bourbonnois and Auvergne,
constable of France, explaining, that in the year 1450, being then lieu-
tenant-general of the county and duchy of Normandy for King Charles VII.,
he had an engagement with the English, the ancient enemies of the crown
of France, in a field near to the village of Formigny, in the diocese of
Bayeux, in which engagement God gave him the victory, so that the
English were defeated, which occasioned the reduction of the whole
duchy and county of Normandy to the obedience of the said king. For
this victory the duke, willing to render his thanks to God, vowed to erect
and dedicate, in the aforesaid field where the victory was won, a chapel to
the honour of *my lord St. Louis, our ancient progenitor and protector of
the crown of France*" (it is the king who speaks), " and to establish two
chaplains as vicars, to celebrate a mass daily, and perform such other
services as may be thought advisable for the salvation of the souls of
those nobles and others who perished in that combat. For the purpose of
this foundation, he had bought of Robert de Mannéville, esquire, lord de
la Vigne, the lands and lordship of Colombiers, in the county and
viscounty of Bayeux, held from his majesty at 20 livres yearly, as a fief
noble, the whole valued at the sum of one hundred livres annual rent,
together with a piece of land, containing about three roods, to build and
erect the said chapel, which fiefs and land the king, by these letters,
grants in mortmain," &c.

others of their relations, to do honour to the corpse of him
who had done them great honour, if they did not deprive
themselves of it by their own faults, as I have before said.

I must mention something more in honour to the good king
St. Louis. I was on a certain day in my chapel of Joinville,
when I thought I saw him resplendent with glory before
me. I was very proud to see him thus in my castle, and said
to him, " Sire, when you shall depart hence I will conduct
you to another of my castles that I have at Chevillon, where
you shall also be lodged. Methought he answered me with
a smile, " Lord de Joinville, from my affection to you, I
will not, since I am here, depart hence so soon." When
I awoke, I bethought myself, that it was the pleasure of
God, and his own, that I should lodge him in my chapel,
and instantly afterward I had an altar erected to the honour
of God and of him. I also founded a perpetual mass for
every day in honour of God and St. Louis. These things
have I told to the king Louis, in order that by my endeavours to please God and my late lord, I might obtain some
part of the relics of the real holy body of St. Louis to
decorate my chapel of Joinville with, to induce those who
shall see his altar to pay greater devotion to the saint.

I now make known to my readers, that all they shall
find in this little book, which I have declared to have seen
and known, is true, and what they ought most firmly to
believe. As for such things as I have mentioned as hearsay.
they will understand them just as they shall please. And
I beseech God, through the prayers of my lord St. Louis,
that it may please him to give us such things as he knows
to be necessary, as well for the body as the soul. Amen.

END OF THE MEMOIRS.

A LIST OF THE KNIGHTS WHO ACCOMPANIED SAINT LOUIS IN HIS EXPEDITION TO PALESTINE.

Underneath are the names of the knights who are to accompany the king, Saint Louis, to the Holy Land, and the terms of agreement entered into between them and the king.

MONSIEUR DE VALERY to be of the expedition, with thirty knights. The king agrees to pay him eight thousand livres tournois. He is to be recompensed by the king for any loss of horses during the passage, but is not to have his meals at court; and he is to remain, he and his people, one whole year, which year is to commence from the day they disembark from the voyage. Should it happen, either by consent or stress of bad weather, that the king and his army pass the winter on an island, and that he remain behind at sea, the year shall commence from the time of his arrival at winter-quarters. In regard to the payment of his knights, he is to pay them one-half of their salaries at the commencement of the year, and the other moiety when the first half-year shall be expired. He is to transport two horses for each banneret, and one horse for such as are not of that rank: with the horses are the boys who take care of them. The banneret to be attended by five persons, and poor knights with two. The Constable will attend with fourteen knights, on the same terms as M. de Valery. He will receive from the king but three thousand livres tournois. Monsieur Florent de Varennes, the admiral, will go on the same conditions as above, himself and twelve knights, and will receive from the king three thousand two hundred fifty-five livres tournois. Monsieur Raoul d'Estrées, the marshal, will go on similar terms, himself and six knights, to receive sixteen hundred livres tournois. Monsieur Lancelot de St. Maart, the marshal, to go on the same conditions, himself and five knights, to receive fourteen hundred livres tournois. Monsieur Pierre de Moleines to go with five knights on the above conditions, excepting that he and his brother in arms have their meals at court, to receive thirteen hundred livres tournois, and four hundred livres as a private gift to them both. Monsieur Collard de Moleines to go on the same terms and manner as his brother. Monsieur Gilles de la Tournelle to go himself and four knights on these same conditions, to receive twelve hundred livres tournois and to eat at court. Monsieur Mahi de Roie to go himself and eight knights on the above conditions, to eat at court, and to receive two thousand livres, and two hundred livres as a private gift. Monsieur Girard de Morbois to go himself and ten knights: three thousand livres tournois. Monsieur Raoul de Neelle, himself and fifteen knights: four thousand livres tournois. He will eat at his own house. Monsieur Amauri de Meulenc, himself and fifteen knights:

on terms the same as the preceding.   Monsieur Ansout d'Offemont, himself and ten knights: two thousand six hundred livres tournois, and their meals at the palace.   Monsieur Raoul le Flamant, himself and six knights: one thousand five hundred livres tournois, and their meals at the palace.   Monsieur Baudouin de Longueval, himself and four knights: eleven hundred livres tournois.   Monsieur Loys de Beaujeu, himself and ten knights: two thousand six hundred livres, and their meals at the palace.   Monsieur Jean Ville, himself and four knights: twelve hundred livres, and their meals at court.   Monsieur Mahi de le Tournelle, himself and four knights: twelve hundred livres: meals as above.   The archbishop of Rheims, four thousand livres.   The bishop of Langres the same.   These two to be attended by thirty knights, and to be embarked on board the same ship.   Monsieur Guillaume de Courtenay, himself and ten knights: two thousand two hundred livres, and their meals at court.   Monsieur Guillaume de Patay, himself and brother: four hundred livres, and their meals at the palace.   Monsieur Pierre de Sarz, himself alone: eight score livres, and his meals at court. Monsieur Robert de Bois-Gencelin, alone, on the same terms as the preceding.   Monsieur Estienne Grancke, alone, on the same terms. Monsieur Maci de Loué, alone, on similar conditions.   Monsieur Gilles de Mailly, himself and ten knights: three thousand livres, transport of horses going and returning, with his meals at the palace.   Monsieur Itier de Maignac, himself and five knights: twelve hundred livres, transport of horses, and his meals as the preceding.   Fouriers de Vernuel, himself and four knights: twelve hundred livres: his meals at court. Monsieur Guillaume de Fresnes, himself and ten knights: two thousand six hundred livres, and their meals at court.   The count de Guignes, himself and ten knights, on similar conditions.   The count de St. Paul, himself and thirty knights, passage and return of horses: twelve thousand livres, including food and all other things, with twelve hundred livres as a private gift.   Monsieur Lambert de Limous, himself and thirty knights in the pay of the king; that is to say, ten sols tournois to each daily for their subsistence, the sum of eighteen hundred and twenty-five livres.   Monsieur Girard de Campendu, himself and fifteen knights at the king's pay, subsisting themselves like to Monsieur Lambert: two thousand seven hundred thirty-seven livres, ten sols.   Monsieur Raimon Aban, himself and five others in the pay of the king, nine hundred twelve livres, ten sols.   Monsieur Jean de Belnes, himself and ten others: three thousand livres, passage and return of his horses, and meals at court.   The marshal of Champagne will go himself with ten others, but will not receive any thing from the king.   Monsieur Guillard d'Arce, himself and five others, in the king's pay, nine hundred twelve livres, ten sols.   Monsieur Guillaume de Flandres, himself and twenty others: six thousand livres, passage and return of their horses, and their meals at the palace.   Monsieur Aubert de Longueval, himself and five more: eleven hundred livres, passage and return of horses, and meals at court.

*Knights of the household who attended the king, Saint Louis, in his
expedition to Tunis.*

Monsieur de Walery.
Ly Boutillera.
Ly Connestables.
Monsieur Guillaume de Flandres
Ly sire de Neelles.
Ly sire de Montmoranci.
Ly sire de Harcour.
Messire Jean ses fils.
Messire Baudouin de Longueval.
Messire Lancelot ly Mareschaux.
Messire Guillaume de Courtenay.
Messire Florant de Vorennes.
Messire Amaury de Mellenc.
Messire Jean de Ville ly estous.
Messire Guillaume de Prunay.
Messire Raoul d'Estrées.
Messire Simon de Contes.
Ly Maistres des Arbalestriers.
Messire Guillaume de Clignes.
Messire Renault de Mormant.
Messire Guilli Bas.
Messire Guinemer de Guimeri.
Messire Jean de Chaumes.
Messire Landry de Bonnay.
Messire Gilles de Brienon.
Messire Pierre de Bailly.
Messire Robert Sansavoir.
Messire Macé de Lyons.
Messire Nebert de Medienne.
Messire Nicolas Routier.
Messire Pierre d'Autoil.
Messire Gautier Descon.
Messire Colars de Molaines.
Messire Pierre de Molaines.
Messire Mahy de Roye.
Messire Jehan de Varennes.
Messire Simon de Falloel.
Messire Gilles de la Tournelle.
Messire Gaufr. de Rinel, ou de Clermont.
Messire Maurice de Craon.
Le comte de Saint Paul.
Le comte de Pontis.
Messire Jean de Neelle.
Messire Raoul de Neelle.
Messire Guillaume de Minieres.
Ly mareschaux de Champaigne.
Le comte de Soissons.
Messire Bonnables.
Messire Guillaume de Fiennes.
Le comte de Dreux.
Messire Jean Malez.
Messire Guillaume de Paroy.
Messire Robert de Girolles.
Messire Lambert de Limous.
Messire Gautier ly Chambellant.
Messire Phelipes de Nemous.
Messire Guillaume de Centegnonville.
Messire Jean l'ainnevaire.
Messire Phelipes d'Autoil.
Messire Hue Gaignars.
Messire Renault Couperiaus.
Messire Henry ly Baacles.
Messire Matheu de Iton.
Messire Jean de Rochefort.
Messire Raoul Flamenz.
Messire Hubert Chesnars.

Messire Robert de Bois-Josselin
Messire Jean Rivellon.
Messire Simon de Menon.
Messire Hue de Villers.
Messire Jean de Bebrete.
Messire Pierre de Bebrete.
Messire Renault de S. Méart.
Messire Pierre de Villenoive.
Messire Geuffroy de Boismenard.
Messire Robert de Boisgautier.
Messire Jean Davion.
Messire Hector Dorillac.
Messire Renault de Precigni.
Messire Guillaume de Aunoy.
Messire Amaut d'Offemont.
Messire Jean de Clery.
Messire Amori de S. Cler.
Messire Johens d'Amiens.
Ly mareschaux de Mirepoix.
Messire Guillaume de Coardon.
Messire Henry de Gaudonvillier.
Messire Goorrem de Lorris, Cosras.
Messire Nesbert de Medion.
Messire Jean de Chambly.
Ly seueschaux de Champaigne.
Messire Engerens de Bailloil.
Messire Jean de Soins.
Messire Pierre de Loon.
Messire Otes de Toucy.
Messire Guillaume de Chasteaunou
Messire Jean Malez.
Messire Guillaume de Sandreville.
Messire Girards de Campendu.
Messire Pierre Rambaus, parent, l'apos-
tole Climent.
Messire Flastre de Henequerque.
Messire Jean de Chastenol.
Messire Pierre de Blemus.
Messire Estienne Granche.
Messire Jean de Soilly.
Messire Jean de Tornebu.
Messire Enfans Chevalier au Connés-
table.
Messire Pregent ly Bretons.
Messire Pierre de Saux.
Messire Jean de Beaumont.
Messire Gaultier ly povre Homme.
Messire Aufroy de Montfort.
Messire Gilles de Boisavernes.
Messire Baudoin de Wandieres.
Messire Raoul de Wandieres.
Messire Gilles de Mailly.
Messire Jean Britaus.
Monsieur Galerens de Yury.
Monsieur Raoul de Jupilles.
Monsieur Guitier ses fils.
Monsieur Roger de Morteigne.
Messire Anguerrans de Jorni.
Messire Pierre de Bautru.
Messire Simon de Baugenci.
Messire Estienne Jaunoy.
Messire Vorez.
Ly Fouriers de Vernoil.
Ly Bruns ses fils.
Messire Guillaume de Precigni.

EXTRACTS FROM AN ARABIAN MANUSCRIPT

ENTITLED

ESSULOUK LI MARISET IL DUVEL IL MULOUK; *that is to say, " The Road to Knowledge of the Reigns of Kings." It is the History of the Sultans* CURDES-EIOUBITES, *of the race of Saladin, and of the two Dynasties that have reigned in Egypt; the one of Turkish slaves, known under the name of* MAMELUKES-BAHABITES, *the other of Circassians. This Work was composed by* MAKRISI, *who was born in the 769th year of the Hegira, or one hundred and twenty years after the expedition* ST. LOUIS.

THE sultan Melikul-Kamil died at Damascus the 21st of the moon Regeb, in the 635th year of the Hegira (March 10, A.D. 1238). Melikul-Adil-Scifeddin, one of his two sons, was proclaimed on the morrow, in the same town, sultan of Syria, and of Egypt. He was the seventh king of the posterity of the Eioubites, who descended from Saladin.

On the 17th day of the moon Ramadan, there arrived an ambassador from the caliph of Bagdad, who was the bearer of a standard and rich robe for the sultan, weak remnants of the vast authority the caliphs who succeeded Mahommed* formerly enjoyed, and of which the sultans had not thought it worth their while to deprive them.

Melikul-Adil, when scarcely on the throne, instead of attending to the government of his kingdoms, gave himself up to all sorts of debauchery. The grandees of the state, who might have reproached him for the dissipated life he led, were banished under various pretexts, and replaced by more complaisant ministers. He believed he could have nothing to fear, if the troops were attached to him; and, in order to gain them, he made them great presents, which, added to those his pleasures required, exhausted the treasures his father had amassed with so much difficulty.

* The caliphs, successors to Mahommed, were formerly masters of Syria. Egypt, and in general of all the conquests made by the Mahommedans. Corrupted by luxury and indolence, they suffered Egypt and Syria to be taken from them by the Fatimites, at the time of the expedition of St. Louis, and they retained Irak-Arabia. They, however, still preserved a shadow of power over the provinces captured from them. The sultans of Egypt submitted to a sort of inauguration on their part, which consisted in the investiture of a dress which the caliphs sent them. This custom is not yet abolished: the grand seignior sends a similar dress to the hispodars of Moldavia and Walachia, when he nominates them to these principalities.

A conduct so unworthy a sovereign made him contemptible, and his subjects offered up vows that his brother Nedjm-Eddin would deprive him of his crown. This prince had no other wish, but he was afraid of intrusting a project of this nature in the hands of a fickle populace. At last all the orders of the state, oppressed by the tyrannies of Melikul-Adil, called Nedjm-Eddin to the throne. He made his entry into Cairo the ninth day of the moon Chuwal, in the year 637 (May 3, A.D. 1240), and was proclaimed sultan of Syria and Egypt. Melikul-Adil was imprisoned, after having reigned two years and eighteen days.

Nedjm-Eddin, on mounting the throne, found only one solitary piece of gold, and one thousand drachms of silver, in the public treasury. He assembled the grandees of the state, and those in particular who had had any share in the administration of the finances, under the reign of his brother, and asked what had been their reasons for deposing Melikul-Adil. "Because he was a madman," they replied. Then, addressing himself to the chiefs of the law, he asked if a madman could dispose of the public money. And on their answering that it was contrary to law, he ordered all who had received any sums of money from his brother to bring them back to the treasury, or they should pay for their disobedience with their heads. By this means, he recovered seven hundred and fifty-eight thousand pieces of gold, and two millions three hundred thousand drachms of silver.

In the year 638 (1240), Salih-Imad-Eddin, who had surprised Damascus, under the reign of Melikul-Adil, fearful that the new sultan would deprive him of this unjust conquest, made an offensive and defensive alliance with the Franks of Syria. He gave them, the better to secure their support, the towns of Safet* and Chakif,† with their territories, half of the town of Sidon, and a part of the country of the

---

* Safet, a moderate-sized town in Palestine. It has a fortress which commands the Lake of Tiberias, and is situated in fifty-seven degrees thirty-five minutes longitude, thirty-two degrees thirty minutes latitude.

† Chakif. Abulfeda mentions two fortresses under the name of Chakif. Chakif-Arnoun, and Chakif-Tiroun : the first, partly cut in a rock, is on one of the roads leading from Sidon to Damascus. It is the second, called Tiroun, which is noticed in the text. It lies towards the sea, in regard to Safet. Chakif-Arnoun is, in like manner, distant from the sea, on the top of Lebanon.

Tiberiad.* He added also the mountain of Aamileb,† and several other places on the sea-shore, permitting them to come to Damascus to purchase arms. This alliance displeased good Mussulmen, who were indignant to see Franks purchase arms in a Mahommedan town, which these infidels might one day turn against the sellers.

Salih-Imad-Eddin resolved to make war on Egypt, and, assembling his troops, joined the army of the Franks. The sultan of Egypt was informed of this movement, and sent, in consequence, a body of men as far as Acre. The two armies met; but the Egyptians corrupted the Mussulman soldiers of Damascus, who, according to their secret conventions, fled on the first attack, and left the Franks singly to bear the shock. They, however, made but a feeble resistance; great numbers were slain, and the rest, loaded with chains, were led to Cairo.

In the 640th year of the Hegira, the Franks surprised the town of Napoulons‡ on a Friday, the 4th day of the moon Djemazilewel, and made slaves of the inhabitants, after they had plundered them of all they had, and committed all sorts of cruelties.

The whole year of 641 (A.D. 1243) was employed in negotiations between Salih-Imad-Eddin and Nedjm-Eddin. The latter consented to allow the former to be master of Damascus, but on condition that the town should be a fief to Egypt, and that the coin should be struck in his name. However, as they could not agree, Imad-Eddin made another treaty with the Franks, by which he gave up to them Jerusalem, the whole country of the Tiberiad, and Ascalon.§

---

* A part of Palestine has been thus called from the town of Tiberias, built on the side of a mountain near to the lake of the same name. The lake is twelve miles long by six wide, and is surrounded by mountains. This town was famous in former times, but Saladin, on reconquering it from the Franks had it destroyed. It owes its name to the emperor Tiberius. There were in its confines many hot springs celebrated for the cure of different disorders. It was but six miles from Tiberias to the well into which Joseph was cast by his brethren.—*Abulfeda.*

† Aamileb, a celebrated mountain of Syria. It spreads eastwardly and southerly from the sea-shore as far as Tyre. It had a fortress on its summit.

‡ Napoulous, a town in Palestine, anciently called Samaria. Jeroboam caused a temple to be built on a mountain near the town to prevent the ten tribes from going to Jerusalem.

§ Ascalon, a town in Palestine, on the Mediterranean shore, six

The Franks took possession of these towns, and instantly
fortified all the castles in the neighbourhood of Tiberias and
Ascalon. They expelled Mussulmen from the mosque
Aksa,* made a church of it, and hung bells in the minaret.

Nedjm-Eddin, on his side, connected himself with the
Kharesmiens,† a people whose lives were passed in war and
plunder. They hastened from the farthest part of the East,
crossed the Euphrates, to the amount of ten thousand combatants, under the command of three generals. One division
fell back upon Balbeck, and another marched to the very gates
of Damascus, pillaging and destroying all that came in their
way. Salih-Imad-Eddin shut himself up in Damascus, without attempting to stop the torrent that inundated his dominions. When they had despoiled all the country near to
Damascus, they advanced to Jerusalem, took it by storm, and
put all the Christians to the sword. The women and girls,
having suffered every insult from a brutal disorderly soldiery,
were loaded with chains. They destroyed the church of the
Holy Sepulchre; and when they found nothing among the
living, to glut their rage, they opened the tombs of the Christians, took out the bodies, and burnt them.

After this expedition, they marched to Gaza, and deputed
some of their principal officers to Nedjm-Eddin. This prince
caressed them much, had them clothed in superb dresses, and
presented them with rich stuffs and horses of great value.
He desired that they would halt their troops at Gaza, where
he proposed making a junction of the two armies, promising
to march them to Damascus. The troops of the sultan were
soon ready to take the field, under the command of the emir
Rukneddin-Bibars, one of his favourite slaves, and in whose

leagues from Gaza. It is built on a rock, but wants a harbour and fresh
water.

* The name of the mosque which the Mahommedans built after the
capture of Jerusalem, on the ancient foundations of the temple of Solomon, and on the stone whence Jacob was said to be have conversed with
God, and which the Mussulmen affirm to be that which this patriarch
named the gate of heaven, in consequence of his vision. The Christians,
when they conquered Jerusalem from the Mahommedans, erected a golden
cross on the top of this temple, but Saladin, on regaining the town, made
them take it down.—*D'Herbelot, Bibl. Orient.*

† Kharesmiens, a people of Khouaresm, which country is situated on
this side the Gion, or Oxus, on the side of Khorassan, and a part beyond
it, bounding the Mawaralnahar, or the Transoxane.

bravery he wholly confided. Bibars joined the Kharesmiens at Gaza.*

Imad-Eddin, on his part, raised troops in Damascus: they marched under the orders of Melik-Mansour, prince of Hemesse.† The Franks were likewise ready to take the field; and the two bodies met at Acre, when they formed but one army. Nasir-Daoud, prince of Karak,‡ and Zahir, son of Songour, also brought some soldiers to the prince of Damascus. This was the first time the standards of the Christians, on which was a cross, were seen intermixed with those of Mussulmen. The Christians formed the right wing, the troops of Nasir-Daoud the left, and the emir Mansour formed the centre with the Syrians.

The two armies met near to Gaza. The Kharesmiens made the first onset, which was but faintly opposed by the Syrians, who instantly fled. Zahir, who commanded the left wing, being made prisoner, there only remained the Franks, who for some time defended themselves, but were soon surrounded by the Kharesmiens: the greater part perished on this occasion, except a few that had the good fortune to escape. Eight hundred prisoners were made; and there lay on the field of battle upwards of thirty thousand dead, as well Christians as Syrian Mussulmen. Mansour returned to Damascus with a few soldiers. The Kharesmiens made an immense booty.

The news of this complete victory arrived at Cairo on the 15th of the moon Gémazilewel, in the year of the Hegira 642 (Oct. 9, A.D. 1244). Nedjm-Eddin was so delighted with it that he ordered public rejoicings to be made, and they were announced to the people by sound of drums and trumpets. The town and the castle of the sultan § were illuminated for several nights. The heads of the enemies that had

* Gaza, a town in Palestine near the sea. Its territory is very fertile, particularly in palm-trees.

† Hemesse or Hems, an ancient town, and one of the principal in Syria. It is situated on a plain, a mile distant from the river Orontes. It is the most fertile country of the whole province.

‡ Kerek or Karak, a celebrated town on the confines of Syria, where it joins Arabia Petræa. This town formerly possessed an impregnable fortress, and was one of the keys to Syria.

§ It was the castle of Cairo built by the sultan Saladin, with stones taken from many small pyramids destroyed near ancient Memphis, opposite to old Cairo. The bashaws, governors of Egypt, make this castle their residence. It is situated at the foot of the Mountain of St. Joseph.

been slain in battle were sent to Cairo, and exposed on the
gates of the town. The captive Franks arrived at the same
time, mounted on camels: as a mark of distinction, horses had
been given to the most considerable among them. Zahir-
ben-Songour, one of the Syrian generals that had been taken,
marched next, with the other officers of the Syrian army.
They were paraded with much pomp through the town of
Cairo, and then confined in prisons.

The emirs Bibars and Abouali had orders from the sultan
to lay siege to Ascalon; but the place was too strong, and
too well defended, to be taken. Bibars remained before
Ascalon, and Abouali advanced to Napoulous.

The other generals of Nedjm-Eddin took possession of
Gaza, Jerusalem, Khalil, Beit-Djebril, and Gaur.* Nasir-
Daoud lost nearly all his territories; for there only remained
to him the fortress of Kerck, Belka, Essalib,† and Adjeloun.

Nedjm-Eddin had promised the Kharesmiens to lead them
to Damascus; for he counted as nothing the last victory, if he
did not regain that town; and he resolved to make so important a conquest in person. The Kharesmiens followed him
with joy, and Damascus was besieged. Battering-rams, and
other machines for casting stones were erected; but the besieged made a vigorous resistance, and the siege lasted upwards of six months without any breach being made. Provisions, however, began to fail in the town; and Mansour,
prince of Hemesse, had a conference with Berket, one of the
Kharesmien chiefs, for the surrender of the place. It was at
length agreed that the town should be surrendered to the
sultan, and that Imad-Eddin, Mansour, and the other Syrian
chiefs, should have liberty to retire with all their riches. The
town of Balbeck, and all its territory, were given to Imad-
Eddin : Hemesse and Palmyra were allotted to Mansour.
The Kharesmiens, who had flattered themselves with the hope
of pillaging Damascus, in despair at being frustrated, quarrelled with the sultan, and, the ensuing year, formed an alliance with Mansour and the other Syrian leaders. They

* Gaur, a deep valley that traverses the country of Jourdan from the
Lake of Tiberias to the Dead Sea.

† Essalib, or, according to some authors, Essolet, is a castle near to,
but on the other side of Jordan. So is Adjeloun.

marched conjointly to the siege of Damascus, and reduced
the town to the utmost distress from want of provision. The
inhabitants, after they had consumed the vilest food, did not
scruple to feed on the bodies of such as died, to preserve
their lives. Nedjm-Eddin had returned to Egypt; but he
hastened to Syria again, with a numerous army, attacked
the Kharesmiens, and totally defeated them in two battles.

In the year 644, the emir Fakreddin won from the Franks
the castle of Tiberias and the town of Ascalon, both of which
he razed to the ground. This year was fatal to the Franks,
from their intestine divisions.

In the year 645, the sultan returned to Egypt, and passed
through Ramlé.* He was there attacked with an abscess,
which turned to a fistula; but in spite of this accident, he
continued his journey, and arrived at Cairo. New troubles,
which had arisen in Syria, called him again into that province;
but having learned at Damascus, † that the French were
preparing to invade Egypt, he preferred defending his own
kingdom in person. In spite of the violence of his sufferings
from pain, he mounted his litter, and arrived at Achmoum-
Tanah,‡ at the beginning of the year 647.

As he had no doubt but that Damietta would be the first
place attacked, he endeavoured to put it in a state of defence,
and formed there magazines of every sort of provision, arms,
and ammunition. The emir Fakreddin was ordered to march
toward that town, to prevent a descent on the coast. Fakreddin encamped at Gizé de Damietta, with the Nile between
his camp and the town.

The disorder of the sultan, however, grew worse; and he
caused proclamation to be made, that all to whom he owed
any thing should present themselves at his treasury, when
they would be paid.§

* Ramlé. Reml signifies sand. Ramla is a town some leagues from
Jaffa or Joppa, on the road to Jerusalem.

† Makrisi, in his description of Egypt, says, that in the year of the
Hegira 647 (A.D. 1249), the emperor sent an ambassador to the sultan
Nedjm-Eddin, who was then ill at Damascus: that this ambassador was
disguised as a merchant, and informed the sultan of the preparations of
the king of France against Egypt.

‡ Achmoum, or Achmoum-Tanah, a town on the Nile, and the capital
of one of the provinces of Egypt called Dahkalié, fifty-four deg. longitude,
thirty-one deg. fifty-four min. latitude.—*Abulfeda.*

§ It is one point of the Mahommedan law to pay all debts before

On Friday, the 21st of the moon Sefer, and in the year of
the Hegira 647 (A.D. 1249, Friday, 4th June), the French
fleet arrived off the coast, at two o'clock of the day, filled
with an innumerable body of troops under the command of
Louis, son to Louis, king of France. The Franks, who were
masters of Syria, had joined the French. The whole fleet
anchored on the strand opposite to the camp of Fakreddin.

The king of France, before he commenced any hostilities,
sent by a herald a letter to the sultan Nedjm-Eddin, conceived
1 the following words :—

"You are not ignorant that I am the prince of those who
follow the religion of JESUS CHRIST, as you are of those who
obey the laws of Mahommed. Your power inspires me with
no fear. How should it ? I who make the Mussulmen in Spain
tremble ! I lead them as a shepherd does a flock of sheep. I
have made the bravest among them perish, and loaded their
women and children with chains. They endeavour by presents to appease me, and turn my arms to another quarter.
The soldiers who march under my standards cover the plains,
and my cavalry is not less redoubtable. You have but one
method to avoid the tempest that threatens you. Receive
priests, who will teach you the Christian religion ; embrace
it, and adore the Cross ; otherwise I will pursue you everywhere, and God shall decide whether you or I be master of
Egypt."

Nedjm-Eddin, on reading this letter, could not restrain his
tears. He caused the following answer to be written by the
cadi Behaedin, his secretary :—

"In the name of the Omnipotent and All-merciful God,
salvation to our prophet Mahommed and his friends ! I have
received your letter ; it is filled with menaces, and you make
a boast of the great number of your soldiers. Are you
ignorant that we know the use of arms, and that we inherit
the valour of our ancestors ? No one has ever attacked us
without feeling our superiority. Recollect the conquests we
have made from the Christians ; we have driven them from
the lands they possessed ; their strongest towns have fallen
under our blows. Recal to your mind that passage of the
Alcoran, which says, 'Those who make war unjustly shall

death, and those who pretend to strictness of doctrine never fail to
observe it.

perish;' and also another passage, 'How often have the most
numerous armies been destroyed by a handful of soldiers!'
God protects the just; and we have no doubt of his protection, nor that he will confound your arrogant designs."

The French disembarked on the Saturday, on the same
shore where Fakreddin had made his encampment, and pitched
a red tent for their king.

The Mussulmen made some movements to prevent their
landing; and the emirs Nedjm-Eddin and Sarimeddin were
slain in these skirmishes.

At the beginning of the night the emir Fakreddin decamped
with his whole army, and crossed the bridge which leads to the
eastern shore of the Nile, whereon Damietta is situated. He
took the road to Achmoum-Tanah, and by this march the
French were left masters of the western bank of that river.

It is impossible to paint the despair of the inhabitants of
Damietta when they saw the emir Fakreddin march away
from their town, and abandon them to the fury of the Christians. They were afraid to wait for the enemy, and quitted
their town precipitately during the night. This conduct of the
Mussulman general was so much the less excusable as the garrison was composed of the bravest of the tribe of Beni-
Kénané, and as Damietta was in a better state of resistance
than when it was besieged by the Franks during the reign of
the sultan Elmelikul-Kamil; for, although plague and famine
afflicted the town, the Franks could not conquer it until after
sixteen months' siege.

On the Monday morning (6th June, 1249), the French
came before the town; but, astonished to see no one, they
were afraid of a surprise. They were soon informed of the
flight of its inhabitants, and, without striking a blow, took
possession of this important place, and all the ammunition
and provision they found there.

When the news of the capture of Damietta reached Cairo,
the consternation was general. They considered how greatly
this success would augment the courage and hopes of the
French; for they had seen an army of Mussulmen timorously
fly before them, and were in possession of an innumerable
quantity of arms of all sorts, with plenty of ammunition and
provision. The disorder of the sultan, which daily grew
worse, and hindered him from acting in this critical state of

affairs, overwhelmed the Egyptians with despair. No one now longer doubted but that the kingdom would be conquered by the Christians.

The sultan, indignant at the cowardice of the garrison, ordered fifty of the principal officers to be strangled. In vain did they allege in their defence the retreat of the emir Fakreddin : the sultan told them they deserved death, for having quitted Damietta without his orders. One of these officers, condemned to death with his son, requested to be executed first ; but the sultan refused him this favour, and the father had the misery to see his son expire before his eyes.

After this execution, the sultan, turning to the emir Fakreddin, asked with an enraged tone, " What resistance have you made ? what battles have you fought ? You could not withstand the Franks one hour. You should have shewn more courage and firmness." The officers of the army, fearing for Fakreddin the rage of the sultan, made the emir understand by their gestures that they were ready to massacre their sovereign. Fakreddin refused his assent, and told them afterward that the sultan could not live more than a few days ; and that, if the prince wished to trouble them, they were able at any time to get rid of him.

Nedjm-Eddin, notwithstanding his melancholy state, gave orders for his departure for Mansoura. He entered his boat of war,* and arrived there on Wednesday the 25th of the moon Sefer (June 9, A.D. 1249). He put the town in a posture of defence by employing his whole army on this service. The boats ordered by the prince before his departure arrived laden with soldiers, and all sorts of ammunition. Every one able to bear arms ranged himself under his standards, and he was joined by the Arabs in great numbers.

While the sultan was making his preparations, the French were adding new fortifications to Damietta, and placed there a considerable garrison.

On Monday, the last day of the moon Rebiulewel (July 12, A.D. 1249), thirty-six Christian prisoners were conducted

---

* *Boat of war.*—The Arabic word signifies properly " fire-work boat." Such were probably made use of to carry the Greek fire, and the machines to throw it. Makrisi, in the history of the first siege of Damietta, speaks much of these fire-ships, saying that the Mussulmen made use of them to set fire to the vessels of the Christians.

to Cairo; they had belonged to the guard of the camp against the inroads of the Arabs, among whom were two knights. The 5th of the same moon, thirty-seven were sent thither; on the 7th, twenty-two; and on the 16th, forty-five other prisoners; and among these last were three knights.

Different Christian princes, who held lands on the coast of Syria, had accompanied the French, by which their places were weakened. The inhabitants of Damascus seized this opportunity to besiege Sidon, which, after some resistance, was forced to surrender. The news of this, when carried to Cairo, caused an excess of joy, and seemed to compensate for the loss of Damietta. Prisoners were made almost daily from the French, fifty of whom were sent to Cairo the 18th of the moon Diemazilewel (Aug. 29, A.D. 1249).

The sultan continued daily to grow worse in health; and the physicians despaired of his recovery, for he was attacked at the same time by a fistula and an ulcer on his lungs. At length he expired, on the night of the 15th of the moon Chaban (Nov. 22), after having appointed as his successor his son Touran-Chah. Nedjm-Eddin was forty-four years old when he died, and had reigned ten years. It was he who instituted that militia of slaves, or of Mamelukes-Baharites,* thus

* Melikul-Salih-Nedjm-Eddin, son to Melikul-Kamil, the last but one of the princes of the dynasty of the Eioubites, opened, if I may so express myself, the road to the throne to these slaves. When this prince was besieging Napoulous, his troops timorously abandoned him, but the Baharite slaves alone supported the enemy's charge, and gave time to Nedjm-Eddin to escape. From that moment this prince gave them his whole confidence. Called some time after by the Egyptians to be sultan, in the place of his brother, Melikul-Adil-Seif-Eddin, he loaded these slaves with his bounties, and elevated them to the highest dignities. He quitted the castle, the usual residence of the sultans, to inhabit one which he had built in the small island of Roudah, opposite to old Cairo. The Baharite slaves had the guard of it, and thence took the name Baharite or Maritime, the Arabs calling all great rivers by the name of sea, as well as the sea itself. These slaves, or Mamelukes-Baharites, amounted to eight hundred at the time of St. Louis's invasion, and it was they who, at the battle of Mansoura, repulsed this prince, who had advanced as far as the palace of the sultan. They contributed greatly to the last victory of the Egyptians over St. Louis; and, as the historian remarks, after these two battles their name and power greatly increased. A short time after they assassinated Touran-Chah, the last prince of the dynasty of the Eioubites, and seized the throne. Azeddin-Aibegh, the Turcoman, was the first who mounted it, and took the name of Melikul-Muez. Chegeret-Eddur, his wife, having caused him to be murdered, his son, who was twelve years old,

called from being quartered in the castle which this prince had built in the island of Roudah, opposite to old Cairo. This militia, in course of time, seized on the throne of Egypt

As soon as the sultan had expired, the sultana Chegeret-Eddur, his spouse, sent for the general Fakreddin and the eunuch Diemaleddin, to inform them of the death of the sultan, and to request their assistance in supporting the weight of government at such a critical period. All three resolved to keep the sultan's death a secret, and to act in his name as if he were alive. His death was not to be made public until after the arrival of Touran-Chah, to whom were sent messengers after messengers.

Notwithstanding these precautions, the French were informed of his death. Their army instantly quitted the plains of Damietta, and encamped at Fariskour. Boats laden with provision and stores came up the Nile, and kept the army abundantly supplied.

The emir Fakreddin sent a letter to Cairo, to inform the inhabitants of the approach of the French, and to exhort them to sacrifice their lives and fortunes in the defence of the country. This letter was read in the pulpit of the great mosque, and the people answered only with sighs and groans. Every thing was in trouble and confusion; and the death of the sultan, which was suspected, added to the consternation. The most cowardly thought of quitting a town which they believed unable to withstand the French; but the more courageous, on the contrary, marched to Mansoura, to join the Mussulman army.

On Tuesday, the 1st day of the moon Ramadan (Dec. 7, A.D. 1249), there were some trifling skirmishes between

---

occupied his place, but reigned only two years. Khotouz succeeded him. Bibars-Elbondukdari, the same who, at the head of the Mamelukes, charged the French cavalry with such fury as forced them to abandon Mansoura, ascended this throne the 658th year of the Hegira, and of our æra 1289, and took the name of Melikal-Daher. After a glorious reign of seventeen years, he died at Damascus. This dynasty reigned in Egypt and Syria during one hundred and thirty-six years, and had twenty-seven sultans. The Mamelukes-Baharites were originally Turks, and had been sold to the sultan Nedjm-Eddin by merchants from Syria. The slaves, or Mamelukes-Circassians, dethroned them in their turn, in the 784th year of the Hegira, and of our æra 1382, and formed a new dynasty, which governed Egypt until the conquest of that kingdom by Sultan Selim, emperor of the Turks, in the 923rd year of the Hegira, A.D. 1517.

different corps of troops of each army. This, however, did not prevent the French army from encamping at Charmesah: the Monday following, being the 7th of the same moon, the army advanced to Bermoun.

On Sunday, the 13th day of the same moon, the Christian army appeared before the town of Mansoura; the branch of the Achmoum was between it and the Egyptian camp. Nasir Daoud, prince of Karak, was on the western bank of the Nile with some troops. The French traced out their camp, surrounding it with a deep ditch surmounted by a palisado, and erected machines to cast stones at the Egyptian army. Their fleet arrived at the same time; so that there were engagements on water and on land.

On Wednesday, the 15th day of the same moon, six deserters passed over to the camp of the Mussulmen, and informed them that the French army was in want of provision.

· The day of Bairam,* a great lord, and relation to the king of France, was made prisoner. Not a day passed without skirmishes on both sides, and with alternate success. The Mussulmen were particularly anxious to make prisoners, to gain information as to the state of the enemy's army, and used all sorts of stratagems for this purpose. A soldier from Cairo bethought himself of putting his head withinside of a watermelon, the interior of which he had scooped out, and of thus swimming toward the French camp; a Christian soldier, not suspecting a trick, leaped into the Nile to seize the melon; but the Egyptian was a stout swimmer, and catching hold of him, dragged him to his general.†

On Wednesday, the 7th day of the moon Chewal (Jan. 12, 1250), the Mussulmen captured a large boat, in which were a hundred soldiers, commanded by an officer of distinction. On Thursday, the 15th of the same moon, the French marched out of their camp, and their cavalry began to move. The troops were ordered to file off, when a slight skirmish took place, and the French left on the field forty cavaliers with their horses.

* The grand Bairam, the 1st day of the moon Chewal, was on Thursday, 6th January, 1250.

† The Egyptians are. at this day, perfect swimmers, and they exhibit extraordinary specimens of their art in this line.

2 N 2

On the Friday, seventy prisoners were conducted to Cairo, among whom were three lords of rank.   On the 22nd of the same moon, a large boat belonging to the French took fire, which was considered as a fortunate omen for the Mussulmen.

Some traitors having shewn the ford over the canal of Achmoum to the French, fourteen hundred cavaliers crossed it, and fell unexpectedly on the camp of the Mussulmen, on a Tuesday, the 15th day of the moon Zilkalde (Feb. 8), having at their head the brother of the king of France.   The emir Fakreddin was at the time in the bath : he instantly quitted it with precipitation, and mounted a horse without saddle or bridle, followed only by some slaves.   The enemy attacked him on all sides, but his slaves, like cowards, abandoned him when in the midst of the French: it was in vain he attempted to defend himself ; he fell pierced with wounds.   The French, after the death of Fakreddin, retreated to Djédilé; but their whole cavalry advanced to Mansoura, and, having forced one of the gates, entered the town: the Mussulmen fled to the right and left.   The king of France had already penetrated as far as the sultan's palace, and victory seemed ready to declare for him, when the Baharite slaves, led by Bibars, advanced, and snatched it from his hands : their charge was so furious that the French were obliged to retreat.   The French infantry, during this time, had advanced to cross the bridge; had they been able to join their cavalry, the defeat of the Egyptian army, and the loss of the town of Mansoura, would have been inevitable.

Night separated the combatants, when the French retreated in disorder to Djédilé, after leaving fifteen hundred of their men on the field.   They surrounded their camp with a ditch and wall, but their army was divided* into two corps: the least considerable body was encamped on the branch of the Achmoum, and the larger on the great branch of the Nile that runs to Damietta.

A pigeon had been let loose to fly to Cairo† the instant the French had surprised the camp of Fakreddin, having a note under its wing, to inform the inhabitants of this mis-

* Joinville speaks of a camp separate from that of the king. commanded by the count of Burgundy.

† This custom is very ancient in the East.

fortune. This melancholy event had created a general consternation in the town, which the runaways had augmented, and the gates of Cairo were kept open all the night to receive them. A second pigeon bearing the news of the victory over the French, had restored tranquillity to the capital. Joy succeeded sorrow ; and each congratulated the other on this happy turn of affairs, and public rejoicings were made.

When Touran-Chah heard of the death of his father, Nedjm-Eddin, he set out from Huns-Keifa.* It was the 15th of the moon Ramadan when he departed, attended by only fifty horsemen, and he arrived at Damascus toward the end of that moon. After receiving the homage of all the governors of the towns in Syria, he set out on a Wednesday, the 27th day of the moon Chewal, and took the road to Egypt. The news of his arrival raised the courage of the Mussulmen. The death of Nedjm-Eddin had not yet been publicly announced : the service of the sultan was performed as usual : his officers prepared his table as if he had been alive, and every order was given in his name. The sultana governed the kingdom, and found, in her own mind, resources for all. The moment she heard of Touran-Chah's arrival, she waited on him, and laid aside the sovereign command, to invest him with it. This prince was anxious to appear at the head of his troops, and set out for Mansoura, where he arrived on the 5th of the moon Zilkadé (Feb. 8).

Boats sent from Damietta brought all sorts of provision to the French camp, and kept it abundantly supplied. The Nile was now at its greatest height.† Touran-Chah caused many boats to be built, which, when taken to pieces, he placed on the backs of camels, and had them thus carried to the canal of Méhalé, when they were put together again, launched on the canal, and filled with troops for an ambuscade.

As soon as the French fleet of boats appeared at the mouth of the canal of Méhalé, the Mussulmen quitted their hiding-place, and attacked them. While the two fleets were

---

* A town of Diarbekir, on the banks of the Tigris.

† How could Makrisi say the Nile was at its greatest height when it was only the 8th of February ? and this river is never in that state but in the month of September. The date is exact, and agrees with Joinville, who notices this same event happening on the Shrove-Tuesday.

engaged, other boats left Mansoura filled with soldiers, and
fell on the rear of the French.   It was in vain they sought to
escape by flight: a thousand Christians were killed or made
prisoners.

In this defeat, fifty-two of their boats laden with provision
were taken, and their communication with Damietta by the
navigation of the Nile was cut off, so that within a short time
the whole army suffered the most terrible famine.   The Mussulmen surrounded them on all sides, and they could neither
advance nor retreat.

On the 1st of the moon Zilhigé (March 7), the French surprised seven boats; but the troops on board had the good fortune to escape.   In spite of the superiority of the Egyptians on
the Nile, they attempted to bring up another convoy from Damietta, but they lost it: thirty-two of their boats were taken
and carried to Mansoura, on the 9th of the same moon.
This new loss filled the measure of their woes, and caused
them to propose a truce and send ambassadors to treat of it
with the sultan.   The emir Zeineddin and the cadi Bedreddin
were ordered to meet and confer with them, when the
French offered to surrender Damietta, on condition that
Jerusalem, and some other places in Syria, should be given in
exchange for it.   This proposal was rejected, and the conferences broken up.

On Friday, the 27th of the moon Zilhijé (April 1), the
French set fire to all their machines of war and timber for
building, and rendered almost all their boats unfit for use.
During the night of Tuesday,* the 3rd day of the moon
Mahasem (April 5), in the year of the Hegira 648, the
whole of the French army decamped, and took the road
to Damietta.   Some boats which they had reserved fell down
the Nile at the same time.   The Mussulmen having, at break
of day of the Wednesday, perceived the retreat of the French,
pursued and attacked them.

The heat of the combat was at Fariskour.   The French
were defeated and put to flight: ten thousand of their men
fell on the field of battle, some say thirty thousand.   Upwards of one hundred thousand horsemen, infantry, trades-
people, and others, were made slaves.   The booty was im-

* Joinville dates this event on the Tuesday evening after the octave of
Easter.

mense in horses, mules, tents, and other riches. There were but one hundred slain on the side of the Mussulmen. The Baharite slaves, under the command of Bibars Elbondukdari, performed in this battle signal acts of valour. The king of France had retired, with a few of his lords, to a small hillock, and surrendered himself, under promise of his life being spared, to the eunuch Djemaddelin Mahsun-Elsalihi : he was bound with a chain, and in this state conducted to Mansoura, where he was confined in the house of Ibrahim-ben Lokman, secretary to the sultan, and under the guard of the eunuch Sahil. The king's brother was made prisoner at the same time, and carried to the same house. The sultan provided for their subsistence.

The number of slaves was so great, it was embarrassing, and the sultan gave orders to Seifeddin-Jousef-ben-tardi to put them to death. Every night this cruel minister of the vengeance of his master had from three to four hundred of the prisoners brought from their places of confinement, and, after he had caused them to be beheaded, their bodies were thrown into the Nile ; in this manner perished one hundred thousand of the French.

The sultan departed from Mansoura, and went to Fariskour, where he had pitched a most magnificent tent. He had also built a tower of wood over the Nile ; and, being freed from a disagreeable war, he there gave himself up to all sorts of debauchery.

The victory he had just gained was so brilliant that he was eager to make all who were subjected to him acquainted with it. He wrote with his own hand a letter in the following terms, to the emir Djemal-Edden-ben-Jagmour, governor of Damascus :

"Thanks be given to the All-powerful, who has changed our grief to joy: it is to him alone we owe the victory. The favours he has condescended to shower upon us are innumerable, but this last is most precious. You will announce to the people of Damascus, or rather to all Mussulmen, that God has enabled us to gain a complete victory over the Christians, at the moment they had conspired our ruin.

"On Monday, the first day of this year, we opened our treasury, and distributed riches and arms to our faithful soldiers. We had called to our succour the Arabian tribes, and

a numberless multitude of soldiers ranged themselves under
our standards.   On the nights between Tuesday and Wednesday, our enemies abandoned their camp with all their baggage,
and marched towards Damietta : in spite of the obscurity of the
night, we pursued them, and thirty thousand of them were left
dead on the field, not including those who precipitated themselves into the Nile.   We have beside slain our very numerous prisoners, and thrown their bodies into the same river.
Their king had retreated to Minieh : he has implored our
clemency, and we have granted him his life, and paid him
all the honours due to his rank.   We have regained Damietta."

The sultan, with this letter, sent the king's cap, which had
fallen in the combat : it was of scarlet, lined with a fine fur.
The governor of Damascus put the king's cap on his own
head when he read to the public the sultan's letter.   A poet
made these verses on the occasion :

" The cap of the French was whiter than paper : our
sabres have dyed it with the blood of the enemy, and have
changed its colour."

The gloomy and retired life the sultan led had irritated the
minds of his people.   He had no confidence but in a certain
number of favourites, whom he had brought with him from
Huns-Keifa, and whom he had invested with the principal
offices of the state, in the room of the ancient ministers of his
father.   Above all, he shewed a decided hatred to the Mamelukes, although they had contributed so greatly to the last
victory.   His debaucheries exhausted his revenue ; and, to
supply the deficiencies, he forced the sultana Chegeret-Eddur
to render him an account of the riches of his father.   The
sultana, in alarm, implored the protection of the Mamelukes,
representing to them the services she had done the state in
very difficult times, and the ingratitude of Touran-Chah, who
was indebted to her for the crown he wore.   These slaves,
already irritated against Touran-Chah, did not hesitate to
take the part of the sultana, and resolved to assassinate the
prince.   To execute this design, they fixed on the moment
when he was at table ; Bibars-Elbondukdari gave him the
first blow with his sabre, and, though he parried it with his
hand, he lost his fingers.   He then fled to the tower which he
had built on the banks of the Nile, and which was but a

short distance from his tent. The conspirators followed him, and, finding he had closed the door, set fire to it. The whole army saw what was passing; but, as he was a prince universally detested, no one came forward in his defence.

It was in vain he cried from the top of the tower, that he would abdicate his throne, and return to Huns-Keifa; the assassins were inflexible. The flames at length gaining on the tower, he attempted to leap into the Nile; but his dress caught as he was falling, and he remained some time suspended in the air. In this state, he received many wounds from sabres, and then fell into the river, where he was drowned. Thus iron, fire, and water contributed to put an end to his life. His body continued three days on the bank of the Nile, without any one daring to give it sepulture. At length, the ambassador from the caliph of Bagdad obtained permission, and had it buried.

This cruel prince, when he ascended the throne, had his brother, Adil-Chah, strangled. Four Mameluke slaves had been ordered to execute this; but the fratricide did not long remain unpunished, and these same four slaves were the most bitter in putting him to death. With this prince was extinguished the dynasty of the Eioubites, who had governed Egypt eighty years, under eight different kings.

After the massacre of Touran-Chah, the sultana Chegeret-Eddur was declared sovereign of Egypt; she was the first slave who had reigned over this country. This princess was a Turk, but others said an Armenian. The sultan Nedjm-Eddin had bought her, and loved her so desperately that he carried her with him to his wars, and never quitted her. She had a son by the sultan, called Khalil, but who died when very young. The emir Azeddin-Aibegh, of the Turcoman nation, was appointed general of the army; and the name of the sultana was imprinted on the coin.

The emir Abou-Ali was nominated to treat with the king of France for his ransom, and for the surrender of Damietta. After many conferences and disputes, it was agreed that the French should evacuate Damietta, and that the king, and all prisoners in Egypt, should be set at liberty, on condition of paying down one half of such ransom as should be fixed on. The king of France sent orders to the governor of Damietta to surrender that town: but he refused to obey, and new orders were necessary.   At last it was given up to the Mussulmen, after having remained eleven months in the hands of the enemy.   The king paid four hundred thousand pieces of gold, as well for his own ransom as for that of the queen, his brother, and the other lords that had accompanied him.

All the Franks that had been made prisoners during the reigns of the sultans Hadil-Kamil, Salih-Nedjm-Eddin, and Touran-Chah, obtained their liberty : they amounted to twelve thousand one hundred men and ten women.   The king, with all the French, crossed to the westward branch of the Nile, and embarked on a Saturday for Acre.*

The poet, Essabib-Giémal-Edden-Ben-Matroub made, on the departure of this prince, the following verses :

" Bear to the king of France, when you shall see him, these words, traced by a partisan of truth : The death of the servants of the Messiah has been the reward given to you by God.

" You have landed in Egypt, thinking to take possession of it.   You have imagined that it was only peopled with cowards ! you who are a drum filled with wind.

" You thought that the moment to destroy the Mussulmen was arrived ; and this false idea has smoothed, in your eyes, every difficulty.

" By your excellent conduct, you have abandoned your soldiers on the plains of Egypt, and the tomb has gaped under their feet.

" What now remains of the seventy thousand who accompanied you ?   Dead, wounded, and prisoners !

" May God inspire you often with similar designs !   They will cause the ruin of all Christians, and Egypt will have no longer to dread any thing from their rage.

" Without doubt, your priests announced victories to you : their predictions were false.

" Refer yourselves to a more enlightened oracle.

" Should the desire of revenge urge you to return to Egypt, be assured the house of Lokman still remains, that the chain is ready prepared, and the eunuch awake."†

Great rejoicings were made at Cairo and throughout Egypt,

* 7th May, 1250.   Joinville says the Saturday after Ascension day.
† The poet, in this stanza, alludes to the prison of St. Louis and the eunuch who guarded him.

for the restoration of Damietta. The army broke up its encampment, and returned to the capital, when the sultana
loaded the officers with presents, and her liberalities extended
to the meanest soldier.

The king of France,* having fortunately escaped from the
hands of the Egyptians, resolved to make war against the
kingdom of Tunis. He chose a time when a horrible famine
ravaged Africa, and sent an ambassador to the pope, whom
the Christians consider as the vicar of the Messiah. This
pontiff gave him permission to take for the support of this
war the wealth of churches. He also sent ambassadors to all
the kings in Christendom, to demand assistance, and to engage
them to unite with him in this expedition. The kings of
England, of Scotland, and of Arragon, the count of Toulouse,
and many other Christian princes, accepted of his invitation.

Abouabdoullah-Muhammed-Elmoustausir-Billah, son to the
emir Abizikeria, then reigned at Tunis. The report of this
intended expedition came to his ears, and he sent an ambassador to the king of France to sue for peace, offering eighty
thousand pieces of gold to obtain it. The king took the
money, but did not the less carry his arms into Africa. He
landed on the shore of the plains of Carthage, and laid siege
to Tunis the last day of the moon Zilkadé, in the 668th year
of the Hegira (July 21, A.D. 1270).

* The Egyptians repented having suffered the king of France to escape
from their hands, for it was commonly reported that he was meditating
another war against Egypt. Makrizi, in the description of this kingdom,
says, that this report was renewed under the reign of Bibars-Albonduk-
dari. This sultan assembled his council, when it was resolved, that, in
order to gain access to succour Damietta, which had lately been rebuilt,
not far from the site of the ancient town, that had been ruined, a bridge
should be constructed from Kiloub to the town. Kiloub was a village two
days' march distant from Damietta, and when the Nile is at its height, the
road to that village is impassable. The emir Achoub, one of the Mameluke chiefs, had the superintendence of it. Thirty thousand men were
employed in building this bridge, and six hundred oxen transported materials and earth. This bridge was finished in a month. It was two days'
march in length, and six horsemen could pass it in front. This bridge,
however, could not be very high, since it was not built over the Nile,
where it would have been impossible to construct one; and this proves it
was erected on the land, and of use only in the time of inundations. It
was rather a causeway than a bridge, and sufficiently high to be above the
country flooded by the Nile. Similar ones are built at this day, to prevent the land from being overflowed.

His army was composed of thirty thousand infantry and
six thousand cavalry.   The siege lasted six months.

On the 15th of the month Muharsem, the first month of
the year 669, there was a bloody battle, in which numbers
were slain on each side.   The Tunisians were on the point of
being destroyed, when the death of the king of France
changed the face of affairs.   The French, after this event,
only thought of making peace and returning to their own
country.

One Ismael-Erreian, an inhabitant of Tunis, made the following verses during the siege :—

" Frenchman, art thou ignorant that Tunis is the sister of
Cairo ?   Think on the fate that awaits thee !   Thou wilt find
before this town thy tomb, instead of the house of Lokman ;
and the two terrible angels, Munkir and Nakir, will take the
place of the eunuch Sahil."*

This king of France had a good understanding, but was of
an artful character.†

---

* *Munkir and Nakir* are two angels who, according to the Mussulman
creed, interrogate the dead the moment they are in the grave. They
begin their interrogatories with these words, " Who is thy Lord ?" and
" Who is thy prophet ?"

† It is disgraceful to Makrisi, otherwise a tolerably faithful historian,
to suffer himself to be blinded by the common aversion of Mussulmen to
Christians.

LONDON: PRINTED BY WILLIAM CLOWES AND SONS, LIMITED,
STAMFORD STREET AND CHARING CROSS.